R. L. Polk

Polk's Indianapolis (Marion County, Ind.) city directory

R. L. Polk

Polk's Indianapolis (Marion County, Ind.) city directory

ISBN/EAN: 9783741106491

Manufactured in Europe, USA, Canada, Australia, Japa

Cover: Foto ©Andreas Hilbeck / pixelio.de

Manufactured and distributed by brebook publishing software
(www.brebook.com)

R. L. Polk

Polk's Indianapolis (Marion County, Ind.) city directory

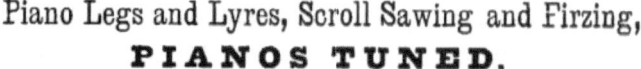

H. D. CARLISLE'S

HOME MILLS

Cor. Maryland Street and Canal,

INDIANAPOLIS, INDIANA.

H. D. CARLISLE,
CHOICE
SNOW FLAKE
FROM
WHITE WHEAT.

Pay strict attention to the supply of the Home trade. All families should try H. D. Carlisle's Snow Flake.

J. E. SHOVER.   W. F. CHRISTIAN.

SHOVER & CHRISTIAN,

CARPENTERS & BUILDERS

Contract for all branches of Buildings of all descriptions. Particular attention paid to building Stores, Show Cases, Desks, fancy and plain Counters and Shelving. Orders from a distance promptly filled and shipped with care.

No. 124 EAST VERMONT ST., BET. DELAWARE & ALABAMA STS.,

P. O. Box 1412.   INDIANAPOLIS, IND.

J. PERRY ELLIOTT'S
CITY
GALLERY OF ART

PHOTOGRAPHER.

ORDERS RESPECTFULLY SOLICITED

NOS. 8 & 10
E. WASHINGTON STREET,
INDIANAPOLIS, IND.

Photographs Copied from Old Pictures, enlarged to any Size desired, Plain or Colored in Oil, Water Colors, or India Ink, in the finest Style of the Art.

A. L. WEBB.   C. A. BATES

Webb & Bates,

GENERAL COMMISSION

MERCHANTS,

DEALERS IN ALL KINDS OF

FLOUR AND FEED

Clover and Timothy Seeds,

AND

FARM IMPLEMENTS.

General Agents for the Massillion, Ohio,

EXCELSIOR

Reaper and Mower,

No. 88

MASONIC HALL,

INDIANAPOLIS, IND.

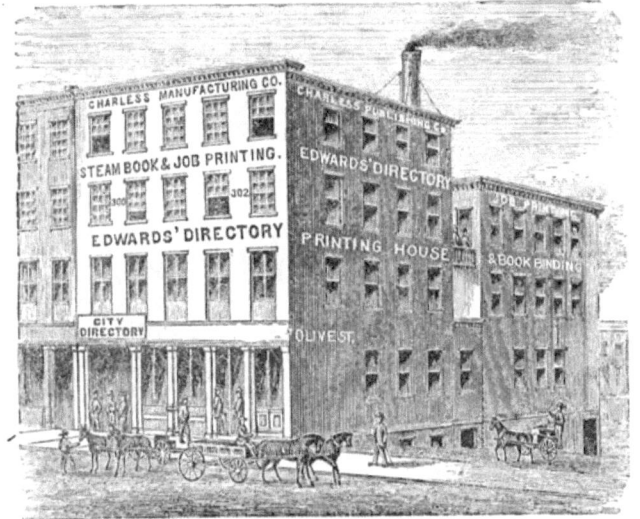

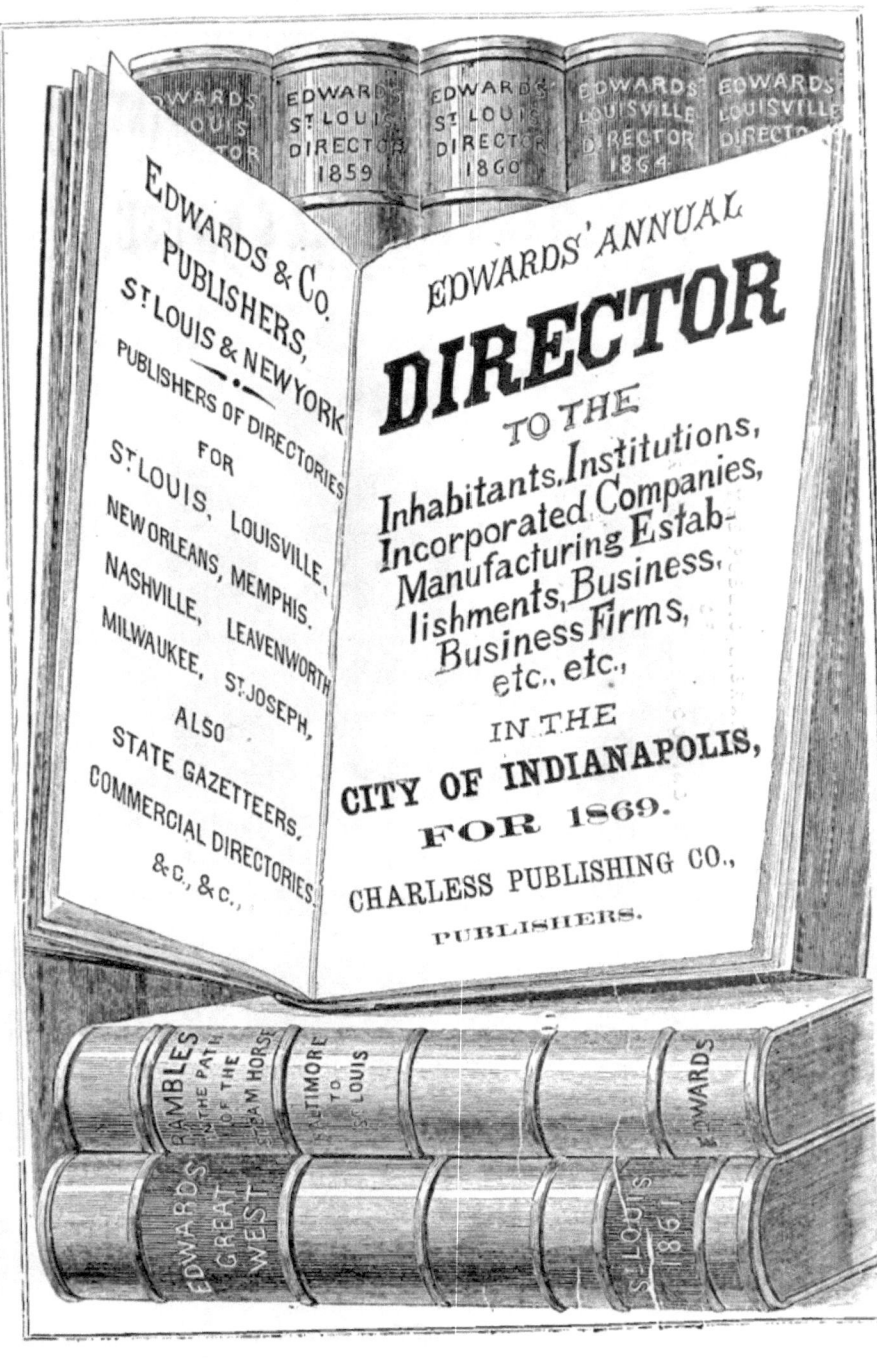

The Evening

COMMERCIAL!

M. E. LEE, - EDITOR.

IS PUBLISHED

Daily, Sundays Excepted,

BY THE

Commercial Company,

CORNER OF

WASHINGTON AND ILLINOIS STS.,

OVER THE CORNER DRUG STORE,

OPPOSITE BATES & PALMER HOUSES.

SUBSCRIPTION TERMS:

By Carriers, to any part of the city, FIFTEEN CENTS per Week, payable semi-monthly. Single copy FIVE CENTS.

HISTORY RECORDING ON TIME THE EVENTS OF NATIONS.

Dedication.

To THE HON. DANIEL MACAULEY,

Mayor of the City of Indianapolis:

The Publishers take the liberty of dedicating to you the Fourth Volume of EDWARDS' ANNUAL CITY DIRECTORY of the City of Indianapolis. Not only as a tribute to your private worth, but as a token of the esteem in which you are held by all who so highly appreciate your exertions, both in time of peace and that of war. As a public benefactor and a civilian your example is well worthy of imitation. Your unrelenting efforts in behalf of the City's good, (in the position of Mayor,) and the high esteem in which you are held by the citizens of Indianapolis, eminently entitle you to the small consideration here bestowed by the publishers of this work.

CHARLESS PUBLISHING CO.,

PUBLISHERS.

THE
Western Fireside,

A MAGAZINE FOR EVERYBODY.

DEVOTED TO

Literature, Agriculture, Horti- culture, Health, Temperance, Education, Etc., Etc.

F. C. HOLLIDAY, D. D.

EDITOR,

DYNES, WEST & CO., - - - **Publishers.**

VINTONS BLOCK.

TERMS, $1.00 PER YEAR.

READ WHAT THE PRESS SAY OF IT:

It presents such a variety and such taste of selections as should make it a favorite everywhere.—*Eagle, Union City, Ind.*

The workmanship is excellent, and the contents are worthy of so neat a setting.—*Commercial, Indianapolis, Ind.*

Try it you who love the West and the way she does things. —*Register, Eaton, Ohio.*

We are very much pleased with the Western Fireside, and wish it abundant success. It looks healthy and its typography will compare favorably with any of the Eastern monthlies. The selections evince considerable taste, while the original articles are all enjoyable.—*National Union, Cincinnati, O.*

The mechanical part is unexceptionable, being neatly gotten up and nicely printed, a feature in itself that will commend it to the favor of all persons of tasts. The contents are varied and interesting, and adapted to the use and information of its locality, touching on almost all subjects, such as general literature, agri- culture, health, education, temperance, &c. Each number con- tains twenty large three column pages of reading matter, and is offered at the low price of $1.00 per year.—*Volunteer, Shelbyville, Indiana.*

INTRODUCTORY.

———o———

OFFICE OF THE CHARLESS PUBLISHING CO., }
ST. LOUIS, JUNE 15th, 1869. }

In presenting this the fourth volume of Edwards' Annual City Directory of Indianapolis to the patrons of the same, we cannot refrain from tendering our thanks for the liberal manner in which they have seconded our efforts in the prosecution of our labors, believing that they will be appreciated and the correctness of our work readily perceived by all who are daily obliged to refer to its pages; as the continual reference by most of our citizens to a work of this nature necessitates correctness and precision, its usefulness and value is readily felt by all business men, more especially as they have for the past year been misguided by a *"skimmed publication."*

In view of this fact we subject our pages to the closest scrutiny, admitting the fact, however, that slight imperfections will unavoidably appear, though the greatest human forethought and precaution may have been exercised. For such slight imperfections we ask the indulgence of a most generous people.

The information has been collected with great care by Reporters who thoroughly understand their business, and no expense nor pains has been spared to give the citizens of Indianapolis a Directory useful as a business guide, and one that will reflect credit upon our beautiful and prosperous city, and at the same time, reflecting great credit upon its publishers for its mechanical execution.

In this connection we deem it proper to state that it is the intent on the part of the publishers, to make an annual publication hereafter, trusting that each succeeding volume will be attended with less difficulties, and that we may be able to merrit the approbation of the patronizing public.

In conclusion, we most heartily return our thanks for the favors and kindness shown us by our friends and patrons.

We are most respectfully yours,

CHARLESS PUBLISHING CO.,

Publishers.

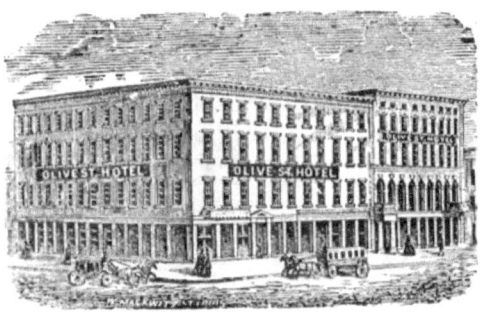

MILLER'S

RESTAURANT!

AND

OYSTER DEPOT,

No. 46 S. MERIDIAN STREET,

UP STAIRS.

Miller would respectfully inform the business men and the traveling public that he has opened the above establishment, which he intends to keep in the very best style, second to no other establishment of the kind in this city, and he hopes by strict attention to the comfort of his customers to deserve their patronage.

ALL THE DELICACIES OF THE SEASON served up in the best style.

A SUPERIOR CUP OF COFFEE with the best FRESH PASTRY can always be obtained here

For persons wishing day board we have the best accommodations Our table always furnished with the BEST THE MARKET AFFORDS. Our charges are moderate. "LIVE AND LET LIVE," our motto.

He also has opened a depot for New York and Baltimore Oysters, WHOLESALE AND RETAIL, kept constantly on hand and shipped to any point in the State. Particular attention paid to city orders.

Private Parties served in best style. Wines and Refreshments furnished.

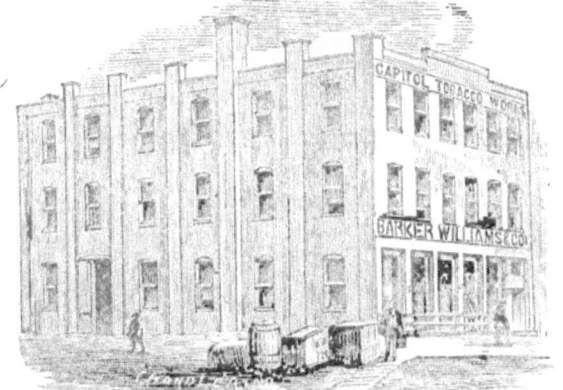

INDICES.

—o—

GENERAL INDEX.

	PAGE.
Abbreviations	32
Academies, Colleges, Institutes, etc.	16
Addition to City Register	10
Banks and Banking Houses	12
Board of County Commissioners	14
Board of Health	12
Business Directory	369-412
Cemeteries	13
Chamber of Commerce	10
Churches	13-14
City Commissioners	12
City Councilmen	11
City Hospital	12
City Officers	11
City Register	11-31
Citizens' Directory	33-356
County Officers	14
Courts	15
Dedication	5
Druids	23
Educational	16
Fair Grounds	12
Fire Alarm Telegraph Signals	15
Fire Department	15
Good Templars	23
Incorporated Companies	19
Indiana Military Agency	20
Indiana State Board of Agriculture	12
Indiana State Government	20
Insurance Companies, (Home)	19
Introductory	7
Libraries	10

	PAGE.
Marion County Agricultural and Horticultural Society	12
Masonic	22
Newspapers and Publications	20-21
Odd Fellows	22-23
Police Department	12
Post Office Department	25-26
Postage, Rates of	26
Pub. Halls, Blocks, Offices & Buildings	21-22
School Board of Trustees	17
School Board of Visitors	17
School property, Statement of	18
School Teachers and number of pupils in each ward	18
School Trustees	12
Schools	17-19
Schools and Teachers	17
Schools Colored	18
Schools Parochial and Private	19
Schools Public	17-18
Secret and Benevolent Societies	22-23
Societies and Associations	23-24
Stamp Duties, Schedule of	357-360
Standing Committees	13
Streets, Avenues and Alleys	27-31
Title Page	3
Too Late for Regular Insertion	31
Township Trustees	15
Trades Union	24-25
U. S. Offices in this city	25
Ward Boundaries	26

INDEX TO ADVERTISERS.

	PAGE.
Aldrich & Gay, wood yard	K
Appleby Robert, house furnishing goods	M
Arden J. Boots and shoes	
	bottom margin lines.
Atkins E. C. & Co. Sheffield Saw Works	415
Baird William, cooper	379
Baldwin J. H. & Co	side margin lines.
Bentley & Chandler, dress & cloak mak'g	O
Bingham W. P. & Co. jeweler	
	top margin lines.
Brackebush C. J. farm machinery	
side margin lines and inset opp.	416
Brolaski & Malin, Laclede Hotel, St. Louis (R. R. Dep't)	409
Bunte & Dickson, lumber	C
Burkhart A. J. ice dealer	366
Byrkitt M. & Son, sash door and blind factory	K
Caldwell G. W. & Co. Aerated Bread Bakery	front cover.
Carlisle H D. flour mill	I
Carr J. M. saddle and harness maker	C
Chapman D. C. painter	364
Charless Publishing Co	2-32

	PAGE.
Cincinnati, Connersville and Indianapolis Junction R. R. (R. R. Dep't)	413
Cleveland, Columbus, Cincinnati and Indianapolis Rw. Co. (R. R. Dep't)	410
Commercial, (newspaper)	4
Coors Aug. F. grocer	bottom margin lines.
Copeland W. J. & Co	bottom margin lines.
Cox Brothers, boiler makers and sheet iron workers	363
Cropper J. H. Furniture, Tin and Hardware Store	N
Culliny Patrick M. dry goods importer and dealer	back cover and top margin lines.
Daggett, R. P. architect	371
Davis I. & Co. Hats, Caps and Furs	
	top margin lines.
Desjardins Joseph, stair builder	O
Elliott J. Perry, photographer	L
Enos & Hueber, architects	366
Ewald Henry, horse shoer & wagon mkr.	E
Fertig Frank, painter	399
Fitzgerald & Carroll, Barnum's Hotel, St. Louis	416

1

	PAGE.
Forbes J. R. jeweler and watchmaker...	
Top margin lines	
Fugit James M. grainer.................	385
Gebhard A. upholsterer and cabinet maker............................	H
Goddard S. & Sons, stone works........	367
Hart Edward F. saloon.................	363
Hess Chas. M. A. ins. agent........	
Side margin lines	
Hildebrand, Keppele & Co. lumber.....	K
Holliday W. & C. F. lamps and lanterns..	364
Indianapolis, Cincinnati & LaFayette R. R. (R. R. Dep't.)	412
Indianapolis & St. Louis R. R. (R. R. Dep't.)............................	414
Ingraham C. B. photographer..........	401
Jackson & Nicoli, grocers ret.......	386
Jeffersonville, Madison & Indianapolis R. R. (R. R. Dep't.)...................	411
Jenison A. F. & Co......*front cover and*	371
Jenkins E. painter...................	E
Jones C. G. ins. agt....*Margin lines and*	391
Kappes J. H. & Co. piano mnfrs.......	415
Kay & Mattern, dress and cloak making.	G
Keller Paul. cabinet maker...........	414
Kemper John M. carpenter and builder.	G
Kindler C. locksmith and bell hanger...	363
Klare & Schroder, saloon and bowling alley...............................	406
Kolb Lonis. wood-turner.............	410
Land Co.'s Indiana & Illinois Central Rw. Co. (John R. Elder)............	414
Lawrence A. V. grocer	365
Lueders Misses, stamping and stamped goods............................	G
Lukens R. L. agricultural implements...	368
Lukens R. L. & Co. Gauze's Ditching Machine............................	368
McFarlane William M. bakery..........	372
McKendry & Lovecraft, stave factory....	N
Meyer Charles & Co. notions, toys and fancy goods......................	365
Mayhew O. F. solicitor of patents....	371
Also front cover	
Meier V. & Bro. Madison Ale..........	362
Meridian Street Bath House	367
Meyer George F. cigars and tobacco....	364
Miller A. R. photographer.............	361
	PAGE.
Miller, Mitchell & Stough	J
Mirror. (newspaper)...................	I
Morse T. A. carpenter and builder......	H
Mueller C. L. tailor and repairer........	K
Mueller Lawrence, architectural carver	R
Munsell Henry. wagonmaker...........	G
Newton Maria S. milliner, dress and cloak maker...........................	366
Perrine T. B. general engraver.........	
Top margin lines	
Pickerill & Cole. physicians.............	402
Reed H A. painter.....................	D
Reynolds N. W. cigars and tobacco.....	J
Robinson Bros. trunks and valises.......	361
Schmidt C. F. brewer............*Front cover*	
Scribner & Smith, soda water..........	362
Shover & Christian, carpenters and builders.................................	I
Smith F. carriage and wagon maker....	D
Smith John B. Chemical Dye Works....	R
Smith, Ittenbach & Co, stoneyard.....	362
Smith N. R. & Co. (Trade Palace)......	413
Spades M. H. dry goods ...*Side margin lines*	
Spring E. Mrs. milliner, cloak and dress maker	365
Stowell M. A. music house..*Side margin lines; also back cover; also*	A
Stumph Joseph	G
Summer Resort. Perry Springs..........	412
Swank M. cancer physician...........	376
Tate Warren, sash and blind factory....	364
Terre Haute & Indianapolis R. R. (R. R. Dep't)..............................	415
The Western Fireside. (newspaper)......	G
Thompson & Cartwright, saloon........	362
Todd, Carmichael & Williams, booksellers and stationers.........*Front cover*	
Trayser F. L. musical instrum't repairer	396
Turner Wm. H. & Co. coal and coke.... *Front cover; also*	378
Turner & Root, coal miners............	C
Van Camp & Jackson, com. mers........	361
Vondersaar, blacksmith and wagonmkr..	D
Webb & Bates, agricultural implements.	O
Weghorst Henry, florist and gardener...	366
Wiegand A. nurseryman and florist.....	M
Wilkinson D. E. grocer..........	365
Wischart & Calvert, flour and feed......	G
Zimmermann C. slate and metal roofer..	363

ADDITIONS TO CITY REGISTER.

CHAMBER OF COMMERCE.

LIBRARIES.

EDWARDS'

1869

INDIANAPOLIS DIRECTORY,

MUNICIPAL RECORD,

—AND—

CITY REGISTER.

CITY GOVERNMENT,

DANIEL MACAULEY.................. ....MAYOR

(Term Expires May, 1871.)

CITY OFFICERS.	CITY COUNCILMEN.
(Offices Glenn's Block.)	FIRST WARD—Leon Kahn and John S. Newman.
CLERK—Daniel Ramsdell.	SECOND WARD—Temple C. Harrison and W. D. Wiles.
DEPUTIES—Jno. G. Waters and Jno. R. Clinton.	THIRD WARD—J. H. Woodburn and W. W. Weaver.
TREASURER—Robert S. Foster.	FOURTH WARD—Erie Locke and Isaac Thalman.
DEPUTY—John W. Coons.	FIFTH WARD—A. H. Brown and James McB. Shepherd.
ATTORNEY—B. K. Elliott.	SIXTH WARD—Henry Gimber and Robert Kennington.
ENGINEER—R. M. Patterson.	SEVENTH WARD—Thomas Cottrell and John Marsee.
ASSESSOR—William Hadley.	EIGHTH WARD—C. E. Whitset and Christopher Heckman.
MARSHALL—George Taffe.	NINTH WARD—John Pyle and Frederick Thoms.
DEPUTY—Augustus Reick.	
STREET COMMISSIONER—Augustus Bruner.	
CHIEF FIRE ENGINEER—Charles Raymond.	
MARKET MASTER—Theodore W. Pease.	
SEALER—S. B. Morris.	
SEXTON—James H. Hedges.	
PRINTER—James G. Douglass.	

STANDING COMMITTEES.

Accounts and Claims—J. H. Woodburn, Leon Kahn and Christian Heckman.

Benevolence and Hospitals—J. H. Woodburn, W. W. Weaver and C. E. Whitset.

Bridges—Eric Locke, John Marsee and Henry Gimber.

Finance—John S. Newman, J. H. Woodburn and Thomas Cottrell.

Fire Department—John Marsee, Isaac Thalman and A. H. Brown.

Gas Light—William D. Wiles, Leon Kahn and Robert Kennington.

Judiciary—John S. Newman, T. C. Harrison and A. Brown.

Markets—John Pyle, Isaac Thalman and Robert Kennington.

Printing and Stationery—Frederick Thoms, T. C. Harrison and James McB. Shepherd.

Public Buildings—W. W. Weaver, John Pyle and Henry Gimber.

Public Schools—Leon Kahn, Eric Locke and C. E. Whitsit.

Railroads—William D. Wiles, Frederick Thoms and James McB. Shepherd.

Revision of Ordinance—T. C. Harrison and Thomas Cottrell.

Streets and Alleys—Isaac Thalman, John Marsee and Christopher Heckman.

---o---

CITY COMMISSIONERS—Pres. S. M. Seibert; Secy. J. N. Russell; W. Braden, John F. Ramsey and Joseph Sutton.

CITY HOSPITAL—Directors: Dr. John M. Kitchen, W. W. Smith, J. C. Geisendorf, W. Braden, George Merritt, Dr. F. S. Newcomer, Charles Glazier, E. J. Holliday, Dr. J. M. Phipps.

BOARD OF HEALTH—Drs. T. B. Harvey, John Comingore and W. Clinton Thompson.

SCHOOL TRUSTEES—Pres. James C. Yohn, Secy. W. H. L. Noble, Treas. John R. Elder.

---o---

POLICE DEPARTMENT.

First Dist.—G. W. Bennett, R. B. Barber, Thomas Horniday.

Second Dist.—James N. Stevens, A. J. Wells, George Buser.

Third Dist.—H. Taffe, J. Cahill, Allen Thornbrough.

Fourth Dist.—William Boler, Michael Murphy, R. M. Boyd.

Fifth Dist.—L. M. Russell, A. P. Wright, John Spellman.

Sixth Dist.—H. Minnick, O. B. Boardman, R. Campbell.

Seventh Dist.—T. S. Wilson, H. Adams, George Sponsel.

Eighth Dist.—William Williams, Abel Catterson, M. Louney.

Ninth Dist.—Jesse Murphy, P. Lendermi, George Thomas.

UNION DEPOT Police force consists of one marshal and three deputies separate from the city organization of police.

POLICE COMMISSIONERS—John Marsee, J. H. Woodburn, William D. Wiles

AGRICULTURE.

INDIANA STATE BOARD OF AGRICULTURE—Hon. A. D. Hamrick, Pres. John Sutherland, Vice Pres. A. J. Holmes, Secy. Carlos Dickson, Treas. Indianapolis, John B. Sullivan, Gen. Supt. Indianapolis. Office State House, Indianapolis.

MARION COUNTY AGRICULTURAL AND HORTICULTURAL SOCIETY—L. W. Hasselman, Pres. John T. Francis, Secy. Office 7 Hubbard's blk.

FAIR GROUNDS, Indiana State Agricultural Society cs. Delaware, north of limits. Seventeenth annual Indiana State Fair will be held at Indianapolis, Monday Sept. 27th, continuing to Oct. 2d.

---o---

BANKS AND BANKING HOUSES

BANK OF THE STATE, incorporated 1857; closing business. James M. Ray, prest., Joseph Moore, cashier.

BRANCH OF THE BANK OF STATE, ne. cor. Washington and Meridian, Oliver Tousey, prest., D. M. Taylor, cashier.

CITIZENS' NATIONAL BANK, 4 E. Washington; organized November 11th, 1864, authorized capital $500,000. W. C. Holmes, pres., Joseph R. Haugh, cashier; John Thomas, J. H. Baldwin, Nicholas McCarty, J. H. Vajen, Wm. Mansur, Geo. B. Yandes, Isaiah Mansur, J. R. Haugh, W. C. Holmes, directors.

FIRST NATIONAL BANK, se. cor. Washington and Meridian; organized 1863, capital $500,000. William H. English, prest., John C. New, cashier; Wm. H. English, John C. New, H. Bates, jr., N. S. Greene, E. G. English, Delos Root, J. McLene, Robt. Browning, J. G. Stitz, E. S. Alvord, T. B. McCarty, directors.

FLETCHER'S BANK, 30 E. Washington; organized 1830, capital, $200,000. S. A. Fletcher & Co., props. Banking hours from 8 A. M. to 4 P. M.

HARRISON'S BANK, 15 E. Washington, established in 1855, capital $100,000. Alfred & John C. S. Harrison, proprs. Banking hours from 8 A. M. to 4 P. M.

INDIANA BANKING CO., 28 E. Washington; organized 1865, capital $100,000. F. A. W. Davis, prest., W. W. Woolen, cashier, Samuel C. Vance, asst. cashier. Banking hours from 8 A. M. to 4 P. M.

INDIANA NATIONAL BANK, 2 E. Washington, cor. Meridian; organized July 1st, 1865, cash capital $400,000 authorized capital $600,000. Geo. Tousey, prest., D. M. Taylor, cashier; Geo. Tousey, Oliver Tousey George Merritt, Wm. Coughlin, Daniel Stewart, Jacob P. Dunn, directors. Banking hours from 8 A. M. to 4 P. M.

INDIANAPOLIS BRANCH BANKING CO. 49 E. Washington, cor. Pennsylvania, capital $200,000. Fletcher & Sharpe, proprs., have been engaged in banking business for 35 years. Deposits received and discounts made daily from 8 A. M. to 4 P. M.

INDIANAPOLIS NATIONAL BANK, under Odd Fellow's Hall, ne. cor. Washington and Pennsylvania, chartered 1864, capital $500,000, surplus fund $184,000. Theodore P. Haughey, prest., A. F. Williams, cashier, Henry Lathani, asst. cashier. S. A. Fletcher, sr., F. M. Churchman, Ingram Fletcher, E. Sharpe and Theodore P. Haughey, directors. Deposits received, discounts made, gold, silver, exchange and government securities bought and sold. Banking hours from 8 A. M. to 4 P. M.

MERCHANTS' NATIONAL BANK, 48 East Washington; organized March 9th, 1865, commenced business June 5th, 1865, capital paid in $100,000, authorized $300,000. John S. Newman, prest., V. T. Malott, cashier. John S. Newman, David Macy, Henry Schnull, H. G Carey, V. T. Malott, directors.

SAVINGS BANK, 14 E. Washington, organized March 25th, 1868; J. B. Ritzinger, propr. Deposits received and discounts made daily from 8 A. M. to 4 P. M.

CEMETERIES.

CITY—West side Kentucky av. adjoining Green Lawn Cemetery, entrance the same. J. H. Hedges, Sexton.

CROWN HILL—Two miles nw. of city, entrance Michigan road. F. W. Chislett, Supt.

GREEN LAWN—West side Kentucky av. bet. Louisiana and the River, entrance Kentucky av. J. H. Hedges, Sexton.

HEBREW—South of city adjoining the Catholic Cemetery.

ST. JOHNS—One mile south of city bet. Bluff and the Notch roads.

CATHOLIC—South of the city, entrance Bluff road.

—o—

CHURCHES.

Baptist.

FIRST BAPTIST CHURCH—northeast corner New York and Pennsylvania.

MISSION CHAPEL—in charge of the First Baptist Church, corner Noble and South.

AFRICAN BAPTIST CHURCH—Michigan, between Indiana av. and West, Rev. Moses Broyles, pastor, residence, 227 Minerva.

Catholic.

CHRIST CHURCH—Meridian, northeast corner Circle. Rev. B. Franklin, pastor, residence, 65 Circle.

ST. JOHN'S CHURCH—(German) south side Maryland, between Pennsylvania and Delaware.

ST. JOHN'S CHURCH—(Roman Catholic), north side Georgia, between Illinois and Tennessee. Rev. A. Bessinones, pastor, residence, north side Georgia, between Illinois and Tennessee. Services, Sabbath at 6, 8, and 10 &. M., Vespers, 3 P. M., Sabbath School, 2 P. M.

ST. MARY'S CHURCH—south side Maryland between Pennsylvania and Delaware. Rev. Father S. Siegrist, pastor, residence, 75 E. Maryland.

ST. PETER'S CHURCH—Dougherty, near Fletcher av. Rev. Joseph Petit, pastor.

Christian.

CHRISTIAN CHAPEL—southwest corner Ohio and Delaware. Rev O. A. Burgess, pastor, residence, 249 N. Alabama.

FOURTH CHRISTIAN CHURCH—330 Indiana av. Rev. J. B. New, pastor, residence, 82 N. Illinois. Hours of service, 10:30 A. M. and 7:30 P. M. Sabbath School, 9 A. M.

MISSION CHAPEL—(African), east side Blackford, between Vermont and Michigan. Rev. Rufus Conrad, pastor, residence, 500 N. Mississippi.

Congregational.

PLYMOUTH CHURCH—northwest corner Meridian and Circle, Rev. E. P. Ingersoll, pastor, residence, 283 N. Pennsylvania.

Episcopal.

CHRIST'S CHURCH—northeast corner Meridian and Circle. Organized August, 1837. Rev. B. Franklin, pastor, residence, 65 Circle.

CHURCH OF THE HOLY INNOCENTS— Fletcher av. northeast corner Cedar. Rev. George B. Engle, rector, residence, 50 S. Tennessee. Services Sunday, 10:45 A. M. and 3 P. M. Wednesday, 7:30 P. M. Sunday School, 4 P. M.

GRACE CHURCH—southeast corner St. Joseph and Pennsylvania.

ST. PAUL'S CHURCH—southeast corner Illinois and New York. Rev. J. H. Stringfellow, pastor, residence, 216 N. Delaware.

Friends.

FRIEND'S CHURCH—southeast corner Delaware and St. Clair. Erected 1856, Enos G. Pray, pastor, residence, 102 Broadway.

German Evangelical.

ST. PAUL'S CHURCH—east side New Jersey between Ohio and Market. Rev. John Kaufman, pastor, residence, rear of the Church.

ZION'S CHURCH—north side Ohio, between Meridian and Illinois. Rev. Herman Quinius, pastor, residence, 36 W. Ohio. Service Sunday, 10:30 A. M. and 7:30 P. M. Sabbath School, 9 A. M.

GERMAN REFORMED—east side Alabama, between Washington and Market. Rev. Henry Eschmeier, pastor, residence, 41 N Alabama.

JEWISH SYNAGOGUE—south side Market, between East and New Jersey.

Lutheran.

DANISH CHURCH—northeast corner East and Georgia. M. F. Wilser, pastor, residence, 66 Huron.

FIRST ENGLISH CHURCH—southwest corner Alabama and New York.

ST. PAUL'S CHURCH.—(German) northeast cor. East and Georgia. Erected in 1861. Rev. Christian Hochstetter, pastor, residence, Ohio, corner East.

Methodist.

ALLEN CHAPEL—(col'd) north side Broadway, between Cherry and Christian av. Rev. Henry DePugh, pastor, residence, 58 Oak.

AMES CHAPEL.—Russell av. near corner Illinois.

ASBURY CHAPEL.—west side New Jersey, between Louisiana and South. Erected 1850. Number of members, 300. Rev. Samuel T. Gillett, pastor, residence, 49 School. Service Sunday, 10:30 A. M. and 7:30 P. M. Prayer meeting, Thursday 7:30 P. M. Class meeting, Sunday, 9 A. M. and 3:15 P. M. Sabbath School, 2 P. M. Dr. William Hanneman, superintendent.

BETHEL CHURCH (col'd)—180 W. Georgia. William Travan, pastor, residence, 214 N. Mississippi.

ROBERTS' CHAPEL.—Vermont, northeast corner Delaware. F. C. Holliday, pastor, residence 131 N. Meridian

STRANGE CHAPEL.—East side Tennessee, between New York and Vermont. Erected in 1842. Rev. George W. Telle, pastor, residence 183 N. Tennessee. Services Sunday 10:30 A. M. and 7 P. M. Class meeting 9 A. M. Sabbath school 2 P. M.

TRINITY CHURCH—Northwest corner Alabama and North. Erected 1865. Rev. J. M. Crawford, pastor; residence 320 N. East

THIRD STREET CHURCH—Third, between Illinois and Tennessee. Erected 1867.

WESLEY CHAPEL—Southwest corner Meridian and Circle. Erected 1827 (a new edifice in course of erection.) Rev. C. M. Sims, pastor.

GERMAN CHURCH—North side Ohio, between East and New Jersey. Erected in 1850. Rev. Gotlob Trefz, pastor, residence 224 East Ohio. Services Sunday 10:30 A. M. and 7:30 P. M.; Sabbath school 9 A. M.

AFRICAN CHURCH—North side Georgia, between Mississippi and the Canal.

Presbyterian.

FIRST CHURCH—Southwest corner Pennsylvania and New York. Erected 1865. Rev. R. D. Harper, pastor, r. 197 N. Illinois.

SECOND CHURCH—Northwest corner Pennsylvania and Vermont. Erected 1867. Rev. H. A. Edson, pastor, residence 151 N. Tennessee. Services, 10:30 A. M. and 7:30 P. M.; Sabbath school 2:15 P. M.

THIRD CHURCH—Northeast corner Illinois and Ohio. Erected 1859. Robert Sloss, pastor, residence 198 N. Illinois.

FOURTH CHURCH—Southwest corner Delaware and Market. Erected 1858. Rev. C. H. Marshall, pastor, residence 104 St. Mary.

FIFTH CHURCH —(German) East side New Jersey, between Washington and Maryland.

SEVENTH CHURCH—Northeast corner Elm and Cedar. Erected 1867. Rev. C. M. Howard, pastor, residence Virginia av. corner Noble.

EIGHTH CHURCH—(Olivet) North side McCarty, between Union and Pennsylvania. Erected 1867. Rev. L. A. Aldrich, pastor, residence 248 S. Meridian.

REFORMED CHURCH OF COVENANTERS—North side of South, between East and Noble. Erected 1863. Organized 1864. Dedicated May 1st, 1864. Building (frame) costs 6,000. Rev. John Crozier, pastor. Hours of service, Sunday 10:30 A. M. and 3:30 P. M.; Sunday school 2:30 P. M. Sunday school superintendent, ———; Number of scholars. 60. Prayer meeting, Thursday 7:30 P. M.

UNITED CHURCH—North side Ohio, between Pennsylvania and Delaware.

UNITED BRETHREN—Southeast corner New Jersey and Ohio. Number of members, 400.

Universalist.

FIRST CHURCH—Meets in Wallace's Hall, southwest corner Delaware and Maryland. Organized 1863.

SECOND CHURCH—Michigan, between Illinois and Tennessee. Organized 1867.

Mission.

ILLINOIS STREET CHURCH—Corner Illinois and Phipps.

—o—

COUNTY OFFICERS.

Clerk—William C. Smock; Deputies, C. F Rooker, D. C. Greenfield, R. W. Smock and S. L. Harvey.

Sheriff—George W. Parker; Deputies, J. Elliott, J. L. Hanna and H. C. Adams.

Treasurer—Arthur L. Wright; Deputy, B. F. Riley.

Auditor—George F. McGinnis; Deputies, F. W. Hamilton and E. M Wilmington.

Recorder—William J. Elliott.

Board of County Commissioners.

Joseph K. English, Center township; Lorenzo VanScyoc, Washington township; Aaron McCray, Wayne township.

Court Bailiffs—J. R. Shea, T. D. Amos, L. L. McFadden, J. M King.

Township Trustees.

Center—Cyrus C. Heizer.
Decatur—J. J. W. Billingsley.
Franklin—James L. Thompson.
Lawrence—Samuel Cory.
Perry—John E. Griffith.
Pike—James H. Kennedy.
Warren—William Hunter.
Washington—H. A. Haverstick.
Wayne—Alexander Jameson.

—o—

COURTS.

County Courts.

MARION CIVIL CIRCUIT COURT meets 3d
Monday in February, 4th Monday in May,
3d Monday in September, and 1st Monday
in December at the Court House; length of
term six weeks. Judge, Cyrus C. Hines;
Prosecuting Attorney, —— Howe; Clerk,
Wm. C. Smock.

MARION CRIMINAL CIRCUIT COURT
meets 1st Mondays in January and July at
the Court House. Judge, George H. Chapman; Prosecuting Attorney, John S. Duncan; Clerk, Wm. C. Smock.

COMMON PLEAS COURT meets 1st Mondays
in February, April, September and November at the Court House; length of term six
weeks. Judge, Solomon Blair; Prosecuting
Attorney; William Irvin, Clerk; Wm. C.
Smock.

Indiana Courts.

SUPREME COURT meets at the Supreme
Court Rooms (State Building) sw. cor. Washington and Tennessee, on the 4th Monday
in May and November. Chief Justice,
Charles A. Ray, Indianapolis; Judges, J. T.
Elliott, Newcastle, James S. Frazer, Warsaw, Robert Gregory, LaFayette; Attorney
General, D. E. Williamson, Greencastle;
Sheriff, Cyrus J. Dobbs, Indianapolis; Deputy, ——; Clerk, Theodore W. McCoy, Jeffersonville; Deputy, J. M. Judah, Vincennes; Reporter, James B. Black, Indianapolis.

UNITED STATES CIRCUIT COURT meets
1st Tuesdays in May and November at the
P. O. building. Circuit court held by Hon.
David Davis, Asst. Justice of the United
States Supreme Court and Hon. D. McDonald District, Judge; Clerk, John D. Howland; Deputy, W. W. Humphreys.

UNITED STATES DISTRICT COURT meets
1st Tuesdays in May and November at the
P. O. building. Judge, Hon. David McDon-
ald; Clerk, John D. Howland; Deputy, W.
W. Humphreys; District Attorney, Thomas
M. Browne; United States Marshal, Gen.
Benjamin J. Spooner; Deputies, J. S. Bige-
low, C. E. McDonald, J. C. Spooner; Land
Office Register, Edward Browing; United

States Commissioners, Edwin A. Davis, J.
W. Raymond, Eben W. Kimball, O. M. Wilson, Fred Kuefler.

—o—

FIRE DEPARTMENT.

Charles Richmond, Chief.
Engine Co. No. 1, south side Washington bet.
West and California.
Engine Co. No. 2, junction New York, Dela-
ware and Massachusetts av.
Engine Co. No. 3, south side South, bet. Del-
aware and Alabama.
Hook and Ladder Co. east side New Jersey
bet. Market and Washington.

Fire Alarm Telegraph Signals.

L. F. Yeagou, Supt.

Signal Nos.
2 No. 2 Engine House, cor. Mass. av. and
New York st.
3 Cor. East and New York st.
4 Hook & Ladder House, New Jersey st.
nr. Wash.
5 Spiegel, Thoms & Cos. factory, East st.
6 Cor. Washington and Noble.
7 Cor. Davidson and New York sts.
1—2 Cor. Noble and Michigan.
1—3 Cor. Noble and Massachusetts av.
1—4 Cor. East and Massachusetts av.
1—5 Cor. New Jersey and Ft. Wayne av.
1—6 Cor. Delaware and Ft. Wayne av.
1—7 Cor. Pennsylvania and Pratt.
1—8 Blind Asylum.
2—1 Cor. Tennessee and St. Clair.
2—3 Michigan bet. Meridian and Illinois.
2—4 Tennessee bet. Vermont and Michigan.
2—5 Cor. Illinois and Indiana av.
2—6 Cor. N. Y. and Canal—Helwig's Mill.
2—7 Cor. West and Indiana av.
3—1 No. 382 Indiana av.
3—2 Cor. Blake and Michigan.
3—4 cor. Douglass and New York.
3—4 Frank Wright's Brewery.
3—5 Cotton Factory near River.
3—6 Geisendoff's Woolen Factory, nr. River.
3—7 No. 1 Engine House, Washington bet.
West and California.
4—1 Cor West and Kentucky av.
4—2 Cor. Georgia and Mississippi, Coburn &
Jones Lumber Yard.
4—3 Cor. Washington and Tennessee.
4—5 Cor. Ills. and Louisiana, Spencer House.
4—6 Ills. and Garden, Osgood & Smith.
4—7 Cor. Illinois and McCarty.
5—1 Cor. Bluff Road and Ray.
5—2 Cor. Delaware and McCarty.
5—3 Cor. East and Dicking.
5—4 Cor. Virginia av. and Bradshaw st.
5—6 Cor. Virginia av. and Noble st.
5—7 Cor. Georgia and Benton.
6—1 No. 131 S. East st. Chief Engr's House.
6—1 Fletcher av.
6—2 No. 2 Engine House, South st., bet. Delaware and Alabama.
6—3 Gas Works.
6—4 Cor. Penn. and Ga. sts., Parley & Sinker.
6—5 Police Office, Glenn's Block.
6—7 Cor. Delaware and Washington.
7—1 No. 185 New Jersey, cor. Virginia av.

EDUCATIONAL.

Academics, Colleges, Institutes, &c.

BRYANT & STRATTON'S BUSINESS COL-
LEGE—C. E. Hollenbeck, principal; Blackford's Block, corner Washington and Meridian.

INDIANA FEMALE COLLEGE—Southwest
corner Meridian and New York. This
building affords accommodations for fifty
boarding and one hundred and fifty day pupils. Thomas Charles, principal. Board
of trustees, Rev. F. C. Holliday, president;
Oliver Tousey, vice-president; John W.
Ray, secretary: T. P. Hanghey, treasurer;
Ingram Fletcher, John W. Holland. W.
Hannaman, James C. Furguson and Jesse
Jones.

INDIANA INSTITUTE FOR THE EDUCA-
TION OF THE BLIND.—This Institution
occupying a healthful and beautiful site in
the northern part of the city, on the north
side of North between Meridian and Pennsylvania, is strictly an educational establishment, having for its object the moral,
intellectual and physical training of the
young blind of both sexes residing in the
State, and is, therefore, neither an asylum
for the aged and helpless, nor a hospital
for the treatment of disease. Trustees,
P. H. Jameson, president; John Beard and
John S. Spann. W. M. Stillwell, secretary;
W. H. Churchman, A. M., superintendent;
Miss M. E. Hanna, Miss S. A. Schofield.
Miss E. D. Starr, and Miss M. D. Naylor,
teachers in literary department; C. H.
Weegmann, G. B. Loomis, and R. A. New-
land, teachers in music department; J. W.
Bradshaw, and Miss P. W. Hawley, teach-
ers in handicraft department; Household
Officers, J. M. Kitchen, physician; W. M.
Stillwell, steward, Miss L. D. Hawley, mat-
ron.

INDIANA INSTITUTION FOR THE DEAF
AND DUMB—East Washington, out of limits. Thomas MacIntire, A. M., superintendent; Horace S. Gillett, A. M., William H.
Latham, A. M., M. D., William S. Marshall,
A. M., Walter W. Angus, Sidney J. Vail,
Harriet N. MacIntire, Annie E. Cooke, William N. Burt, A. B., John L. Houdyshell,
and Naomi S. Hiatt, Instructors; P. H.
Jameson, physician; Chapin C. Foster,
steward; Julia A. Taylor, matron. G. L.
Strang, master shoe shop; P. Jane Stiers,
mistress of tailor shop; John Hack, gardener; M. W. E. Doran, master cabinet
shop. Board of Trustees, P. H. Jameson, M.
D. president, John M. Kitchen, M. D., Jas.
C. Burt, M. D.

INDIANAPOLIS FEMALE INSTITUTE.—
This Institute is delightfully situated on the
corner of Pennsylvania and Michigan sts.,
one block north of University Park, in the
centre of a plot of ground of more than an
acre, and most beautifully shaded; making
it a most desirable location for a literary
institution. The Institute was established
to impart to its students sound learning,
to encourage thorough mental and moral
culture, by faithfully inculcating those
truths which should ever govern the moral
being without sectarian prejudice or bias.
The school-rooms are the finest in the State.
There are accommodations for one hundred
and twenty-five boarding pupils and three
hundred day pupils. The entire buildings
are warmed by means of new and improved
methods, so that all the rooms and halls are
kept in a uniform temperature, day and
night. In the improvements a large
and commodious Callstheneum has been
fitted up, so that regular and pleasant exercise under a competent teacher is secured
for the pupils at all times. Officers, Rev.
C. W. Hewes, president of the Institute;
Board of Trustees, Rev. Henry Day, president; E. C. Atkins, secretary; J. R. Osgood, treasurer. Board of Intruction;
Rev. C. W. Hewes, A. M., president, professor of Mental and Moral Philosophy;
Prof. Adrian J. Ebell, Ph. B., lecturer on
Natural History and Geology; Prof. Carl
Zoneada, teacher of Modern Languages
and Piano; Prof. J. S. Black, teacher of
the art of singing; Miss Jennie Woodbury,
teacher of Geometry, Latin, Botany, Physiology, etc.; Mrs E. Earl, teacher of French
and German, Logic, English Literature, etc.;
Miss M. E. Grafton, principal of the Primary Department; Miss Hattie J. McLure,
teacher of Grammar, Arithmetic, Geogra-
phy, etc.; Miss Eulalia Bailey, assistant
teacher in the English Department; Edward Bruel and R. J. Rabjohn, Directors of
Music, assisted by Clara J. Sawyer and
Libbie Hood; Mrs. S. S. Starling and Miss
Emma D. Wood, Teachers of Painting,
Drawing, Wax Work, Embroidery, etc.;
Mrs W. McGibbon, matron

INDIANAPOLIS LAW COLLEGE—Presi-
dent, John T. Elliott; Secretary, S. E. Perkins, Jr.; Treasurer, David McDonald;
Trustees, J. E. McDonald, F. M. Finch, M.
B. Taylor, T. A. Hendricks, A. G. Porter
and R. B. Duncan; Professors, Hon. Samuel E. Perkins, Hon. Lucien Barber.

MEDICAL COLLEGE—Faculty—Professor of
the principles and practice of Surgery, J.
S. Bobbs, M D.; Professor of Clinical and
Operative Surgery, J. A Comingore, M. D.;
Professor of Obstetrics, George W. Mears.
M. D.; Professor of the Diseases of Women
and Children. T. B. Harvey, M. D.; Pro-
fessor of Anatomy, L. D. Waterman, M.D.;
Professor of the Theory and Practice of
Medicine, R. N. Todd, M. D.; Professor of
Chemistry and Toxicology, R. T. Brown,
M. D.; Professor of Materia Medica and
Therapeutics, F. S. Newcomer, M. D.; Pro-
fessor of Physiology, W. B. Fletcher, M.
D., Demonstrator of Anatomy, Charles E.
Wright, M. D. These gentlemen, together
with Judge Samuel E. Perkins and John D.
Howland, Esq., are the Trustees of the In-
stitution. George W. Mears, M. D., Dean
of the Faculty.

N. W. C. UNIVERSITY—Corporate limits,
northeast part of the city. O. Butler, president Board of Directors, A. B. Cole, secre-

tary and treasurer. Faculty, President O. A. Burgess, A. M., Professor of Bible Department, S. K. Hoshour, A. M. Professor of Ancient and French Languages; R. T. Brown, A. M., M. D., Professor of Natural Science; W. M. Thrasher, A. M., Professor of Mathematics; H. W. Wiley, A. B., Adjunct Professor of Languages and Principal of Preparatory Department; Miss Catharine Merrill, (Demia Butler) Professor of English Literature and the German Language; Mrs. Henry C. Guffin, Teacher of Music; W. M. Thrasher, Secretary of the Faculty.

NATIONAL BUSINESS COLLEGE—A. Hollingsworth & Co., Hendrix & Koerner in charge, entrance, 24½ E. Washington.

NORMAL INSTITUTE OF PENMANSHIP—(National Business College) J. R. Goodier in charge, entrance, 24½ E. Washington.

INDIANA NORMAL ACADEMY OF MUSIC —Charles Hess, Principal; Miss Emma Wesselhoeft, assistant Teacher; 35½ E. Washington.

——o——

SCHOOLS.

Public.

The city free schools are under the general management of a Board of three Trustees, elected by the Common Council; A. C. Shortridge being clerk of the Board and Superintendent of the Public Schools. Office of the Board and Superintendent, in High School Building, corner West Market street and the Circle

BOARD OF TRUSTEES.

James C. Yohn, president, John R. Elder, secretary, and W. H. L. Noble, treasurer.

BOARD OF VISITORS.

Are appointed by the Board of Trustees, and have special supervision over the educational interests of the schools in the different wards, during the terms, and at the semi-annual and annual examinations. Marie E. Cole, secretary.

HIGH SCHOOL—W. P. Fishback and Rev. E. P. Ingersoll.

FIRST WARD—Dr. J. M. Gaston and Charles P. Jacobs.

SECOND WARD—Dr. W. B. Fletcher and Isaac C. Hays.

THIRD WARD—Rev. C. H. Marshall and Rev. R. D. Robinson.

FOURTH WARD—Rev. H. A. Edson and Hon. O. B. Hord.

FIFTH WARD—Simon Yandes and Rev. L. H. Jameson.

SIXTH WARD—A. H. Brown and A. Seidensticker.

SEVENTH WARD—Charles Secrest and S. V. B. Noel.

EIGHTH WARD—Rev. L. G. Hay and Samuel Merrill.

NINTH WARD—Rev. B. F. Rawlings and J. H. Kappes.

SCHOOLS AND TEACHERS.

There are twelve School Buildings and seventy-eight teachers. The Schools are divided into three departments: Primary, Intermediate and High School, with four grades in each department. A new School building is contemplated, and will be erected in the extreme northern portion of the city, in some elligible location, which, with the present large number of school buildings now completed, will afford accommodations equal to any city in the West, compared to the population of the city.

FIRST WARD—Southwest corner New Jersey and Vermont. Miss Henrie Colgon, principal; Mary Colgon, Chloe Murphy, Ibbie Green, Maggie Elder, Mary Cropsey, Kate Coffin, teachers.

SECOND WARD—Delaware between Vermont and Michigan. Ella S. Tysen, (Mrs.) Principal; Lutie M. Brouse, Pauline Conde, Vina A. Tedrowe, teachers.

THIRD WARD—New York between Illinois and Tennessee. Jennie Lindley, Mary Taylor, Emma Root, teachers.

FOURTH WARD—(Old House) Market west of West, (New House) Michigan northeast corner Blackford. W. J. Button, principal; Amanda P. Funnelle Emma Laird, Annie Tyler, Ella Coffin, Hannah Collins, Annie Barbour, Marie Bradshaw, teachers.

FIFTH WARD—Maryland between Mississippi and Missouri. Eliza T. Ford, principal; Mary Kelley, Augusta Brown, Laura Ford, Mattie McEnnally, Anna Winder, Bette Jameson, Alice Wilson, teachers.

FIFTH WARD BRANCH (Colony School)— South side Root near River. Miss M. A. McEnnally, in charge.

SIXTH WARD—Union between Merrill and McCarty. Helen A. Davis, principal, Mattie A. Robinson, Mrs. Emma Colwell, Mary E. Laughlin. Mary E. Wilson, Etta Bradshaw, Lizzie Murphy, Belle Crawford Sarah Sloan, Alice Gray, Grace D. Wilson, teachers; Louise Seeberger, and Mrs. E. S. Miller, teachers German department.

SEVENTH WARD—East between Georgia and Louisiana. Mary Ingersoll, Alice Secrest, teachers.

EIGHTH WARD—Virginia avenue corner Huron. Maria H. Jones, principal, Mrs. Sarah C. Wirt, Abbie Davis, Mattie Campbell, Julia Stevens, Alvina Nichols, Clara Harlan, teachers.

NINTH WARD—(Old House) corner Vermont and Davidson, (New House) corner Michigan and Davidson. Mary E. Perrott, Mrs. Mary Aborn, Ada Khem, Mrs. Nannie Noble, Linnie Doxon, Mrs. Mary Curry, Mattie Gregory, Sarah Beck, Amanda Shoemaker, Flora Finch, Jennie Newton, teachers; Dora Miller, Kate Oechles, teachers German department.

2

A. GRADE, Intermediate Department—High School Building. Fidelia Anderson, Maggie Bell, teachers.

HIGH SCHOOL.—Market northwest corner Circle. Wm. A. Bell, principal, Eliza Cammell, Emily Johnson, Mary Kreutzer, Mrs. E. A. Green, Sarah Kelley, teachers. Special Teachers—George B. Loomis, Music; Miss N. Cropsey, Primary Astronomy; Annie Griggs, Gymnastics; Selma Ingersoll, Writing.

NUMBER OF TEACHERS AND PUPILS IN EACH WARD.

See the following Schedule:

Wards.	NUMBER OF PUPILS.			TEACHERS.		
	Boys.	Girls.	Total.	M.	F.	Total
1	200	196	396		7	7
2	119	127	246		4	4
3	95	89	184		3	3
4	301	306	607	1	7	8
5	208	174	382		8	8
6	303	357	660		14	14
7 & 8	309	300	609		9	9
9	321	304	625		13	13
A. Int.	38	53	91		2	2
H. S.	59	81	140	1	5	6
	1853	1987	3840	2	72	74
Special Teachers				1	3	4
				3	75	78

STATEMENT OF SCHOOL PROPERTY.

The estimated value of improvments, includes buildings, fences and furniture,

FIRST WARD SCHOOL HOUSE—Corner of Vermont and New Jersey streets. Size of lot, 90 by 195 feet. Building, brick, two stories, five school rooms. Capacity for 293 pupils. Value of lot, $7,000; value of improvements, $6,000; total, $13,000.

SECOND WARD SCHOOL HOUSE—Delaware street, between Vermont and Michigan. Size of lot, 101 by 195 feet. Building, brick, two stories, four school rooms. Capacity for 234 pupils. Value of lot, $3,000; value of improvements, $4,000; total $13,000.

THIRD WARD SCHOOL HOUSE—New York street, between Illinois and Tennessee. Size of lot, 82.6 by 195 feet. Building, brick, two stories, three school rooms. Capacity for 168 pupils. Value of lot, $5,000; value of improvements, $6,000; total, $11,000.

FOURTH WARD SCHOOL HOUSE—Market street between West and California. Size of lot, 67.6 by 204 feet. Building, brick, one story, two school rooms. Capacity for 154 pupils. Value of lot, $3,000; value of improvements, $3,000; total, $6,000.

FOURTH WARD, NEW SCHOOL HOUSE—Corner of Michigan and Blackford streets. Size of lot, 157.4½ by 210 feet. Building, brick, two stories and attic, nine school rooms. Capacity for 500 pupils. Value of lot, $4,000; value of improvements, $32,000; total, $36,000.

FIFTH WARD SCHOOL HOUSE—Maryland street, between Mississippi and the Canal. Size of lot, 67.6 by 195 feet. Building, brick, two stories, five school rooms. Capacity for 285 pupils. Value of lot $4,000; value of improvements, $9,000, total, $13,000.

FIFTH WARD, NEW SCHOOL HOUSE—Root street, between West and White River. Size of lot—north front on Root street, 144 feet; east on alley, 231; south on Kingan street, 291; West on the river, 300 feet. Building, frame, one story, two school rooms. Capacity for 128 pupils. Value of lot, $3,500; value of improvements, $2,000; total, $5,500.

SIXTH WARD SCHOOL HOUSE—Union street, between Merrill and McCarty. Size of lot, 233.4½ by (average of) 160 feet. Building, brick, four stories. Capacity, 800 pupils. Value of lot, $6,500; improvements, $10,000; total, $46,500.

SEVENTH WARD SCHOOL HOUSE—East street, north of Louisiana. Size of lot, 90 by 202 feet. Building, brick, one story, two school rooms. Capacity for 107 pupils. Value of lot, $5,000; value of improvements, $2,500; total, $7,500.

EIGHTH WARD SCHOOL HOUSE—Virginia avenue, corner of Huron street. Size of lot, on Virginia avenue, 238.6 feet; on Huron street, 163 feet; north line, 134.5 feet; south side, 123.4 feet. Building, brick, three stories, six school rooms. Capacity for 364 pupils. Value of lot, $5,500; value of improvements, $10,000; total, $15,500.

NINTH WARD SCHOOL HOUSE—Corner of Vermont and Davidson streets. House rented. Capacity for 200 pupils.

NINTH WARD, NEW SCHOOL HOUSE—Corner of Michigan and Davidson streets. Size of lot, 140 by 150 feet. Building, two stories and an attic, nine school rooms. Capacity for 500 pupils. Value of lot, $4,000; value of improvements, $32,000; total, $36,000.

TOTAL VALUATION—Total value of the school property, $213,000.

Schools Colored.

ALLEN CHAPEL DAY SCHOOL—S. A. Elbert, principal; north side Broadway, bet. Cherry and Christian avenue.

FOURTH WARD DISTRICT SCHOOL.—South side Market, between West and California. George H. W. Stewart, teacher,

PUBLIC SCHOOL.—180 West Georgia. Melinda Lawrence, teacher.

SCHOOL—642 North Mississippi. J. M. Williams, teacher.

RUFUS CONRAD, (col') teacher, Second, near Lafayette Railroad.

Schools Parochial and Private.

GERMAN-ENGLISH SCHOOL—Established 1859. Theodore Dingeldey, principal. North side Maryland, between Delaware and Alabama.

GERMAN EVANGELICAL SCHOOL—South East, opposite Stevens. M. G. I. Stern, principal.

GERMAN LUTHERAN SCHOOL—Herman Fruchtenicht, principal. North side Georgia, between East and Liberty.

NORTH OHIO, between Delaware and Pennsylvania. Minnie Jewell, principal.

PENNSYLVANIA, southwest corner South. Maurice Ferriter, teacher.

ST. JOHN'S SCHOOL, FOR BOYS—Brothers of the Sacred Heart, in charge. North side Georgia, between Illinois and Tennessee.

ST. JOHN'S SCHOOL FOR GIRLS—Located South Tennessee, ne. cor. Georgia. Sisters of Providence, in charge.

STAINT MARY'S GERMAN CATHOLIC SCHOOL—Alley between Pennsylvania and Delaware, Maryland and Georgia.

ST. PETER'S CATHOLIC SCHOOL—Dougherty, near Virginia avenue.

49 NORTH ALABAMA—Mrs. Sarah A. Smith, principal.

——o——

INCORPORATED COMPANIES.

——

BUILDERS AND MANUFACURERS ASSOCIATION. Organized April 1st 1867. Capital Stock $50,000. C. Eden, Pres. James Hassen. Sec. J. L. Avery, Treas.
BOARD OF DIRECTORS.—C. Eden, Pres. J. L. Avery, Treas. James Hassen, Sec. John B. Many, H. W. Hildebrand, T. W. Brouse, E. Daly.

CITIZENS STREET RAILWAY COMPANY. Office ns. Louisiana bet. S. Illinois and S. Tennessee. Incorporated June 4th 1861. Authorized capital $250,000. E. S. Alvord, Pres. W. H. English, Treas. R. F. Fletcher, Supt. J. C. Alvord, Sec.
DIRECTORS.—E. S. Alvord, W. H. English, J. B. Slosson, E. G. English, R. F. Fletcher.

INDIANAPOLIS COAL AND MINING COMPANY. Office No. 19 Circle street. Incorporated April 1st 1866.
OFFICERS.—Dr. W. S. Pierce, Pres. Edwin Carpenter, Sec. Nathaniel Carpenter, Treas. and Supt. Prof. R. T. Brown. Mineralogist and Geologist, W. H. Turner & Co. Lessees.
DIRECTORS.—Dr. W. S. Pierce, Wm. Braden, Delosa Root, John C. Green, John M. Todd, Wm. L. Pyle, Ezra Carpenter.

INDIANAPOLIS COTTON MANUFACTURING COMPANY. Washington, (Nat. Road) north of the bridge. Capital Stock $150,000.
OFFICERS.—John Thomas, Pres. Wm. Rowe, Treas. Wm. Wilson, Sec. R. P. Duncan, Supt.

DIRECTORS.—John Thomas J. C. Geisendorff, W. W. Leathers, Wm. Wallace, Wm. Rowe, Nathan Kimball.

INDIANAPOLIS GAS LIGHT AND COKE CO. S. A. Fletcher, Jr. Pres. S. A. Fletcher Sr. Treas. L. VanLaningham, Sec., Pennsylvania ne. cor. Maryland.

INDIANAPOLIS PIANO MANUFACTURING COMPANY. Office and Factory 159 and 161 E. Washington. Incorporated January 1868. Capital Stock $100,000. J. A. Geisendorff, Pres. Isaac Thalman, Sec. and Treas. W. H. Robinson, Supt.

INDIANAPOLIS PRINTING AND PUBLISHING HOUSE. Incorporated Feb. 1869. Capital Stock $20,000.
OFFICERS,—W. W. Dowling, Pres. Scott Butler, Sec. and Treas.
DIRECTORS.—W. W. Dowling, J. E. Downey, Elijah Goodwin, John Doughty, Ovid Butler, Sr.

INDIANAPOLIS ROLLING MILL CO. capital $600,000.
OFFICERS.—John M. Lord. Pres. and Supt. C. B. Parkman, Sec. A. Jones, Treas. John Thomas, Manager.
DIRECTORS.—J. M. Lord, John Thomas, Wm. O. Rockwood, E. J Peck, A. Jones.

INDIANAPOLIS AND ST. LOUIS SLEEPING CAR COMPANY, H. Q. Sanderson, President; Charles J. Sanderson Secretary and Treasurer. Office Union Depot.

INDIANAPOLIS WAGON AND AGRICULTURAL WORKS. Incorporated, December 1866. Authorized capital, $100,000. Office and factory, No. 172 S. Tennessee st.
OFFICERS.—W. H. Jones, Pres, George T. Moore, Sec. and Treas. W. A. Pattison, Agent.

UNION NOVELTY WOKS MANUFACTURING COMPANY. Organized Jan. 1869. Capital $45,000. Located W. St. Clair, cor. Canal, office same.
OFFICERS—S. C. Frink, Pres. R. S. Dorsey, Sec. and Treas. H. A. Moore, Supt.
DIRECTORS.—S. C. Frink, R. S. Dorsey, H. A. Moore, E. O. Frink.

WHITE RIVER AND BIG EAGLE CREEK GRAVEL ROAD CO. OFFICERS.—John H. Wiley, Pres. W. P. Clements, Sec.

——o——

INSURANCE COMPANIES.

(Home Companies.)

EQUITABLE, a mutual company, incorporated 1861, now closing business. Wm. Manlove, receiver; office, room 4, Eden's block, Market street.

FRANKLIN LIFE INSURANCE COMPANY, organized August 1st 1866, office cor. Illinois and Kentucky av. James Ray, Pres. Wm. S. Hubbard, Vice Pres. and Treas., Edward P. Howe, Secy., Bennet F. Witt. Gen. Supervising Agent.

GERMAN MUTUAL FIRE INSURANCE CO. Organized 1854. Cash capital $38040. A. Seidensticker, Pres. Valentine Butsch, Vice President, Fred. Ritzinger, Sec, 16 S. Delaware.

HOME, a mutual company organized in 1864, now closing business, under the management of a receiver. Charles W. Smith, Jr., room 5, Yohn's blk., N. Meridian.

INDIANA FIRE, originally a mutual company, organized 1862, now doing business on the stock system, with a capital of about $200,000. J. S. Harvey, Pres., W. T. Gibson, Sec., office, room 5 Odd Fellows' Hall, over Indianapolis National Bank, cor. Washington and Pennsylvania.

INDIANAPOLIS, a stock company, chartered 1836, authorized capital, $500,000; office in old bank building, cor. Virginia av. and S. Pennsylvania. Wm. Henderson, Pres., Alexander C. Jameson, Secy.

SINNISSIPPI, a mutual company, organized in ——, now closing business under the management of a receiver, T. W. Whittman, over 87 E. Market.

UNION, a stock company, organized 1865, with a cash capital of $200,000, has lately retired from business by reinsuring her risks in the Home Insurance Co., of New York.

—o—

INDIANA STATE GOVERNMENT.

Governor—Conrad Baker, Indianapolis.
Lieut Governor — Will Cumback, Greensburg.
Governor's Private Secy.—John Commons.
Secretary of State—Max F. A. Hoffman.
Auditor of State—John D. Evans.
Treasurer of State—Nathan Kimball, Indianapolis.
Superintendent of Public Instruction—Barnabas C. Hobbs, Indianapolis.
State Librarian—Moses G. McClain.
Attorney General—D. E. Williamson.
Adjutant General—To be appointed.

—o—

Indiana Military Agency.

Office cor. Tennessee and Market. General Agent, William Hannaman, Indianapolis; John G. Greenawalt, Notary Public.

—o—

NEWSPAPERS AND PUBLICATIONS.

AMERICAN HOUSEWIFE, Mrs. M. M. B. Goodwin, editor and propr. Issued by the Indianapolis Printing and Publishing House.
BEHARRELL'S BIBLICAL BIOGRAPHY, Donney & Brouse, publishers. Issued by the Indianapolis Printing and Publishing House.

COMMERCIAL, (Daily Evening), M. T. Lee, editor and propr. Illinois, ne. cor. Washington.
FUTURE, (German Weekly), issued by the Gutenberg Co. Meridian, se. cor. Circle.
HEART AND HAND, (monthly), Rev. E. P. Ingersoll, editor; A. A. Barnes & Co., publishers; office, 33 E. Washington.
INDEPENDENT, (monthly) S. T. Montgomery, editor, 104 S. Pennsylvania.
INDIANA MASONIC HOME ADVOCATE, (monthly), F. M. Blair, editor and publisher. 44 N. Pennsylvania, Vinton's Block.
INDIANA SCHOOL JOURNAL, (monthly), G. W. Hoss and Thomas Charles, editors and props. Issued by the Indianapolis Printing and Publishing House.
INDIANA TEACHER, (monthly), John B. Allen, editor and propr. Issued by the Indianapolis Printing and Publishing House.
INDIANA VOLKSBLATT, (weekly), J. Boetticher, editor and propr. 164 E. Washington.
INDIANAPOLIS JOURNAL, Republican, (daily except Sunday, weekly, Friday). Douglass & Conner, publishers, Market, ne. cor. Circle, (Journal bldg.)
JOLLY HOOSIER, (monthly), A. C. Roach, editor and publisher. Issued by the Journal office, Market, ne. cor. Circle.
LADIES' CHRISTIAN MONITOR, (monthly) Mrs. M. M. B. Goodwin, editor and propr. Issued by the Indianapolis Printing and Publishing House.
LADIES OWN MAGAZINE, (Monthly), Mrs. M Cora Bland, editor. Bland & Taylor, publishers, 19 N. Meridian.
LITTLE CHIEF, (monthly), Shortridge & Alden, editors and proprs. Issued by the Indianapolis Printing and Publishing House.
LITTLE SOWER, (weekly), W. W. Dowling, editor and propr. Issued by the Indianapolis Printing and Publishing House.
MIRROR, (daily, Sundays excepted, weekly Saturday), independent, Harding. Morton & Finch, publishers, 19 N. Meridian.
MOCKING BIRD, (German weekly, Sunday) issued by the Gutenburg Co., Meridian, se. cor. Circle.
MORNING WATCH, (monthly) W. W. Dowling, editor and propr. Issued by the Indianapolis Printing and Publishing House.
MOTHER'S MONITOR, (monthly) Mrs. M. M. B. Goodwin, editor and propr. Issued by the Indianapolis Printing and Publishing House.
NORTHWESTERN, (monthly), Martin & Hopkins, editors and publishers, Market, ne. cor. Circle, (Journal bldg.)
NORTHWESTERN FARMER, (monthly), Bland & Taylor, editors and proprs., 19 N. Meridian
ODD FELLOWS' TALISMAN, (monthly) R. J. Strickland, editor and publisher, 30 S. Meridian.
OLD OAKEN BUCKET, (monthly), Cowen & Protzman, publishers and proprs. Issued by Sentinel office, 16 E. Washington.

ROACH'S WESTERN MUSEUM, (monthly).
A. C. Roach, editor and publisher. Issued
by *Journal* office, Market, ne. cor. Circle.

SPARKLING GEM, (monthly), Mrs. M. M. B.
Goodwin, editor, A. Q. Goodwin, publisher,
30 S. Meridian.

STATE SENTINEL, (daily, except Sunday,
weekly, Wednesday), R. J. Bright, propr.;
J. J. Bingham, editor in chief; J. H. Holliday, local editor; John Schley, night editor.
16½ E. Washington.

SUNBEAM, (monthly), William Travis, editor. Issued by the Indianapolis Printing
and Publishing House.

TELEGRAPH, (German), published daily and
weekly by the Gutenburg Co., C. Beyschlag,
editor. Office Meridian, *ne.* cor. Circle.

THE INVENTOR AND MECHANIC, a journal of industrial art, published monthly by
Charles Werbe, propr., 81 E. Market.

WESTERN FIRESIDE, (monthly) F. C. Holliday, editor; R. R. City Printing Co.,
proprs., 35½ E. Market, Vinton's Block.

WESTERN MANUFACTURER'S REVIEW
AND RAILROAD JOURNL, (semi-month-
ly), A. L. Logan, editor and propr., 30 S.
Meridian.

WESTERN MUSICAL REVIEW, (monthly),
H. L. Benham & Co., editors and publishers, No. 1 Martindale's Block, Market, ne.
cor. Pennsylvania. Issued at *Journal* office.

—o—

PUBLIC HALLS, BLOCKS, OF-
FICES AND BUILDINGS.

ACADEMY OF MUSIC, se. cor. Illinois and
Ohio.

ÆTNA BUILDING. es. Pennsylvania bet.
Washington and Market.

ALVORD'S BLOCK. sw. cor. Meridian and
Georgia.

BATES HOUSE BLOCK, Illinois nw, cor.
Washington.

BISMARK HALL, Virginia av. nr. McCarty.

BLACKFORD'S BLOCK, Washington se.
cor. Meridian.

BLAKE BLOCK, ss. Washington bet. Illinois
and Tennessee.

BROWN'S BLOCK, Pennsylvania nw. cor.
Washington.

CHAMBER OF COMMERCE, Vinton's Block,
Pennsylvania sw. cor. Market.

CITY OFFICES, Glenn's Block.

COLLEGE HALL, sw. cor. Washington and
Pennsylvania.

COMMERCIAL BUILDING, cor. Meridian
and Circle.

COUNTY BUILDINGS, Court House Square,
ns. Washington bet. Delaware and Ala-
hama.

COUNTY OFFICES, Court House Square,
ns. Washington bet. Delaware and Alabama.

DAUBENSPECK'S BLOCK, 17 to 27 Massachusetts av.

EDEN'S BLOCK, ss. Market bet. Pennsylvania and Delaware.

EMENEGGER HALL, ss. Washington bet.
Delaware and Alabama.

FATOUT'S BLOCK, ss Washington bet.
Mississippi and Canal.

GALLUP'S BLOCK, Tennessee se. cor.
Market.

GLENN'S BLOCK, ss. Washington bet.
Meridian and Pennsylvania.

GOOD TEMPLAR'S HALL, sw. cor. Meridian and Washington.

GYMNASIUM HALL, nw. cor. Meridian and
Maryland.

HERETH'S BLOCK, N. Delaware opposite
Court House.

HUBBARD'S BLOCK, Washington, sw. cor.
Meridian.

JOURNAL BUILDING, Market, ne. cor.
Circle.

MARMONT HALL, H. Marmont, propr. 102,
104 and 106 S. Illinois.

MARTINDALE'S BLOCK, Pennsylvania ne.
cor. Market.

MASONIC HALL, W. Washington se. cor.
Tennessee.

METROPOLITAN THEATRE, 84 W. Washington.

MILLER'S BLOCK, nw. cor. Illinois and
Market.

MILLER'S HALL, cor. Delaware and Pearl.

MORRISON'S BLOCK, Meridian, nw. cor.
Maryland.

MORRISON'S OPERA HALL, Meridian ne.
cor. Maryland.

MOZART HALL, es. Delaware bet. Washington and Maryland.

MUSIC HALL, ns. Court bet. Delaware and
Pennsylvania.

NEWS BLOCK, 10 and 12 E. Washington.

NORWOOD BLOCK, ws. Illinois bet. Washington and Market.

ODD FELLOWS' HALL & BUILDING, ne.
cor. Pennsylvania and Washington.

PALMER HOUSE BLOCK, ne. cor. Illinois
and Washington.

POST OFFICE, Pennsylvania se. cor. Market.

REVENUE DETECTIVE, (State) J. T. Bryer,
No. 4 Vinton's Block.

ROBERT'S BLOCK, ns. Louisiana opposite
Depot.

SCHNULL'S BLOCK, sw. cor. Meridian and
Maryland.

SEIDENSTICKER'S BLOCK, opposite ss.
Union Depot.

SHERMAN HOUSE BLOCK, Louisiana opposite Depot.

STATE HOUSE, full square bet. Washington
and Market and Tennessee and Mississippi.

SUPERVISOR OF INTERNAL REVENUE,
(State) G. B. Williams, room 4 Vinton's
Block.

SUPREME COURT AND STATE OFFICE
BUILDING, sw. cor. Washington and
Tennessee.

TALBOTT & NEW'S BLOCK, es. Pennsylvania bet. Washington and Market.

TEMPERANCE HALL, ns. Washington bet.
Illinois and Meridian.

THORP'S HALL & BLOCK, ss. Market bet.
Pennsylvania and Delaware.

TILFORD'S BUILDING, Meridian se. cor. Circle.

TURNER HALL, ns. Maryland bet. Delaware and Alabama.

UNION DEPOT, Louisiana bet. Illinois and Meridian.

UNION HALL, ss. Washington bet. Delaware and Alabama

UNITED STATES OFFICES AND COURT ROOM, in Post Office Building se. cor. Pennsylvania and Market.

VINTON'S BLOCK, Pennsylvania sw. cor. Market.

WALLACE'S HALL, 54 S. Delaware

WASHINGTON HALL, Philip Fahrback propr. 78 and 80 W. Washington.

WILEY'S BLOCK, ws. Pennsylvania bet. Market and Washington.

YOHN'S BLOCK, Meridian ne. cor. Washington.

———o———

SECRET AND BENEVOLENT SOCIETIES.

MASONIC.

Ancient and Honorable Order of Free and Accepted Masons.

THE GRAND LODGE—Meets in the city of Indianapolis, at the Grand Masonic Hall, West Washington street, southeast corner Tennessee, Tuesday after the fourth Monday in May, annually. Grand Secretary's office in Grand Masonic Hall. Martin H. Rice, M. W. G. M. of Plymoth; Geo. W. Potter, R. W. G. D. M. of New Albany; Wm. T. Clark, R. W. S. G. W. of Indianapolis; Christian Fetta, R. W. J. G. W. of Indianapolis; John M. Bremwell, R. W. G. S. of Indianadolis; Charles Fisher, R. W. G. T. of Indianapolis.

THE GRAND CHAPTER—Meets annually on the third Wednesday in October.

GRAND COUNCIL—R. and S. Masters—Meets annually on Tuesday before the third Wednesday in October.

GRAND COMMANDERY—Meets on the first Tuesday in April. Thomas Newby, of Cambridge City, M. E. G. Commander; David P. Wheden, of Fort Wayne, R. E. D. G. C.; Thomas Pattison, of Aurora, G. G.; Elbridge G. Hamilton. of Laporte, G. C. G.; Charles Fisher, of Indianapolis, G. T.; John M. Bramwell, of Indianapolis, G. R.; Rev. Thomas H. Lynch, of Brookville, E. G. P.; George A. Johnson, of Cambridge City, G. S. W.; George V. Howk, of New Albany, G. I. W.; George H. Fish, of Evansville, G. Staudard B.; W. F. Cushing, of South Bend, G. W.; William M. Black, of Indianapolis, G. C. G.

Subordinate Lodges in Indianapolis.

The six following Subordinate Lodges meet in the Grand Masonic Hall, West Washington street, corner Tennessee.

CENTRE LODGE, NO. 23—meets on the first Wednesday in each month. Benjamin C. Darrow, W. M.; Joseph Solomon, S. W.; George W. Tucker, J. W. (pro tem.); Henry Daumont, Treas.; Charles Fisher, Sec.

MARION LODGE, NO. 35—Meets on the third Wednesday in each month. John Ebert, W. M.; J. Saylor, S. W.; John M. Bramwell, Sec.

TEUTONIA LODGE, NO. 178—Meets on the second Wednesday in each month. Officers elected June. J. C. Brinkmeyer, Meridian.

CAPITAL CITY LODGE, NO. 312—Meets on the first Tuesday in each month. W. H. Ireland, W. M.; J. H. Colclazer, S. W.; W. Kitzmiller, J. W.; Fred. Baggs, Treas.; G. H. Fleming, Sec.: A. L. Stoner, S. D.; Wm. Weir, J. D.; H. Seibert, S.; M. D. Stacy, S.; Thomas Vance, T.

ANCIENT LANDMARKS LODGE, NO. 319 —Meets on the first Thursday in each month. George Warren, W. M.; Julius C. Walk, S. W.; Charles A. Bates, J. W.; Barton D. Jones, Treas; Ephraim Hartwell, Sec.; W. H. Valentine, S D.; Arthur Galbraith, J. D.; Thomas C. Tilt, S.; Chas. McGuire, S.; Charles John, T.

MYSTIC TIE LODGE, W. D.—Meets on the fourth Monday in each Month. John Craven, W.; George Engle, jr., S. W.; ——Smith, M. D ; Wm. Cone, Sec.; John Reynold, Treas.

INDIANAPOLIS CHAPTER, NO. 5—Meets on the first Friday in each month. Roger Parry, H. P.; Ephraim Colestock, K.; Jacob King, S.; John Ebert, C. H.; W. S. Cone, P. S.; Charles A. H. Bates, R. A. C.; Thomas C. Rout, G. M. 3d V.; Joshua R. McKibbon, G. M. 2d V.; Henry Daumont, G. M. 1st V.

INDIANAPOLIS COUNCIL, NO. 2—Meets on the first Monday in each month. John Ebert, I. G. M.; Roger Parry, Dep. I. G. M.; Ephraim Colestock, P.C. W.; J. R. McKibbon, C. G.; H. Daumont, Treas.; C. Fisher, R.

RAPER COMMANDERY, NO. 1—Meets on the fourth Wednesday in each month. Roger Parry, E. C.; Alfred L. Webb, G.; Wm. H. Bullard, C. G ; John Ebert, P.; Geo. H. Fleming, S. W.; W. S. Cone, J. W.; H. Daumont, Treas.; C. Fisher, R ; H. S. Bighan. W.

———o———

ODD FELLOWS.

———

Independent Order of Odd Fellows.

THE GRAND LODGE OF INDIANA,—Holds its semi-annual communication at Odd Fellows' Hall, in the city of Indianapolis, on the third Tuesdays of May and November of each year.

CAPITAL LODGE, NO. 124—John B. Kelley, Noble Grand; Carlin Hamlin, Vice Grand; Henry C. Adams, Secretary; John F. Wallick, Permanent Secretary; John McElwe, Treasurer; James H. Hodges and M. R. Barnard, Representatives to Grand Lodge; Henry W. McCune, R. S. to N. G., Frederick J. Prail, L. S. to N. G.; Ben. D. House, R. S. to V. G.; Calvin F. Rooke Warden; A. R. Miller, Conductor; Artemus Morris, I. S.; Paul Sherman, O. S.; Eli Thompson, R. S. S.; Henry Nichols, L. S. L.; Moses R. Bernard, Chaplain.

LODGE NO. 18, — Noble Grand, E. M. Byrkitt; Vice Grand, E. A. Ferguson; Recording Secretary, Charles Maguire; Permanent Secretary, George P. Anderson; Treasurer, John G. Waters; Representatives to Grand Lodge, Samuel W. Cochran and John A. Buchanan; Trustees, Henry Allen, James H. Perry, and John G. Pendergast.

METROPOLITAN ENCAMPMENT, NO. 5— A. B. Howard, Chief Patriarch; V. G. Dickhout, High Priest; Charles Maguire, Senior Warden; Philip H. Oyler, Junior Warden; Samuel P. Daniels, Scribe; Geo. D. Staats, Per. Scribe; John Reynolds, Treasurer; Samuel W. Cochran. William Kitzmiller and Henry M. Mounts, Representatives to the Grand Encampment.

OLIVE BRANCH REBECCA DEGREE LODGE, NO. 6—Joseph S. Watson, Noble Grand; Jonathan Elliott, Vice Grand; Geo. D. Staats, Secretary; Mrs. Jona Elliott, Treasurer; Cal. Rooker, Chaplain; John McCloskey, Warden; Mrs. Frank Glazier, Conductor; Brother Noe, I. G.; Sister Raymond, R. S. to N. G.; Sister Noe, L. S. to N. G.; Sister Ellms, R. S. to V. G.; Sister Prail, L. S. to V. G.; Visiting Committee—Sisters A. McLane, F. Glazier, and S. P. Daniels.

——o——

GOOD TEMPLARS.

Independent Order of Good Templars.

RIGHT WORTHY GRAND LODGE OFFICERS—R. W. G. T., J. Orne, of Marblehead, Mass. R. W. G. C., H. H. Giles, of Stoughton Wis. R. W. G. V. T., Miss Rebecca J. Reed, West Va. R. W. G. S., J. A. Spencer. Ohio. R. W. G. T., John Campbell, Missouri. R. W. G. C., Rev. S. H. Platt, New York. R. W. G. M., M. M. Earle, Sand Creek, N. Y. R. W. G. D. M., Mrs. A. H. Leonard, Minn. R. W. G. I. G., J. Norwood, Iowa City, Iowa. R. W. G. O. G., S. S. King. Pennsylvania. P. R. W. G. T., Samuel D. Hastings, Wis. GRAND LODGE OFFICERS—G. W. C. T., S. T. Montgomery, Indianapolis. G. W. C., M. H. Mendenhall, Indianapolis. G. W. V. T., Maggie M. Gray, Memphis. G. W. S., D. R. Pershing, Warsaw. G. W. T., S. Johnson, Centreville. P. G. W. C. T., Miss A. M. Way, Indianapolis. G. W. Chaplain, D. C. Benjamin, Carthage. G. W. M., J.

Knight, Anderson. G. W. D. M., Cassie Davis, Renolds, Indiana. G. W. I. G., Bell Rossman, Winchester G. W. O. G., W. R. Shepperd, Martinsville
CENTRE LODGE No. 322—Meets every Tuesday evening at Wood's Hall, 64 E. Washington; F. M. Hawkins, W C. T.
CHARITY LODGE—Meets every Friday evening at Berg's Hall, ne. cor. Smith and Tennessee, Rev. L. A. Aldrich, W. C. T.
GOUGH LODGE No, 178—Meets every Monday evening at Moore's Hall, 64 E. Washington, Lea M. Lemmons, W. C. T.
JULIAN LODGE No. 178 (col'd)—Meets every Wednesday evening at Temperance Hall, 30 W. Washington
MARION LODGE—Meets Friday evening at Baptist Chapel, sw. cor. South and Noble.
NORTHERN STAR LODGE (col'd)—Meets Wednesday evening of each week at Wood's Hall 64 E. Washington, William Walden, W. C. T.
WAY LODGE—Meets Saturday evening of each week se. cor. Washington and Meridian, C. G. Coffin, W. C. T.

——o——

DRUIDS.

OCTAVIAN GROVE No. 3, U. A. O. D.— Meets every Monday evening at 27 S. Meridian; H. Hofman, E. E., D. Grier, E. E., F. Lange, U. E., A. Dikmann, Secy., F. Damme, Financial Secy., A. Kaiser, Treas.
HUMBOLDT GROVE No. 8 U. A. O. D.— Meets Wednesday evening of each week at 27 S. Meridian; Joseph Viernikel, E. E., Frederick Fels, U. E.. Herman Gruenert, Secy., John Goebel, Financial Secy., Wm. Shoeneman, J. W., Geo. Fahrian, Schatzen.

——o——

SOCIETIES AND ASSOCIATIONS.

BETHOVEN SOCIETY (Amateur)—Organized February 1st, 1869. Regular meetings are on Monday night of each week, at the rooms of the Indiana Normal Academy of Music, No. 35 E. Washington. J. B. Follet, pres.; M. H. Spades, vice pres.; U. T. Woodbury, sec.; R. Russell, treas.; A. M. Kuhn, librarian; Charles Hess, director.

BUTCHERS' ASSOCIATION—William Shoensberger, pres.; David Wexler, treas.; F. Borst, sec. Meets Thursday evening of each week.

ECLECTIC MEDICAL ASSOCIATION—D. H. Prank, pres.; J. F. Ridgeway, 1st vice; G. W. Pickerill, sec.; L Abbott, treas.

GERMAN BENEVOLENT SOCIETY—Meets first Friday evening of each month, in Emmenegger's Hall, opposite Court House. George Ferling, sec.

GERMAN TURNERS' GYMNASTIC ASSOCIATION—Chas. Koehne, pres; Peter Lieber, vice pres.; I. W. Loeper, cor. sec.; Dr M. Loeper, rec. sec.; F. W. Schliebitz,

1st master of exercises; Ad. Barthels, 2d master of exercises; Charles Stierle, treas.; O. Schindler, librarian; B. Bamvart, janitor; C. I. M. Koster, John Haehle, Jacob Huber, trustees. Meets first Wednesday in every month, for business; Monday and Thursday, for exerciser, at Turner Hall, Maryland between Delaware and Alabama.

GERMAN TURN-VEREIN (Gymnastic Society)—John Rosenberg, pres.; Henry Bauer, vice pres.; Lorenz Schmidt, treas.; Herrmann Brandt, sec.; Albert M. Behrendt, corresponding sec.; Louis Fleury, 1st turnwart. Meets in Mozart Hall—S. Delaware—Monday and Thursday, for exercises; first Wednesday of each month for business.

HARMONIA (German Musical)—Meets on Monday and Wednesday evening of each week, at Marmont Hall. Aug. Mueller, director.

HOME FOR FRIENDLESS WOMEN.—Pennsylvania north of limits. Officers—James Smith, superintendent; Sarah J. Smith, city missionary; Susan L. Horney, matron. Officers of the Board of Managers—Mrs. John S. Newman, president; Mrs. J. L. Ketcham, Mrs. Hannah Hadley, vice presidents; Mrs. C. N. Todd, treasurer; Mrs. Charles W. Moores, corresponding secretary; Mrs. J. H. Kappes, recording secretary; Mrs. J. M. Ray, auditor. Officers of the board of trustees—James M. Ray, president; Samuel Merrill, vice president; William S. Hubbard, treasurer; James Nevill, M. D., clerk; D. E. Snyder, auditor.

INDIANAPOLIS ACADEMY OF MEDICINE—Meets at the rooms of the Young Men's Christian Associaton. Tuesday evening of each week. J. A. Comingore, pres.; F. S. Newcomer, vice pres.; Chas. Wright, Sec.; J. M. Kitchen, treas.

INDIANAPOLIS FEMALE BIBLE SOCIETY—Mrs. M. Given, pres.; Mrs. —— Rockwood, vice pres.; Miss J. A. Bassett, sec.; Managers: Mrs. E. Wilkins, Mrs. F. C. Holliday, Eliza Newman, Mrs. Amanda Bassett, Mrs. James M. Ray, Mrs. C. Todd, and others. Depository at Todd, Carmichael & Williams', 35 E. Washington.

INDIANAPOLIS MANNAENCHOR SOCIETY (German Musical)—Theodore Dingeldey, pres.; Charles Frese, vice pres.; F. Merz, Sec.; H. Reese, treas.; Max Loeper, librarian. Meets at Miller's Hall, corner Delaware and Pearl, on Tuesday evening of each week.

LADIES' WORKING BAND (Connected with the Y. M. C. A.)—Mrs. R. C. Wiles, pres.; Mrs. Givan, vice pres.; Mrs. S. Behymer, vice pres.; Mrs. A. Clark, sec.; Mrs. Dr. Parry, treas.

MENDELSSOHN SOCIETY (Musical.)—Organized September, 1867. Regular meetings Wednesday evening, at room 11 Martindale's Block. W. H. Churchman, pres.;

W. H. Harris, 1st vice pres.; Daniel Macauley, 2d vice pres.; H. L. Benham, sec. and treas.; Carl Bergstein, conductor and librarian; G. R. Chilian, pianist.

MERCHANTS AND MANUFACTURERS; EXCHANGE—W. C. Farrington, pres. James Greene, sec. 10 and 11 Blackford's Block.

ORPHAN ASYLUM—Mrs. Anna M. Johnson, matron. 711 N. Tennessee.

ST. JOHN'S HOME FOR INVALIDS—Under charge of Sisters of Providence. 127 and 129 S. Tennessee.

YOUNG MEN'S CHRISTIAN ASSOCIATION—Rooms 16, 17, 18 and 19 Vinton's Block, opposite Postoffice. Organized November, 1854. W. A. Bell, pres.; F. H. K.'Enos, rec. sec.; E. P. Ingersoll, cor. sec.; E. T. Sinker, treas.; John R. Brandt, supt. 1600 volumes books.

COMMITTEES.

Finance—Joseph G. McDowell, chairman.
Library and Rooms—Field, chairman; C. P. Wilson, chairman.
Temperance—Wm. Armstrong, chairman.
Lecture and Sermon—E. P. Ingersoll, chairman.
Music and Concert—I. C. Hays, chairman.
Hotel and Boarding House—Edward A. Cobb, chairman.
Statistical—W. H. Hay, chairman.
Library, Exercise and Meeting—L. G. Hay, chairman.

The monthly meeting of the Association is held on the third Monday evening of each month. The reading room is open from 7 o'clock A. M. to 9 o'clock P. M. Number volumes in the library of the Association, 1,600. Catalogues can be obtained of the librarian. Books can be taken from the library between 6 and 11 o'clock A. M., or from 2 to 3 P. M., by calling on the librarian, at the rooms.

——o——

TRADES UNION.

CIGAR MAKERS' PROTECTIVE UNION—pres. Joseph Unger; vice pres. Aug. Holzhacker; rec. sec. John Jacques; cor. sec. H. E. Durham; fin. sec. A. A. Andrews; treas. Peter Uhl. Meets at Millers Hall, first Tuesday of each month.

CONTRACTING BRICK-LAYERS UNION—Meets first Tuesday in each month, room 5, Hubbards Blk. Washington sw. cor. Meridian Thomas Theodore pres.; G. W. Lucky sec

EDITORS UNION—pres. T. H. B. McCan, (Crawfordsville) ; vice pres. R. Spicer (Shelbyville); treas. W. H. Draper, (Indianapolis); sec. J. N. Sceare, (Danville.) J. W. Foster, (Evansville *Journal*) A. Bushwalter, (Lawrenceburg *Register*) J. M. Cumback, (Shelby *Union*); E. W. Callis, (Morgan County *Gazette*) I. N. Brown Sulivan *Union*) D. E. Caldwell (Lebanon *Patriot*) J. R. Willard, (Fort Wayne *Gazette*) M. E.

Pleas(New Castle *Courier*.) Meets subject to call of President.

PAPER HANGERS UNION—John Coen, pres.; R. C. Dain, sec.; Committee of Investigation—John Coen, N. F. Marshall.

TYPOGRAPHICAL UNION—pres. Wm. M. Meredith ; vice pres. W. W. Davy ; cor. sec. M. G. Henry; rec. sec. Henry Feary; Fin. sec. H. F. Garner; treas. N. R. Ruckle; guard, A. Barns. Executive Committee—Geo. J. Schley, W. H. McFarland T. McClure, T. Monroe, T. Brower, C. O. Sackett, John Hargin, W. H. H. Haines, D. M. Cantrill, E. J. Marsh, J. H. Love, — Atherton.

---o---

UNITED STATES OFFICES IN THIS CITY.

United States Arsenal.

Located one-half mile from city corporation east. The grounds consist of about seventy-five acres. There is already completed a main store-house, one building for storing artillery, one magazine for storing powder, one set of officers' quarters and one office. Other buildings, for manufacturing and storing ammunition and for other purposes, will be put up from year to year, as fast as it is possible to do so. Brevet Lieutenant Colonel W. Y. Wylie, Colonel Commanding.

United States Internal Revenue Sixth District, Indiana.

Assessor——William M. Wiles.
Assistants—L. M. Phipps and Love H. Jameson.
Chief Clerk—H. J. Craft. Office room 14, P. O. building.
Collector—Charles F. Hogate.
Deputy—James King. Office, room 15, P. O. building.
Register—Edmund Browning. Office, room 8, P. O. building.
Receiver—G. M. Ballard.

United States Marshal's Office.

(Room 6 P. O. building.)
United States Marshal—Benjamin J. Spooner.
Deputies—I. S. Bigelow, C E. McDonald, W C. David, John C. Spooner, H. N. Bigelow.
UNITED STATES COMMISSIONER, Eben W. Kimball; office 46 E. Washington.
UNITED STATES REVENUE DETECTIVE (For Indiana), James T. Bryer; office 4, Vinton's blk.
SUPERVISOR INTERNAL REVENUE, (For Indiana), G. R. Williams; office room 4, Vinton's blk.

---o---

POST OFFICE DEPARTMENT.

Indianapolis Post Office.

POST OFFICE BUILDING.

Located southeast corner Pennsylvania and Market. Open from 7:30 A. M. to 6:30 P. M. Sundays from 9 A. M. to 10 A. M.

Post Master—W. R. Holloway.
Assistant Post Master—John F. Wood.
Money Order Clerks—E. P. Thompson and H. C. Holloway.
Local Mail Agent—William Boaz.
Registry Clerks —B. F. Conner and J. H. Williams.

Mail Carriers.

FREE DELIVERY SYSTEM TO BE INAUGURATED JULY 1st, 1869.

T. P. Vance, Henry J. Brittain, Newman Hume, N. B. Meek, J. M. Holloway, Wm. B. Downey, Andrew J. Wells, J. B. Selgrove, M. D. Hamilton, E. M. Spicer, D. W. Brouse, W. H. Wainwright, J. D. Eagle, J. McHugh, F. Wiles, T. B. Stapp.

Time of Arrival and Closing of Mails.

All mails are assorted for delivery immediately upon their arrival at the office.

EAST.

VIA COLUMBUS & INDIANAPOLIS R. R.—New York, Washington, Philadelphia, Harrisburg, Pittsburg, close 6:30 and 10:00 P.M. Wheeling and Baltimore, close 10:00 P. M. Richmond, Columbus, O., and Dayton, O., close 11:30 A. M and 10:00 P. M.

VIA BELLEFONTAINE R. R.—Cleveland, Buffalo, Albany, Boston, all of New England and Northern Ohio, close 9:00 A. M. and 6:30 P. M.

WEST.

VIA TERRE HAUTE R. R.—St. Louis, all Kansas, Colorado, Arizona, Idaho, New Mexico, California, Missouri, Southern and Central Illinois, Terre Haute, close 6:30 A. M. and 6:30 P. M.

TERRE HAUTE WAY.—Evansville, Vincennes and Southwestern Indiana, close 10:00 and 12:30 P. M.

NORTH.

VIA PERU R. R.—All Michigan, Iowa, Wisconsin, Minnesota, Oregon, Montana, Utah, Chicago, Northern Illinois, Nebraska. Peru, Kokomo, Logansport, Detroit and Canada, close 10:30 A. M., and 6:30 P. M.

VIA LAFAYETTE R.R.—Quincy, Springfield, Decatur, Bloomington, Peoria, Jacksonville Attica, Covington, close 10:30 A. M. and 6:30 P. M.

LaFayette, Fort Wayne and Toledo, close 6:30 P. M.

SOUTH.

VIA JEFFERSONVILLE R. R.—All Texas, Louisiana, Alabama, Georgia, Mississippi, South Carolina, Arkansas, Louisville, New Albany, Jeffersonville, Madison and Seymour, close 9:00 A.M. and 6:30 P.M.

VIA CINCINNATI R. R —All Southern Ohio and Eastern Kentucky, close 9:00 A. M. and 6:30 P. M.

VIA VINCENNES R. R.—Martinsville, West Newton, Valley Mills, Spencer, Gosport, Mooresville, Brooklyn, &c. close 12:30 P. M.

VIA JUNCTION R. R.—Connersville, Rush-
ville, Beech Grove, Morristown, Hamilton,
O., Oxford, O., Sugar Creek, Davisville,
Carrsville, and Kinder, close 12:30 P. M.

HORSE MAILS.

WAVERLY WAY.—Waverly, Bluff Creek,
and Glenn Valley, Daily, close 7:00 A. M.
CRAWFORDSVILLE WAY. — Brownsburg,
Clermont Daily, close 12:00 M.
New Ross, New Elizabeth Junction, Pitts-
boro and Orth. Tuesdays and Fridays,
close 12:30 P. M.

——o——

Instructions have been given the clerks to
deliver letters from the boxes only to persons
renting the same, or on their written orders,
or to those known by the clerk to be authorized to receive them.

The rules of the office, made in pursuance
of instructions from the Post Office Department, forbid persons not in its immediate
employ, or otherwise connected with its offi-
cial transactions, from entering upon the
floor. It is hoped that no one, whatever his
position, will attempt to violate these rules.

Persons having grievances against the office, on any account, will please report the
fact in writing, or in person, to the Postmaster or Chief Clerk.　W. R. HOLLOWAY,
Post Master.

Rates of Postage.

Letters to any part of the United States, 3
cents for each ½ ounce or part thereof.

Drop Letters, 2 cents per each ½ ounce.

Advertised Letters, 1 cent in addition to
the regular rates.

Valuable letters may be registered on ap-
plication at the office of mailing, and the
payment of a registration fee not exceeding
20 cents.

Transcient Newspapers, Periodicals,
Pamphlets, Blanks, Proof-sheets, Book Man-
uscripts, and all mailable printed matter, (except circulars and books,) 2 cents for each
and every 4 ounces. Double these rates are
charged for books.

Unsealed Circulars, (to one address) not
exceeding 3 in number, 2 cents, and in the
same proportion for a greater number.

Seeds, Cuttings, Roots, &c., 2 cents for each
4 ounces or less quantity.

All Packages of Mail Matter not charged
with letter postage must be so arranged that
the same can be conveniently examined by
Postmasters; if not, letter postage will be
charged.

No package will be forwarded by mail
which weighs over 4 pounds.

All Postage Matter, for delivery within the
United states, must be PREPAID by stamps, except duly certified letters of soldiers and
sailors.

Weekly Newspapers, (one copy only) sent
to actual subscribers within the county where
printed and published, free.

Letters to Canada and other British North
American Provinces, when not over 3000
miles, 10 cents for each ½ ounce. When over
3000 miles, 15 cents, payment optional.

Letters to Great Britian or Ireland, 12 cents.
Prepayment optional.

Letters to France, 15 cents for each ¼
ounce. Prepayment optional.

Letters to other foreign countries vary in
rate according to the route by which they are
sent, and the proper information can be obtained of any postmaster in the United States.

——o——

WARD BOUNDARIES.

FIRST WARD.—All that part of the city
bounded on the south by New York street,
on the north by North street, (from Meridian street east to the termination of North
street, thence east on the continuation of
the line from the center of North street to
the corporation line) and on the east by the
corporation line shall constitute the First
Ward.

SECOND WARD.—All that part of the city
bounded on the south by the northern
boundary of the First Ward, on the west
by Meridian street, and on the north and
east by the corporation line, shall constitute the Second Ward.

THIRD WARD.—All that part of the city
bounded on the south by Washington street,
(from Meridian street to Mississippi street,)
on the west by Mississippi street from
Washington street north to the intersection
of Indiana avenue; thence northwest by
Indiana avenue to West street, thence north
by West street to the corporation line and
on the east by Meridian street and Circle
street, (running east of the Governor's circle,) shall constitute the Third Ward.

FOURTH WARD.—All that part of the city
bounded on the south by Washington street,
on the West by White river and the corporation line, and on the east by the western
boundary of the Third Ward, shall constitute the Fourth Ward.

FIFTH WARD.—All that part of the city
bounded on the north by Washington street,
from White river to Delaware street, running south to Merrill street, running
west from Delaware street to Illinois street;
thence north by Illinois street to Garden
street; thence west by Garden street to
Mississippi street; thence north by Mississippi street to Henry street; thence west by
Henry street to Missouri street; thence
north by Missouri street to South street;
thence west by South street to Kentucky
avenue; thence southwest by Kentucky Avenue to White river, and on the west by
White river and the corporation line shall
constitute the Fifth Ward.

SIXTH WARD.—All that part of the city
bounded on the north by the southern
boundary of the Fifth Ward, on the east by
Delaware street, south to Madison avenue;
thence south by Madison avenue to the corporation line; on the south by the corporation line; and on the west by White river,
north to Kentucky avenue, shall constitute
the Sixth Ward.

SEVENTH WARD.—All that part of the city bounded on the north by Washington street, on the east by East street, on the south by the corporation line, and on the west by Madison avenue and Delaware street, shall constitute the Seventh Ward.

EIGHTH WARD.—All that part of the city bounded on the north by Washington street, on the east and south by the corporation line, and on the west by East street, shall constitute the Eighth Ward.

NINTH WARD.—All that part of the city bounded on the south by Washington street, (from the corporation line west to Meridian street), on the west by Meridian street, and Circle street (running east of the Governor's circle), on the north by New York street, and on the east by the corporation line, shall constitute the Ninth Ward.

ALPHABETICAL DIRECTORY

— OF —

STREETS, AVENUES AND ALLEYS

IN INDIANAPOLIS.

The principal streets crossing Washington Street are divided into North and South; those crossing Meridian Street into East and West. The four principal Avenues extend in four diagonal directions, from near the center to the extreme limits of the city.

AGNES, north and south from New York to North, twelve blocks west of Meridian.

ALABAMA, north and south, three blocks east of Meridian.

ALLEGHANEY ALLEY, east and west from Tennessee, bet. Vermont and Michigan.

ANN, from Macauley to Catherine, bet. Tennessee and Mississippi.

ARCH, east and west bet. Jackson and Noble nine blocks north of Washington.

ARCHER, from Michigan to St. Clair, four blocks east of corporation.

ARSENAL, from east National road to Michigan, one half mile east of corportion.

ASH, from Massachusetts av. to Home av., bet. Bellefontaine and Oak.

ATHON, north and south, from Rhode Island to Indiana av., ten blocks west of Meridian.

BARNHILL, north and south from Elizabeth to Coe, sixteen blocks west of Meridian.

BATES, east and west, from noble to corporation east, four blocks south of Washington.

BEATY, from Buchanan to McCarty, bet. Noble and Greer.

BELLEFONTAINE, from corporation to Home av., bet. Peru and Ash.

BENTON, north and south, from Harrison to Market, bet. Noble and Cady.

BICKING, east and west from Delaware to East, two blocks south of McCarty.

BIDDLE, east and west, bet. Winston and corporation east, seven blocks north of Washington.

BLACKFORD, north and south, from National road, to North, seven blocks west of Meridian.

BLAKE, north and south, from National road to Indiana av., ten blocks west of Meridian.

BLUFF ROAD, terminus south Meridian.

BRADSHAW, east and west from Beaty to Virginia av., bet. Buchanan and McCarty.

BRETT, east and west, beyond corporation, west of Michigan road.

BRIGHT, north and south, from Ohio to North, eight blocks west of Meridian.

BROADWAY, from St. Clair to Home av., bet. Plum and Jackson.

BROOKS, north and south, from First to Drake, bet. Michigan and Fall creek.

BUCHANAN, east and west, from East to Virginia av., bt. Dougherty and McCarty.

BUTLER, east and west, from Ft. Wayne av. to College av., twelve blocks north of Washington.

CADY, north and south, from Harrison to Market, one block east of Benton.

CALIFORNIA, north and south from Washington to St. Clair, six blocks west of Meridian.

CAMPBELL, east and west, east of corporation six blocks north of Washington.

CATHARINE, east and west, from Mississippi to West, bet. Merrill and McCarty.

CEDAR, north-east and south-west, from Dillon to Virginia av., bet. Grove and Pine.

CENTER, east and west, from Douglas to Ellen, bet. North and Elizabeth.

CHADWICK, from McCarty to city limits south, bet. Missouri and West.

CHATHAM, from Massachusetts av. to St. Clair, bet. East and Noble.

CHERRY, east and west, bet. Ft. Wayne av. and Charles, ten blocks north of Washington.

CAESTNUT, from Georgia to Morris, bet. Delaware and Pennsylvania.

CHESAPEAKE ALLEY, east and west, from Mississippi to West, bet. Maryland and Georgia

CHOPTANK ALLEY, from Washington to St. Clair, bet. New Jersey and East.

CHRISTIAN AVENUE, east and west from Ft. Wayne av. to Peru R. R., eleven blocks north of Washington.

CIRCLE, crossing of Meridian and Market one block north of Washington.

COBURN, east and west, from East to Short, bet. Dougherty and corporation south.

COE, east and west, west of corporation line, ten blocks north of Washington.

COLLEGE AVENUE, from Christian av. to Home av., bet. Ash and Broadway.

COLUMBIA ALLEY, north and south, from Georgia to Michigan, bet. West and Missouri.

COTTRELL, from Louisiana to Georgia, bet. Missouri and West.

COURT, east and west, bet. Washington and Market, from Pennsylvania to Delaware.

CRANE, east and west, from Arsenal to Seymour, two blocks north of Washington.

CROSS, east and west, bet. Peru and Bellefontaine R. R. eleven blocks north of Washington.

DACOTA, from Rockwood to city limits south, bet. West and White river.

DAVIS, north-east and south-west, from Indiana av. to Fall creek, twelve blocks north of Washington.

DELAWARE, north and south, two blocks east of Meridian.

DILLON, north and south, from Harrison to corporation south, on corporation line east.

DORMAN, from Michigan to St. Clair, one block east of corporation.

DOUGHERTY, east and west, from East to Virginia av., bet. Buchanan and Coburn.

DOUGLAS, north and south, from Ohio to Indiana av., nine blocks west of Meridian.

DOWNEY, east and west, from Bluff road to Japan, fourteen blocks south of Washington.

DRAKE, east and west, beyond corporation, west of Michigan road.

DUNCAN, east and west, from Delaware to New Jersey, bet. south and Merrill.

DUNLOP, east and west, from Bluff road to Japan, fifteen blocks south of Washington.

EAST, north and south, five blocks east of Meridian.

EAST CUMBERLAND, east and west, from Delaware to East, one-half block south of Washington.

EAST NATIONAL ROAD, terminus east Washington.

ECKERT, from Kentucky av. to Merrill, bet. West and Kentucky av.

EDDY, from Merrill to South, bet. Illinois and Tennessee.

EIGHTH, east and west, eighteen blocks north of Washington.

ELIZABETH, east and west, from Blake to Ellen, eight blocks north of Washington.

ELK, north-east and south-west, from Dillon to Virginia av., bet. Dillon and Virginia av.

ELLEN, north and south, from North to Indiana av., eight blocks west of Meridian.

ELLIS, from Georgia to Maryland, bet. West and Helen.

ELLSWORTH, north and south, from New York to Vermont, bet. Missouri and Mississippi.

ELM, north-west and south-east, from Noble to Dillon, bet. Virginia av. and Huron.

ERIE ALLEY, from Washington to St. Clair, bet. Alabama and New Jersey.

FAYETTE, north and south, from North to St. Clair, bet. Missouri and West.

FIFTH east and west, fifteen blocks north of Washington.

FIRST, east and west, west of Meridian eleven blocks north of Washington.

FLETCHER AVENUE, north-west and south-east, from Noble to Dillon, bet. Forest av. and Huron.

FOREST AVENUE, north-west and south-east, from Harrison to Dillon, bet. Harrison and Fletcher av.

FORT WAYNE AVENUE, north-east and south-west, from Pennsylvania and north to city limits north-east.

FORT WAYNE ROAD, terminus Ft. Wayne av.

FOURTH, east and west, fourteen blocks north of Washington.

FRANKLIN, from Morris to city limits south, bet. Wallace and Japan.

GARDEN, east and west, from Mississippi to Pennsylvania, bet. South and Merrill.

GEISENDORFF, north and south, from National road to New York, nine blocks west of Meridian.

GEORGIA, east and west, two blocks south of Washington.

GRANT, bet. West and Kentucky av., one block south of Merrill.

GREER, from Buchanan to Stevens, bet. East and Beaty.

GREGG, east and west, bet. New Jersey and Jackson, nine blocks north of Washington.

GROVE, north-east and south-west from Dillon to Virginia av., bet. Elk and Cedar.

HARRISON, east and west, from Noble to corporation east, four blocks south of Washington.

HELEN, from Maryland to Louisiana, bet. Ellis and White river.

HENDERSON, north and south, terminus of north Illinois.

HENRY, east and west, from Missouri to Mississippi, bet. South and Merrill.

HIGH, from McCarty to corporation south, bet. New Jersey and Alabama.

HOME AVENUE, east and west, from Fort Wayne av. to Peru R. R., thirteen blocks north of Washington.

HOSBROOK, north-west and south-east, from Cedar to Dillon, bet. Virginia av. and Elm.

HOWARD, north and south, from First to Seventh, bet. Lafayette and Mill.

HUDSON ALLEY, from Ohio to Walnut, bet. Delaware and Alabama.

HURON, east and west, from Virginia av. to Noble, one block south of South.

HURON, north-west and south-east, from Noble to Dillon, bet. Fletcher av. and Elm.

ILLINOIS, north and south, one block west of Meridian.

INDIANA AVENUE, north-west and south-east, from corner Ohio and Illinois to city limits north-west.

JACKSON, from St. Clair, to Home av. bet. Broadway and East.

JAPAN, north and south, extension of south East.

JOHN, east and west, bet. Peru and Bellefontaine R. R., ten blocks north of Washington.

JONES, east and west, from West to Dacota, six blocks south of McCarty.

KANKOKEE ALLEY, from Michigan to North, bet. Illinois and Tennessee.

KANSAS, east and west, from Meridian to Minnesota, thirteen blocks south of Washington.

KENTUCKY AVENUE, north-east and south-west, from corner Washington and Illinois to city limits south-west.

KINGAN, east and west, from West to White river, two blocks south of McCarty.

LAFAYETTE, north and south, from First to city limits, bet. Mississippi and Howard.

LAFAYETTE ROAD, terminus Indiana av.

LENOX, north and south, from Seventh to Ninth, bet. Lafayette and Mill.

LIBERTY, north and south, six blocks east of Meridian.

LOCKERBIE, east and west, from East to Liberty, bet. New York and Vermont.

LOCUST, from McCarty to Morris, bet. Meridian and Union.

LORD, east and west, from Noble to corporation east, bet. Louisiana and Harrison.

LOUISIANA, east and west, three blocks south of Washington.

MACAULEY, east and west, from Ann to Missouri, one block south of McCarty.

MADISON AVENUE, north-west and south-east, from corner South and Meridian to city limits.

MADISON ROAD, terminus Madison av.

MAPLE, from Ray to Morris, bet. Tennessee and Illinois.

MARGARETT, east and west, south of City Hospital.

MARIA, east and west, east of City Hospital.

MARKET, east and west, one block north of Washington.

MARYLAND, east and west, one block south of Washington.

MASSACHUSETTS AVENUE, north-east and south-west, from corner of Ohio and Pennsylvania, to city limits north-east.

MAXWELL, north and south, from Elizabeth to Davis, fourteen blocks west of Meridian.

MAYHEW, east and west, beyond corporation, west of Michigan rd.

MEEK, east and west from Noble to corporation east, two blocks south of Washington.

MEIKLE, from McCarty to city limits south, bet. Mississippi and Missouri.

MERIDIAN, north and south, through Govenor's circle, bet. Pennsylvania and Illinois, south terminus per canvass, McCarty st.

MERRILL, east and west, six blocks south of Washington.

MIAMI ALLEY, east and west, bet. Ohio and New York.

MICHIGAN, east and west, five blocks north of Washington.

MICHIGAN ROAD, terminus north-west.

MICHIGAN ROAD, (east,) east terminus, Washington, ten blocks east of Meridian.

MILL, north and south, from Fifth to city limits, bet. Howard and Michigan road.

MINERVA, north and south, from Ohio to North, eleven blocks west of Meridian.

MINNESOTA, from Morris to city limits south, bet. Tennessee and West.

MISSISSIPPI, north and south, three blocks west of Meridian.

MISSOURI, north and south, four blocks west of Meridian.

MOBILE ALLEY, east and west, from Meridian to Mississippi, bet. Georgia and Louisiana.

MORRIS, east and west, twelve blocks south of Washington.

MORRISON, east and west, bet. Delaware and Alabama, twelve blocks north of Washington.

MULBERRY, from McCarty to Morris, bet. Union and Chestnut.

MUSKINGUM ALLEY, from Louisiana to First, bet. Tennessee and Illinois.

McCARTY, east and west, eight blocks south of Washington.

McGILL, from Louisiana to South bet. Mississippi and Missouri.

McGINNIS, from McCarty to Ray, bet. Tennessee and Mississippi.

McINTIRE, east and west, beyond corporation, west of Michigan road.

McKERNAN, from Buchanan to corporation south, bet. Short and Wright.

McNABB, east and west, from Illinois to Meridian, bet. Louisiana and south.

NEW JERSEY, north and south four blocks east of Meridian.

NEW YORK, east and west, three blocks north of Washington.

NINTH, east and west, fourteen blocks north of Washington.

NORTH, east and west, six blocks north of Washington.

NOBLE, north and south, seven blocks east of Meridian.

OAK, from Massachusetts av. to Christian av., bet. Ash and Plum.

OHIO, east and west, two blocks north of Washington.

OREGON, north and south, from first to Pratt, bet. Brooks and Michigan road.

OSAGE ALLEY, north and south, from Georgia to Pratt, bet. Missouri and Mississippi.

OXFORD, east and west, bet. Charles and corporation east, nine blocks north of Washington.

PATTERSON, north and south, from Vermont to Elizabeth, thirteen blocks west of Meridian.

PEARL, east and west, from Illinois to Pennsylvania, half block south of Washington.

PECK, bet. old and new cemetery, terminus Kentucky av.

PENDLETON PIKE, terminus Massachusetts av.

PENNSYLVANIA, north and south, one block east of Meridian

PERU, from North to Home av., nine blocks east of Meridian.

PHIPPS, east and west, from Meridian to Pennsylvania, bet. Merrill and McCarty.

PINE, north-east and south-west, from Harrison to Virginia av., one block east of Noble.

PLUM, from St. Clair to Christian av., bet. Oak and Broadway.

POPLAR, east and west, from Union to Chestnut, two blocks south of McCarty.

POTOMAC ALLEY, east and west, bet. Washington and Market.

PRATT, east and west, nine blocks north of Washington.

RAILROAD, from Market to Massachusetts av., bet. Spring and Davidson.

RAY, east and west, from McGinnis to Chestnut, two blocks south of McCarty.

RHODE ISLAND, east and west, eight blocks north of Washington.

RIVER, south of old cemetery.

ROANOKE ALLEY, north and south, from Ohio to First, bet. Tennessee and Mississippi.

ROCKWOOD, east and west, from West to Dacota, three blocks south of McCarty.

ROOT, east and west, from West to White river, one block south of McCarty.

ROSE, between West and White river, two blocks south of Merrill.

RUSSELL, north and south, from Meridian to Illinois, bet. McCarty and Merrill.

SAND, south-east, from Kentucky av., to White river, one block west of West.

SANDERS, east and west, from Shelbyville road to terminus of Wright, terminus Virginia av.

SCHOOL, north and south, from South to Huron, bet. Noble and Virginia av.

SCIOTO ALLEY, from Washington to New York, bet. Meridian and Pennsylvania.

SECOND, east and west, twelve blocks north of Washington.

SEVENTH, east and west, seventeen blocks north of Washington.

SEVERN ALLEY, north and south, from Louisiana to Second, bet. Meridian and Illinois.

SEYMOUR, from east National rd. to Crane, one-half mile east of corporation.

SHARPE, east and west, from Eckert to Missouri, bet. South and Merrill.

SHELBYVILLE ROAD, terminus Virginia av.

SHORT, from Dougherty to city limits south, bet. McKernan and Virginia av.

SINKER, east and west, from Alabama to East, one block north of McCarty.

SIXTH, east and west, sixteen blocks north of Washington.

SMITH, north and south, from Rhode Island to Indiana av., eleven blocks west of Meridian.

SOUTH, east and west, four blocks south of Washington.

SPRING, from Market to St. Clair, bet. Noble and Railroad.

STEVENS, east and west, from East to Virginia av., one block north of McCarty.

SUSQUEHANNA ALLEY, from Washington to North, bet. Pennsylvania and Delaware.

ST. CLAIR, east and west, eight blocks north of Washington.

ST. JOSEPH, east and west, ten blocks north of Washington.

TENNESSEE, north and south, two blocks west of Meridian.

TENTH, east and west, twenty blocks north of Washington.

THIRD, east and west, thirteen blocks north of Washington.

THOMAS, east and west, from West to Dacota, five blocks south of McCarty.

TINKER, east and west, seventeen blocks north of Washington.

TIPPECANOE ALLEY, east and west, from Tennessee to Illinois, bet. New York and Vermont.

TORBET, east and west, from Fall Creek to Michigan road, beyond corporation.

UNION, from Merrill to Morris, bet. Meridian and Chestnut.

VERMONT, east and west, four blocks north of Washington.

VINE, east and west, bet. Jackson and Charles, nine blocks north of Washington.

VINTON, east and west, from West to Dacota, four blocks south of McCarty.

VIRGINIA AVENUE, north-west and south-east, from corner Washington and Pennsylvania, to city limits.

WABASH ALLEY, east and west, bet. Market and Ohio.

WALLACE, from Morris to city limits south, bet. Madison road and Franklin.

WALNUT, east and west, seven blocks north of Washington.

WASHINGTON, east and West, length of city, first street south of Governor's Circle.

WATERS, from Stevens to McCarty, bet. Greer and Virginia av.

WESSON, east and west, from Arsenal to Seymour, one block north of Washington.

WEST, north and south, five blocks west of Meridian.

WEST CUMBERLAND, east and west, from Tennessee to White river, one-half block south of Washington

WEST NATIONAL ROAD, east and west, west White river bridge.
WESTFIELD PIKE, terminus north Illinois.
WILKINS, east and west, from Tennessee to Chestnut, three blocks south of Mc-Carty
WILLARD, from Merrill to Garden, bet. Tennessee and Mississippi.
WILLARD, north and south, south side east National road, one-half mile east of corporation.
WILSON, north and south, from Elizabeth to Davis, fifteen blocks west of Meridian.
WINSTON from Ohio to Walnut, ten blocks east of Meridian.

WISCONSIN, east and west, from West to Meridian, fourteen blocks south of Washington.
WOOD, north and south, from Michigan to North, bet. Missouri and Mississippi.
WRIGHT, from Buchanan to corporation south, one block west of McKernan.
WYOMING, east and west, from Delaware to East, one block south of McCarty.

YEISER, east and west from Bluff road to Japan, thirteen blocks south of Washington.

TOO LATE FOR REGULAR INSERTION.

AMERICAN SAW WORKS, Pennsylvania cor. Georgia

Barker M. I. (Barker, Williams & Co.) r. 163 N. Tennessee
Bowman Peter, (Carter & Bowman,) r. 9 W. Washington
Bullard Wm. carpenter and builder, shop ns. Washington bet. Canal and Mississippi, r. 52 Indiana av.

Carter J. F. (Carter & Bowman,) r. 252 N. Mississippi
CARTER & BOWMAN, (J. F. Carter and Peter Bowman,) proprs. Gem Billiard Saloon, 9 W. Washington
COLLINS JOSEPH G. propr. Richmond Temperance House, 35 W. Georgia, r. same

Feigeland C. R. salesman A. Kaufman
Feller George, watchmaker 114 S. Illinois, r. same
FRIEDGAN C. boots and shoes 36 W. Washington, r. 36 N. East

Hall Alfred, photograph gallery 16½ E. Washington
Harbin T. N. physician and surgeon, office 26 N. Illinois
Harper R. D. pastor 1st Presbyterian Church, r. 197 N. Alabama
Hunt L. C. (R. R. City Printing Co.) r. North nr. Blake
Indianapolis and St. Louis Sleeping Car Co. H. Q. Sanderson, Pres. C. J. Sanderson, Secy. and Treas. Office Union Depot
Justis James M. hostler, r. 26 N. Illinois

Montgomery S. T editor *Independent* 10½ S. Pennsylvania, r. same
Payne William, bartender, r. 26 N. Illinois
Pershing D. R. editor *Independent*, 10½ S. Pennsylvania
Rasner Henry, (Rasner & Rittew,) r. Illinois cor. 6th
Rasner & Rittew, (Henry Rasner and J. P. Rittew,) house and sign painters 61 Kentucky av.
Rittew J. P. (Rasner & Rittew,) r. Mississippi cor. North
Rockwell Silas, boarding house, 87 and 89 E. Market
SINKER ALFRED T. American Saw Works, r. Ft. Wayne rd. out of city
Stacy M. D. jeweller, 34 Virginia av. r. 42 N. New Jersey
Way A. M. Miss, editor *Independent*, 10½ S. Pennsylvania, r. same

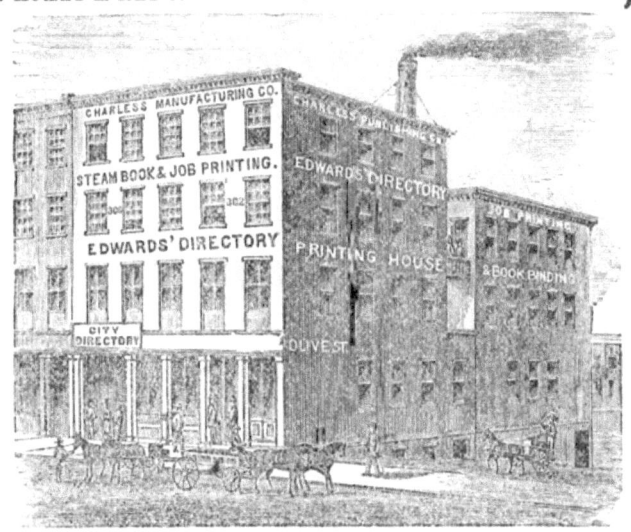

CONFIDENCE
—IN—
EDWARDS' CITY DIRECTORIES,
THE STANDARD AND OFFICIAL DIRECTORIES OF THE SOUTH and WEST.

Resolution of the Indianapolis Chamber of Commerce.

Be it Resolved, That the Indianapolis Board of Trade appreciate the enterprise of Mr. Edwards in issuing our City Directory on a scale and style that will command respect and attention at home and abroad, and to show forth in an influential manner the population and resources of our flourishing city, that we recommend the undivided support of our business men be given Edwards' Directory.

JAS. C. FERGUSON, President.   J. BRAINERD, Secretary.

☞ *From the Chicago Daily Tribune.*

Edwards' Directory combines all the qualities needed in a work of this kind, and has the entire confidence of the business men of all classes. The highest testimonials have been bestowed upon it. It has been pronounced "unsurpassed for beauty and correctness;" **"THE STANDARD BOOK OF THE CITY;"** "an indispensable requisite to every business office;" "highly appreciated by the business community and travelers generally;" "an institution in the West, and its annual visit always welcome," &c., &c.

Resolution of the City Council of Indianapolis.

Be it Resolved, That the CITY COUNCIL of Indianapolis, feeling the want, and knowing the value of such a work to their fellow-citizens, and appreciating the enterprise of Mr. Edwards in issuing the Indianapolis Directory for the last two years in a manner creditable to the city and himself, and that we recommend our citizens to give their support to Edwards' Directory, thus securing the annual publication of a standard work.

JOHN CAVEN, Mayor.   CYRUS S. BUTTERFIELD, City Clerk.

☞ *From the Chicago Evening Journal.*

As Edwards' Directories have been pronounced the best **EVER PUBLISHED IN CHICAGO,** and as they have been **THOROUGHLY TESTED BY ALL CLASSES OF CITIZENS,** we can fully rely upon the forthcoming work as being in every particular correct and reliable.

Merchants' Exchange Resolution of St. Louis.

WHEREAS, The merchants, manufacturers and business men of St. Louis regard the publication of an annual Directory of our city a great convenience and a business necessity, and that our fellow citizen, Mr. Richard Edwards, has for many years issued such a work as has shown from time to time our growth and the greatness of St. Louis; be it

RESOLVED, That the Union Merchants' Exchange of St. Louis appreciate the enterprise and public spirit of Mr. Edwards, in permanently establishing a standard annual Directory of the city, and that we recommend our fellow citizens to give such annual encouragement, by subscription and otherwise, as will enable him to issue such a Directory as will be justly entitled the Model Directory of the West, and that the Secretary be instructed to forward a copy of the Directory, with the compliments of the President and Directors of the Exchange, to the various Exchange Rooms and Board of Trade Rooms of the large cities of the country.

GEO. H. MORGAN, Secretary.

☞ Hundreds such Resolutions and Editorials could be added from the various Cities for which we publish.

TO MY FRIENDS AND THE PUBLIC:

Having been frequently solicited by friends and patrons, during the last twelve years, to issue in my publications a good likeness of myself, and presuming it will gratify the curious, with an eye to business, I present the above as a faithful representation engraved from a photograph. As a business policy, and believing in advertising, I am in hopes the presentation of the likeness will not be without its good effect. Having studied and labored for over fifteen years in making the publication of city directories a business, I am proud to say that I have accomplished what thousands have attempted and failed. As there are always unprincipled persons ready to use the reputation of others, I hope the above likeness will aid in protecting my friends and the public against bogus adventurers, and also against the numerous irresponsible persons, who are constantly soliciting patronage to Bogus Directories and other advertising mediums, some of them having represented themselves as MR. EDWARDS, others as his agent, thereby enabling them to collect money, and impose upon the public. I would caution all persons against subscribing or paying any money to any person who does not show his responsibility and authority for whom he is acting.

Richard Edwards

(*Established at St. Louis in 1853.*)

Please turn over.

EDWARDS'
INDIANAPOLIS DIRECTORY
1869.

ABBREVIATIONS.

ABB	33	ACH

Abbett Charles H. (L. & C. H. Abbett) r. 35 Virginia av.

Abbett John B. r. 164 Virginia av.

Abbett Lawson, (L. & C. H. Abbett) r. 35 Virginia av.

ABBETT L. & C. H. (Charles H. and Lawson Abbett) physicians and surgeons 35 Virginia av.

Abbot Frederic, salesman Trade Palace, bds. Pyle House

Abbott John W. (col'd) lab. r. 177 W. 2d

Abel Charles, teamster Schmidt's Brewery, r. 401 S. Delaware

Abker William, student National Business College

Abner John, varnishmkr. r. 310 S. East

Aborn Mary J. Mrs. 1st asst. principal 9th Ward School, r. 116 Broadway

Aborn Orin, physician, 74 E. Market, r. 116 Broadway

Abrams David, hostler Holmes & Rains

Abrams John, bookkeeper J. George Stilz, r. 129 N. Noble

Abrams John, (col'd) porter, r. 129 N. California

Abrams Milton, engineer Journal Office

Abrams William J. carpenter, r. 419 N. East

ABROMET ADOLPH, agt. Ætna Fire and Life and Howard's Fire Ins. Co.'s room 1 Ætna Bldg. r. 21 W. North

ACADEMY OF MUSIC, Butsch, Dickson & Dell, proprs. W. H. Lake, lessee, Ohio se. cor. Illinois

Achey Americus, carpenter Builders and Mnfrs. Association

Achey James, bds. 17 Kentucky av.

Achey John, bds. 17 Kentucky av.

Achey Mary, wid. Henry, r. 17 Kentucky av.

ACH	34	AFF

Achillas Thomas, turner L. Kolb, r. 28 W. Georgia

Ackerman Andrew, (Western Furniture Co.) r. ws. Noble bet. Market and Ohio

Ackerman August, compositor Gutenberg Co.

Ackert George F. clk. Asher, Adams and Higgins, bds. Pyle House

Ackles Mary, dressmaker, r. 152 W. Washington

Adam William, teamster, r. ws. Jackson nr. St. Clair

Adams A. T. physician, bds. Little's Hotel

Adams Aaron, (col'd) whitewasher, bds. 460 S. Missouri

Adams Alexander, boarding house 268 E. St. Clair, r. same

Adams Andrew J. bds. 268 E. St. Clair

Adams D. O. operator Miller's Photograph Gallery, r. 197 N Illinois

Adams George F. lumber dealer 169 Bates, r. 175 E. Market

Adams George H. (Asher, Adams & Higgins,) r. Brooklyn, New York

Adams George S. salesman J. W. Adams, bds. 430 N. Illinois

Adams Harvey, cooper, r. 164 Pattison

Adams Henry C. deputy sheriff, r. 115 S. New Jersey

Adams Hubbard S. policeman, r. ns. Louisiana, bet. New Jersey and Alabama

Adams Jefferson, clk. bds. 9 S. Mississippi

Adams Jesse, brick yard, r. 346 N. New Jersey

Adams John Q. carpenter, r. 9th cor. Lenox

Adams John W. boots and shoes 49 and 53 W. Washington, r. 430 N. Illinois

Adams Lafayette, r. 165 N. Alabama

Adams Lida Miss, bds. 268 E. St. Clair

Adams Mary M. wid. Reuben, r. 115 S. New Jersey

Adams Samuel, lawyer 19 W. Washington, r. 297 N. Delaware

Adams Samuel C. brickmkr. r. 297 N. Delaware

Adams Thomas H. cooper D. Burton & Co. r. 248 N. Blake

Adams William, porter, r. ws. Jackson bet. Arch and St. Clair

Adams William L. (Hume, Adams & Co.) r. 165 N. Alabama

Adkins Martin V. B. conductor, r. 346 N. Noble

Adsit Charles S. salesman Geo. K. Share & Co. bds. 234 S. Alabama

Adsit Henry B. clk. Geo. K. Share & Co. bds. 332 N. Alabama

Aebker Henry, wks. Cabinet Maker's Union

Aebker William, wks. Cabinet Maker's Union

Aehr Joseph, r. Bluff rd. nr. Wisconsin

Aess Sebastian, lab. r. 505 N. Illinois

Ætna Building, es. Pennsylvania bet. Washington and Market

Ætna Fire Ins. Co. of Hartford, Conn. A. Abromet, agt. R. L. Douglass, State agt. room 1 Ætna Bldg.

Ætna Life Ins. Co. of Hartford, Conn. A. Abromet, agt. room 1 Ætna Bldg

Affantranger, S. J. blacksmith 191 Indiana av. r. 215 W. North

AFT	35	ALE

Aftung Anton, books and notions 26 S. Delaware, r. 277 S. New Jersey

Agnew William, sawyer, r. es. Mississippi nr. **1358747**

Ahenfeld William, carpenter W. H. Henschen

Ahern Michael, fireman Gas Works, r. Illinois sw. cor. Wilkins

Ahlders Ahlrich, collarmkr. D. Schwegel, bds. South cor. Pennsylvania

Aiken J. B. ins. agt. r. 649 N. Tennessee

Aiken Louis G. salesman L. Ludorff & Co. bds. 649 N. Tennessee

Aikens Daniel, cooper, r. 393 S. Missouri

Aikman John B. (Kimble, Aikman & Co.) 382 N. Tennessee

Aker Ellis L. carpenter H. H. Wheatly, r. 116 Elm

Akins Milton, teamster, bds. 121 Huron

Alanstraw William, lab. Rolling Mill

ALBANY CITY FIRE INS. CO. of New York, R. E. Beardsley, State agt. 11 N. Meridian

ALBERSHARDT HENRY F. boots and shoes, 139 E. Washington, r. same

Albersmeier Daniel, lab. Terre Haute & I. freight depot, r. 172 Union

Albersmeier Henry, clk. bds. 299 S. Delaware

Albert John W. carriage trimmer Miller, Mitchell & Stough, r. Ash bet. Vine and Cherry

Albert Lawson H. baggageman, r. 211 N. Missouri

Albertson Charles, printer Journal Job Room, bds. 98 N. East

Albro Henry O. foundry foreman Phœnix Machine Works, r. 160 Blackford

Alcon Albert, gold and silver plater room 22 Talbott & News Block, bds. 22 W. Ohio

Alcoron Sarah Miss, asst. matron Home of the friendless, r. same

Aldag August, shoemkr. Charles Aldag, r. 581 E. Wshington

Aldag Charles, boots and shoes 175 E. Washington, r. same

Aldag Charles L. shoemkr. r. Cumberland bet. New Jersey and Alabama

Aldag Louis, shoemkr. Charles Aldag, r. 78 N. Liberty

Alden John B. (Shortridge & Alden) and publisher of the Indiana Teacher, bds. 20 S. Pennsylvania

Alden Lydia T. clk. J. B. Alden, bds. 20 S. Pennsylvania

Aldred Salina, wid. r. South nw. cor. Noble

Aldrich Alexander W. carpenter, r. 308 Winston

Aldrich Chauncey, carpenter, r. 425 E. St. Clair.

Aldrich Frank, (Aldrich & Gay) r. 366 N. West

Aldrich John D. stair builder, r. 244 Davidson

Aldrich L. A. porter Olivet Presbyterian Church, r. 248 S. Meridian

ALDRICH & GAY, (Frank Aldrich and Alfred Gay) wood yard Indiana av. cor. Canal

Aldridge I. N. bds. 10 W. Georgia

Alexander Alfred M. clk. r. 550 N. Tennessee

Alexander Christinia, wid. John, r. West Indianapolis
Alexander Elvira, wid. Archibald, r. 319 S. Delaware
Alexander Emma B. wid. James C. r. 332 E. Ohio
Alexander George, clk. Dury & Hawk, bds. 173 Huron
Alexander George W. (col'd) barber W Artis, r. 181 W. Washington
Alexander George W. (G. W. Alexander & Co.) r. 550 W. Tennessee
Alexander J. D. trav. salesman Hays, Rosenthall & Co. rooms 62 S. Meridian
Alexander Joseph, carpenter, r. 173 Huron
Alexander Michael, salesman L. I. Mossler & Bro. r. 37 E. Washington
Alexander Norton E. traveling agt. *State Sentinel*, bds. 119 W. Maryland
Alexander Theodore T. salesman L. H. Tyler & Co. r. 289 W. Vermont
Alexander William, r. 233 Winston
Alexander G. W. & Co. (George W. Alexander and ——) real estate agts. 2 W Washington
Alford Henry A. bookkeeper H. F. West & Co. r. 175 N. Alabama
Alford Thomas G. (Alford, Talbot & Co.) r. 175 N. Alabama
Alford William H. marblewrkr. T. S. James & Co. bds. 229 S. Alabama
ALFORD, TALBOT & CO. (T. G. Alford, R. L. Talbot, W. H. Morrison, J. P. Patterson and J. A. Moore) wholesale grocers 2 Morrison Blk. S. Meridian
Algeo John, salesman Pettis, Dickson & Co. r. 67 N. Alabama
Algeo Samuel, porter Foster & Wiggins, r. 359 E. Market
Allaire Andrew, (Stirk & Allaire) r. es. Clinton alley bet. New York and Ohio
Allaire James P. traveling agt. r. 95 Jackson
Allbright Francis, barber R. Harding, bds. same
Allbright George, varnisher Cabinet Maker's Union, r. 182 N. Davidson
Allen A. C. Rev. missionary, r. 181 N. Delaware
Allen Abner, shoemkr. Adolph Shafer, r. 345 N. Alabama
Allen Austin W. agt. Lamb's Knitting Machine, 18 N. Delaware, bds. 30½ N. Pennsylvania
ALLEN CHAPEL, (African) Henry Depugh, (col'd) pastor, ns. Broadway bet. Cherry and Christian av.
Allen Chapel Day School, (African) S. A. Elbert, principal, ns. Broadway bet. Cherry and Christian av.
Allen Edward, (col'd) car cleaner, r. 173 Douglass al.
Allen Edward G. clk. Louis Hollweg, bds. 213 N. Pennsylvania
Allen Eliza, wid. r. 89 N. West
Allen Firman, salesman Wiles Bro. & Co. r. 316 N. Illinois
Allen George, (col'd) brickmkr. r. 224 Huron
ALLEN HENRY, livery and sale stable, 25 and 27 E. Pearl, r. 130 W. Vermont

Allen Henry S. salesman Trade Palace, bds. 9 S. Mississippi
Allen James, pressman H. C. Chandler & Co. r. 31 W. Georgia
Allen James A. carpenter, r. 57 Huron
Allen James R. coppersmith C. C. C. & I. R. R.
Allen John H. (col'd) farmer, r. 44 Harris
Allen Josephine, wid. James, r. 83½ E. Washington
Allen Martha, wid. William, r. 134 Virginia av.
Allen Mary, wid. Larew, r. 159 Meek
ALLEN N. M. MRS. dress and cloak making 36½ E. Washington bds. Palmer House
Allen Robert, moulder, r. 31 W. Georgia
Allen Stella Mrs. bds. Stanridge House
Allen Thomas C. r. 181 N. Delaware
Allen William A. bds. Palmer House
Allison Joseph, plasterer, r. 30 Fletcher av.
Allison Mary, wid. Dr. L. r. Pennsylvania nw. cor. Market
Allred Garrison W. sexton City and Green Lawn Cemeteries, office and entrance ws. Kentucky av. bet. Louisiana and River, r. 215 N. South
Alstrod Henry, cabinetmkr. r. 184 Winston
Alt John, carpenter, r. 463 N. Alabama
Altenburger Jacob, wks. Wheat, Fletcher & Co. r. es. Blake 6 s. New York
Alters A. bds. Jefferson House
Althoff James, wks. Indianapolis Paper Co. r. 300 S. Missouri
Althoff James B. r. 300 S. Missouri
Altland Hiram, constable, r. 150 Ft. Wayne av.
Altland Samuel T. carpenter, r. 179 N. Spring
Altman Hermann, (H. Altman & Co.) r. Bluff rd. cor. Ray
Altman H. & Co. (H. Altman, W. Sogemuer and W. Mayer) grocery and Saloon, Bluff rd. cor. Ray
Alum John, saw grinder, bds. 75 S. Pennsylvania
Alvey James H. (Carr & Alvey) r. 548 N. Tennessee
Alvord Elijah S. prest. Citizen's Street R. R. Co. r. 92 N. Pennsylvania
Alvord James C. sec. Citizen's Street R. R. Co. r. 92 N. Pennsylvania
Alvord Mary, wid. E. B. r. 334 N. Illinois
Alward Samuel, (Stoneman, Pee & Co.) r. 247 N. East
Amack Anna, wid. r. 83½ E. Washington
Amberg Charles, shipping clk. Spiegel & Thoms, r. 186 Davidson
Amberg George, r. 168 Davidson
Ambrose Franklin, (col'd) lab. r. opp. City Hospital
Ambrose Morris, lab. I. C. & L. R. W.
American House Wife, Mrs. M. M. B. Goodwin, editor and propr. Meridian se. cor. Circle
American Leg and Arm Co. Haywood & Co. props. 172 E. Washington
AMERICAN MERCHANTS' UNION EXPRESS CO. E. W. Sloane supt. J. Butterfield agt. 42 and 44 E. Washington
AMES CHAPEL, Russel av. nr. Illinois

AMM	38	AND

Ammon George, wks. J. S. Cary & Co.

Amos —— r. ss. 2d bet. Illinois and Meridian

Amos Isaac, gas fitter, r. Missouri nr. First

Amos James, spinner Hoosier Woolen Factory, r. 408 W. Washington (nat. road)

Amos Robert C. salesman, Pettis, Dickson & Co. bds. 218 E. Market

Amos Samuel, wks. Hoosier Woolen Factory

Amos Thomas D. court bailiff, r. 218 N. Davidson

Amos William, brick layer, r. Missouri nr. First

Amsler Frederick, trunkmkr. M. Burton, bds. California House

Amthor William, bookkeeper, r. 253 N. Noble

ANCHOR LIFE INSURANCE COMPANY OF NEW YORK, A. H. Turner State agt. office No. 1 Wiley's Block N. Pennsylvania nr. Washington

Anders E. S. r. 36 Rose

Anders Henry, (col'd) lab. r. 225 N. Ohio

Anderson ——, brakeman, bds 58 Benton

Anderson August, lab. Rolling Mills

Anderson Bell, artist, r. 186½ W. Washington

Anderson Caroline, wid. Henry S. r. ns. E. North bet. New Jersey and East

Anderson Charles, wks. Emerson, Beam & Thompson, r. 28 N. New Jersey

Anderson Charles, (col'd) cook Sherman House

Anderson Cynthia, wid. George, r. 177 E. Market

Anderson David, salesman Pettis, Dickson & Co. bds. Macey House

Anderson David, wks. Emerson, Beam & Thompson, r. 70 Indiana av.

Anderson Edward, lab. Rolling Mills

Anderson Edward, plasterer, r. 82 N. Pennsylvania

Anderson Edward, puddler Indianapolis Rolling Mill

Anderson Fidelia, r. 418 N. Tennessee

Anderson George, carpenter in al. rear 177 E. Market, r. 191 E. Market

Anderson George P. real estate and patent right agt. and notary public, 2 Wiley's Block ws. Pennsylvania nr. Washington, r. 279 E. South

Anderson H. P. (Anderson & Scott) r. New Palestine

Anderson Harry, lab. r. 160 Huron

Anderson Henry, r. 177 E. Market

Anderson J. N. clk. Browning & Sloan

Anderson James r. 177 E. Market

Anderson James T. (Anderson, Bullock & Schofield) r. 367 N. New Jersey

Anderson Jerome S. salesman J. N. Conklin, r. 163 N. Tennessee

Anderson John, wks. Emerson, Beam & Thompson, r. 34 N. New Jersey

Anderson Randolph W. carpenter Hill & Wingate, r. 435 E. Georgia

AND	39	APP

Anderson Robert, brick mason, r. 351 E. Market
Anderson Robert, cook Union Depot Dining Hall, r. 189 S. Illinois
Anderson Thomas, carpenter, r. 413 N. Mississippi
Anderson William, clk. J. F. Wingate, r. 177 E. Market
Anderson William, conductor, bds. 58 Benton
ANDERSON, BULLOCK & SCHOFIELD, (James T. Anderson, James B. Bullock and Nathaniel N. Schofield) importers and whole-sale dealers in Hardware, 62 S. Meridian
ANDERSON & SCOTT, (H. P. Anderson and E. P. Scott) flour and feed, 180 E. Washington
Andra John, harness and saddle mkr. 178 E. Washington, r. same
Andrews Alfred A. cigar mkr. r. 126 N. Mississippi
Andrews George W. (col'd) cooper, r. 177 Indiana av.
Andrews John B. confectioner, bds. Neiman House
ANDREWS LYMAN N. gen'l freight agt. Indianapolis, Peru & Chicago R. R. r. 444 N. Tennessee
Andrews Philip, (col'd) lab. r. 239 N. Tennessee
Andrews Robert, heater Rolling Mill, r. 236 S. Missouri
Andrews Samuel B. photographer 94 E. Washington, r. 82 Ft. Wayne av.
Angle Abraham R. conductor R. R. r. 34 N. Delaware
Angus Walter W. teacher Indiana Deaf and Dumb Institute, r. Washington e. of Limits
Anhorn Eibert, painter, r. ss. St. Clair bet. Noble and Railroad
Anhorn Gottlieb, painter, r. Court bet. East and New Jersey
Ankenbrook Henry, drayman Ryan & Holbrook, r. 351 S. Delaware
Anker Aristides, (Haebl & Anker) r. 182 E. Washington
Annan Charles, (J. W. Copeland & Co.) bds. Pyle House
Ante Jacob, blacksmith, r. 426 S. Illinois
Anthony J. carpenter T. J. Morse, r. 256 Blake cor. Michigan
Anthony John, hostler Citizens' Street R. R. Co. bds. Globe House
Antlees Esther A. wid. r. 373 E. Georgia
Anton Andrew, news dealer, r. 277 S. New Jersey
Anton K. pedler, r. 82 E. South
Antrim James, blacksmith, R. A. Darbon, r. Plum nr. Vine
Antrim Levi, r. ws. Plum nr. Vine
Antrim William H. driver Express Co. r. ws. Plum bet. Cherry and Vine
Apperson Isaac H. driver Citizens' Street R. R. Co. r. 256 Madison av
Apperson Isaac M. clk. Kiefer & Vinton, bds. 256 Madison av.
Apperson Mary, dressmkr. Mrs. N. M. Allen, r. 256 Madison av.
Apperson Sarah, presser H. Malpas, r. 256 Madison av.
Apple John H. clk. David Hanna, bds. 203 Massachusetts av.
APPLEBY ROBERT, furniture dealer, 83 N. Illinois, r. same
Applegate A. W. traveling agt. r. 175 E. Washington
Applegate Berg, (Severin Schnell) r. Fletcher rd. ne. city limits nr. Arsenal

C. J. BRACKEBUSH, Farm Machinery, Hardware and Seeds, Nos. 75 and 77 W. Washington st., Indianapolis.

Applemade Adolph, agt. Ætna Ins. Co. office Ætna Bldg, r. 23 W. North

Appleton W. P. printer, bds. Little's Hotel

Appollo Garden, Kentucky av. cor. S. Tennessee

Arbuckle Matthew, (Witt & Arbuckle) r. N. Delaware n. of city limits

Archer William, salesman, r. 780 N. Illinois

ARDEN J. boot and shoe mnfr. and dealer 65 S. Meridian r. same

Armacost Ellis, carpenter, r. 337 N. Noble

Armbruster Frank E. White River Saloon ss. W. Washington 2 e. the bridge, r. same

Armbruster John J. saloon 215 W. Maryland, r. 79 S. West

Arms —— Mrs. wid. r. 126 N. Mississippi

Armstead James, wizard oil mnfr. r. 362 N. West

Armstrong George F. messenger A. M. U. Ex. Co.

Armstrong George, agt. Howe Sewing Machine, r. 162 S. Illinois

Armstrong Henry, clk. bds. 338 W. Washington

Armstrong Mary Miss, r. 268 E. Washington

Armstrong Mary, wid. Charles, r. 78 Fayette

Armstrong William, clergyman, r, 35 W. St. Clair

Armstrong William, (col'd) lab. r. Rhode Island nr. Blake

Armstrong William S. (Vinnedge, Jones & Co.) r. 180 N. Illinois.

Arnett Spencer, (col'd) lab. r. 179 Eddy

Arnholter Henry, (Henry Arnholter & Bro.) r. 323 E. Ohio

Arnholter William, (Henry Arnholter & Bro.) r. 323 E. Ohio

Arnholter Henry & Bro. (Henry and William Arnholter) harness and saddle mnfrs. 225 E. Washington

Arnold Emma, wid. William, r. 222 N. New Jersey

Arnold John, lab. r. Michigan nr. junction Washington

Arnold Martha J. wid. Willis, r. Michigan rd. nr. Washington

Arnold Peter, clk. Richards & Thomas, r. 17 N. New Jersey

Arnold Peter, lab. Union Novelty Works, r. 17 N. New Jersey

Arnold Taylor, lab. r. Michigan rd. nr. Washington

Arnouil Leopold, lab. r. 320 S. West

Aron Adolphus, salesman J. H. Baldwin & Co. r. 54 and 56 W. New York

Arthur Thomas, moulder Greenleaf & Co. r. 75 Norwood

Arthur William stonecutter, r. 21 Pitt

Arthur William A. moulder Union Novelty Works, bds. 75 Norwood

Artis William H. (col'd) hair dresser and barber 197 W. Washington, bds. 181 W. Washington

ASBURY METHODIST EPISCOPAL CHURCH, ws. New Jersey bet. Louisiana and South, Samuel T. Gillett, D. D. pastor

Ashe William, porter, r. 111 N. Spring

Asher John R. (Asher, Adams & Higgins) r. Davenport, Iowa

ASHER, ADAMS & HIGGINS, (John R. Asher, George H. Adams and Charles J. Higgins) book and map publishers and wholesale dealers in books, maps and school apparatus 76 E. Market

Bingham's Jewelry Store, cor. Pennsylvania and Washington Sts.

ASH   41   AVE

Ashley Thomas, foreman Bunte, Dickson & Co. r. 402 E. Michigan

Ashmead Jacob N. r. 240 N. Noble

Ashmead John S. carpenter, r. 240 N. Noble

Ashmead Seely W. engineer C. C. & I. C. R. R. r. 240 N. Noble

ASMUS LOUIS, saloon and billiard hall 199 Indiana av. r. same

Astly Samuel C. salesman A. F. Coors, r. 14 S. Mississippi

Astor Saloon, (Joseph Deschler) 15 N. Pennsylvania

Atherton Fenton, brakeman, bds. 58 Benton

Atherton William F. printer R. R. City Printing Co. r. 477 N. New Jersey

ATHON JAMES S, physician and surgeon. rooms 5 and 7, 26 Kentucky av. r. N. Meridian ne. cor. 1st

Atkins Elias C. (E. C. Atkins & Co. and J. H. Kappes & Co.) r. Idaho Territory

Atkins George W. sawmkr. Sheffield Saw Works, bds. Pyle House

ATKINS E. C. & CO. (E. C. Atkins, J. H. Kappes and H. Knippenberg) proprs. Sheffield Saw Works, 210 to 226 S. Illinois

Atkinson Joseph H. r. 237 S. Delaware

Atkinson Thomas J. painter, r. 181 Virginia av

Attison Henry, (col'd) lab. r. Missouri nr. 7th

Attridge Richard master car repairs C. C. & I. C. R. R. r. 236 Winston

Aubrey Clinton, painter, bds. 427 N. Mississippi

Auch, Andrew varnisher Cabinet Maker's Union

Aufderheide Gottfried, painter, r. 275 Davidson

Aufderheide Henry, carpenter, r. 241 Davidson

Aufderheide John H. r. 241 Davidson

Aufderheide Joseph, expressman, r. 432 E. Vermont

Aufderheide William, turner Cabinet Maker's Union

Aughinbaugh Edward L. (Aughinbaugh & Bro.) and prescription clk. Browning and Sloan, r. 88 W. Ohio

Aughinbaugh Perry, (Aughinbaugh & Bro.) r. 88 W. Ohio

Aughinbaugh Sarah, wid. Perry, r. 88 W. Ohio

Aughinbaugh William M. Longsdorf & Co. bds. 88 W. Ohio

Aughinbaugh & Bro. (Edward L. and Perry Aughinbaugh) dealers in fancy goods, etc. 7 Martindale's Block opp. P. O.

Angstein Charles, varnisher Cabinet Maker's Union r. 344 Railroad

Aukonbrock Henry, drayman, r. 351 S. Delaware

Ault Elizabeth, wid. Christopher. r. ws. Blake 2 s. New York

AURORA FIRE INS. CO. OF COVINGTON, KY. Tobias M. Murphy agt. room 9 (2d floor) Martindale's Block

Austermiller Otto, engineer T. H. & I. R. R. r. 157 W. South

Austin George T. adjuster Howe Sewing Machine, r. 160 E. St. Joseph

Austin Margaret Mrs. dressmkr. 32 N. Delaware, r. same

Austin Mary, wid. Thomas W. r. 314 N. East

Austin Samuel C. cabinetmkr. r. 166 N. Delaware

Avels George, salesman J. H. Avels, r. 257 S. Delaware

Avels Joseph H. flour, feed and produce 61 N. Illinois, r. same

AVE	42	BAG

Avels Margaret, wid. Henry, r. 357 S. Delaware
Averill Joseph, checkman T. H. & I. R. R. r. 103 W. South
Avery John L. treas. Builder's and Manufacturer's Association r. East nw. cor. Walnut
Avery John P. physician and surgeon 1 Massachusetts av. r. 256 N. Alabama
Avery Joseph, carpenter, r. 123 E. Ohio
Avis Samuel, bds. Nagle House
Axum William, lab. Osgood, Smith & Co. r. 213 W. McCarty
Ayeres Lucy, wid. E. S. r. 240 N. Meridian

B

Baar B. J. tailor 174 E. Market, r. same
Baas John, lab. brick yard, r. 241 Union
Baatling John, bds. Jefferson House
Babbitt Alonzo P. compositor Journal News Room, r. 23 Pitt
Babbitt Samuel, shoemkr. r. 179 N. Noble
Bach Casper, lab. Hair and Bristle Works, r. Bluff rd. s. of limits
Bach John, eating house, 30 W. Louisiana, r. same
Back Clemens, (Back & Wenken) r. Market cor. Noble
Back Hubbard, shoemkr. F. Robinius
Back John, lab. Bellefontaine Freight Depot, bds. 233 Union
Back & Wenken, (Clemens Back and Erust Wenken) tobacconists, 209 E. Washington
Backemeier Frederick, baggageman Union Depot, r. 235 Union
Backman Ester, wid. William, r. 408 W. North
Backus Vic. helper Ind. Coach Works, bds. 124 S. Meridian
Bacon Albert, painter, r. 75 N. Pennsylvania
Bacon Cora Miss, music teacher, bds. 62 S. Pennsylvania
Bacon E. H. physician, Washington sw. cor. Meridian
Bacon Eliza J. wid. Elisha, r. 307 N. Alabama
Bacon George, helper B. F. Haugh & Co. r. 307 N. Alabama
Bacon John L. blacksmith B. F. Haugh & Co. r. 307 N. Alabama
Bacon Joseph E. engineer, r. 22 Bates
Bacon Robert D. clk. John E. Fawkner, r. 75 N. Pennsylvania
Bacon Theodore, bookkeeper, bds. 510 N. Delaware
Bacon William, painter, r. 174 E. North
Bacon William, keeper Toll Gate, Indiana av. r. same
Bade Antony, checkman Central Freight Depot, r. 209 S. Alabama
Bade Charles, clk. Edward Sexauer, bds. 125 E. Washington
Bade John, teamster, bds. 65 S. East
Bade William, bds. 209 S. Alabama
Badger Theodore, notions, 175 W. Washington, r. same
Baenake Frederick, lab. r. S. East, s. of limits
Baer Powell, r. 113 Indiana av.
Baggs Frederick, bookkeeper Kennedy, Byram & Co. r. 125 E. Ohio
Bagley Charles, cigarmkr. bds. 160 E. Market

Bagley Jane Mrs. boarding house, 36 W. Maryland, r. same
Bagley Sophia, wid. r. 431 N. Tennessee
Bailer John, driver Street Car, r. 116 Bluff rd.
Bailey George W. painter, r. 225 N. New Jersey
Bailey Julius M. carpenter, r. 22 Bates
Bailey Martha, chambermaid Institute for the Blind, r. same
Bailey Robert, engineer J. G. Hanning, r. 50 Fletcher av.
Bailie Hamilton, coal dealer, r. 348 W. Washington
Bain James, student, bds. 398 N. New Jersey
Bainbridge Mahlon S. plasterer, r. 248 E. Louisiana
Baine Jennie Mrs. dressmkr. 20 W. Maryland, r. same
Bair Leonidas, harnessmkr. Daniel Sellers, bds. 20 E. Market
BAIRD WILLIAM, cooper, Helen sw. cor. W. Maryland, r. 112 N.
     Pennsylvania
Bakemeier Henry, lab. r. 419 Virginia av.
Baker A. H. (Baker & Surbey) r. 228 E. South
Baker Albert R. printer H. C. Chandler & Co. bds. 84 Massa-
     chusetts av.
Baker Anna Mrs. milliner, 42 S. Illinois, r. same
Baker Catherine, wid. Frederick, r. 317 N. Illinois
Baker Charles, clk. J. Wissert, bds. 180 S. Meridian
Baker Charles, madison ale, 211 Massachusetts av. r. same
BAKER CONRAD, governor of the State of Indiana, office State
     House, r. 173 N. Tennessee
Baker Edward, pressman H. C. Chandler & Co. bds. 2 Indi-
     ana av.
Baker Frederick, plasterer, r. 317 N. Illinois
Baker Henry, lab. B. F. Haugh & Co. r. 208 N. Illinois
Baker Henry, lab. r. 317 N. Illinois
Baker James, brakeman, bds. 58 Benton
Baker James P. law student, bds. Avenue House
Baker Jesse A. bookkeeper J. C. McIver, r. 244 E. Wash-
     ington
Baker John, machinist Sinker & Co. r. 194 E. McCarty
Baker John H. boot and shoemkr. 63 Massachusetts av. r. ss.
     New York, bet. Delaware and Alabama
Baker Nathan S. (N. S. Baker & Co.) r. 75 S. Noble
Baker N. S. & Co. (Nathan S. Baker and ——) furniture and
     matresses, 73 E. Washington
Baker S. W. salesman Pettis, Dickson & Co. r. 244 E. Wash-
     ington
Baker Thomas M. saloonkeeper, r. 64 Oak
Baker & Surbey, (A. H. Baker and J. S. Surbey) grocers, 199
     Virginia av.
Baking William, r. 1 Eden's Block 77½ Market
Baldwick Fred. R. eating house 32 W. Louisiana, r. same
Baldwin B. L. engineer, r. 301 E. Georgia
Baldwin Hattie, dressmkr. S. Coles, r. 197 N. Illinois
Baldwin James, clk. r. 289 Virginia av.
Baldwin J. Herman, (J. H. Baldwin & Co.) r. 396 N. Me-
     ridian

BAL	44	BAN

BALDWIN J. H. & CO. (J. Herman Baldwin, George S. Warren) importers of German, French and English fancy goods, notions, toys, &c. Fancy Bazaar, 6 E. Washington

Balior Rachael, wid. James, r. 68 Plum

Balke Charles, saloon 231 E. Washington, r. same

Ball Fletcher, (col'd) lab. r. 241 W. Ohio

Ball John E. telegraph operator Union Depot, r. 135 W. Maryland

Ball Matilda, wid. Edwin, r. 91 S. Illinois

Ball William, carpenter, John Fearnley, r. 135 W. Maryland

Ballard Austin, seal engraver, r. 28 Circle

Ballard G. M. receiver Internal Rev. office room 8, P. O. bldg. r. 356 N. Alabama

Ballard James M. r. 52 Indiana av.

Ballard Owen (col'd) lab. Osgood, Smith & Co

Ballard Samuel, boarding house, 70 E. Market

Ballard Thomas, (col'd) farmer, r. al. bet. Noble and Benton, Georgia and Meek

Ballard William, carpenter, r. 52 Indiana av.

Ballard William, shoemkr. L. Siersdorfer, r. 45 S. Illinois

Ballard William P. ins. agt. r. 487 N. Mississippi

BALLENGER JOHN H. reporter Charless Publishing Co. St. Louis, bds. Sherman House

Ballett Leaven, (col'd) carpenter, r. Missouri nr. 7th

Ballinger Elijah M. carpenter, r. 161 St. Mary

Ballman Herman, tailor, 200 S. Illinois, r. 400 S. Illinois

Balls Antony, baker, 178 S. Illinois, r. same

Ballweg Ambrose mnfr. and dealer in guns, rifles and pistols, 129 W. Washington, r. 26 Ft. Wayne av.

Ballweg Frederick, saloon, 131 W. Washington, r. same

Bals Charles H. G. (Hahn & Bals) r. 110 E. St. Joseph

Bals Christ, tender John Frick, r. 107 E. St. Joseph

BALTIMORE & OHIO R. W. Sam'l P. Hazzard, western freight agt. office Virginia av. cor. Alabama

Balz Frederick, clk. P. Balz, bds. 425 N. Illinois

Balz Peter, (Sponsel & Balz) r. Madison rd. nr. city limits

Balz Philip, butcher, 427 N. Illinois, r. 425 N. Illinois

BAMBERGER HERMAN, hats, caps, furs and straw goods, 16 E. Washington, r. 1 Ft. Wayne av.

Bamberger Isaac, salesman H. Bamberger, bds. 18 Circle

Banard Timothy, lab. r. rear Rolling Mill

Banes James, bds. 144 N. Tennessee

Bangs E. lab. McKendry & Lovecraft

Bangs J. engineer McKendry & Lovecraft

Banks James, (col'd) lab. r. 3d nr. Lafayette R. R.

Banks John H. carpenter C. C. & I. C. R. R. r. 526 E. Georgia

Banna Matthew, blacksmith Eagle Machine Wks, r. 217 S. Illinois

Bannister W. shoemkr. r. 65 S. Illinois

Bannon James, lab. Gates, Pray & Co. r. 487 Virginia av

Bannon Matthew, blacksmith, bds. 217 S. Illinois

Bannwuarth Benjamin, shoemkr. 48 Massachusetts av. r. same

Banta John, P. (Indiana Banking Co.) r. Franklin, Ind

Baptist Church, (col'd) ns. Michigan bet. Indiana av. and West
BAPTIST MISSION CHURCH, ws. Noble bet. South and Huron
Barnard Gust, machinist, bds. 65 S. East
Barbee Henry, engineer Indianapolis Printing and Publishing House
Barbee Isadore, student, r. 385 N. East
Barbee Robert B. policeman, r. 385 N. East
Barbee Sampson, moulder D. Root & Co. r. 32 Dougherty
Barbee Sampson, r. 125 E. North
Barber Edward, carpenter, r. 75 Elizabeth
Barber James H. (col'd) lab. r. 340 Indiana av.
Barbour Annie Miss, teacher Fourth ward School, r. Meridian cor. 5th
Barbour Linus, student, r. N. Meridian cor. 5th
Barbour Lucian, (Barbour & Jacobs) r. N. Meridian cor. 5th
Barbour Samuel, clk. post office, r. 216 N. West
Barbour Thomas, civil engineer, r. 216 N. West
Barbour Thomas F. sawmkr. Sheffield Saw Works, bds. Pyle House
BARBOUR & JACOBS, (Lucian Barbour and Charles P. Jacobs) lawyers, 14 N. Delaware
Barclay James, stone cutter, r. 206 E. Market
Baret Caspar, rag dealer, r. 270 S. Delaware
Barfuss G. watchmkr. and jeweler, 79 S. Illinois, r. same
Barger George W. lab. r. 183 Maple
Barker —— bds. Circle se. cor. Market
Barker John, watchman, r. 149 Winston
Barker Kate, cloak and dressmkr. 19 Massachusetts av. r. same
Barker Mary T. wid. Enoch. r. 227 E. Market
Barker Myron I. (Barker, Williams & Co.) r. 269 E. South
Barker Samuel, meat market, ss. St. Clair bet. East and New Jersey, r. same
Barker William W. (W. W. Barker & Co.) r. 19 Massachusetts av.
Barker W. W. & Co. (William W. Barker and John E. Redford) cigars and tobacco, 22 N. Pennsylvania and 21 Massachusetts av.
BARKER, WILLIAMS & CO. (M. T. Barker, W. Williams and C. J. Veith) proprs. Capitol Tobacco and Cigar Works, mnfrs. and wholesale dealers in cigars and tobacco, 42 W. Washington. factory 19 to 23 N. Tennessee
Barkley William S. law student, Parker & Bloome, bds. 75 N. California
Barkman Frank, soapmkr, r. S. West nr. Jones
Barkus Sarah E. wid. William, r. 9 S. Mississippi
Barlow Liberty, (col'd) shoemkr. r. 141 W. Washington
BARLOW THOMAS J. saloon, 79 E. Washington, r. 84 S. Mississippi
Barmeier Bernhard, clk. Clemens Vonnegut, bds. 180 E. Washington
Barnaby Catherine, wid. William, r. 181 Elizabeth

BAR	46	BAR

Barnard Eugene E. clk. L. H. Tyler & Co. bds. 35 Cherry

BARNARD J. gen. ins. agt. and secy. Chamber of Commerce, Vinton's Block Pennsylvania sw. cor. Market, r. 419 N. Illinois

Barnard M. R. bookagt. Bowen, Stewart & Co. r. 35 Cherry

Barneclo Henry, fireman C. C. & I. C. R. R. r. 53 Bates

Barneclo Lorenzo, machinist Eagle Machine Works, r. 156 S. Noble

Barneclo Rebecca, wid. John, M. r. 53 Bates

Barnes ——, conductor, bds. 58 Benton

Barnes A. A. propr. City Picture Palace, 39 E. Washington, r. 782 N. Illinois

Barnes Andrew, printer *Journal* Job Rooms, bds. 98 N. East

Barnes George H. carpenter. r. 326 E. Vermont

Barnes Henry F. physician and surgeon, room 6 McOuat Block Kentuckey av. r. 197 N. Alabama

Barnes Jerome B. cooper D. Burton & Co. r. 264 Indiana av.

Barnes R. A. physician, 66 Virginia av. r. same

Barnes Wesley N. compositor *Sentinel* News room, r. 144 N. Mississippi

Barnet Annie, wks. Caledonia Paper Mill

Barnet Edward, lab. r. 277 S. West

Barnet Francis, cloak and dressmkr. 11 Massachusetts av. r. same

Barnet Thomas, r. 19 W. Pratt

Barnett Nathaniel, carpenter, bds. 61 S. Noble

Barnett P. rag dealer, r. 115 W. McCarty

Barney Chester, asst. foreman *Sentinel* News room r. 70 N. Liberty

Barney Jacob, physician and surgeon, 81 S. Illinois, r. 245 N. Davidson

Barnitz Charles, real estate agt. 115 E. Washington, r. 177 S. Noble

Barnitz Jacob W. taxidermist, 115 E. Washington, r. 177 S. Noble

Barns Alexander, bds. 377 N. Illinois

Barns William, patent right dealer, r. 377 N. Illinois

Barr Jacob, blind mnfr. 424 N. Delaware, r. same

Barr Jacob, sawyer Rolling mill

Barr Lorenzo D. lab. Rolling mill, r. 233 S. Tennessee

BARR MARION J. grocer 233 S. Tennessee, bds. 169 S. Tennessee

Barr William, lab. bds. 27 Rose

Barrett Charles E. carriage painter, r. 666 N. Mississippi

Barrett Edward, lab. Rolling Mill

Barrett E. lab. r. 338 E. Washington

Barrett E. G. solicitor, *Evening Mirror*, r. 123 Huron

Barrett Henry, bartender J. Karny, bds. 36 W. Maryland

Barrett James, lab. bds. 425 S. Tennessee

Barrett James, lab. r. 126 Stevens

Barrett James Jr. wks. J. C. Ferguson & Co.

Barrett John, lab. r. Morris nr. New Jersey

Barrett Lucretia, wid. r. 123 Huron

BAR	47	BAS

Barrett Michael, wks. J. C. Ferguson & Co.
Barrett P. D. lab. r. Virginia av. nr. Bradshaw
Barrett Patrick, lab. r. 174 Meek
Barrett William, shoemaker, r. 47 S. Illinois
Barrett ——, r. 232 W. Georgia
Barrick George, lab. bds. 350 Spring
Barrit Patrick, lab. C. & I. J. R. R.
Barritt Frank, apprentice B. F. Hetherington & Co. r. 390 N. Mississippi
Barritt Michael, lab. r. 425 S. Tennessee
Barrow James M. medical student, r. 52 Indiana av.
Barrow Samuel, teamster G. W. Caldwell & Co. r. Indiana av.
Barry ——, stonecutter, r. 136 N. Spring
Barry Charles L. clerk Stewart & Morgan, bds. 528 N. Tennessee
Barry Edward, scroll sawyer Helwig & Co.
Barry Edward H. grand sec. I. O. G. T. office No. 2 Odd Fellows Hall, r. Tennessee nw. cor. 1st
Barry Ellen, wid. r. 368 S. Delaware
Barry John, gardener, r. 145 Huron
Barry John, scroll sawyer Helwig & Co.
Barry Patrick, lab. r. 203 W McCarty
Barry Thomas G. with Stewart & Morgan, r. 197 N. Delaware
Barth Charles, salesman Charles Mayer & Co. r. 387 N. West
Barth George, clerk J. W. Copeland & Co. bds. 387 N. West
Barth John W. salesman J. H. Vajen & Co. r. 387 N. West
Barth Louis A. news stand Union Depot, r. 233 Virginia av.
Barth Sebastian, Ins. agt. r. 387 N. West
Barthel Bernhard, (Barthel & Kaufmann) r. High nr. Smith's Brewery
Barthel & Kaufmann, (Bernhard Barthel and Louis Kaufmann) meat market, 32 Virginia av.
Barthels A. confectioner F. P. Becker & Bro. bds. 17 N. Pennsylvania
Bartholomew H. M. traveling agent Lines, Snelser & Co.
Bartholomew John C. millwright, r. 191½ E. Washington
Bartholomew P. W. lawyer, room 1, 20½ N. Delaware, bds. 160 N. Meridian
Bartholomew Thomas, cooper, r. 33 Ellen
Bartlett Alice, wid. Dewitt C. r. 237 N. New Jersey
Bartlett Arthur, salesman W. H. Sullivan r. 720 N. Illinois
Bartley Abraham, (col'd) r. rear 247 W. Ohio
Bartley Lydia, (col'd) r. ws. Geisendorff nr. New York
Bartley Thornton, (col'd) lab. r. 164 Douglas al.
Bartollas William, carpenter, r. 321 S. Delaware
Base Ernst, boardinghouse, 65 S. East, r. same
Bash Marshall, student, bds. 365 N. Alabama
Baskett John, (col'd) barber M. Mason
Bass J. (Henderson & Bass) r. 168 N. East
Bass John, lab. r. 170 Union
Bass Lovel, (col'd) cook, r. 126 S. Benton
Bassett Amanda, wid. Horace, r. 46 E. Ohio

| BAS | 48 | BEA |

Bassett Horace H. with B. D. Jones, r. Ohio nw. cor. Pennsylvania

Baster Edward, r. 187 Davidson

Basy A. H. machinist B. F. Haugh & Co. r. 79 E. Elm

Bates A. wks. J. S. Carey & Co.

Bates Caroline, Mrs. (col'd) r. 143 Bright

Bates Charles A. (Webb & Bates) r. 135 W. New York

Bates Daniel, moulder Eagle Machine Works, r. 134 S. East

Bates Harvey, r. 190 E. Market

Bates Harvey jr., assistant cashier First National Bank of Indianapolis, r. 185 N. Delaware

BATES HOUSE, N. D. Keneaster, propr. Illinois nw. cor. Washington

Bates House Block, Illinois nw. cor. Washington

Bates Mattie, wid. B. r. 44 Massachusetts av.

Bates Samuel, carpenter, bds. 356 N. West

Batey Elizabeth, wid. Abraham, r. rear 2 Ann

Batler Robert, clerk F. Seitz, bds. 117 S. Illinois

Batty Edwin, carpenter, r. ws. Broadway bet. Cherry and Christian av.

Batty George W. clerk D. E. Wilkinson, bds. n. end Broadway

Batty John, clerk Recorders office, r. 228 E. Louisiana

Batz William, blacksmith, r. 131 Bluff rd.

Bauer Adolph, printer, r. 348 S. Meridian

Bauer B. wid. George, r. ns. Kansas w. Bluff rd.

Bauer Frank, lab. r. 329 W. Market

Bauer Gottleib, tailor, r. 285 N. Noble

Bauer Henry, pres. Cabinet Makers Union, r. ns. Market nr. City limits

Bauer Jacob, lab. r. es. Camp nr. 1st

Bauer Mary, wid. George, r. 77 N. Illinois

Bauer Nicholas, stone mason, r. Bluff rd. nr. Wisconsin

Baugher F. W. salesman John Fishback

Baughn William, carpenter, r. Merrill cor. Eckert

Baum Levi H. r. 82 W. South

Bauman Andrew, policeman. r. Elizabeth se. cor. Douglas

Bauman Henry, tailor Frederick Scheldmeier, r. 237 N. Liberty

Baumhofer Henry, carpenter, r. 236 Madison av.

Baur Adolph, foreman Gutenberg Co. r. 348 S. Meridian

Bawler Thomas, helper Rolling Mill, bds. 300 S. Tennessee

Baxter John, school teacher, r. 85 Maple

Baxter John G. clk. Baxter & Davis, bds. 250 W. Washington

Baxter Peter D. (Baxter & Davis) r. 250 W. Washington

Baxter William, (col'd) lab. r. 247 Howard

Baxter & Davis, (Peter D. Baxter and Able F. Davis) groceries and provisions, 250 W. Washington

Baylor Albert E. salesman G. E. Gordon, bds. 24 West Georgia

Beach Daniel W. compositor *Journal* News Room, r. 126 E. Michigan

Beal Jerome, traveling agt. J. Sweetser

Beal Joshua, paper hanger Gall & Rush, r. 77 W. Walnut

Beal William, butcher, r. 306 W. Washington
Beam David (Emerson, Beam & Thompson) r. 187 S. Tennessee
Bear —— harnessmkr. bds. 70 E. Market
Beard Amos, wagonmkr. Ind. Agricultural Works, r. 443 S. Illinois
Beard Benjamin F. plowmkr. N. Kimball, r. 80 S. Mississippi
Beard Solomon, manager Kimball Plow Manufatory, r. 80 S. Mississippi
Beardsley H. Millard, clk. R. E. Beardsley, bds. 336 N. Alabama
BEARDSLEY R. E. gen'l ins. agt. 11 N. Meridian, r. 336 N. Alabama
Bearman Henry, lab. C. C. C. & I. R. R. Outer Freight Depot
Beasler Thomas, boot and shoemkr. 137 N. Tennessee, bds. 144 N. Tennessee
Beaty David S. r. 194 E. Michigan
Beaty John, wks. Simms & Hoskins
Beaven Samuel W. salesman Pettis, Dickson & Co. bds. 218 E. Market
Beaver Elisha, teamster, r. 380 N. West
Beaver John, teamster, r. 259 E. McCarty
Beaver Kate, packer Barker, Williams & Co.
Beaver Leonidas, draughtsman J. Hodgson, bds. Pyle House
Beaver R. I. bookbinder *Journal* Bindery, r. 380 W. West
Beaver Thomas F. r. 74 Massachusetts av.
Beavers John W. driver City R. R. r. 338 E. Washington
Becher Henry, meat market, 122 Bluff rd. r. same
Beck Albert T. attorney at law and notary public, 4 Brown's Block, Pennsylvania nr. Washington, bds. 132 N. Mississippi
Beck Andrew, bds. 103 W. South
Beck Benedict, butcher, r. 407 S. Illinois
Beck Benedict, railshearer Rolling Mills
Beck Charles, railshearer Rolling Mills
Beck Christian, gunsmith, 12 S. Pennsylvania av. r. 154 N. New Jersey
Beck Clemens, cigars and tobacco, r. 108 S. Noble
Beck Conrad, r. rear 222 Union
Beck Conrad, brewer Harting & Bro.
Beck Conrad, baker Fred. C. Bollman, bds. 107 E. Washington
Beck David, bds. 154 N. New Jersey
Beck Edward, saloon and restaurant, 44 W. Washington, r. 27 W. Maryland
Beck Frederick, meat market, Meridian sw. cor. McCarty, r. 7 W. McCarty
Beck Henry, baker, 88 Ft. Wayne av.
Beck Herman, r. 331 S. Meridian
Beck James A. shipping clk. A. V. Lawrence
Beck John, railshearer, Rolling Mill
Beck Joseph W. clk. George K. Share & Co. bds. 152 N. Mississippi
Beck Michael, barber B. Fisher, r. 35 W. Georgia
Beck Michael, cigarmkr. r. 141 Union

BEC	50	BEL

Beck Rupert, r. rear 222 Union
Beck Samuel, gunsmith, 63 E. Washington, r. 152 Mississippi
Beck Samuel T. watchmkr. 43 S. Illinois, bds 152 N. Mississippi
Beck Sarah E. Miss. teacher 9th Ward School, r. 154 N. New
    Jersey
Beckel Jacob, bds. 575 S. Illinois
Becker F. P. (F. P. Becker & Bro.) r. 17 N. Pennsylvania
Becker George, surgical instrument mkr. August Piscator, bds.
    Meridian nr. Union Depot
Becker Henry, lab. Butsch & Dickson, r. 324 Madison av.
Becker Jacob, (Becker & Huber) r. 180 N. New Jersey
Becker Jacob, cigarmkr. Henry Schulz, bds. 176 S. Delaware
Becker John, r. 180 N. New Jersey
Becker Joseph, (F. P. Becker & Bro.) r. 17 N. Pennsylvania
Becker F. P. & Bro. (F. P. and Joseph Becker) confectioners
    and ladies' restaurant, 17 N. Pennsylvania
BECKER & HUBER, (Jacob Becker and Jacob Huber) merchant
    tailors, 77 E. Washington
Becket Theophilus M. engineer C. C. & I. C. R. R. r. 473 E.
    Georgia
Beckley James S. produce dealer, r. 258 Bluff rd.
Beckman Christiana, wid. William, r. 332 S. Alabama
Beckmann J. W. engraver, 46 Virginia av. r. same
Beckwith Frank, (col'd) lab. r. 177 St. Mary
Beeler Lorenzo D. carpenter, r. 99 Benton
Beeman Truman, carpenter, r. 262 N. East
Beemer Mary, wid. August, 44 Virginia av
Beerbower E. J. upholsterer C. C. C. & I. R. R.
Beeson J. W. lab. Osgood, Smith & Co.
Beeson William r. 51 Maple
Beethooven Society, Charles Hess, director, 35½ E. Washington
Behler Louis, saddler, r. ns. McCarty 1 s. of East
Behrent Henry, teamster. r. 187 Harrison
Behrig Ernst, teamster, r. 472 S. West
BEHRINGER JOSEPH, saloon, 145 W. Washington, r. same
Behrmann William, shoemkr. Charles Rehling, bds. 218 E.
    Washington
Behymer Simeon, lumber dealer, r. 247 N. New Jersey
Beiter Matthias, machinist Spiegel & Thoms
Belcer George, lab. r. 141 St. Mary
Belcher Edward, teamster, r. 174 N. Davidson
Belcher William, teamster, r. 139 Huron
Belk Fred. railshearer Rolling Mill, r. 16 Chadwick
Belke Henry, pianomkr. Indianapolis Piano Mnfg. Co. r. 16
    Chadwick
Bell Alfred R. compositor *Daily Evening Commercial*, r. Tennessee
    se. cor. New York
Bell Amanda, r. ns. New York 2 e. Minerva
Bell Andrew, (col'd) shoemkr. r. 345 N. Alabama
Bell James B. propr. Pattison House, 63 N. Alabama, r. same
Bell John S. druggist, 212 E. Washington, r. same

Bell Miletus, druggist, 261 Massachusetts av. r. 484 N. East
Bell Samuel, checkman Freight Depot C. C. & I. C. R. R. bds. 426 S. Tennessee
Bell William, (col'd) barber Knox & Embers
Bell William, expressman, r. 248 Blackford
Bell William, principal High School, bds. Pyle House
Bell William H. painter Ryan Bros. r. 51 Dougherty
Bellis John R. machinist Sinker & Co. bds. Ray House
Beltz Harry A. cigars and tobacco ret. and newspapers, Spencer House, r. 175 Stevens
Beltz Jacob, plasterer, r. 175 Stevens
Belzer George, machinist Eagle Machine Works, r. 141 St. Mary
Belzer Joseph, carpenter, r. 332 E. New York
Belzer William, machinist Eagle Machine Wks. bds. 141 St. Mary
Benauer, Usef. wood yard, r. 132 Huron
Benaway A. cigarmkr. r. 370 E. New York
Benaway Emily, wid. r. 370 E. New York
Bence Robert F. physician, r. 86 Ash
Bender George A. chairmkr. r. 168 N. Noble
Bender Louis L. compositor W S. Cameron, bds. Commercial Hotel
Bender Tobias (Tobias Bender & Co.) r. 192 E. Market
BENDER TOBIAS & CO. (Tobias Bender and John B. Stumpf) rectifiers and wholesale dealers in wines and liquors, 189 E. Washington
Benham Azel W. (Sochner & Benham) r. 235 E. Vermont
Benham Henry L. (H. L. Benham & Co.) r. 235 E. Vermont
BENHAM H. L. & CO. (Henry L. Benham and E. Sharpe) music dealers and publishers of the *Western Musical Review*, No. 1 Martindale's Block, Market ne. cor. Pennsylvania
Benner Arthur, porter Wiles Bro. & Co. r. 13 Henry
Bennerschild August, machinist Sinker & Co. r. rear 259 S. Pennsylvania
Bennett Anna, dressmkr. r. 67 W. Georgia
Bennett F. F. carpenter, r. 117 Indiana av.
Bennett Frank F. salesman C. J. Brackebush, bds. 117 Indiana av.
Bennett George W. policeman, r. 286 E. St. Clair
Bennett H. W. paternmkr. Sinker & Co. r. 23 Chatham
Bennett Homer A. fireman, bds. 56 Bates
Bennett John B. telegraph operator Union Depot, r. Georgia cor. Tennessee
Bennett Lavina, wid. Charles, bds. 56 Bates
Benruer Benedict, tailor, r. 53 Coburn
Benson Aaron, sexton Jewish Synagogue, r. rear of Synagogue
Benson David S. second hand store, 206 S. Illinois, r. same
Benson John A. toll gate keeper White River Bridge, r. same
Benson John S. r. 61 Ft. Wayne av.
Benson Richard, wood worker Miller, Mitchell & Stough
Bentley Benjamin, machinist, bds. 169 S. Tennessee
Bentley Mary, (Bentley & Chandler) r. 44 Indiana av.

BENTLEY & CHANDLER, (Mary Bentley and **Mrs.** Maggie Chandler) dress and cloak making, 44 Indiana av.

Bentz Nicholas, lab. J. M. & I. R. R.

Benzil George, lab. Union Starch Factory, r. 282 N. Winston

Berendes Joseph, clerk N. Jose, r. 8 S. Pennsylvania

Berg Frederica, wid. Charley, r. 171 E. South

Berg Gustave, piano maker Indianapolis Piano Mnfng. Co. bds. 171 E. South

Berg Henry, (Berg & Waterman) r. 19 S. Tennessee

Berg S. V. Mrs. r. 92 E. New York

Berg William, reel driver Engine No. 3

Berg & Waterman, (Henry Berg and Christian Waterman) grocers, 193 S. Tennessee

Bergen Bridget, wid. William, r. 80 Maple

Bergener Gustav, bookkeeper Indianapolis Branch Bkg. Co. bds. 109 W. Washington

Bergenthal David C. bookkeeper E. Over & Co. r. 333 S. Alabama

Berger J. H. brakeman C. C. & I. C. R. R.

Bergitt Peter, lab. r. 89 Elm

Bergmann Francis, soap mnfr. s. end S. West, r. same

Bergstein Carl, **Prof.** teacher of German, French and Italian singing, 2 floor, room 11 Martindale's blk. bds. Emennegger Hotel

Berhamus John T. salesman Donaldson & Stout, r. 27 W. 1st

Berkhofer George, show case maker George Berkhofer, r. 354 Virginia av.

BERKHOFER GEORGE, show case mnfr. 5 Virginia av. r. 354 Virginia av.

Berkshire Life Ins. Co. of Pittsfield, Mass. Green & Tilford State agts. 21 N. Meridian

Bernauer Benedict, (Steinmann & Bernauer) r. Coburn nr. S. East

Bernd Daniel, blacksmith Ind. Coach Work, r. 435 S. Illinois

Berndt Bruno, clerk German Pharmacy, bds. 187 E. Washington

Berner Charles, salesman A. V. Lawrence, r. 248 Blake

Berner Frederick, (B. F. Hetherington & Co.) r. 373 S. Illinois

Berner John, expressman, r. 185 Davidson

Bernhamer W. F. A. law student, bds. 174 W. New York

Bernhamer William, plasterer, r. 284 N. West

Bernhard John, stone mason, r. 355 Spring

Bernhardt Ernst, clerk C. Schwomeyer, bds. 297 S. Meridian

Bernhardt William, cabinet maker, Helwig & Co.

Berran Kittie Miss, teacher German English school, r. 290 E. Ohio

Berry Andy, (col'd) lab. r. 6th nr. LaFayette R. R.

Berry Austin F. comp. *Journal* news room, bds. 126 N. Tennessee

Berry C. A. wid. Frank, r. 315 Wabash

Berry C. B. bricklayer, bds. Ray House

Berry Charles, bds. Macy House

Berry Charles, saw maker, Sheffield Saw Works

Berry Corinthia A. wid. Frank, r. rear 228 W. Georgia

Berry Daniel M. with Elliott & Mott, 87 E. Market

Berry G. W. brickmaker, r. 320 E. Washington

Berry John, tender J. Whitcomb, bds. 18 W. Georgia
Berry John, r. 310 Blake
Berry John, r. Wisconsin nr. Mill
Berry Marion, carpenter and builder 23 n. Noble, r. 272 Virginia av.
Berry Mary, wid. Edward, r. St. Clair nw. cor. Davidson
Berry M. machinist Sinker & Co.
Berryman James, machinist, r. 88 S. Noble
Berryman John, wagonmaker se. end Virginia av. r. 88 S. Noble
Berryman William, cooper, 88 S. Noble
Bershea Daniel, saloon 294 E Washington, r. same
Bert Henry L. solicitor A. C. Roach
Bertelsmann Fred, watch maker Theodore Zumbusch, r. 264 Massachusetts av.
Bertelsmann Lisette, wid. Henry, r. 264 Massachusetts av.
Berth William, lab. Greenleaf & Co.
Bertling John, rectifier Hahn & Bals, bds. Jefferson House
Bese Fred, lab. r. 324 E. Vermont
Bess William K. saloon, 284 W. Washington, r. same
Bessiones Augustus, pastor St. John's Church, r. ns. Georgia bet. Illinois and Tennessee
Best John, basket maker, r. Washington east of limits
Beston Michael, lab. r. 1 Elm
Bethel, Methodist Church, (African) 180 W. Georgia, William Travan pastor
Bethel Sunday School, Blake nw. cor. New York
Betts Henry, moulder Eagle Machine Works, bds. Nieman House
Beyer F. wid. Adam, midwife, 78 N. Noble, r. same
Beyer Josephine, wid. Casper, 180 E. Washington
Beyschlag Charles, editor Guttenberg Co. r. 227 S. Delaware
Beyschlag Charles, salesman H. H. Lee, r. 227 S. Delaware
Beyschlag George, clk. r. 227 S. Delaware
Bick Abbey, (col'd) wid. Harvey, r. 248 W. Ohio
Bicking House, W. Hebble prop. 89 S. Illinois
Biddy James M. lab. Gas Works, r. 526 S. Illinois
Bidleman Edward, lab. Osgood, Smith & Co.
Bidleman S. G. shoemaker C. Friedger, r. 259 S. Mississippi
Biedenmeister Charles A. ins. agt. 96 E. Washington, r. 149 N. East
Bieler Jacob L. (Franer, Bieler & Co.) r. McCarty nw. cor. East
Biener George, bookbinder Julius H. C. Smith, bds. Illinois House
Bienzen George, bds. 282 Winston
Biermann Henry, lab. r. 502 S. New Jersey
Biersdorfer George, saloon, Illinois cor. Indiana av. r. 7 Massachusetts av.
Bigelow I. S. Dep. Marshal, r. 161 Massachusetts av.
Bigelow Ira P. plasterer, r. 141 N. New Jersey
Bigelow James K. (Todd & Bigelow) r. 326 N. Illinois
Bigelow John S. plasterer, r. es. Clinton al. bet. E. Ohio and New York

BIG	54	BLA

Bigger Samuel S. salesman Trade Palace, r. 311 N. Delaware

BIGHAM HEYDEN S. flour, feed, and commission mer. 149 E. Washington cor. Alabama, r. 510 E. Washington

Billing Andrew, machinist, r. 136 S. East

Billings William, lab. Long & Joseph, r. ws. Minerva 2 S. Vermont

Bills J. M. lawyer, room 2 20½ N. Delaware, bds. Pyle House

Bingham J. W. clk. P. O.

Bingham James, stone cutter, r. Michigan rd. nr. junction Washington

BINGHAM JOSEPH J. editor in chief *State Sentinel*, r. 148 W. Maryland

Bingham Joseph W. student, bds. 148 W. Maryland.

Bingham Wheelock P. clk. W. P. Bingham & Co. r. 32 N. California

Bingham William, r. 32 N. California

BINGHAM W. P. & CO. (Wheelock P. Bingham & ——) Watches, Diamonds, Jewelry and Silver Ware, 50 E. Washington

Binkley Benjamin R. machinist Ind. Agricultural Works, bds. 169 S. Tennessee

Binkley Samuel, blacksmith, r. 230 S. Pennsylvania

Birch Richard E. pilot, r. 114 Broadway

Birchard Amos, (J. E. Robertson & Co.) r. 189 E. Ohio

Birchard G. A. clk. bds. 189 E. Ohio

Birchfield Lewis, driver J. Carlisle

Bird Abram, r. 129 N. Illinois

Bird Frank, r. 129 N. Illinois

Bird Henry, (col'd) barber, r. 75 W. Georgia

Bird James, lab. r. 280 Madison av.

Bird John C. (Spickelmeyer & Bird) r. 127 Indiana av.

Bird Mary, wid. Pratt, r.406 W. North

Birth William H. moulder, bds. 103 S. New Jersey

Bisbel Thomas, machinist C. C. & I. C. R. R.

Bisbing Jacob J. depot marshall Union Depot, r. 212 N. West

Bishop George M. fireman Fire Engin No. 3 r. 221 S. Alabama

Bishop J. W. engineer, r. 27 Massachusetts av.

Bishop James, driver Steamer No. 1, bds. 23 N. West

Bishop Jessie, (col'd) lab. r. 490 S. Illinois

Bishop Louis, lab. r. rear 391 N. New Jersey

Bishop Sarah, wid. John, r. 391 N. New Jersey

Bishop William, roller Rolling Mill, r. 270 S. Illinois

Bishop William, lab. r. 77 W. South

Bisking ——, carpenter, Eagle Machine Works, r. Ft. Wayne nr. St. Clair

Bisking Henry, machinist Eagle Machine Works, r. 140 Huron

Bisking William, moulder, r. 76 Fort Wayne av.

Bisplinghoff Herman, r. 189 E. Washington

Biter Mathias, wks. Speigle & Thoms, r. 71 S. Liberty

Bixler John, rope maker, r. 371 W. New York

Black C. W. traveling agt. bds. 2 Indiana av.

Black Charles, engineer, bds. 56 Bates

Black Charles H. blacksmith S. W. Drew, bds. 206 E. Ohio
Black Eagle Pharmacy, A. Metzner, propr. 127 E. Washington
Black G. lab. McKendry & Lovecraft
Black George, Carpenters, Builders and Mnfrs. Association, r. 390 N. West
Black George H. carpenter, r. 206 E. Ohio
Black J. S. Musical Institute, 25, 26 and 27 Talbott & News blk. r. 219 E. North
Black James B. reporter Supreme Court State bldg. rooms over 46 E. Washington, bds. Oriental House
Black Jerry, (col'd) lab. r. 10 Blaker
Black John H. employee A. M. U. Ex. Co.
Black Joseph, pump maker Thomas Davis, r. 402 N. West
Black Joshua, bds. 248 N. West
Black Julius, r. 390 N. West
Black Matthew, carpenter, r. 390 N. West
Black Peter, bds. 62 S. Pennsylvania
Black William, janitor Masonic Hall
Black William, tanner, r. 114 W. Georgia
Blackburn George W. (col'd) barber, r. 303 E. Washington
Blackford's Block, Washington se. cor. Meridian
Blackwell Michael, puddler Indianapolis Rolling Mill
Blackwell Thomas, puddler Rolling Mill, r. 131 Maple
Blain Thomas, machinist, Greenleaf & Co. r. 175 W. New York
Blain Thomas M. Sr. coremaker Eagle Machine Works, r. 175 W. New York
Blair A. V. auctioneer, bds. 166 E. Market
BLAIR FURGES M. state agt. Brooklyn Life Ins. Co. of Brooklyn, New York, also editor and publisher *Indiana Masonic Home Advocate*, 44 N. Pennsylvania, Vinton's blk. r. 294 N. Pennsylvania
Blair J. W. student Bryant & Strattons College, bds. 152 N. Meridian
Blair Joseph M. advertising agent *Indiana Masonic Home Advocate*, bds. 294 N. Pennsylvania
Blair Lydia, wid Thomas, r. 79 N. Tennessee
Blair Napoleon B. painter, r. 79 N. Tennessee
Blair Solomon, judg Court Common Pleas, office room 5, 14 N. Delaware, r. 254 N. East
Blake Albert E. omnibus agent, Bates House, bds. same
Blake Augustus, lab. r. 15 Williard
Blake Block, ss. Washington bet. Illinois and Tennessee
Blake James, r. 308 N. Tennessee
Blake James R. (James R. Blake & Co.) r. 86 W. North
Blake John G. delivery clerk W. W. T. Co. bds. 308 N. Tennessee
Blake John W. lawyer and genl. collection agt. 45 E. Washington, r. 268 W. Vermont
Blake Samuel, r. 308 N. Tennessee
Blake Walter A. with John W. Blake, r. 308 N. Tennessee
Blake William M. (J. R. Blake & Co.) r. 327 N. Tennessee

BLA	56	BLY

BLAKE J. R. & CO. (James R. Blake and ——) flour, feed and commission, 15 S. Delaware

Blakemore John, (col'd) lab. r. 175 N. 2d

Blalock Mattie, cloak and dressmaker, 9 Massachusetts av. r. same

Blanchard Charles, cigarmaker, bds. 13 S. Mississippi

Blanchard Henry, pastor First Unitarian church, r. 283 N. Alabama

Bland F. D. Rev. ins. agt. r. 32 N. East

Bland George, driver Aldrich & Gay

Bland George W. carpenter, r. 442 W. North

Bland M. Cora Mrs. editor *Ladies Own Magazine*, r. 171 Fort Wayne av.

Bland Thomas A. (Bland & Taylor) r. 171 Ft. Wayne av.

BLAND & TAYLOR, (Thomas A. Bland and Timothy B. Taylor) publishers *North Western Farmer*, also *Ladies Own Magazine*, 19 N. Meridian

Blank Anton, clk. Clemens Vonnegut, r. 180 E. Washington

Blank August, machinist, bds. California House

Blankenship Louis, lab. r. rear 300 W. Maryland

Blase Henry, porter Crossland Hanna & Co. r. 173 Union

Blattner John, blacksmith Eagle Machine Works, r. 284 E. Louisiana

Blatz Katy, wid. Anderson, groceries 108 Bluff rd. r. 414 S. Illinois

Blauvelt D. C. salesman, r. 271 W. Vermont

Blauvelt James, cooper, r. 427 E. Vermont

Blenk Rudolph, painter, r. 5 Elm

Bless Eliazer, r. 346 N. New Jersey

Blettner, John, blacksmith, r. 234 E. Louisiana

Bletzinger H. gardner, r. West Indianapolis

Block Henry, foreman painter C. C. C. & I. R. R.

Block Julius, carpenter, r. 261 Davidson

Block W. lab. I. C. & L. R. W.

Blodan John, cabinet maker Helwig & Co

Blodau John, saloon 231 S. Delaware, r. same

Blodau John H. bookkeeper John P. Meikel, bds same

Blood Lucius, bds. 83 W. Louisiana

Bloomendale Bell Mrs. r. 388 Indiana av.

Bloomer Francis, contractor, r. 27 W. St. Clair

Bloomer Isaac L. (Parker & Bloomer) r. 155 N. New Jersey

Bloomstock John, driver Citizen's Street R. R. Co.

Blowvalt James, fireman C. C. & I. C. R. R.

Blue Charles G. gas fitter John G. Hanning, r. 365 N. East

Blue Cyrus, carpenter, r. 365 N. East

Blue Gerard, farmer, r. 498 N. Illinois

Blue W. J. bds. Western House

Blue William, brakeman, r. 498 N. Illinois

Blume William, lab. I. P. & C. R. R. r. Madison av.

Bly Jacob, watchman, r. 77 N. Liberty

Bly John, teamster, r. 399 S. East

Bly Oliver H. P. r. 34 N. New Jersey
Blyble August, cabinet maker Spiegel & Thoms
Blyble Charles, asst. shipping clk. Spiegel & Thoms
Blythe Samuel, engineer, r. 187 S. Alabama
Blythe William M. engineer, r. Alabama ne. cor. St. Clair
Boachmiller Leonard, blacksmith Bremerman & Benner
Boahm Frederick, r. 398 N. West
Boardinghammer William, printer *Journal* job rooms, bds. 75
    Kentucky av.
Boardman Omer B. policeman, r. 211 Union
Boase Ellen, wid. Gottlieb, r. 267 N. Liberty
Boaz William, local mail agt. r. 321 S. Pennsylvania
Bobbs Elizabeth, wid. Conrad, r. 195 N. Pennsylvania
Bobbs John S. physician, 15 E. Washington, r. nr. E. Michigan
    bet. I. & C. and C. C. & I. C. R. R.
Bochert Frederick, coppersmith, r. 282 E. Washington
Bochmont Bernard, foreman Henry Weghorst, r. same
Bode Henry, lab. r. 260 N. Noble
Bodmer Charles, meat market, 276 W Market, r. same
Boealar George, brewer, r. 22 Wyoming
Boedeker Henry, (Boedeker & Niemann) r. 418 E. North
Boedeker & Niemann, (Henry Boedeker and Henry Niemann)
    carpenters and builders, 418 E. North
Boehm Ferdinand, teacher Zions School
Boehming William, lab. r. 470 E. Georgia
Boerum Joseph S. carpenter, r. 414 N. Delaware
Boetticher Julius, editor and prop. *Indiana Volksblatt*, r. 166 E.
    Washington
Boetticher Otto, printer Julius Boetticher, r. 166 E. Washington
Bogan Joseph, watchmaker, r. 24 McCarty
Bogardus William B. carpenter, r. 199 Harrison
Bogert James, trunk mnfr. 2 N. Meridian, r. 490 N. Mississippi
Bogert William J. trunkmakr. James Bogert, bds. 490 N. Mis-
    sissippi
Boggess Henry H. r. 612 N. Illinois
Boggs Elizabeth, wid. William, r. 82 Garden
Boher August, machinist Eagle Machine Works, r. 326 S. Dela-
    ware
Bohl Charles, cabinet maker Spiegel & Thoms Furniture Co.
    r. 295 E. Georgia
Bohlen Diederich A. architect, room 19 Talbott & New's Blk. r.
    71 N. Noble
Bohn Gustave, machinist, r. 326 S. Delaware.
Bohn P. Mrs. midwife, 72 E. Maryland
Bohning William, lab. C. C. C. & I. R. W
Boight David, belt maker John Fishback, r. Bluff rd.
Bokearn Joseph, jeweler Charles Dietrichs, r. 200 Davidson
Bolan Michael, lab. Rolling Mill, r. 43 Henry
Boland John, lab. F. L. Farnam, r. 232 S. Missouri
Boland Matilda, wid. Jordan, r. 386 W. New York
Boland William, policeman, r. 386 W. New York

C. J. BRACKEBUSH, Farm Machinery, Hardware and Seeds, Nos. 75 and 77 W. Washington st., Indianapolis.

Boller Peter, painter, F. Fertig, r. 185 N. Vinston

Bollinger James, (Dreher & Bollinger) bds. 112 S. East

Bollman Fred C. Cincinnati Bakery 107 E. Washington, r. same.

Bollmann Charles, blacksmith William Hillman, bds. E. Georgia bet. Noble & Liberty

Bolser Andrew, cooper, Helen se. cor. Maryland

Bolser George, carriage painter, r. 125 Bluff rd.

Bolser George A. wagon maker Indiana Agricultural Works, r. 471 S. Illinois

Boltey Henry, lab. C. & I. J. R. R. r. Michigan cor. Noble

Bolton James P. Yard Master C. & I. J. R. R. r. College av. out of limits

Bolz Peter, (Sponsel & Bolz) r. rear Union Brewery

Boman William, painter, W. B. Milender

Bombarger David, carpenter, r. 287 Indiana av.

Bombarger Jacob E. clerk, bds. 287 Indiana av.

Bond Abraham V. foreman A. I. Knodle, r. 273 N. Tennessee

Bond Alonzo, engineer, r. 56 Bates

Bond Edward, carpenter C. C. C. & I. R. R.

Bond Edward, cigars and tobacco, 262 E. Washington, r. same

Bond Riley, (J. J. Graham & Co.) r. Brookfield Ind.

Bone William M. (Thomas Wills & Co.) r. 305 E. New York

Bonegute Clemens, r. E. Market e. of limits

Bonner ——, r. 229 E. South

Bons Samuel, (col'd) barber Russell & Gulliver

Bonse William, wagon maker East bet. South and Louisiana, r. 193 S. East

Booms John, bds. Jefferson House

Boone Daniel, (col'd) lab. r. 598 N. Mississippi

Boone Eva, dress maker, r. 10 Bates House Block

Borchers J. F. harness maker Henry Arnholter, r. N. East

Bordman Owen B. policeman, r. 209 Union

Borgert Anton, lab. Western Furniture Co.

Boring Ephram, plasterer, r. 345 N. West

Borman Ernst, lab. freight depot C. C. & I. C. R. R. r. al. rear 131 Union

Borst Frederick, butcher, r. ns. Kansas nr. Canal

Borst George, tanner, r. s. end Tennessee

Bosart Timothy L. salesman A. F. Coors, r. 14 S. Mississippi

Bosderfer George, grocer, r. 168 Winston

Bose Christian, carpenter, r. 297 E. Georgia

Bossart John, baker, 112 Bluff rd. r. same

Boston Bakery, Joseph Virnickel, propr. 285 E. Washington

Boston Jacob A. bds. 169 S. Tennessee

Boston Store, Wm. H. Close & Co. proprs. 10 E. Washington

Boston Washington, bds. 198 S. Illinois

Boswell John, carpenter, r. 24 Wright

Boswell John K. fruit dryer and room heater, 16 S. Pennsylvania, bds. 20 S. Pennsylvania

Boswell Joseph E. (Boswell & Fleming) r. 177 Massachusetts av.

Boswell William, turner, r. 123 Maple

Boswell & Fleming (Joseph E. Boswell and John Fleming) grocers, 211 Massachusetts av.

Bosworth Isaac D. carpenter, r. 136 N. Winston

Botenmiller Leonard, blacksmith, r. 140 St. Mary

Bothwell Henry, saloon and grocery, 536 N. Mississippi r. 557 N. Mississippi

Bott Gottleib, baker Indiana Bakery

Bottoms Micagah, r. 218 Union

Bouchet S. Mrs. dyeing and cleaning, 42 Kentucky av. r. same

Bourgonne Stephen, (S. Bourgonne & Co.) bds. California House

Bourgonne S. & Co. (Stephen Bourgonne and P. Kretoch) saloon, 139 S. Illinois

Bourkemer Fred. baggage man Union depot

Bouser Henry, (col'd) lab. r. 207 W. 2d

Bovey Adrian, tinsmith D. r. Pine bet. Harrison and Forest

Bowen Cornelius, engineer C. C. & I. C. R. R. r. 141 Meek

Bowen Curtis J. fireman C. C. & I. C. R. R. r. 141 Meek

Bowen Edward machinist C. C. & I. C. R. R.

Bowen John F. huckster, r. Indiana av. nr. Toll Gate

Bowen Oliver T. painter, r. Mississippi sw. cor 6th

Bowen Patrick, lab. Rolling Mill

Bowen Silas T. (Bowen, Stewart & Co.) r. 82 W. Vermont

Bowen William, painter, r. 118 N. Liberty

BOWEN, STEWART & CO. (Silas T. Bowen, Mrs. S. W. and Charles G. Stewart) whol. and ret. booksellers and stationers, 18 W. Washington

Bower Caroline, wid. Frederick, r. 318 Winston

Bower George, teamster, McKendry & Lovecraft

Bower Jacob, baker and confectioner, 147 W. Washington

Bowers Fred. wks. Indianapolis Paper Co.

Bowes William R. special mail agt. P. O. bds Bates House

Bowker Clarence B. clk. r. 154 S. New Jersey

Bowker Harrison, (H. Boker & Co.) r. 154 S. New Jersey

Bowker Henry, (Bowker & Co.) r. 154 S. New Jersey

Bowker Willis L. bookkeeper, r. 154 S. New Jersey

Bowker H. & Co. (Harrison Boker and Cary McFarland) grocers and com. mers. 50 Virginia av. cor. Delaware

Bowker & Co. (Henry Bowker and C. A. and J. L. McFarland) flour and feed mers. 146 Virginia av.

Bowlby Samuel H. brakeman, r. 164 S. East

Bowles Thomas H. lawyer, 4 W. Washington, r. 493 N. Meridian

Bowman Henry, r. 122 S. Noble

Bowman James S. spoke turner Osgood, Smith & Co. r. 211 S. Illinois

Bowman Peter clk. P. Fahrbach, r. 176 N. Mississippi

Bowman William, lab. bds. 326 Virginia av.

Bowser Levi C. clk. r. 277 Virginia av.

Boyd ——, huckster, r. James nr. 1st

Boyd David M. r. 177 S. Alabama

Boyd Frank A. (Wood & Boyd) bds. 230 N. Tennessee

BOY	60	BRA

Boyd Gabriel, (col'd) lab. bds. 172 W. Georgia
Boyd George W. clk. C. C. & I. C. R. R. r. 177 S. Alabama
Boyd Hester, wid. James, r. 94 N. California
Boyd James M. engineer, r. 200 Bates
BOYD JAMES T. physician and surgeon, 5 Martindale's blk. r. 117 Massachusetts av.
Boyd Richard M. rimmer Osgood, Smith & Co. r. 182 N. Missouri
Boyd William H. telegraph operator T. H. & I. R. R. bds. Spencer House
Boyer B. F. shoemkr. 1. N. Rose, bds. Stanridge House
Boyle Catherine, wid Francis, r. 175 S. New Jersey
Boyle Eliza, bookbinder Journal Book Bindery
Boyle James J. (A. Reed & Co.) r. 225 W. Washington
Boyle M. W. (F. Smith & Co.) r. 83 Ash
Boyles Barney, lab. Osgood, Smith & Co. r. 151 High
Brackebush Alfred, bds. 126 E. Ohio
BRACKEBUSH CHARLES J. agricultural store, 75 and 77 W. Washington, r. 220 N. Tennessee
Bracken Lizzie, wid Ratliff, r. 177 Meek
Bracken Susan, wid James A. r. 28 Rose
Bracken Thomas, engineer M. Byrkit & Sons
Brackin Thomas E. (Isgrigg & Brackin) r. 403 W. New York
Bradeau Thomas, r. 80 Elm
Brademeir Charles, teamster McCord & Wheatley
Brademier Christ, lab. C. C. C. & I. R. R. r. 279 Davidson
Brademier John F. teamster, r. 315 E. New York
Braden James, (W. & J. Braden, Indianapolis Paper Co.) r. 469 N. Illinois
Braden William, (W. &. J. Braden and Brett, Braden & Co.) r. 473 N. Illinois
BRADEN W. & J. (William and James Braden) blank book mnfrs. printers, stationers, lithographers, etc. 24 W. Washington
Bradford John, (col'd) fireman Sherman House
Bradley E. railroad man, r. 143 N. Pennsylvania
Bradley Jeptha W. mill wright, r. 186 N. Mississippi
Bradley Joseph, ins. agt. bds. 17½ Virginia av.
Bradley William, lab. Schmidt's Brewery, r. Bicking cor. East
Brado Joseph, clerk, r. 25 Fletcher av.
Brado Thomas, porter James Frank
Bradshaw Etta Miss, teacher Sixth Ward School, bds. 226 E. Merrill
Bradshaw George, carpenter, r. 309 Winston
Bradshaw J. W. contractor of shops Institute for the Blind, r. same
Bradshaw James M. bds. Bates House
Bradshaw John, r. 26 E. Vermont
Bradshaw Margaret, wid. r. 264 N. Tennessee
Bradshaw Marie Miss, teacher Fourth Ward School
Bradshaw William A. gen'l agt. North American Life Ins. Co. room 14 Talbott & New's Block, r. Western av. w. of limits
Brady George, baker, r. Blake nw. cor. New York

BRA 61 BRA

Brady John, bricklayer, r. 251 S. Alabama
Brady John, driver Citizen's Street R. R. Co. r. 128 S. Tennessee
Brady Joseph, (col'd) r. Douglas Alley bet. New York and Ohio
Brady Michael, bricklayer, r. 673 N. Illinois
Brady Oliver H. P. groceries and dry goods, 546 E. Washington, r. same
Brake John S. engineer C. C. & I. C. R. R. r. 424 E. Maryland
Bramble Hamilton, bricklayer, r. 239 Massachusetts av.
Bramble Oneis N. salesman A. F. and J. H. Jenison, bds. 19 W. Ohio
Bramer William F. pattern maker, r. 347 S. Pennsylvania
Bramkamp Elizabeth, wid. Henry, r. 120 W. Maryland
Bramley John, miller, r. 196 E. Washington
Bramley Mary, wid. John (Bramley & Chapman) r. 28 N. East
Bramley & Chapman, (Mary Bramley and Caddie Chapman) dress makers, 28 N. East
Brammel Edward, apprentice B. F. Hetherington & Co. r. S. Pennsylvania
Bramotter ——, r. 329 W. Market
Bramwell John M. Grand Masonic Secretary, office Masonic Hall, Washington se. cor. Tennessee, r. 68 S. Mississippi
Brand John G. dealer in cider, r. 62 W. South
Brand Julius, upholsterer P. Dohn
Brandt August, clerk Emmerich & Co.
Brandt Augustus, locksmith B. F. Haugh & Co. bds. S. East
Brandt Herman, draughtsman D. A. Bohlen, bds. 173 E. Washington
BRANDT JOHN B. Supt. Y. M. C. A. and City Missionary, 16, 17, 18 and 19 Vinton's Block, r. 230 S. Alabama
Branham Edward, (Mayhew & Branham) r. 240 N. Tennessee
Brannan Daniel, hostler Exchange Stables, bds. 101 S. Illinois
Brannan John, cooper 362 W. New York, r. same
Brannan John, janitor P. O. r. 489 Virginia av.
Brannan Patrick, porter Sherman House, r. 392 S. Missouri
Branson David A. traveling agt. Lines, Smelser & Co.
Branyan James, patcher Rolling Mill, r. 278 S. Mississippi
Branyan Robert, asst. engineer Rolling Mill
Branyan Sarah, wid. Andrew, r. 278 S. Mississippi
Branyan William, fireman T. H. & I. R. R.
Braster William, carpenter Boedeker & Mimann
Brattan Henry, huckster, r. Buchanan nr. Virginia av.
Bratain John W. teamster, r. Tennessee cor. 4th
Bratain Jonathan, teamster, r. Tennessee cor. 4th
Brattain Silas, bookbinder Julius H. C. Smith, bds. 85, Buchanan
Brattain William, huckster, r. 70 N. Delaware
Braumer William, patternmkr. D. Root & Co.
Braun William P. lithograph printer W. & J. Braden, bds. California House
Bray John S. cabinetmkr. r. 240 N. East
Bray Peter L. plasterer, r. 176 Massachusetts av.
Bray William H. clk. J. F. Wingate, r. 240 N. East

Brayan Louis, wks. Miller & White, bds. Orient rear Deaf and Dumb Asylum

Breckenseick Frederick, cigarmkr. bds 2 Indiana av.

Bredehop Diedrich, expressman, r. 213 Virginia av.

Breedlove Sarah wid. Bales, r. 143 N. Davidson

Breedlove Thomas J. (J. M. Poe & Co.) r. 35 Bright

Breon James, lab. r. 339 Winston

Breese Isaac, carpenter, r. 436 E. St. Clair

Brehl Joseph, upholsterer A. Gebard, r. 18 S. Delaware

Brekenseik Frederick, cigarmkr. W. H. Wallace

Bremerman Benjamin, carriagemkr. Bremerman & Renner, r. 127 E. St. Joseph

Bremerman Casper, (Bremerman & Renner) r. Illinois nr. Tinker

Bremerman Frederick, wagonmkr. r. 295 N. Alabama

BREMERMAN & RENNER, (Casper Bremerman and John B. Renner) carriage makers, 123 E. Washington

Breneler August, pedler, r. Kentucky av. opp. Cemetery

Brenk William tailor, I. N. Winter, r. 393 E. Michigan

Brenker William, cooper, ss. Walnut bet. East and New Jersey, r. 343 N. New Jersey

Brennan Daniel, porter, Trade Palace, r. 27 Thomas

Brennan John, lab. r. 73 Maple

Brennan Thomas, painter, Ind. Coach Works, r. 204 Buchanan

Breman William, lab. P. O. r. 204 Buchanan

Brenning Frederick, drayman, r. 139 Bluff rd.

Brensell Henry, lab. D. Root & Co.

Brenton Oliver, r. 216 Winston

Brestlin Timothy, lab. freight depot, T. H. & I. R. R.

Bretney Eugene, carder Hosier Woolen Factory

Brett Matthew L. (Brett Braden & Co.) r. 2 E. Michigan

Brett, Braden & Co. (Matthew L. Brett, William Braden and ——) McIntire Flouring Mills, Michigan rd. nw. cor. Mill

Bretz Adam, grocer, 44 W. Louisiana and 118 N. Illinois, r. 118 N. Illinois

Breuer Harry, cigarmkr. bds. 2 Indiana av.

Breunig George, pastor German Methodis church Hamilton, Ind. r. Jackson se. cor. Forest Home av.

Brewer ——, musician, bds. Stanridge House

Brewer Catherine, wid. Charles, r. ns. Market e. Blackford

Brewer D. M. student, bds. 164 S. New Jersey

Brewster J. H. propr. Sleeping Car Line, Peru & Chicago R. R. bds. Spencer House

Briggs Albert, farmer, r. 456 S. New Jersey

Briggs Erastus, carpenter Shover & Christian, bds. 36 Cherry

Briggs Fred, machinist Sinker & Co.

Briggs James, wks. Hoosier Woolen Factory

Briggs James, stove moulder A. D.Wood, bds. 456 S. New Jersey

Briggs Luther, conductor, bds. 58 Benton

Briggs William, carpenter, r. 638 N. Mississippi

Brigham Charles E. with W. & J. Braden, r. 37 Indiana av.

Bright Charlotte E. wid. Charles Henry, r. 37 Ellen

Bright David, teamster, r. 319 N. East
Bright George A. boilermkr. Eagle Machine Works, r. 124 E. Duncan
Bright Mattie Miss, bookbinder Sentinel bindery
BRIGHT MICHAEL G. r. 292 N. Meridian
BRIGHT RICHARD J. editor and propr. *State Sentinel*, daily and weekly, 16½ E. Washington, r. 21 S. Pennsylvania
Brill John, carpenter, r. Illinois ne. cor. Ray
Brink Frederick, teamster, r. Madison rd. s. of limits
Brink William, tailor, r. 393 E. Michigan
Brinker August, grocer, 174 W. New York, r. same
Brinker Henry, machinist Eagle Machine Works, r. 174 W. New York
Brinker William, cooper, r. 343 N. New Jersey
Brinkman Charles, Livery and Sale stable, 23 S. Delaware, r. 131 N. New Jersey
Brinkmann Frank H. carpenter Fred Stelhorn, r. E. Washington out of limits
Brinkmeyer Fred, rectifier, r. 234 Davidson
Brinkmeyer George H. (I. C. Brinkmeyer & Co.) r. 238 N. Davidson
Brinkmeyer John C. (J. C. Brinkmeyer & Co.) r. 288 N. Liberty
Brinkmeyer John F. porter J. C. Brinkmeyer & Co. r. 234 N. Davidson
BRINKMEYER J. C. & CO. (John C. Brinkmeyer, Charles Kemker and George Brinkmeyer) distillers and wholesale dealers in bourbon, rye and wheat whiskeys, 80 S. Meridian
Brison Drusilla, bookbinder *Journal* bookbindry
Brison J. D. lab. r. 46 Thomas
Brison Johnathan, r. 46 Thomas
Bristol Anthony I. druggist, r. 59 W. Maryland
Bristor Samuel M. r. 135 N. Delaware
Bristor William A. boots and shoes 75 E. Washington, r. 135 N. Delaware
Britt Thomas, lab. J. S. Carey & Co. r. West se. cor. Georgia
Brittenham Frank, salesman E. A. Elder, r. 39 N. Illinois
Brittingham Mary Miss, clk Trade Palace, bds 16 S. Mississippi
Britton John (col'd) barber 181 W. Washington r. same
Broadhurst Isaac, piano maker Indianapolis Piano Mnfg. Co. r. 22 W. St. Clair
Brobston Charles, lab. r. 135 W. Michigan
Brock James M. blacksmith Indiana Agricultural works, bds. Nagle House
Brock Robert, carpenter Warren Tate, r. 352 Virginia av.
Brocken John, bds. Jefferson House
Brocking Augusta, wid. Christian, r. 143 Union
Broden James, machinist, r. ns. Sinker nr. New Jersey
Broden James, moulder Sinker & Co. r. 271 E. New York
Broden John, moulder Phœnix Machine Works
Broden John, sheet iron worker Cox & Brothers, bds. East cor. Georgia

BRO 64 BRO

Broden Michael, printer *Journal* job room, r. 296 E. New York
Broden Patrick, r. 2 Henry
Brodie George H. pastry cook Bates House
Brodrick John, machinist C. C. & I. C. R. R. r. 421 E. Georgia
Brodrick Mary, wid. r. 142 Indiana av.
Broking Deidrich, checkman Indiana Transfer Co.
Broking Frederick, teamster Indiana Transfer Co.
Bromer Frederick, painter, r. 570 E. Washington
Broner Roman, lab. r. 26 W. McCarty
BRONSON ANDREW W. manf. and dealer in boots and shoes whol. and ret. 17 W. Washington, bds. 373 N. Delaware
Bronson Rufus, grafter, r. 174 N. Davidson
Bronson Horace, grafter, r. 174 N. Davidson
Brookens Lucy, (col'd) wid. r. 179 Indiana av.
Brooker Thomas, grocery and meat market, 774 N. Tennessee, r. same
BROOKLYN LIFE INSURANCE CO. of Brooklyn, New York, F. M. Blair State Agent, 44 N. Pennsylvania, Vinton's Block
Brooks Bennett, carpenter, r. 178 Massachusetts av.
Brooks George, r. 231 E. South
Brooks George W. wks. rolling mill, bds. 310 S. Illinois
Brooks Henry, carpenter, r. West Indianapolis
Brooks Joseph, stone cutter F. L. Farman, bds. es. Kentucky av. nr. Illinois
Brooks Linsey G. (col'd) office boy A. E. Pursell
Brooks Nancy, weaver Hoosier Woolen Factory
Brooksmith, Henry, blacksmith Eagle Machine Works, r. 122 Huron
Brooksmith Lewis, machinist Eagle Machine Works, r. 122 Huron
Brother Elizabeth, wid. John, r. 560 E. Washington
Brough George, butcher, r. 296 N. Noble
Brough John W. reporter *Daily Sentinel*, r. 333 S. Alabama
Brouse Andrew, carpenter 130 E. New York, r. 138 E. New York
Brouse Charles W. r. 126 E. New York
Brouse David W. salesman Tatewiler Bros. r. 138 E. New York
Brouse Lutie M. teacher 2d Ward School, r. 92 E. Market
Brouse John A. (Indianapolis Printing and Publishing House, Downey & Brouse) r. 92 E. Market
Brouse Thomas W. r. 274 N. Alabama
Brower George W. printer *Journal* job room, r. 58 Massachusetts av.
Brower Theodore, foreman printing dept. W. & J. Braden, r. 58 Massachusetts av.
Brown Albert, groceries and saloon 387 S. Delaware, r. same
Brown Augusta, assistant principal Fifth Ward School
Brown Austin H. revenue collector, r. 290 S. Meridian
Brown Benjamin, saloon, r. 44½ W. Louisiana
Brown Benjamin F. (Logan & Brown) r. 294 W. St. Clair
Brown Charles H. architect and carpenter, r. 96 Fletcher av.

Brown Charles W. (col'd) barber Russell & Gulliver, bds. 345 N. Alabama
Brown Chris. (col'd) lab. r. 163 Indiana av.
Brown Daniel R. (Fortner, Floyd & Co.) r. Noblesville Indiana
Brown D. F. heater and helper Rolling Mill
Brown D. James, paper hanger W. H. Roll
Brown Eathen A. salesman Fortner Floyd & Co. bds. 32 W. Maryland
Brown Edmund, register U. S. land office, r. 109 Virginia av.
Brown Elison, painter, r. 564 N. Illinois
Brown Elizabeth, r. ws. Douglas 2 s. New York
Brown Francis M. grocer 59 W. Washington, r. 163 N. Illinois
Brown George, r. 392 N. Alabama
Brown Henry, clerk, bds. Pyle House
Brown Henry, (col'd) lab. r. 251 N. Liberty
Brown Henry, (col'd) lab. r. Missouri nr. Tinker
Brown Henry C. carpenter Phœnix Machine Works, r. 22 Kansas
Brown Henry P. salesman Hume, Adams & Co. bds. Pyle House
Brown Henry T. (col'd) porter I. L. Frankem & Co.
Brown I. I. groceries retail 292 E. Washington, r. same
Brown Ignatius, lawyer 8½ E. Washington, r. 243 E. South
Brown J. B. R. R. agt. r. 88 Plum
Brown J. L. blacksmith Buchanan & Hoover, r. 87 S. East
Brown James, paper hanger, r. 352 N. Alabama
Brown James B. plasterer, r. 229 Massachusetts av.
Brown James H. druggist Kiefer & Vinton, r. 181 Massachusetts av.
Brown James J. carpenter, r. 274 Madison av.
Brown James W. engineer, r. 115 N. Meridian
Brown Jeremiah, (col'd) expressman 349 N. Alabama
Brown Jervis, r. 22 Fletcher av.
Brown Jessie, blacksmith Greenleaf & Co. bds. 167 Eddy
Brown John, lab. Rolling Mill, r. 567 S. Illinois
Brown John, plasterer, r. 229 Massachusetts av.
Brown John, policeman, r. 30 W. Maryland
Brown John, sheet iron worker Cox & Brothers
Brown John, shoemaker, r. 61 Indiana av.
Brown John, (col'd) lab. r. rear 391 N. New Jersey
Brown John A. plasterer, r. 229 Massachusetts av.
Brown John P. carpenter, r. 65 James
Brown John G. grocer 300 N. New Jersey, r. 302 N. New Jersey
Brown John H. F. tinner, r. 366 N. Alabama
Brown John W. grocer, r. 401 N. New Jersey
Brown John W. r. 302 N. New Jersey
Brown Joseph, plasterer, r. 327 N. New Jersey
Brown Joseph J. shoemaker L. Siersdorfer, bds. Martin House
Brown Julia A. wid. Philip, r. 351 Massachusetts av.
Brown Kinsey (col'd) teamster J. L. & M. D. Fatout, r. 107 S. Noble
Brown Lizzie, wid. George, r. 388 N. Alabama

BRO	66	BRU

C. J. BRACKEBURH, Farm Machinery, Hardwrre and Seeds, Nos. 75 and 77 W. Washington Street, Indianapolis.

Brown Mary C. wid. John J. r. 302 N. New Jersey
Brown Mary F. City Laundry, r. 69 Ann
Brown Merrill O. clk J. S. Dunlop & Co. bds. 82 N. East
Brown Michael, marble polisher, r. James nr. cor. 1st
Brown N. A. Mrs. r. 30 W. Maryland
Brown Obediah Rev. r. 208 N. Alabama
Brown P. lab. r. 341 S. Delaware
Brown R. H. student National Business College
Brown R. J. blacksmith Rolling Mill, r. 131 Union
Brown R. T. prof. naturel science N. W. C. University, r. Western av. head Ft. Wayne av.
Brown Roland, buggyman Rolling Mill
Brown Samuel, (col'd) cook Stanridge House bds. same
Brown Solomon, clk. T. B. Brown, bds. Western House
Brown T. B. saloon 125 S. Illinois r. 45 S. Illinois
Brown Valorious J. clerk E. E. Case, r. 564 N. Illinois
Brown W. H. clk. express office
Brown William (Goth, Brown & Co.) r. 401 N. New Jersey
Brown William, express, Madison road s. of limits
Brown William, lithographer, bds. California House
Brown William, messenger, bds. depot C. C. & I. C. R. R.
Brown William, (col'd) porter Stanridge House, bds. same
Brown William H. agent *Journal*, bds. 241 N. Tennessee
BROWN WILLIAM H. (col'd) asst. pastor Bethel Methodist (African) church, r. 79 N. Missouri
Brown William J. inspector and guager, bds 258 S. Meridian
Brown William J. plasterer, r. es. University bet. Christian av. and Forest Home av.
Brown William J. plasterer, r. ws. College bet. Christian av. and Butler
Brown William M. clk. r. 327 N. New Jersey
Brown William N. driver, bds. Neiman House
Brown William P. hat manfr. 61 E. Washington
Brown William P. clk. Wiles & Reynolds, bds. 327 N. New Jersey
Brown William S. (col'd) barber, r. rear 247 W. Ohio
Brown William T. puller Rolling Mill
Brown Willis (col'd) farmer, r. 170 W. Georgia
Brown's Block, Pennsylvania nw. cor. Washington
Browning Frank, clk Browning & Sloan, bds. Pyle House
Browning G. clk. P. O. bds. Macy House
Browning John W. checkman T. H. and I. R. R. bds 25 E. Ohio
Browning Robert (Browning & Sloan) r. 172 N. Illinois
BROWNING & SLOAN, (Robert Browning and George W. Sloan) whol druggists 7 and 9 E. Washington
Brownley John Q. lawyer, bds 162 N. New Jersey
Broyles Moses, (col'd) pastor 2nd Baptist (African) church, r. 227 Minerva
Brubaker H. W. clk. Browning and Sloan, r. 43 Kentucky av.
Bruce Henry, (col'd) r. 98 S. Delaware
Bruce Robert, moulder Greenleaf & Co. r. 257 S. Alabama
Bruening Edward, (E. & J. Bruening) r. 180 E. Washington

Bruening Fred, drayman Stewart & Morgan
Bruening Frederick, carpenter, r. 379 S. Delaware
Bruening Joseph (E. & J. Bruening) r. 180 E. Washington
Bruening E. & J. (Edward and Joseph) photographers, 6 E. Washington
Bruggmann William, teacher German Lutheran school, r 65 N. Noble
Bruin Newton, teamster Isgrigg & Bracken, r. 195 W. Ohio
Brummer Charles, music teacher, r. 26 N. Noble
Brummer William F. policeman, r. 384 W. North
Brundage Edward C. livery stable 223 E. Washington, r. 339 E. Market
Bruner Adam, carpenter, r. 129 Massachusetts av.
Bruner Augustus, clk. James Loucks, bds. 402 N. New Jersey
Bruner Jacob M. carpenter, r. 202 E. Michigan
Bruner John, (Bruner & Comer) r. Tennessee sw. cor. 4th
Bruner Ramond, machinist Eagle Machine Works, r. 26 W. Mc-Carty
Bruner William, watchman, r. 22 Douglas
Bruner & Comer, (John Bruner and Stephen Comer) grocers and saloon Tennessee sw. cor. 4th
Brunnerman Casten, carriage mnf. r. es. Illinois s. Tinker
Bruno William, clk Hendricks, Edmunds & Co. bds. 171 W. New York
Bruns Henry, teamster City Brewery, r. same
Bryan A. H. physician and surgeon 68 E. Market, r. 420 N. Delaware
Bryan Felix A. druggist Massachusetts av. cor. Vermont, r. same
Bryan James W. druggist 48 W. Louisiana, r. 420 N. Delaware
Bryan John M. clk. J. W. Bryan, r. 420 N. Delaware
Bryan Joseph, wks. Sohl, Gibson & Co. r. 320 W. Washington
Bryan Peter, harness and saddlemkr. Daniel Sellers, bds. 26 Kentucky av.
Bryant James, G. law book agt. bds. 225 S. New Jersey
Bryant John S. conductor Bellefontaine R.R. r.138 N.New Jersey
Bryant Mary, (col'd) wid. Aaron, r. Douglas al. nr. cor. Michigan
Bryant Theodore R. state agt. New Jersey Mutual Life Ins. Co. 17½ W. Washington, r. 205 E. Market
Bryant William, brakeman, bds. 138 N. New Jersey
BRYANT & STRATTON BUSINESS COLLEGE, C. E. Hollenbeck, principal, Washington se. cor. Meridian
BRYER JAMES T. revenue detective, No. 4 Vinton's blk. bds. Sherman House
Buchanan Andrew A. blacksmith Buchanan & Hoover, r. 316 E. Washington
Buchanan Catharine, wid. Thomas, r. 314 E. Washington
Buchanan Charles, blacksmith Buchanan & Hoover, r. 316 E. Washington
Buchanan George W. foreman and supt. John T. Pressly's saw mill, r. 131 S. East

BUC	68	BUG

Buchanan James, machinist, bds. 312 S. Illinois

Buchanan James M. (Buchanan & Hoover) r. 314 E. Washington

Buchanan John, carpenter, r. 125 Duncan

Buchanan John, wks. Indianapolis Paper Co. r. 298 S. Missouri

Buchanan Oliver H. mason, r. 70 Indiana av.

Buchanan & Hoover, (James M. Buchanan and William H. Hoover) plow mnfrs. 25, 27 and 29 S. East

Buchhorn Christopher, wagonmaker Louis Miller

Buchhorn William, chairmaker H. Schilling & Bro. r. 294 S. Alabama

Buchter George, groceries and provisions, 54 S. California r. same

Buck Charles, r. 30 Biddle

Buck Christian, carpenter, r. 166 E. Michigan

Buckeye Fire Ins. Co. of Cleveland, O. J. S. Dunlop & Co. agts. 2 W. Washington

Buckley Dennis Mrs. weaver Hoosier Woolen factory

Buckley John, breakman, r. 32 Lord

Buckley Timothy, lab. r. al. bet. Noble and Benton, Georgia and Meek

Buckner Louis, (col'd) lab. r. 6 nr. Lafayette R. R.

Bucksot William, propr. Gem Billiard Hall, 9 W. Washington, r. 482 N. Illinois

Buckstahler Charles, clk. J. W. Bryan, r. 72 W. South

Budd John R. (Budd & Hinsley) r. 234 N. East

BUDD & HINSLEY, (J. R. Budd and A. J. Hinsley) produce dealers, 18 W. Pearl

Buddenbaum Henry, (Charles Prange & Co.) r. 396 E. Ohio

Buddenbaum John A. (G. C. Krug & Co.) bds. East st. House

Budenz Henry, tailor, 266 S. Pennsylvania

Budenz Louis, tailor, 168 E. Washington, r. 229 Union

Buechner Frederick, blacksmith, Virginia av. sw. cor. Dougherty, r. same

Buehler John, brewer Schmidt's Brewery, r. same

Buehrig Henry E. saloon, 37 E. South, r. same

Buell C. H. mnfr. Buell's family medicines, 75 E. Market, r. Vermont cor. Noble

Buell Jared R. lawyer, 68 E. Washington, r. 15 Madison av.

Buell's Family Medicines, C. H. Buell mntr. and propr. 75 E. Market

Buemagen Frederick, baker, r. 308 E. Ohio

Buennagel Charles, stone cutter Smith, Ittenbach & Co. r. Wabash nr. Noble

Buescher Jacob, lab. r. 432 S. East

Buffalo City Ins. Co. of Buffalo, New York, J. Barnard agent, Vinton's blk. Pennsylvania sw. cor. Market

Bug Browny, (col'd) white washer, r. 215 W. 2d

Bug Nathan, (col'd) lab. r. 215 W. 2d

Bugg Samuel, (col'd) r. 451 E. Georgia

Bugby Mary A. wid. Lyman M. r. 262 N. Noble

Bugby Parker E. engineer C. C. C. & I. R. R. r. 262 N. Noble

Bugett Patrick, lab. 113 N. West

Buhler George, butcher Charles Kuhn, bds. same
Buhler John, apprentice E. F. Steffers, bds. 183 Blake
Builders and Mnfrs. Association, lumber yard 343 Massachusetts av.
Builders and Mnfrs. Association planing mill, Charlton Eden, pres. J. L. Avery, treas. James Hasson, sec. 225 N. Delaware
Buist Missouri, wid. Thomas, r. 60 N. California
Bull George W. clerk Star Union Line, bds. Meridian nw. cor. Circle
Bullard A. Miss, wks. Indianapolis Paper Co.
Bullard Emily, wid. Charles, r. 278 W. McCarty
Bullard Mary, wks. Indianapolis Paper Co.
Bullard Miller, operator W. U. T. Co. bds. 346 N. Meridian
BULLARD WILLIAM R. physician and surgeon, 72 E. Market, r. 175 E. Ohio
Bullock Conrad, bartender, r. Wabash nr. cor. Noble
Bullock James B. (Anderson, Bullock & Schofield) r. 276 N. Tennessee
Bulock John, bartender John Grosch, r. Wabash nr. Noble
Bultemaear William, lab. r. 339 E. McCarty
Bulsterbaum Elenore, wid. grocer, 312 N. Meridian, r. same
Bundy John P. carpenter, r. 137 St. Mary
Bunker Alexander, blacksmith, r. 129 E. Walnut .
Bunte John B. (Bunte & Dickson) and (Bunte, Dickson & Co.) r. 415 E. Washington
Bunte, Dickson & Co. (John Bunte, William B., J. F. and Thomas M. Dickson) stave mnfrs. Railroad n. of Market
BUNTE & DICKSON, (John B. Bunte and William B. Dickson) lumber dealers, 387 E. Washington
Burbank John A. (Scott, West & Co.) r. 125 E. Ohio
Burbeck Walter, baker G. W. Caldwell & Co. r. Coburn bet. East and Virginia av.
Burbridge John, clerk Globe House, r. same
Burbridge John, clerk H. Gruenard, bds. 164 S. Illinois
BURCH LEONARD B. groceries and provisions, 223 W. Ohio, r. same
Burchfield Louis, deliveryman Carlisle's Mill, r. 290 W. Washington
Buress William, saloon Washington se. cor. New Jersey, r. 285 W. Michigan
Burford William, clk. W. & J. Braden, bds. 24 W. Washington
Burger John, fireman Union Starch factory, r. New York cor. Winston
Burgess C. C. (Burgess & Faries) r. 429 N. Pennsylvania
Burgess C. N. printer *Journal* office, r. 89 N. East
Burgess Ezra T. painter Howe & Converse, r. California cor. Vermont
Burgess O. A. pres. North Western Christian University, bds. 249 N. Alabama
Burgess & Faries, (C. C. Burgess and T. C. Faries) dentists, room 1, Odd Fellows Hall

BUR 70 BUR

Burgner Charles, cigarmkr. r. 31 Chatham
Burk George, pressman *Journal* office, bds. 31 W. Ohio
Burk George, saloon 154 Indiana av. r. 141 S. New Jersey
Burk Henry, boot and shoemkr. 68½ E. Market r· 94 N. East
Burk John, coal dealer, 23 Virginia av. r. 254 N. Tennessee
Burk John, turner, bds. 177 S. New Jersey
Burk John R. clk. John Burk, r. 162 W. South
Burk Lemuel, r. 165 E. St. Joseph
Burk William C. (Burk, Ernshaw & Co.) r. Mississippi bet. Vermont and Michigan
BURK, ERNSHAW & CO. (W. C. Burk, Joseph Ernshaw and J. H. Turner) wholesale mnfrs. of furniture 67 and 69 W. Washington
Burke Henry, sawer Osgood, Smith & Co.
Burke Henry, stone mason, r. 344 S. Delaware
Burke Henry, with Union Starch Factory, r. 344 S. Delaware
Burke J. W. lab. Osgood, Smith & Co.
Burke Martin, soapmaker, r. 112 Dacotah
Burke Matilda, wid. Anderson, r. 172 Eddy
Burkert Edwin A. asst. bookkeeper William Sumner & Co. r. 353 N. New Jersey
Burkert Winfield S. bookkeeper Scott, West & Co. bds. 454 N. Tennessee
Burket Erastus, bds. 170 E. Walnut
Burket Jacob, cabinet maker, r. 384 S. West
Burket John, chairmaker H. Schilling & Bro. r. 171 Madison av.
BURKHART ANDREW J. ice dealer, whol. and ret. N. Mississippi sw. cor. Michigan, r. same
Burkhart John, blacksmith, r. West Indianapolis
Burkhart Mary, wks. cotton factory, r. West Indianapolis
Burkhart Thomas, lab. r. W. Indianapolis
Burkit Albert, sawer, bds. 111 W. South
Burkit Frank, moulder, bds. 111 W. South
Burkitt Charles, tailor, r. 408 Virginia av.
Burkitt David, carpenter Gilkey & Jones
Burkitt George W. doorkeeper Skating rink, r. 161 W. Madison
Burkitt S. r. 117 N. Missouri
Burks Henry S. carpenter, r. 315 E. Merrill
Burnam Samuel W. real estate broker, 17½ W. Washington, r. ss. 2d bet. Tennessee and Mississippi
Burnes John B. engineer C. C. & I. C. R. R. r. 462 E. Georgia
Burnett Edward, lab. Greenleaf & Co.
BURNETT JEROME C. deputy State Auditor, Insurance and Bank department office, r. 284 N. Tennessee
Burnett John J. bricklayer, r. 284 N. Tennessee
Burnham N. G. (Burnham & Tisdale) r. 38 W. Market
BURNHAM & TISDALE, (N. G. Burnham and T. P. Tisdale) physicians and surgeons, office 38 W. Market
Burns Christopher, lab. r. 117 Oak
Burns David V. (Burns & Carter) bds. Pyle House
Burns George, conductor I. M. & I. R. R. bds. 319 S. Delaware

Burns James, wks. Mooney & Co. r. Mississippi cor. Henry
Burns James, engineer J. Marseo & Son, r. 107 S. New Jersey
Burns John, cooper, bds. 259 S. West
Burns John, student National Business College
Burns John, teamster Gas Works
Burns John, teamster R. Simpson
Burns John F. clk. r. 324 N. Noble
Burns Michael, lab. freight depot T. H. & I. R. R. r. 252 S. West
Burns Owen, lab. Osgood, Smith & Co. r. 251 S. Tennessee
Burns Patrick, pork packer, bds. 191 W. Maryland
Burns Patrick, r. 1 Willard
Burns Patrick, r. 13 Henry
Burns Philip, wks. Goas & Co. r. ss. Mayhew nr. Michigan rd.
Burns William, fireman, bds. 56 S. Noble
Burns William, printer, r. 208 W. Ohio
Burns William, porter Bates House, bds. same
Burns William, r. 259 S. West
BURNS & CARTER, (David V. Burns and Vinson Carter) lawyers, 74 E. Washington
Burnside Henry Mrs. r. 280 N. Mississippi
Burnworth Jennie, bookbinder J. II. C. Smith
Burnworth Mary, wid. r. 22 Elm
Burr Charles, cigarmaker Louis Young, bds. 77 S. Illinois
Burr N. B. real estate agt. bds. Stanridge House
Burress William, saloon 201 E. Washington, r. 285 W. Michigan
Burruss Luke, (col'd) porter Kettenbach, Newmeyer & Co.
Burrows Asa W. clerk W. W. Northrop, r. Beach Tree Cottage near Deaf and Dumb Asylum
Burrows Charles W. clk. bds. Stanridge House
Burrows George F. clk. J. H. Baldwin & Co. bds. Pyle House
Burrows Louis (col'd) whitewasher, r. ss. Wabash al. bet. New Jersey and East
Burs Thompson, (col'd) r. 446 W. North
Burt A. S. agt. r. 264 E. Ohio
Burt William N. teacher Indiana Deaf and Dumb Institute, r. E. Washington out of limits.
Burtch O. clk. bds. Macy House
Burton Daniel, (D. Burton & Co.) r. 427 W. New York
Burton George H. cooper, r. 138 N. Mississippi
Burton John C. (John C. Burton & Co.) r. 445 N. New Jersey
BURTON MARTIN, mfr. and dealer in trunks, valises and traveling bags, 39 S. Illinois, r. 346 N. Illinois
Burton D. & Co. (Daniel Burton and Sohl Gibson & Co.) coopers, West End New York
BURTON JOHN C. & CO. (John C. Burton and William A. Pfaff,) whol. dealers in boots and shoes 114 S. Meridian
Busath Charles L. chief cook Bates House, r. 164 W. Maryland
Busch Adam, carpenter, r. 342 S. Delaware
Busch Christian, boot and shoemkr. 248 W. Washington, r. same
Busch Jacob, saloon 251 W. Washington, r. same
Buscher Henry, saloon 89 E. South, r. same

Buschke Gustav, lab. r. 140 Huron
Buschmann William, (Lewis Meier & Co., also Goth Brown & Co.) r. 469 N. New Jersey.
Buser George, policeman, r. 148 Indiana av.
Buser Jacob, policeman, r. 74 W. Louisiana
Buser John, policeman, bds. 74 W. Louisiana
Buser Samuel, policeman, r. 163 W. Maryland
Bush David, (col'd) lab. r. al. bet. Noble and Benton, Bates and Georgia
Bush George, weaver 20 and 22 S. East, r. same
Bush Hannah, wid. Jacob, r. 163 Davidson
Bush Jerry, fireman C. C. & I. C. R. R.
Busher Henry, r. 26 S. Alabama
Busher Mary, wid. Herman H. r. 189 S. Alabama
Busher William, teamster H. S. Bigham, r. 26 S. Alabama
Bushnell Daniel W. printer *Mirror* job rooms
Bushnell J. printer, bds. 2 Indiana av.
Bushrong George L. carpenter, r. Fayette se. cor. Walnut
Busking Christopher, lab. Coburn & Jones
Busking Chris. shoemaker, r. 136 Huron
Buson John, policeman, r. S. Illinois
Bussell Bev, printer R. R. City Printing Co. bds. 239 N. New Jersey
Bussell Erastus T. r. 239 N. New Jersey
Bussell William M. with R. R. City Printing Co. and *Western Fireside*, r. 239 N. New Jersey
Butler Charles C. printer, bds 107 N. Noble
Butler James O. comp. *Journal* news room, bds. 107 N. Noble
Butler Ovids, (Indianapolis Printing and Publishing House and prest. board directors N. W. C. University) r. Forest Home av. near Cottage av.
Butler Ovid D (Butler, Smith & Harlan) r. 257 N. East
Butler Randall (col'd) lab. r. 753 N. Mississippi
BUTLER SCOTT, sec. Indianapolis Printing and Publishing House, r. Ft. Wayne av. ne. cor. Home av.
Butler, Smith & Harlan, (Ovid D. Butler, Butler K. Smith and George W Harlan) grocers Massachusetts av. ne. cor. New Jersey
Butsch George M. r. 247 S. Delaware
Butsch Joseph, ice dealer, r. 68 W. South
Butsch Mary, wid. Peter, r. 893 S. East
Butsch Valentine, (V. Butsch & Dickson) vice prest. German Mutual Fire Ins. Co. r. 553 N. Meridian
BUTSCH V. DICKSON & DELL, (V. Butsch, James Dickson and William Dell) coal, lime, plaster and cement and prop. Academy of Music and Metropolitan Hall, 27 E. Georgia
Butterfield Cyrus S. (Knotts & Co.) r. 78 W. Market
Butterfield Frank H. clk. express office, bds. 175 N. Tennessee
BUTTERFIELD JEREMIAH, agt. American Merchants' Union and United States Ex. Cos. 42 and 44 E. Washington, r. 475 N. Pennsylvania

Butterfield Newton J. upholsterer, r. 473 N. East
Butterfield S. A. physician, 366 N. East, r. same
Butterfield W. Webster, physician 382 N. East, r. same
Button Emma, wid. r. 173 Madison av.
Button Gertrude Miss, clk Frank J. Medina 34 W. Washington
Button William J. principal Fourth Ward School, r. 174 W. Ohio
Byer Edmund, lab. bds 68 S. West
Byers George W. clk. A. C. Roach, bds. 23 N. West
Byers W. C. clk. Institute for the Blind, r. same
Byington William W. (Byington & Erringer) r. 65 W. Michigan
Byington & Erringer, (W. W. Byington and J. R. Erringer)
    State agts. New York Life Ins. Co. 11 S. Meridian
Byram Norman S. (Kennedy Byram & Co.) r. 466 N. Meridian
Byrd Henry, barber (col'd) 63 S. Illinois, r. 75 W. Georgia
Byrkit Albert, machinist M. Byrkit & Sons, bds. Tennessee nw.
    cor. Georgia
Byrkit Davis Y. bookkeeper M. Byrkit & Sons, r. Tennessee
    nw. cor. Georgia
Byrkit Edwin M. (M Byrkit & Sons) r. 118 W. Georgia
Byrkit Frank, moulder Sinker & Co.
Byrkit Hiram, candy mkr. Daggett & Co. r. 143 Ft. Wayne av.
Byrkit John W. (M. Byrkit & Co.) r. 71 Norwood
BYRKIT M. & SONS, (John W. and Edwin M. Byrkit) planing
    mills, sash, door and blind factory, Tennessee nw. cor.
    Georgia

C

Cabel Charles, cabinet maker Cabinet Maker's Union
CABINET MAKER'S UNION, Henry Bauer tres. Gustavus Stark,
    sec'y, E. Market cor. Winston
Cady A. A. Mrs. r. 24 Circle
Cady D. (D. Cady & Co.) r. 227 S. New Jersey
CADY ELMER E. grocer 523 N. Illinois, bds 346 N. Mdridian
Cady D. & Co. (D. Cady and ——) boots and shoes ret. 9 Odd
    Fellows' Bldg.
Cafe Du Pueple, Eugene Renard prop. 299 E. Washington
Caffey O. salesman bds. 126 E. Ohio
Caffey John H. (Kolyer & Caffey) r. 315 E. Ohio
Cahill James, pressman *Sentinel* office, bds. 128 Bluff rd,
Cahill John, policeman, r. 81 W. St. Clair
Cahill John, boss weaver Merritt & Coughlen
Cahill John S. r. 519 S. Illinois
Cahill Joseph, spinner Hosier Woolen Factory
Cahill Mary, wid. Hugh, r. 347-9 W. Washington
Cahm Barnhard, engineer, r. 113 Benton
Cain Eliza, wid. John r. 77 Kentucky av.
Cain G. W. bookbinder *Journal* bindry, bds. ns. East nr. cor.
    Pennsylvania
Cain Hattie C. clk. Trade Palace, r. 77 Kentucky av,

Cain Michael, bartender Thos. S. Barlow, bds. 84 S. Mississippi
Cain Morris, horseshoer J. Hitchens, bds. 126 Christian av.
Cain Samuel, carpenter John M. Kemper, r. 144 E. Stephens
Calder John D. salesman Pettis, Dickson & Co. bds. Macy House
Caldwell Albert W. law student Ritter & Irvin, bds. Pyle House
Caldwell Andrew, (G. W. Caldwell & Co.) r. 232 S. Alabama
Caldwell George L. mnfr. ærated bread, r. 11 E. South
Caldwell George W. (G. W. Caldwell & Co.) r. 11 E. South
Caldwell H. W. grocer, 149 Indiana av. r. 180 W. Michigan
Caldwell J. W. com. mer. 61 S. Illinois, r. same
Caldwell John M. (Crossland, Hanna & Co.) r. Mississippi sw. cor.
    Market
Caldwell Samuel, r. 5 Peru
Caldwell Thomas G. tailor, r. 292 E. Michigan
CALDWELL G. W. & CO. (George W. and Andrew Caldwell)
    proprs. Aerated Bread Bakery, 14 and 16 E. South
Cale Howard, notary public, with Porter, Harrison & Fishback,
    room 6, Yohn's blk. Meridian ne. cor. Washington, r. Hanna
    Gravel Pike, 1½ mi. e. of city
CALEDONIA PAPER MILL, Field, Locke & Co. proprs. E. Locke,
    supt. w. end Market, office 265 W. Washington
California House, A. Kestner propr. 184 S. Illinois
Callaghan Daniel, lab. r. 423 W. Washington
Callahan James, carpenter, r. 68 Fayette
Callahan John P. driver Engine No. 3, r. 167 E. South
Callahan Michael, r. ws. Missouri cor. Walnut
Callahan Michael, checkman freight depot I. C. & L. R. R.
Callahan Michael, lab. r. 36 Lord
Callahan Patrick, lab. r. 130 S. Noble
Callihan Bridget, wks. Cotton Factory
Callihan M. works J. S. Carey & Co.
Callinan Daniel J. D. r. Massachusetts av. sw. cor. St. Clair
Caloern Thomas, coal agent, bds. 191 W. Maryland
Callon James, fire department, r. 104 Massachusetts av.
Calvert Charles L. (La Dow & Calvert) r. 375 N. West
Calvert James, (La Dow & Calvert) r. 375 N. West
Calvert Redmon, (Wischart & Calvert) bds. 375 N. West
Cameron George K. brickmaker, r. 413 S. East
Cameron John J. physician, 15 E. Washington, r. same
Cameron William, teamster McCord & Wheatly
Cameron William D. pressman W. S. Cameron, r. 278 N. Alabama
Cameron William S. book and job printer 8 E. Pearl, r. 278 N.
    Alabama
Cammel Eliza, wid. William, r. 337 N. New Jersey
Cammel George, collarmaker Ad Hereth
Cammel Mary, wid. r. 161 W. Maryland
Campbell Andrew, tailor, r. 334 W. Washington
Campbell Carter, (col'd) carpenter, r. 179 Indiana av.
Campbell Charles C. r. 2 W. North
Campbell Daniel, bds. 16 Willard
Campbell Dennis, peddler, bds. 116 Oak

CAM	75	CAP

Campbell George, clerk, r. Meridian nw. cor. North
Campbell George H. lawstudent, r. 2 W. North
Campbell Hezekiah, carpenter, r. 51 Wyoming
Campbell J. W. agt. Bee Line R. R. r. 156 N. Illinois
Campbell James S. Pattison House
Campbell Jerry, carpenter C. F. Resener, r. 36 Dougherty
Campbell John, harnessmkr. Daniel Sellers, bds. 26 Kentucky av.
Campbell John, pastor Christian Church, r. 23 Bright
Campbell John T. (Campbell & Green) bds. 180 N. Mississippi
Campbell Maria Mrs. (col'd) r. 115 Ash
Campbell Mary F. wid. Henry, dressmaker, 113 Massachusetts av. r. same
Campbell Mattie, teacher 8th Ward Dist. School, r. Bethel Pike
Campbell Morris, driver street car, r. 16 Willard
Campbell Richard C. sexton 3d Pres. Church, r. 34 Union
Campbell Robert, policeman, bds. 438 S. Illinois
Campbell Robert L. saddler, r. 191 Huron
Campbell Samuel, bookbinder, r. 10 Bates House Block
Campbell Samuel, messenger Indianapolis Branch Banking Co. r. Washington sw. cor. Pennsylvania
Campbell Samuel L. bookbinder *Journal* Bindery, r. 2. W. North
Campbell Thos. S. bookbinder *Sentinel* Bindery, r. 246 N. Illinois
Campbell William, blacksmith, r. 297 S. Tennessee
Campbell William, teamster, r. 338 E. Washington
CAMPBELL WILL M. reporter Southern Publishing Co. N. O. bds. Sherman House
Campbell William W. teamster, r. 85 N. Noble
CAMPBELL & GREEN, (John T. Campbell and Perry M. Green) druggists, 149 W. Washington
Canadee John, teamster, r. ws. Illinois nr. Ray
CANAN JOHN W. propr. Spencer House, Illinois nw. cor. Louisiana, r. same
Canan William S. clerk Spencer House, bds. same
Candee John B. clerk Freight Office T. H. & I. R. R. bds. 188 S. Mississippi
Cane James, r. 16 Root
Canella Luke, lab. r. 246 S. West
Cannell Eliza C. 1st asst. teacher High School, r. Christian av. ne. cor. College
Cannon L. G. clerk P. & C. Rw. bds. Pyle House
Cantlon Thomas, lab. r. 94 Fayette
Cantrill Daniel M. (Ferree & Cantrill) r. 132 W. Vermont
Cantwell M. foreman Sinker & Co. r. 132 N. Winston
Capen Nathan B. stonemason, r. 37 W. McCarty
CAPITOL CITY VARNISH WORKS, Mears, Lilly & Co. proprs. office and factory Kentucky av. cor. Mississippi
Capitol Drug Store, F. A. Bryan propr. Massachusetts av. cor. Vermont
CAPITOL TOBACCO AND CIGAR WORKS, Barker, Williams & Co. proprs. manufactory, 19, 21 and 23 N. Tennessee, salesroom 42 W. Washington

Capp Abraham B. writingmaster, r. 323 Virginia av.
Cardwell Ellen Mrs. r. 31 Center
Cardwell James E. carpenter, bds. 198 S. Illinois
Carr Henry, shoemaker J. N. Rose, bds. Bicking House
Carey Harvey G. (J. S. Carey & Co.) r. 284 N. Meridian
Carey Jason S. (J. S. Carey & Co.) r. 191 N. Delaware
Carey Patrick, fireman papermill, r. 365 S. Missouri
Carey William shoemaker, bds. 58 S. Alabama
Carey J. S. & Co. (Jason S. and Harvey G. Carey) machine
    cooperage, mnfrs. of staves, headings and barrels, Geor-
    gia bet. West and the river
Carleton George T. clerk, r. 174 E. New York
Carleton James M. r. 174 E. New York
Carleton Philip J. agent A. M. U. Express Co. at Union depot,
    r. 174 E. New York
Carley George, miller James & Killen, r. 52 Bright
Carlisle Ann M. wid. Daniel, r. 117 N. Mississippi
CARLISLE HENRY D. flouring mills, Maryland cor. Canal, r. 77
    W. Ohio
Carlisle Hugh, compositor *Journal* news room, bds. Commer-
    cial House
Carlisle John, Flouring Mills cor. Market street and Canal, r.
    260 W. Washington
Carlisle John, student National Business College
Carlisle's Model Mills, John Carlisle prop. Market cor. Canal
Carlon John, printer, bds. 36 W. Maryland
Carlton George, clerk W. & J. Braden, r. 174 E. New York
Carmichael Jessie D. (Todd, Carmichael & Williams) r. 456 N.
    Meridian
Carmichael John, (col'd) whitewasher, r. 251 N. Liberty
Carnahan A. M. clerk, C. & I. J. R. R., r. 410 N. Delaware
Carnet Edward, lab. Greenleaf & Co.
Carpenter Benjamin O. marbleworker and granite dealer, 36 E.
    Market, r. 244 N. Illinois
Carpenter Frank, stewart Oriental Hotel
Carpenter Ira H. entry clerk Landers, Conditt & Co. bds.
    234 S. Alabama
Carpenter John, bds. 369 N. New Jersey
Carpenter John, physician, 31 N. Delaware, r. 369 N. New
    Jersey
Carpenter John, marshal Union Depot, r. 351 N. Pennsylvania
Carr Charles, wks. Piano Mn'f'g Co. bds. Pattison House
Carr Charles W. bricklayer, bds. Ray House
Carr Ellen Mrs. r. 117 Oak
Carr George, machinist C. C. & I. C. R. R.
Carr George W. lab. r. 420 E. Maryland
Carr James, peddler, r. 96 Oak
Carr James M. saddle and harness mnfr. 9 Bates House Block,
    r. 490 N. Meridian
Carr John, lab. bds. 232 Blackford
Carr John A. photographer, r. 211 E. Market

Carr Joseph, r. 113 N. Davidson
Carr Mary, wid. Moses, r. 35 W. Georgia
Carr Omer B. salesman Carr & Alvey, bds. 490 N. Meridian
Carr Patrick, lab. r. 26 John
Carr Richard, street contractor, r. 349 E. McCarthy
Carr Roland S. (Carr & Alvey) r. 490 N. Meridian
CARR THOMAS, grocery and saloon, 276 S. Missouri, r. same
CARR & ALVEY, (Roland S. Carr and James H. Alvey) hats,
    caps, furs and straw goods, whol. 6 W. Louisiana, (Roberts
    Block)
Carrick M. lab. bds. 245 W. Maryland
Carroll Michael, lab. T. H. & I. freight depot, r. 369 S. Missouri
Carroll Thomas, lab. freight depot T. H. & I. R. R.
Carroll William, lab. T. H. & I. R. R. bds. 389 S. Missouri
Carroll William M. compositor *Sentinel* news room, bds. 30½ N.
    Pennsylvania
Carson Peter, pork packer, r. 199 W. Maryland
Carson Pryor G. constable, 83½ E. Washington, r. 11 S. Meridian
Carter A. Mrs. dressmaker Mrs. N. M. Allen, r. 540 N. Mississippi
Carter Albert, (col'd) barber Henry Byrd, r. 63 S. Illinois
Carter Brice, carpenter, r. 540 N. Mississippi
Carter Carrie, dressmaker Mrs. N. M. Allen, r. 62 Grant
Carter Charles, candy maker, r. 123 N. West
Carter Enoch D. carpenter, r. S. Pennsylvania
Carter Edward, (col'd) barber Hill & Carter, r. 780 N. Tennessee
Carter George, (Lathers & Carter) r. 544 N. Tennessee
Carter George, bds. 169 N. Illinois
Carter George B. clerk Sherman House saloon, bds. same
Carter James F. clerk W. Bucksot, r. 254 N. Mississippi
Carter John (John S. Spann & Co.) r. 440 N. New Jersey
Carter John, watchmkr. and jeweler, 125 W. Washington, r. 158
    W. Washington
Carter John W. bookkeeper, r. 199 S. New Jersey
Carter Joshua, carpenter, r. 412 N. East
Carter Louisa S. Miss, teacher Indianapolis Female Institute
Carter Mary L. Mrs. asst. teacher Indianapolis Female Insti-
    tute, r. same
Carter Robert, (col'd) waiter, r. 67 Howard
Carter Sanford, engineer J. M. & I. R. R. r. 31 Madison av.
Carter Vinson, (Burns & Carter) r. 21 E. St. Joseph
Carter W. M. (col'd) barber Hill & Carter, r. 26 Illinois
Carter William, (col'd) lab. r. rear 115 N. Davidson
Carter William E. Saloon, 87 S. Illinois, bds. Commercial
Carton Andrew, lab. r. 406 S. West
Barts John, shoemaker, r. rear 175 E. Market
Cartwright Tom. E. (Cartwright & Thompson) r. 597 N. Illi-
    nois nr. 2d
CARTWRIGHT & THOMPSON, (Tom. E. Cartwright and John T.
    Thompson) saloon, 33 N. Illinois
Carty Charles P. clerk E. Over & Co. bds. Bates House
Carvett Charles, tinner, bds. Nieman House

CAR	78	CAV

Carvin Armel, clerk Wilkens & Hall, 84 and 86 E. Market
Carvin James, physician, r. 138 Bluff road
Case Elon E. (Case, Parker & Co.) r. 246 N. Meridian
Case Harvey, lab. Edward C. Brundage
Case John B. engineer F. P. Rush, r. 338 E. Ohio
Case John L. engineer, r. 128 Bates
Case Lyman, ins. agent, r. 25 N. Mississippi
CASE, PARKER & CO., (E. E. Case, J. F. Parker, and P. Sharpless) Agricultural Implements, Stoves and Tinware, 84 W. Washington
Casey John, r. 438 S. West
Casey John, lab. r. es. Camp, nr. First
Casey John, drayman W. P. & E. P. Gallup
Casey John, pegmaker, bds. 38 S. Tennessee
Casey Michael, harnessmaker, r. Sinker nr. New Jersey
Casey Michael, lab. bds. 501 E. Georgia
Casey Patrick, lab. r. 432 E. Georgia
Casey Patrick, lab. bds. 300 S. Tennessee
Casey Rachel, wid. Samuel r. 42 Massachusetts av.
Casey Thomas, woodsawer, r. 235 N. West
Cash A. O. student National Business College
Cashen William, works Emerson, Beam & Thompson
Caskey J. fireman C. C. C. & I. R. R. bds. 454 E. Michigan
Cassidy F. C. Miss, clk. William Sumner & Co. bds. 170 E. Walnut
Cassin Michael, lab. Rolling Mill
Cassin John, engineer Bates House, r. 91 S. West
Cassin Peter, wks. Scott & Nicholson
Cassin William, lab. r. 317 W. Market
Casteel Charles E. Osgood, Smith & Co. r. 142 Union
Casteel Harmon, cigarmaker, r. 347 N. Noble
Castetter Hiram D. clk. Stewart & Morgan, bds. Palmer House
Castile J. C. spoketurner Osgood, Smith & Co.
Castin Christ, lab. Greenleaf & Co.
Castor E. A. carpenter Warren Tate
Catany James, pianoforte maker J. H. Kappes & Co.
Cathcart Andrew, engineer, r. 258 S. New Jersey
Cathcart Robert W. salesman Merrill & Co. r. 258 S. New Jersey
Catherwood Joseph, (Gapen, Catherwood & Co.) bds. Bates House
CATLIN M. J. MRS. milliner and millinery goods, 46 W. Washington, r. 44 N. Mississippi
Catlin Martha, wid. Edward, r. 298 W. Market
Catlin William W. r. 44 N. Mississippi
Catt Milton, bleacher, r. 239 S. Alabama
Catterson Abel E. policeman, r. 276 E. South
Catterson David, lab. r. 166 Buchanan
Catterson Elizabeth, wid. Robert, r. 57 Maple
Catterson Horrace, r. 276 E. South
Catterson Robert, collector, r. 80 S. Mississippi
Cauffmann George H. saddler Frauer, Bieler & Co. r. Liberty bet. Market and Ohio
Cava Mary, wid. John, r. 280 E. Washington

Cavan Michael, lab. r. 124 S. Noble
Cavanaugh Edward, lab. r. 280 S. Tennessee
Cavanaugh Larra, helper, r. al. bet. Pennsylvania and Delaware, South and McCarty
Cavanaugh Lawrence, blacksmith C. C. & I. C. R. R.
Cavanaugh Matthew, r. 55 Eddy
Cavanaugh Matthew, wks. Osgood, Smith & Co.
Cavin John, state senator, bds. Bates House
Caylor Henry, wks. Indianapolis Paper Co.
Caylor I. r. 321 N. West
Caylor Jacob, stockdealer, r. 321 N. West
Caylor Otho, r. 272 Rail Road
Celia Jefferson, lab. r. 247 Minerva
Ceiter Cassimer, cooper, r. 183 Madison av.
Cepf Mathew, car inspector C. C. & I. C. R. R.
Cepf Mathias, lab. r. 19 Meek
Cepf Sebastian, varnisher, r. 19 Meek
CHAMBER OF COMMERCE, Vinton's Blk. Pennsylvania sw. cor. Market
Chamberlain James H. carpenter, r. 374 W. Vermont
Chamberlain William B. pastor fifth Presbyterian church, r. 35 N. California
Chambers Annie, r. 201 E. Market
Chambers Thomas, teamster W. W. Weaver, bds. 233 N. Illinois.
Champeigh Albert, porter Anderson, Bullock & Schofield, r. Illinois cor. Vermont
Champie Joseph, clerk Gall & Rush, r. 130 N. Illinois
Champion William, pressman *Sentinel* office, r. 347 S. Meridian
Chance Harry C. clerk Browning & Sloan, bds. Martin House
Chandler Charles, engineer C. C. & I. C. R. R.
Chandler Eliza, wid. Sylvester, r. 119 Indiana av.
Chandler Frank, general ticket agent C. C. & I. C. R. R. office Virginia av. cor. Delaware, bds. 109 Virginia av.
Chandler George, printer W. & J. Braden, r. 119 Indiana av.
Chandler Henry C. (H. C. Chandler & Co.) r. 278 N. Vermont
Chandler Maggie Mrs. (Bentley & Chandler) r. 260 W. Vermont
Chandler Thomas E. (Chandler & Taylor) r. 34 N. California
Chandler William, (Chandler & Field) bds. 278 W. Vermont
Chandler William E. foreman Phoenix Machine Works, r. 293 W. Vermont
Chandler William G. carpenter Phoenix Machine Works, r. 276 W. Vermont
CHANDLER H. C. & CO. (H. C. Chandler and George Merritt) engravers and book and job printers, 25 and 27 S. Meridian
CHANDLER & FIELD, (William Chandler and Edward S. Field) whol. and com. paper dealers, 24 S. Meridian
CHANDLER & TAYLOR, (Thomas E. Chandler and Franklin Taylor, proprs. Phoenix Machine Works, 370 W. Washington
CHAPEL OF HOLY INNOCENTS, (Episcopal) George Engle, pastor, Fletcher av. cor Cedar

Chapin Foster C. steward Indiana Deaf and Dumb Institute, r. E. Washington out of limits

Chapman Caddie, wid. (Bramley & Chapman) r. 28 N. East

CHAPMAN DAVID C. house and sign painter, Virginia av. cor. Washington, r. 33 Ellsworth

CHAPMAN GEORGE H. judge criminal circuit court, office room 3 14 N. Delaware, r. Meridian n. of limits

Chapman John C. foreman Indianapolis Cotton Manufacturing Co. bds. 366 W. Washington

Chapman John W. wagonmkr. W. Indianapolis, r. same

Chapman T. S. wks. Emerson, Beam & Thompson, r. 75 James

Charles Abram B. carpenter, r. 311 N. West

Charles John, farmer, r. Michigan rd. nr. 1st

Charles Thomas, hackman, r. 109 S. Noble

Charles Thomas, (Hoss & Charles) and principal City Academy, bds. Pyle House

Charter Oak Life Ins. C. of Hartford, Conn. W. H. Day, gen. agt. 6 Blackford's Block

Charters William, michanic Rolling Mill

Chase A. Sydney, piano maker, r. 304 E. New York

Chase Henry B. piano maker, r. 326 E. New York

Chasteen Charles V. coooper, r. ws. Minerva 1 s. New York

Chearman Henry, fireman C. C. & I. C. R. R.

Cheatham Joseph, lab. bds. 217 S. Illinois

Cheeley George W. driver Citizens St. R R. Co.

Chellenbaum ——, wks. J. S. Carey & Co.

Cheney George E. clerk supts. office W. U. T. Co. bds. 17½ Virginia av.

Cheney William G. foreman *Journal* news room, bds. 183 N. Tennessee

Chenoweth Charles M. traveling agent Barker, Williams & Co. r. 54 W. New York

Chester Albert A. stairbuilder, r. 275 Winston

Chester C. C. student Bryant & Stratton College, bds. 749 W. Illinois

Chetester William G. moulder D. Root & Co. r. 465 S. New Jersey

Chevalier A. house and sign painter, r. 125 N. Noble

CHILD M. JR. gen. ins. agent, 25 W. Washington, r. 106 N. Broadway

Childers Eliza J. wid. John P. r. 235 S. Noble

Childers Jacob, lab. McCord & Wheatley, r. W. Indianapolis

Childers John R. agent Guardian Mutual Life Ins. Co. of N. Y. 4 Blackford's block, r. 60 Fletcher av.

Childers Joshua, lab. r. 128 E. Merrill

Chilian R. prof. of music, 198 E. Washington, r. same

Chill Thomas, carpenter, r. 302 N. Madison av.

Chill William, bds. 302 Madison av

Chipman Leander, r. 334 N. Illinois

Chison Robert, (col'd) cook, r. 350 W. North

Chissel C. C. sawmaker Sheffield Saw Works

Chitty S. C. salesman M. A. Stowell, r. 213 N. Pennsylvania

Chivers Enos, shoemaker, r. ns. New York 3 E. Minerva,

Chives James A. shoemaker, 63 Indiana av. r. same

Chrisman John, clerk National Hotel

CHRIST CHURCH, (Episcopal) Benjamin Franklin pastor, Meridian ne. cor. Circle

CHRISTIAN CHAPEL, Delaware sw. cor. Ohio

Christian John E. lab. rolling mill, r. 430 S. Tennessee

CHRISTIAN W. F. (Shover & Christian) r. 146 E. Vermont

Christman Ferdinand, teller Merchants' National Bank, bds. 27 W. Maryland

Christy Albert, saloon, 206 W. Washington, r. 13 W. South

Christy Israel, (col'd) lab. r. 39 Harris

Christy James A. cook, r. al. bet. Meridian and Pennsylvania, North and Michigan

Christy William, (col'd) porter 71 W. Washington, r. 344 N. Blake

Chultheis Jacob, carpenter, r. al. bet. Pennsylvania and Delaware, Maryland and Georgia

Church B. F. lab. J. P. Evans & Co.

Church Fannie, wid. Edward, r. 121 N. West

Church Henry E. Southern Route Agent *Journal*, r. 121 N. West

Church Joseph, wks. American saw works, r. 347 S. Alabama

Church Richard, varnisher, bds. 225 E. Market

Churchill David, (col'd) lab. r. Missouri nr. 7th

Churchman Francis W. (S. A. Fletcher & Co.) r. 130 N. Alabama

Churchman W. H. Supt. Indiana Institution for the Education of the Blind, r. same

Chroick William, tailor, r. 356 S. Alabama

Cimmerman George, drayman, r. 74 Lockerbie

Cincinnati Bakery, Fred C. Rollman proprietor, 107 E. Washington

Cincinnati Mutual Life Insurance Company of Cincinnati, C. G. Jones State Agent, Vinton Block

CINCINNATI & INDIANAPOLIS JUNCTION R. R. General office 64 E. Washington, J. M. Ridenour, Vice Prest.

Cincinnatti & Indianapolis Junction R. R. Freight office, W. C. Lynn freight agent, 112 Virginia av.

Cincinnati & Indianapolis Junction R. R. Machine Shops, A. Van Tuyl, foreman, E. Maryland at limits

Cismer P. M. clk. r. al. bet. Washington and Market, Alabama and New Jersey

CITIZENS' CARRIAGE AND WAGON MANUFACTORY, Fuller Smith, proprietor, Liberty se. cor. Washington

CITIZENS' NATIONAL BANK, W. C. Holmes prest., Joseph R. Haugh, cashier, 4 E. Washington

Citizens' Street Railroad Co. R. F. Fletcher, Supt. office ns. Louisiana between Illinois and Tennessee

City Academy, Thomas Charles principal, 13 and 15 E. New York

Bingham's Jewelry Store, cor. Pennsylvania and Washington Sts.

CIT 82 CLA

City Assessor's office, Glenn's Block
City Brewery, P. Lieber & Co. proprs. 213 S. Pennsylvania
City Cemetery, J. M. Hedges, sexton, entrance ws. Kentucky av. bet. Louisiana and River
CITY CLERK'S OFFICE. 8 Glenn's Block
CITY COUNCIL ROOMS, Glenn's Block
City Engineer's Office, Glenn's Block, R. M. Patterson, engineer
City Grocery Store, J. N. Conklin, propr. 31 W. Washington
City Hospital, Margaret cor. Locke, w. end Indiana av. G. V. Woolen, supt.
City Library, room 5, 2d floor, Martindale's Block
CITY OFFICES, GLENN'S BLOCK, ss. Washington bet. Meridian and Pennsylvania
City Treasurer's Office, Glenn's Block.
Claffey Christian, drayman, r. 328 N. Noble
Claffey Frederick, carpenter, r. 38 Dougherty
Claflin Charles C. (Treat & Claflin,) r. 489 Meridian
Claflin David B. operator Ingraham's Art Gallery, bds. 89 Indiana av.
Clainsmith J. r. 478 N. Tennessee
Clark Addison L. dealer in woolen waste, rear of 164 W. Maryland
Clark Charles, clerk, bds. 269 E. South
Clark Charles, roller Barker, Williams & Co.
Clark Charles, r. 69 Ann
Clark Davis L. photograper J. W. Winder, r. 111 Stevens
Clark Frank, (col'd) lab. r. Elizabeth nr. Pattison
Clark Frank Miss, 207 S. Tennessee
Clark Frank J. (Rakestraw & Co.) rooms 71 N. Pennsylvania
Clark George, salesman W. P. & E. P. Gallup, bds. 78 N. Tennessee
Clark Hampton, grocer, r. 266 Indiana av.
Clark Henry W. clerk J. W. Caldwell, r. 249 N. Davidson
Clark Hugh, wagonmkr. r. 312 W. Washington
Clark J. F. clerk C. C. C. & I. Rw. r. 27 Lockerbie
Clark James, clerk Sherman House
Clark John, blacksmith, r. 68 Plum
Clark John T. horseshoer, 27 N. Tennessee, r. 370 S. Illinois
Clark John T. miller C. Orm & Bro, r. S. Illinois n. w. cor. Ray
Clark Levi, bartender William Buress, bds. Little's Hotel
Clark Levi, produce dealer 49 S. New Jersey, bds. 133 New Jersey
Clark Maria, wid. James B. r. 177 W. Vermont
Clark Milton L., heater rolling mill, r. 312 S. Illinois
Clark P. bds. Jefferson House
Clark Patrick, lab. Rolling Mill
Clark Reuben, carpenter r. 176 W. Michigan
Clark Sarah, milliner and dressmaker 199 N. Illinois r. same
Clark Selden, r. 708 N. Tennessee
Clark Thomas, lab, r. 7 Dacotah
Clark Timothy, engineer C. C. & I. C. R. R. bds. 58 Benton

Clark W. H. cutter William Clark bds. 180 W. Ohio
Clark William, frt. agt. Bellefontaine R. R. r. 27 Lockerbie
Clark William, merchant tailor 31 S. Illinois, r. 180 W. Ohio.
Clark William H. (col'd) barber W. Porter
Clarke Samuel, lab. Bunte, Dickson & Co.
Clary James, lab. Rolling Mill, r. 127 N. Maple
Clary Jasper N. drayman Sinker & Co. r. 63 E. McCarty
Clary Patrick, porter Palmer House
Claudfelter Henry, carpenter Shover & Christian
Clausai E. hooker Rolling Mill
Clawson J. C. (Clawson & Woods) r. Western House
Clawson & Woods, (J. C. Clawson and William Woods) proprs.
    Western House, 127 S. Illinois
Clay Benjamin, (col'd) lab. r. 8 Blake
Clay H. r. 240 N. Meridian
Clay Henry, (col'd) cook Ray House, bds. same
Clay Henry, (col'd) lab. r. Missouri nr. Tinker
Clay John H. (col'd) moulder James Hamilton
Clayton C. J. carpenter, r. 43 Fletcher av.
Clayton Leonidas W. salesman D. Root & Co. r. 131 E. New York
Cleffy William, carpenter C. C. & I. C. R. R.
Clear Jane Miss, asst. cook Institute for the Blind, r. same
Clear Jeremiah, lab. r. 241 S. Tennessee
Clear Mary, laundress Institute for the Blind, r. same
Clearwater C. H. messenger Express Co.
Cleary James, wks. Rolling Mill
Cleaveland John B. (John S. Spann & Co.) r. ns. Christian av.
    2 E. Broadway
Cleaver Jefferson, bricklayer, r. 318 E. New York
Clem Aaron, (Clem & Bro.) 173 Massachusetts av.
Clem William F. (Clem & Bro.) r. 266 N. Alabama
Clem A. & Bro. (Aaron and William F. Clem) groceries and pro-
    visions, junction Massachusett av. and Delaware
Clemens G. engineer, r. 138 N. Davidson
Clemens William, cooper, r. 5 Cary's Row, Helen st.
Clements A. R. engineer C. C. C. & I. R. R.
Clements Frank H. lab. r. 135 W. Michigan
Clements George W. (col'd) lab. r. 247 Howard
Cleveland Calvin C. painter Thomas Cook, bds. same
Cleveland Ins. Co. of Cleveland, O. J. Barnard agt. Vinton's
    blk. Pennsylvania sw. cor. Market
Cleveland John B. real estate agt. r. Christian av. bet. Broad-
    way and Plum
CLEVELAND, COLUMBUS, CINCINNATI & INDIANAPOLIS Rw.
    J. L. Cozad, supt. Indianapolis Div. Edward King, gen.
    agt. office 53 S. Alabama
Cleveland, Col., Cin. and Ind. Rw. freight depot, Virginia av.
    ne. cor. Alabama. Passenger depot at Union Depot, R. W.
    Geiser, agt.
Cleveland, Col. Cin. and Indianapolis R. R. machine shops,
    North cor. Winston

CLI	84	COF

Clifford E. student, bds. 268 E. St. Clair
Clifford Jesse, lab. Bunte, Dickson & Co.
Clifford Patrick, lab. Bunte, Dickson & Co.
Cline C. wks. Kingan & Co.
Cline Peter, planer Hill & Wingate, r. 116 S. East
Cline William E. cooper, r. 4 Carey's Row, Helen st.
Clines Isaac, painter, r. 234 S. Missouri
Clines Peter, machinist, r. 116 S. East
Clinton James, (col'd) waiter, r. 228 N. Noble
Clinton John R. clk. City Clerk, r. 369 N. Alabama
Clippenger G. W. physician and surgeon, 64½ E. Washington, r.
        335 N. Pennsylvania
Cloffie Conrad, drayman, r. 69 Huron
Cloffy Fred, carpenter C. C. & I. C. R. R.
Close William H. (Wm. H. Close & Co.) r. 154 S. New Jersey
CLOSE WM. H. & CO. (Wm. Rowe) dry goods, 10 E. Washington
Cloud David, (col'd) wks. Phineas G. C. Hunt, bds. same
Cluck William, lab. r. 87 S. West
Clune Mary, wid. John, r. 372 S. Tennessee
Clune Patrick, r. 454 S. Illinois
Cobal Alexander, cooper, r. 84 Benton
Cobb Edward A. (Hay & Co.) r. 369 W Vermont
Cobb George, student National Business College
Coble David, (D. & G. Coble) r. 265 N. Mississippi
Coble George, carpenter, r. es. Blake 2 s. New York
Coble George, (D. & G. Coble) r. 386 N. Mississippi
Coble George, student, r. 265 N. Mississippi
COBLE D. & G. (David and George Coble) grocers and com. mers.
        152 W. Washington
Cobour Catherine, wid. Daniel, r. 50 Huron
Coburn Henry, (Coburn & Jones) r. 125 E. New York
Coburn John, jr. salesman Coburn & Jones, r. Vine cor. Oak
Coburn Mary, wid. Augustus, r. Oak ne. cor. Vine
Coburn Samuel, machinist Sinker & Co., bds. Ray House
COBURN & JONES, (Henry Coburn and William H. Jones) lum-
        ber dealers, n. of. Terre Haute freight depot
Cochran Cyrus, wks. Rolling Mill, r. 42 Rose
Cochran Jesse H. bkpr. Sohl, Gibson & Co. r. 322 W. New York
Cochran Thomas, cripple, r. W. Indianapolis
Cochran William A. carpenter, bds. 420 S. Illinois
Cochrane Samuel W. carpenter and builder, Tennessee cor.
        Michigan, r. 424 N. Mississippi
Coddington James, plasterer, r. 66 Indiana av.
Coe John, salesman Pettis, Dickson & Co. r. 218 E. Market
Coen John, paper hanger, r. 169 S. Tennessee
Coen Mollie Miss, clk Frank J. Medina, 34 W. Washington
Coffey Sarah, r. 57 Douglas al.
Coffield John, engineer C. & I. J. R. R. r. 56 S. Noble
Coffield Lucy A. wid. Arthur, r. 237 E. South
Coffin Abram, lab. Osgood, Smith & Co. r. 161 Stevens
Coffin Barnabas, (Wheat, Fletcher & Co.) r. 410 N. Pennsylvania

COF	85	COL

Coffin Caroline, wid. Erastus, r. 262 N. East
Coffin Carrie Mrs. dressmaker S. A. Mulliken, r. 262 N. East
Coffin Charles E. bookkeeper Luther R. Martin, bds 84 Massachusetts av.
Coffin David W. (Wiles, Bro. & Co.) r. 432 N. Pennsylvania
Coffin Ella, milliner E. Kirk, bds. 65 Liberty
Coffin Ella P. Miss, teacher fourth ward school
Coffin John R. retired, bds. 2 Indiana av.
Coffin Julius V. clk Wiles, Bro. & Co. bds. Sherman House
Coffin Kate, teacher first ward school
Coffin R. M. clk R. R. Parker, r. 81 Massachusetts av.
Coffman C. W. clk. Vinnedge, Jones & Co. bds. 10 E. Michigan
Coffman Henry, saddler, r. 65 N. Liberty
Coffman Jacob, carpenter and builder, r. 255 S. New Jersey
Coffman John, lab. Bunte & Dickson.
Coffman Samuel J. carpenter, r. 305 Virginia av.
Cogan William, salesman, bds 320 N. Illinois
Cogle Ellen, wid. Stephen, r. 233 Huron
Cogle William, contractor, r. 223 Virginia av.
Coiner Martin, civil engineer, r. 31 W. Ohio
Cola Fred, wks. Cotton Factory
Colclazer J. H. jeweler W. P. Bingham & Co. bds. nw. cor Meridian and Circle
Colden John E. real est. agt. room 11, Talbott and News Block, r. 129 Union
Cole Albert M. engineer, r. 605 E. Washington
Cole Albert V. secy. and treas. N. W. C. University, r. 31 Cherry
Cole B.W. clk. freight office T. H. & I. R.R. bds. Palmer House
Cole Charles W. conductor, bds. 605 E. Washington
Cole Eliazer B. r. es Western av. bet. Christian and Forrest Home av.
Cole Ernest B. clk. John Furnas & Co. bds. 68 E. Washington
Cole James, asst. doorkeeper State House, bds. 30 N. Maryland
Cole James S. carpenter, r. 397 E. Georgia
Cole Maria E. clk. supt. of Public Schools, r. 31 Cherry
Cole Oscar F. clk. T. H. & I. R. R. frt. office, bds. Pyle House
Cole William, (col'd) r. Missouri nr. Tinker
Cole Zina, (Pickerill & Cole) bds. 30½ N. Pennsylvania
Coleman Allen, teamster, r. Blake nw. cor. Elizabeth
Coleman Benjamin F. lab. r. Blake cor. Elizabeth
Coleman Christine, wid. Henry, r. 105 Bluff rd.
Coleman Elizabeth J. r. Blake nw. cor. Elizabeth
Coleman Franklin, sexton, r. Blake nw. cor. Elixabeth
Coleman Harvey, cigarmkr. A. W. Sharpe, bds. 182 E. Georgia
Coleman Henry, messenger Gov. Baker, r. opp. State House
Coleman Herman, meat Market, 267 N. East, r. same
Coleman Ruhamah, wid. Henry, r. Blake nw. cor. Elizabeth
Coleman William, brakeman, r. 382 E. Michigan
Coles Georgia, dressmkr. S. Coles, r. 199 N. Illinois
Coles Susan Miss, dress and cloakmkr. 199 N. Illinois, r. same
Colestock Ephram, carpenter, r. 250 N. Illinois

Colestock George, binder W. & J. Braden, bds. 250 N. Illinois
Coley J. M. heater Rolling Mill
Coley John, (col'd) carpenter, r. 196 W. 2d
Colgan Henrie, prin. First Ward school, r. College av. cor. Christian
Colgan Henry, supt. r. 81 Christian av.
Colgan Mary, teacher First Ward school, r. College av. cor. Christian
Coljee George, brewer, r. 370 S. Delaware
Coll Hugh, peddler, r. 116 Oak
Collett Moses M. (John Furnas & Co.) r. 413 N. New Jersey
Colley Simes, lawyer, r. 338 N. New Jersey
Collier William, r. 277 N. East
COLLINS ALPHEUS R. C. reporter Charless Publishing Co. St. Louis, bds. Sherman House
Collins Cadwalader Jones, machinist William Sumner & Co. bds. National Hotel
Collins Cornelius, lab. r. 223 S. West
Collins Daniel, sawmkr. Am. Saw Works, r. 46 S. East
Collins Hanna Miss, teacher 4th Ward School, bds. 218 N. Illinois
Collins James L. brakeman, r. 452 E. Georgia
Collins Jeremiah, lithograph printer W. & J. Braden, bds. East Street House
Collins Jerry, lab. Sinker & Co. r. 239 Buchanan
Collins John W. student, bds. 164 S. New Jersey
Collins Joseph, r. 52 S. Pennsylvania
Collins Martin, wks. Kingan & Co. bds. 245 W. Maryland
Collins Thomas, hostler Citizens' St. R. R. Co. r. 20 N. Noble
Collins William, wks. J. S. Carey & Co.
Collins William B. student, r. 126 E. North
Collord Isaac, moulder, Phœnix machine works
COLONY SCHOOL, ss. Root, nr. River Miss M. E. McEnally in charge
Colter George, tobacconist W. H. Wallace, r. 256 S. Delaware
Colton Elijah, lab., r. rear 2 Ann
COLUMBUS, CHICAGO & INDIANA CENTRAL R. R., J. M. Lunt, Gen'l Sup't, Virginia av cor Delaware
Columbus, Chicago & Indiana Central R. R. machine shops, Thomas V. Losee master mechanic, Noble, near cor. Washington
Columbus, Chicago & Indiana Central R. R. freight office, Delaware, south of Georgia, W. M. Graygon, freight agent
Colwell Emma Mrs. teacher Sixth Ward School, r. 5 Peru
Combs Job S. huckster, r. 422 S. New Jersey
Comegys Levi, carpenter, r. Illinois, cor. Sixth
Comer Stephen, (Bruner & Comer) r. Mississippi, n. w. cor. Fourth
Comingor John A. physician and surgeon, 1 Massachusetts av, r. 335 N. Liberty
Comingore William H. r. 164 S. New Jersey

COMLEY WILLIAM J. reporter Southern Publishing Co. N. O. bds. Sherman House.

Comly David J. clk: r. 165 Meek

Commerce Insurance Co. of Albany, New York, Martin, Hopkins and Ohr agts. Market, n. e. cor. Circle (Journal bldg)

COMMERCIAL, (daily evening) M. G. Lee, editor and proprietor, Illinois, n. e.cor. Washington

Commercial Hotel, T. C. Miles prop. Illinois ne. cor. Georgia

Commons John M. private sec. Gov. Baker, r. 363 N. Alabama

COMMONWEALTH LIFE INS. CO. of New York, Gibson Bros. agts. for Indiana and Ohio, room 5 Odd Fellows' Hall

Compton A. B. bds. 27 Indiana av.

Compton E. M. student Bryant & Stratton's College, bds 167 Ft. Wayne av.

Compagne Joseph, lab. D. Root & Co. r. 118 Huron

Compagne Louis, carpenter, r. 118 Huron

Conant ———, engineer, bds. 47 N. East

Conaty James B. millinery goods, 44 S. Illinois, r. same

Conaway James, printer, bds. 75 Kentucky av.

Concordia House, Ferdinand Mottery prop'r, 200 S. Meridian

Conde Charles, machinist Sinker & Co.

Conde Henry T. bookkeeper C. Dickson & Co., bds. Pyle House

Conde Pauline M. teacher second ward school, r. 84 E. Michigan

Condenbar John, engineer Calidonia paper mill

Condit John D. 1 Blackford's blk. r. 54 Circle

Condon John, r. 54 Circle

Condor Christ, tailor H. Euggass, r. 328 S. Delaware

Conduitt Alex. (Landers, Conduitt & Co.,) r. Mooresville, Ind.

Condy Jerome (col'd) teamster, r. opp. city hospital

Cone William S. clk J. M. & I. R. R., bds. 207 W. Maryland

Cones Charles E. clk. Murphy, Johnston & Co. bds Pyle House

Congrove Michael, puddler Indianapolis rolling mill

Conklin August, carpenter P. Routier

Conklin Henry N. (Durfeld & Conklin, r. 252 N. Mississippi

Conklin J. N. grocery, 31 W. Washington, bds. Palmer House

Conklin Jennie, dressmaker, r. 148 Indiana av.

Conlen Michael, r. 323 Indiana av.

Conley Charles, wks. Indianapolis Paper Co.

Conley Michael, lab. r. rear Rolling Mill

Connal Hugh, lab. gas works

Connecticut General Life Insurance Company of Hartford, Conn. Cowen & Potzman Agents Central Indiana, 16½ E. Washington

CONNECTICUT MUTUAL LIFE INSURANCE COMPANY OF HARTFORD, CONN. E. S. Green State Agent, room 4 (2d floor) Martindale's Block

Connell Bettie, wks. Marshall & Sweeny, r. 364 S. Delaware

Connell Daniel lab. Bunte, Dickinson & Co.

Connell Morris, lab. r. 336 S. West

Connell Thomas, r. Benton nr. Maryland

Connelland Jerry, printer, bds. 65 S. East

CON	88	COO

Connelley A. J. engineer C. C. C. & I. C. R. R. r. 114 S. East
Connelley Patrick, beam hand J. Fishback
Connelly Patrick, clk. bds. 40 N. Pennsylvania
Connelly Patrick, tanner, bds. 148 Indiana av.
Connelly Robert, merchandise broker, 27 S. Meridian, r. 296 N. Alabama
Conner Alexander H. (Douglas & Conner), r. 515 N. Pennsylvania
Conner Benjamin F. reg. clk. P. O. r. 425 N. Pennsylvania
Conner Eliza L. wid. Robert, r. 177 S. New Jersey
Conner Herbert, bds. 425 N. Pennsylvania
Conner James H. (Shaw, Lippincott & Conner) r. Greensburg
Conner John, lab. r. 75 Fayette
Conner Mary, wid. William, r. 73 N. Illinois
Conner Patrick, lab. r. 525 N. Mississippi
Connor H. J. student National Business College
Connor John, lab. r. 247 S. Delaware
Connor John, lab. r. 14 N. Noble
Connor M. lab. r. 1 Elizabeth
Connor Morris, lab. Rolling Mill
Connors John, lab. r. 288 S. Delaware
Connors Larry, brakeman, bds. 58 Benton
Conrad Rufus, (col'd) pastor 2d Christian Church, (African) r. 500 N. Mississippi
Conrades Hugh, lab. r. 783 N. Illinois
Conroy Daniel, tailor, bds. 72 S. West
Conroy Patrick, tailor, r. 72 S. West
Conti Antonia, foreign & domestic fruits, 22 N. Illinois, r. same
Continental Fire Ins. Co. of New York, Martin, Hopkins & Ohr, agents, Market ne. cor. Circle (Journal bldg.)
Continental Life Ins. Co. of Hartford, Conn. Ransford & Denton, state agt's, Washington sw. cor. Meridian
Continental Life Ins. Co. of N. Y. Daniel W. Grubbs gen'l agt. 7 Blackford's blk.
CONTRACTING BRICKLAYERS UNION, room 5 Hubbard's blk.
Convers Joel, carpenter, r. 128 S. East
Conway James, compositor, Sentinel news room
Conway Thomas, porter, Express office, bds. 217 S. Illinois
Conwell Emma, dressmaker Mrs. N. M. Allen r. 120 S. New Jersey
Conwell Maria Miss, music teacher, bds. 334 N. Illinois
Conwell John S. r. 120 S. New Jersey
Coober Isaac, r. 80 Huron
Cook Andrew, packer, Judson & Dodd r. 84 S. Liberty
Cook Charles, teamster, r. 84 S. Liberty
Cook Charley, clerk, Emerich & Co.
Cook Christian, baggageman, r. 26 Bicking
Cook Frank, lab. Rolling Mill
Cook George W. painter, John Tull bds. 365 North
Cook Henry, bricklayer, r. 38 Chatham.
Cook Henry, wks. Omer T. Porter r. 22 John

Cook Ignatius, machinist Osgood, Smith & Co.
Cook John, machinist Sinker & Co. r. 38 Chatham
Cook John V. trav. salesman Ryan & Holbrook, r. 87 S. Benton
Cook John W. millwright, r. 194 Virginia av.
Cook Mary, wid. John, r. 38 Chatham
Cook Samuel M. machinist M. Byrkit & Sons, r. 194 Virginia av.
Cook Thomas V. sign painter, 58 N. Pennsylvania, r. Fallcreek gravel rd. ¾ mile beyond city limits
Cook W. G. bookkeeper Andrew Wallace, r. 88 N. Delaware
Cook William, (col'd) lab. r. al. bet. New York and Vermont, West and California
Cook William, (William Cook & Co.) r. 83 S. East
Cook William, sawer McKendry & Lovecraft
COOK WILLIAM & CO. (William Cook and Charles Dammeier) dry goods and groceries, 249 E. Washington
Cooke Annie E. teacher Indiana Deaf and Dumb Institute, r. E. Washington out of limits
Cooke Jane Miss, r. 24 Indiana av.
Coombs C. C. lab. Osgood, Smith & Co.
Coon Alice Miss, music teacher, bds. Stanridge House
Coon Peter, bds. Stanridge House
Cooney D. moulder Sinker & Co. r. 27 N. East
Cooney George, bds. 225 E. Market
Cooney T. drayman E. Over & Co. r. E. Market
Coons John W. clk. bds. 79 Massachusetts av.
Coons John W. deputy city treas. r. 274 E. St. Clair
Cooper Hamilton, tailor J. Mitchell, r. 260 St. Clair
Cooper Jane, wid. Hamilton, r. 260 W. St. Clair
Cooper John J. farmer, r. 422 N. Illinois
Cooper Joseph M. physician, 160 Indiana av. r. 217 W. Michigan
Cooper R. W. bagmkr. M. Burton, bds. Stanridge House
Cooper Rebecca J. wid. John, r. 257 E. McCarty
Cooper William H. clk. W. P. & E. P. Gallup, r. 155 W. Maryland
COORS AUGUST F. whol. and ret. grocer and agt. American and China Tea Co. 151 W. Washington, r. 14 S. Mississippi
Coots Edwin, moulder D. Root & Co.
Copeland Joshua W. (J. W. Copeland & Co.) r. 372 N. Meridian
Copeland Margaret B. Mrs. (J. W. Copeland & Co.) r. 372 N. Meridian
Copeland William J. (W. J. Copeland & Co.) notary public, r. 27 Massachusetts av.
COPELAND J. W. & CO. (J. W. Copeland, M. B. Copeland and Charles Annan) whol. dealers in straw and millinery goods, 39 S. Meridian and ret. 8 E. Washington
COPELAND W. J. & CO. (William J. Copeland) gen'l ins. and real estate agts. 5 Martindale's Block. See margin bottom lines
Corbaley Samuel B. (Corbaley & Cossel) r. 414 W. Washington, (nat. road)
Corbaley Will H. clk. B. F. Witt, r. 15 Fayette

COR	90	COU

CORBALEY & COSSEL, (Samuel B. Corbaley and Willliam Cossel) groceries and provisions, 414 W. Washington, (nat. rd.)

Corbett Charles, turner C. Cox

Cord Fred, jr. wks. paper mill, bds. 475 W. Michigan

Corden John, porter Spencer House

Corey J. A. plasterer, bds. 82 E. St. Clair

Coridan Mary, dressmaker Mrs. N. M. Allen, r. 340 S. West

Corigan John G. clk. bds. 20 S. Pennsylvania

CORLISS CORYDON T. homœopathic physician, office No. 5 Miller's Block, Illinois, nw. cor. Market, bds. 169 N. Illinois

Cornelius Cassius, plasterer, r. 254 S, Alabama

Cornelius Edward, bds. 254 S. Alabama

Cornelius Edward G. (Kennedy, Byram & Co.) r. 138 E. Pratt

Cornelius Wilbur F. (Cornelius & McElvano) r. 112 Huron

Cornelius & McElvano, (Wilbur F. Cornelius and John McElvano) house and sign painters, 46 Kentucky av.

Cornwell Carlos, engineer, r. 333 Davidson

Corriden Thomas, saloon, 350 S. West r. same

Corrigan John, teamster, r. 311 W. Market

Corrigan John D. salesman, Pettis, Dickson & Co. bds. 20 S. Pennsylvania

Corson Henry L. conductor, bds. 58 Benton

Cortapeter William, tailor, (Becker & Huber) r. S. East

Cortney William, hackdriver, r. 315 Blake

Cosby Charles E. comp. *Mirror* news room, bds. Little's Hotel

Cosby Richard M. carpenter and builder, 32 Christian av. r. same

Cosgrove Patrick, blacksmith, Sinker & Co.

Cosgrove Rose, wid. Domonic, r. 356 S. Tennessee

Cossel William, (Corbaley & Cossel) r. nr. Mount Jackson

Cossler Dav. carpenter, Builders & Mnfrs. Union, r. 195 Davidson

Cost Anthony, carpenter, Academy of Music, bds. 31 Indiana av.

Costello J. F. clerk, bds. Stanridge House

Costello John, boiler maker, r. 114 Meek

Costello John, machinist Sinker & Co. r. 276 W. Maryland

Costello Martin, fireman, r. 483 E. Georgia

Costello S. puddler, Indianapolis Rolling Mill

Costello William, office boy, *Mirror* news room

Costigan Frank, propr. Oriental House, 71 to 75 S. Illinois

Costigan T. J. clerk Oriental House, bds. same

Coston Henry, (col'd) teamster, r. 38 Bates

Cotter James, tailor Moritz Bros. r. 23 Kentucky av.

Cotter John, cigar maker Jacob Garrott, bds. Union Hall

Cottman David, bds. 176 Virginia av.

Cotton Perry W. r. 22 Gregg

Cottrell Thomas, (Cottrell & Knight) r. 160 S. New Jersey

COTTRELL & KNIGHT, (Thomas Cottrell and John Knight) tin plate, copper and sheet iron, 179 E. Washington

Coughlen ——, engineer, bds. 74 N. Pennsylvania

Coughlen Frank, clk. Merritt & Coughlen, bds. 282 W. New York

Coughlen William, (Merritt & Coughlen) r. 282 W. New York

Coulon Charles, tobacco and cigars ret. 11 Pennsylvania, r. Arsenal road nr. Arsenal

Coulon Charles G. clk. T. Theobald, bds. 60 S. Delaware

Coulter Archibald, r. 256 S. Delaware

Coulter James, (Coulter & White) r. 376 Alabama, cor. McCarty

Coulter John, straightner Rolling Mill, r. 213 S. Tennessee

Coulter Margaret, wid. Charles, r. 191½ W. Washington

Coulter William, boilermaker Sinker & Co.

COULTER & WHITE, (James Coulter and Charles H. White) gas fitters and plumbers, 47 S. Pennsylvania

Council John F. (W. R. Hogshire & Co.) r. Jackson, sw. cor. Cherry

County Appraiser's office, room 6, 20½ N. Delaware

COUNTY BUILDINGS, Court House Square, ns. Washington, bet. Delaware and Alabama

COUNTY OFFICES, County Buildings, Court House Square

Courtney C. wks. Caledonia Paper Mill

Courtney John, fireman Caledonia Paper Mill

Covault Erastus J. clk. Rickard & Talbott, bds. Bates House

Covenanter Church, ns. South, bet. East and Noble

Cover Isaac, car repairer C. & I. J. R. R. r. 27 S. New Jersey

Coverdill Thomas, teamster, r. 229 W. Merrill

Covert William, carpenter, r. 6th Ward School House

Covington Emily, bookbinder J. H. C. Smith

Covington Susan, wid. William, r. 12 N. California

Cowan Harriett, wid. William, r. 319 W. Merrill

Cowan Robert, clk. bds. 320 N. Illinois

Cowen James, (col'd) wks. J. S. Carey & Co. bds. same

Cowen Martin V. B. (Cowen & Protzman, r. 40 S. Illinois

COWEN & PROTZMAN, (Martin V. B. Cowen and Ferdinand Protzman) Western Publishing Co. directories, subsbription books, and editors and proprs. *Old Oaken Bucket*, and agts. for central Indiana of the Connecticut General Life Ins. Co. of Hartford, Conn. 16½ E. Washinton

Cowgill John G. sewing machine agt. r. 320 N. Alabama

Cox A. G. clk. Murphy, Johnston & Co. r. 69 S. Meridian

Cox Albert W. (Lukens, Gause & Cox) r. 174 E. Walnut

Cox Andrew G. salesman Dessar Bro. & Co. r. 76 N. Noble

Cox A. William, salesman J. W. Adams, r. ws. James bet. First and St. Joseph

Cox Charles, stoves and tinware, 57 W. Washington, r. 71 S. Meridian

Cox Charles H. salesman C. Cox, r. 71 S. Meridian

Cox Crittenden A. baggage master, r. 18 Chatham

Cox David, tinner C. Cox, bds. 71 N. Meridian

Cox Edward, finisher Woolen Mill, r. ws. Douglas, 5 s. New York

Cox Edward T. State Geologist, office State House

Cox Grand A. clk. r. 69 S. Meridian

Cox Henry C. carpenter and builder, r. 224 W. Washington

Cox J. F. wks. Osgood, Smith & Co. bds. 30½ N. Pennsylvania

COX	92	CRA

Cox Jacob, artist, 26 and 28 W. Washington, r. 69 S. Meridian
Cox John A. M. (Cox & Brother) r. 264 S. Alabama
Cox John F. carpenter, r. 105 Bradshaw
Cox Lydia Mrs, r. 250 Minerva
Cox Milton L. (Landers, Conduitt & Co.) bds. Palmer House
Cox Sophia, wid. Nathaniel, r. 252 W. Market
Cox Thomas, carpenter, r. 128 N. Illinois
Cox Thomas C. (Cox & Brothers), r. 320 E. Louisiana
Cox Thomas T. sheetiron worker, r. 298 E. Louisiana
Cox William, painter W. B. Milender, r. 27 S. New Jersey
Cox William B. (R. L. Lukens & Co.) r. 262 N. East
Cox William C. (Tomlinson & Cox) r. 30 W. St. Clair
COX BROTHERS, (Thomas C. Cox and John A. M. Cox) sheet-
iron workers, 24 E. Georgia
Coy Daniel, carriage trimmer Ind. Coach Works, r. 304 N. Illinois
Coy Simeon, painter Ind. Coach Works
Coyle Bernard, bds. 130 W. New York
Coyle Hannah, wid. Michael, r. 130 W. New York
Coyner J. S. r. ws. Illinois, bet. 2d and 3d
Coyner J. V. clk. Anderson & Scott, r. 449 E. St. Clair
Coyner John V. contractor, r. 449 E. St. Clair
Coyner Martin L. asst. city engineer, bds. 31 W. Ohio
Coyner Martin L. contractor, r. 449 E. St. Clair
COZAD J. L. Div. Supt. C. C. C. & I. R. R. and Chief Engineer
I. & St. L. R. R. 53 S. Alabama, r. n. end Massachusetts av.
Cozzens Mary (col'd), wid. John, r. 179 W. 2nd
Craber ——, lab. Bunte, Dickson & Co.
Crabtree A. (col'd) watchman McKendry & Lovecraft
Craft Anna, saleslady Mrs. E. I. Fisk
Craft Frost P. r. 496 N. Tennessee
Craft Hiram J. dep. int. rev. assessor, bds. 17 W. Maryland
Craft John P. bookkeeper Sinker & Co. r. 496 N. Tennessee
Craft Lewis, brewer Indianapolis Brewery, r. 72 S West
Craft R. P. machinist Sinker & Co. r. 496 N. Tennessee
Craft Smith, blacksmith J. M. Van Blaricum, r. 286 Indiana av.
Craft Werner P. salesman Dury & Hawk, bds. 496 N. Tennessee
CRAFT WILLIAM H. watches, jewelry, silver and plated ware, 36
E. Washington, r. 163 N. Alabama
Craig Alexander, salesman Alford, Talbot & Co. r. 218 Huron
Craig Gustavus, clerk, bds. 36 N. Pennsylvania
Craig Samuel A. (W. I. Haskit & Co.) bds. Pyle House
Craig William, clerk, bds. 36 N. Pennsylvania
Craig William, (William Craig & Co.) Delaware n. of limits
Craig Wm. R. bookkeeper Alford, Talbot & Co. r. 66 Fletcher av.
CRAIG WILLIAM & CO. (William Craig & George R. Kirkpatrick)
Flour and Feed, 78 Massachusetts av.
Craighead Robert D. medical student, bds. 230 N. Tennessee
Crail William, teamster J. R. Marot
Crain W. N. (Crain & Needham, r. Tennessee ne. cor. N. York
CRAIN & NEEDHAM, (W. N. Crain & William Needham) mer-
chant tailors, 3 Bates House blk.

Cramer George H. (Cramer & Newton) r. Morrison
Cramer Jacob, helper Ind. Coach works, r. 199 Liberty
CRAMER & NEWTON, (George H. Cramer & I. Jesse Newton) Billiard Hall, 63 N. Illinois
Crane Dennis, porter Union depot, r. 6 Henry
Crane George W. blacksmith, r. 378 N. Delaware
Crane James F. photographer. ns. Washington, bet. the canal and West, r. 256 S. Mississippi
Crane John, wks. Rolling Mill
Crane Len, wks. Rolling Mill
Crane William, r. 153 N. Tennessee
Crane William H. blacksmith Ind. Agricultural Works, bds. 78 S. Illinois
Crane James T. bookkeeper E. S. Folsom, bds. Palmer House
Crape R. P. looking glasses, frames, pictures, etc. 196 E. Washington, r. same
Crauly John, puddler Rolling Mill
Craven Anna, dressmkr. Mrs. S. L. Forbey, r. 278 W. Greer
Craven Cornelius, clk. Muehlenbeck & Obermeyer, r. 3 Ann
Craven John, lab. r. Greer bet. Mississippi and Missouri
Craven William, wks. Rolling Mill
Cravens June E. dental student P. G. C. Hunt, bds. Pyle House
Crawford Belle Miss, teacher 6th Ward, r. 256 S. Pennsylvania
Crawford Eli, moulder, r. 256 S. Pennsylvania
Crawford J. M. pastor Trinity M. E. Church, r. 320 N. East
Crawford Susan, (col'd) r. 177 Douglas al.
Crawley James, boilermkr. Eagle machine works, r. 54 Bicking
Crawley Patrick, hostler Citizens St. R. R. Co.
Crawley Thomas, lab. J. M. & I. R. R.
Crawley Timothy, lab. City R. R. bds. Globe House
Crayon Patrick, lab. r. 60 S. Alabama
Creedan Jerry, pipe layer Gas Works
Cregan Patrick, lab. Gas Works
Crehea Thomas, lab. r. 288 S. Delaware
Cress John B. (V. B. Cress & Son) r. 9 Fletcher av.
Cress Valentine B. (V. B. Cress & Son) r. 9 Fletcher av.
CRESS V. B. & SON, (Valentine Band, John B. Cress.) real estate agts. nw. cor. Delaware
Cretan Jerry, foreman gas works, bds. 217 S. Illinois
Cretchfield Stableton, (col'd) lab. r. Missouri nr. Tinker
Criley William W. pastor Lutheran Evangelical Church, r. 109 N. Pennsylvania
Crillman David, machinist, r. 351 E. Market
Crobb Jacob, gardner, r. W. Indianapolis
Crobb John, r. W. Indianapolis
Crockett Frank, South Side livery stable, bds. 198 S. Illinois
Croghan Henry, (col'd) porter S. A. Fletcher & Co. r. 181 Elm
Cronch Angeline, r. 242 W. Market
Cronch John, plasterer, r. 42 Helen
Cronin John, lab. r. 85 W. McCarty
Cronin Michael, lab. bds. 272 S. Tennessee

Bingham's Jewelry Store, cor. Pennsylvania and Washington Sts.

CRO   94   CUL

Cronin Timothy, lab. bds. 85 W. McCarty
Cronin William, puddler Indianapolis Rolling Mill
Cronley John, lab. r. 372 S. Tennessee
Crookston James H. salesman, bds. Commercial Hotel
Cropper James, r. 776 N. Tennessee
Cropper James, watchman C. C. C. & I. R. R. r. 210 Winston
CROPPER JAMES H. prop. Great Western Stove and Tin House 169 and 171 W. Washington, r. 776 N. Tennessee
Cropper John, r. Illinois se. cor. Tinker
Cropper John B. prop. city bath house 16 W. Pearl and saloon 24 W. Pearl, r. 526 N. Meridian
Cropper Joseph, carpenter Osgood, Smith & Co.
Cropper Joseph, carpenter, r. 372 E. New York
Cropsey Ann, wid. James E. r. 359 N. Alabama
Cropsey James M. r. 359 N. Alabama
Cropsey Mary, teacher 1st Ward School, r. 359 N. Alabama
Cropsey Nebraska Miss, teacher, r. 359 N. Alabama
Crosby J. P. printer, bds. Little's Hotel
Crosby John, expressman, r. 69 W. Maryland
Crosby John, teamster, r. 69 E. Maryland
Crosgrove Michael lab. rolling mill, r. 29 Henry
Crossland Jacob A. (Crossland, Hanna & Co.) r. 39 N. Illinois
CROSSLAND, HANNA & CO. (Jacob A. Crossland, Samuel C. Hanna and John M Caldwell), whol. grocers Meridian sw cor. Maryland
Crossley Thomas B. saddler, bds. Pattison House
Crosson John D. (col'd) barber, 395 N. New Jersey, r. same
Crouch George W. plasterer, r. 218 S. East
Crouch John D. cooper W. Baird
Crow Jacob, deliveryman Meikel's Brewery, r. 239 W. Maryland
Crowley Daniel, fireman gas works, r. 271 E. Market
Crowley Patrick, lab. r. 338 E. Washington
Crowley Thomas, engineer, r. 54 Bicking
Crowley Timothy, teamster, r. 40 Elizabeth
Crowley William, lab. r. 376 N. Missouri
Crozeer ——, night watchman, r. 350 N. Meridian
Crull Eliza Miss, bds. 199 N. Pennsylvania
Crull Jacob R. horsedealer, r. 32 Massachusetts av.
Crullman David, machinist C. C. & I. C. R. R.
Crum ——, tailor, bds. 64 W. Maryland
Cruse Solomon, farmer, r 122 E. Pratt
Cschech Gustavus, eagle machine works, r. 251 S Meridian
Culbert Patrick, lab. Rolling Mill, r. 436 S. West
Culings Owen, carpenter, r. Sixth, cor. Canal
Culley Daniel B. bkpr. Cottrell & Knight, r. 486 N. Pennsylvania
Culley David V. r. 193 E. Ohio
Culley William, scroll sawer M. Byrkit & Sons, r. 71 Norwood
Culligan John, lab. r. 338 E. Washington
Culliger William, lab. r. 27 S. Alabama
CULLINY PATRICK M. dry goods importer, 98 E. Washington, r. 40 N. Pennsylvania.

Cullum Eberle, pressman W. & J. Braden, r. 219 N. Mississippi
Culvis Lizzie Miss, student National Business College
Culver Thomas student, rooms 109 Massachusetts av
Cummings Charles, clk. A. Bretz, bds. 118 S. Illinois
Cummings Charles R. works Osgood Smith & Co. r. 56 Eddy
Cummings James, pump maker, r. 234 s Pennsylvania
Cummings Lewis (col'd) barber W. Porter, r. 130 N. Missouri
Cummings Richard, r. 234 S. Pennsylvania
Cummings Waldo F. teamster Emerson, Beam & Thompson, bds. 239 W. Market
Cunnigan John, hostler Citizens' Street R. R. Co
Cunningham Frank, bds. Bates House
Cunningham James, drayman T. F. Ryan, bds. Tennessee
Cunningham, John clk. Simpson & Dugan, bds. 16 Willard
Cunningham John, farmer. r. LaFayette road
Cunningham John, lab. r. Fifth, near LaFayette R. R.
Cunningham John, lab. r. 73 Maple
Cunningham John, lab. D. Root & Co.
Cupples Mary, wks. Caledonia Paper Mill
Care Rilla, wid. Harry, r. 230 E. Washington
Curley John, lab. D. Root & Co.
Curran John, lab. r. 167 Dougherty
Curran Michael, lab. r. 192 Bates
Curran Michael, r. 487 E. Georgia
Curran Patrick, (Lawless & Curran) r. 56 Huron
Curran Patrick, sr. lab. r. 56 Huron
Curran Thomas, lab. r. 56 Huron
Currans Michael, lab. I. C. & L. Rw.
Currie Mary P. Mrs. teacher 9th Ward School, r. Pennsylvania bet. Delaware and Meridian
Currlen Fred, cabinetmkr. Western Furniture Co.
Curry E. (col'd) teamster Caledonia Paper Mill, r. rear 265 W. Washington
Curry Hamilton, (col'd) lab. r. 588 N. Mississippi
Curry Robert, lumberyard, r. 246 Blake
Curry Thomas W. salesman H. Rothschild, bds. Bicking House
Curtis Andrew, justice of the peace, 834 E. Washington, r. 27 Fort Wayne av.
Curtis Charles, engineer, r. 2 Carey's row, Helen
Curtis Charles E. engineer, r. 79 Massachusetts av.
Curtis Joseph, (col'd) whitewasher, r. W. North cor. canal
Curtis Ruth, wid. Thomas, r. 222 N. New Jersey
Curtis Truman, clk. r. 65 S. California
CURZON JOSEPH, architect, room No. 4 Blake blk. 55 W. Washington, r. 376 N. Illinois
Cusick Joseph, groceries and liquors, 73 and 75 S. West, r. 71 S. West
Cussen Garrett, flagman, cor. Missouri and W. Washington, r. 158 Indiana av.
Cussen Garrett, jr. dry goods ret. 158 Indiana av. r. same

CUT	96	DAN

Cutsinger John, I. M. & I. R. R. R. r. Merrill, bet. Delaware and Alabama

Cutting F. B. Vice Pres. I. P. & C. R. R. r. New York

Cutpeter Henry, car inspector T. H. & I. R. R.

Cuykendall W. A. engineer C. & I. J. R. R. r. 330 E. Louisiana

D

Dabney Joseph, lab. r. ns. Kansas, 3 W. Bluff road

Dacy Patrick, lab. Rolling Mill, r. 17 Maple

Dade Tonnson, (col'd) lab. r. 232 N. Missouri

DAGGETT ROBERT P. architect and superintendent, room 6 Wiley's Block ws. Pennsylvania nr. Washington, r. 280 N. New Jersey

Dagget William, (Daggett & Co.) r. 280 N. New Jersey

DAGGETT & CO. (William Daggett, G. C. Webster and J. W. Smither) confectioners and foreign fruits, 26 S. Meridian

Daglish John, clk. P. M. Culliny, r. 504 N. Mississippi

Dahn Charles, flour and feed, bds. 65 S. East

Dahna William, clerk, r. 215 N. Davidson

Daily D. A. harnessmkr. Ad. Hereth

Daily Edward, blacksmith Greenleaf & Co. bds 217 S. Illinois

Daily Harrison H. r. cor. St. Mary's and Western av.

Daily Jennie, r. 36 S. New Jersey

Daily Laura, wks. Cotton Factory

Daily Michael, r. 27 S. Alabama

Dain Robert, paper hanger, r. 370 N. Alabama

Dain T. pumpmkr. 57 Massachusetts av. r. 114 N. Delaware

Dalby Lawrence, plaster, r. 211 W. Maryland

Dale Alfred, carpenter, r. al. rear Blake bet. Michigan and Vermont

Dall Peter, cleaner Sinker & Co. r. 131 E. McCarty

Dallas Bell, salesman R. Sedgewick, r. 170 W. Ohio

Dallas William, wks. N. Kellog, r. 366 W. Washington

Dalton F. lab. Sinker & Co.

Dalton Michael, lab. frt. depot T. H. & I. R. R. r. 389 S. Missouri

Dalton Thomas, lab. r. 214 Buchanan

Daly David N. varnisher, r. 328 E. New York

Daly Eugene, foreman Builders' and Mnfrs. Association's lumber yard, r. 343 Massachusetts av.

Daly George, harnessmaker, r. 328 E. New York

Daly John, varnisher Spiegel & Thoms, bds. 328 E. New York

Dame Jason, (Dame & Greenlee) r. 287 S. New Jersey

DAME & GREENLEE, (Jason Dame and E. A. Greenlee) marble workers and dealers, 69 E. Washington

Damme Albert, student National Business College

Damme Frank, lab. r. 327 S. East

Dammeier Charles, (William Cook & Co.) r. 310 E. Georgia

Danacker Paul, cabinetmaker, r. 89 Buchanan

Dane ——, wid. r, 114 St. Mary

Dane Thomas, pump maker, r. 114 St. Mary

DAN	97	DAV

Danford Isaac, pump maker, bds. Ray House

Danforth Albert J. r. 352 N. New Jersey

Daniel Adam, engineer, r. S. New Jersey 1 s. South

Daniel Henry, (col'd) lab. r. 170 Douglas al.

DANIELS LEWIS H. carpenter, 129 S. New Jersey, r. 350 S. East

Daniels Samuel P. tailor, r. 108 New Jersey

Dannahe Peter, lab. r. 108 Bluff rd.

Dannar John, lab. freight depot C. C. & I. C. R. R. r. S. New Jersey, 1 s. South

Dannar M. wid. picker Paper Mill, r. 373 W. Washington

Danninburg James, teamster, r. 424 S. East

Danninburg Margaret, wid. Christian, r. 175 E. South

Dannmeyer Anthony, grocer, E. Washington out of limits

Darby Adrian, brickmason, r. 444 W. North

Darby John, (John Hauck & Co.) r. 227 W. New York

Darby P. M. bds. Bates House

Darby Samuel F. sawmkr. Sheffield Saw Works, r. 476 N. Alabama

Dark Charles, teller Indianapolis Branch Banking Co. r. Walnut se. cor. Tennessee

Dark Jonathan, blacksmith, r. 572 West North

Darnall William W. carpenter, r. 342 E. New York

Darnell Calvin F. carpenter, r. 738 N. Illinois

Darnell Lewis, boxmkr. Pfaendler & Zogg, r. 738 E. New York

Darnes William, (col'd) barber, bds. 212 W. Vermont

Darrow Benjamin C. clk. J. C. Burton & Co. r. 545 N. Illinois

Darrow Milton, printer, bds. Western av. se. cor. Christian av.

Darrow James, grocer, r. Western av. se. cor. Christian av.

Darter Amos R. pumpmkr. r. 128 N. Tennessee cor First

Darter Jasper, r. 129 W. Market

Dasher Mary, wid. r. 339 N. Illinois

Daubenspeck Nelson, (Myers & Daubenspeck) r. 121 N. Delaware

Daubenspeck's Block, 17 to 27 Massachusetts av.

Daugherty E. Miss, dress and cloak maker, room 12 2d floor Martindale's blk. r. 222 N. Delaware

Daugherty Morris, lab. r. Maryland ne. cor. Benton

Daumont Henry, (H. Daumont & Co.) r. 439 N. Pennsylvania

Daumont Peter A. mnfr. of fine jewelry, 47 S. Illinois, r. same

DAUMONT H. & CO. (Henry Daumont & William M. Wheatly) whol. and ret. dealers in gilt and rosewood mouldings, pictures and picture frames, clocks, looking-glasses, etc. 15 W. Washington

Davenport Daniel, (col'd) fireman Sherman House

Davenport Malinda, wid. John, r. ws. Minerva 4 s. New York

Davenport Samuel, wks. Cotton Factory

Davenport Thomas, lab. r. 115 Huron

Davenport Thomas, saw maker Sheffield Saw Works, 136 W. 1st

Davenport William, wks. W & J Braden, bds. ws. Minerva 4 s. New York

Davenport Wm. pattern maker Sinker & Co. bds. 111 W. South

David Anna, wid. William, r. 273 E. Market

7

DAV	98	DAV

David George F. checkman C. C. C. & I. R. R. outer freight depot, r. 273 E. Market

David Thomas, butcher, r. 210 Union

Davidson C. B. rector Grace Episcopal Church, r. 373 N. Pennsylvania

Davidson George, carpenter P. Routier

Davidson James, compositor *Journal* news room, bds. Pennnsylvania nw. cor. Market

Davidson John, northern route agt. *Journal*, r. 170 Davidson

Davis Abbie C. teacher 8th ward district school, r. 97 Buchanan

Davis Abel E. (Baxter & Davis) r. 325 N. West

Davis Ann (col'd) wid. George, r. 126 N. Missouri

Davis Benjamin, r. 249 E. Louisiana

DAVIS BENJAMIN, grocer and dealer in flour and feed, Indiana av. cor. West, r. same

Davis Charles (col'd) lab. r. 570 N. Mississippi

Davis Charles B. gen. agt. Imperial Fire Insurance Co. room 6 Odd Fellows' Hall, r. 139 Indiana av.

Davis Charles E. scenic painter, bds. 144 N. Tennessee

Davis Charles S. Butcher, r. 129 N. Pennsylvania

Davis Daniel, machinist Sinker & Co.

Davis, David, puddler, r. 281 S. Tennessee

Davis Alexander, lab. Union Novelty Works

Davis Edward, deputy constable, office 83½ E. Washington, r. Westfield gravel road, out of limits

Davis Edward W. butcher Harvey D. Davis, r. 129 N. Pennsylvania

Davis Edwin A. (Voss & Davis) bds. Bates House

Davis Earnst G. clk. C. B. Davis, r. 139 Indiana av.

Davis Ellen A. Miss, Principal Sixth Ward School, bds. 290 S. Meridian

Davis F. A. W. (Indiana Banking Co.) r. Merrill, se. cor. New Jersey

Davis G. M. (col'd) blacksmith 252 Indiana av. r same

Davis G. W. brass founder & gas fitter, r. 221 N. Tennessee

Davis George (col'd) porter, r. 79 Ann

Davis George, watchmaker and jeweler, 37 W. Washington, r. 40 N. California

Davis George F. checkman, r. 273 E. Market

Davis George W. traveling agt. J. W. Smith, bds. 123 N. Illinois

Davis Greer W. painter, r. 172 S. Tennessee

Davis Harrison, engineer B. F. Haugh & Co. r. 150 S. Alabama

Davis Harvey, (Davis & Donovan) r. 126 Virginia av.

DAVIS HARVEY D. meat market 71 E. Washington, r. 129 N. Pennsylvania

Davis Henry, machinist, bds. 73 Kentucky av.

Davis Horace H. machinist, r. 139 Indiana av.

Davis Isaac, (Isaac Davis & Co.) r. 426 N. Pennsylvania

Davis J. W. steam and gasfitter and brass founder, 110 S. Delaware, r. 221 N. Tennessee

Davis Jacob, carpenter, r. 100 James

DAV	99	DAY

Davis James E. boot and shoemaker, 239 E. Washingtsn, r. 299 N. Liberty

Davis John, day watchman, C. C. C. & I. R. R.

Davis John, (col'd) barber shop, 14 S. Pennsylvania, r. 231 N. Tennessee

Davi John R. shoemaker James E. Davis, r. 299 N. Liberty

Davis Levi L. butcher, r. 129 N. Pennsylvania

Davis M. C. wid. r. 147 W. Maryland

Davis Margaret, wid. Ira, r. ns. 1st nr. Mississippi

Davis Mary Mrs. (col'd) milliner, 252 Indiana av. r. same

Davis Mary, (col'd) wid. r. rear 239 N. Tennessee

Davis Milton, carpenter, r. 45 E. McCarty

Davis Nancy J. wid. James, r. 83½ E. Washington

Davis P. L. millwright, r. Broadway se. cor. Cherry

Davis Quincy A. student, bds. Broadway nw. cor. Vine

Davis Richard A. r. 308 E. New York

Davis Robert, engineer, r. 308 S. Illinois

Davis Robert F. saw maker Sheffield Saw Works

Davis Rufus P. carpenter, r. 215 Massachusetts av.

Davis Samuel, well digger, r. 81 Huron

Davis Thomas J. photographer, r. 150 W. New York

Davis Wells W. engineer C. C. & I. C. R. R. r. 37 Bates

Davis Wesley, carriage trimmer, r. Westfield Pike

Davis William, bricklayer, r. 120 N. Davidson

DAVIS WILLIAM H. pump mnfr. 133 N. Tennessee, r. 128 W. 1st

Davis William M. (Davis & Jones) r. 430 N. New Jersey

DAVIS ISAAC & CO. (Berry Self) hats, caps, furs, straw goods, robes, gloves, umbrellas, &c. 12 E. Washington

DAVIS & DONOVAN, (Harry Davis and John E. Donovan) groceries and com. mer. 342 E. Washington

DAVIS & JONES, (William M. Davis and W. W. Jones) auctioneers 88 E. Washington

Davison George, carpenter, r. 188 Dougherty

Davison John, engineer, r. 174 N. Davidson

Davison Rufus, millright, r. 148 Blackford

Davolls John, traveling agent, r. 303 S. Meridian

Davy Daniel, machinist, bds. 217 S. Illinois

Davy John, porter John Sweetser, bds. 217 S. Illinois

Davy Walter W. comp. *Mirror* newsroom, r. 60 Massachusetts av.

Dawson C. works J. S. Carey & Co.

Dawson George, varnisher Western Furniture Co.

Dawson James, engineer, r. 268 N. Merrill

Dawson Lewis, works Indianapolis Paper Mill Co.

Dawson Luther, lab. r. 273 S. West

Dawson Thomas B. r. 161 Maple

Dawson T. works J. S. Carey & Co.

Dawson William, driver Express Co. r. 62 Fletcher av.

Day Elisha M. lab. r. 348 Indiana av.

Day Hannah, wid. Thomas D. r. 91 S. Pennsylvania

Day John, (col'd) wks. S. W. Patterson, r. Elizabeth bet. Patterson and Minerva

DAY	100	DEL

Day John, (col'd) teamster Sohl, Gibson & Co.
Day R. L. r. 547 N. Illinois
Day William, butcher, r. 438 E. St. Clair
Deal Harvy, genl. freight agt. bds. 73 W. Maryland
Deallor Charles, lab. bds. 65 S. East
Dean Charles, bricklayer, r. 320 S. West
Dean Charles, moulder Rolling Mill
Dean Charles, (Dean & Bro.) bds. East St. House
Dean King, lab. r. 317 Massachusetts av.
Deane Charles H. bds. 154 S. Noble
Deane Fieldon, (col'd) lab. r. 166 Elm
Deane Harrison, (col'd) lal. r. 176 Elm
Deane Harry, surveyor, bds. 154 S. Noble
Dearinger Simeon, plasterer, r. 313 E. Georgia
Deaver Charles, delivery clk. Express Co.
Deaver George W. clk. r. 14 E. Michigan
Debershire D. B. carpenter, bds. 10 W Georgia
Decker Conrad, blacksmith C. C. C. & I. R. R. r. 248 Winston
Decker Laura, wid. John B. r. 181 N. Noble
Decker Lewis H. (Gardner & Decker) r. 296 Virginia av.
Deckman Andrew, carpenter, r. ns. Kansas, 2 w. Bluff rd.
Deey Patrick, lab. r. 17 Maple
Deder W. check clk. C. C. C. & I. Rw. r. Michigan rd e. of limits
Dedrich Frank, varnisher, r. 295 E. Georgia
Dedrick George, clk. P. O. bds. 194 N. Illinois
Deebig Fredericke, wid. Christian, r. 418 S. East
Deer George, lab. r. 55 Dacotah
Deer Henry, varnisher Spiegel & Thoms
Deer L. varnisher, Spiegel & Thoms
Deery Bridget, wid. Edward, r. es. Jackson bet. Cherry and
    Christian av.
Deery John, expman. r. es. Jackson bet. Cherry & Christian av.
Deffaugh Louis, pianoforte maker J. H. Kappes & Co. r. 259
    N. Liberty
De Fonfride Joseph, traveling agt. bds. 147 W. Maryland
Degering Christian, clk. E. Rentoch, bds. 174 S. Illinois
DE GRAY THOMAS, baker and confectioner 59 N. Illinois, r. same
De Haven Andrew J. foreman paper dept. Hume, Adams & Co, r.
    174 Madison av.
Dehart David, teamster, r. Ellen, sw. cor Indiana av.
De Hoff James A. painter Ryan Bros.
Dehue Charles (Dehue & Bro.) bds. S. East, nr. the railroad
Dehue William (Dehue & Bro.) r. 215 N. Davidson
DEHUE & BRO. (William and Charles Dehue) flour and feed, 300
    E. Washington
Deiner Carry, wks. Caledonia Paper Mill
Deitch Charles, salesman F. Deitch, bds. 173 E. Market
Deitch Clarence, salesman F Deitch, bds. 173 E. Market
Deitch Felix, dry goods rct. 162 W. Washington, r. 173 E. Market
Deitch Joseph, r. 85 N. Alabama
DeLaney John, lab. r. 384 S. Delaware

T. B. Perrine, Engraver on Jewelry & Silver Ware, 34 Virginia av.

DEL   101   DEP

DelaneyMichael, lab. r. 133 N. Noble
Delaney Michael, lab. r. ss. Merrill, nr. Grant
Delaney Peter, lab. Rolling Mill, r. 511 S. Tennessee
Delaney William, wks. Rolling Mill, r. 189 High
Delano Joel A. constable, office Yohn's blk. r. 349 E. McCarty
Delbrook William, shoemaker John Matz
Delks Franklin, teamster, bds. 151 Bluff rd.
Dell Edward, clk. William Dell, r. 135 Washington
DELL WILLIAM, saloon and boardinghouse, 135 E. Washington
Dell William H. collecting agent, r. 135 E. Washington
Deller Frederick, printer, r. 184 N. Noble
Dellfield Myer, r. 258 S. Delaware
DeLong M. lab. Union Novelty Works
DeLong John D. cooper, r. 314 E. Georgia
Delvo Eugene, stonemason, r. 471 Virginia av.
Delvo John, machinist Eagle Machine Wks. r. 471 Virginia av.
Delzell Samuel, moneybroker, r. 276 N. Delaware
De Martz Hanton, bds. Jefferson House
Deming W. H. driver Citizens' R. R. Co.
Demmy Martin, saddler, r. 219 W. North
Demmy William H. harnessmaker, r. 206 Huron
Demmitt John, carpenter, bds. Little's Hotel
De Moss Leander, checkmstr. T. H. & I. R. R. r. 123 W. South
De Munn George T. r. 111 Meek
Denech August, shoemkr. C. Halterman, bds. 172 S. Illinois
Deneen James W. tailor, r. 27 Vine
Denk Andrew, vinegar mnfr. r. 183 Indiana av.
De Night David, works *Journal* press room
Denis Charles D. jr. r. 171 Virginia av.
Dennis Charles C. bookkeeper Hume, Adams & Co. r. 70 W. New York
Dennis Charles C. (Swiney & Dennis) bds. 17½ Virginia av.
Dennis E. R. wid. John, bds. 17½ Virginia av.
Dennis Frank Miss, clk. bds. 78 W. North
Dennis James M. oil painter A. R. Miller, bds. 140 N. East
Dennis M. P. trav. agt. Lines, Smelser & Co.
Dennis Peter, bricklayer, r. 26 Buchanan
Denning O. H. painter Ind. Coach Works, bds. 24 W. Georgia
Denning Samuel, bds. 173 S. Tennessee
Denny A. F. lawyer, 94 E. Washington, rooms same
Denny John E. carpenter, 50 Kentucky av. r. 136 Blackford
Denny Joseph W. millwright, r. 60 Fayette
Denny Robert, claim agt. 98 E. Washington, r. 18 Bates
Denton A. B. (Ransford & Denton) r. 283 E. South
Denwiddie Hugh, painter, r. 76 Indiana av.
Denzelman Henry, pianoforte mkr. J. H. Kappes & Co. bds. 135 Delaware
Department of Public Instruction, B. C. Hobbs, supt. office 45 N. Tennessee
Depugh Henry, (col'd) pastor Allen Chapel, r. 58 Oak
Deputy Clark, dental student M. Wells, bds. Pyle House

DER	102	DIC

Derdert William, lab. r. Michigan rd. nr. junction Washington
Dermody Thomas, lab. r. ss. Sinker nr. Alabama
Dorringer David, carpenter, r. 437 N. Mississippi
Dersh John, lab. r. 157 Winston
DeRuiter Derk, (W. DeRuiter & Bro.) bds. 65 S. Illinois
DeRuiter White, (W. DeRuiter & Bro.) bds. 65 S. Illinois
DeRuiter W. & Bro. (White and Derk DeRuiter) oyster and
  fruit depot, 65 S. Illinois
Deschler John, (Western Furniture Co.) r. St. Joseph nw. cor.
  Alabama
Deschler Joseph, saloon, 15 N. Pennsylvania, r. 26 Cherry
Deshong Jemima, wid. Hiram, r. 457 E. Georgia
DES JARDINS JOSEPH, stairbuilder 191 Virginia av. r. 464
  Virgiania av.
Des Jardins Prim, carpenter, r. 426 E. Georgia
DE SOTO MUTUAL LIFE INSURANCE CO. OF ST. LOUIS, MO.
  Wilcox & Means, State agents, office rooms 3-4 Wiley's
  block opposite Odd Fellows' Hall
Despa Ernst, painter, r. 50 Lockerbie
Despa Wilhelmina (wid. Ernst) r. 50 Lockerbie
Despo Esidore, carpenter, r. ns. Harrison nr. stone yard
Despo Odiel, carpenter P. Routier
Dessar A. (Dessar Bro.& Co.) r. New York city
Dessar David (Dessar Bro. & Co.) r. New York city
Dessar Joseph B. (Dessar Bro. & Co.) r. 213 N. Illinois
Dessar Lewis (Dessar Bro. & Co.) r. 172 E. Ohio
DESSAR BRO. & CO., (Joseph B. Lewis, Adolwhers and David
  Dessar) clothing wholesale, 60 S. Meridian
Devsner William, carriagemaker, bds. 225 E. Market
Devel James, grocer, r. 139 N. Davidson
De Vennish Collin F. r. 219 E. South
De Vennish Solomon, r. 219 E. South
De Vennish Solomon B. r. 219 E. South
Devere Charles, teamster, bds. 62 Massachusetts av.
Devine William, tailor, r. 160 S. Noble
Dewald Frank, clerk Henry Greenewald, bds. Pattison House
Dewald Mathias, drayman, Holland, Ostermeyer & Co. r. 236
  Railroad
Dewdney William H. r. 176 E. South
Denin Thomas, lab. r. Chespeak bet. West and the Canal
Dial Frank A. (Lindley & Co.) conveyancer and notary. r. 376
  N. Tennessee
Diaz Antony, tailor A. Kelly, bds. Pyle House
Dickens ——, Mrs. r. 28 W. Ohio
Dicker Harriett, wid. James, r. 70 N. California
Dicker Sophia, r. 70 N. California
Dickert Jacob, Cabinet Makers Union, r. 22 N. West
Dickey J. B. watchman Greenleaf & Co. r 47 Dougherty
Dickey Thomas W. carpenter, 34 S. Pennsylvania, bds. 74 N.
  Pennsylvania
Dickhout Valentine G. trunk maker r. 165 N. Mississippi

Dickinson James L. r. 460 S. New Jersey
Dickinson Jefferson (col'd) lab. r. Rhode Island nr. Blake
Dickinson John C. r. 235 E. South
Dickison Frank, hostler John Smither
Dickmann Charles, saloon 208 E. Washington, r. same
Dickmann Francis, r 775 N. Illinois
Dickson ——, r. 172 Buchanan
Dickson Andrew, (Pettis, Dickson & Co.) bds. Bates House
Dickson Carlos, (C. Dickson & Co.) r. 74 W Vermont
Dickson George, (col'd) carpenter, r. 225 W. Ohio
Dickson James, (V. Butsch & Dickson) r. N. Pennsylvania bet. First and Second
Dickson James B. treasurer Academy of Music, bds. N. Pennsylvania bet. First and Second
Dickson James C. (C. Dickson & Co.) r. 110 Indiana av.
Dickson James P. clk. bds. N. Pennsylvania n. of limits
Dickson John, yardmaster Bunte, Dickson & Co. bds. 196 N. Tennessee
Dickson John T. (Bunte, Dickson & Co.) r. N. Pennsylvania n. of First
Dickson Sarah, wid. Charles, r. rear 241 W. Ohio
Dickson Thomas M. bookkeeper Bunte, Dickson & Co. r. 172 Buchanan
Dickson Wallace E. (C. Dickson & Co.) r. 110 Indiana av.
Dickson William B. (Bunte, Dickson & Co. and Bunte & Dickson) r. 196 N. Tennessee
DICKSON C. & CO. (Carlos, James C. & Wallace Dickson) woolen factory supplies and dye stuffs, 47 and 49 N. Tennessee
Diefenbach Jacob, carpenter, r. 472 N. Alabama
Diehl H. C. agt. P. C. & St. L. R.R. r. 74 W. Maryland
Diekmann Fred. Jr. carpenter F. Diekmann, bds. 71 N. East
Diekmann Frederick, carpenter and builder, Wabash nr. cor. East, r. 91 N. East
Dietel Charles, expressman, r. 273 N. Liberty
Dieten Ernst, shoe maker George Fisher, r. 25 Biddle
Dietrich Jos. cigar maker Henry Schulz, bds. 176 S. Delaware
Dietrichs Charles, jeweler and silversmith, 66 N. Pennsylvania, r. ws. Liberty 3 n. Michigan
Dietrichs William, salesman Todd, Carmichael & Williams, r. 36 N. Pennsylvania
Dietz Adam, barber, 116 Fort Wayne av. r. same
Dietz August, baker Fred. C. Bollman
Dietz Ferdinand (Dietz & Reissner) r. 390 E. Market
Dietz Fred. (Fred. Dietz & Co.) and saloon 255 E. Washington, r. in country
Dietz Jonn A. barber J. G. Klein, bds. 68 Ft. Wayne av.
Dietz Peter, saloon and propr. Washington House, 181 S. Meridian, r. same
Dietz Fred. & Co. (Fred. Dietz, John Houck & Geo. Eberhardt) saloon 133 E. Washington

DIETZ & REISSNER, (Ferdinand Dietz & Albert Reissner) leather, hides, oil and findings, 17 S. Delaware

Diffey Thos. machinist Schneider & Co. r. 225 W. Washington

Dill Benjamin, cooper, bds. 127 S. New Jersey

Dill Charles, painter, r. 751 N. Mississippi

Dill E. B. blacksmith R. A. Durbon, r. 98 Broadway

Dill Gertrude, wid. r. 328 N. Illinois

Dill John P. compositor *Sentinel* news room, r. 328 N. Illinois

Dille Jasper, teamster H. H. Lee

Dille Jasper, clerk G. Douglass, r. 60 S. Pennsylvania

Dille S. L. wid. r. 147 W. Maryland

Dillon Bridget, r. 30 Willard

Dillon Daniel, lab. A. D. Wood, r. 61 Maple

Dillon John, lab. r. 360 S. Delaware

Dillon Patrick, machinist, r. 30 Willard

Dillon Thomas, bricklayer, r. 461 N. East

Dilly John, engineer, bds. 217 S. Illinois

Dilts Sarah, wid. H. W. r. 7 Massachusetts av.

Dingeldey Theodore, prin. German English School, r. 124 N. Alabama

Dippel Edward, carpenter, r. 497 S. New Jersey

Dippel F. pianofortemkr. J. H. Kappes & Co.

Dippel Henry, varnisher Helwig & Co. r. 497 S. New Jersey

Dippel John, carpenter, r. 425 E. Vermont

Dippel Joseph, lab. r. 195 N. Noble

Dippel Lebricht, cabinetmaker Spiegel & Thoms

Dishon James, billposter, r. 222 Noble

Dishon William, painter, r. James nr. 1st

Dittrich Christian G. cabinetmkr. Cabinet Makers' Union, r. 77 W. Davidson

Dixon George F. wagonmkr. r. 149 Winston

Dixon Emily C. wid. John, r. Georgia cor. Liberty

Dixon James, apprentice B. F. Hetherington & Co. r. 262 S. Missouri

Dixon James W. r. 262 S. Missouri

Dixon John, bookkeeper Trade Palace, bds. Bates House

Dixon Minerva L. dressmkr. Mrs. N. M. Allen

Dixon Prophet, (col'd) porter Merrill & Co.

Dixon William, (col'd) lab. r. 225 W. Ohio

Dobbs Cyrus J. sheriff of the Supreme Court, bds. Bates House

Dobson James, hostler D. Ricketts, r. same

Dockweiler Jacob, engineer C. C. C. & I. R. R. r. 501 E. Market

Dodd E. patternmkr. Phœnix machine works, bds. 23 N. West

Dodd John W. (Judson & Dodd) r. 214 N. Illinois

Dodd Richard, brakeman, bds. 58 Benton

Dodd W. S. clk. Judson & Dodd, r. 214 N. Illinois

Dodge Emma Miss, bds. 19 E. St. Joseph

Dodson James, engineer T. H. & I. R. R. r. 151 W. South

DOEPFNER CHARLES F. justice of the peace, 139½ E. Washington, r. 52 S. Alabama

Doerbecker John, barber, r. 77 N. New Jersey

Doerbecker Jacob, barber, bds. 77 N. New Jersey
Doerfel Herman, propr. Grant House, South, ne. cor. Illinois, r. same
Doerr George, boardinghouse, 267 E. Washington, r. same
Dohart Gehart, stonemason, r. es. Minerva bet. Vermont and Michigan
Doherty Francis, salesman L. H. Tyler & Co. bds. Palmer House
Dohn Peter, cabinetmkr. r. ss. Kansas, w. of Bluff rd.
DOHN PHILIP, mnfr. and dealer in furniture, 246 S. Meridian, r. same
Dold Pierce, wks. railroad, bds. Ray House
Dold Ferdinand, wks. Eagle Machine Works, r. 275 E. New York
Dold P. lab. Sinker & Co. bds. 275 E. New York
Domon Jacob, r. 18 S. Delaware
Domon Jacob, r. 414 S. Illinois
Domon Oliver, r. 385 E. Georgia
Domon Peter E. saloon 18 S. Delaware, r. same
Donahue Patrick, lab. Gates, Pray & Co.
Donahue Patrick, hostler Citizens' Street R. R. Co.
Donahue Patrick, lab. r. 499 E. Georgia
Donahue Patrick, lab. r. 340 E. Washington
Donahue Timothy, lab. r. 480 E. Georgia
Donaldson Claybourn S. (Donaldson & Stout) bds. 180 N. Illinois
Donaldson Edwin C. clk. (Donaldson & Stout) bds. 180 N. Illinois
DONALDSON & STOUT (Claybourn S. Donaldson and David E. Stout) hats, caps and furs wholesale, 54 S. Meridian
Donillin Michael, lab. Gas Works
Donlan Michael, lab. r. 399 S. West
Donlan Peter, brakeman, bds. 199 W. Maryland
Donnan Barbara, wid. David, r. 126 N. Tennessee
Donnan Theodore, clk. Hendricks, Edmunds & Co. r. 126 N. Tennessee
Donnan Wallace, tinner, J. H. Cropper, bds. 126 N. Tennessee
Donnang Henry W. r. ss. 5th bet. Tennessee and Mississippi
Donnelly Francis, grocer, 347 S. Delaware, r. same
Donnelly John, carpenter, P Routier
Donnelly John, lab. r. 66 S. West
Donnelly Michael, boilermaker, r. Sinker nr. New Jersey
DONOUGH DANIEL R. asst. ticket agt. Union depot, r. 335 S. Meridian
Donovan James, drayman, r. 360 W. North
Donovan John, r. Benton ne. cor. Maryland
Donovan John E. (Davis & Donovan) r. 126 Virginia av.
Donovan Lawrence, lab. r. 142 S. Noble
Donovan Obediah, painter, r. ss. E. Michigan nr. Davidson
Doogan John, lab. r. 37 Dougherty
Doogan Neal, saloonkeeper, r. 60 Oak
Doolittle Sarah, wid. r. 90 N. Mississippi
Doran Henry, porter D. Root & Co. r. 21 Pine
Doran John, importer and whol. dealer in linen, 69 S. Illinois, r. New York City

DOR　　　106　　　DOU

Doran M. W. E. master cabinet shop Indiana Deaf and Dumb Institute
Doremus George C. carriagemkr. r. 217 Massachusetts av.
Dorhart Ambrose, works Cotton Factory
Dorhart Henry, works Cotton Factory
Dorland A. Mrs. dressmkr. 9 E. New York, r. same
Dorney Edward, clk. R. Hollywood, bds. 62 W. Maryland
Dorr William, bricklayer, r. 532 E. Georgia
Dorsch Paul, clerk City Brewery, r. same
Dorsey George, (col'd) lab. Builders and Mnfr. Association
Dorsey R. S. sec. and treas. Union Novelty Wks. Mnfr. Co. office St. Clair cor Canal, r. 495 N. Mississippi
Doster Fletcher, fireman C. & I. J. R. R. bds. 149 S. New Jersey
Doty A. driver Aldrich & Gay, bds. 240 W. Market
Doty Carey, bds. 240 W. Market
Doty Harriet, wid. Carey, r. 240 W. Market
Doty Oliver, bds. 240 W. Market
Doty Richard M. clk. H. Daumont & Co. r. 129 W. Maryland
Dauboch John, blksmith Eagle Machine Wks. r. 65 S. East
Doud John, lab. C. & I. J. R. R. r. 178 Meek
Dougherty Andrew, tanner, r. Bluff rd. cor Kansas
Dougherty Aquilla J. bds. Palmer House
Dougherty Bernard, hostler, r. 126 S. Tennessee
Dougherty Bernard, tanner, r. Kansas, w. of Bluff rd.
Dougherty Charles, lab. r. 383 S. Delaware
Dougherty Francis clk. Bee Hive, bds. Palmer House
Dougherty Frank L. wk. Merritt & Coughlen, bds. Nagle House
Dougherty James, lab. r. 14 Willard
Dougherty John, r. 227 E. South
Dougherty Margaret, dressmaker Mrs. S. L. Forby r. N. Illinois
Dougherty Mary, wid. William, r. Kansas, w. of Bluff rd.
Dougherty Michael, r. Wisconsin, opp. mill
Dougherty William, lab. C. C. C. & I. R. R.
Dougherty William, local editor daily evening *Commercial*, bds. Palmer House
Doughty John G. supt. Indianapolis Printing and Publishing House, r. 27 Indiana av.
Douglass Andrew, lab. r. 323 S. East
Douglass Clifton, telegraph operator C. C. C. & I. R. R. bds. ns. Michigan, bet. Winston and Railroad
Douglass Frank D. ins. agt. r. 144 E. New York
Douglass George, grocer 157 W. Washington, r. 129 W. N. York
Douglass James G. (Douglass & Conner) r. 129 W. New York
Douglass Robert L. state agt. Ætna Fire Ins. Co. room 1, Ætna bldg. r. 182 S. New Jersey
Douglass Samuel M (Douglass & Conner) r. 129 W. New York
DOUGLASS & CONNER, (James G. Douglass, Samuel M. Douglass, Alexander A. Conner, William R. Holloway) publishers and proprietors Indianapolis (daily evening) *Journal*, Market, ne. cor. Circle, *Journal* bldg.
Douty A. B. Mrs. teacher of Gymnastics Institute for the Blind

Dowdney W. blacksmith Sinker & Co.
Dowling James, lab. r. 313 N. Merrill
Dowling William W. (Indianapolis Printing & Publishing House) also editor and prop. *Little Sower* and the *Morning Watch*, Meridian se. cor. Circle, r. 488 N. Mississippi
Downey Dennis, lab. Rolling Mill
Downey James E. (Indianapolis Printing & Publishing House) and Downey & Brouse, r. 355 N. Alabama
Downey John, r. 277 E. Georgia
Downey John, lab. r. alley bet. East and Liberty and Georgia and R. R.
Downey John, porter P. O.
Downey John, fireman Gas Works
Downey Robert, r. 92 E. Market
Downey & Brouse, (James E. Downey, John A. Brouse) publishers Beharrell's Biblical Biography, Meridian se. cor. Circle
Downing Clarissa A. (wid. William) r. 102 N. Missouri
Downing Thomas, carpenter, bds. 144 S. Tennessee
Downs M. wks. Kingan & Co.
Downs Peter, night watchman State House, r. 10 Mississippi
Downs Thomas, lab. Rolling Mill, r. 52 Maple
Dox William A. clk. Kennedy, Byram & Co. bds. Spencer House
Doxey Edward O. travelling salesman Mayhew & Branham, bds. Spencer House
Doxon Linnie Miss, teacher 9th Ward School, r. 104 Delaware
Doyle —— Mrs. wks. Indianapolis Paper Co.
Doyle Andy, lab. r. 309 W. Merrill
Doyle Thomas, moulder Greenleaf & Co. bds. Illinois House
Drake Chester B. switchman C. C. & I. C. R. R. r. 77 S. East
Drake Edward B. cigar and tobacco dealer, r. 28 S. Mississippi
Drake F. harnessmaker Ad. Hereth, bds. Pattison House
Dransfield Ezra, wks. Cotton Factory, r. Geisendorff bet. Washington and New York
Drapier Ariel E. reporter, r. Market ne. cor. Tennessee
Drapier William H. job printer and reporter, 21 N. Meridian, r. Market ne. cor. Tennessee
Draper Anna, packer Barker, Williams & Co.
Draper Joseph M. carpenter, r. 101 E. St. Joseph
Draper Mollie, packer Barker, Williams & Co.
Draper Thomas, porter Wiles Bro. & Co. r. 85 W. Maryland
Drayer M. dry goods, r. 82 N. Liberty
Drechser Andrew, shoe maker, r. 344 Railroad
Dreepe Henry, turner, r. 118 Bluff rd.
Dreher Matthias, (Dreher and Bollinger) r. 82 N. Liberty
DREHER & BOLLINGER, (Matthias Dreher and James Bollinger) staple and fancy dry goods, 250 E. Washington
Dresker Mary, milliner J. W. Coppeland & Co.
Dreskins I. moulder Sinker & Co.
Drew Harry, conductor, r. 88 Massachusetts av.

Drew John A. (Sullivan & Drew) r. 88 Massachusetts av.

DREW SAMUEL W. mnfr. of carriages, buggies and spring wagons, East Market Square, bet. Delaware and Alabama, r. same

Drier Pater, blacksmith, r. 70 Elm

Driftmeyer Henry, drayman W. J. Holliday & Co. r. 176 S. Noble

Driggs Nat. S. clk. Browning & Sloan, bds. Spencer House

Drinkot William, lab. r. 113 S. Noble

Driscoll Jeremiah, lab. Rolling Mill, r. 26 Willard

Drorge Charles J. salesman C. P. Wilder, bds. 17 W. Maryland

Droessler William, lab. Schneider & Co.

Droping A. D. Indiana Transfer Co. r. 77 E. McCarty

Drotz Emile, (Drotz & Steinhauer), r. 258 S. Pennsylvania

DROTZ & STEINHAUER, (E. Drotz and M. Steinhauer) mnfrs. of files and rasps, 136 S. Pennsylvania

Drout John, lab. r. 109 Elm

Drum Robert, railroadman, r. 224 S. East

Drummond Hugh, watchman Rolling Mill

Drummond Hugh J. lab. Rolling Mill, r. es. Missouri n. of Merrill

Drummond Joseph, lab. r. 96 Green

Drury Charles, cooper McKendry & Lovecraft

Drury John, carpenter, bds. 6 Willard

Drusler William, lab. r. 276 W. Michigan

Dryer George W. photographer, 2. W. Washington, bds. Pyle House

Dryer James W. druggist, 344 E. Washington, r. 522 E. Washington

Dryer Peter, (Van Antwerp & Dryer) r. 7. Elm, cor. Cedar

Dubach John, wks. Washington Foundry, bds. 65 S. East

Duchene Charles, baker, r. 310 E. Georgia

Dudley T. car service dept. C. C. & I. C. R. R. bds. Bates House

Duell Thomas Walton, engineer, r. 433 E. Vermont

Duesner William, woodworker S. W. Drew

Duff Alexander W. painter, r. 207 Union

Duffy James, lab. r. St. Clair cor. Missouri

Duffy John, tailor, r. 57 S. California

Duffy Joseph, student National Business College

Duffy Michael, tailor, r. es. Clinton al. bet. Ohio and New York

Dugan John, wks. Rolling Mill

Dugan Neil, saloon, 62 S. Illinois, r. 60 N. Oak

Dugan Thomas, boot and shoe mnfr. 136 S. Illinois, r. 305 S. Pennsylvania

Dugdale William, shoemaker, r. 243 S. Mississippi

Dunaway Albert, (col'd) chairbottomer, r. 187 Elm

Dunbar John M. driver Citizens' Street R. R. Co. r. 276 W. Washington

Dunbar M. student Nation Business College

Dunbar Sarah, wid. Melzar, r. 254 S. Pennsylvania

Duncan A. W. lab. r. 253 S. West

Duncan David W. carpenter, bds. Ohio ne. cor. Mississippi

Duncan James R. plasterer, bds. Ohio ne. cor. Mississippi

Duncan John, bricklayer, r. 426 E. North

Duncan John S. (R. B. & J. S. Duncan) and prosecuting attorney Criminal Court, r. Western av. nw. cor. Forest Home av.

Duncan Maria, (col'd) wid. Matthew, r. 172 W. Georgia

Duncan Robert, lab. r. 137 W. Michigan

Duncan Robert B. (R. B. & J. S. Duncan) Indianapolis Cotton Mnfg Co. r. ws. Western av. cor. Forest Home av.

Duncan Robert P. supt. Indianapolis Cotton Mnfg. Co. w. end Washington, north of bridge, r. Western av. nw. cor. Forest Home av.

DUNCAN R. B. & J. S. (Robert B. and John S.) attorneys at law, 3 Brown's blk. Pennsylvania nw. cor. Washington

Duncomb Albert, varnisher Burk, Earnshaw & Co. bds. 144 N. Tennessee

Dunham S. T. driver Citizens' Street R. R. Co. r .128 S. Tennessee

Dunlap D. M. wid. Livingston, r. 25 Virginia av.

Dunlap J. M. physician, 77½ E. Market, r. same

Dunlea Charles, driver Express Co.

Dunlop Elizabeth, wid. John, r. 297 N. Meridian

Dunlop J. S. (J. S. Dunlop & Co.) r. 288 N. Pennsylvania

Dunlop Joshua (col'd) lab. r. 190 N. Missouri

DUNLOP JOHN S. & CO. (John S. Dunlop, Martin V. M'Gilliard and Silas W. Williams, gen. ins. agts. 2 W. Washington

Dunmeyer Christian, boardinghouse, 217 S. Illinois, r. same

Dunmeyer Frederick, drayman, r. 266 E. Ohio

Dunn Charles, bookkeeper J. N. Conklin, r. First nr. Illinois

Dunn Edward, lab. r. 275 S. Pennsylvania

Dunn George T. clerk Warren Tate, r. 410 N. Tennessee

Dunn George W. r. 25 W. First

Dunn Jacob P. (William Love & Co.) r. 410 N. Tennessee

Dunn John, plumber, r. 544 N. Mississippi

Dunn John E salesman L. H. Tyler & Co. r. 426 N. East

Dunn Martha Mrs. (Dunn & Franco) r. 77 S. Mississippi

Dunn Oliver, carpenter, r. 385 E. Georgia

Dunn William, wks. Rolling Mill

Dunn William A. janitor state house, r. 77 S. Mississippi

Dunn & Franco (Mrs. Martha Dunn and Mrs. Sarah Franco) milliners and millinery goods, 85 N. Illinois

Dunning James, wks. *Journal* press room, bds. 144 N. Tennessee

Dunning M. S. wks. R.R. r. 73 W. McCarty

Dunning Robert B. lab. bds. 104 N. California

Dunning William, sawer McKendry & Lovecraft, bds. 400 N. Mississippi

Dunnington William, (col'd) plasterer, r. 127 W. Fourth

Dunson Madison, farmer, r. Sharp e. of Meridian

Durbin Dav. S. bookkeeper Lawyer & Hall, bds. 346 N. Meridian

Durbon J. H. with R. A. Durbon, bds. East cor. Ohio

DURBON R. A. pump mnfr. 97 & 99 S. Meridian, r. East cor. Ohio

Durfeld John F. attorney at law and notary public and (Durfeld & Conklin) r. 2½ miles nw. city, Crawfordsville rd.

DUR	110	EAR

Durfeld & Conklin, (John F. Durfeld, Henry N. Conklin) solicitor of patents, real estate agents, 16½ E. Washington

Durgin Lyman W. foreman C. C. C. & I. R. R. Machine shops, r. 452 E. Michigan

Durham H. A. cigarmkr. r. 17 E. North

Dury John, (Dury & Hawk) r. 184 Massachusetts av.

DURY & HAWK, (John Dury and William V. Hawk) mnfrs. and dealers in boots and shoes, 3 E. Washington

Dutton George, blacksmith Gas Works

Duvall David C. clk. W. H. Roll, r. 159 N. Illinois

Du Vall Ely, r. 337 S. Alabama

Du Vall P. Joseph, policeman, r. 260 Madison av.

Du Vall Sarah, wid. Joseph, r. 337 S. Alabama

Dux Jacob, confectioner F. P. Becker & Bro. bds. 17 N. Pennsylvania

DUZAN W. N. physician and surgeon, r. 418 N. Tennessee

Dwyer Daniel R. carpenter, r. 226 N. East

Dwyer Thomas, lab. r. 36 Bicking

Dwyer William, shoemkr. A. W. Bronson, r. 74 Bicking

Dye John T. (Dye & Harris) r. s. end Virginia av.

DYE & HARRIS, (John T. Dye and A. C. Harris) lawyers, rooms 8 and 9 Talbott & New's block

Dyer Edward, lab. r. ss. Sinker nr. Alabama

Dyer Frank, r. 376 N. Tennessee

Dyke Joseph, horsedealer, r. 382 W. New York

Dynes John F. R. R. City Printing Co. bds. 477 N. New Jersey

Dynes Joseph A. printer R. R. City Printing Co.

Dynes Leonidas G. supt. R. R. Printing Co. 351 E. Market, Vinton's blk. r. 364 N. Mississippi

E.

Eaerd Joseph, stonemason, r. 239 Bluff rd.

Eagle Brass Works, Stierle & Loepper proprs. 94 S. Delaware

Eagle John, messenger A. M. U. Ex. Co. r. 205 Union

Eagle John D. (Eagle & Son) r. 340 N. Delaware

Eagle John H. (Eagle & Son) r. 340 N. Delaware

EAGLE MACHINE WORKS, Frederick Ruschhaupt, pres. George W. Penn, sec'y, Louisiana se. cor. Meridian opp. east end Union Depot

Eagle William O. clerk Eagle & Son, bds. 340 N. Delaware

EAGLE & SON, (John H. & John D. Eagle) groceries, ret. 340 N. Delaware

Earl Simon, wks. Osgood Smith & Co. r. 370 N. West

Earls A. (col'd) wks. McKendry & Lovecraft

Early James, lab. r. 280 E. Washington

Early William A. trav. salesman Lesh, Tousey & Co. r. 69 S. East

Earnshaw Frank, wks. Burk, Earnshaw & Co. bds. Ray House

Earnshaw Joseph, (Burk, Earnshaw & Co.) r. 257 S. Pennsylvania

Earwig ——, r. 19 Buchanan

Eastman F. N. harnessmaker, r. 191½ W. Washington
Eastman Frank M. harnessmaker J. M. Huffer & Son, bds. 23 S. Meridian
Eaton George A. (N. R. Smith & Co.) bds. Bates House
Eaton George A. salesman, bds. 203 N. Illinois
Eaton John W. r. 37 Chatham
Eaton John R. teamster G. W. Caldwell & Co.
Eaves Samuel, engineer T. H. & I R. R. bds. Nagle House
Eberhardt George (Fred. Dietz & Co.) r. 133 E. Washington
Eberhart John, carpenter, r. S. West nr. cor. Jones
Eberline G. cabinetmaker Speigle & Thoms
Eberline William, cabinetmaker, bds. 117 S. Illinois
Ebert John, carpenter and builder and (Ebert & Owens) 44 Kentucky av. r. 240 W. South
Ebert & Owens (John Ebert and Benjamin F. Owens) lumber-dealers 44 Kentucky av.
Eberts John, ice collector, r. 62 W. South
Ebner John, varnishmaker Mears, Lily & Co. r. 310 S. East
Eccles William, dry goods ret. 22 W. Washington, r. 241 N. Alabama
Echols William, conductor, r. 187 Meek
Eck Joseph, machinist Spiegel & Thoms, r. Ohio, e. of limits
Eckel Edward, gunsmith, r. 280 E. Washington
Ecksler John, teamster, r. 692 N. Tennessee
Eddy Harrison, fireman R. R. r. 250 S. Missouri
Eddy Marshal W. brakeman r. 225 S. West
Eddy Morris R. gen'l bkpr. Ind. Nat. Bank, bds. Bates House
Eden Asa, brickmason, r. 448 N. New Jersey
Eden Charlton, pres. Builders and Manufacturers Association, r. 340 N. Meridian
Eden Samuel C. carpenter Builders and Manufacturers Association, r. 178 E. Vermont
Eden William H. cigarmkr. W. H. Wallace, bds. 160 E. Market
Eden's Block, ss. Market bet. Pennsylvania and Delaware
Edmonds John, bookbinder *Journal* Office
Edmunds Edward, galvanizer Sinker & Co. r. 363 S. Missouri
Edmunds William, (Hendricks, Edmunds & Co.) r. 222 N. Illinois
Edson Hanford A. pastor Second Presbyterian Church, r. 157 N. Tennessee
Edwards ——, wks. J. S. Cary & Co.
Edwards Edward, saddle and harness mnfr. 16 W. Maryland, r. 75 Kentucky av.
Edwards John, blacksmith Phœnix Machine Works
Edwards John, (col'd) lab. r. 39 Harris
Edwards John G. operator W. U. T. Co. bds. 75 Kentucky av.
Edwards Martha, wid. John, boardinghouse, r. 75 Kentucky av.
Edwards Richard, r. 398 S. West
Edwards William, farmer, bds. 29 Grant
Edwards William B. stockdealer, bds. 75 Kentucky av.
Edwards William T. machine hand, wks. Cabinetmakers' Union, r. 525 E. Market

EDW	112	ELL

Edwards Willis R. (col'd) physician, r. 805 N. West

Edwardt John, hooker Rolling Mill.

Egan Edward C. cutter Treat & Claflin, bds. 14 W. Maryland

Egan Patrick, lab. r. 52 Fayette

Egan T. P. cutter E. A. Hall, bds. 17 W. Maryland

Egelus Daniel, clk. Tomlinson & Cox, bds. 130 N. Noble

Egelus Frederick, carpenter, r. 130 N. Noble

Egger John, (Egger & Muecke) r. 54 S. Alabama

Egger Samuel, lab. r. 35 Jones

EGGER & MUECKE, (John Egger and William Muecke) house,
   sign & ornamental painters, 152 E. Washington cor. Alabama

Eggerhorst ——, r. 88 E. Pratt

Eggert William, physician, 75 E. Ohio, r. same

Egleston Daniel W. varnisher. r.Wabash bet. Liberty and Noble

Ehrensperger Frank, clk. Vinnedge, Jones & Co. r. 266 N. East

Ehrich Wm. G. tinsmith I. L. Frankem & Co. bds. 19 Buchanan

Ehrman Louis, brewer Schmidt's brewery, r. same

Eichner William, lab. r. 19 Chadwick

Eichner William, bellboy Bates House, bds. same

Eichole August, cigarmaker H. Speckman, bds. 108 S. Illinois

Eighth Ward District School, Miss Maria H. Jones, principal,
   Virginia av. cor. Huron

Einatz Anthony, tollgate keeper, Lafayette rd. r. same

Einhams Carl, wks. Rolling Mill

Einsman William, lab. C. C. C. & I. R. R.

Eix Henry, saloon, 228 E. Washington

Elbecker John, woodwkr. John Feil, bds. South, sw. cor. Illinois

Elber Daniel, wiper T. H. & I. R. R.

Elbert Lawson, porter Union depot r. N. Missouri

Elbert Samuel A. (col'd) prin. Allen Chapel Day School, r. 229
   N. Tennessee

Elbrecht August, clk. F. W. Rosebrook, bds. 486 Virginia av.

Elder ——, farmer, r. Merrill cor. Eckert

ELDER ELI A. grocer, 52 N. Illinois, r. 133 W. New York

Elder James, salesman Pettis,Dickson & Co. bds. Oriental House

ELDER JOHN R. land agt. of the Indiana & Illinois Central R.
   R. Co. 21 S. Pennsylvania, r. 150 N. New Jersey

Elder Maggie, teacher 1st Ward School, r. 150 N. New Jersey

Elder William G. agt. *Sentinel*, r. 27 W. Ohio

Eldridge Jacob, 'real estate agt. room 8, 30 W. Washington, r.
   74 S. Mississippi

Eleck Lucy, wid. Jacob, r. 293 Winston

Elff Frank, barber, 135 S. Illinois, r. 273 S. New Jersey

Elgin William, pastor Mission Chapel, bds. 149 S. East

Ellenwood Emma, wid. r. 205 Huron

Ellerby James, veterinary surgeon, 10 E. Pearl, bds. Pyle
   House

Elliott Byron K. (Elliott & Holstein) r. 221N. California

Elliott C. J. presser Barker, Williams & Co.

Elliott Calvin A. r. 180 N. West

Elliott Flora Miss, matron City Hospital, r. same

ELLIOTT J. PERRY, City Art Gallery, 8 and 10 E. Washington, r. 293 N. Delaware

ELLIOTT JEHU T. Judge Supreme Court, State bldg. bds. Bates House

Elliot John, room 2, 77½ E. Market

Elliot John S. tobacconist, bds. Stanridge House

Elliott John M. with T. F. Ryan, bds. Commercial Hotel

Elliott Jonathan, deputy sheriff, r. 77 N. Noble

Elliott Joseph T. notary public and abstract of titles in real estate, office, recorders officeCourt House Square, r. 22 Chatham

Elliott Meiggs M. lab. Osgood, Smith & Co. r. 374 S. West

Elliott N. K. conductor C. & I. C. R. R. bds, Bates House

Elliott Russell, clk. Ed. King, I. & St. L. R. R. r. 38 W. St. Clair

Elliott T. B. physician and surgeon, r. w. end Michigan

Elliott Thomas B. (Elliott & Mott) r. w. end Michigan, city limits

Elliott William D. clk. County Recorder office, r. 426 N. Pennsilvania

ELLIOTT WILLIAM J. County Recorder office, county buildings, Court House Square, r. n. end Tennessee

Elliott William S. clk. P. O. r. 361 E. Market

ELLIOTT & HOLSTEIN, (Byron K. Elliott and Charles L. Holstein) attorneys at law, 24½ E. Washington

ELLIOTT & MOTT, (Thomas B. Elliott and Charles E. Mott) com. mers. flour, grain and provisions, 37 E. Market

Ellis Camel, (col'd) farmer, r. 6th nr. La Fayette R. R.

Ellis Ellen, wid. James, r. 32 Helen

Ellis James, (col'd) lab. r. Rhode Island nr. Blake

Ellis John, clk H. F. West & Co. bds. Palmer House

Ellis Mary, weaver Hoosier Woolen Factory, bds. 32 Helen

Ellis Mattie Miss, bds. 18 W. Georgia

Ellis Thomas, fireman, r. 35 Bradshaw

Ellis Thomas, moulder Sinker & Co.

Ellison Frederick, clk. Bellefontaine frt. office, r. 369 S. Alabama

Ellms Charles H. engineer C. C. C. & I. R. R. r. 219 Davidson

Elmer John W. shipping clk. Patterson, Moore & Talbot, r. 192 E. McCarty

Elmore Thomas, (col'd) lab. Osgood, Smith & Co. r. 67 Eddy

Elschlager Benjamin, machinist, r. 424 E. St. Clair

Elstrod George, varnisher, Cabinetmaker's Union

Elstrod Henry, trustee and foreman, Cabinetmaker's Union, r. 184 N. Winston

Eltzroth John, confectioner, C. A. Woelz, bds. 149 N. Delaware

Elvin Gardner W. night watchman, r. 500 S. East

Ely Joseph, constable, r. 130 E. St. Joseph

Ely R. H. furdealer, bds. Ray House

Embers Thomas, (col'd) Knox & Embers, r. Indiana av. cor. Blake

Emenegger John, brewer, r. Wyoming sw. cor. High

EMENEGGER MATHIAS, propr. Emenegger's Hotel, 111 and 113 E. Washington

EME   114   ENG

Emenegger's Hotel, Mathias Emenegger, prop. 111, 113 E. Washington

Emerick Henry, r. 224 W. Maryland

Emerson John B. bookkeeper Emerson, Beam & Thompson, bds. 239 W. Market

Emerson Roswell B. (Emerson, Beam & Thompson) r. 239 W. Market

EMERSON, BEAM & THOMPSON, (Roswell B. Emerson, David Beam, Eli Thompson) mfrs. of sash, doors and blinds, mouldings, frames, brackets, &c., and planers and lumber dealers, 225, 229 W. Market

Emile Max, painter, 143 S. New Jersey, r. same

Emis Elizabeth, r. ss. National rd. w. end bridge

Emmerich Henry, cabinetmaker, Helwig & Co.

Emmerich Henry (Emmerich & Co.) r. 118 W. Maryland

EMMERICH & CO. (Henry Emmerich, Fred Faut and John Osterman) flour and feed merchants, 86 W. Washington

Emmett Margaret, wid .Robert, r. 82 E. South

Emmons John, carpenter, bds. 149 Winston

Emmons John B. sawmaker, Sheffield Saw Works, r. 169 Eddy

Empire Fast Freight Line, J. A. Murray, agt. 96 Virginia av.

Emrich Nicholas, agt. Guardian Mutual Life Ins. Co. of New York, 4 Blackford's blk. r. 444 Indiana av.

Ender Anna M. wid. John, r. 327 S. Pennsylvania

Endicott Henry, (col'd) r. 182 Douglas alley

Endicott Isom, (col'd' r. rear 25 St. Clair

Endicott Mary, (col'd) r. 182 Douglas alley

Engelde John, lab. r. ns. Missouri, s. end

Engelhardt W. boot and shoemkr. 286 E. Washington, r. same

Enggass Henry, tailor, 113 S. Illinois, r. same

ENGINE HOUSE NO. 1, ss. Washington bet. West and California

Engine House No. 2, junction Massachusetts av. New York and Delaware

England George, carpenter, r. 226 W. New York

Engelbach Herman, notions, bds. 135 E. Washington

Engle George B. rector Church Holy Innocents (Episcopal) r. 80 S. Tennessee

Engle George B. Jr. frt. agt. T. H. & I. R. R. r. 89 S. Tennessee

Engle John, tinsmith, bds. 458 E. Georgia

Engle Tracy, wid. John, r. 97 Bates

Engle Willis D. clk. frt. office T. H. R. R. r. 80 S. Tennessee

Engleking Frederick, teamster Butsch & Dickson, r. 143 Bluff rd.

Engleking William, teamster Butsch & Dickson, r. 208 Union

Engleman Mary, wks. Cotton Factory

English Alonzo printer *Journal* job room

English Benjamin, cattle drover, r. 38 Center

English Benjamin, lab. Long & Joseph

English David W. compositor *Commercial*, r. 267 N. West

English Elijah G. vice pres. C. S. R, R. r. 48 Circle

English Nettie Miss, clerk Frank J. Medina, r. 34 W. Wash'ton

English William, painter, bds. 21 E. North

English William E. r. 38 Circle
ENGLISH WILLIAM H. President First National Bank of Indianapolis, r. 48 Circle
Ennars Henry, bricklayer, r. 287 Massachusetts av.
Ennars W. wid. Philip, r. 287 Massachusetts av.
Ennars William, saloon 387 N. Noble, r. 369 N. Noble
Ennes Louis, butcher, r. 367 N. Noble
Ennes Louis, painter S. W. Drew
Enos Benjamin H. architect, 397 N. Alabama
Enos Benjamin V. (Enos & Huebner) r. 397 N. Alabama
Enos Robert C. carpenter, r. 397 N. Alabama
Enos Trovillo H. K. bookkeeper Browning & Sloan, r. 236 S. Alabama
ENOS & HUEBNER, (Benjamin V. Enos and Henry R. Huebner) architects and superintendents 1-2 Eden's block 77½ E. Market
Ensey John, engineer C. C. C. & I. R. R. r. 144 N. Winston
Ensey Samuel, fireman C. C. C. & I. R. R. r. 144 N. Winston
Enterprise Fire Insurance Co. of Cincinnati Ohio, R. H. Ewing state agent, Market ne. cor. Circle, *Journal* building
Enterprise Fire Ins. Co. of Cincinnati Ohio, Martin, Hopkins & Ohr, agents, Market ne. cor. Circle
Entwistle George, wks. Cotton Factory
Enwald Henry, tender J. Whitcomb, r. Illinois cor. Georgia
Epperd Francis M. teamster, r. 295 N. Alabama
Equitable Life Insurance Co. of New York, J. S. Dunlop & Co. general agents for Indiana 2 W. Washington
Erb Solomon, cooper, r. north end Grant
Erdelmeyer Frank, druggist 91 E. Washington, r. same
Erevin Thomas, lab. Rolling Mill, r. 337 S. Missouri
Erhardt J. confectioner Bernhard Martin
Ernst Frederick, r. 137 Union
Ernst Louis, driver A. F. & J. H. Jenison, r. 137 Union
Erran ——, salesman, r. 54 W. New York
Erringer John R. (Byington & Erringer) r. 259 N. Illinois
Erwin ——, printer, bds. 30½ N. Pennsylvania
Erwin Thomas, sawyer Rolling Mill
Ervin Edward P. agent, r. 405 S. East
Eschmeier Henry Rev. r. 41 N. Alabama
Esemann Joseph, dairyman, r. 330 Madison av.
Esmus Christian, r. 15 Lord
Esmus Fred. lab. r. 15 Lord
Essigke August, meat market, 295 E. Washington, r. same
Essigke Richard, meat market, 170 S. Illinois, r. same
Essman Louis, student National Business College
Essmann William, proprietor Illinois House, 183 S. Illinois, r. same
Etherton Samuel, carpenter, r. 23 Center
Etsler ——, lab. r. Mayhew near Michigan rd.
Ettinger Gustave, flagman Terre Haute Depot, r. Draper near Kentucky av.

Eubanks Roland R. painter Brenneman & Renner, r. N. Pennsylvania, city limits

Euller Margarette, wid. Philip, r. 232 Railroad

Eurich John, saloon, 17 N. Illinois, r. Madison rd.

Euwie Johnson H. real estate agent 161 W. Washington

EVANGELICAL CHURCH, (German) es. New Jersey bet. Ohio and Market, J. Kauffman pastor

Evans Adolphus G. salesman Fortner, Floyd & Co. bds. Sherman House

Evans Frank A. entry clk. Hibben, Tarkington & Co. bds. Sherman House

Evans George, fireman, r. 25 Lord

Evans George A. bookkeeper Fortner, Floyd & Co. r. 259 Virginia av.

Evans George T. (I. P. Evans & Co.) r. 548 N. Meridian

Evans H. W. carpenter, r. 25 Lord

Evans Isaac P. (I. P. Evans & Co.) r. Richmond, Ind

EVANS JOHN D. state auditor, office, State Building, and (Fortner, Floyd & Co.) bds. 30 W. Maryland

Evans John J. shoemaker, r. 232 W. Michigan

Evans Joseph R. (I. P. Evans & Co.) r. 360 N. Alabama

Evans London, (col'd) lab. r. 385 N. New Jersey

Evans Louis, lab. Hill & Wingate

Evans Robert, bricklayer, r. 476 N. Meridian

Evans Thomas, brickmason, r. 496 N. Mississippi

Evans Thomas, (Rev.) r. 166 N. Liberty

Evans William, bricklayer, r. 674 N. Mississippi

Evans William R. (I. P. Evans & Co.) r. 23 Ft. Wayne av.

Evans Zebedee, (col'd) engineer J. Carlisle

EVANS I. P. & CO. (Isaac P. George T. William R. and Joseph R. Evans) mnfrs. of linseed oil, 124 S. Delaware

Evanston Henry, lab. r. 10th sw. cor. Pittsfield

Everest Samuel, patternmaker Sinker & Co.

Everling Amos, hauler, r. 38 Center

Everson Erastus, clk. Levi Wright, bds. 158 E. Michigan

Everson Margaret, wid. boardinghouse 98 E. New York

Everett David T. blacksmith Indiana Agricultural Works, bds. 64 W. Maryland

EVERTS EVERT, saloon 137 Ft. Wayne av. r. 139 Ft. Wayne av.

Eves Samuel, engineer John T. Pressly

EWALD HENRY, blksmith and wagonmkr, 299 Massachusetts av. r. 10 Arch (See advt page)

Ewald Robert, music teacher, r. 271 N. Liberty

Ewing Johnson H. dist. agt. Travelers' Ins. Co. 2 W. Washington, r. 164 W. Maryland

EWING D. B. physician, 33 Virginia av. bds. Palmer House

Ewing Jacob D. clk. r. 78 Indiana av.

Ewing John S. traveling agent, r. 48 W. Market

Ewing R. H. gen. state agt. Enterprise Ins. Co. of Cincinnati, O. Market ne. cor. Circle, *Journal* bldg. r. 67 W. Michigan

Ewing William, carpenter, 2 Indiana av. r. 78 Indiana av.

EWI	117	FAR

Ewing William M. trunkmkr, R. L. Smith & Co. r. 78 Indiana av.
Exchange Stables. William Hinesley propr. 35 N. Illinois
Eyman John H. shoemaker, r. ss. Cumberland bet. the Canal and West

F

Fagin J. works Kingan & Co.
Fahls Henry, engineer Eagle Foundry, r. 127 E. Merrill
Fahnley Frederick, (Fahnley & McCrea) r. 86 S. Illinois
FAHNLEY & McCREA, (F. Fahnley and R. H. McCrea) whol. millinery and fancy goods, 131 S. Meridian
Fahrion Christian, (Western Furniture Co.) r. 363 N. Noble
Fahrion J. George, flour and feed, 90 and 92 E. South, r. same
FARBACH PHILIP, propr. Washington Hall Saloon, 78 and 80 W. Washington, r. same
Fahralent Joseph, cabinetmaker Spiegel & Thoms
Failey John W. foreman Osgood, Smith & Co. bds. National Hotel
Fairbanks George P plasterer. r. s. end New Jersey
Fairbanks John J. (Fairbanks & Co.) r. Illinois n. First
Fairbanks Philip E. (Fairbanks & Co.) r. 598 N. Illinois
FAIRBANKS & CO. (Philip E. and John J. Fairbanks) notions and fancy goods, 22 W. Washington
Fairchild Thomas, carpenter, bds. 9th cor. Lenox
Faling Fred, machinist, Spiegel & Thoms
Falkening C. H. salesman McCord & Wheatley
Fallen James J. news agent, r. in rear of 175 E. Market
Fallon James J. with Cowen & Protzman, 16½ E. Washington, r. 22 Potomac
Faning Thomas, lab. r. 112 Meek
Fanning Thomas, lab. r. Maryland nr. Benton
Faris H. V. engineer, r. 226 E. Merrill
Faries T. C. (Burgess & Faries) bds. Jackson nr. cor. Butler
Farley Michael, lab. Rolling Mill, r. 301 Kentucky av.
Farley Richard, lab. r. 189 W. 2nd
Farman F. L. prop. stoneyards, Kentucky av. cor. Louisiana, r. 149 W. South
Farman John H. stonecutter F. L. Farman, r. 49 S. Mississippi
Farmer Albert A. fireman, r. 289 Winston
Farmer J. B. wks. Bellefontaine shops, r. 289 Winston
Farmer Richard (col'd) bricklayer, r. rear 243 W. Ohio
Farnesworth Charles O. r. 170 Walnut
Farnesworth George, bds. 248 E. Louisiana
Farnsworth T. W. physician and surgeon, 21½ W. Maryland, r. 317 E. Ohio
Farnsworth Thomas, Western route agent Mirror office, r. 431 N. Tennessee
Farr Henry L. moulder Greenleaf & Co. bds. 310 S. Illinois
Farr Robert, teamster, r. 55 Jones

Farrall Patrick, r. 246 Indiana av.
Farrar John, mnfr. and dealer in boots and shoes, 191 W. Washington, r. same
Farrell E. patternmaker Sinker & Co.
Farrell Fergus, porter Hibben, Tarkington & Co. r. 77 W. St. Clair
Farrell Henry, carpenter, r. Michigan road above 8th
Farrell Mary, wid. John, r. 169 Davidson
Farrell Michael, lab. C. C. C. & I. R. R.
Farries Milton H. carpenter, r. N. Pennsylvania n. of limits
Fast Erastus E. bookkeeper J. H. Varjen, & Co. bds. Macy House
Fatout H. B. student rooms, 109 Massachusetts av.
Fatout J. L. (J. L. & M. K. Fatout) r. 238 N. West
Fatout Moses K. (J. L. & M. K. Fatout) r. 238 N. West
Fatout Percy, carpenter, r. 336 N. West
FATOUT J. L. & M. K. carpenters and builders, La Fayette nr. La Fayette freight depot
Fatout's Block, W. Washington cor. canal
Faulkner Eugene H. machinist Howe & Converse
Faulkner George, machinist, r. 297 W. Vermont
Faulkner George S. woodworker Howe & Converse, r. California cor. Vermont
Faulkner Joseph, supt. Loom Works, r. ns. W. Washington nr. the river
Faust E bookkeeper, bds. Macy House
Faut Frederick, (Emmerich & Co.) r. 222 N. East
Fawsett Alpheus H. machinist Phoenix Machine Works, bds. 215 W. Ohio
Fawkner John, groceries ret. 338 W. Washington, r. same
FAWKNER JOHN E. coal and lime dealer, 24 W. Maryland, r. 338 W. Washington
Fay Amos F. merchant, r. 255 N. East
Fay Henry, clerk, r. 255 N. East
Fay John J. traveling agt. r. 107 Massachusetts av.
Feary Henry J. compositor *Sentinel* news room, r. 129 Stevens
Feary Jeremiah E. carpenter, rear 318 E. North, r. 318 E. North
Fearey John, bricklayer, r. 477 N. East
FEARNLEY JOHN, carpenter, builder and store furniture, and manufacturer of Mills Corn Sheller, 23 Circle, r. 25 Circle
Featherlin William, lab. r. 199 N. East
Featherson William E. auction and commission merchant, 194 and 196 W. Washington, r. 165 Massachusetts av.
Feely Daniel, turner, bds. 400 N. Mississippi
Feely Daniel, stave cutter McKendry & Lovecraft
Feemeyer Andrew, moulder D. Root & Co.
Fehi Kate, waiter Institute for the Blind, r. same
Fehr Christian, carpenter, r. Tennessee cor. 7th
Fehr Henry, tailor Hetz & Co. bds. 21 S. Illinois
Fehre Ernst, cabinet maker, bds. Michigan rd. nr. Junction of Washington
Fehre Fred. lab. bds. Michigan rd. nr. Junction of Washington

FEH	119	FER

Fehrensback John, machinist, C. C. & I. C. R. R.
Fehring Ernst, cabinetmaker Cabinetmakers' Union
Fehring Frederick, lab. wks. Cabinetmakers' Union
Feibelman A. L. merchant, r. 180 Virginia av.
Feil Augustus, clk. A. M. U. Ex. Co. r. 43 Madison av.
Feil Gebhardt, teamster Schmidt's Brewery, r. same
Feil John, wagonmaker 123 Bluff rd. r. 396 S. Illinois
Feiner Julius, salesman J. George Stitz, r. 223 N. Noble
Felbaum William, engineer, r. Mississippi sw. cor. North
Feld G. painter, 249 W. Maryland, r. same
Feldbusch Conrad, lab. r. 426 E. Vermont
Feldbusch John, lab. r. 168 Davidson
Feller Charles, jeweler George Feller, bds. 114 S. Illinois
Feller George, watchmkr and jeweler 55 S. Illinois
Fells Frederick, teamster J. Marsee & Son, r. 185 Harrison
Feltman Hermann, shoemaker L. Siersdorfer, r. 396 S. Delaware
Felz Charles, (col'd) lab. r. 227 E. Washington
Fennelle Amanda, teacher, bds. 60 N. California
Fenneman W. H. teacher German Evangelical School, r. country
Fennerty Jennie Miss, dressmaker Kay & Mattern, r. Illinois
    cor. Maryland
Fenrich Jacob, tinner I. L. Franken & Co. bds. La Fayette
    House
Fenton Franklin, saw maker Sheffield Saw Works, r. 131 E. St.
    Joseph
Fenton John, machinist Sinker & Co. r. 124 S. Meridian
Fenton John H. machinist Sinker & Co. bds. 124 S. Meridian
Ferdz Conrad, butcher, r. 8th cor. Lenox
Ferger Charles, baker and confectioner 96 E. South, r. same
Ferguson A. V. wid. Glenn, r. 31 W. Ohio
Ferguson C. A. watchmaker and jeweler 7 W. Washington, r.
    Meridian cor. 7th
Ferguson David, carpenter, bds. 78 W. North
Ferguson Edward H. bricklayer, r. 463 N. Meridian
Ferguson G. W. machinist, r. 175 E. Washington
Ferguson George, carpenter, bds. Nagel House
Ferguson James, bookbinder *Sentinel* Bindery, r. 78 W. North
Ferguson James C. (J. C. Ferguson & Co.) r. 139 N. Meridian
Ferguson Jeremiah F. bds. 463 N. Meridian
Ferguson John A. (W. J. Holliday & Co.) r. 270 N. Tennessee
Ferguson Kilby, r. 251 E. McCarty
Ferguson Revin, clk. Trade Palace, r. 155 N. Illinois
Ferguson Robert, plasterer and cistern builder, r. 27 W. Pratt
FERGUSON J. C. & CO. (J. C. Ferguson, E. B. Howard, A. M.
    Neeld) pork packers and commission merchants west end
    Georgia
Feriter James, lab. r. alley bet. Noble and Benton and Georgia
    and Meek
Ferley Michael, bds. Jefferson House
Ferling George, barber under 1st Nat. Bank, r. 124 E. Maryland
Ferran Frank, machinist Phœnix Machine Works

FER	120	FIN

Ferree Francis M. physician, 31 N. Delaware, r. 369 N. New Jersey

Ferree Jarred D. (Ferree & Cantrill) r. 83 N. Pennsylvania

Ferree & Cantrill, (J. D. Ferree and D. M. Cantrill) cigars and tobacco, ret. 11 N. Illinois

Ferrell E. J. r. 27 Massachusetts av.

Ferrell Francis J. tailor Wm. F. Rupp, bds. 131 E. Washington

Ferriter Margaret, wid. John, r. 331 E. Louisiana

Ferriter Morris, school teacher, r. 142 Bluff rd.

Ferry Jane, wid. Hugh, r. 26 Gregg

Fertig Francis, painter F. Fertig, bds. California House

FERTIG FRANK, house, sign and ornamental painter, 6 E. Washington, r. 65 W. South. See card business directory

Fertig Louis, painter F. Fertig, bds. same

Ferver August, grocer, r. 416 S. West

Fesler James M. carpenter H. H. Wheatly, r. 216 S. East

Fesler William B. carpenter, r. 212 Bluff rd.

Fetherston William, auctioneer, r. 165 Massachusetts av

Fette Charles, machinist Sinker & Co. r. 250 S. Alabama

Fette George, cleaning and repairing, 38 Virginia av. r. 123 Duncan

Fetty A. H. saddler, r. 442 Virginia av.

Fetty Conrad, tailor, room 16 Miller's blk. r. same

Fetty Henry, harnessmkr. Frauer, Bieler & Co. r. Noble cor. Fletcher av.

Fey Conrad, lab. r. Illinois ne. cor. Ray

Foy Henry, teamster City Brewery, r. 315 Virginia av.

Fibleman C. B. liquor dealer, r. 18 S. Mississippi

Fibelman C. R. L. bookkeeper, r. 7 Lockerbie

Fichtner Mary Miss, r. 273 S. West

Fichtner Rachel, wid. Godlib, r. 273 S. West

Fidel Simeon, saloon 211 W. Washington, r. same

Fieber William, bookkpr. Schmidt's Brewery, r. 359 S. Alabama

Field Edward S. (Chandler & Field and Field, Locke & Co.) r. 613 N. Illinois

FIELD, LOCKE & CO. (Edward S. Field, E. Locke, B. Scanlin) proprs. Caledonia Paper Mill west end Market, business office 265 W. Washington

Fifer Maria, clerk, r. 19 Douglass

Fifth Ward School, 181 W. Maryland, Miss E. T. Ford principal

Fig John, brickmaker, r. 30 Helen

Fike Peter, r. 318 Madison av.

Filbeck Lena, wid. John, r. 11 Buchanan

Filer S. salesman, bds. 78 W. North

Filer Samuel J. salesman Bowen, Stewart & Co. 18 W. Wash'ton

Finch Charles, clerk, r. 323 W. Washington

Finch Elmira, wid. tailoress, bds. 144 N. Tennessee

Finch Flora Miss, teacher 9th Ward School, bds. 286 E. Ohio

Finch Fabius M. (Finch & Finch) and (Harding, Morton & Finch) r. 286 E. Ohio

Finch John A. (Finch & Finch) r. 286 E. Ohio

FINCH & FINCH, (F. M. & John A. Finch) lawyers, room 6, Talbott & New's block

Finke Mary, wid. John, r. 51 E. McCarty

Finley B. (col'd) plasterer, r. 263 N. West

Finn John, cooper, r. 126 Union

Finn John, lab. r. 33 Doughety

Finn John, yardman Bates House

Finnegan D. porter Express Co.

Finneran James, lab. r. 399 S. West

Finney E. H. cooper Parrott, Nickum & Co.

Finney Jasper, salesman Murphy, Johnston & Co. r. 430 Virginia av.

Finney William, lab. Bunte, Dickson & Co.

Finter Frederick, baker, r. 115 Ft. Wayne av.

FIRST BAPTIST CHURCH Pennsylvania, ne. cor. New York

FIRST ENGLISH LUTHERAN CHURCH, Alabama, sw. cor. New York

First National Bank of Indianapolis, John C. New, cashr. Washington, se. cor. Meridian

First National livery and board stables, ns. Court nr. cor. Pennsylvania

FIRST PRESBYTERIAN CHURCH, Pennsylvania, sw. cor New York

FIRST REFORM CHURCH, N. Alabama nr. cor. Market, Rev. Henry Eschmeier, pastor

First Ward School, Miss Henrie Colgan, principal, Vermont sw. cor. New Jersey

Fischer Benjamin, barber, r. 189 S. Illinois

Fischer Charles, cooper, r. 123 N. Spring

Fischer Franklin, stone mason, r. 243 Bluff rd.

Fischer Sarah, wid. Adam, r. 114 Bluff rd.

Fiscus Andrew, brick mason, r. East se cor. Walnut

Fiscus John R. brick mason, r. 372 F. New Jersey

Fiscus Thomas, bricklayer, r. 280 E. St. Clair

Fiscus William, bricklayer, r. 1 Vine

Fish Byron E. printer H. C. Chandler & Co. r. 178 N. Mississippi

Fish John L. bookkeeper Mayhew & Brenham, r. 78 E. Hratt

Fish Oliva M. ice cream saloon, 80 S. Illinois, r same

Fish William S. printer Indianapolis Printing and Publishing House, r. 267 N. East

Fishback Charles, r. 353 N. Illinois

FISHBACK JOHN, leather, hides, oils, belting and mnfr. of oak leather belting, 125 S. Meridian, r. Walnut cor. Illinois

Fishback William P. (Porter, Harrison & Fishback) r. ns. E. Washington, 4 e. city limits

Fisher Andrew, salesman, r. 406 N. East

Fisher Benedict, prop. Union dpt. barber shop, r. 189 S. Illinois

Fisher Charles, photographer J. F. Crane, bds. 30 N. East

FISHER CHARLES, Justice of the Peace, room 3 Yohn's block, Meridian, ne. cor. Washington, r. 26 W. North

Fisher Elwood, cashboy, L. H. Tyler & Co. bds. 172 N. Meridian

FIS	122	FLA

Fisher George, shoemaker, 119 Fort Wayne av. r. same

Fisher H. machinist, Sinker & Co.

Fisher John, barber, 374 Virginia av.

Fisher John, barkeeper, Pearson & Co. r. 78 W. Washington

Fisher Louis, tender, W. A. Smith, bds. 40 W. Louisiana

Fisher Mark, lab. r. ss. 2d bet. Illinois and Meridian

Fisher Phillip, lab. Edward C. Brundage, bds. Little's Hotel

Fisher Samuel A. tailor, 26 Virginia av. r. 30 N. East

Fisher W. wks. Kingan & Co. pork packers

FISK E. I. MRS. hoopskirt mnfr. and dealer in fancy goods and notions, 62 N. Illinois, r. same

Fitch Asa M. hostler Citizens' Street R. R. Co. bds. Globe House

Fitch Daniel H. bartender A. M. Mortland, bds. 23 N. Illinois

Fitch Grant, bartender, A. M. Mortland, bds. 23 N. Illinois

Fitchey Michael G. carpenter, r. 378 S. Illinois

Fitz John, lab. Rolling Mill, bds. 426 S. Tennessee

Fitzgerald Edmond, lab. r. 156 Meek

Fitzgerald Edward, boilermaker C. C. & I. C. R. R.

Fitzgerald Fanny, wid. Michael, r. 247 S. Missouri

Fitzgerald James, carpenter, r. 71 La Fayette

Fitzgerald Joseph, cabinetmaker, r. 158 Blackford

Fitzgerald Joseph, stonemason, bds. 158 Blackford

Fitzgerald Joseph H. engineer, r. 316 E. Georgia

Fitzgerald John, tinsmith Munson & Johnston, r. 399 S. Delaware

Fitzgerald Nathan, lawyer and notary public, 5 Vinton's Blk.

Fitzgerald Patrick, lab. r. 298 S. Delaware

Fitzgerald William, watchman Rolling Mill, r. 224 N. Merrill

Fitzgerald William, wks. Rolling Mill, r. 188 Maple

Fitzgibbon John, wks. Rolling Mill

Fitzgibbon M. bds. Bates House

Fitzhugh Lee M. clk. Murphy, Johnston & Co. r. 139 N. Alabama

Fitzpatrick James, tailor, bds. 66 S. West

Fitzpatrick Joseph, carpenter, r. 240 W. New York

Fitzpatrick Peter, tailor, r. 66 S. West

Flaber John, r 295 Coburn

Flack Samuel, carpenter, r. 40 Thomas

Flager Jacob, carpenter Boedeker & Neimann

Flaherty George, cabinetmkr. Indianapolis Piano Mnfg. Co. bds. 63 Delaware

Flaherty James, wks. *Journal* office, r. 329 W. Maryland

Flaherty Joseph, lab. bds. 283 E. Georgia

Flaherty John, lab. r. 690 N. Illinois

Flaherty Sarah, wid. Michael, r. 329 Maryland

Flaherty Thomas, clerk, bds. Ray House

Flaig Andrew, cabinetmkr. Helwig & Co.

Flaig David, cabinetmkr. Helwig & Co.

Flaig Mathew V. carpenter Warren Tate, r. 136 N. New Jersey

Flanders H. teamster McKendry & Lovecraft

Flanner Frank, clk. A. Rosengarten

Flanner Orpha A. wid. Henry V. r. ss. Vine bet. Broadway and Jackson

Flanner Tyler, salesman S. Kahn & Bro. r. 47 E. Washington

Flathers James B. carpenter, r. 151 Maple

Flatley Patrick B. porter Patterson, Moore & Talbot, r. 39 Bright

Fleet John, (col'd) whitewasher, r. 276 E. North

Flegger Ryman, gunsmith, r. 483 E. Georgia

Flegherty Joseph, blacksmith C. C. & I. R. R.

Fleitz Charles, blacksmith, 187 Bluff rd. r. same

Fleming David, expressman, r. 92 Bradshaw

FLEMING GEORGE H. city gas inspector, office 60 N. Illinois, r. 230 E. Vermont

Fleming John, (Boswell & Fleming) bds. 177 Massachusetts av.

Fleming John, printer, bds. 191 W. Maryland

Fleming John P. r. 485 E. Georgia

Fleming John T. printer, r. es. Winston nr. cor. Biddle

Fleming T. R. W. telegraph operator, bds. 84 Massachusetts av.

Flenner M. B. conductor Junction R. R. bds. Bates House

Fleshman Lawrence, wks. Phœnix Machine Works, r. 271 N. Noble

Fleshman Theodore, machinist Phœnix Machine Works

Fletcher Albert E. teller Indianapolis Branch Banking Co. (F. and S.) r. 239 N. Pennsylvania

Fletcher Bishop, mechanic Rolling Mill

Fletcher Calvin, asst. treas. I. & O. R. R. r. College av. se. cor. Forrest Home av.

Fletcher Charles, (col'd) carriage painter, 178 Indiana av. r. Michigan bet. West and Canal

Fletcher David, r. 121 N. Noble

Fletcher Elijah T. r. 410 N. Delaware

Fletcher Elizabeth, wid. John, r. 308 Madison av.

Fletcher Henry, F. exp. clk. r. 189 E. Market

Fletcher Ingram, asst. cashier Indianapolis Branch Banking Co. (F. & S.) r. 46 N. Pennsylvania

Fletcher J. J. clk. frt. office C. C. & I. C. R. R. bds. Pyle House

Fletcher John B. teamster, r. 326 Virginia av.

Fletcher L. W. (Wheat, Fletcher & Co.) r. Franklin, Ind.

Fletcher Lucinda, wid. Richard, r. 72 N. Liberty

Fletcher Mary Mrs. dressmaker, 509 E. New York, r. same

Fletcher Richard F. supt. Citizens' Street R. R. Co. r. 477 N. Tennessee

Fletcher S. A. Jr. pres. Indianapolis Gaslight & Coke Co. r. Virginia av. and South

Fletcher Stephen K. farmer, r. 24 Ft. Wayne av.

Fletcher Stoughton A. (S. A. Fletcher & Co.) r. 180 E. Ohio

Fletcher Stoughton J. clerk S. A. Fletcher & Co. bds. 180 E. Ohio

FLETCHER S. A. & CO. (Stoughton A. Fletcher, Francis M. Churchman) Fletcher's Bank, 30 E. Washington

Fletcher T. A. livery stable ns. Court, bet. Pennsylvania & Delaware, r. 329 Alabama

FLE	124	FOL

C. J. BRACKEBUSH, Farm Machinery, Hardware and Seeds, Nos. 75 and 77 W. Washington St. Indianapolis.

Fletcher W. B. (Fletcher & Wright,) r. 105 N. Alabama
Fletcher Walker, wks. Rolling Mill
Fletcher William H. r. 326 Virginia av.
Fletcher Z. r. 189 E. Market
Fletcher's Bank, S. A. Fletcher & Co. proprietors, 30 E. Washington
FLETCHER & WRIGHT, (W. B. Fletcher and C. E. Wright) physicians and surgeons, 107 N. Alabama
Fleury Louis, tailor, bds. 18 S. Delaware
Flocken Jacob, barber F. Elff
Florence Sewing Machine, J. W. Smith agt. 27 N. Pennsylvania
Flowers Jennie, twister Hoosier Woolen Factory
Flowers Naomi, wid. S. W. II. r. 248 W. Market
Flowers Sam. V. P. blksmith King & Pinney, r. 98 Kentucky av.
Floyd Mahlon H. (Fortner, Floyd & Co.) r. Noblesville, Ind.
Floyd William T. (col'd) engineer, r. 553 N. Mississippi
Flynn Byron P. clk. Munson & Johnston, r. 37 Dougherty
Flynn Byron, teamster, r. 21 Dougherty
Flynn David, lab. Gas Works, r. 227 Union
Flynn Dennis, bricklayer and plasterer, r. 69 Maple
Flynn Thomas, metersetter Gas Works, r. 336 S. Delaware
Flynn William, lab. bds. 267 E. Washington
Fogerty John, r. rear 498 E. Georgia
Foland Frederick, bds. 124 N. Alabama
Foland Vollentine, carpenter, r. 299 E. Merrill
Foley Henry, machinist Eagle Machine Works, r. 71 E. Merrill
Foley James, bartender, r. 223 W. Washington
Foley James W. (J. W. Foley & Co.) bds. Pyle House
Foley Jerry, lab. bds. 267 E. Washington
Foley Michael, moulder Union Novelty Wks. r. 132 N. Winston
Foley Murty, lab. r. 284 S. Delaware
Foley Patrick, r. 296 Louisiana
Foley Patrick, lab. freight depot C. & L. R. R.
Foley Patrick, lab. Union Novelty Wks. r. 132 N. Winston
Foley Patrick, lab. r. 128 N. Winston
Foley Patrick, lab. r. 91 Fayette
Foley Thomas, moulder Union Novelty Wks. r. 132 Winston
Foley Timothy, blksmith C. C. C. & I. C. R. R.
Foley W. W. physician and surgeon, office 53 Indiana av. bds. Pyle House
Foley J. W. & Co. (James W. Foley and —— Long) packers of produce and provisions, 188 W. Washington
Foljambe George B. express mes. r. 238 Vermont
Folkening Charles, lab. r. 21 Coburn
Folking Henry, wks. A. H. Connor, bds. 515 N. Pennsylvania
Follett J. B. special agt. Imperial Fire Ins. Co. of Liverpool, office *Journal* bldg. r. College av. nr. Christian av.
Follett John C. bookkeeper Martin, Hopkins & Ohr, r. 224 N. East
FOLSOM E. S. gen. agt. Phœnix Mutual Life Ins. Co. room 14 Talbott & New's blk. bds. Palmer House

FOL	125	FOS

Foltz Howard M. (Olin & Foltz) r. 279 N. Alabama
Foos Peter, engineer, r. 82 James
Foote Charles, machinist, bds. Stanridge House
Foote Maria W. wid. Jeremiah, r. 16 E. Michigan
Forander Neil, lab. Rolling Mill
FORBES JOSEPH A. watchmaker and jeweler 34 Virginia av. r. 233 S. East
Forby Charles II. trunkmfr. and dealer 109 S. Illinois, r. 34 S. Illinois
Forby Sarah L. Mrs. dressmaker 34 S. Illinois, r. same
Ford Eliza T. principal 5th Ward School, r. 188 W. Ohio
Ford Frank, bds. Pattison House
Ford Fletcher W. carpenter, r. 305 E. Washington
Ford Henry, salesman, r. 225 N. Mississippi
Ford Irvin S. carpenter, r. 228 Winston
Ford John, r. 188 W. Ohio
Ford L. E. carpenter, r. 149 N. Noble
Ford Laura, teacher 5th Ward School, r. 188 W Ohio
Ford Michael, shoemaker, r. 326 N. West
Ford Peter, teacher, bds. 48 Indiana av.
Ford Phœbe Mrs. boarding house 78 S. Illinois
Ford William, compositor *Sentinel* news room, bds. W. Ohio near the Canal
Forgus W. clerk, bds. Pyle House
Forsha Thomas, cigarmaker 66 Massachusetts av. r. 191 N. Alabama
Forsyth E. J. agt. r. 414 S. East
Fortenbury James M. telegraph operator T. H. & I. R. R. r. 41 Russel av.
Fortner Alfred J. (Fortner, Floyd & Co.) bds. 30 W. Maryland
FORTNER FLOYD & CO. (A. J. Fortner, M. H. Floyd, J. D. Evans and D. R. Brown) whol. notions and white goods, etc. 75 S. Meridian
Forwald John, lab. I. C. & L. R. W. r. 314 N. Noble
Foster Andrew J. r. 51 Dacotah
Foster Arnica S. foreman boilershop Eagle Machine Works, r. 33 Fletcher av.
Foster Benjamin, clergyman, r. 408 N. Illinois
Foster Edgar J. (Hume, Adams & Co.) r. 339 N. Pennsylvania
Foster Emma, wid. Daniel, dressmkr. 323 E. Washington, r. do.
Foster George A. carpenter, r. 367 S. Missouri
Foster Isaac, carpenter, r. 76 S. Tennessee
Foster James, lab. r. Rockwood nr. River
Foster John, brakeman, bds. 58 Benton
Foster John E. carpets, &c. bds. 339 N. Pennsylvania
Foster Riley, r. 339 N. Pennsylvania
Foster Robert, baker W. K. McFarlane, bds. 12 S. Meridian
Foster Robert S. (Foster & Wiggins) and City Treasurer, r. 452 N. Delaware
Foster Wallace, (Smith & Foster) r. 24 E. Pratt
Foster William N. sawfiler, 71 Jackson, r. same

FOSTER & WIGGINS, (Robert S. Foster and Joseph P. Wiggins) wholesale grocers, 68 and 70 S. Delaware

Foudray John, harnessmaker Frauer, Bieler & Co. bds. Pennsylvania bet. Washington and Market

Foudray John E. (Wood & Foudray) r. 215 N. New Jersey

FOURTH PRESBYTERIAN CHURCH, Market sw. cor. Delaware

Fourth Ward School, William J. Button, principal, Michigan ne. cor. Blackford

Fourth Ward District School (col'd) ss. Market bet. West and California

Foust C. J. porter Foster & Wiggins, bds Pratt cor. Delaware

Fout Frederick, flour and feed, r. 222 N. East

Fout Henry, teamster, r. 349 Winston

Fowler James, carpenter, r. 258 N. East

Fowler William H. r. 325 N. Liberty

Fox ——— Mrs. boardinghouse, r. 191 W. Maryland

Fox Arthur B. bookkpr. John G. Hanning, r. 174 W. Michigan

Fox James, engineer Rolling Mill, r. 140 E. McCarty

Fox Jennie Miss, sewer W & J. Braden, r. 261 E. Washington

Fox John, bartender Charles Lauer, r. 70 Hossbrook

Fox Judson, lab. Warren Tate, bds. 32½ N. Pennsylvania

Fox Martin, clk. Spencer House saloon, bds. 280 E. Market

Foxcraft Francis (Woodson & Foxcraft) r. Second bet. Illinois and Meridian

Foy Owen, machinist Sinker & Co. r. 88 Benton

Fraley ———, teamster, r. 167 High

Fraley Michael, R. R. flagman, bds 191 W. Maryland

Fraley Joseph, frt. conductor, T. H. & I. R. R. r. 178 Madison av.

Francis Alonzo E. (Francis & Bro.) r. 65 S. Illinois

Francis George, clk. James Francis, r. 99 Massachusetts av.

Francis George, r. 249 N. Davidson

Francis George, lab. r. 528 N. Mississippi

Francis H. N. (Francis & Bro) r. 65 S. Illinois

Francis Hilman (col'd) lab. r. 249 Howard

Francis Jacob, porter Maxwell, Fry & Thurston

Francis James, grocer, 99 Massachusetts av. r same

Francis James B. tinner, r. 271 Indiana av.

Francis William (Francis & Bro.) r. 65 S. Illinois

Francis & Bro. (William H. N. and Alonzo E. Francis) oyster and fruit depot, 67 S. Illinois

Franck Henry, bartender Emenegger's Hotel, bds. 111 E. Washington

Franco Daniel lastmkr. r. es. Illinois co.r Russell av.

Franco Sarah Mrs. (Dunn & Franco) r. 77 S. Mississippi

Frank Adam, carpenter, bds 267 E. Washington

Frack Anthony, porter Union depot, r. 176 Union

Frank D. varnisher Spiegel & Thoms

Frank George H. engineer, bds. 149 S. New Jersey

Frank H. pres. Spiegel & Thoms' Furniture Co. r. Quincy, Ill.

Frank James, real estate and com. agt. 35½ E. Washington, r. 461 N. Tennessee

Frankem Isaac L. (I. L. Frankem & Co.) r. 235 N. Illinois
Frankem Jonathan, r. 249 N. Illinois
Frankem I. L. & Co. (Isaac L. Frankem and Joseph Kline) stoves, tinware, mantles, grates, house furnishing goods, 34 E. Washington
Frankenstein George, barber Henry Weiss, r. 401 E. Washington
Frankenstein Jacob, barber, 326 S. Delaware, r. same
Frankenstein Kate, wid. George, r. 118 Bluff rd.
Franklin Benjamin, pastor Christ Episcopal Church, r. 65 Circle
Franklin Benjamin, student, bds. 268 E. St. Clair
Franklin Benjamin, (col'd) lab. r. 85 Eddy
Franklin J. E. law student, bds. N. Pennsylvania opp. P. O.
FRANKLIN LIFE INSURANCE CO. of Indianapolis, James M. Ray pres. Wm. S. Hubbard, vice pres. and treas. E. P. Howe, sec. B. F. Witt, gen'l agt. office S. Illinois cor. Kentucky av.
Franklin William, (col'd) whitewasher, r. 161 Indiana av
Franklin William T. carpenter, r. es. Illinois, above 6th
Franky Anthony, lab. Union depot, r. 176 Union
Franz Peter, well digger, r. 222 N. Noble
Franz William, lab. Bunte, Dickson & Co.
Franzie J. H. carpenter C. C. & I. C. R. R.
Franzman Mrs. Amelia Mrs. r. 293 E. Market
Frary John, printer *Journal* job room
Frauer Albert G. (Thayer & Frauer) r. New York bet. East and Liberty
Frauer Emanuel, druggist, r. 257 E. New York
Frauer Herman E. clerk, bds. 257 E. New York
Frauer I. C. druggist, 246 E. Washington, r. 257 E. New York
Frauer Rudolph, saddler, r. 265 E. New York
Frauer Rudolph, (Frauer, Beiler & Co.) r. 87 N. New Jersey
FRAUER, BEILER & CO. (Rudolph Frauer, Jacob L. Beiler and Frank Rottler) mnfrs. and whol. dealers in saddles and harness, 109 E. Washington
Fraulet Peter, chairmaker Speigel & Thoms
Frawley John, brakeman, bds. 58 Benton
Frazee Amanda, wid. Aaron, r. 344 Indiana av.
Frazee Elizabeth, wid. Moses, r. 303 N. Delaware
Frazee John, clerk, r. 303 N. Delaware
Frazee Samuel E. paymaster I. & St. L. R. R. 53 S. Alabama, r. 176 N. Illinois
Frazor Dav. salesman Pettis, Dickson & Co. bds. 218 E. Market
Frazer Jas. S. Judge Supreme Court, state bldg. bds. Bates House
Frazer William, carpenter, r. 82 James
Frazier J. H. carpenter, r. 271 E. Market
Freas Martin, baker, r. 134 Bluff rd.
Frech Henry, saloon and groceries, ns. Nat. road west of the bridge, r. same
Frecker Jacob, r. Morris, nr. cor. New Jersey
Fredenburg Sylvester, cooper A. L. Furguson, r. 43 Hossbrook
Frederick George, lab. D. Root & Co.
Fredericks Godfrey, wks. Rolling Mill, r. 9 Willard

Frederick John, brakeman, bds 113 Benton

Free Frederick, machinist, r. Cumberland bet. New Jersey and Alabama

Free Herman, varnisher, bds. Cumberland bet. New Jersey and Alabama

Free John, machinist, r. alley bet. East and Liberty and Georgia and R. R.

Freedman Joseph, lab. r. 117 W. McCarty

Freed Fred. machinist Spiegel & Thoms

Freelove William, student, bds. 89 N. Delaware

Freeman David II. lab. r. 285 Madison av.

Freeman Geo. W. salesman G. K. Share & Co. rooms 11 Gas bldg.

Freeman Henry, machinist Eagle Machine Works, bds. 341 S. Pennsylvania

Freeman Joseph, carpenter, r. 94 S. Liberty

Freeman Michael, patternmaker Eagle Machine Works, r. 341 S. Pennsylvania

Freitaz John M. carpenter, 264 Railroad, r. same

FRENCH CHARLES G. jewler and dealer in watches, 13 N. Meridian, r. ns. E. Washington city limits

French E. M. student Bryant & Stratton's college, bds. 84 Massachusetts av.

French George W. traveling agt. r. 177 N. Delaware

French Richard, (col'd) lab. 224 Huron

Frendlman Christ. lab. C. C. C. & I. R. R.

Frenzel John P. (Frenzel & Simon) and hide and leather dealer, 104 S. Illinois, r. 42 N. East

Frenzel John P. Jr. messenger Merchants National Bank, bds. 48 N. East

Frenzel & Simon, (John P. Frenzel and John P. Simon) tanners, Benton cor. E. Washington

Frese Charles, (C. Frese & Co.) r. 27 W. Washington

FRESE C. & CO. (Charles Frese and C. F. Hahn) whol. and ret. dealers in hardware and cutlery, 27 W. Washington

Frey Adolphus, bookkeeper *Daily Telegraph*, r. 350 S. Meridian

Frey Albert, (col'd) hostler Wood & Mansur, r. 85 Eddy

Frey William, iron dealer, r. N. Meridian n. of limits

Freye William, brass finisher Schneider & Co. r. 267 S. Alabama

Frick John, saloon, 155 Ft. Wayne av. r. Massachusetts av. cor. St. Clair

Frick Peter, clk. John Frick, r. St. Clair junc. Massachusetts av. and Plum

Frick Philip, tinner, r. 15 S. Alabama

Fricker Jacob, (Schmedel & Fricker) r. Morris bet. East and New Jersey

Fridley W. R. r. 10 E. Michigan

Friechet Charles, baker Henry Beck, bds. 88 Ft Wayne av.

Friedgen C. II. tailor, 41 N. Illinois, r. 123 W. Market

Friedgen Cornelius, boots and shoes ret. 36 W. Washington, r. 36 N. East

Friege Paul, tanner, r. 4th near Howard

FRI	129	FUL

FRIENDS CHURCH Delaware se. cor. St. Clair
Fries Martin, baker Parrott, Nickum & Co.
Fries Paul, lab. J. Fishback
Friese Joseph, painter C. C. C. & I. R. R.
Frink E. Otis, wks. Union Novelty Works, r. 203 Massachusetts av.
Frink H. S. tailor, wks. 8 S. Meridian, r. 353 S. Delaware
Frink Samuel C. pres. Union Novelty Works Mnf. Co. Office St. Clair cor. Canal, r. N. Mississippi sw. cor. Tinker
Friscus Frank, r. 415 N. East
Fritch Louis, cabinet maker Helwig & Co.
Fritche Charles, clk. bds. 467 N. Delaware
Fritz Charles L. clk. S. H. Vajen & Co. r. 137 Massachusetts av.
Frizzell Allen, carpenter, r. 55 Ellen
Froelking John T. r. 449 N. New Jersey
Froesdorff Ferd. engineer 71 S. California
Froghaure A. tanner Frenzel & Simon, bds. 518 E. Washington
Fromacar Henry, salesman, r. 134 N. Mississippi
Fromhold, Peter, turner, r. 167 Bluff rd.
Frosahouir Casper, stone mason, r. 228 S. New Jersey
Frost Bushrod T. farmer, r. 157 W. Maryland
Frost Daniel V. r. 157 W. Maryland
Fruchtenicht Herman, principal German Lutheran school r. 88 S. Liberty
Frusler T. J. r. es. Western av. bet. Christian av. and Forest Home av.
Fry Archibald, (col'd) r. rear. 25 St. Clair
Fry John, basket maker, r. Washington east of limits
Fry R. N. Miss, r. 204 N. Illinois
Fry William H. (Maxwell, Fry & Thurston) r. Fifth, cor. N. Meridian
Fuchsloch Aloes, shoemaker W. Engelhardt, bds. 286 E. Washington
Fruhr Henry, tailor, bds. 117 S. Illinois
Fugate James L. (J. H. Vajen & Co.) r. 169 W. New York
FUGIT JAMES M. grainer, 18 S. Meridian, bds. 160 E. St. Joseph
Fuller Alonzo, Indiana Agricultural Works, r. 78 S. Illinois
Fuller Emma, wid r. 793 N. Tennessee
Fuller Joseph, lab. r. 793 N. Tennessee
Fuller Joseph A. operator W. U. T. Co. bds. 75 Kentucky av
Fullwaker John, lab. r. 26 Center
Fulmer Charles H. machinist, bds. 146 Bates
Fulmer David P. silver plater, bds. 236 E. Market
Fulmer Frederick,(F. Fulmer & Son) r. 236 E. Market
Fulmer Lee A. (F. Fulmer & Son) r. 236 E. Market
Fulmer Otto P. r. 311 E. St. Clair
Fulmer F & Son, (Frederick and Lee A. Fulmer) silver platers, 30 Virginia av.
Furnell Amanda P. Miss, teacher Fourth Ward School
Fulton Felix M. cabinet maker, r. 214 Union
Fulton H. H. bds. Macy House

9

FUL	130	GAL

Fulton Homer, clk. bds. 214 Union
Fulton John F. cabinet maker Burk, Earnshaw & Co. r. ws. Union, nr. cor. McCarty
Fulton W. H. piano maker, bds. 30½ N. Pennsylvania
Fultz Eliza, wid. Jacob, r. 231 W. South
Fultz John W. Rolling Mill, r. 11 Willard
Funk Amer, watchman Rolling Mill
Funke F. W. stocking mnfr. 90 E. Washington, bds. 135 E. Washington
Funkhouser David, (Jameson & Funkhouser) r. 40. N. Misissippi
Furchtenicht Albert, apprentice Cabinet Makers' Union
Furchtenicht Ernst, cabinetmkr. Cabinet Makers' Union
FURGISON ALBERT L. cooper, 321 E. Georgia, r. 123 S. Noble
Furgison Charles, fireman C. C. & I. C. R. R. r. 321 E. Georgia
Furnas John, (John Furnas & Co.) r. 518 N. Delaware
Furnas John & Co. (John Furnas, Moses M. Collett and Moses H. McKay) dry goods whol. and ret. 68 E. Washington

G

Gabel Charles, blksmith Bremermann & Renner
Gabel Conrad, lab. Osgood, Smith & Co. r. 221 Bluff rd.
Gabel Conrad, wagonmkr. r. 194 N. Noble
Gabel John, lab. r. 126 Osbrook
Gage Mary, wid. John, r. 94 N. Tennessee
Gagle Ernest, wks. Indianapolis Paper Co.
Gagnon George F. compositor *Sentinel* news room
Gahn John, groceries ret. r. 196 Indiana av. r. same
Gaines George B. millwright S. Tagart, r. 274 W. Market
Gains P. U. lab. I. P. Evans & Co.
Gaither George (col'd) r. 8 Anthony
Galbraith Arthur N. clk. Pettis, Dickson & Co. r. 50 W. New York
Gall Albert, (Gall & Rush) r. 217 E. Ohio
Gall Caroline, wid. A. D. r. 65 N. New Jersey
Gall Edmond, clk, F. P. Rush, r. 65 N. New Jersey
GALL & RUSH, (Albert Gall and Charles Rush) carpets, wall paper and window shades, 101 E. Washington cor. Delaware
Gallagher Francis, peddler, r. 62 Massachusetts av.
Gallagher Mary, wid. Martin, wks. Indianapolis Paper Co. r. 59 N. Alabama
Gallagher Patrick, peddler, r. 330 Railroad
Gallagher Patrick C. lab. r. ns. West nr. cor. Merrill
Gallagher Patrick C. clk. Pettis, Dickson & Co. r. 66 W. New York
Gallahue W. C. whol. notions, r. 261 Virginia av.
Gallahue P. M. clk. Murphy, Johnston & Co. r. 261 Virginia av.
Galliton John, (col'd) lab. bds. 171 Blake
Galliton Sarah, (col'd) wid. Albert, r. 73 Bright
Gallivan John, fireman Gas Works, bds. 217 S. Illinois

GAL	131	GAR

Gallivan Michael, lab. r. 148 S. Noble

Gallivan Patrick, fireman Spencer House

Galloway Catherine, wid. Jonathan, r. 204 W. Vermont

Galloway Frank, conductor, bds. 204 W. Vermont

Galloway Kizzie, wid. John, r. 204 W. Vermont

Gallup Edward P. (W. P. & E. P. Gallup) r. 78 N. Tennessee

Gallup William P. (W. P. & E. P. Gallup) r. 78 N. Tennessee

GALLUP W. P. & E. P. commission merchants and general agents Fairbanks' Scales, 43 and 45 N. Tennessee

Gallup's Block, Tennessee se. cor. Market

Galmyer Conrad, carpenter, r. ns. Stephens, 3d w. of Virginia av.

Galvin A. bds. Little's Hotel

Galvin Michael, lab. r. 169 Davidson

Gambold Thomas E. clk. Wm. Craig & Co. r. 140 Bluff rd.

Gamilenger Jacob, blksmth C. C. C. & I. R. R. r. Washington e. city limits

Gangrich John, woodworker Indianapolis Coach Works

Gansberg Frederick, baggagemaster Union dpt. r. 69 S. Liberty

Ganter Daniel, lab. Skating Rink

Ganter Daniel, newspapers and periodicals, 338 E. Washington, r. same

Gapen Philip M. (Gapen, Catherwood & Co.) r. w. s. Bluff rd. s. of city limits

GAPEN, CATHERWOOD & CO. (P. M. Gapen and J. Catherwood) wholesale liquor dealers, 118 S. Meridian

Garden Mission Sabbath School, 196 W. Washington

Gardner C. L. wid. r. 96 Fletcher av.

Gardner Charles, butcher John Yorger & Bro.

Gardner Eunice F. Miss r. 41 Fletcher av.

Gardner Joseph, frmn. R. L. & A. W McOuat, r. 118 Indiana av.

Gardner Julia, (co,'d) wid. r. 202 W. 2nd

Gardner Samuel, cooper, r. 375 W. New York

Gardner T. A. printer, bds. 169 S. Tennessee

Gardner Vinder, sashmaker M. Byrkit & Sons, r. 31 James

Gardner William H. (Gardner & Decker) r. 220 S. East

Gardner Windell, carpenter, r. 31 James

Gardner & Decker, (William H. Gardner and Lewis H. Decker) tinners, 308 Virginia av.

Garhart N. K. tailor, r. 29 W. Pratt

Garlick E. C. Rolling Mill, r. es. Meridian bet. 2nd and 3d

Garman Thomas, blksmth. r. Chesapeake bet. West and the Canal

Garner Horatio S. foreman *Sentinel* newsroom, r. 119 Maryland sw. cor. Tennessee

Garratt Aaron (A. Garratt & Son) r. 257 E. Washington

Garratt Jacob, cigar manfr. also (A. Garratt & Son) 257 E. Washington, r. same

Garratt A. & Son (Aaron & Jacob Garratt) second-hand clothing 257 E. Washington

Garrett Benjamin D. Carpenter, r. 61 James

Garrett David, carpenter 353 E. Market, r. same

Garring Frank, blacksmith, r. 19 Willard

| GAR | 132 | GEI |

Garrison Edward, carpenter, r. 39 Massachusetts av.
Garrison William L. shoemaker, bds. 202 Blake
Garshwiler William I. salesman D. A. Lemon, r. 92 S. West
Gartner Conrad, butcher ns. Nat. Road west of the bridge
Garvey Charles, bds. 217 S. Illinois
Garvey John, lab. Rolling Mill
Garvin Joseph, stovemoulder A. D. Wood
Gass Andrew, meat market 118 E. St. Joseph, r, 116 same
Gaston Delilah wid. H. R. r. 289 W. Vermont
Gaston Edward, coachmaker, r. 49 Kentucky av.
Gaston Edward, jr. r. 47 Kentucky av.
Gaston John M. physician and surgeon 66 E. Market, r. 147 N. New Jersey
Gaston Simpson P. r. 35 N. Alabama
Gas Works, es. Pennsylqania cor. Poge Run
Gatch Con. B. bookkeeper John Fishback, bds. Sherman House
Gates Alfred B. (Ripley & Gates) r. 322 N. Illinois
Gates Austin B. (Gates, Pray & Co.) r. 91 N. Delaware
Gates Charles, brakeman, bds. 262 E. Washington
Gates John J. blacksmith 26 S. New Jersey, r. 223 E. Market
GATES, PRAY & CO. (B. G. Kelley, A. B. Gates and William Pray) livery, feed and sale stable E. Market Square bet. Delaware and Alabama
Gath Frederick, car cleaner T. H. & I. R. R.
Gattonby John B. wks. J. C. Ferguson & Co.
Gause William (R. L. Lukens & Co.) r. 262 N. East
Gausepohl Fred. cabinetmaker, r. 164 S. Noble
Gauss Caroline, wid. Charles, r. 65 W. McCarty
Gauss Charles, r. 8 Fletcher av.
Gauss Eugene, clk. Charles Mayer & Co. bds. California House
Gauvison Lewis, cooper, bds. Nagle House
Gay Alfred (Aldrich & Gay) r. 38 N. West
Gaybar Jonathan, wks. Paper Mill, r. W. Indianapolis
Gaynor Henry, porter, bds. Ray House
Gearn Daniel, lab. r. 96 N. Railroad
Gebert Frederick, lab. C. C. C. & I. Rw. r. 228 Union
GEBHARD AUGUST, upholster and furniture dealer, 67 E. Washington, r. same
Gebhardt Henry, cigarmkr. George Roswinkel, r. 152 Greer
Gehring Conrad, books and stationery, 147 E. Washington, r. same
Gehring Fred, local editor Gutenberg & Co. r. 119 St. Joseph
Geiger George W. salesman Landers, Conduitt & Co. r. 434 N. Tennessee
Geiger John W. salesman Pettis, Dickson & Co. r. 219 E. Market
Geiger R. W. agt. C. C. & I. Rw. r. Meridian nw. cor. Circle
Geiger William, shoemkr. r. 237 W. Ohio
Geis Frank, foreman Journal book bindery, r. 163 Uion
Geis John, saloon, 62 S. Delaware, r. same
Geis Joseph, brewer City Brewery, r. 184 Madison av.
Geis Lawrence A. (Geis & Weaner) r. 99 E. Washington

Geis & Weaner, (Lawrence A. Geis and John Weaner) saloon, 99 E. Washington

Geisel Christian, carpenter C. C. C. & I. R. R. r. 222 Davidson

Geisel Henry, blacksmith Eagle Machine Works, bds. 83 N. Missouri

Geisel Henry, blacksmith, r. 291 Massachusetts av.

Geisendorff Albert, student Bryant & Stratton College, bds. 328 W. New York

Geisendorff Christian E. (C. E. Geisendorff & Co., Geisendorff, Richards & Co. and Indianapolis Cotton Mnfg. Co.) r. 328 W. New York

Geisendorff J. C. (Indianapolis Cotton Mnfg. Co.) and pres. Indianapolis Piano Mnfg Co. r. 191 N. New Jersey

Geisendorff Louis, clk. Hoosier Woolen Factory, bds. [328 W. New York

Geisendorff Sarah H. (C. E. Geisendorff & Co. and Geisendorff, Richards & Co.) r. 191 N. New Jersey

Geisendorff C. E. Co. (Christian E. and Sarah H. Geisendorff and Isaac Thalman) proprs. Hoosier Woolen Factory, and dealers in woolen goods, ns. Washington, (nat. rd.) near White river bridge

Geisendorff, Richards & Co. (C. E. Geisendorff, D. A. Richards Sarah H. Geisendorff and Isaac Thalman) proprs. Hoosier State Flouring Mill, ns. W. Washington, (nat. rd.) nr. the bridge

Geitz John, lab. r. 165 Stevens

Geitzentanner Anna, wid. John, r. 319 N. Noble

Gele John, stonecutter, r. 81 N. Liberty

Gelzenleuchter George, clk. Philip Lehr, bds. 246 N. Noble

Gelzenleuchter John, lab. r. 340 Railroad

Gelzenleuchter Peter, clk. Fred Simon, hds. 188 N. Noble

Gensberg Fred, baggage master, r. Liberty cor. Meek

Genter C. bakery and confectionery, 233 E. Washington, r. same

George ——, machinist, bds. 20 S. Pennsylvania

George Austin R. salesman R. George, bds. 24 N. Mississippi

George James, painter Ryan Bros. r. 161 W. Maryland

George Robert, grocer, 184 W. Washington. r. 24 N. Mississippi

Gerber Henry, lab. r. 112 S. Benton

Gerdts Henry, packer Scott, West & Co. r. 75 E. McCarty

Gerdts John, car cleaner T. H. & I. R. R.

Gererdy Nicholas, tailor, 313 E. Washington, r. same

Gerhardt L. J. druggist, 96 Russel av. r. same

Germ Jeremiah, wks. Caledonia Paper Mill, r. 354 S. West

German English School, Theodore Dingeldey prin. ns. Maryland bet. Delaware and Alabama

GERMAN EVANGELICAL CHURCH, S. East opp. Stevens, M. G. I. Stern, pastor

GERMAN EVANGELICAL ZIONS CHURCH, Herman Quinius, pastor. 26 W. Ohio

GERMAN LUTHERAN CHURCH, Christian Hochstetter, pastor, East cor. Georgia

German Lutheran School, Herman Fruchtenicht, prin. ns. Georgia bet. East and Liberty

GERMAN M. E. CHURCH, 220 E. Ohio, Gottlob Fretz, pastor

German Mutual Fire Ins. Co. Adolph Seidensticker, pres. Valentine Butsch, vice-pres. Fred. Ritzenger, sec. 16 S. Delaware

Gerstner Anthony, mer. tailor, 173 E. Washington, r. ns. Cumberland bet. Alabama and New Jersey

Gerstner H. A. clothier Cumberland bet. New Jersey and Alabama

Gertzmein Charles, porter Browning & Sloan

Germania Fire Insurance Co. of Cincinnatti, O., J. S. Dunlop & Co. agts, 2 W. Washington

Gettier George W. moulder, r. McCauley cor. Ray

Geyer David (W. E. Mick & Co.) r. Kansas nr Bluff rd.

Gibbons John, stonemason, r. 365 E. Market

Gibbon Theodore, dentist, bds. Stanridge House

Gibbs Duncan, (col'd) barber Henry C. Mann, r. 165 Indiana av.

Gibbs Wm P. furniture rep'rer, 78 E. Market, r. 102 N. Missouri

Giberson James, lab. r. 29 James

Giblin David, lab. frt. depot C. C. & I. C. R. R. r. 60 Bates

Giblin John, lab. frt. depot C. C. & I. C. R. R.

Gibson Adam, baker W. K. McFarlane, bds. 12 S. Meridian

Gibson David, (Sohl, Gibson & Co. and D. Burton & Co. r. 322 W. New York

Gibson Harvey, blacksmith, 291 Kentucky av. r. 56 Bright

Gibson James, marble cutter, r. 36 Fayette

Gibson Louis H. r. 322 W. New York

Gibson Lucinda, wid. r. head of Fletcher av.

Gibson Thomas shoemaker, r. Sharp e. of Merrill

Gibson William, carpenter, r. Union nw. cor. Phipps

Gibson William T. secy. Indiana Fire Ins. Co. room 5 Odd Fellow's Hall, r. 140 N. Alabama

Gieff John, boilermaker Sinker & Co.

Gieseking Christenia, wid. Frederick, r. 381 Virginia av.

Gieseking Christopher, carpenter, r. 83 N. Davidson

Gieseking Frederick, machinist Eagle Machine Works, bds. Concordia House

Gieseking Gottlieb, cigar maker Back & Wenker

Gieseking Henry, lab. C. C. & I. C. R. R. r. 53 Harrison

Gizendanner William, (Hespelt & Co.) r. 150 W. Vermont

Gilbert Edward, genl. agt. Guardian Mutual Life Ins. Co. of N. Y. 2 & 4 Blackford's blk. r. 307 Indiana av.

Gilbert Joseph, (col'd) lab. Barker, Williams & Co.

Gilbrecht Jacob, shoemkr. 168 Virginia av. r. East cor. Virginia

Gilchrist David, stonemason, r. 195 N. Tennessee

Gilkey Oliver B. (Gilkey & Jones) r. 32 W. Maryland

Gilkey & Jones, (Oliver B. Gilkey and Julius Jones) carpenters and builders, 48 Kentucky av.

Gilkison William F. compositor *Journal* news room, r. 127 Meek

Gillespie Jane, wid. James, r. 116 N. Delaware

Gillespie William J. r. 124 N. Delaware

Gillet Horace S. teacher Indiana Deaf and Dumb Institute, r. 478 N. Pennsylvania

Gillett Omer T. physician and surgeon, 64 E. Washington, r. 49 School

GILLETT SAMUEL T. D. D. pastor Asbury Church, (Methodist) r. 49 School

Gilmore Daniel, bricklayer, r. 329 Virginia av.

Gilmore Samuel H. shoemaker, 195 Indiana av. r. 94 Douglass

Gilmore Thos. H. wks. W. & J. Braden, bds. 329 Virginia av.

Gimbel Michael, grocer, 329 S. East, r. same

Gimber Henry, teamster, r. 132 Bluff rd.

Ginkle George, currier Mooney & Co. r. 75 Garden

Ginrich John, carriage maker, bds. 135 E. Washington

Gintensperger Vinzenz, stone cutter, r. 349 S. Alabama

Ginz Henry, (M. & H. Ginz) r. 297 E. Ohio

Ginz Michael, (M. & H. Ginz) r. 227 Virginia av.

Ginz Michael & Henry, saloon, 185 E. Washington

Gipe Silvester, brakeman, bds. 58 Benton

Gipe William, fireman C. C. & I. C. R. R. bds. 58 Benton

Girard Charles, r. 286 Winston

Girard Fire Ins. Co. of Philadelphia, J. Barnard, agt. Vinton's blk. Pennsylvania, sw. cor. Market

Givan Margaret, wid. James, r. 246 E. Market

Given George W. machinist, r. 21 Peru

Givins Alonzo, bds. 2 Meek

Givins Charles, brakeman, bds. 2 Meek

Glaoff Lucy, wks. Cotton Factory

Glascock William, carpenter, Phœnix Machine Works, r. 54 Bright

Glass Henry, watchman Caledonia Paper Mill, r. 321 W. Market

Glass, Odd, wks. Indianapolis Paper Co.

Glaven Edward S. moulder Sinker & Co. r. 144 E. McCarty

GLAZIER CHARLES, commission merchant, dealer in flour, grain and hay, and manufacturer of corn meal, 146 S. Pennsylvania, r. 129 Virginia av.

Glazier Daniel, engineer fire engine No. 3, r. 185 S. New Jersey

Glazier Frank, engineer steamer No. 1, r. 273 W. Washington

Glazier Peter, fireman steamer No. 1, r. 273 W. Washington

Gleason Henry, lab. r. ns. Nat. road west of the bridge

Gleason John, Messenger Indianapolis Ins. Co. cor. Virginia av. and Pennsylvania

Gleason T. track foreman T. H. & I. R. R. r. 396 S. Wisconsin

Gleason Thomas W. clk. M. Rhodius, bds. same

Gleason John, lab. r. ns. Mayhew, nr. Brooks

Glenn Amanda, wid John, r. 793 N. Tennessee

Glenn Michael, expressman r. 150 Douglas

Glenn Michael, helper Rolling Mill, bds. 300 S. Tennessee

Glenn Robert, driver Citizens' R. R. Co. r. 128 S. Tennessee

Glenn's Block, ss. Washington, bet. Meridian and Pennsylvania

Glessing T. B. scenic artist Academy of Music, r. 237 W. New York

GLI   136   GOL

Glick Herman, (Glick & Schwartz) r. 161 Massachusetts av.

GLICK & SCHWARTZ, (Herman Glick and Joseph Schwartz) manfr. hoop skirts and dealers in notions and fancy goods, Miller's blk. 54 N. Illinois

Glickert John, shoemaker, bds. Bicking House

GLOBE MUTUAL LIFE INSURANCE CO. OF NEW YORK, R. E. Beardsley, state agt. J. C. Smith, local agt. 11 N. Meridian

Glutz John, carpenter, r. 413 S. Illinois

Glynn Michael, puddler Indianapolis Rolling Mill

Goas J. H (Goas & Co.) r. country

Goas & Co. (J. H. Goas and Joseph Nure) glue manufacturers, Michigan road, opp. Camp Carrington

Goddard Samuel, (Goddard & Sons) r. 100 S. Mississippi

Goddard Samuel, jr. (Goddard & Sons) r. 100 S. Mississippi

Goddard Thomas, (Goddard & Sons) r. 100 S. Mississippi

GODDARD & SONS, (Samuel, Samuel jr., and Thomas Goddard] stoneyards, Kentucky av. cor. Georgia

Godley Patrick, wks Caledonia Paper Mill

Goe H. N. confectioner, r. 354 W. New York

Goe H. N. grocer, Illinois, se. cor. St. Clair, r. 352 W. New York

Goe Henry S. spoketurner Osgood, Smith & Co. r. 15 Henry

Goebel John G. cabinetmaker P. Dohn, r. 221 S. Meridian

Goebler William, tailor and repairer, 182 Bluff rd. r. same

Goedker Rudolph, tailor, r. 128 N. Noble

Goeke A. carpenter P. Routier

Goeken William, foreman J. Marsee & Son, r. 43 New Jersey

Goepper Frederick (F. Goepper & Co.) r. Meridian w. of city limits

GOEPPER F. & CO. (Frederick Goepper and George Mannfeld) clothiers and merchant tailors, 17 E. Washington

Goets Charles, clk. M. Rhodius, bds. same

Goff Eliza A. (col'd) wid. Samuel, r. 213 N. West

Goff William, (col'd) painter, r. 213 N. West

Goff William W. painter Charles Fletcher, r. 327 N. West

Gogan Mary, wid. Richard, r. Dougherty ne. cor. Short

Gogan James, printer, 462 Virginia av.

Gogen Kate, saleswoman J. W. Copeland & Co.

Gogen Michael, lab. r. 460 S. East

Gohl John G. carpenter, r. 161 High

Gohl John J. carpenter, r. 161 High

Gohn James, clk. bds. 242 N. Illinois

Gohn Jerry, sawer Smith, Ittenbach & Co. r. 498 Georgia

Gohn William J. clk. L. Q. Sherwood, bds. 242 N. Illinois

Goines Manson, (col'd) wks. John B. Smith, bds. cor. West and Ohio

Goines Simeon, (col'd) whitewasher, r. 247 W. Ohio

Golay A. M. bds. 320 N. East

Gold Adam, grocery, meatmarket and saloon, 405 & 407 N. Mississippi, r. same

Gold John, carpenter W. H. Henschen

Golden Dennis, helper, r. 373 Virginia av.

T. B. PERRINE, Engraver on Wood and Metal, 34 Virginia av.

| GOL | 137 | GOR |

Golder Howard, engineer, bds. 75 Kentucky av.
Golding Andrew J. painter, bds. 400 S. Tennessee
Golding James E. blacksmith, r. 266 S. Illinois
Golding Patrick, watchman, r. 68 N. Davidson
Golding William G. painter, r. 400 S. Tennessee
Goldman Jacob, second-hand clothing, r. 277 S. Delaware
Goldsberry Bayless S. hats, caps and furs 32 W. Washington, r. 129 N. Illinois
Goldsberry L. D. r. 240 N. Mississippi
Goldsberry S. S. watchmkr. McLene & Herron, r. 241 Virginia av.
Goll John, machinist, r. es. S. Illinois cor. Russell av.
Golligher Michael, lab. r. 394 S. West
Golly James, watchman, r. 86 Bates
Goodall John, bds. 329 E. New York
Goodhart Benjamin F. (Smith & Goodhart) r. 236 N. East
Goodier J. R. Prof. penmanship A. Hollingsworth & Co.'s National Business College, bds. Neiman House
Goodman Charles, cabinetmaker, r. 2 Cumberland
Goodman George R. clk. r. 274 E. Louisiana
Goodman Phillip W. lab. Osgood, Smith & Co. r. 198 S. Illinois
Goodperle Peter, clerk, r. 204 N. Noble
Goodrich Nancy (col'd) wid. John, r. Howard sw. cor. 3d.
Goodspeed Henry, r. 205 Huron
Goodwiler Frank, varnisher Spiegel & Thoms
GOODWIN A. Q. publisher of *Sparkling Gem* and book and job printer 30 S. Meridian, r. same
Goodwin Elijah (Indianapolis Printing and Publishing House) and pastor Christian Church, r. 173 Jackson
Goodwin M. M. B. Mrs. editor and publisher *Ladies' Christian Monitor, Mothers' Monitor, and American House Wife*, 21 N. Meridian, r. 171 Jackson
Goodwin Robert M. attorney at law and notary public, room 6 Vinton's block Pennsylvania sw. cor. Market, bds 282 N. Pennsylvania
GOODWIN THOMAS A. real estate agt. broker and dealer 35 E. Market, r. Nat. road 2 miles east city
Goodwin William, engineer C. C. & I. C. R. R.
Gooth Edward, machinist Eagle Machine Works, r. 364 S. Illinois
Gopp John, tailor, r. 284 N. Liberty
Gordan James, saloon, r. 81 Indiana av.
Gordan William, barber Harry Guetig, r. 202 Indiana av.
GORDAN GEO. E. dry goods whol. and ret. 3 Odd Fellows bldg. also lawyer, room 6 Odd Fellows' Hall, r. 230 N. Pennsylvania
Gordon J. W. lawyer room 4 Talbott & New's block, r. 439 N. New Jersey
Gordon M. bartender John Enrich, r. 83 Indiana av.
Gordon Robert, (Gordon & Wilson) r. sw. cor. Broadway & Vine
Gordon & Wilson, (Robert Gordon and George W. Wilson) photographic Temple of Art, 36½ E. Washington
Gore James, bds. 206 N. Delaware

Gorham William H. awning mnfr. slate 16 E. Washington, r. 289 N. Mississippi
Gorman Daniel, coal dealer, r. 266 Union
Gorman James, lab. r. 56 Lord
Gorman John, driver street cars, r. 338 E. Washington
Gorman Thomas, blacksmith Citizens' St. R. R. Co.
Gorrell A. Willis, (H. F. West & Co.) r. 91 Fletcher av.
Goshwaller William clk. r. 32 S. West
Gosney Newton J. switchman, r. 127 S. New Jersey
Goss William, lab. Bunte, Dickson & Co.
Gossett Thomas F. salesman Hendricks, Edmunds & Co. r. Circle nw. cor. Meridian
Gossman William, carpenter, r. 123 W. 4th
Goth George, porter Alford, Talbot & Co. r. 449 N. New Jersey
Goth J. L. tinsmith D. Root & Co. bds. 451 N. New Jersey
Goth Jacob, tinsmith D. Root & Co. r. 451 N. New Jersey
Goth Peter, (Goth, Brown & Co.) r. 453 N. New Jersey
Goth, Brown & Co. (Peter Goth, William Brown and William Buschmann) grocers, 489 N. New Jersey
Gotlische Henry, carpenter Spiegel, Thoms & Co. r. 181 Madison av.
Gotpeler Henry, lab. r. 162 Buchanan
Gott Thomas, r. 219 S. Tennessee
Gotschall John, foreman car dept. C. C. & I. C. R. R. r. 165 Meek
Gotz John, lab, r. 332 E. New York
Goudy Hugh, student National Business College
Grabb Carl, lab. Helwig & Co.
Grabb William, farmer, r. W. Indianapolis
Grabhorn Henry, varnisher, r. ws. Jackson bet. Arch and St. Clair
Grace Church, (Methodist) East ne. cor. Market
GRACE EPISCOPAL CHURCH, Pennsylvania se. cor. St. Joseph
Grady Martin, lab. r. 28 Helen
Graeb Gottlieb, stonemason, r. 334 Railroad
Grafenstein Frederick, meat market, 660 N. Tennessee, r. same
Grafenstein William, butcher and drover, r. 491 N. Alabama
Graff L. D. blacksmith John J. Gates, bds. Jefferson House
Graft Joseph, gardener A. Wiegand, r. same
Grafton John Jr. Pennsylvania ne. cor. Maryland
Grafton M. E. Miss, teacher Indianapolis Female Institute same
Graham ———, law student, bds. 70 E. Market
Graham John A. (Graham & Yewell) r. Louisville, Ky.
Graham John J. (J. J. Graham & Co.) r. 244 S. New Jersey
Graham Michael, mounter D. Root & Co.
Graham Samuel J. conductor, r. 337 N. Tennessee
Graham William, r. 141 Huron
Graham J. J. & Co. (John J. Graham, Riley Bond, J. B. Gray,) flour and feed, 62 N. Pennsylvania
Graham & Yewell, (John A. Graham and Thomas Yewell) proprs. Parcel Express, 20 S. Meridian

Graley Michael, lab. r. 279 W. Merrill
Gramling Adam, salesman J. & P. Gramling, r. ws. Union bet. Meridian and Pennsylvania
Gramling Anton, r. 210 N. Noble
Gramling John, (J. & P. Gramling) r. 210 N. Noble
Gramling Peter, (J. & P. Gramling) r. 212 N. Noble
GRAMLING J. & P. (John and Peter Gramling) merchant tailors and gents' furnishing goods, 35 E. Washington
Graney Dennis, lab. r. 331 E. Louisiana
Graney Hannah, r. 331 E. Louisiana
Graney John, drayman, r. 276 S. Tennessee
Grass Adam, grainer D. C. Chapman, r. 121 W. Vermont
Grassow William, clk. Kiefer & Vinton, bds. 128 N. Noble
Graves Kate, wks. City Laundry
Graves Charles, conductor, r. 23 N. California
Graves Highland, carpenter King & Pinney, r. 52 Fletcher av.
Graves Highland, Jr. crpntr. King & Pinney, r. 28 Fletcher av.
Graves James P. D. (col'd) wks. John T. Pressly, r. 75 Missouri
Graves Richard, confectioner 50 Kentucky av. r. same
Gravey Charles, fireman Gas Works
Gravis Charles, brickmason, bds. 74 N. Pennsylvania
Gravis Charles M. medical student D. Wiley, bds. 74 N. Penn.
Gray Alice Miss, teacher Sixth Ward School, r. 235 N. Illinois
Gray C. B. moulder D. Root & Co.
Gray Cyrus, shoemaker F. W. Schomberg, r. Stephenson bet. Virginia and East
Gray Columbus D. moulder, r. 480 New Jersey
Gray George, gold and silversmith, 498 E. Washington, r. same
GRAY GEORGE W. tailor, 27 Kentucky av. r. same
Gray J. B. (J. J. Graham & Co.) r. Brookfield
Gray James W. clk. Spencer House, bds. same
Gray John, eggpacker, bds. Neiman House
Gray John, machinist Sinker & Co. r. 28 Lord
Gray Jonathan, bricklayer, r. 224 Winston
Gray Robert, carpenter, r. 78 E. St. Clair
Gray Robert, engineer, r. 28 Lord
Gray Robert, clk. Kimble, Aikman & Co. bds. 30 W. Maryland
Gray Robert P. agt. Wheeler & Wilson, r. 52 Greer
Gray S. F. agt. Star Union Freight Line, r. 70 E. St. Clair
Gray Stephen, cutter Crain & Needham, bds. Pyle House
Gray Thomas, cutter, bds. Pyle House
Gray Thomas, bookkeeper Todd, Carmichael & Williams, bds. 235 N. Illinois
Gray William, conductor, bds. 177 S. New Jersey
Gray William, engineer Builders and Mnfrs. Ass. r. 120 S. Noble
Gray William, salesman H. H. Lee, r. 235 N. Illinois
Gray William H. painter, r. 127 Stevens
Graybill Howard, miller J. Carlisle
Graydon Andrew, clk. frt. office C. C. & I. C. R. R. r. 232 E. Ohio
Graydon Jane C. wid. Alexander, r. 332 E. Ohio

GRA	140	GRE

Graygon William M. freight agt. C. C. & I. C. R. R. r. Sycamore se. of city limits
Grayson LaFayette, brakeman, bds. 319 S. Delaware
Grayson S. W. freight conductor J. M. & I. R. R. bds. 319 S. Delaware
GREAT WESTERN DESPATCH, T. A. Lewis, agt. 82 Virginia av.
Great Western Express Co. T. A. Lewis, supt. 82 Virginia av.
Greble Eliza, wid. James, r. 215 W. Ohio
Greegor A. baker Boston Bakery, bds. 285 E. Washington
Greegor Jeremiah W. check clk. r. 76 Bates
Greene ——, wid. r. 39 Maple
Greene A. Mrs. hat bleacher, 162 N. Delaware, r. same
Green Allen T. chair painter, r. 199 Huron
Green B. S. student Bryant & Stratton College
Green David, clk. bds. 364 N. Meridian
Greene E. insurance agt. bds. 31 W. Ohio
Green E. A. teacher High school, r. 87 E. Michigan
GREEN E. S. state agt. Connecticut Mutual Life Ins. Co. of Hartford, Conn. room 4, second floor, Martindale's blk. Pennsylvania ne. cor. Market, bds. 87 E. Michigan
Green Elizabeth A. bds. 162 N. Green
Green George, merchant tailor, 32 N. Pennsylvania, r. Mississippi se. cor. 5th
Green Henry, cabinetmkr. Spiegel & Thoms
Green Henry F. bookkeeper Geisendorff, Richardson & Co. bds. Palmer House
Green Ibby, teacher First Ward school, r. Western av. n. limits
Green J. N. ins. agt. r. 84 Plum
Green James, ins. agt. r. 364 N. Meridian
Green John, gen'l R. R. contractor, r. 203 Huron
Green John, (col'd) lab. r. 125 N. California
Green John C. (J. C. Green & Co.) r. East sw. cor. St. Clair
Green Joseph, (col'd) lab. r. 688 N. Illinois
Green Perry M. (Campbell & Green) r. 130 N. Mississippi
Green Scott, clerk, bds. 364 N. Meridian
Green Thomas, r. 364 N. Meridian
GREEN J. C. & CO. (J. C. Green and J. T. Houston) druggists and whol. dealer in tobacco and cigars, 100 E. Washington
Greenawalt John G. clk. Claim office, r. 29 W. Michigan
Greenawalt William, r. 29 W. Michigan
Greene Davies M. salesman A. W. Bronson, r. 364 N. Meridian
Greene Henry F. bookkeeper, bds. 45½ N. Tennessee
Greene James, (Green & Royse) r. 364 N. Meridian
Greene John N. (Green & Tilford) r. ss. Cherry nr. cor Plum
Greene N. Scott, bookkeeper First National Bank of Indianapolis, r. 364 N. Meridian
Greene Thomas C. clk. Greene & Royse, bds. 364 N. Meridian
GREENE & ROYSE, (James Greene and W. T. Royse) gen'l Ins. agts. 10 Blackford's blk.

GRE	141	GRI

GREENE & TILFORD, (John N. Greene, James M. Tilford) state agts. Berkshire Life Ins. Co. of Pittsfield, Mass. also loan agency, 21 N. Meridian

Greenen Michael, fireman, bds. 58 Benton

Greenewald Henry, dry goods and notions ret. 174 E. Washington, r. same

Greenfield Daniel C. deputy county clerk r. 328 W. Washington

Green Lawn Cemetery, J. M. Hedges, sexton, office and entrance ws. Kentucky av. bet. Louisiana and River

Greenleaf Allen, machinist, r. 314 S. Illinois

Greenleaf Clements A. (Greenleaf & Co.) r. 312 S. Illinois

Greenleaf Edward, foreman pattern shop Greenleaf & Co. r. 416 S. Tennessee

Greenleaf William, machinist, r. 416 S. Tennessee

GREENLEAF & CO. (C. A. Greenleaf, E. and J. Peck and J. L. Mothershead) founders and machinists, 325 S. Tennessee

Greenlee E. A. (Dame & Greenlee) r. Fall Creek rd. out of limits

Greenrod Timothy, stonecutter F. L. Farman, r. 76 S. Missouri

Greenstreet Jason H. bookkeeper Wheat, Fletcher & Co. r. 110 Broadway

Greenwald John, r. 506 S. New Jersey

Greenway James shoemaker, r. 64 S. Alabama

Greenwoldt Albert, (Rikhoff & Bro.) r. 448 S. Illinois

Greenwoldt Albert J. salesman Rikhoff & Bro. r. 448 S. Illinois

Greenwood B. bookkeeper J. Carlisle, bds. 260 W. Washington

Greer Elisha, clk. r. ss. McCarty bet. East and Water

Greer James, cabinetmaker 249 S. Mississippi, r. 242 same

Greger C. F. carpenter, r. 83 James

Greger George W. teamster, r. 83 James

Gregg J. A. wagonmaker 191 Indiana av. r. 327 N. West

Gregg Joshua, conductor, r. 348 N. Alabama

Gregoire August, tailor and repairer 129 S. Illinois, r. same

Gregory Robert C. Judge Supreme Court state bldg. bds. Bates House

Gregory Mattie Miss, teacher 7th Ward School, bds. 143 S. East

Grely Michael, wks. Gas Works, r. 279 Merril

Grely Dennis, lab. r. 175 Meek

Gremleng Adam, clk. r. ws. Union 1 n. of Phipps

Greny Patrick, bds. 101 S. New Jersey

Gresh B. F. teacher of music, r. 282 E. St. Clair

Gresh Samuel, carpenter, r. 265 N. West

Gresel Michael, lab. r. 34 Cherry

Grouzard Louis S. artist, r. 454 Virginia av.

Grieb John, teamster, r. 172 E. Market

Griener John, shoemaker, r. ws. Douglas 3 s. New York

Grieshaber Sebastian, boilermaker Washington Foundry, r. 349 S. Alabama

Griesheimer Louis, (M. Griesheimer & Bro.) bds. 15 N. Meridian

Griesheimer Morris, (M. Griesheimer & Bro.) bds. 15 N. Meridian

Griesheimer M. & Bro. (Morris and Louis Griesheimer) clothing and gents' furnishing goods 1 W. Washington

| GRI | 142 | GRI |

Grieshopper John, boilermaker Eagle Machine Works, r. Alabama cor. Sinker

Grienlich John, cabinetmaker W. P. Gibbs, bds. 23 Kentucky av.

Grieves Clarrence, printer, bds. 314 W. Merrill

Grieves Mary A. Miss, dressmaker, bds. 313 W. Merrill

Grieze Frank R. turner Helwig & Co.

Griffin Dennis, lab. r. 252 S. Missouri

Griffin George, tender T. Griffin, r. 376 Delaware

Griffin James, lab. r. 2 Walter

Griffin John, lab. Rolling Mill, r. rear 84 Vinton

Griffin John, wks. Scott & Nicholson

Griffin Mary, wid. Thomas, r. 142 S. Noble

Griffin Martin, lab. r. 115 Elm

Griffin Michael, drayman, r. 90 Fayette

Griffin Michael, drayman, r. 95 Fayette

Griffin Patrick, lab. r. 376 S. Delaware

Griffin Patrick, lab. r. 388 Indiana av.

Griffin Peter, compositor *Sentinel* news room, bds. Palmer House

Griffin Sarah, wid. James, r. 362 S. Delaware

Griffin Timothy, saloon, 48 Pennsylvania, r. 376 S. Delaware

Griffin Timothy, stonecutter Scott & Nicholson

Griffin William D. clerk Kettenbach, Newmeyer & Co. bds. N. East bet. Walnut and St. Clair

Griffith A. writingmaster, bds. Stanridge House

Griffith C. A. patternmaker Sinker & Co. r. 23 Short

Griffith Edward, dentist, room 3, 77½ E. Market, r. 474 N. Pennsylvania

Griffith Edward, helper Rolling Mill, bds. 300 S. Tennessee

Griffith Frederick, bookkeeper, bds. 126 E. Ohio

Griffith George W. mail agent, r. 645 N. Tennessee

Griffith Humphrey, r. 78 N. Illinois

Griffith J. J. F. bookkeeper, Patterson, Moore & Talbot, bds. 126 E. Ohio

Griffith J. R. Mrs. wid. r. 42 S. Mississippi

Griffith James, engineer, bds. 47 Bates

Griffith John, switchman C. C. & I. C. R. R.

Griffith Pleasant H. r. 78 N. Illinois

Griggs Abigal, wid. r. 80 N. Mississippi

Griggs Annie Miss, bds. 199 N. Pennsylvania

Grigsby Jas. gardener, r. Michigan rd. nr. junction Washington

Grimes Henry, wks. Emerson, Beam & Thompson

Grimes Joseph, miller, r. ns. Stevens 3 w. of Virginia av.

Grimes L. Moore, cooper W. Baird, r. rear 225 W. Ohio

Grimes William H. carpenter, r. 325 N. West

Grimm Casper, painter, r. 174 E. St. Joseph

Grimm Jacob, carriagesmith Miller, Mitchell & Stough, r. 174 St. Joseph

Grimm Jacob, cistern builder, r. 174 E. St. Joseph

Grimm John, brewer Schmidt's Brewery, r. High, cor. Wyoming

Grimm Wendelin, cabinet maker, Cabinet Makers' Union

Grine C. baker and confectioner, 264 E. Washington, r. same

GRI	143	GUS

Griner John, shoemaker Christ. Karle & Co. r. Douglas, bet. Ohio and New York

Grinon Michael, fireman C. C. & I. C. R. R.

Grinsteiner George, undertaker 276 E. Market, r. same

Grion Nicholas, carpenter, r. 317 Davidson

Griswold Malinda, wid. James, r. es. Douglas, 1 n. New York

Griswold T. E. traveling salesman Patterson, Moore & Talbot, bds. Oriental House

Grobe Charles, restaurant, 12 W. Louisiana, r. same

Groff Daniel, ins. agt. r. 256 N. East

Grogan G W. harness maker, Ad. Hereth, r 35 Circle

Crooms Ansel C. bookkeeper *Journal* office, r. 412 N. New Jersey

GROSCH JOHN, prop. Mozart Hall Restaurant, wines and liquors, 39 S. Delaware, r. same

Groschel August, tailor, r. 175 E. Washington

Grose Charles, baker, Charles Grine, bds. 264 E. Washington

Grove Benjamin, agt. r. 329 E. New York

Groove Samuel, clk. Will. W. Wallace, r.329 E. New York

Grove Samuel A. grocery, r. 329 E. New York

Grubbs Daniel W. gen. agt. Continental Life Ins. of New York, 7 Blackford's blk. r. 282 N. Illinois

Grube Jacob, carpenter, r. 355 S. Illinois

Gruenard, H. prop. Globe House, 164 S. Illinois, r. same

GRUENERT JOHN H. prop. Jefferson House and saloon, 61 E. South, r. same

Grund George, striker Washington foundry, r. 137 Bluff rd.

Guard David, clk. bds. 17½ Virginia av.

GUARDIAN MUTUAL LIFE INSURANCE CO. of New York, Edward Gilbert, gen. agt. 2 & 4 Blackford's blk.

Guetig Henry, barber, Washington, ne. cor. Pennsylvania, r. 280 E. Market

Guetig Henry, Spencer House saloon, r. 280 E. Market

Guetz Charles, barkeeper, r. 340 E. Market

Guezet A. house and sign painter, 297 S. Delaware, r. same

Guffin Henry C. (Guffin & Parker) r. nr. University

GUFFIN & PARKER (Henry C. Guffin and Robert P. Parker) lawyers room 10-11 Talbott & New's blk.

Guinn Eliza, wid. Seth, r. 31 Henry

Guinn John, brakeman, bds. 31 Henry

Guisinger John, machinist Academy of Music

Gulick John F. mail agt. r.310 Indiana av.

Gullion Leo. (col'd) lab. r. ws. Blackford nw. cor. Market

Gulliver Aaron (col'd) barbershop W. Washington sw. cor. Kentucky av. r. 69 Kentucky av.

Gulliver William (Russell & Gulliver) r. 79 Kentucky av.

Gundelfinger Benjamin, men and boys' clothing whol. and ret. 6 W. Washington, r. 260 E. Ohio

Gundelfinger Max, salesman Benjamin Gundelfinger

Gustetter Frederick, r. 435 N. New Jersey

Gustin Frank, wks. Indianapolis Paper Co.

GUS	144	HAG

Gustin George, telegraph operator, r. 275 N. New Jersey
Gustin John, auctioneer G. W. McCurdy, r. 27 E. North
Gustin Levi, physician 44½ W. Louisiana, r. 275 N. New Jersey
Gustin Lewis Q. insurance solicitor Whitcomb & Potter, bds. 275 N. New Jersey
Gustin Robert, carpenter, r. 275 N. New Jersey
Gutenberg Co. publishers, Adolph Frey, supt. 13 W. Maryland
Guth Egbert, machinist, r. 364 S. Illinois
Guthperle Peter, salesman 71 W. Washington, r. 204 N. Noble
Guthrie E. A. comp. *Journal* news room, r. 124 N. Missouri
Gutknecht John, painter, r. 157 Fort Wayne av.
Gutknuht Rudolph, shoemaker, r. 560 N. Mississippi
Gutur George, stovemoulder A. D. Wood
Gutzweiller Frank, r. 251 Virginia av.
Guy James C. bds. 121 N. Delaware
Guyre D. real estate agt. r. 161 Huron
Guysinger John, stage carpenter, bds. 144 N. Tennessee
Gwynn Thomas, fireman T. H. & I. R. R.

H.

Haag Charles, peddler, r. 274 Massachusetts av.
Haag William, clk. T. W. Farnsworth, bds. 274 Massachusetts av.
Haas George, baker Parrott, Nickum & Co. r. 134 N. Penn.
Habeny Henry, student Nat. Business College, r. 185 W. New York
Hack George, blacksmith C. Wehling, r. 90 S. East
Hack John, gardener Indiana Deaf and Dumb Institute, r. E. Washington out of limits
Hacke Charles, patternmkr. Sinker & Co.
Hackelmann Andrew, varnisher, r. 66 N. Noble
Hacker A. P. tobacconist, r. 465 E. Georgia
Hacker James, sawer, r. 273 W. Merrill
Hacker Lida, bookbinder J. H. C. Smith
Hackett William, lab. r. 64 S. Liberty
Hadley Evan, med. student T. B. Harvey, 58 E. Market
Hadley William, city assessor, office Glenn's Block, r. 381 N. Delaware
Haeffner Fred, r. ss. Nat. rd. west of the bridge
Haehl John, (Haehl & Anker) r. 170 E. Washington
HAEHL & ANKER, (John Haehl and Aristides Anker) inssurance agts. 20 S. Delaware
Haerle William, ladies dress trimmings, 4 W. Washington, r. 312 N. Illinois
Haess John, bds. Jefferson House
Haffield Uriah, farmer, r. 83 N. Missouri
Haft Julius, porter D. Root & Co. bds. 441 N. Meridian
Hagar E. C. bookkeeper S. A. Fletcher & Co. bds. 17 W. Maryland
Hagedon William H. salesman Trade Palace, r. 84 E. Michigan

T. B. Perrine, Engraver on Jewelry & Silver Ware. 34 Virginia av.

HAG   145   HAL

Hagedorn Henry, watchman, r. 7 Buchanan
Hagentucher William, shoemkr. bds. California House
Hagerdon Henry, car cleaner T. H. & J. R. R.
HAGERHORST CHRISTIAN L. groceries and provisions, 223 W. Ohio, r. same
Hagerhorst William, machinist Eagle Machine Works, r. 115 W. South
Hagerty Cornelius, wks. porkhouse, r. 32 Helen
Hagerty James, wks. John Fishback, bds. ws. Bluff rd. nr. Kansas
Hagerty Patrick, teamster, r. 261 S. Tennessee
Haggerty James, puddler Rolling Mill
Haggerty Timothy, wks. Rolling Mill
Hahler William, coffee stand, r. 106 N. Davidson
Hahn A. shoemkr. H. F. Albershardt, bds. 135 E. Washington
Hahn Charles F. (Hahn & Bals and C. Frese & Co.) r 79 N Alabama
Hahn Henry, musician, r. 67 S. East
Hahn Hiram, printer, bds. 60 W. Market
Hahn Jacob, butcher, bds. 227 S. Tennessee
Hahn John F. clk. John Shafer, r. 115 N. Tennessee
Hahn Louis, meatmarket 229 S. Tennessee, r. 227 S. Tennessee
HAHN & BALS, (Charles F. Hahn and Charles H. G. Bals) importers and wholesale liquor dealers, 25 S. Meridian
Hahnemann Life Ins. Co. of Cleveland, Ohio, W. J. Copeland state agt. 5 Martindale's blk.
Hahnenstein Siezfried, (Western Furniture Co.) r. 142 Fort Wayne av.
Haie Frank, switchman, r. 2 Meek
Hainebach Samuel, compositor Gutenberg Co. r. 144 Stevens
Haines William, printer, bds. Oriental House
Haisch John, printer Julius Boetticher
Halahan Jeremiah, lab. r. 44 Elizabeth
Halbert Joseph D. clk. r. 108 N. Plum
Halderman Charles, shoemaker, r. 17 Willard
Halderman Joseph, house mover, bds. 11 S. Mississippi
Halderman John M. salesman, bds. 11 S. Mississippi
Hale Alfred, r. 500 Virginia av.
Hale H. J. machinist, r. 196 W. Vermont
Hale H. J. mchnst Eagle Mchne Works, r. 81 Massachusetts av.
Hale Henry, brakeman, r. 281 E. Georgia
HALE JUDSON, physician for diseases of the throat and lungs, office No. 1 Miller's blk. Illinois nw. cor. Market, r. 572 N. Tennessee
Hale Margaret J. Mrs. bds. 65 N. East
Haley Dennis, lab. Rolling Mill
Haley John, lab. r. 215 S. Missouri
Haley Oliver, engineer, r. 180 Dougherty
Haley Patrick, wks. Rolling Mill
Halford E. W. r. 118 St. Mary
Halford James, clk. bds. 363 N. New Jersey

10

Hall Adam, porter Institute for the Blind, r. same
Hall Allen G. lab. r. 278 Railroad
Hall Andrew W. miller, r. 302 W. Washington
Hall C. E. clk. E. A. Hall, bds. Illinois n. of limits
Hall C. M. wid. r. 704 N. Tennessee
Hall Charles F. clk. Greene & Tilford, bds. 140 W. Market
Hall Charles T. r. 123 N. Tennessee
Hall E. A. merchant tailor, 31 N. Pennsylvania, r. Illinois n. of limits
Hall E. K. (Lawyer & Hall) r. Noblesville, Ind.
Hall Earls A, carpenter, r. 248 N. Illinois
Hall Frank, fireman I. C & L. R. W. r. 8 Lord
Hall Franklin, farmer, r. ss. Fifth bet. Mississippi and Tennessee
Hall George, salesman J. McIntyre, bds. 117 Morrison
Hall George W. (col'd) driver, r. 218 W. Second
Hall H. (Jones & Hall, col'd) 16 S. Meridian
Hall H. E. teamster C. Orff & Brothers
Hall Harry, brakeman, r. 327 S. Alabama
Hall Harry L. supt. LaFayette R. R. bds. Bates House
Hall Henry, engineer, r. 8 Lord
Hall Henry, lab. Sinker & Co.
Hall J. W. paperhanger, bds. Stanridge House
Hall James, (col'd) bds. Douglas alley bet. New York and Ohio
Hall John K. blacksmith, bds. 301 S. Pennsylvania
Hall John W. paperhanger Gall & Rush
Hall L. A. mnfr. Stitch Spring Bed 83 E. Market, r. 10 Henry
Hall M. M. Miss, governess Orphan Asylum, r. 711 N. Tennessee
Hall Reginald H. (Rand & Hall) r. 210 N. Meridian
Hall Robert, carpenter Citizens' R. R. Co.
Hall Sarah C. Mrs. physician, office 248 N. Illinois, r. same
Hall Thaddeus, fireman, r. 8 Lord
Hall Thomas Q. (Wilkins & Hall) and salesman Mitchell & Rammelsberg Furniture Co. r. 125 Walnut
Hall William, (col'd) carpenter, r. 129 Bright
Hall William, patternmaker Sinker & Co. r. 197 Bates
Hall William, tinsmith, C. C. & I. C. R. R.
Haller Leon, clk. r. 25 S. Delaware
Hallihan Jeremiah, wks. Cotton Factory
Hallihan Mary, wks. Cotton Factory
Hallin Thomas, lab. r. Coburn nr. cor. New Jersey
Halpin M. H. compositor *Journal* news room, r. 233 N. Liberty
Halsker Benjamin, lab. r. 505 S. Tennessee
Halter Christ, butcher Charles Kuhn, bds. same
Halterman Charles, shoemaker 168 S. Illinois, r. 17 Willard
Hamburg Henry, cook Spencer House, r. Union nw. cor. Phipps
Hamill Michael, lab. Rolling Mill, r. w. end McCarty
Hamilton Alexander, cooper, r. 390 N. West
Hamilton Alfred, clk. A. G. Willard & Co. bds. 89 Indiana av.
Hamilton Augustus A. medical student J. T. Boyd
Hamilton Benjamin, moulder D. Root & Co. r. 343 S. East
Hamilton C. wid. Kinard, boarding house, 89 Indiana av.

J. R. Forbes Dealer in Watches, Clocks & Jewelry, 34 Virginia av.

HAM 147 HAN

Hamilton Charles, wks. Caledodia Paper Mill
Hamilton David P. engineer, r. 379 E. Georgia
Hamilton Emma, tel. operator, bds. 39 Indiana av.
Hamilton Frank W. deputy auditor, r. 191 S. New Jersey
Hamilton J. machinist, C. C. & I. R. R.
Hamilton James, foundery, Kentucky av. cor. Mississippi, r. 517 S. Maple
Hamilton James, fireman, C. & I. J. R. R.
Hamilton James, moulder, r. 17 Maple
Hamilton James, lightning rod agt. bds. Western House
Hamilton Patrick, lab. r. ns. Market, 2 e. Blackford
Hamilton Robert, machinist, King & Pinney, r 517 S. Maple
Hamilton Samuel A. machinist, r. Michigan road near junction Washington
Hamilton Sarah Mrs. housekeeper Sherman House, bds. same
Hamilton T. D. clk. W. L. Munson, r. 166 E. Market
Hamilton Thomas J. wks.Warren Tate, r. out of city limits
Hamilton William, bookbinder Wm. Sheets r. 80 S. Mississippi
Hamilton William, bookbinder *Journal* bindery, bds 17½ Virginia av.
Hamilton William S. machinist, r. 74 S. Noble
Hamlin Carlin, (Hamlin & Wright) lawyer, 62½ E. Washington, bds. 17 W. Maryland
Hamlin Richard, wks. Osgood, Smith & Co. r. 24 S. Illinois
Hamlin, William H. tel. operator I. C. & L. R. R. r. 129 Bates
Hamlin & Wright (Carlin Hamlin and Jacob T. Wright) claim agts. 62½ E. Washington
Hamman Edward, heater Rolling Mill
Hammel Andrew, blacksmith, ss. Seventh, bet. Tennessee and Mississippi, r. Mississippi, cor Seventh
Hammel George, cigarmkr. A. W. Sharpe, bds. 193 S. N. Jersey
Hammel George, cigar maker, r. Mississippi, cor. Seventh
Hammel Peter, carriage maker, r. Mississippi, cor. Seventh
Hammerly George J. lab. Starch Factory, r. 461 S. New Jersey
Hammil Bernard, drayman, r. 493 N. Mississippi
Hammil Peter, blacksmith S. W. Drew
Hammond Joseph W. clk. Little's Hotel, bds. same
Hammond John, clk. bds. Little's Hotel
Hammond, U. S. ins. agt. r. 279 W. Michigan
HAMMOND UPTON J. attorney at law and notary public 8 E. Washington, r. 569 N. Pennsylvania
Hampton Frank, clerk W. H. Hay, r. 365 W. Vermont
Hampton J. B. coachmkr. 186 W. Market, r. 365 W. Vermont
Hampton Stephen, clerk, bds. 163 N. Tennessee
Hampton Stephen L. salesman J. Woodbridge, bds. Pyle House
Hanck Nicholas, lab. r. 404 S. Illinois
Hand Adolphus C. bricklayer, r. Madison road s. of limits
Hand Emma, wid. r. 164 Huron
Hand Hiram, printer, *Journal* job room
Hand William, brickmaker, r. Nebraska nr. Madison road
Handrchan Frank, lab. r. 362 S. Tennessee

Haneman John, (J. & T. Haneman) r. 135 Massachusetts av.
Haneman Theodore (J. & T. Haneman) r. 135 Massachusetts av.
Haneman J. & T. (John & Theodore Haneman) grocers 135
    Massachusetts av.
Haney Mary wid. John, r. 334 S. Delaware
Hanh David, r. 466 E. Georgia
Hanh George W. cooper, r. 466 E. Georgia
Hanhoerster William, cabinetmaker Helwig & Co.
Hanley James, clk. bds. Pyle House
Hanley John, grocer clk. 322 Virginia av. r. same
Hanly Patrick, gluemaker Goas & Co.
Hanlin Catherine wid. William, r. 19 S. West
Hann Elizabeth A. wid. Bradford, r. 27 Massachusetts av.
Hannah David G. grocer 203 Massachusetts av. r. same
Hanna Jerusha Mrs. clk. Trade Palace, r. 77 Kentucky av.
Hanna John (Hanna & Knefler) r. Greencastle, Ind.
Hanna John L. deputy sheriff, r. 427 E. St. Clair
Hanna Mary E. Miss, teacher Indiana Institution for the Blind
Hanna S. C. (Crosland Hanna & Co.) r. 388 N. Illinois
Hanna Samuel, r. 131 N. Meridian
Hanna Valentine C., U. S. Paymaster, r. 172 N. Meridian
Hanna & Knefler (John Hanna and Frederick Knefler) lawyers
    room 4, 204 N. Delaware
Hannah George W. cooper A. L. Furgason, r. 466 E. Georgia
Hannahan J. P. clk. bds. Little's Hotel
HANNAMAN WILLIAM, military claim agt. State of Indiana, N.
    Tennessee se. cor. Market, r. National Road
Hannan Edward, r. 183 High
Hannemann Jacob, peddler, r. Wabash ne. cor. Noble
Hannerhan Lawrence, lab. C. C. C. & I. R. R.
Hannesy Jesse, lab. Rolling Mill
Hanniger John, carpenter, r. 124 Osbrook
HANNING JOHN G. plumber and gas fitter, 82 W. Washington
    (also Pearson & Co.) r. 135 E. St. Joseph
Hanover Christian, r. 2 Arch
Hanover Arthur J. storekeeper, Bates House, bds. same
Harrahan Kate, dressmaker Mrs. F. Jarrell, r. 272. S. Tennessee
Hanrahan L. lab. r. 30 John
Hanrahan Michael, moulder Union Novelty Works
Hanrahan Michael, switchman T. H. & I. R. R. r. 272 S. Ten-
    nessee
Hanrahan Michael J. salesman Pettis, Dickson & Co. bds. Little's
    Hotel
Hanrahan Thomas, fireman T. H. & I. R. R.
Hanrahan Patrick G. r. 263 S. Tennessee
Hanson Charles, clerk, r. Illinois ne. cor. Ray
Hanson Joseph, coachmaker, bds. 166 E. Market
Hanson John, wks. Burk, Ernshaw & Co. bds. 203 S. West
Hanson John, lab. Rolling Mill
Hanson Mat. boot and shoemaker, 359 S. Delaware, r. same
Hanway Samuel, r. 435 N. East

Hanway Thomas H. bricklayer, r. 465 N. East
Hapenny T. S. publisher, r. 32 W. St. Clair
Harbison Alexander, engineer *Journal* office, r. 136 W. Vermont
Harbison Robert, foreman Am. U. Ex. Co. at Union depot, bds. 136 W. Vermont
Harcourt Theodore, cabinetmaker, r. 287 E. Georgia
Hardee Alexander, (col'd) lab. bds. 66 N. Missouri
Harden R. E. carpenter, 237 E. Washington, r. 225 E. Market
Harden Samuel, carpenter R. E. Harden, r. 225 E. Market
Harden T. G. N. harnessmaker, r. Washington ne. cor. East
Hardesty E. J. trainmaster J. M. & I. R. R. r. 335 S. Penn.
Hardin Albert G. jailor county jail Court House Square, r. same
Hardin E. C. carpenter, r. 231 E. Market
Hardin E. R. carpenter, r. 229 E. Market
Hardin James S. confectioner, r. 231. E. Market
Hardin Thomas, carriage trimmer, r. 179 S. Illinois
Harding George C. (Harding, Morton & Finch) r. 127 W. First
Harding Jacob, clk. *Mirror* office, r. 331 N. Alabama
Harding J. Oscar, compositor *Mirror* news room, bds. 331 N. Alabama
Harding Richard, (col'd) barber 255 W. Washington, r. 288 W. Washington
Harding William P. *Mirror* job rooms 21 N. Meridian, r. 269 E. Market
HARDING, MORTON & FINCH, (George C. Harding, J. R. Morton, F. W. Finch) publishers daily and weekly *Mirror* 19 N. Meridian
Hardline George, cabinet maker Spiegel & Thoms
Hardwick John, carpenter, r. 318 E. Market
Hardwick Nellie, bookbinder *Journal* Book Bindery
Hardy Edward A. bookkeeper W. A. Bristor, bds. 17½ Virginia
Hare Marcus L. trader, r. 121 N. Delaware
Hargin John, compositor *Journal* news room
Hargt Fred. meat market 234 E. Washington, r. 345 same
Hargus William F. carpenter, r. 299 Indiana av.
Harkness A. wid. r. 346 N. Meridian
Harkness John, painter, r. 179 N. Pennsylvania
Harkworth Theodore, machinist Spiegel & Thoms
Harlan Clara, teacher 8th Ward District School
Harlan George W. (Butler, Smith & Harlan) r. 191 Mass. av.
Harlan L. D. physician 142 Virginia av. r. same
Harland Susan, wid. George W. r. 136 N. Tennessee
Harman Lawrence, wks. Phœnix Machine Works
Harmening Christian, drayman, r. 76 N. Railroad
Harmening Christian, grocer 283 S. Delaware, r. same
Harmon Charles, clk. J. Rupp
Harmon John, carpenter, r. 124 N. Winston
Harmon Lawrence, lab. r. 44 Michigan rd.
Harmuth August, wks. Burk, Earnshaw & Co. r. 131 Bluff rd.
Harnebom Barney, lab. Hair and Bristle Works, bds. same
Harness Amos, wks. Cotton Factory

Harness Solomon, lab. r. 18 Douglas
Harness William, heater Rolling Mill
Harney Robert, wks. Schneider & Co. bds. Jefferson House
Harold Isaac W. salesman Wm. H. Close & Co. bds. 70 E. Market
Harper Henry, cooper, r. 162 Bluff rd.
Harper James, chief engineer Indianapolis & Vincenness R. R.
 Co. office Kentucky av. cor. Illinois, r. 434 N. Delaware
Harper James, (col'd) (Pearson & Harper) r. 325 E. Washington
Harper John L. asst. engineer, r. 379 N. Pennsylvania
Harper Laura Mrs. dress and cloakmkr. 69 E. Maryland, r. same
Harris Addison C. (Dye & Harris) r. N. Meridian cor. 5th
Harris Bug, (col'd) whitewasher, r. 231 Minerva
Harris Charles E. constable, 74 E. Washington, r. 140 E. North
Harris D. lab. Sinker & Co. r. 30 Helen
Harris D. wks. Kingan & Co.
Harris Elizabeth, wid. Isaac, r. 37 Kentucky av.
Harris Frank Miss, clk. Trade Palace, r. 244 S. New Jersey
Harris James, lab. bds. Western House
Harris John, night watchman freight depot T. H. & I. R. R.
Harris M. (col'd) lab. r. 125 N. California
Harris Thomas W. plasterer, r. 380 S. West
Harris William, (col'd) whitewasher, r. 19 Center
Harrison A. Irwin, agt. Western Insurance Co. 79 W. Washing-
 ton, r. Westfield rd.
Harrison Alfred, (A. & J. C. S. Harrison) r. 252 N. Meridian
Harrison Benjamin, (Porter, Harrison & Fishback) r. 299 N. Al-
 abama
Harrison Edward G. clk. Harrison's Bank, bds. 252 N. Meridian
Harrison George, lab. Rolling Mill
Harrison John, watchman, r. 24 Lord
Harrison John C. S. (A. & J. C. S. Harrison) r. 262 N. Meridian
Harrison R. E. lawyer, 17½ W. Washington, r. Oak ne. cor. Cherry
Harrison Sarah, wid. r. 123 N. Tennessee
Harrison Temple C. lawyer, 17½ W. Washington, r. 23 Cherry
Harrison Thomas, lab. Rolling Mill, r. 6 Willard
Harrison Thomas, (col'd) dyer J. Prosser, r. Douglas al. bet.
 New York and Ohio, Missouri and West
Harrison Urbane C. collector Daily *Evening Commercial*, r. 49 Ann
Harrison W. H. (col'd) cook Palmer House
Harrison William, lab. Union Novelty Works
HARRISON A. & J. C. S. (Alfred and John C. S. Harrison) props.
 Harrison's Bank, 15 E. Washington
HARRISON'S BANK, A. & J. C. S. Harrison, proprs. 15 E. Wash
 ington
Harrold Isaac, clk. Boston Store, bds. 70 E. Market
Harrold Jacob, railsbearer Rolling Mill
Harst Fred, butcher, r. 405 E. Washington
Hart A. T. traveling agent, r. 45½ N. Tennessee
Hart Abram, junk dealer, r. 320 Railroad
Hart Charles, lab. J. W. Whitney
Hart Edward F. saloon 132 S. Illinois, r. 30 S. West

HAR   151   HAR

Hart Michael, lab. r. 57 Dougherty
Hart T. J. (Hart & Mathews) r. 799 N. Tennessee
Hart Thomas, (col'd) lab. r. Indiana av. nr. toll gate
Hart Thomas, porter Murphy, Johnston & Co.
Hart & Mathews, (T. J. Hart and C. Mathews) carpenters and builders, Maryland, se. cor. Pennsylvania
Harter John, baker, bds. 47 N. East
Harter John A. (Parrott, Nickum & Co.) bds. East, se. cor. Market
Hartford Fire Ins. Co. of Hartford, Conn. Snyder & Hays, agts. 17 N. Meridian
Harting Frederick, (Harting & Bro.) r. 62 Russell av.
Harting Henry, (Harting & Bro.) r. 363 S. Illinois
Harting William, drayman, r. 230 Union
Harting & Bro. (Frederick and Henry Harting) lager beer brewers, 7 Norwood
Hartline George, r. 381 E. Georgia
Hartmann C. foreman F. P. Rush, r. ss. Ohio, bet. East and Liberty
Hartman Charles, clk. J. George Stitz, r. 119 N. New Jersey
Hartman Christian, lab. r. 279 E. Ohio
Hartman Christopher, lab. r. 80 N. Railroad
Hartman Frederick, wagonmaker 377 Virginia av. r. 479 E. Georgia
Hartman Henry, lab. Central depot, r. 13 N. Union
Hartman Henry, packer Kiefer & Vinton, r. 123 N. New Jersey
Hartman Herman, porter Screrin & Schnull, bds. 119 N. New Jersey
Hartman Mathew, plasterer, r. 262 N. Alabama
Hartman W. carpenter C. Miller, r. 77 Way
Hartman W. compositor, bds. 213 N. Pennsylvania
Hartnett Patrick E. (O'Hara & Hartnett) bds. 101 S. Illinois
Hartney Michael, lab. r. rear 242 S. Mississippi
Hartpence Walter, fruit dealer, r. 48 W. Market
Hartrot Hermann, saloon 249 W. South, r. same
Hartstein Marks, clk. J. & M. Solomon, r. 25 S. Illinois
Hartrodt Charles, cooper, r. 182 Blake
Harvey Alfred, telegraph operator, r. 205 W. McCarty
Harvey Alonzo D. ins. agt. r. 73 N. Liberty
Harvey James R. bricklayer, r. 302 Blake
Harvey Jonathan S. (Harvey & Horn) pres. Indiana Fire Ins. Co. room 5 Odd Fellows Hall, r. 23 E. New York
Harvey Marion, teacher Fifth Ward School, bds. 169 N. Illinois
Harvey Silas L. deputy County Clerk, bds. 230 E. New York
HARVEY THOMAS B. physician and surgeon 58 E. Market, r. 302 N. Delaware nw. cor. North
HARVEY & VAN HORN, (Jonathan S. Harvey and Nicholas Van Horn) lawyers 101 E. Washington cor. Delaware
Hartwell E. chief clerk Bates House, bds. same
Hartwig John, porter, Crossland, Hanna & Co. r. 290 S. Alabama
Harwood Alice Miss, dressmaker S.A. Mulliken, r. 67 Madison av.

HAR	152	FAU

Harwood Irwin M. cabinetmaker, r. 67 Madison av.
Haselbeck Chris, r. 86 Eddy
Haskit William I. (W. I. Haskit & Co.) r. 647 N. Meridian
HASKIT W. I. & CO. (William I. Haskit, E. B. Martindale and S. A. Craig) 14 W. Washington
Haslep Isiah, mechanic, r. 255 Virginia av.
Haslup J. D. machinist, C. C. & I. C. R. R.
Hass Louis, hackman, r. Court bet. East and New Jersey
Hassalbirg Chris, lab. Rolling Mill
Hasselman J. W. student Bryant & Stratton's College, bds. Meridian cor. Vermont
Hasselman Otto H. mer. broker, Meridian sw. cor. Vermont
Hasselt Ernest, varnisher Spiegel & Thoms
Haslinger Leonard, blacksmith, r. 578 E. Washington
Hassman Henry, car cleaner, T. H. & I. R. R.
Hasson C. E. clk. Isaac Davis & Co.
Hasson Charles, r. 423 N. New Jersey
Hasson James, sec. Builders and Mfrs. Association, r. 423 N. New Jersey
Hasson William with Patterson, Moore & Talbot, r. 444 N. Meridian
Hastings Edwin L. supt. Journal office, r. 550 N. Illinois
Hasty John, line repairer W. U. T. Co. r. 239 S. Delaware
Hatfield James, bds. 774 N. Tennessee
Hathaway Alfred, (col'd) hostler Gates, Pray & Co. r. 130 N. East
Hathaway E. W. painter, r. Indiana av. opp. toll gate
Hatney J. Mrs. r. 162 S. Illinois
Hattendorf Henry, mer. tailor 317 E. Washington, r. same
Hattman John G. lab. r. Noble nw. cor. North
Hatton Ellmaza, milliner E. Kirk, bds. 75 N. Pennsylvania
Hatton Florence, dressmaker S. Coles, r. 313 E. Georgia
Haubold Nicholas, locksmith C. Kindler, bds. 326 S. Delaware
Hauck John (John Hauck & Co.) r. 373 N. East
Hauck John & Co. (John Hauck and John Darby) Farmers' Grocery 11 W. Washington
Haueisen Robert, salesman Charles Mayer & Co. bds. 32 N. Mississippi
Haueisen William, (Charles Mayer & Co.) r. 32 N. Mississippi
Hauf Henry, boilermkr. Eagle Machine Works, bds. Cumberland bet. New Jersey and Alabama
Hauf Valentine, expressman, r. 138 N. Davidson
Haufler John, machinist Helwig & Co. r. 452 Indiana av.
Haugh Adam, r. 208 N. Alabama
Haugh Alex. finisher B. F. Haugh & Co. bds. 244 E. Vermont
Haugh Benjamin F. (B. F. Haugh & Co.) r. 504 N. Pennsylvania
Haugh Emanuel, bookkeeper B. F. Haugh & Co. r. 244 E. Vermont
Haugh Joseph R. (B. F. Haugh & Co.) and cashier Citizens' Nat. Bank r. 175 N. New Jersey
Haugh Wm. A. finisher B. F. Haugh & Co. bds. 244 E. Vermont

HAUGH B. F. & CO. (B. F. Haugh and J. R. Haugh) mnfrs. of wrought and cast iron railing, 74 S. Pennsylvania

HAUGHEY THEODORE P. pres. Indianapolis National Bank, r. 242 N. Pennsylvania

Hauk John, bartender Fred. Dietz, r. 255 E. Washington

Hauk Nick, moulder D. Root & Co.

Haupt Robert, notions 151 E. Washington, r. 17 Chatham

Hausbrook John, cigarmkr. bds 301 N. Pennsylvania

Hanshill C. compositor Gutenberg Co.

Hansoman John W. agt. bds. 19 N. East

Havens Ann wid. Churchill, r. 191½ W. Washington

Hawk William V. (Dury & Hawk) r. College av. ne. city limits

Hawkey Nathan B. bricklayer, r. 138 N. Winston

Hawking Eliza J. Miss, r. 173 Jackson

Hawkins James, engineer Spiegel & Thoms, bds. 189 Virginia av.

Hawkins Jesse F. salesman J. L. Sailors, r. 268 N. Blake

Hawkins John, carpenter, r. 186 Meek

Hawkins Mary Mrs. (col'd) r. 116 Ash

Hawkins Mattie wid. William, r. 6, 3d floor Martindale's Block

Hawkins Thomas (col'd) barber W. Porter, r. 221 N. Missouri

HAWKINS WILLIAM M. propr. Sherman House, Louisiana opp. Union Depopt, r. same

Hawkins William M. Jr. first clk. Sherman House, r. same

Hawley Louisa D. Miss, Matron Institute for the Blind, r. same

Hawley Philoma W. Miss, teach. Institute for the Blind, r. same

Hawthorn Charles E. r. 132 N. Alabama

Hawthorn Nancy A. wid. William, r. 188 E. Washington

Hay Campbell, (Hay & Co.) 79 E. St. Joseph

Hay John C. bkpr. William Sumner & Co. bds. Sherman House

Hay Lawrence G. rec. sinking fund State Auditor's office, r. 128 S. Meridian

HAY WILLIAM H. general agent Charter Oak Life Ins. Co. of Hartford, Conn. 6 Blackford's blk. r. 222 N. Tennessee

HAY & CO. (C. Hay and E. A. Goble) druggists, 48 W. Washington

Hayden John, r. 378 N. Meridian

Hayden William, (col'd) lab. r. 47 Peru

Hayer Charles, r. 317 S. Pennsylvania

Hayes John, fireman C. C. & I. C. R. R.

Hayes T. (Indianapolis Paper Co.) r. 83 W. St. Clair

Hayes Thomas, with T. F. Ryan, r. 83 W. St. Clair

Haynes William, printer W. & J. Braden, bds. Oriental House

Haynes Charles, clk. Landers, Conduitt & Co. r. 129 E. Walnut

Haynes Charles, clk. r. Morrison 3 e. of Delaware

Haynes George E. student Bryant & Stratton's College, bds. 169 N. Illinois

Haynes James, (col'd) bathtender George M. D. Mitchell

Haynes Martha, wid. r. 39 Elm

Haynes Philip, confectioner, r. 169 N. Illinois

Haynes Thomas, fishdealer, bds. 24 W. Pearl

Haynes William, cooper, r. 20 N. California

HAY	154	HEI

Hays B. S. portrait painter, room 24 Talbott & New's blk. r. 41 Madison av.

Hays David, wks. J. Marsee & Son, r. 135 Huron

Hays E. M. (Hays, Rosenthal & Co.) r. 223 E. Ohio

Hays Frank H. r. 340 N. Alabama

Hays Isaac C. (Snyder & Hays) r. 340 N. Alabama

Hays John, lab. Rolling Mill, bds. 454 S. Illinois

Hays Samuel, r. 281 Indiana av.

Hays Walter, carpenter, r. 281 Indiana av.

HAYS, ROSENTHAL & CO. (E. M. Hays, Henry and Moses Rosenthal) clothing wholesale, 64 S. Meridian

Haywood A. (Haywood & Co.) r. 237 E. Washington

HAYWOOD & CO. (A. Haywood and Henry Roney) artificial limbs, 172 E. Washington

Hazelton William H. clk. r. 348 N. Alabama

Hazelrig ——, auctioneer, bds. 30½ N. Pennsylvania

Hazleden Charles, shoemaker J. A. Chives, r. 63 Indiana av.

Hazleton W. H. clerk Joseph Wiggins

Hazzard Wiley, Ins. agt. No. 2 Blake blk. bds. 112 N. Penn.

HAZZARD SAMUEL P. western frt. agt. B. & O. R. R. 100 Virginia av. r. 166 N. West

Head Charles N. clerk Commercial Hotel, bds. same

Heaf August, propr. New York Dye House, 65 N. Illinois, r. same

Healy Jeremiah, hodcarrier, r. 68 Coburn

Healy Morris, plasterer, r. 223 Dougherty

Healy Patrick, Rolling Mill, r. 252 S. Tennessee

Hearth A. saddler, bds. Pyle House

Hearth Henry, carpenter, r. 248 W. New York

Heath A. G. salesman Carr & Alvey, bds. 548 N. Tennessee

Heath John, r. 35 Chatham

Heath Sylvester, student, r. 35 Chatham

Heaton Eli, r. 378 Indiana av.

Hebble W. propr. Bicking House, 89 S. Illinois, r. same

Heck Peter, tilecutter Drotz & Steinhauer, r. 119 Buchanan

Heckman C. (Heckman & Sheesley) r. 413 E. Washington

Heckman Henry, lab. r. 282 N. Liberty

HECKMAN & SHEESLEY, (C. Heckman & Eli Sheesley) millers, 354 E. Washington

Hedden Albert, carpenter, bds. 144 N. Tennessee

Hedderich Peter, cabinetmaker, r. 231 N. Noble

Heddrech John, cabinetmaker, r. 120 N. Noble

Hedgepeth John, (col'd) lab. Union Novelty Works, r. 206 W. 2d

Hedges Elijah, foreman William W. Weaver, r. 39 N. Illinois

Hedges Francis M. lab. r. 317 W. Washington

Hedges James, wks. Emerson, Beam & Thompson, r. 140 N. Tennessee

Hedrich John, machinist Spiegel & Thoms r. 120 N. Noble

Hefkin Samuel, billiards, bds. 18 W. Georgia

Hehl John, Ins. agt. r. 178 E. Washington

Heiber T. L. clerk John Furnas & Co. r. 408 N. New Jersey

Heid Frederick, butcher, 59 N. Noble, r. National rd.

| HEI | 155 | HEL |

Heid John, butcher F. Heid, bds. National rd.
Heid Louis, butcher, r. 171 N. Spring
Heider Hermann, wks. E. F. Steffens, r. 200 W. Washington
Heider Paulina, wid. Julius, r. 200 E. Washington
Heidlinger John A. manfr. and dealer in cigars and tobacco, 39 W. Washington, r. 14 N. Mississippi
Heidmann W. cabinet maker P. Dohn
Heihmann Mathias, saw filer, 63 S. Pennsylvania, bds. California House
Heim Henry C. butcher, r. Washington, cor. Michigan rd.
Heim Jacob F. Washington, cor Michigan rd.
Heim John R. Washington, cor. Michigan rd.
Heiman Robinson, peddler, r. 191 N. Liberty
Hein Charles, lab. r. 160 N. Liberty
Heinbuch Henry, lab. r. 287 N. Noble
Heins Henry, butcher John Gorger & Bro.
Heiner Andrew, watchman, r. 60 S. Noble
Heiner George P. r. 38 Christian av.
Heiner John, engineer Charles Glazier, r. Bradshaw
Heiney Henry, shoemaker A Knodle, r. 304 Virginia av.
Heinrichs Charles, porter Severin & Schnull
Heinrich Joseph, wks. Cabinet Makers' Union
Heiser Charles, saloon, 76 S. Delaware, r. same
Heiser Henry, plasterer, r. 356 N. Noble
Heiser John, r. 350 Railroad
Heiser William L. carpenter, r. 113 N. Davidson
Heiskell William S. dentist, rooms 13, 14, 15 and 16 (2d floor) Martindale's blk. bds Pyle House
Heisler Jacob, lab. I. C. & L. R. R.
Heisler John lab. rear 43 Harrison
HEISSER JACOB H. agt. for brushes, locks, moulders' tools, blow pipes, 24 N. Pennsylvania, r. 508 N. Mississippi
Heitcomb John, musician, r. 87 S. Pennsylvania
Heitkam George H. merchant tailor, 8 W. Washington, r. 154 N. Winston
Heitkam Henry, barber Henry Goetig, r. 310 E. New York
Heitkam John, cabinet maker, Cabinet Makers' Union, r. 112 N. Noble
Heitz Louis, file grinder Drotz & Steinhauer, r. 62 Hosbrook
HEIZER CYRUS C. township trustee, office 13 & 14 N. Delaware, r. 78 Lockerbie
Helcher Charles, carpenter, r. 72 Coburn
Held Louis, machinist Eagle Machine Works, r. 165 S. Meridian
Helle Louis, painter and glazier, 248 S. Pennsylvania, r. same
Heller Jacob, cabinet maker C. Williams, r 40 Douglas
Heller James E. ins agt. bds. 109 Virginia av.
Helley John, fireman Gas Works
Hellmick John, r. 347 N. New Jersey
Helm Adam, carpenter and builder, North nr. cor. Liberty, r. 296 N. Liberty
Helm Henry, stonemason, r. Washington east of limits

Helm John, grocer, 272 Winston, r. same

Helman Mary, wid. Michael, r. 18 S. East

Helman Michael, lab. r. 18 S. East

Helmich George, baker A. Balls, bds. 178 S. Illinois

Helmick John, porter P. O. r. 347 N. New Jersey

Helms Lewis A. (Kilgore & Helms) bds. 31 W. Ohio

Helms Thomas M. chairmkr. r. 107 N. Noble

Helmstetter John, tailor, r. 221 W. Washington

Helt Aug. machinist Spiegel & Thoms

Helton James, gunsmith, bds. 149 Winston

Helwig Charles, (Helwig & Co. r. 224 W. New York

Helwig Charles & Co. (Charles Helwig, George E. Woodman and T. M. Jackson) furniture mnfrs. and dealers, 115 and 117 E. Washington, factory New York cor. Canal

Hemrich Henry, cabinetmkr. r. 109 N. Davidson

Henderson James, fireman I. C. & L. R. R. bds. Ray House

Henderson John, (Henderson & Bass) r. 168 N. East

Henderson William, pres. Indianapolis Ins. Co. r. 134 N. Meridian

Henderson William, porter J. K. Marot

Henderson William J. spoke turner, r. 404 S. Missouri

HENDERSON WILLIAM R. attorney at law and notary public, Indianapolis Ins. Co.'s bldg. es. Pennsylvania bet. Washington and Maryland, bds. 134 N. Meridian

Henderson & Bass, (John Henderson and Joseph Bass) flour and feed store, 145 N. Delaware

Hedricks Abram W. (Hendricks, Hord & Hendricks) r. 296 N. Meridian

Hendricks J. Blythe, prescription clk. W. I. Haskit & Co. r. 331 N. Pennsylvania

Hendricks James C. carpenter, r. ws. Blake bet. New York and Vermont

Hendricks Michael, lab. r. 385 E. Ohio

Hendricks Sarah E. wid. James, r. 175 E. South

Hendricks Thomas A. (Hendricks, Hord & Hendricks) r. East s. of city limits

Hendricks Victor K. (Hendricks, Edmunds & Co.) r. Meridian ne. cor. Pratt

HENDRICKS, EDMUNDS & CO. (Victor K. Hendricks, William Edmunds and T. S. Stone) boots and shoes whol. 56 S. Meridian

HENDRICKS, HORD & HENDRICKS, (Thomas A. and Abram W. Hendricks and Oscar B. Hord) attorneys at law, 24½ E. Washington

Hendrix D. M. (Hendrix & Koerner) National Business College, bds. 20½ N. Pennsylvania

Hendrix James, carpenter Shover & Christian

Hendrix & Koerner, (D. M. Hendrix and Conrad Koerner) in charge A. Hollingsworth & Co.'s National Business College, entrance 24½ E. Washington

Henleng Bernard, tailor, r. 225 Winston

Hennegar M. machinist Sinker & Co.

T. B. PERRINE, Engraver on Wood and Metal, 34 Virginia av.

HEN   157   HER

Henneman Anton, medical student Dr. J. Hale, r. 52 N. Illinois
Hennessy Daniel, lab. **r. 270 S. Alabama**
Hennessey Jerry, lab. bds. 213 S. Tennessee
Hennessey John, lab. r. 14 Walter
Hennessey John, switchman T. H. & I. R. R. bds. 217 S. Illinois
Hennessey Patrick, lab. r. ws. Union, 3 n of limits
Henning Fred. A. barber Vondergotton & Satorius, 357 E. Market
Henning G. F. german clerk P. O. r. Wabash, bet. Noble and Liberty
Henning H. R. carpenter Hubert Reeker, r. 357 E. Market
Henninger Edward, (G. & E. Henninger) r. 115 S. Illinois
Henninger Gustavus, (G. & E. Henninger) r. 115 S. Illinois
HENNINGER G. & E. (Gustavus and Edward Henninger) groceries and fancy goods, 115 S. Illinois
Hennis Sarah, laundress Institute for the Blind, r. same
Henri Guidio, plasterer, r. 528 N. Mississippi
Henry Anna, wid. George, r. 141 N. Noble
Henry Charles G. compositor *Sentinel* news room, bds. Little's Hotel
Henry Francis, milliner E. Kirk, bds. 75 N. Pennsylvania
Henry George W. salesman Kennedy, Byram & Co. bds. Sherman House
Henry J. printer, bds. Little's Hotel
Henry Joseph, lab. r. ss. Cherry, bet. Plum and Oak
Henry John, lab. Osgood, Smith & Co.
Henry Lawrence, lab. r. 286 S. East
Henry Marshall G. comp. *Journal* news room, r. 322 E. Market
Henry Peter, lab. Osgood, Smith & Co. r. 282 S. East
Henry W. lab. bds. Western House
Henschen Franz, lab. Woolen Mill, r. al. nr. 131 Union
HENSCHEN WILLIAM H. carpenter and builder 252 E. South, r. same
Hensel Samuel T. carpenter, r. 485 S. Illinois
Henshaw Jerry, (col,d) lab. r. 81 S. Missouri
Hensley James, carpenter Greenleaf & Co.
Hensley John T. carpenter, r. Merrill, 1 w. of East
Henson Peter, shoemaker, bds. 258 S. Delaware
Hentges Joseph, lab. D. Root & Co.
Hepp, John K. carpenter, r. ss. E. Michigan, 2 e. Liberty
Hereth Ad. saddle and harness maker and dealer in whips, collars &c. 24 N. Delaware, r. same
Hereth John C. harness and saddle maker, r. 268 N. Alabama
Hereth John G. carpenter, r. 263 N. East
Hereth Peter, carpenter, r. 64 Bates
Hereth Philip, harnessmakr. r. 161 Davidson
Hering Philip, pianotuner, r. 269 S. New Jersey
Herken Christian, bds. Jefferson House
Herman Charles, r. ws. Douglas 4 s. New York
Heroff P. watchman, r. 155 N. Spring
Herr John, carpenter, bds. 31 S. Illinois

HER	158	HET

Herrmann F. J. (F. J. Herrmann & Son) r. 272 E. Market

Herrmann Gabrel (F. J. Herrmann & Son) r. 272 E. Market

Herrmann George, cabinetmkr. wks. Cabinet Makers' Union, r. Ohio east of limits

Herrmann Ignatz, lab. r. 328 S. Delaware

Herrmann Jacob, carpenter Union Starch Factory, r. 277 N. Winston

Herrmann John, cabinetmkr. Cabinet Makers' Union

Hermann John, lab. r. 222 Winston

HERRMANN F. J. & SON (F. J. Herrmann and Gabrel Herrmann) undertakers 36 S. Delaware

Herreth Henry, carpenter Hill & Wingate, r. 241 W. New York

Herreth Peter, carpenter Hill & Wingate, r. 64 Bates

Herring Philip, tuner Sochner & Benham

Herrorn F. M. (McLene & Horrorn) r. 416 N. Illinois

Herron Michael, lab. r. 27 S. Alabama

Hershey John W. varnisher, r. 249 W. McCarty

Herspel Andy, butcher J. Roos, r. W. Georgia

Hert William, engineer, r. 383 E. Michigan

Hertweck Lucas, r. Tennessee cor. McCauley

Herzsch Ferdinand, modelmkr. Charles Werbe, bds. Alabama cor. Court

Hesler Jacob, lab. r. 122 S. Noble

Hespelt Charles (Hespelt & Co.) r. 150 W. Vermont

Hespelt & Co. (Charles Hespelt and William Giesendanner) bakers and confectioners 150 W. Vermont

Hess August, bookbinder, r. 126 W. Ohio

Hess Casper, lab. Sinker & Co.

Hess Charles, principal Normal Academy of Music, r. 263 S. Meridian

HESS CHARLES M. A. special agt. Providence Life and Trust Company 8 E. Washington, r. 263 S. Meridian. See margin side lines

Hess E. Aug. bookbinder Meikel Bros. r. 126 W. Ohio

Hess Godfrey, lab. r. 126 W. Ohio

Hess Gustave, confectioner, r. 288 Madison av.

Hess J. W. supt. G. E. Gordon, r. 385 N. Illinois

Hess Julius, bds. 26 W. Washington

Hesse George, cabinetmaker, r. 376 Virginia av.

Heston Charles R. r. 309 E. New York

Heston Thomas, (cold') lab. r. 179 Eddy

Hetherington B. F. (B. F. Hetherington & Co.) r. 264 S. Pennsylvania

Hetherington Christopher, machinist I. C. & L. Rw. r. 101 Bates

HETHERINGTON B. F. & CO. (B. F. Hetherington, F. Berner and J. Kindel) foundry and machine shops, 244 S. Pennsylvania

Hetselgesser Lucian W. (L. W. Hetselgesser & Co.) bds. 595 E. Washington

Hetselgesser Samuel, (L. W. Hetselgesser & Co.) r. 595 E. Washington

HETSELGESSER L. W. & CO. (L. W. and S. Hetselgesser) South Side livery and sale stable, South nw. cor. Illinois

Hewes Charles W. pres. Indianapolis Female Institute, r. Michigan ne. cor. Pennsylvania

Hewes Charles W. Jr. salesman Bowen, Stewart & Co. r. Michigan ne. cor. Pennsylvania

Hewling Clara, wid. Alexander, r. 233 N. West

Hewy M. S. foreman varnisher Spiegel & Thoms

HEYMANN HERMAN, wholesale dealer in wines, liquors, cigars, etc. 193 W. Washington, r. 18 S. Mississippi

Hiatt Naomi S. teacher Indiana Deaf and Dumb Institute, r. E. Washington out of limits

Hibbard Horace W. general frt. agent T. H. & I. R. R. bds. Bates House

Hibben Ethelbert C. r. 176 N. East

Hibben James S. (Hibben, Tarkington & Co.) r. 435 N. Tennessee

HIBBEN, TARKINGTON & CO. (J. S. Hibben, W. C. Tarkington, C. B. Pattison, W. S. Webb and Augustus E. Pattison) dry goods and notions wholesale, 112 S. Meridian

Hickey James, driver Citizens' Street R. R. Co.

Hickey Joseph, stonecutter, r. 30 Grant

Hickey John, lab: r. 23 Willard

Hickman John W. r. 126 Blackford

Hicks Charles, farmer, r. rear 19 Maria

Hicks D. C. carpenter, r. 125 Broadway

Hicks Frances, wid. M. W. r. 79 W. South

Hicks Joseph M. patent rights, r. 175 Eddy

Hieber Theodore, elk. r. 408 N. New Jersey

Hiedmerich Chris. tailor, r. 130 Huron

Hierholzer Benjamin, carpenter, bds. Washington House

Hiener Sarah Miss, hoopskirtmaker Pauline Newman, r. 60 S. Noble

Hiet George, cooper A. L. Ferguson, r. 378 E. Georgia

Hiet Louis, meat market 71 S. Noble, r. 171 Spring

Higdon William, r. East s. of limits

Higel Christian, woolworker, r. 175 E. Washington

Higgins Charles J. (Asher, Adams & Higgins) r. 15 E. Ohio

Higgins Mary Miss, waiter Institute for the Blind, r. same

Higgins Monroe, porter, r. 289 E. New York

Higgins Patrick H. r. 286 E. Louisiana

Higgins William, paperhanger W. H. Roll, r. 426 N. Meridian

Higgins William, roller Barker, Williams & Co.

Higgins, William, tobacconist, bds. 121 W. New York

Higgins William B. silverplater 8 W. Washington, r. Plum bet. Vine and Cherry

Highland Conley, cabinetmaker, r. 31 Bradshaw

High School, W. A. Bell, prin. Circle nw cor. Market

Hight Ferdinand, actor Academy of Music, r. 196 N. Mississippi

Hight William, (col'd) teamster, r. 338 W. North

Hildebrand Clayton S. watchmaker McLene & Herron, r. 51 Madison av.

Hildebrand Henry W. (Hildebrand, Keppele & Co.) r. 308 N. Delaware

Hildebrand John J. clk. H. Bowker & Co. r. Virginia av. cor. Delaware

HILDEBRAND, KEPPELE & CO. (H. W. Hildebrand, John Keppele and Milton Hoover) saw mill and lumber yard, office Indiana av. cor. Canal. See advertisement

Hilden Minnie, dressmaker Marshall & Sweeney, r. Mississippi cor. North

Hilderbrand Jacob S. (J. H. Vajen & Co.) r. 51 Madison av.

Hilderbrand John, clk. bds. 304 N. Pennsylvania

Hiles Isaac, carpenter, bds. 126 N. Tennessee

Hilgemeyer Christian, (C. Hilgemeyer & Co.) r. 41 Wyoming

Hilgemeyer Christian & Co. (C. Hilgemeyer and D. Megge) groceries ret. 367 S. Delaware

Hilger Christian, tailor 42 S. Liberty, r. same

Hilkenbach Wm. porter Wiles, Bro. & Co. r. 494 N. Mississippi

Hilkene Jacob, clk r. 163 E. St. Joseph

Hilker Henry, gardener Institute for the Blind, r. 124 E. St. Joseph

Hill A. whitewasher, r. Vine sw. cor. Plum

Hill Ellison C. (Hill & Vinnedge) r. 577 N. Tennessee

Hill Frank, stock dealer, r. 50 Cherry

Hill George W. (Hill & Wingate) r. 110 S. East

Hill J. B. grocer 192 E. Washington, r. in country

Hill James, (col'd) barber Hill & Carter, r. 190 Missouri

Hill James, groceries ret. New York ne. cor. Douglas, r. same

Hill James R. paperhanger, r. 314 N. New Jersey

Hill John B. artist, bds. 84 N. Alabama

Hill John F. propr. Beechwood Nurseries, r. 84 N. Alabama

Hill John F. (col'd) (Hill & Carter) r. 756 N. Tennessee

Hill Nathan, lab, r. 72 Massachusetts av.

Hill Samuel, printer *Journal* job room, r. 183 W. New York

Hill W. O. r. 40 N. Pennsylvania

Hill & Carter, (John F. Hill & Edward Carter) barber shop, 14 N. Illinois

Hill & Vinnedge, (E. C. Hill & G. W. Vinnedge) dealers in boots and shoes, 3 W. Washington

HILL & WINGATE, (George W. Hill and William L. Wingate) planing mill and mnfrs. of sash, doors and blinds, East se. cor. Georgia

Hillis Jennie Miss, music teacher, bds. 346 N. Meridian

Hillman Frederick, section boss, r. 36 Walter

Hillman Charles, carpenter Eagle Machine Works, r. 32 Walter

Hillman John, drayman Wiles Bro. & Co. r. 238 Union

Hillman Joseph, stove moulder A. D. Wood

Hillman S. wid. Noah, r. 298 S. Illinois

Hillman William, blacksmith, 377 Virginia av. r. 44 Walter

Hillman William, porter J. E. Robertson & Co. r. 225 Bluff rd.

Hills Lucien, gen'l frt. agt. C. C. C. & I. R. R. office 53 S. Alabama, r. 208 N. Illinois
Hilt August, lab. r. 287 Davidson
Hilt Frank L. machinist B. F. Haugh & Co. r. 159 N. Spring
Hiltebrand Jacob M. marble cutter, r. 317 Indiana av.
Hiltebrand Molissa, groceries and confectionery, 46 Massachusetts av. r. same
Hiltebrand William, groceries, 46 Massachusetts av. r. same
Hine William, moulder D. Root & Co.
Hindman Robert F. news stand Palmer House, bds. same
Hinds Frank, bricklayer, bds 63 E. St. Clair
Hinds Jesse, bricklayer, r. 83 E. St. Clair
Hinds Robert M. bricklayer, r. 83 E. St. Clair
Hine Charles, machinist Spiegel & Thoms
Hine Henry, painter C. C. C. & I. R. R.
Hine Henry, shoemaker, r. 304 Virginia av.
Hiner F. fireman C. C. C. & I. R. R.
Hines Andrew, lab. r. 321 Davidson
Hines C. wks. J. S. Carey & Co.
HINES CYRUS C. Judge Civil Circuit Court, office room 6, 14 N. Delaware, r. 428 N. Tennessee
Hines Henry, lab. r. Minerva nw. cor. Michigan
Hines Sarah J. wid. John, r. 79 N. California
Hinesley Andrew Jackson, produce shipper, r. 491 N. Tennessee
Hinesley William, prop. Exchange Stables, 35 N. Illinois, r. 469 N. Tennessee
Hinkle Christopher, spinner Merritt & Coughlen
Hinkley Oliver W. bookkeeper Indianapolis Branch Banking Co. rooms 8 Vinton blk.
Hinninger Michael, machinist, r. 295 S. East
Hinsdale E. milliner, 197 W. Washington, r. same
Hinsley A. J. (Budd & Hinsley) r. 491 N. Tennessee
Hinton James S. (col'd) barber, r. 229 N. West
Hipler William, peddler, r. 409 S. East
Hirch Nathan, stock dealer, r. 139 N. Delaware
Hirt Albert, sawmkr. Sheffield Saw Works, r. 383 S. Illinois
Hische John, printer, bds. 135 E. Washington
Hitchcock Alexander, r. 186 E. St. Joseph
Hitchcock Jesse, teamster Coburn & Jones
Hitchen T. G. bookkeper Charles Glazier, r. 267 S. New Jersey
Hitchens John, horseshoer, 44 E. Maryland, r. 126 Christian av.
Hitchins John, blacksmith, r. 126 Broadway
Hite Charles W. machinist r. 82 N. Market
Hite William, (col'd) lab. Builders and Mnfrs. Association
Hoagland G. wks. J. S. Carey & Co.
Hoagland Israel, dealer in patent rights, 16½ S. Meridian, r. New York nw. cor. Bright
Hoagland Jacob, farmer, r. LaFayette rd.
Hoagland John, wks. J. S. Carey & Co.
Hoagland John B. messenger Am. Ex. r. 389 N. West
Hoagland William, wks. J. S. Carey & Co.

11

Hobbs Barnabas C. supt. Public Instruction, 45 N. Tennessee, r. 187 E. Ohio
Hobbs Charles, clk. bds. 70 E. Market
Hobbs Solomon, prod. dealer, 49 S. New Jersey, r. 384 N. West
Hobbs William H. clk. dept. Public Instruction, r. 187 E. Ohio
Hochstotter Christian, pastor German Lutheran Church, r. Ohio cor. East
Hocket Benjamin, r. Rockwood near River
Hockey Samuel, lab. Bunte, Dickson & Co.
Hocksmith Thomas, r. 136 S. Noble
Hockstein Christian, lab. Rolling Mill, r. 166 Union
Hodapp William, pianomaker, bds. 18 S. Delaware
Hodge Joseph, carpenter, r. 81 E. McCarty
Hodges Ambrose, carpenter, r. 267 Davidson
Hodges James, r. 127 Huron
HODGSON ISAAC, architect, room 1-2 Brown's block, Washington, nw. cor. Pennsylvania, r. 433 N. Illinois
Hodgson Thomas, paper hanger, r. 119 Massachusetts av.
Hodler Gottlieb, porter Kiefer & Vinton, r. McCarty
Hoefgen Emanuel, janitor Gymnasium Billiard Hall, r. 64 Indiana av.
Hoefgen S. B. 16½ E. Washington, bds. 18 W. Georgia
Hoefler G. A. R. piano maker Indianapolis Piano Mnfrg Co. r. 178 S. Illinois
Hoereth John L. clk. A. Metzger, r. 155 Spring
Hoerner Emanuel, turner, r. 35 W. Georgia
Hofacker Charles, bakery 277 N. Noble, r. same
Hofecker Gotlieb, shoemaker, r. 70 Virginia av.
Hoff James D. painter, r. 309 E. New York
Hoff Louis, puddler rolling mill, r. 270 Madison
Hoffenberther Kate, wks. Cotton Factory
Hoffer George, shoemaker, r. 392 S. Missouri
Hoffman Ephraim, wagonmkr. r. 383 S. Delaware
Hoffman George W. student Bryant & Stratton's College, bds. 263 E. Washington
Hoffman Henry, shoemaker, 122 S. Illinois, r. 173 Bluff rd.
Hoffman John H. tannner, r. 263 E. Washington
Hoffman Man, wks. Emerson, Beam & Thompson
Hoffman Samuel, wks. Emerson, Beam & Thompson
Hoffman Caspar, r. 534 N. Alabama
HOFFMAN MAX F. A. Secretary of State, office State building, r. 80 N. New Jersey
Hoffman Michael, grocer, and saloon, 170 Bluff rd. r. same
Hoffman Philip, grocer and saloon, 775 N. Tennessee, r. same
Hoffman Valentine, lab. r. 110 S. Noble
Hoffmeyer Frederick, drayman, r. 224 Davidson
Hoffmeyer Henry, drayman. r. 195 N. Liberty
Hoffmeyer William, teamster City Brewery, r. 376 New York
Hoffner Samuel, checkman freight depot C. C. & I. C. R. R.
Hoffrogge Joseph, finisher B. F. Haugh & Co. r. 339 Virginia av.
Hofmeister Nicholas, grocer 150 N. Noble, r. same

Hogan Jane, wid. r. 380 S. West
Hogan Kate Mrs. forewoman Barker, Williams & Co.
Hogan Philip, r. 45 S. Illinois
Hogan Philip, r. 47 S. Illinois
HOGATE CHARLES F. collector Internal Revenue, office room 15 Post Office Bldg. bds. Palmer House
Hogerty Michael, stone cutter, r. 225 Virginia av.
Hogle Samuel N. wagonmaker, bds. Stanridge House
Hogshire William R. (W. R. Hogshire & Co.) r. 287 N. Meridian
HOGSHIRE W. R. & CO. (W. R. Hogshire, Earl Reid and J. F. Council) boots and shoes retail 25 W. Washington
Hohl C. G. bookkeeper Hahn & Bals, r. 265 Massachusetts av.
Hohmann Bertha, cigar maker V. Hohmann, bds. 74 Virginia av.
Hohmann Louis, cigar maker V. Hohmann, bds. 74 Virginia av.
Hohmann V. cigars and tobacco, 51 S. Illinois, r. 74 Virginia av.
Hoke Lewis A. salesman J. H. Vajen & Co. bds. Macy House
Holbrook Henry C. (Ryan & Holbrook) r. 314 W. New York
Holbrook Preston, (D. Cady & Co.) r. 293 S. New Jersey
Holbrook Thomas E. r. 157 N. Alabama
Holden J. M. r. 93 S. Noble
Holderman J. M. salesman H. Daumont & Co.
Holer Philip, watchman C. C. & I. C. R. R.
Holern Thomas, lab. r. 160 Meek
Holl William H. driver 71 W. Washington
Holla William, r. 228 Madison av.
Holland Arsa, box maker Pfaendler & Zogg, r. 239 S. Mississippi
Holland Charles, fireman C. C. C. & I. R. R.
Holland Charles, farmer, bds. 393 Massachusetts av.
Holland Emma, dressmaker Mrs. N. M. Allen
Holland George B. r. 126 W. Sixth
Holland George G. gardener, r. 771 N. Mississippi
Holland George L. painter, r. 44 Coburn
Holland Isaiah, r. 239 S. Mississippi
Holland J. pressman Indianapolis Printing & Publishing House
Holland John, carpenter, r. 303 S. Delaware
Holland John, car inspector T. H. & I. R. R.
Holland John, lab. r. 291 S. East
Holland John, Jr. clk. J. Cusick, bds. 303 S. Delaware
Holland John W. (Holland, Ostermeyer & Co.) r. 112 W. Pennsylvania
Holland Theodore F. bookkeeper Holland, Ostermeyer & Co. r. 383 N. Illinois
Holland Thomas, lab. C. & I. J. R. R.
HOLLAND, OSTERMEYER & CO. (J. W. Holland and F. Ostermeyer) wholesale grocers, 27 and 29 E. Maryland
Holle Charles, lab. Rolling Mill, r. 146 Union
Holle Herman C. stonemason, r. 343 E. Market
Hollenbeck C. E. principal Bryant & Stratton's Business College, bds. 169 N. Illinois
Holler August, piano forte maker J. H. Kappes & Co.
Holler George P. cabinetmaker, bds. 348 N. Alabama

Holler Gottlieb, hostler Charles Brinkman
Holler Philip, r. 205 N. Noble
Holler Philip H. stonemason, r. 349 N. Noble
Holler William, cabinetmaker, r. 292 S. Illinois
Holliday Cort F. (W. & C. F. Holliday) r. 131 N. Meridian
Holliday E. teamster Ripley & Gates, r. 44 S. Illinois
Holliday Eliza Mrs. wid. r. 44 S. Illinois
Holliday F. C. pastor Roberts Chapel and editor *Western Fireside*,
	r. 131 N. Meridian
Holliday Francis T. clk. r. 242 N. Alabama
Holliday J. Duncan, clk. W. J. Holliday & Co. r. 398 N. Delaware
HOLLIDAY JOHN H. local editor *State Sentinel*, r. 242 N. Ala-
	bama
Holliday Lucia, wid. William, r. 242 N. Alabama
Holliday W. J. (W. J. Holliday & Co. and Murphy, Johnston &
	Co.) r. 131 N. Meridian
Holliday Wilbur, (W. & C. F. Holliday) r. 131 N. Meridian
Holliday William D. r. 398 N. Delaware
HOLLIDAY W. J. & CO. (W. J. Holliday, John W. Murphy, John
	A. Ferguson and Henry W. Voight) iron, steel, nails, springs,
	axles, bolts and blksmiths tools, 59 S. Meridian
HOLLIDAY W. & C. T. (Wilbur and Cort T. Holliday) wholesale
	dealers in lamps, oils, etc. 15 S. Meridian
Hollingsworth A. (Hollingsworth & Co.) r. Covington, Ky.
Hollingsworth Daniel, r. 286 E. St. Clair
Hollingsworth Jeph (Mills & Hollingsworth) bds. Nagel House
Hollingsworth A. & Co. (Hendrix & Koerner in charge) National
	Business College, entrance 24½ E. Washington
Hollis Edward, machinist, bds. Stanridge House
Hollis Ephram, clk. r. 172 Virginia av.
Hollis John E. machinist King & Pinney, bds. Wyles House
Hollman John, hostler Sullivan & Drew, bds. S. Pennsylvania
Holloway Allen, clerk P. O. bds. 119 W. Marylad
Holloway Henry C. money order clk. P. O. r. 432 N. Delaware
Holloway J. M. clerk P. O. bds. 4 S. Mississippi
HOLLOWAY WILLIAM R. (Douglass, Conner & Co.) and Post-
	master, r. 287 N. Alabama
Hollowell Amos K. bookkeeper Budd & Hensley, bds. 441 N.
	Mississippi
Hollowell Calvin, clerk E. Hollowell, bds. same
Hollowell Edwin, groceries and provisions, 430 W. Washington,
	(Nat. rd.) r. 404 W. New York
Hollweg Louis, china, glass and queensware whol. 90 S. Meri-
	dian, r. 213 N. Pennsylvania
Holly Henry, machinist, r. 428 S. East
Holly Martha, r 2d nr. LaFayette R. R.
Holly Theodore, shoemaker, r. es. Blake 5 s. New York
Hollywood Richard, White House Saloon, 66 W. Maryland, r.
	same
HOLMAN G. G. gen'l com. mer. 6 Bates House blk. r. ws. Wes-
	tern av. 2d house s. Tinker

T. B. PERRINE, Engraver on Wood and Metal, 34 Virginia av.

HOL   165   HOM

Holman John A. lawyer, room 12 Talbott & New's block, r. Western av. w. of limits
Holman Merritt S. salesman Merrill & Co. r. 163 N. Illinois
HOLMES ANDREW J. Sec. State Board Agriculture, office State House, bds. Bates House
Holmes Erastus, painter, r. 239 McCarty
Holmes Henry, r. 20 N. California
Holmes Henry A. plasterer, r. 64 S. California
Holmes James carpenter, r. 181 N. Liberty
Holmes John B. (Holmes & Rains) r. Holmes Station
Holmes Mary M. wid. Truesdel, dress and cloak maker, 30 S. Delaware
Holmes Sophia Miss, restaurant 75 S. Illinois, r. same
Holmes W. Canada, President Citizens' National Bank, r. Wayne Township
Holmes & Rains, (John B. Holmes and M. S. Rains) livery stable, 163 W. Washington
Holsbach John, cigarmaker A. W. Sharpe, bds. 32 N. Pennsylvania
Holscher Charles, cabinet maker Spiegel & Thoms
Holsker Benjamin, lab. frt. depot C. C. & I. C. R. R.
Holsker Henry, lab. frt. depot C. C. & I. C. R. R.
Holst John, lab. I. M. & I. frt. depot, r. 338 Madison av.
Holstein Charles L. (Elliott & Holstein) r. 155 N. Tennessee
Holstein Isaac, lab. r. 276 W. Washington
Holztein Louis, hostler Indianapolis Brewery
Holt Alexander, confectioner, 3 Indiana, av. r. same
Holt Charles, machinist, Eagle Machine Works
Holt J. F. clk. Indianapolis Gas Light and Coke Co. r East cor. Vermont
Holt Louisa, wid. Joshua, r. ns. Vermont bet. East and Liberty
Holt W. S. check clk. Star Union Line, bds. Meridian cor. Circle
Holtka Andrew, hostler, Ind. Transfer Co. bds. S. Delaware
Holtmann John H. lab. r. 335 N. Noble
Holtoof John, delivery clk. Express Office, bds. Pyle House
Holtz John, lab. J. M. & I. R. R.
Holtzkom Charles, harnessmkr. W. S. Marsh, r. 180 W. Washington
Holtzman Isaac, r. 223 S. West
Holzbacher August, cigarmkr. G. F. Mayer, bds. 86 Indiana av.
Holzwart Gottlieb (Holzwart & Wernbeck) r. 132 St. Joseph
Holzwart & Wernbeck (Gottlick Holzwart and George Wernbeck) blacksmiths Alabama bet. Washington and Market
Homan Jeremiah (W. J. & J. Homan) r. 130 S. East
Homan W. J. (W. J. & J. Homan) r. 130 S. East
Homan W. J. & J. (W. J. and Jeremiah Homan) cistern builders 82 W. Washington
Homburgh R. physician 194½ E. Washington, r. same
Homburgh William, clk. room 194½ E. Washington
Home Fire Ins. Co. of New York, E. B. Martindale agt. room 2, 2d floor, Martindale's Blk.

Home Insurance Co. of New Haven, Con. C. A. Biedenmeister agt. 96 E. Washington

HOME INSURANCE CO. OF NEW YORK, Henry H. Walker State agent, room 3, 2d floor, Martindale's Blk. Pennsylvanda ne. cor. Market

HOME LIFE INSURANCE CO. OF NEW YORK, Tobias M. Murphy general agt. room 9, 2d floor, Martindale's Blk.

Home Mutual Fire Ins. Co. of Indianapolis, Charles W. Smith, Jr. receiver No. 5 Yohn's Blk. Meridian ne. cor. Washington

Home of the Friendless, James Smith supt. N. Pennsylvania, n. of limits

Homes Joseph, carpenter Bœdeker & Niemann

Homyer Frederick, tinner C. Zimmerman, bds. 65 S. East

Homyer William, slater C. Zimmerman, bds. 65 S. East

Homuat Frederick, drayman, r. 3 Charles

Hook and Ladder Co. es. New Jersey bet. Market and Washington, J. H. Webster driver

Hooker Edwin, printer, r. 215 W. Michigan

Hooker H. wid. Henry, r. 258 S. Meridian

Hoosier State Flouring Mills, Geisendorf, Richardson & Co. propr. ns. W. Washington (Nat. Road) near bridge

Hoosier Woolen Factory, C. E. Geisendorff & Co. propr. ns. Washington (Nat. Road) near White river bridge

Hoover Daniel, grocer, r. 149 Blake cor. New York

Hoover Isaac N. telegraph operator C. C. C. & I. R. R. 53 S. Alabama, bds. 17½ Virginia av.

Hoover Jacob, farmer, r. 311 W. Washington

Hoover Jacob B. farmer, r. 503 N. Mississippi

Hoover John W. boiler maker, r. 241 N. Liberty

Hoover William H. (Buchanan & Hoover) r. 228 E. Louisiana

Hope Christenia, bds. ws. Blake 2 n. New York

Hope J. (col'd) porter Tutewiler & Bros. r. 300 E. Walnut

Hopkins David H. clk. county clerk's office, bds. 218 N. Alabama

Hopkins H. foreman bindery W. & J. Braden, r. 340 W. Washington

Hopkins Hannibal, grafter, r. 174 N. Davidson

Hopkins Henry C. (Martin, Hopkins & Ohr) also (Martin & Hopkins) r. 218 N. Alabama

Hopkins J. H. bookbinder, bds. 340 W. Washington

Hoppe George, propr. LaFayette House, 179 S. Meridian r. same

Hoppe John W. tinner R. L. & A. W. McOuat, r. 58 S. Hosbrook

Hoppe Louisa, wid. E. P. r. 54 S. California

Hoppe Louis M. carpenter, r. es. Jackson, 2 n. of Christian av.

Hoppe William, sawer Helwig & Co.

Hoppeng Fred. cabinet maker, bds. 65 S. East

Hoppeng William, cabinet maker, bds. 65 S. East

Horan Daniel, fireman C. C. C. & I. R. R.

Horan James, wagon maker, Washington junc. National rd. r. 36 Douglas

Hord Oscar B. (Hendricks, Hord & Hendricks) r. New York nw. cor. California

Horen James, stonecutter, r. 10 Willard
Horeth Adam, carpenter, r. 474 N. Alabama
Horn Henry J. salesman J. N. Conklin, r. 72 N. Mississippi
Horn Patrick, blacksmith C. C. & I. C. R. R.
Hornady John E. carpenter, r. 365 N. Alabama
Hornady Thomas B. policeman, r. 365 N. Alabama
Hornberger Andrew, wks. C. Kuhn, bds. same
Hornberger Christian, carpenter, r. 70 Jackson
Hornedy Thomas B. policeman, r. 365 N. Alabama
Horney Susan A. Mrs. matron Home of the Friendless, r. same
Horning John, brewer, r. 385 S. Delaware
Horsley Joseph, painter Ind. Coach Works, bds. 73 N. Illinois
Horst Hermann, tailor, r. 317 S. Pennsylvania
Horstmann Henry, drayman, r. 186 Harrison
Hortoway Henry, drayman, 128 N. Davidson
Hosbrook Daniel B. surveyor and engineer, r. 439 N. Illinois
Hoshour Samuel K. teacher N. W. C. University, r. 172 N. East
Hoskins Robert S. (Simms & Hoskins) r. 159 Meek
Hoslinger Leonard, blacksmith r. 578 E. Washington
Hospel Andreas, butcher, r. 39 W. Georgia
Hoss David, lab. I. P. C. Rw. r. 433 Virginia av.
Hoss G. W. (Indianapolis Printing and Publishing House, also
    Hoss & Charles) r. Bloomington, Ind.
Hoss Nelson, deputy assessor, r. 476 N. East
Hoss & Charles, (G. W. Hoss, Thomas Charles) editors and
    proprs. Indiana *School Journal,* Meridian se. cor. Circle
Hottman George, cabinetmaker Helwig & Co.
Hotz George, (Hotz & Co.) r. 124 S. Illinois
Hotz & Co. (George Hotz and William Pope) merchant tailors
    124 S. Illinois
Houck Jacob, r. 373 N. East
Houck John, (Fred. Deitz & Co.) r. 255 E. Washington
Houder Jacob, currier John Fishback, bds. 130 S. Meridian
Houdyshell John L. teacher Indiana Deaf and Dumb Institute,
    r. E. Washington out of limits
Houg Michael, saloon 138 S. Pennsylvania, r. same
Hough Charles, pianomaker, bds. 22 W. St. Clair
Hough James, pianomaker, bds. 22 W. St. Clair
Houghtaling Hiram, conductor, bds. 58 Benton
Houghten J. N. sawer J. Marsee & Son
Houk Andrew, varnisher, r. 186 N. Davidson
Houlihen Daniel, lab. r. 343 Winston
Houlihen Jerry, lab. Gas Works, r. 424 S. Tennessee
Houlihen Patrick, lab. Gas Works, r. 424 S. Tennessee
House Ben D. clk. Hamlin & Wright, r. 193 S. New Jersey
Housen Albert, r. 184 Madison av.
Housten Hiram, lab. r. 255 E. McCarty
Houston John T. druggist, r. East sw. cor. St. Clair
Houston Robert, r. East sw. cor. St. Clair
HOWARD AZEL B. grocer, Virginia av. cor. New Jersey, r. 160
    Virginia av.

HOW	168	HUB

Howard C. M. pastor Seventh Presbyterian Church, r. Virginia av. cor. Noble

Howard David W. lab. Osgood, Smith & Co.

HOWARD EDWARD, cancer physician 92 S. Illinois, r. same

Howard Edward B. [J. C. Ferguson & Co.] r. 141 N. Meridian

Howard Eliza (col'd) r. 163 Cedar

Howard Elizabeth, wid. J. W. r. 298 S. Illinois

Howard Fire Ins. Co. of New York, A. Abromet, agt. room 1 Ætna building

Howard Frank, saloon, r. 39 W. McCarty

Howard Frank, tinsmith Munson & Johnston, r. 109 N. West

Howard George W. lab. Osgood, Smith & Co., bds. Ray House

Howard Lewis N. cancer physician, r. 92 S. Illinois

Howard Liberty, clerk Azel B. Howard, r. Virginia av. cor. New Jersey

Howard Mary, dressmaker 50 S. Illinois, bds. 35 S. Illinois

Howard William O. cancer physician, r. 92 S. Illinois

Howe A. bookkeeper. bds. Martin House

Howe Edward P. sec. Franklin Life Ins. Co. r. 420 S. Pennsylvania

Howe John W. deliv. clk. L. H. Tyler & Co. bds. 33 Forest av.

Howe Robert, r. 176 W. Ohio

Howe Sewing Machine, Olin & Foltz agts. 12 N. Pennsylvania

Howell Elizabeth, wid. George, saloon and grocery ns. Nat. rd. west of the bridge, r. same

Howell Frank, telegraph operator, bds. 237 E. South

Howell J. W. bookkeeper Foster & Wiggins, r. 96 W. 1st

Howell Joseph W. sign and ornamental painter, 12 S. Pennsylvania, r. 576 S. Illinois

Howell T. F. engineer Osgood, Smith & Co. r. 393 N. West

Howes Charles, (C. & H. Howes) r. 76 Huron

Howes Henry, (C. & H. Howes) r. 78 Huron

Howes C. & H. (Charles and Henry Howes) meat market, 150 Virginia av. cor. New Jersey

Howey James, carpenter Greenleaf & Co.

Howie James, patternmaker, r. ns. Stevens 2 w. of Virginia av.

Howie William, machinist, r. 453 E. Market

Howland J. C. dentist John F. Johnston, bds. Pyle House

Howland J. D. Clerk U. S. and Circuit Court, r. 98 W. Vermont

Howland James, dentist, bds. 126 N. Tennessee

Howland Livingston, attorney at law and notary public 8 E. Washington, bds. 109 Virginia av.

Howlett Edward C. clk. Vinnedge, Jones & Co. bds. Bates House

Howsley David (col'd) farmer, r. 239 N. Tennessee

Hoyle Clinton D. (Hoyle & Moore) r. 312 E. Louisiana

HOYLE & MOORE, (C. D. Hoyle and J. L. Moore) pump mkrs. 14 Virginia av.

Hoyt Harriet, wid. Benajah, r. 84 Massachusetts av.

Hoyt Walter D. r. 84 Massachusetts av.

Hubbard George, cabinetmkr. J. R. Marot, r. Virginia av. beyond city limits

Hubbard William, lab. Rolling Mill, r. 266 S. Illinois
Hubbard William H. student, r. Meridian nw cor. 2d
Hubbard William S. vice pres. and treas. Franklin Life Ins. Co.
    r. N. Meridian out of limits
Hubbard's Block, Washington sw. cor. Meridian
Huber Jacob, (Becker & Huber) r. 77 E. Washington
Huber William, tailor Becker & Huber, r. 77 E. Washington
Huckry Ernst, carcleaner T. H. & I. R. R.
Huckshire R. boots and shoes, r. es. Meridian bet. North and
    Michigan
Hudson James W. paver, r. Dacotah cor. Jones, see map
Hudson Simeon, blksmith, r. 246½ W. Washington
Huebner Henry R. (Enos & Huebner) r. 362 Massachusetts av.
Huegele John, billiard hall and saloon, 39 E. Washington, r. 40
    N. New Jersey
Huey Milton S. painter, r. 293 Winston
Huff Andrew L. brakeman, r. 329 N. Noble
Huff J. T. groceries, 298 N. Pennsylvania, r. same
Huff John E. confectioner, r. 331 N. Noble
Huffer D. F. harnessmkr J. M. Huffer & Son, r. 69 Fletcher av.
Huffer James M. (J. M. Huffer & Son) r. 69 Fletcher av.
Huffer John J· (J. M. Huffer & Son) r. 69 Fletcher av.
HUFFER JAMES M. & SON, (James M. and J. J. Huffer) harness-
    mkrs. 23 S. Meridian
Huffington Manlove A. teamster, r. 31 Dougherty
Hug C. wid. r. 81 N. New Jersey
Hug Martin, apprentice *Sentinel* bindery
Hug Mary, wid. Joseph, r. 66 N. Noble
Huger Andrew, lab. r. 77 S. East
Huger John, saloon, r. 40 N. New Jersey
Hughes Ishum, engineer, r. 337 S. Delaware
Hughes Joseph, hostler Exchange stables
Hughes Lizzie Miss, r. 169 N. Noble
Hughes Mary, Miss, bds. 27 N. Noble
Hughes Missouria, wid. Andrew, r. 27 N. Noble
Hughes Samuel A. con. C. & I. C. R. R. bds. Bates House
Hughes William, patentright dealer, bds. 74 N. Pennsylvania
Hughey D. N. varnisher, bds. 208 W. Ohio
Hughey Temperance, wid. William, r. 310 E. Louisiana
Hughs T. M. express messenger, rear 239 N. Tennessee
Hughs James, (col'd) lab. r. Rhode Island nr. Blake
Hugley Samuel (col'd) lab. r. 130 Massachusetts av.
Hugo Charlotte Mrs. r. 81 N. Noble
Hugo Henry, plasterer, r. 359 S. East
Huit John H. photographer R. P. McCoy, r. 139 W. Washiagton
Hukins Jennie Mrs. dressmaker, r. 186½ W. Washington
Hull Armstrong, teamster, r. 748 N. Tennessee
Hull Emma Mrs. dressmaker, 44½ W. Louisiana, r. same
Hull William H. teamster, r. ns. Wabash alley, bet. N. New Jer-
    sey and N. East
Hume Eliza, wid. Rev. Madison, r. 673 N. Tennessee

Hume James M. (Hume, Adams & Co.) r. 25 E. Ohio
Hume Newton, clerk, r. 673 N. Tennessee
Hume Thomas M. farmer, r. 6 Pitt
Hume, Adams & Co. (James M. Hume, William L. Adams, and
    Edgar J. Foster) carpets, oil cloths, wall paper whol. and
    ret. 26 and 28 W. Washington
Humphrey Charles A. traveling salesman Stewart & Morgan,
    bds. Palmer House
Humphrey J. wks. McKendry & Lovecraft
Humphrey John W. cooper, r. 294 Indiana av.
Humphreys W. W. deputy clerk District Court, bds. 126 N. Tennessee
Hunnington James N. carpenter, r. 476 N. Mississippi
Hunt Aaron L. auction and com. mer. r. 320 N. Illinois
Hunt Albert, machinist, r. 119 W. South
Hunt Amelia, wid. William, r. 309 E. Merrill
Hunt Ase, r. 390 N. Delaware
Hunt Charles, engineer Barker, Williams & Co, r. 139 W. South
Hunt Charles C. cigars and tobacco, 61 E. Washington, r. 366 S.
    Alabama
Hunt Elisha W. printer Indianapolis Printing and Publishing
    House
Hunt Gideon S. bds. 390 N. Delaware
Hunt Jennie Miss, dressmkr. L. H. Tyler & Co. bds. Pyle House
Hunt Jesse L. bds. 390 N. Delaware
Hunt Julia A. wid. David, r. 13 Miller's Block cor. Illinois and
    Market
Hunt L. C., R. R. City Printing Co. r. 125 N. Liberty
Hunt Mary, wid. John, r. 520 S. Illinois
Hunt Phineas G. C. dentist 76½ E. Market, r. 172 N. Delaware
Hunt Phoebe A. Miss, teacher City Academy, bds. 410 N. Pennsylvania
Hunt Walter W. bookkeeper, r. 320 N. Illinois
Hunter James (col'd) whitewasher, r. 135 Bright
Hunter Marcellus, lab. Osgood, Smith & Co. bds. Ray House
Hunter Thomas, cooper, bds. 67 S. California
Hanley I. N. r. 19 E. North
Huntley Nellie Mrs. dressmaker, 19 E. North, r. same
Hupp Aaron, peddler, r. Wabash bet. Liberty and Noble
Hupp Abner C. grainer, r. 338 E. Washington
Hupp Albert, varnisher, Cabinetmakers' Union
Hurd C. L. wid. Daniel B. r. 144 N. Tennessee
Hurd Gertrude, wid. bds. 67 Indiana av.
Hurley Frank, hackman, r. 132 Maple
Hurley Michael, teamster Ind. Trans. Co. bds 29 Ellen
Hurley Patrick, hackdriver, r. California ne. cor. Michigan
Hurley Richard, hackman, bds 101 S. Illinois
Hurley Timothy, expressman, r. 22 Pitt
Hurrle Ignatz, mercht. tailor, 168 E. washington, r. 63 N. Noble
Hurt David, bell boy Bates House, bds. same
Hurt James R. brakeman, r. 212 E. Washington

HUR   171   IGO

Hurt Louisa, r. 383 S. Illinois
Husband Lindsley, (col'd) whitewasher r. 165 Indiana av.
Huskinson Thomas, carpenter, r. 145 N. New Jersey
Hussey Edward, wks. Caledonia Paper Mill, r. 356 S. West
Hust George C. meat market, 564 E. Washington, r. same
Hurst Jacob butcher R. Essigke, bds. 170 S. Illinois
Husted Hiram C. sawer Osgood Smith & Co. r. 255 E. McCarty
Husted J. T. lab. Osgood, Smith & Co. r. 255 E. McCarty
Huston Angeline, forewoman printing office; 10 Bates House blk.
Huston Cephas B. salesman D. Root & Co. r. 77 E. St. Joseph.
Huston Eunice, wid. r. 107 Huron
Huston F. (col'd) r. 75 Bright
Huston George, r. Louisiana cor. McGill
Huston Joel, engineer J. Fishback, 552 N. Mississippi
Hutchins Henry H. bookeeper, J. R. Sharpe, r. E. Market, out of
    limits
Hutchins, Hezekiah S. grocer, 407 N. Alabama, r. St. Clair,
    bet. Alabama and Delaware
Hutchinson B. con. C. C. & I. C. R. R. bds Spencer House
Hutchinson Charles P. supt. State *Sentinel*, r. 289 N. New Jersey
Hutchinson E. B. clk. supt. C. C. & I. C. R. R. bds. 80 N. Miss-
    issippi
Hutchinson John, cooper, bds. 314 E. Georgia
Hutchinson W. T. trav. agt. William Sumner & Co. bds. Nation-
    al Hotel
Hutchison Annie, dress and cloakmkr. r. 299 N. East
Hutchison David, engraver, r. 196 E. McCarty
Hutchison William, machinist, r. 383 Massachusetts av.
Hutton Edward L. (E. L. Hutton & Co.) r. 52 W. Ohio
Hutton Eliza, wid. William, r. 655 N. Tennessee
Hutton George, carpenter, r. 180 Dougherty
HUTTON E. L. & CO. (Edward L. and——) groceries and provis-
    ions, 94 N. Illinois
Hyase Samuel, brakeman, r. 36 Henry
Hyatt John, bartender Bates House
Hyde N. A. state agt. American Home Missionary Society, r.
    116 N. Alabama
Hyer Frank, switchman C. C. C. & I. R. R.
Hyland J. r. Illinois cor. 5th
Hyland Michael, contractor, r. 673 N. Illinois
Hyman Abraham, cigarmkr. A. W. Sharpe, bds. 32 N. Penn.
Hyne William H. moulder, r. 257 Coburn

I.

Iding William P. printer, r. 269 E. Market
Idler Clinton, foreman, T. H. & I. R. R. Shops, r. 171 W. South
Igoe Martin, (Igoe & Johnston) r. 34 Lockerbie
IGOE & JOHNSTON, (Martin Igoe and John M. Johnston) law-
    yers, 83½ E. Washington

Igou John W. stockdealer, r. 119 W. Maryland
Ihndriss John, carpenter, r. 429 N. East
Ilg George, propr. Union House, 202 S. Illinois, r. same
Iliff Charles E. clk. H. Bamberger, bds. 73 N. Alabama
Iliff L. S. clerk, bds. 73 N. Alabama
Illinois House, W. Essmann propr. 183 S. Illinois
Imboden Isaac, cigarmkr. bds. 135 E. Washington
Imelli Max. house and sign painter, 143 S. New Jersey, r. same
Ince Thomas, soldier, r. 228 Massachusetts av.
Indiana Bakery, William Kuhn propr. 150 N. East
INDIANA BANKING CO. (F. A. W. Davis, Willis S. Webb, John L. Ketcham, William W. Woollen, Samuel C. Vance, John P. Banta, William Needham) a general banking business 28 E. Washington
INDIANA FIRE INSURANCE CO. of Indianapolis Ind. J. S. Harvey pres. W. T. Gibson sec. room 5 Odd Fellows' Hall
INDIANA INSTITUTE FOR THE EDUCATION OF THE BLIND, W. H. Churchman supt. ns. North bet. Meridian and Pennsylvania
INDIANA INSTITUTION FOR THE EDUCATION OF THE DEAF AND DUMB, Thomas MacIntire supt. E. Washington out of limits
INDIANA MASONIC HOME ADVOCATE (monthly) F. M. Blair editor and publisher 44 N. Pennsylvania, Vinton's Blk.
Indiana Military State Claim Office, W. Hannaman agt. N. Tennessee opp. State House
INDIANA NATIONAL BANK, George Tousey pres. D. M. Taylor cashier, 2 E. Washington
INDIAN NORMAL ACADEMY OF MUSIC, 35½ E. Washington, Charles Hess principal
Indiana School Journal, G. W. Hoss and Thomas Charles editors and proprietors, Meridian se. cor. Circle
Indiana State Agricultural Fair Grounds, es. Delaware n. limits
INDIANA TELEGRAPH INSTITUTE, C. E. Hollenbeck propr. Washington se. cor. Meridian
Indiana Transfer Co. 42 E. Maryland, Fred. Meyer supt.
INDIANA VOLKSBLAT, (German) Julius Bœtticher editor and proprietor, 164 E. Washington
INDIANAPOLIS BRANCH BANKING CO. (Fletcher & Sharpe) Thomas H. Sharpe cashier, Washington sw. cor. Pennsylvania
Indianapolis Brewery, John P. Meikel propr. ss. W. Washington, junction Nat. Road
Indianapolis, Cincinnati and LaFayette Rw. Cattle Yards, Vincent Fagan supt. Louisiana out of limits.
Indianapolis, Cincinnati and LaFayette R. R. Freight Depot, Louisiana cor. Delaware, J. D. Morris freight agt.
Indianapolis, Cincinnati and LaFayette Railway Machine Shops, Theodore Mosher foreman, Louisiana east of limits
Indianapolis Coach Works, Shaw, Lippincott & Conner proprs. 26, 28 and 30 E. Georgia

INDIANAPOLIS COPPER LIGHTNING ROD WORKS, David Munson propr. 62 E. Washington

Indianapolis Cotton Manufacturing Co. (Robert P. Duncan supt.) west end Washington (Nat. Road) north of the bridge

Indianapolis Female Bible Society Depository, Todd, Carmichael & Williams, Glenn's Blk.

INDIANAPOLIS FEMALE INSTITUTE, Charles W. Hewes pres. Michigan ne. cor. Pennsylvania

Indianapolis File Works, Drotz & Steinhauer proprs. 136 S. Pennsylvania

INDIANAPOLIS GAS LIGHT AND COKE CO. S. A. Fletcher, Jr. pres. S. A. Fletcher, Sr. treas. L. Van Lannigham sec. H. Tracy supt. Pennsylvania ne. cor. Maryland

Indianapolis Hair and Bristle Works, south end of West, F. Miller supt.

Indianapolis Insurance Co. William Henderson pres. Alex. C. Jameson sec. Virginia av. cor Pennsylvania

Indianapolis Insurance Co. Savings Bank, Wm. Henderson pres. Alex. C. Jameson sec. Virginia av. cor. Pennsylvania

INDIANAPOLIS JOURNAL, (daily except Sunday, weekly Friday) Douglass & Conner publishers Market ne. cor. Circle

Indianapolis Marble Works, La Dow & Calvert proprs. 120 S. Illinois

Indianapolis Mission Sunday School Chapel, Union cor. Madison av.

Indianapolis National Bank, Theodore P. Haughey pres. A. F. Williams cashier, Washington ne. cor. Pennsylvania, Odd Fellows' Hall

Indianapolis, Peru and Chicago Railway gen. office 101 E. Washington, freight depot New Jersey nr. Washington passenger depot, Union dep.

INDIANAPOLIS PIANO MANUFACTURING CO. 159 and 161 E. Washington, J. C. Geisendorff pres. Isaac Thalman sec. and treas.

INDIANAPOLIS PRINTING AND PUBLISHING HOUSE, W. W. Dowling pres. Scott Butler sec. John Doughty supt. Meridian se. cor Circle

Indianapolis Rolling Mill Co. John M. Lord pres. A. Jones treas. C. B. Parkman sec. office No. 8 Bates House blk. Mill bet. Tennessee and Mississippi

Indianapolis Skating Rink, E. S. Alvord pres. W. H. English treas. Tennessee sw. cor. Georgia

Indianapolis Steam Laundry, 22-24 S. New Jersey

INDIANAPOLIS AND ST. LOUIS R. R. T. A. Morris pres. E. King sec. and treas. J. D. Herkimer, supt. office 53 S. Alabama, ticket office Union Depot

INDIANAPOLIS AND VINCENNES RAILROAD CO. A. E. Burnside pres. Calvin Fletcher sec. and treas. J. P. Harper chief engineer, office Kentucky av. cor. Illinois

Indianapolis Wagon and Agricultural Works, 172 S. Tennessee, W. A. Pattison, agent

ING	174	ISG

Ingersoll Charles H. foreman Indianapolis Piauo Mnfg. Co. bds. 163 E. Washington

Ingersoll Edward P. pastor Plymouth Church, r. 283 N. Pennsylvania

Ingersoll Frank, turner, r. 131 E. South

Ingersoll Martha S. Miss, writing teacher city school, bds. 333 S. Alabama

Ingersoll Mary Miss, teacher Eighth Ward School, bds. 333 S. Alabama

Ingham James, engineer Goddard & Sons

Ingle Jacob, lab. r. Chadwick 2 s. of McCarty

Ingle Mark W. salt and coal whol. and ret. 28 S, Meridian, bds. 17 W. Maryland

Ingles John, tinsmith C. C. & I. C. R. R.

INGRAHAM C. B. Ingraham's Art Gallery, 32¼ E. Washington, opp. Glenn's block, r. same. See advertisement in business directory opp. photographers

Inkelkee George, wks. J. S. Carey & Co.

Inkelkee William, wks. J. S. Carey & Co.

Insurance Co. of North America of Philadelphia, Martin, Hopkins & Ohr agents, Market ne. cor. Circle, *Journal* bldg.

Insurance Co. of North America of Philadelphia, W. H. Seiders state agent, Market ne. cor. Circle

Intermediate School, (A. grade) Fidelia Anderson, pirncipal, High School building

International Fire Ins. Co. of New York, Martin, Hopkins & Ohr, agents, Market ne. cor. Circle, *Journal* bldg.

Inwalle Benjamin J. saloon and propr. Inwalle's Garden, 367 Virginia av.

Inwalle's Garden, Benjamin J. Inwalle, propr. 367 Virginia av.

Ireland William H. stair builder, r. 52 Fletcher av.

Irens Catharine, wid. Stephen, r. 193 W. Maryland

Irens Harry, bookbinder, r. 193 W. Maryland

Irick Charles C. r. 326 N. New Jercy

Irick Morris C. painter, r. 133 Fort Wayne av.

Irick William, pressman *Journal* office, bds 31 W. Ohio

Irick William H. bricklayer, r. 326 N. New Jersey

Irons Harry, bookbinder *Journal* bindery, r. 193 W. Maryland

Irvin Benjamin, teamster, r. ss. Nat. rd. west of the bridge

Irvin William, (Ritter & Irvin) bds. Morrison 3d e. of Delaware

Irving Alexander B. salesman, r. 96 E. New York

Irving Cornelius L. salesman, r. 96 E. New York

Irving Jacob R. traveling agent William Sumner & Co. r. Broadway below Christian av.

Irwin Rollin, printer, r. 24 Kentucky av.

Isensce Albert, bellhanger and locksmith 24 N. Pennsylvania, r. 72 N. California

Isgrigg James A. (Isgrigg & Brackin) r. 413 W. New York

ISGRIGG & BRACKIN, (James A. Isgrigg and Thomas E. Brackin) dealers in lumber, laths and shingles, office and yard 180 W. Market

Ishman Frederick, lab. r. 3rd nr. Howard
Iske Christian, lab. Eagle Machine Works, r. 427 Virginia av.
Iske William, bartender Frederick Jasper, r. 333 Virginia av.
Ittenbach Frank, (Smith, Ittenbach & Co.) r. ns. South bet. Virginia av. and Noble
Ittenbach Gerhard, (Smith, Ittenbach & Co.) r. ns. South bet. Virginia av. and Noble
Ivory Peter, r. Ash se. cor. Winston

J

Jachmann A. Mrs. midwife, r. 312 E. Washington
Jachman Hermann, tailor, r. 312 E. Washington
Jack Charles, sheetiron worker Cox & Brothers, r. 320 E. Louisiana
Jack Henry, bds. 74 W. Pennsylvania
Jack Matthew B. 2nd clk. Bland & Taylor, bds. 74 N. Pennsylvania
Jack Matthew W. boardinghouse 74 N. Pennsylvania, r. same
Jack Matthew W. Jr. *Northwestern Farmer* office, bds. 74 N. Pennsylvania
Jacks Isaac, r. 308 E. Washington
Jackson ——, wks. J. S. Cerey & Co.
Jackson Andrew, lab. Budd & Hensley, r. 293 Blake
Jackson Elizabeth M. wid. Charles, r. 152 E. St. Clair
Jackson George, brakeman, bds. 58 Benton
Jackson James, sectionmaster, r. 74 Wilkins
Jackson John, lab. r. 157 High
Jackson John O. (Jackson & Nicoli) bds. 222 W. Ohio
Jackson Maggie V. wid. William, r. 25 Dacotah
Jackson Rachel, (col'd) wid. r. 207 W. North
Jackson T. M. (Charles Helwig & Co.) r. es. East foot Vermont
Jackson Thomas, clk. Luther R. Martin, bds. 79 E. Michigan
Jackson Thomas, currier Mooney & Co. r. 191 W. Maryland
Jackson Thomas B. (Van Camp & Jackson) r. 172 W. Ohio
JACKSON W. N. sec. treas. and gen'l ticket agt. Union Railway Co. office Union depot, r. 82 W. North
Jackson William, slate roofer, r. 186 N. Davidson
Jackson Willis, (col'd) lab. r. 177 Indiana av.
JACKSON & NICOLI, (John O. Jackson, Lewic Nicoli) groceries, provision, meat, &c. 221 W. Ohio
Jacobi F. r. 67 Wyoming
Jacobs A. Mrs. wid. Joseph, r. 156 N. East
Jacobs Charles, (Barbour & Jacobs) r. 83 Christian av.
Jacobs John, carpenter T. J. Morse
Jacob Joseph, notions and fancy goods, 131 E. Washington, r. 156. N. East
Jacobs Milton, r. 145 S. New Jersey
Jacobs Richard, box maker M. Burton, r. 109 N. Illinois
Jacobs Richard, carpenter, Maryland e. of Illinois, r. 164 S. East

JAC	176	JEN

Jacobs Stephen, carpenter, bds. 116 S. East
Jacobs Stephen S. carpenter, bds. 129 S. East
Jacobs Valentine, r. 145 S. New Jersey
Jacoby J. H. candy maker Daggett & Co. r. 35 W. Georgia
Jacquemin Francis, foreman City Brewery, r. 213 S. Pennsylvania
Jacques John, cigar maker G. F. Meyer, r. 13 S. Mississippi
Jaegers Charles, (col'd) barber, r. 177 Indiana av.
Jaguey Guillon, beam hand J. Fishback
James Evan, puddler Indianapolis Rolling Mill
James Frank, (col'd) lab. r. 410 S. Tennessee
James John, (col'd) lab. r. 410 S. Tennessee
James John, patternmaker Sinker & Co. bds. 24 W. McCarty
James Lindsley (col'd) barber M. Mason
James Michael C. clk. Pettis, Dickson & Co. r. 66 W. New York
James Oliver H. plasterer, r. 362 W. Vermont
James Seth C. marble worker T. S. James & Co. r. 46 Fletcher av.
James Thomas S. (T. S. James & Co.) bds. Ray House
James T. S. & Co. (T. S. James and H. P. Speer) marble workers and dealers, 136 S. Meridian
Jameson Alex. C. sec. Indianapolis Ins. Co. bds. Alabama nw cor. Michigan
Jameson Bettie Miss, teacher Colony School, r. 139 W. South
Jameson Frank, (col'd) porter Palmer House
Jameson L. H. r. 189 W. South
Jameson Lillie Mrs. cigars and fruit, 35. S. Illinois, r. same
Jameson Patrick H. (Jameson & Funkhouser) r. 249 N. Alabama
Jameson & Funkhouser, (P. H. Jameson and David Funkhouser) physicians, 19 S. Meridian
Janaway John, machinist, bds. Stanridge House
Jarrell F. E. Mrs. dress and cloak maker, 36 N. Illinois, r. 148 Indiana av.
Jasper Frederick, groceries and saloon, 333 Virginia av. r. same
Jasper Herman, rubber, r. 493 S. New Jersey
Jasper Oliver, (col'd) lab. r. 204 W. 2d
Jeffers James, soldier, r. 474 E. Washington
Jefferson Benjamin, (col'd) lab. r. Rhode Island nr. Blake
Jefferson Thomas, roller Barker, Williams & Co.
JEFFERSONVILLE, MADISON & INDIANAPOLIS R. R. Horace Scott, gen. supt. J. G. Whitcomb, agt., freight office ss. South bet. Delaware and Pennsylvania, ticket office, Union depot
Jeffree Mary, r. W. Indianapolis
Jeffrey John, lab. r. Massachusetts av. ne. cor. Plum
Jeffreys Lucinda, weaver Hoosier Woolen Factory
Jeffries Thomas W. carriage painter, r. 47 Rose
Jemison John, (Jemison & Mitchell) r. 147 S. Union
Jemison & Mitchell, John Jemison and James T. Mitchell) harness and saddle makers, 138 Bluff rd.
Jencks George W. engineer, r. 212 E. Washington
Jenison Alexander F. (A. F. and J. H. Jenison) r. 19 W. Ohio

Jenison Frank, engraver and silversmith, r. 356 N. Illinois
Jenison John H. (A. F. & J. H. Jenison) r. 19 W. Ohio
JENISON A. F. & J. H. (Alexander F. and John H. Jenison) grocers ret. 89 N. Illinois
Jenkins A. W. wood measurer, r. 394 N. Delaware
Jenkins Andrew, painter, bds. 23 N. West
Jenkins Charles, switchman C. C. & I. C. R. R.
Jenkins D. H. express messenger, bds. Spencer House
JENKINS EBENEZER, house and sign painter, 43 Massachusetts av. r. 74 Ft. Wayne av.
Jenkins Edward H. clk. Lindley & Co. bds. 394 N. Delaware
Jenkins Henry, (col'd) lab. r. opp. City Hospital
Jenkins J. Wood, student Bryant & Stratton's College, bds. 129 E. North
Jenkins Jesse W. telegraph operator, bds. 72 Ft. Wayne av.
Jenkins John, moulder Union Novelty Works, r. 294 E. Market
Jenkins John R. painter E. Jenkins, bds. same
Jenkins R. (col'd) wks. McKendry & Lovecraft
Jenkins Robert, lab. r. 228 W. Vermont
Jenkins Thomas, (col'd) lab. r. 157 Maple
Jenkins William, baker W. K. McFarlane, bds. 12 S. Meridian
Jenkins William F. stockdealer, 30½ W. Washington, r. 512 N. Illinois
Jennings George, switchman J. M. & I. R. R. r. 312 Madison av.
Jennings Patrick, r. 248 Davidson
JENNINGS WILLIAM T. tin, copper and sheet iron worker, 60 E. Market, r. 277 W. Michigan
Jerum Joseph, car inspector C. C. & I. C. R. R.
Jessie Samuel H. fireman, bds. 319 S. Delaware
Jesterson Andrew, lab. Rolling Mill
Jewell Minnie, select school, ns. Ohio bet. Delaware and Pennsylvania
Jewett Samuel, moulder Eagle Machine Wks. r. 42 Henry
Jewish Synagogue, ss. Market bet. New Jersey and East
Jewitt William, bds. Ray House
Jillson J. M. frt. clk. C. C. C. & I. R. R. bds. Pyle House
Jines William, carpenter, r. 35 Kentucky av.
Joachim John C. meat market, 88 Fort Wayne av. r. same
Job Alzine, wagonmkr. Virginia av. nr. cor. Dougherty, r. same
Jocelyn Charles D. carpenter, r. 244 Davidson
Johantgen George, blksmith, r. 210 E. Louisiana
Johantgen Nicholas, engineer, r. 63 Harrison
John Charles, r. 273 N. Mississippi
Johnes Eugene, architect, room 33 Blackford's Blk. bds. Palmer House
Johns Jennie, dressmkr. M. Shepard. r. 128 N. Spring
Johns Samuel, binder W. & J. Braden, r. 318 N. Alabama
Johnson A. lab. Osgood, Smith & Co.
Johnson Aaron, lab. r. Rockwood nr. River
Johnson Aaron R. huckster, r. 458 S. West
Johnson Abijah, room 8, 30 W. Washington

JOH   178   JOH

Johnson Albert H. bkpr. A. V. Lawrence, r. 167 W. Maryland
Johnson Alexander, carpenter, r. 394 N. West
Johnson Alexander W. (Monroe & Johnson) r. Huron se. cor. Noble
Johnson Anna, wid. Henry, r. 2d nr. LaFayette R. R.
Johnson Anna E. dressmkr. 231 Massachusetts av. r. same
Johnson Anna M. Mrs. matron Orphan Asylum, r. 711 N. Tennessee
Johnson B. F. 33 W. Washington, r. 800 N. Tennessee
Johnson B. N. clk. Hibben, Tarkington & Co. bds. Sherman House
Johnson Benjamin, (col'd) driver, r. 217 W. 2nd
Johnson Benjamin, hackman, r. 243 N. West
Johnson Benjamin, railshearer, rolling mill, r. 279 S. Tennessee
Johnson Benjamin F. saw mill, r. 231 Massachusetts av.
Johnson C. works J. S. Carey & Co.
Johnson Charles, r. 95 Benton
Johnson Charles, carpenter, r. 73 Huron
Johnson Charles F. r. 23 E. North
Johnson Charles R. fish dealer, 397 Virginia av. r. same
Johnson Cynthia A. wid. of Robert, r. 434 W. North
Johnson Edmund C. r. 341 S. Meridian
Johnson Elias (E. Johnson & Co.) r. 191 S. Alabama
Johnson Elizabeth, wid. John B. r. 167 W. Maryland
Johnson Emily, asst. teacher High School, r. 138 Massachusetts av.
Johnson Emma, dress maker, r. 194 N. Mississippi
Johnson Gabriel (col'd) lab. r. 6th near LaFayette R. R.
Johnson George H. r. 20 Fletcher av.
Johnson George H. clk. J. T. Layman & Co. r. 370 S. Alabama
Johnson George W. bds. 62 S. Pennsylvania
Johnson Green C. (col'd) barber, 267 Washington, r. same.
Johnson Howard A. grocer, 399 N. New Jersey, bds. 372 N. New Jersey
Johnson Henry, (col'd) brick maker, bds. 228 Huron
Johnson Isaac B. r. 246½ E. Washington
Johnson Jacob A. stock dealer, r. 132 N. Tennessee
Johnson James, carpenter, r. 394 N. West
Johnson James, bds. Ray House
Johnson James, carpenter, bds. 64 W. Maryland
Johnson James A. wks. Warren Tate, r. se. cor. Noble and Huron
Johnson Jennie Mrs. dressmaker, 68 S. Illinois, r. same
Johnson Jesse, salesman H. J. Prior, r. 246 E. Washington
Johnson Joel M. r. 386 N. New Jersey
Johnson John, works Cotton Factory
Johnson John, carpenter, bds. 38 S. Tennessee
Johnson John, (col'd) barber, 303 E. Washington, r. same
Johnson John S. carpenter, r. 341 S. Meridian
Johnson John W. bookkeeper Daggett & Co. r. 491 N. Mississippi
Johnson Lewis, hostler Sullivan & Drew, r. 225 N. Tennessee
Johnson Marcus L. insurance solicitor, r. 546 N. Illinois
Johnson Marietta Mrs. bds. 474 N. Pennsylvania

Johnson Mary J. wid. T. A. r. 23 E. North
John Noah, (col'd) lab. r. Missouri nr. Tinker
Johnson P. A. carpenter Builders & Mnfrs. Association
Johnson P. DuBois, clk. Trade Palace, bds. 132 N. Tennessee
Johnson Peter, (col'd) lab. r. 6. Athon
Johnson R. J. asst. paymaster C. C. C. & I. R. R. 53 N. Alabama
Johnson Robert, (col'd) barber Russell & Gulliver, bds. Pyle House
Johnson Samuel L. comp. *Sentinel* news room, r. 37 Fletcher av.
Johnson Sarah Mrs. (col'd) r. 149 Bright
Johnson Sidney H. ret. grocer, 143 N. Delaware, r. New Jersey cor. St. Joseph
JOHNSON T. E. atty. at law, 42 E. Washington, r. 355 N. East
Johnson Thomas, r. ss. Louisiana bet. New Jersey and Alabama
JOHNSON THOMAS E. lawyer, room 9, Blackford's Blk. r. 474 N. Pennsylvania
Johnson W. W. printer, r. 236 E. Vermont
Johnson William, farrier, r. 328 Blake
Johnson William, (col'd) lab. bds. 174 Douglas alley
Johnson William, (col'd) waiter, r. 68 Eddy
Johnson William G. clk. John Furnas & Co. r. 711 N. Tennessee
Johnson William H. (col'd) r. 196 Minerva
Johnson William H. H. r. 135 Union
JOHNSON E. & CO. (Elias Johnson, Julius Smith, and Lambert S. Ayers) tin, glassware and produce dealers, 108 S. Delaware
Johnston Elizabeth, wid. r. al. bet. Delaware and Pennsylvania Maryland and Georgia
Johnston George W. bookkeeper Citizens' National Bank, bds. S. Rockwell
Johnston John C. clerk, r. 185 N. Liberty
Johnston John F. dentist, 19 W. Maryland, r. Pennsylvania cor. King
Johnston John Milton, (Igoe & Johnston) r. 185 N. Liberty
Johnston McL. bricklayer, r. 267 Davidson
Johnston R. J. supt's. clk. express office, bds. 54 S. Pennsylvania
Johnston Robert, clerk, bds. 38 St. Clair
Johnston Samuel A. clk. Munson & Johnston, r. 220 N. New Jersey
Johnston W. W. (Murphy, Johnston & Co.) r. 546 N. Meridian
Johnston William J. (Munson & Johnston) r. 86 E. Vermont
Jolly Hoosier, (monthly) A. C. Roach editor and publisher, *Journal* Bldg.
Jolly James, watchman I. C. & L. R. R.
Jolly John, lab. r. 14 Lord
Jones Agilla, Jr. (Vinnedge, Jones & Co.) r. 187 N. Pennsylvania
Jones Albert, farmer, r. ws. Missouri nr. 1st
Jones Alexander, (col'd) farmer, r. 824 N. Illinois
Jones Alfred, boots and shoes, r. 306 N. Delaware
Jones B. wks. J. S. Carey & Co.

JON	180	JON	

Jones Barton D. real estate agt. r. 188 N. Delaware

Jones Braxton, (col'd) lab. r. Maple ne. cor. Ray

Jones C. baggagemaster, r. 3 Arch

Jones Casper M. Jr. clk. Parrott, Nickum & Co. r. 188 E. Wash.

Jones Charles, (col'd) lab. r. 558 N. Mississippi

Jones Charles, salesman Wm. H. Close & Co. r. 187 N. Penn.

JONES CYRUS G. gen. state agt. Cincinnati Mutual Life Ins. Co. office No. 7 Vinton's blk. r. same

Jones E. B. engineer C. C. C. & I. R. R.

Jones E. F. engineer I. C. & L. R. R.

Jones Edward, clk. r. 323 N. Delaware

Jones Edward, (col'd) expressman, bds. 205 N. West

Jones Elisha, bds. 187 N. Pennsylvania

Jones Evan C. expressman, r. 339 S. Pennsylvania

Jones F. J. broommaker, r. Illinois se. cor. Tinker

Jones George W. teamster, r. es. Illinois above 6th

Jones Harry, brakeman, bds, 58 Benton

Jones Harry, (col'd) r. 134 W. Michigan

Jones Hester, wid. William, r. Rockwood nr. River

Jones J. W. clk. J. E. Robertson & Co. r. 187 N. Pennsylvania

Jones J. W. night clk. Spencer House, bds. same

Jones James, lab. r. 169 Eddy

Jones James, wks. J. S. Carey & Co.

Jones Jesse, clk. bds. 148 Indiana av.

Jones Jesse, real estate agt. 19 W. Washington, r. 488 N. Illinois

Jones Jesse M. clk. Moody Bros. r. 488 N. Illinois

Jones John, bds. 187 N. Pennsylvania

Jones John, carpenter, r. 156 Huron

Jones John, (col'd) (Jones & Hall) r. 16 S. Meridian

Jones John L. r. 430 N. New Jersey

Jones John W. r. 412 S. West

Jones John W. yardmaster T. H. & I. R. R. r. 132 W. First

Jones Joseph H. (col'd) barber, r. 214 W. New York

Jones Julius, (Gilkey & Jones) bds. 85 W. Maryland

Jones L. N. B. ins. agt. bds. Bates House

Jones L. W. salesman Kimble, Aikman & Co. bds. Sherman House

Jones Margaret, (col'd) r. Douglas alley bet. New York and Ohio

Jones Mariah H. prin. Eighth Ward School, bds. 333 S. Alabama

Jones Marshall, (col'd) lab. r. S. Tennessee nr. Ray

Jones Mary A. wid. r. 188 S. Mississippi

Jones Olive, wid. r. 129 W. Market

Jones R. L. (col'd) barber Hill & Carter, r. ws. Missouri, bet. Ohio and Market

Jones Ralph H. carpenter, r. 225 N. New Jersey

Jones Robert A. stair builder, r. 209 Winston

Jones Sallie, clerk, bds. 11 S. Mississippi

Jones Spicer, farmer, r. 136 N. Tennessee

Jones Sullivan, (col'd) lab. r. 168 W. Georgia

Jones Susan, wid. Dillon, r. Chesapeak, bet. West and the Canal

Jones T. wks. J. S. Carey & Co.

JON	181	JUS

Jones Thomas, (col'd) hostler south side livery stable, bds. 198 S. Illinois

Jones W. B. switchman, r. es. New Jersey nr. R. R. track

Jones W. E. messenger freight office T. H. & I. R. R. bds. 325 N. Delaware

Jones W. W. (Davis & Jones) r. 70 N. East

Jones William, (col'd) coachman, r. 68 N. Missouri

Jones William, (col'd) lab. r. 6th, nr. LaFayette R. R.

Jones William B. ins. agt. bds. 127 S. New Jersey

Jones William H. (Coburn & Jones) r. 278 N. Illinois

Jones William M. grain dealer, r. es. Jackson, bet. Christian av, and Forest Home av.

Jones William T. clerk, r. 324 N. Alabama

Jones William T. foreman bending dept. Osgood, Smith & Co. r. 35 Fletcher av.

Jones & Hall, (J. Jones and H. Hall, (col'd) barbers, 16 S. Meridian

Jonston Scott, lab. Bunte, Dickson & Co.

Jordan Ella Miss, dressmaker, 186½ W. Washington

Jordan Gilmore, r. 186 N. Tennessee

Jordan H. L. ins. agt. bds. 98 E. New York

Jordan John, grocer, 158 W. Washington, r. 172 N. Mississippi

Jordan Phineas, r. 492 N. Mississippi

Jordan William F. barber, r. 210 Indiana av.

Jordan Anna Miss, clk. r. 290 E. Ohio

JORDAN LEWIS, lawyer, room 1 Talbott & New's blk. r. 352 Meridian

Jordan Thomas, lab. Osgood, Smith & Co. bds. 213 S. Illinois

Jordan Nicholas, carpenter P. Routier

Jorman Frank, bds. Jefferson House,

Jose Nicholas, furniture dealer, 8 S. Pennsylvania, r. country

Joseph George W. (Long & Joseph) r. 29 N. California

Joseph J. G. salesman Mayer & Rheimheimer, bds. Palmer House

Joseph R. C. ins. agt. 81 E. Market, r. 29 N. California

Josey A. frame maker H. Daumont & Co.

Journal Building, Market ne. cor. Circle

Jowitt Wm. sawmkr. Sheffield Saw Works, r. 70 E. Maryland

Judah John M. deputy clk. Supreme Court, bds. Pyle House

Judd Frederick, boss carder Merritt & Coughlen, r. 233 Blake

Judge James R. roller Rolling Mill, r. 47 Wyoming

Judge Thomas, puddler Rolling Mill, r. 508 S. Illinois

Judson Andrew, brickmason, r. 201 N. Davidson

Judson Charles E. trav. salesman Holland, Ostermeyer & Co. r. 135 N. Illinois

Judson Henry, clk. Judson & Dodd, r. 297 N. Mississippi

Judson William, (Judson & Dodd) r. 152 N. Meridian

Judson & Dodd, (William Judson and John W. Dodd) coffee and spice mills, 251 and 253 E. Washington

Justice James N. mechanic, r. 10 Bates House Block

Justin John, auctioneer, r. 27 E. North

K

Kader John, huckster, r. 310 W. Washington
Kael Conrad, lab. r. 199 N. East
Kaeser Adam, shoemkr. H. Hoffman
Kaeser Charles, meat market, 4th bet. Tennessee and Mississippi, r. same
Kafader Joseph, stonecutter, r. 461 S. Illinois
Kahlor Frank, salesman Smith & Goodhart
Kahn Abram, r. 226 E. New York
Kahn Adolphus, commercial clothing store, 95 S. Illinois, r. 184 Virginia av.
Kahn Isaac, (S. Kahn & Bro.) r. 139 N. Delaware
Kahn Jacob, r. 193 N. East
Kahn Leon, dry goods, r. 164 N. East
Kahn Lyon, clerk P. Kaufman, bds. Commercial Hotel
Kahn Samuel, (S. Kahn & Bro.) r. 283 E. Market
Kahn S. & Bro. (Samuel and Isaac Kahn) dry goods and notions ret. 45 and 47 E. Washington
Kaiban John, lab. George F. Adams
Kalb Fred. grocer, 310 Winston, r. same
Kalb Henry, gaslighter. r. 164 E. St. Joseph
Kalb Henry Jr. tinner R. L. A. & W. McOuat, r. 164 E. St. Joseph
Kalb John, tinner R. L. & A. W. McOuat, r. 164 E. St. Joseph
Kalb Philip, lab. 127 St. Mary
Kalb William, student Bryant & Stratton's College, bds. 164 E. St. Joseph
Kaler Frank, teamster, r. 136 N. Noble
Kalkhoff Charles, drayman, r. 25 Coburn
Kamm Gottlieb, saloon, 70 Virginia av. r. 505 S. New Jersey
Kanaur John, teamster, r. 65 N. East
Kane Dennis, blacksmith, r. 400 E. Georgia
Kane James, teamster, r. 755 N. Mississippi
Kane Patrick, boilermaker Sinker & Co.
Kappes J. Henry, (E. C. Atkins & Co. and J. H. Kappes & Co.) r. 132 E. North
Kappes J. H. & Co. (J. H. Kappes, H. Knippenberg and E. C. Atkins) piano-forte mnfrs. 210 to 216 S. Illinois
Karch John E. shoemaker John H. Ezmann, r. 2 Court
Karkoff Fred. tally clerk J. M. & I. R. R.
Karle Christ (Christ Karle & Co. Schneider & Co. and Indianapolis Cotton Mnfrg. Co.) r. 82 S. Delaware
Karle J. J. shoemaker, 160 Bluff rd. r. same
Karle Joseph, bookkeeper Schneider & Co. r. 82 S. Delaware
Karle Christ & Co. (Christ Karle and Michael Mode) boot and shoe dealers and mnfrs. 83 E. Washington
Karney John, com. mer. and grocer, 56 S. Illinois, r. 307 S. Delaware
Karras Joseph, carpenter I. C. & L. R. R.

| KAS | 183 | KEE |

Kasberg Peter, (Russell & Kasberg) r. 71 Hossbrook
Kasburgh Joseph, bookkeeper William Sheets
Kaspar George, tanner, r. Michigan Road cor. 10th
Kattenhorn John, r. 220 Noble
Kattmann Ernst, groceries and saloon, 1 Buchanan, r. same
Kauffman Abram, r. 153 W. Maryland
Kauffman John, currier John Fishback, bds. Washington House
Kaufman A. salesman S. Kaufman, r. 389 N. Pennsylvania
Kaufman Adam, collarmkr. r. 76 S. Delaware
Kaufman Charles (M. Kaufman &. Bro.) r. Maryland cor. Mississippi
Kaufman John, clothing dealer 24 W. Louisiana, r. 263 E. Market
Kaufmann John, pastor Evangelical Church (German) r. rear of church
Kaufman Louis (Barthel & Kaufman) r. 171 High
Kaufmann Moritz, meat market, North cor. West, r. same
Kaufman Moses (M. Kaufman & Bro.) r. 119 N. Illinois
Kaufmann Peter, clothing dealer, r. 23 Madison av.
Kaufman Solomon, hats, caps and furs whol. and ret. 16 W. Washington and (Lines, Smelser & Co.) r. N. Pennsylvania near 2d
KAUFMAN M. & BRO. (Moses and Charles Kaufman) whol. dealers wines and liquors and sole proprs. Dr. Kaufman's world premium and Blue Jacket Bitters 116 S. Meridian
Kavanaugh Edward, blacksmith Rolling Mill
Kavanaugh Philip, wks. Indianapolis Paper Co.
Kay Hannah, dressmaker Kay & Mattern, r. Walnut cor. Missouri
Kay Mary Miss (Kay & Mattern) r. Walnut cor. Missouri
Kay Robert (Trucks & Kay) r. Missouri sw. cor. Walnut
Kay Sarah, wks. Indianapolis Paper Co.
KAY & MATTERN (Miss Mary Kay and Mrs. Martha C. Mattern) dress and cloak makers 68½ E. Market
Kealey Sarah Miss, music teacher, bds. 169 N. Illinois
Keating Joseph J. Prof. of Music, r. 90 S. Illinois
Keating Jeff, roller Rolling Mill
Keating Lucy Miss, teacher St. Peters School
Keay William, stonecutter, r. 378 N. East
Keay William, Jr. clk. r. 378 N. East
Keck Reason W. clk. Cabinet Saloon, bds. Palmer House
Keefe Arthur, lab. r. 368 S. Tennessee
Keefe M. moulder, Sinker & Co. r. ss. Sinker nr. Alabama
Keefer Augustus, druggist, r. 483 N. Illinois
Keefer Jacob, retired, r. 484 N. Illinois
Keegan Hubert, plasterer, r. 49 Bradshaw
Keely Arthur, carpenter Wm. C. McLain, bds. Ohio bet. East and Liberty
Keely Catharine, wid. Samuel, r. 291 E. Ohio
Keely Daniel, bricklayer, r. 321 N. Noble
Keely Eliza, bookbinder Journal bookbindery

C. J. BRACKEBUSH, Farm Machinery, Hardware and Seeds, No. 75 and 77 W. Washington st., Indianapolis.

Keely Henry S. bricklayer, r. 146 N. Winston
Keely Isaac, bricklayer, r. 321 N. Noble
Keely John, bricklayer, r. 124 N. East
Keely Josie, milliner E. Kirk
Keely Louisa, wid. Alfred, r. 152 W. Washington
Keely Mary, bookbinder *Journal* bookbindery
Keely Oliver, bricklayer, r. 391 E. Ohio
Keely William, r. 158 E. Michigan
Keely William H. bricklayer, r. 309 E. Ohio
Keemer James, (col'd) lab. 181 W. Washington
Keen John, clk. Spencer House saloon, bds. 280 E. Market
Keen Lorence, shoemaker, r. 203 S. Alabama
Keenan Barnard, peddler, bds. 36 W. Maryland
Keenan Phelix, peddler, bds. 36 W. Maryland
Keer George, painter Indiana Coach Works, bds. 52 S. Pennsylvania
Keers James, packer Sohl, Gibson & Co. r. Michigan rd. city limits
Keers Samuel, wks. Hoosier State Mills, r. 25 Blake
Keers W. J. cooper, r. opp. City Hospital
Keers William, packer Sohl, Gibson & Co. r. Michigan rd. city limits
Kees Hiram, engineer, r. 68 Bates
Kees Hiram W. engineer, r. 165 Bates
Keesee George, carpenter, r. ws. Mayhew nr. Michigan rd.
Keesee George, r. 122 Blackford
Keeting Jeffrey, lab. r. 107 High
Keffe John, carpenter, r. 43 Harrison
Keffer Jacob, machinist Sinker & Co. r. 177 Union
Kegel Mary, saleslady Glick & Schwartz, r. 168 N. Davis
Keherer Louisa, wid. Gottleib, r. 156 E. St. Joseph
Kehling Henrietta, wid. Andrew, r. 163 E. St. Joseph
Kehling William, butcher, r. 163 E. St. Joseph
Keifer J. machinist Sinker & Co.
Keightley John A. clk. Patterson, Moore & Talbot, bds. Pyle House
Keilman William, school teacher, bds. 238 S. New Jersey
Keiser Catherine, wid. Christian, r. 68 Massachusetts av.
Keiser Charles A. cigarmaker W. H. Wallace, r. 86 Indiana av.
Keiser George, plumber, bds. 23 N. West
Keiser Jacob, clk. F. Mottery, bds. Concordia House
Keiser John, carpenter, bds. 23 N. West
Keiser John, machinist Sinker & Co.
Keising Joseph, tanner Frenzel & Simon, bds. 518 E. Washington
Keitley ——, drug clk. bds. Pyle House
Kelesch Martin, butcher, r. 140 Madison av.
Kelleher James, boot and shoe maker Coburn bet. East and Virginia av. r. same
Kelleher John, carpenter, r. 347 S. Missouri
Kelleher P. works J. S. Carey & Co.
Kellenger John G. carpenter, 326 E. Market, r. 328 E. Market

Keller David, stone cutter, r. 466 S. East
Keller George, painter, W. Whitridge
Keller Jacob, lab. r. 326 S. Delaware
KELLER PAUL, cabinet maker, manufacturer of office and store furniture, 21 Circle, bds. 18 Pennsylvania
Keller Paul, piano-forte maker, J. H. Kappes & Co.
Keller Robert, book keeper, bds. 42 N. East
Keller William, lab. r. 247 S. Delaware
Keller Z. P. engineer, r. 102 Meek
Kellermier Henry, lab. frt. depot C. C. & I. C. R. R., r. 249 S. Alabama
Kelley ——, lab. r. 240 S. Mossouri
Kelley Andrew, comp. *Sentinel* job room, bds. 24 Buchanan
Kelley Anthony, tailor, 28 S. Meridian, r. South nr. cor. Illinois
Kelley Benjamin G. (Gates, Pray & Co.,) bds. 91 N. Delaware
Kelley C. painter, S. W. Drew
Kelley Catharine, wid. Patrick, r. 24 Buchanan
Kelley Elijah, (col'd) lab. r. 318 W. North
Kelley Ellen, laundress, Institute for the blind, r. same
Kelley Jerry, hostler Wood & Mansur, bds. 99 S. New Jersey
Kelley John B. painter, r. ss. Cherry near cor. East
Kelley Mary Miss, teacher, bds. 204 N. Illinois
Kelley P. Henry, clerk Moody Bros., bds. 126 W. Vermont
Kelley Patrick, lab. F. L. Farnam, r. country
Kelley Patrick, apprentice *State Sentinel* job room, bds. 24 Buchanan
Kelley Robert, wks. Rolling Mill, r. 153 W. South
Kelley Sarah Miss, teacher, bds. 204 N. Illinois
Kelley Laura, (col'd) wid. John, r. 225 W. Ohio
Kelley Thomas, butcher, bds. 24 Indiana av.
Kelley Thomas, porter Commercial Hotel, bds. same
Kelley Walter, brick mason, r. 153 W. South
Kelley William, harness maker, r. 338 E. Washington
Kellogg Amos V. engineer, r. 377 E. Georgia
Kellogg Daniel W. messenger Am. Ex. Co. r. 397 W. New York
Kellogg George, lab. bds. 198 S. Illinois
Kellogg Newton, edge tool manufacturer 411 W. Washington (Nat. Road), r. 47 N. West cor. Market
Kelly Cornelius, painter, r. 140 Massachusetts av.
Kelly Hugh, lab. Budd & Hinsley, r. 216 E. Washington
Kelly James, huckster, r. 128 Bluff road
Kelly John, lab. r. 430 S. Illinois
Kelly Michael, r. 39 S. West
Kelly Thomas, butcher, 34 Kentucky av. r. 24 Indiana av.
Kelsner W. P. painter W. Whitridge, bds. 74 N. Pennsylvania
Kemker Charles (J. C. Brinkmeyer & Co.) r. 190 N. East
Kenneet George, teamster, r. 279 S. Meridian
Kemp A. (col'd) lab. r. 79 N. California
Kemp Jasper, heater Rolling Mill
KEMPER JOHN M. carpenter and builder, 184 E. South, r. 192 S. New Jersey

KEM	186	KEP

Kemper Lorenzo D. carpenter John M. Kemper, r. 192 S. New Jersey

Kemper William H. r. 45 Madison av.

Kempf Robert, harness maker Frauer, Briler & Co. bds. Washington cor. East

Kenan John, teamster, r. 105 S. Noble

Kenani Margarett, wid. Thomas, r. 105 S. Noble

Kenan William, teamster, r. 105 S. Noble

Kendall Henry, salesman Pettis, Dickson & Co. r. 86 N. Mississippi

Kendall John A. clerk Moritz Bro. bds. Kentucky av.

Kendall John McD. printer, r. 41 Grant

Kendell Joseph, foundry, r. 19 Madison av.

Kendle James, painter, r. 1 Thomas

Kendrick Robert, artist, 73 N. East, r. same

Kendrick R. fireman C. C. C. & I. R. R.

Kendrick W. H. physician, 73 N. East, r. 75 N. East

KENEASTER N. D. propr. Bates House, Illinois nw. cor. Washington, r. same

Keneaster Peter, cigar stand Bates House, bds. same

Kenig Christian, carpenter, r. 123 E. McCarty

Kennedy Daniel, blacksmith Greenleaf & Co. r. 165 High

Kennedy Frank, whol. dry goods, r. 247 N. Meridian

Kennedy James, wks. Miller & White, bds. Orient nr. Deaf and Dumb Asylum

Kennedy James, blacksmith, r. Maryland, ne. cor. Benton

Kennedy James, gardner, bds. 245 W. South

Kennedy John, boilermaker, 245 W. South

Kennedy John, compositor *Journal* news room

Kennedy Patrick, lab. r. 151 S. Alabama

Kennedy R. Frank, (Kennedy, Byram & Co.) r. 247 N. Meridian

Kennedy Thomas, r. 179 E. South

Kennedy William A. salesman Kennedy, Byram & Co. bds. 17½ Virginia av.

KENNEDY, BYRAM & CO. (R. Frank Kennedy, N. S. Byram, E. G. Cornelius and Oliver Tousey) dry goods and notions whol. 104 S. Meridian

Kennengton John, teamster Gas Works

Kenney Catharine, wid. r. rear 144 Stevens

Kenney Michael, lab. frt. depot C. C. & I. C. R. R.

Kenney Thomas, cutter G. H. Heitkam, r. 58 S. West

Kenney Walter, lab. r. 486 E. Georgia

Kennington Robert, saloon and hand ball alley, 178 S. Delaware, r. 325 S. Pennsylvania

Kenower John, teamster Coburn & Jones

Kentman Mathias, lab. r. 236 Massachusetts av.

Kenton James, blksmith, r. 41 Ellen

Kenyon Wallace B. painter, r. 83 W. Market

Kenzle George, grocer, 233 W. McCarty, r. same

Keppel Daniel, wks. Rolling Mill, bds. 270 S. Tennessee

Keppel Henry, heater Rolling Mill, r. 272 S. Illinois

Keppel Jesse, mechanic Rolling Mill
Keppele John, (Hildebrand, Keppele & Co.) r. Morgan Co.
Keppele Josiah, Rolling Mill, r. 270 S. Tennessee
Keppel Martin, eatinghouse, 36 W. Louisiana, r. same
Kercheval William J. bkpr. J. T. Layman & Co. r. 75 E. Pratt
Kerfoot L. B. r. 78 N. New Jersey
Kerfoot Richard A. clerk Smith & Foster, bds. 78 N. New Jersy
Kerins Mary, wid. James, r. 38 Douglas
Kerkoff Frederick C. lab. J. M. & I. R. R. r. 271 Union
Kern Casper, cabinetmaker, r. 392 E. Michigan
Kern Charles, wks. Scribner & Smith, bds. 392 E. Michigan
Kern Jacob, r. 288 E. Michigan
Kern Louis, wks. Scribner & Smith, bds. 392 E. Michigan
Kern N. R. machinist Greenleaf & Co.
Kerper Charles, r. 73 W. Maryland
Kerr Charles, baker A. Ball, bds. 178 S. Illinois
Kerr George, painter, bds. Richmond Temperance House
Kersch John, lab. r. 144 Union
Kersey Oliver, joiner W. Tate, r. 240 Union
Kershaw George, bookkeeper, bds. 2. Indiana av.
Kershaw J. D. bookkeeper M. Kaufman & Bro. bds. Indiana av.
    cor. Ohio
Kesee Mary, wid. William, r. 296 Blake
Kesheirnan Martin, lab. A. D. Wood
Kesler N. driver Citizens' R. R. Co. bds. Globe House
Kessler Fred. lab. r. St. Clair junc. Massachusetts av. and Plum
Kessner Henry, shoemaker, r. 144 Indiana av.
Kester Joseph, driver Citizens' Street R. R. Co.
Kester Laban, streetcar driver, bds. 266 S. Illinois
Kestler Rosa Mrs. confectioner, 173 W. Washington, r. same
Kestner Adam, prop. California House, 184 S. Illinois, r. same
Kestner Henry, driver City R. R. bds. Globe House
Ketcham William A. (Newcomb, Mitchell & Ketcham) r. 164 E.
    Merrill
Kettenbach Edward, (Kettenbach, Newmeyer & Co.) r. 279
    Massachusetts av.
Kettenbach Eliza, wid. Henry, r, 279 Massachusetts av.
Kettenbach F. W. (Kettenbach, Newmeyer & Co.) r. 279 Mas-
    sachusetts av.
Kettenbach, Newmeyer & Co. (Edward and F. W. Kettenbach
    and Julius A. Newmeyer) grocers, 273, 275 and 277 Massa-
    chusetts av.
Kettler Herman, varnisher, r. 193 Bates
Keuhn Ernest, watchman Eagle Machine Works
Keutzer Peter, lab. Schmidt's Brewery, r. same
Kevers John H. grocer, 525 N. Mississippi, r. same
Keveux Julius, painter S. W. Drew
Keyser George, plumber J. G. Hanning
Keyser John, carpenter, bds. 23 N. West
Kiefer Augustus, (Kiefer & Vinton) r. 483 N. Illinois
Kiefer L. A. (L. F. Kiefer & Son) bds. 463 N. Delaware

Kiefer L. F. (L. F. Kiefer & Son) r. 463 N. Delaware

Kiefer L. F. & Son, (L. F. and L. A. Kiefer) watchmakers and jewelers, 2 Odd Fellows bldg.

KIEFER & VINTON, (Augustus Kiefer and Almus E. Vinton) whol. druggists, 68 S. Meridian

Kieger John, driver City railroad, r. al. bet. Pennsylvania and Delaware, Maryland and Georgia

Kierst A. cabinetmkr. Helwig & Co.

Kiker J. C. driver Citizens R. R. Co.

Kiler John, engineer, bds. 61 S. Noble

Kiley Daniel, engineer, r. 115 N. Davidson

Kilgore John D. (Kilgore & Helms) bds. 31 W. Ohio

Kilgore John, boot and shoemkr. 64 S. Delaware, r. same

KILGORE & HELMS, (John D. Kilgore and Lewis A. Helms) dentists, office 19 Miller's block, 70 N. Illinois

Kilian Louis, tender Louis Lang, bds. 29 S. Meridian

Killay Mathew, lab. r. 155 Meek

Killorin Michael, teamster D. B. McDonough, bds. 199 W. Maryland

KIMBALL EBEN W. attorney at law, notary public and U. S. commissioner, 46 E. Washington, r. 382 N. Meridian

Kimball George H. carpenter, r. 61 Russell av.

Kimball James N. deputy State treas. State bldg. r. 475 N. Illinois

KIMBALL NATHAN, state treas. office State bldg. and mnfr. of plows, es. Tennessee bet. Washington and Kentucky av. r. 475 N. Illinois

Kimble Thomas V. (Kimble, Aikman & Co.) r. 275 Indiana av.

KIMBLE, AIKMAN & CO. (Thomas V. Kimble, John B. Aikman and D. J. Stile) hardware and cutlery whol. 108 S. Meridian

Kincaide Harry, r. 228 W. Ohio

Kindel Joseph, (B. F. Hetherington & Co.) r. 19 Madison av.

Kinder Mariah W. wid. Isaac, r. 27 Lockerbie

KINDLER CHARLES, locksmith and bellhanger, 60 N. Pennsylvania, r. 215 N. Noble

Kindley Samuel J. r. 11 Dacotah

King Adam, hostler, r. 483 S. New Jersey

King Christian, carpenter Eagle Machine Works, r. 123 E. McCarty

King Cornelius, lumber dealer, es. Western av. nr. Forrest Home

King David, ice dealer and carpenter, r. 261 N. Mississippi

KING EDWARD, gen'l agt. C. C. C. & I. R. R. and sec'y and treas. I. & St. Louis R. R. 53 S. Alabama, r. Nat. rd. 2 miles west of City

King Eli, lumber dealer, 448 E. St. Clair

King George, carpenter, r. 272 E. St. Clair

King Harry, baggage master, bds. 175 S. New Jersey

King Harry, tender, bds. Western House

King Ira S. r. 313 S. East

King Jacob, (King & Pinney) r. 186 E. McCarty

King James H. boots and shoes, 156 Indiana av. r. 111 Indiana av.
King James M. deputy Collector Internal Revenue, room 15 P. O. bldg. r. 196 Davidson
King John H. blacksmith, r. 51 Peru
King John, salesman Hayden S. Bigham, bds. 200 S. Alabama
King John, student Bryant & Stratton's College, bds. 374 S. West
King John B. teamster, r. 386 N. Mississippi
King Jonn W. wool buyer Hoosier Woolen Factory, r. Circle se. cor. Market
King Lovie Miss, dressmkr. Mrs. A. Dooland, bds. 9 E. New York
King Mary Miss, clk. William Haerle, r. 111 Indiana av.
King Peter, moulder, r. 385 S. Delaware
King Sarah, wid. r. 261 N. Mississippi
King Thomas, lab. bds. Illinois House
KING & PINNEY (Jacob King and Frank W. Pinney) founders and machinists, Kentucky av. cor. Mississippi
Kingan Samuel, (Nofsinger, Kingan & Co. also Kingan & Co.) r. New York
Kingan Thomas D. (Nofsinger, Kingan & Co. also Kingan & Co.) bds. Bates House
KINGAN & CO. (Thomas D. and Samuel Kingan) pork packers and com. mers. west end Maryland
Kingham Alice, student National Business College
Kingham John, student National Business College
Kingham Joseph, broommaker, r. 253 Massachusetts av.
Kingman Nelson, bookkeeper D. Root & Co. r. 510 N. Delaware
Kingsbury John E. watchmaker, 237 Massachusetts av. r. same
Kingston Samuel, painter F. Fertig, r. 231 S. Mississippi
Kinkler Henry, baggageman Union depot, bds. California House
Kinney Cornelius, switchman, r. 270 W. St. Clair
Kinnister Henry, cigarmaker J. Miller
Kinsley Martha, wks. paper mill, r. 311 W. Market
Kintz Adam, hostler Charles Brinkman
Kipp Albrecht, traveling agt. Charles Mayer & Co. bds. Emenegger's Hotel
Kirby Bettie, tailoress Smith's Chemical Dye Works, r. 173 E. New York
Kirby Henry, salesman Kimble, Aikman & Co. bds. Sherman House
Kirby J. M. painter E. Jenkens, r. 660 N. Mississippi
Kirby James, r. 627 N. Illinois
Kirby Joseph, moulder Union Novelty Works
Kirby Samuel, r. 27 Chatham
Kirby William L. salesman Fahnley & McCrea, bds. Sherman House
Kirk Daniel, carpenter, r. 191½ W. Washington
Kirk Daniel, turner, r. 131 Meek
Kirk E. Mrs. milliner, 75 N. Pennsylvania, r. same

KIR	190	KLI

Kirk McClellan, carpenter, r. 232 W. Georgia

Kirk Nathaniel, r. 75 N. Pennsylvania

Kirkpatrick George A. (William Craig & Co.) r. Broad Ripple

KIRKPATRICK JOHN, physician and surgeon, 26½ N. Illinois, r. 204 N. Illinois

Kirkwood Adam, fireman, r. 40 Lord

Kirlin James, dry goods 186 W. Washington, r. 526 N. Illinois

Kirsbaum Henry, wks. V. Meier & Bro.

Kirsey P. Miss, dressmaker S. A. Mulliken, r. 372 E. New York

Kirsch John, lab. Osgood, Smith & Co.

Kirshner Frederick, salesman John Fishback, r. 311 N. Pennsylvania

Kirtland G. A. lawyer, bds. Little's Hotel

Kirtz ———, blacksmith, bds. 258 N. Mississippi

Kise Elisha S. teamster, r. Maria nw. cor. Smith

Kise John W. clk. r. 162 Indiana av.

Kissel Frederick, saloon 98 Russel av. r. same

Kissell Jacob W. saloon, r. 22 S. West

Kissinger Charles M. painter, r. 171 Bluff rd.

Kissour Gustavus H. bds. Illinois House

Kistner Fred, painter D. C. Chapman, r. 336 S. Meridian

Kistner John G. boots and shoes 83 S. Illinois, r. 336 S. Meridian

Kitchel Celeste Miss, r. 18 W. Georgia

Kitchel M. boardinghouse 18 W. Georgia, r. same

Kitchel Priscilla Miss, bds. 18 W. Georgia

Kitchen John M. physician and surgeon Vinton's blk. opp. Post Office, r. 145 N. Pennsylvania

Kitzmiller William, engineer Emerson, Beam & Thompson, r. 246 W. Washington

Klare Frederick, (Klare & Schroeder) r. ws. Bluff rd. 2 w. limits

KLARE & SCHROEDER, (Fred Klare and William Schroeder) saloon and bowling alley Bluff rd. cor. city limits

Klefers Henry, machinist, bds. Washington House

Klein John G. barber shop 2 Martindale's blk. r. nw. cor. Missouri and 3d

Klein Madison C. watchmaker C. A. Ferguson, bds. Pyle House

Kleine Richard, clk. C. H. Schwomeyer, bds. 297 S. Meridian

Kleiner Frederick, teamster Indianapolis Transfer Co. r. 222 Bluff rd.

Kleinschmidt Christian, teamster, r. 284 E. Market

Kleinsmith Fred teamster Fred C. Bollman

Kleis Frederick, r. 476 E. Georgia

Kleis Henry, lab. r. 528 E. Georgia

Kline Frederick, r. 222 Bluff rd.

Kline Frederick, engineer, r. 530 E. Georgia

Kline George, machinist Eagle Machine Works, r. 105 S. Meridian

Kline Joseph, (I. L. Frankem & Co.) r. 295 S. New Jersey

Kline Nicholas, shoemaker 283 Massachusetts av. r. 361 Spring

Klingensmith Israel, lawyer 115 E. Washington, bds. 478 N. Tennessee

Klink Mathias, lab. r. 67 Harrison

Klotz John, carpenter, r. 413 S. Illinois
Klum Ada B. Miss, teacher 9th Ward School, bds. 171 Davidson
Klump Fred, foreman Indianapolis Brewery, r. same
Klusman Antony, baker A. Balls, bds. 178 S. Illinois
Klussman Fred, helper Ind. Coach Works, r. 123 St. Marys
Klussmann Louis, tailor, r. 123 St. Mary
Knapp Gardner, r. 50 Ellsworth
Knauf Adam, bakery 257 Massachusetts av. r. same
Knaus C. G. lab. r. 450 Indiana av.
Knauss W. J. lab. r. 297 E. New York
Knarzer George, bds. 60 S. Delaware
Knatzer Philip, bartender M. Wenger, bds. 60 S. Delaware
Knefler Charles, bookkeeper Hays, Rosenthal & Co. 64 S. Meridian
Knefler Frederick, (Hanna & Knefler) r. 466 N. Pennsylvania
Kneip John, lab. r. 294 N. Liberty
Knieriem Henry, painter F. Fertig
Knight J. Newton, painter, r. 666 N. Tennessee
Knight John, (Cottrell & Knight) r. 304 N. Delaware
Knight O. wks. J. S. Carey & Co.
Knight William, moulder D. Root & Co.
Knighton C. J. carpenter and builder, E. Market cor. Davidson,
    r. 78 N. Illinois
Knipe William, driver Pettis, Dickson & Co.
Knippenberg Henry, (E. C. Atkins & Co. and J. H. Kappes &
    Co.) r. 497 N. Meridian
Knippenberg Jacob, salesman Crain & Needham, bds. Oriental
    House
Knippenberg John, clerk, bds. Oriental House
Knodle A. mnfr. and dealer in boots and shoes, 32 E. Washington, r. 8 Indiana av.
Knodle George, clerk A. Knodle, r. 80 Ohio
Knotts Nim. K. (Knotts & Co.) r. 76 W. Market
KNOTTS NIM. K. & CO. (N. K. Knotts & C. S. Butterfield) saloon
    and restaurant, 72 W. Washington
Knowlton Benjamin, head waiter Bates House, bds. same
Knox Francis A. (col'd) (Knox & Embers) r. es. Howard nr. 2d
Knox J. W. lab. Union Starch Factory
Knox Joseph, engineer, r. Geisendorff bet. Washington & N. York
Knox & Embers, (col'd) (Fracis Knox, Thomas Embers) barbers,
    Washington ne. cor. Meridian
Koallesch Martin, (Lake & Co.) r. 140 S. Madison av.
Koble Elizabeth, wid. Jacob, r. Minerva 1 s. Vermont
Koble Samuel H. wks. Capital Brewery, bds. ws. Minerva 1 s.
    Vermont
Koch Christian, porter Union Depot
Koch Frank, lab. Rolling Mill, r. 237 W. South
Koch Frederick, porter Hahn & Bals
Koch Geo. shoemaker C. Neermann, bds. 271 Massachusetts av.
Koch H. H. porter Stoneman, Pce & Co. r. South cor. Noble
Koch Henry, teamster, r. 22 John

KOC	192	KOU

Koch Henry H. grocer, 192 S. Noble, r. same
Koch Ignatz, lab. r. 491 S. Illinois
Koch Thomas, lab. r. 16 Lockerbie
Koch William, clerk Fahnley & McCrea, r. 192 S. Noble
Koch William, apprentice Helwig & Co.
Kochel Thomas, hostler south side livery stable, r. 198 S. Illinois
Koebler Gottlieb, painter L. Helle, bds. 228 S. Pennsylvania
KOEHL PETER, grocer, 188 S. Illinois, bds. Califoania House
Koehn Ernest, watchman, r. 503 N. Illinois
Koehne Charles, (H. Sieber & Co.) r. 467 N. Delaware
Koehring Bernhard, cooper, 287 N. Liberty, r. same
Koeniger George, saloon, 338 S. Meridian, r. same
Koepper William, lab. Union Starch Factory
Koerner Conrad, (Hendrix & Koerner) National Business College, bds. Ray House
Koerner Michael, lab. r. Court bet. East and New Jersey
Koester D. lab. C. C. C. & I. Rw.
Koester Theodore, lab. C. C. C. & I. Rw.
Kohl Peter, grocer, bds. California House
Kohler Henry, (col'd) lab. r. 227 N. West
Kohler John, grocer and saloon, 247 N. Noble, r. 244 N. Noble
Kohlscheek George, brewer Schmidt's Brewery, r. S. Delaware
Kohs Charles, porter Kennedy, Byran & Co.
Kolb Adam, buckster, r. 177 Union
KOLB LOUIS, job turning, 23 E. South, r. 17 E. South
Kolb William, boarding house, 23 Kentucky av. r. same
Kolb William, salesman H. Reese, bds. 113 W. Washington
Kolthoff Fred. r. Union opp. 6th Ward School
Kolthof Frederick, machinist Burk, Earnshaw & Co.
Kolyer J. W. (Kolyer & Caffey) bds. 72 E. Market
Kolyer & Caffey, (J. W. Kolyer and J. H. Caffey) sale and feed stable, Wabash alley bet. Pennsylvania and Delaware
Konntz Harman, cook Bates House
Kooh Frederick, r. 79 S. Liberty
Kopper Frederick, cabinetmaker Spiegel & Thoms
Korn Martin, tanner, r. 32 S. Alabama
Korpeter William, tailor, r. 430 S. East
Koser John, locksmith, 18 Virginia av. r. 256 Pennsylvania
Koss Caroline, wid. William, r. 275 N. Noble
Koss Louis, stonemason, r. 329 Davidson
Kostenbader Charles, stonecutter Smith, Ittenbach & Co.
Koster C. J. M. cigar mnfr. and dealer, 141 E. Washington, r. 181 Blake
Koster Joseph, baker, r. rear 435 S. Illinois
Koster Richard, lab. Bellefontaine frt. depot, r. 225 Bluff rd.
Kothe Henry, pianomkr. Indianapolis Piano Mnfg. Co. r. 187 E. Washington
Kothe William, bookkeeper Clemens Vonnegut, r. 113 Davidson
Kothe William, groceries ret. 130 N. Davidson, r. same
Kouster Joseph, pastry cook Palmer House
Kouvtz George W. clk. P. O. r. 218 E. Market

Kown Alexander, r. 300 E. St. Clair
Kown William, street contractor, r. 169 N. East
Kathiman William, varnisher Wilkens & Hall 84-86 E. Market
Kræger Henry, beltmkr. r. 331 E. Georgia
Kraft Henry, lab. Lash, Tousey & Co. r. Madison rd. s. of limits
Kragar Frederick, lab. J. M. & I. R. R.
Kragg August P. salesman J. H. Baldwin & Co. bds. 32 N.
    Pennsylvania
Kragg William A. salesman Holland, Ostermeyer & Co. bds. 32
    N. Pennsylvania
Kramer Andrew, shoemaker Charles Aldag, r. 199 N. Liberty
Kramer George, billiard hall, r. Morrison 2 east of Delaware
Kramer Henry, meat market 80 Fort Wayne av; r. same
Kramer Jacob, wagonmkr. r. 199 N. Liberty
Kramer Michael, bartender Abdon Singel, bds. 176 E. Wash-
    ington
Kramer William, lab. r. 333 S. East
Kramer William H. meat market 306 Virginia av. r. 321 Vir-
    ginia av.
Krass S. wid. William, r. ns. Wabash alley bet. N. New Jersey
    and N. East
Kraus Christian, machine hand Cabinet Makers' Union
Kraus Jacob, teamster, r. 27 Center
Krause Christ, carpenter C. C. & I. C. R. R.
Krause J. sawmkr. Sheffield Saw Works
Krause R. (Krause & Riemenschneider) r. 456 E. Michigan
Krause & Riemenschneider (R. Krause and Herman Riemen-
    schneider) stocking mnfrs. 84 E. Washington
Krause Charles, messenger Citizens' National Bank
Krauss Paul, messenger Indiana National Bank
Krefker Henry, tailor Becker & Huber, r. 53 E. Harrison
Kregelo Charles E. salesman D. N. Mitchell, r. 52 Indiana av.
Kregelo David (Long & Kregelo) r. 228 N. West
Kreger Frederick, lab. r. 398 S. East
Kreger Henry, beltmkr. Mooney & Co. r. 331 E. Georgia
Kreger William, currier Mooney & Co. r. 393 S. East
Kreglo Jacob, carpenter C. F. Rafert, r. 82 E. St. Clair
Kreglo Mary, boarding house 82 E. St. Clair, r. same
Kreider Ruben G. clk. r. 218 E. South
Kreis Philip, r. 327 S. Delaware
Kreitzer Fred, lab. r. 197 Harrison
Kreitzer Henry, lab. r. 197 Harrison
Krentler Frederick C. clk. Dessar Bro. & Co. r. Elm cor. Cedar
Kretsch Peter, mfr. and dealer in cigars and tobacco 141 S.
    Illinois, r. 325 S. Meridian
Kreutzer Mary, teacher German High School, r. Illinois se. cor.
    South
Krider Reuben, clk. r. 218 E. South
Kring John L. carpenter, r. 378 S. West
Krister Theodore, lab. Bellefontaine frt. depot, r. 265 Union
Kroeber Frederick, tanner, r. 31 N. East

13

Krome August, teacher German Lutheran School, r. 280 E. Georgia
Krame Fred, mason, r. 148 Huron
Kroenberger William, musician, r. al. bet. Pennsylvania and Delaware, Maryland and Georgia
Krouse Christian, deck hand, r. Ohio, e. of limits
Krug George C. (G. C. Krug & Co.) r. 67 S. Noble
Krug G. C. & Co. (George C. Krug and John A. Buddenbaum) grocers, Georgia cor. Liberty
Kruger Charles, clk. Ripley & Gates, r. 362 W. New York
Kruger Christian, (Schrader & Kruger) r. 343 E. McCarty
Kruger Henry, brewer Harting & Bro. r. 355 S. Illinois
Kruger Henry, tailor, r. 221 N. Noble
Kruger Joseph, r. 266 E. Market
Krumm Joseph, tailor George Green
Krummels ——, wid. r. Illinois ne. cor. Wilkins
Kruse Christian, carpenter, r. 15 E. McCarty
Kruse Henry, drayman, r. 55 Harrison
Kruse John, saloon, 222 E. Washington, r. same
Kruse R. stocking mnfr. r. 456 E. Michigan
Krytzer John, tailor, r. 690 N. Tennessee
Kuerst Henry, carpenter, r. 182 Madison av.
Kugelman William, salesman G. F. Meyer, r. 134 N. Maryland
Kuhleman Henry, r. Market cor. Tennessee
Kuhlinberg Barney, butcher R. Essigke, bds. 170 S. Illinois
Kuhlman Charles, pianomaker, r. 118 N. Noble
Kuhlman Conrad, varnisher Cabinet Maker's Union
Kuhn August M. clk. Fahnley & McCrea, bds. National Hotel
Kuhn Charles, meat market, 207 W. Michigan, r. same
Kuhn John, blacksmith W. Vondersaar, r. 160 Fort Wayne av.
Kuhn Philip, blksmith B. F. Haugh & Co. r. 160 Ft. Wayne av.
Kuhn Philip J. grocer, Ft. Wayne av. junction New Jersey,
Kuhn William, propr. Indiana Bakery, r. 150 N. East
Kuhn William, messenger Indiana Banking Co.
Kunkel Augustus, lab. Osgood, Smith & Co.
Kunkel Benjamin, cigarmaker, r. 451 S. Illinois
Kunkel Charles, miller Heckman & Sheesley, r. 434 Virginia av.
Kunkel Henry, carpenter, r. 431 Virginia av.
Kunkel Jacob, belt maker John Fishback, r. E. Maryland rear St. Mary's Church
Kunkel John, lab. r. rear St. John's Catholic Church
Kuntz Jacob, carpenter, r. 27 Lord
Kunz Hellen, milliner M. A. Kunz, r. 9 S. Alabama
Kunz M. A. milliner, 9 S. Alabama, r. same
Kupper Frederick, carpenter, r. 81 S. Liberty
Kurn Dennis, lab. r. 354 Winston
Kurts H. P. blacksmith, 178 Indiana av. r. 258 N. Mississippi
Kurtz L. K. paperhanger, bds. 340 N. Delaware
Kuser Daniel, lab. r. 44 Dougherty
Kutemeyer Charles, carpenter, r. 317 E. Market
Keutzleb Robert, painter, r. alley rear 120 Union

L

Laag Henry, blacksmith Phœnix Machine Works
Labarre Louis, moulder, r. 79 Elm
Label Henry, wheeler Rolling Mill
Lack Rudolph, clk. Harrison's Bank, r. 184 W. Ohio
Lackey Joseph, (Snider & Lackey) r. 496 Virginia av.
Lacy A. C. comp. *Journal* newsroom, r. 234 W. Michigan
Lacy Julia A. Mrs. r. 12 Indiana av.
Ladd Harrison, bds. 554 N. Illinois
Ladd Robert, bds. 554 N. Illinois
Ladd William H. bookkeeper, r. 554 N. Illinois
Ladies' Christian Monitor, Mrs. M. M. B. Goodwin editor and
    propr. Meridian se. cor. Circle
Ladies' Own Magazine, Mrs. M. Cora Bland editor, Bland & Tay-
    lor publishers, 19 N. Meridian
La Dow Daniel, (La Dow & Calvert) r. Dayton, Ohio
La Dow & Calvert, (Daniel La Dow and James Calvert) Indi-
    anapolis Marble Work 120 S. Illinois
La Fayette House, George Hoppe propr. 179 S. Meridian
Laha Timothy, lab. r. 493 E. Georgia
Lahman Frederick, shoemaker. r. 203 N. Winston
Lahman W. drayman Anderson, Bullock & Schofield, r. 85
    Union
Laing David, r. 223 W. South
Laing Samuel, tinner, r. 223 W. South
Laing William W. bookbinder Meikel Bros. bds. 223 W. South
Lair Jacob, cooper, r. 61 E. McCarty
Laird Charles P. ins. solicitor Martin, Hopkins & Ohr, r. 36
    Cherry
Laird Emma Miss, teacher 4th Ward School
Laird William, bookkeeper Kiefer & Vinton, r. 554 N. Illinois
Lake Ellis, r. 265 Bluff rd.
Lake John, drover, r. ws. Bluff rd. nr. Kansas
Lake John, (Lake & Co.) r. Bluff rd.
Lake Joseph P. carpenter J. L. & M. K. Fatout, r. 161 Indiana av
Lake & Co. (John Lake and Martin Koallesch) butchers 22 N.
    Illinois
Lakin Joseph D. brakeman, r. 68 S. Noble
Lamb Amos S. clk. r. 102 E. Pratt
Lamb Peter, lab. r. 253 S. Tennessee
Lamb Samuel, detective, r. 102 E. Pratt
Lamb William, bds. 102 E. Pratt
Lamb William C. librarian Supreme Court Library, State Bldg.
    r. 204 N. Illinois
Lambert J. M. propr. Ray House, r. same
Lambert Joseph, teamster, r. 373 W. Washington
Lame John, conductor Bellefontaine R. R. bds. 207 W. Maryland
LAMOTTE CHARLES, saloon 100 S. Illinois, and (Joseph La-
    motte & Son) r. 192 Massachusetts av.

LAM	196	LAN

Lamotte Joseph, (Joseph Lamotte & Son) r. 192 Massachusetts av.

LAMOTTE JOSEPH & SON, (Joseph and Charles Lamotte) stoves and tinware, 192 Massachusetts av.

Landauer N. J. gen'l agt. Sycamore Woolen Mills, office 164 W. Washington, r. same

Landers A. C. wid. Joseph, r. 89 W. Market

Landers Franklin, (Landers, Conduitt & Co.) r. 402 N. Pennsylvania

Landers James, engineer, r. 153 Winston

Landers John, exp. messenger, r. 200 E. McCarty

Landers Thomas, lab. r. 200 E. McCarty

Landers, Conduitt & Co. (Franklin Landers, Alexander B. Conduitt and Milton S. Cox) dry goods and notions whol. and ret. 58 S. Meridian

Landgraff Bertha Mrs. r. 44 Douglas

Landgraff Joanna, wks. Cotton Factory

Landgraff Norbert, wks. Cotton Factory

Landis Jacob, livery and sale stable, 30 S. Pennsylvania, r. 128 W. Maryland

Landis James, engineer C. & I. J. R. R.

LANDIS MILTON M. agt. White Line (fast frt.) office Wallace's block, r. 506 N. Meridian

Landormie Ernst, fireman C. C. & I. R. R.

Landragan Michael, fireman, r. 327 E. Georgia

Lane Ida. (col'd) wid. David, r. 23 Vine

Lane Mary J. milliner, r. 428 N. East

Lane Thomas S. sawmaker Am. Saw Works, bds. 75 S. Penn.

Lane Uriah, carpenter, r. 428 N. East

Lang Daniel, carpenter, r. 15 Madison av.

Lang Frederick, janitor State bldg.

Lang Julius clerk Joseph Langbein, bds. 300 E. Washington

LANG LOUIS, dealer in bottled liquors and cigars, 29 S. Meridian, r. 221 E. Ohio

Lang Samuel, tinner W. T. Jennings

Langbein Joseph, groceries, toys and fancy goods, 200 E. Washington cor. New Jersey, r. same

Langdon Caroline, wid. r. 21 Maria

Lange Louis, painter, r. 330 S. Delaware

Langenberg —— Mrs. r. 225 W. Washington

Langenberg Henry H. (H. H. Langenberg & Co.) r. ws. Bluff rd. city limits

LANGENBERG H. H. & CO. (Henry H. Langenberg, Frederick J. Vogt and Aaron Rozier) groceries, provisions, flour, feed, grain, etc. 244-6 W. Washington

Langford Ann M. wid Albert F. r. 58 Cherry

Langhorn A. T. telegraph operator C. C. & I. C. R. R. bds. 17½ Virginia av.

Langhorn W. A. telegraph operator C. C. & I. C. R. R. bds. 17½ Virginia av.

Langley L. Cornell, clerk A. Abromet, bds. 2 Indiana av

Langsdale J. M. W. r. 225 E. Ohio

T. B. Perrine, Engraver on Jewelry & Silver Ware. 34 Virginia av.

LAN   197   LAW

Langsdale Mary, wid. John, bds. 325 E. New York
Langsdale Robert, bds. 225 E. Ohio
LANGSENKAMP WILLIAM, coppersmith 96 S. Delaware r. 184 S. Delaware
Lanihan John, lab. r. 374 S. Illinois
Lanners David G. clk. r. 143 N. Delaware
Laport Millard J. sawer Osgood, Smith & Co. r. 34 Vinton
Lappert Leopold, tailor, r. 184 S. Delaware
Large Michael, lab. r. 332 Indiana av.
Larger Jerome, brakeman, bds. 58 Benton
Larimore Jerimiah, physician and surgeon, office 172½ W. Washington, r. same
Larkens John, trackman Citizens' Street R. R. Co.
Larkin John, lab. r. 31 Ellen
Larner James, lab. r. 113 N. West
Larsen Anders, tailor A. J. Gerstner, r. 173 E. Washington
Larsen Jens, tailor A. J. Gerstner, r. 173 E. Washington
Larsn Peter, H. straightner, Rolling Mill
La Rue Clarence, telegraph operator, r. 429 E. St. Clair
La Rue Isaac S. r. 429 E. St. Clair
La Rue Leslie, tinner, r. 429 E. St. Clair
La Ruff Thomas B. painter Ind. Coach Works, bds. 20 W. Georgia
Lary James, lab. r. 82 Bates
Lasley Martha, wid. Simon, r. 254 Massachusetts av.
Latham Charles, clerk S. A. Fletcher & Co. bds. ns. E. Washington, 3 e. city limits
Latham George A. salesman E. A. Elder, bds. Wiles House
Latham George W. clerk, bds. Stanridge House
Latham Henry, bookkeeper Indianapolis National Bank, r. E. Washington nr. Corporation
Latham William H. teacher Indiana Deaf and Dumb Institute, r. Washington e. of limits
Lather John, bartender Henry Eix
Lathrop ——, salesman, bds. 10 E. Michigan
Latshaw John F. real estate agent, r. 92 S. Mississippi
Laubheimer August, r. 347 N. Noble
Lauck John, apprentice, bds. 391 S. Delaware
Lauck Mary, wid. Michael, r. 391 S. Delaware
Lauderback Peter, farmer, r. Sharp e. of Merrill
Lauer Charles, saloon, r. 15 Russell av.
Lauer Charles, saloon and restaurant, 202 E. Washington,
Lauer John, moulder D. Root & Co.
Lauer William, starchmaker, r. 52 Bicking
Laughlin Dennis, lab. freight depot I. C. & I. R. R.
Laughlin James, lab. C. C. C. & I. R. R.
Laughlin Jennie, r. 34 W. Ohio
Laughlin Mary E. Miss, teacher 6th Ward School, r. 34 W. Ohio
Laughner Joseph, lab. Hair and Bristol Wks. r. s. end S. West
Laupheimer August, saloon, 191 E. Washington, r. same
Lawhurn George, (col'd) medical student R. Lawhurn, 163 Indiana av.

LAW	198	LEA

Lawler William, engineer, r. 289 S. East

Lawless Michael, (Lawless & Curran) r. 138 S. Noble

LAWLESS & CURRAN, (Michael Lawless and Patrick Curran) grocers, 138 S. Noble

LAWRENCE ARTHUR V. grocer, 173 W. Washington, r. 211 W. Ohio

Lawrence David F. canvasser, bds. 74 N. Pennsylvania

Lawrence Jacob, bds. 35 Ellen

Lawrence James H. (col'd) barber W. Porter, r. 441 S. Illinois

Lawrence M. (col'd) wid. Thomas, r. 441 S. Illinois

Lawrence Melinda, principal Colored School

Lawrence Thomas, paperhanger, bds. Stanridge House

Lawrie William, salesman Pettis, Dickson & Co. bds. 204 E. Market

Lawson ——, lab. r. 516 S. Illinois

Lawson Aaron P. farmer, r. 222 Union

Lawson Elizabeth, wid. Israel, r. 374 S. Tennessee

Lawton Henry W. transfer clk. C. C. C. & I. R. R. bds. ns. Michigan bet. Winston and Railroad

Lawyer P. C. (Lawyer & Hall) bds. Little's Hotel

LAWYER & HALL, (P. C. Lawyer and E. R. Hall) dealers in grain, flour, eggs and poultry, 49 S. New Jersey

Lax Elizabeth, wid. Andrew, r. 191 N. East

Lax Henry, baker E. Meier, bds. 131 S. Illinois

Lax Jacob, printer, r. 191 N. East

Lax Louis, printer, r. 191 N. East

Laycock C. F. carpenter, r. 167 Eddy

LaFayette & Indianapolis Rail Road Freight Depot, ws. Mississippi bet. Walnut and North

Layman James T. (James T. Layman & Co.) r. 85 E. Pratt

Layman John, wks. W. P. Bingham, bds. same

LAYMAN JAMES T. & CO. (James T. Layman, Jonathan M. Ridenour and George W. Clippinger) importers and whol. dealers in hardware, cutlery, window glass, &c. 64 E. Washington

Layton F. M. sleeping car conductor, bds. 317 E. Ohio

Layton Timothy, conductor, r. 45 Virginia av.

Leach James, lab. r. 288 S. East

Leach Joshua G. lab. T. H. & I. R. R. bds. Nagel House

Leahy Michael, shoemaker Thomas Dugan

LEAKE W. H. Lessee Academy of Music and Metropolitan Theatre, r. 75 N. Illinois

Leaman A. B. book agt. r. 405 N. New Jersey

Lean Goodspeed (col'd) painter, bds. 247 Howard

Leanty August, gunsmith A. Ballwey

Learned Charles, mnfr. lath machines, 304 W. Washington, r. 630 N. Illinois

Learned Charles C. r. 630 N. Illinois

Learsch William. butcher Julius Queisser, bds. Virginia av.

Leary Edward, lab. r. 42 Bicking

Leary Patrick C. lawyer, 85 E. Market, bds. 126 E. Ohio

Leary William, boilermaker Sinker & Co.

| LEA | 199 | LEL |

Leash Aaron, grocer, r. 94 N. California
Leash Isabell A. wid. Lewis, r. 94 N. California
Leathers William W. (Leathers & Carter) and Indianapolis Cotton Manufacturing Co. r. 273 N. New Jersey
Leathers & Carter, (William W. Leathers and George Carter) lawyers, room 3 Odd Fellows Hall
Leavitt William, carpenter, r. 302 E. North
Le Baron S. C. lab. C. C. C. & I. Rw.
Le Barre Louis, stove moulder A. D. Wood
Leck Robert M. book keeper, r. 480 N. Mississippi
Leddy John, lab. Rolling Mill
Lee Arch, carpenter, r. 232 N. Noble
Lee Charles N. solicitor Ind. Fire Ins. Co. bds. 138 N. New Jersey
LEE H. H. wholesale dealer in teas, 7 Odd Fellows building and druggist 18 and 20 Bates House blk. r. 189 N. Illinois
Lee James, (Lee & Replogle) r. 161 N. Spring
LEE MANDAVILLE G. editor and pulisher of *Daily Evening Commercial*, r. Ellsworth sw. cor. Vermont
Lee William E. saloon; 48 Virginia av. r. 173 S. Tennessee
Lee & Replogle, (James Lee and John Replogle) saloon, Noble near cor Washington
Leeds Francis M. lab. Osgood, Smith & Co. r. 32 Henry
Leeds George, r. 256 N. Mississippi
Leeds Learner, r. 20 W. Georgia
Leerkamp George, cooper J. S. Carey & Co. bds. Nagel House
Leerkamp John, clk. John Helm, bds. 272 Winston
Leers L. B. lab. Osgood, Smith & Co.
Le Ferver Samuel, street contractor, r. 145 W. South
Legrand Hubert L. physician and surgeon, 192 Massachusetts av.
Lehein Thomas, lab. r. 498 E. Georgia
Lehman Charles, wks. brewery, r. 68 S. California
Lehman John, porter W. P. Bingham, bds. same
Lehr Ferdinad A. real estate agt. 83 E. Washington, r. 419 N. New Jersey
Lehr Henry, carpenter, r. 347 E. New York
Lehr Philip, grocer and saloon, 246 N. Noble, r. same
Lehrritter Conrad, r. 213 E. Ohio
Lehrritter George, saloon, 143 E. Washington, r. same
Lehrritter Lizzie, milliner Bertha Baker, r. 143 E. Washington
Leibald John, lab. Helwig & Co.
Leibardt Joseph, dyer Merritt & Coughlen
Leible George, shoe maker Daniel Vielhaber, r. 134 Spring
Leisemann William, lab. r. 9 Peru
Leistner William, r. 223 W. Washington
Leitz Theobald, oil painter Miller's photographic gallery, r. 83 N. East
Lelewer David, (D. Lelewer & Bro.) r. 229 S. Delaware
Lelewer Isador, (D. Lelewer & Bro.) r. 229 S. Delaware
Lelewer D. & Bro. (David and Isador Lelewer), importers and dealers in ladies and gents furs, 39½ S. Meridian

Lelly Thomas, tailor, r. 225 W. South
Leming Marshall, miller Sohl, Gibson & Co. r. ws. Douglass 1 s. New York
Lemka Herman, music teacher, r. 193 Huron
Lemman Jennie, wid. John, r. 72 E. Ohio
Lemman Lander A. clk. bds. 72 E. Ohio
Lemmons William, bricklayer, r. 158 Winston
Lemon A. E. clk. Indiana Fire Ins. Co. r. 68 N. Liberty
Lemon C. fireman C. C. & I. C. R. R.
Lemon Daniel A. groceries and provisions 187 W. Washington, r. 46 N. Mississippi
Lemon P. H. r. 68 N. Liberty
Lendormi Desiree, wid. Basil, r. 434 E. North
Kendormi Ernest, fireman, r. 434 E. North
Lendormi Joseph, fireman, r. 434 E. North
Lendormi Paulin, policeman, r. 434 E. North
Lenk Mathias, foreman Schmidt's Brewery, r. same
Lennanan Bernhard, lab. r. 273 N. Noble
Lennelan John, fireman Gas Works
Lennert Ferdinand G. embroidery stamping, r. 38½ S. Illinois
Lennert Sarah, embroidery stamping and fancy goods 76 N. Pennsylvania, r. 38 S. Illinois
Lenox Edward, merchant tailor 20 N. Pennsylvania, r. same
Lenox John C. shoemkr. Rakestraw & Co. bds. 460 Virginia av
Lensann Henry, clk. r. 382 E. Michigan
Lensman Henry, clk. John Kohler, r. ns. Michigan bet. Noble and Railroad
Lentz G. gardner, r. ws. Western av. north of limits
Lentz William F. packer H. F. West & Co. r. East se. cor. Stevens
Lentzen William, grocer 249 W. McCarty, r. same
Leog John O. bds. Jefferson House
Leonard Abigail, wid. James, r. 183 N. Liberty
Leonard Frank, printer *Journal* job room, bds. Commercial Hotel
Leonard James (Leonard & Victor) r. 65 W. Washington
Leonard Michael, r. West nr. cor. Merrill
Leonard Michael, hostler Gates, Pray & Co.
Leonard Morris, lab. r. 81 Maple
LEONARD & VICTOR (James Leonard and Julius A. Victor) proprs. Emmett Saloon 65 W. Washington
Leopard Enzo B. fireman C. C. & I. C. R. R. r. 33 Meek
Lepp Henry, tailor r. 320 E. Ohio
Leppert Nicholas, blacksmith, r. 23 Lord
Lesh Aaron B. (Lesh, Tousey & Co.) bds. 94 N California
LESH, TOUSEY & CO. (A. B. Lesh and Wood G. Tousey) pork packers 72-74 S. Delaware
Le Shane Charles, shoemaker A. Knodle, r. 60 S. Alabama
Le Shane Eugenie, milliner J. W. Copeland & Co.
Leshman Fred. baker E. Miers, bds. 131 S. Illinois
Lesman August, r. 413 Virginia av.
Lesman Simon, lab. r. 144 Huron

Leser John, tailor, r. 191 E. Washington
Levering Matilda Miss, milliner, 140 Bluff rd. r. same
Levette Gilbert M. modelmkr. room 5, Blake block, r. same
Levin Seigmund, traveling agt. r. 212 E. Vermont
Levy Henry, clothing, 199 E. Washington, r. same
Lewellyn Francis, wid. r. 39 Ellsworth
Lewellyn Luther, carpenter W. H. Vincent
Lewis A. M. clk. G. W. Despatch, r. First nw. cor. Meridian
Lewis Alfred, (col'd) lab. r. 2d near LaFayette R. R.
Lewis Anderson, (col'd) blacksmith J. S. Affenstranger, r. North cor. Minerva
Lewis C. B. shipper Wiley & VanBuren, bds. 17 S. Pennsylvania
Lewis Charles, (col'd) lab. r. Missouri near 7th
Lewis Curtis H. moulder B. F. Haugh & Co. r. 26 Henry
Lewis Dallas, moulder B. F. Haugh & Co. bds. 26 Henry
Lewis F. C. Mrs. clairvoyant, 70 E. Ohio, r. same
Lewis Frederick C. teacher of languages, r. 70 E. Ohio
Lewis George W. Rev. r. 269 E. North
Lewis Henry, teamster John Lewis, bds. 151 Bluff rd.
Lewis Hiram M. teamster, r. 407 S. East
Lewis James, brickmaker, r. 228 Winston
Lewis John, (col'd) waiter Bates House, bds. same
Lewis John H. teamster, r. 151 Bluff rd.
Lewis Paul, lab. F. L. Farnam, r. country
Lewis Silas, (col'd) r. ws. Canal bet. Maryland and Georgia
Lewis Susan, (col'd) wid. David, r. Vine se. cor. Oak
Lewis Tomkins A. supt. G. W. Ex. Co. 82 Virginia av. r. First nw. cor. Meridian
Lewis Walter W. moulder B. F. Haugh & Co. bds. 75 Norwood
Lewis William B. porter Hume, Adams & Co. r. 433 E. Vermont
Lewis William H. H. compositor *Sentinel* book and job room, r. 67 Indiana av.
Lewy Edward, lab. r. 19 Willard
Lex Jacob, pressman Indianapolis Printing and Publishing House
Lex Louis, pressman Indianapolis Printing and Publishing House
Leydon William, lab. Rolling Mill
Liantey John, shoemkr. H. F. Albershardt, r. 60 Delaware
Lickerd Simon, expressman, r. 393 S. East
Liddy John, lab. r. 51 Wyoming
Lieber Herman, (H. Lieber & Co.) r. 404 N. Delaware
Lieber Peter, (P. Lieber & Co.) r. 246 S. Pennsylvania
LIBER H. & CO. (H. Lieber and Charles Cochne) mnfrs. picture frames, looking glasses and artists' materials, 21 N. Pennsylvania
Lieber P. & Co. (P. Lieber and ———) brewers of lager beer, 213 S. Pennsylvania
Liebrich Louis, porter Browning & Sloan, r. 234 W. North
Lietz Theobold, portrait painter, r. 83 N. East
Lightfoot Thomas, (col'd) lab. r. Missouri nr. Tinker
Lightford James, foreman Sinker & Co. r. 71 S. Pennsylvania
Likert H. Mrs. r. 395 S. Delaware

LIK	202	LIN

Likert Simon, expressman, r. 271 N. Liberty
Lillienkamp Ernst, tailor. r. 126 N. Noble
Lilly Eli. chemist Patterson, Moore & Talbot
Lilly John O. D. (Mears, Lilly & Co.) r. ws. Tennessee bet. 2d and 3d
Lilly Mary, wid. James, r. 73 W. Maryland
Lilley Samuel, (col'd) lab. r. 154 Douglas alley
Linas Daniel, stonecutter, r. Kentucky av. opp. Cemetry
Linas David G. clerk Clem & Bro.
Lince John, lab. r. 112 Stevens
Linch Jacob H. lab. Bunte, Dickson & Co.
Lincoln Charles, clk. G. H. Heitkam, bds. 212 E. Washington
Lincoln Henry, (col'd) blksmith, r. 218 W. 2d
Lincolnfelter John, plasterer, r. 267 N. Mississippi
Lindemann Frank, grocer, 206 E. Washington, r. 15 N. New Jersey
Lindemann William, moulder, r. 109 Benton
Lindenbower William H. real estate agt. r. 682 N. Mississippi
Lindley Calvert, bds. 74 E. Pratt
Lindley H. J. bookkeeper J. H. McKernan, r. 74 State
Lindley Hiram, (Lindley & Co.) and notary public, r. 134 E. St. Joseph
Lindley Jennie Miss, teacher 3d Ward School
LINDLEY & CO. (Hiram Lindley and Frank A. Dial) real estate agents, brokers and dealers, notaries public and conveyancers, 8 E. Washington
Lindner Fred. clerk W. Rhodius, bds. same
Lines James W. (Lines, Smelser & Co.) bds. National Hotel
LINES, SMELSER & CO. (J. W. Lines, Frank Smelser and S. Kaufman) whol. dealers in tobacco and cigars, 4. W. Louisiana
Lingenfelter A. carpenter B. F. Haugh & Co. r. Shelbyville pike
Lingenfelter Ashford, carpenter, r. 271 Davidson
Lingenfelter Ashford, Jr. carpenter, r. 271 Davidson
Lingenfelter Jefferson, carpenter, r. 271 Davidson
Link Albert, lab. Sinker & Co.
Link Nathan, (col'd) cook Bates House
Link Orlando, r. 77 W. McCarty
Linn Robert, farmer, r. 124 Osbrook
Linnahan Ellen, carcleaner C. & I. J. R. R.
Linnahan Thomas, lab. C. & I. J. R. R.
Linnens Daniel, brakeman, bds. 58 Benton
Linsel George, lab. Rolling Mill
Lintner Abraham, clerk C. H. Lintner, bds. 269 N. West
Lintner Amos H. groceries ret. 182 Indiana av. r. same
Lintner Christian H. dry goods, boots and shoes, hats and caps, 184 Indiana av. r. 285 Indiana av.
Lintner Daniel H. groceries ret. 400 W. North, r. same
Lintner John, r. 269 N. West
Linton Abbie, milliner J. W. Copeland & Co.
Linton James W. drover, r. 270 N. Liberty

LIN	203	LOD

Lintz Benjamin, clerk Stewart & Morgan
Lintz Delia, wid. Anthony, r. 322 E. New York
Lintz G. gardener, West Indianapolis
Lintz John K. r. 322 E. New York
Lipp Emanuel, carpenter Shover & Christian, bds. 64 W. Maryland
Lipp Henry, carpenter, r. Tennessee se. cor. 3d
LIPP HENRY, merchant tailor, 13 Massachusetts av. r. 320 E. Ohio
Lippert Elizabeth, wid. Henry, r. 222 Rail Road
Lippincott Samuel R. (Shaw, Lippincott & Conner) r. Richmond
Lippus William, stone cutter, r. 418 N. East
Lippus William C. clerk Phipps Bros. bds. 84 Massachusetts av.
Liscom Josephine, wid. bds. 78 W. North
Listner William, moulder Phœnix Machine Works
Little Chief (monthly) Shortridge & Allen publishers, 18 S. Penn.
Little Emma, dressmaker S. A. Mulliken, r. 237 E. South
Little Joseph C. roller Rolling Mill, r. 255 S. Mississippi
Little Robert E. salesman Pettis, Dickson & Co. r. 54 S. Penn.
Little Sarah, r. 74 N. Liberty
Little Sower, W. W. Dowling, editor, Meridian se. cor. Circle
Little's Hotel, (Mrs. R. Pryor) Washington se. cor. New Jersey
Litton Preston, mason, r. 325 E. Walnut
Lively George, shoemaker, r. 134 N. Spring
Livingston H. B. salesman J. Mitchell, r. 78 N. Pennsylvania
Livingston William, (W. C. Lupton & Co.) r. 326 W. Maryland
Lloyd Gideon, real estate agt. 45 E. Washington, r. 241 N. Tennessee
Lloyd Spencer C. salesman Hildebrand, Keppele & Co. r. 241 N. Tennessee
Llybrand C. C. machinist Rolling Mill
Locke Eric, (Field, Locke & Co.) supt. Caledonia Paper Mills, office 265 W. Washington, r. 76 N. California
Locke James, r. 444 S. Illinois
Locke John, huckster, r. 319 Virginia av.
Locke Josiah, lightning rods, r. 463 N. Pennsylvania
Locke Stephen, painter, r. 444 S. Illinois
Locke William M. r. 211 S. Illinois
Lockhart William, student, bds. Jackson sw. cor. Cherry
Lockhart Wilson, physician, bds. 381 N. Delaware
Locklayer Benjamin, (col'd) lab. r. 218 W. 2d
Locklayer Lavina, (col'd) wid. r. ws. Missouri nr. 1st
Lockwood Henry, cooper, r. ns. New York 1 e. Minerva
Lockwood Isaac, peddler, r. es. Clinton alley, bet. E. Ohio and New York
Lockwood James, cooper D. Burton & Co.
Lockwood Matthew, r. 376 S. West
Lockwood Nelson, cooper, bds. New York ne. cor. Minerva
Lockwood William A. teamster, r. es. Blake 3 s. New York
Lody James, bookkeeper Landers, Conduitt & Co. r. 297 N. Delaware

LOE	204	LON

Lochmann Charles, brewer Indianapolis Brewery, r. 68 S. California

Lœper F. W. physician 192 E. Washington, r. same

Lœper Jacob W. (Stierle & Lœper) r. 80 S. Delaware

Lœper Max, prof. of music, r. 192 E. Washington

LOGAN ABRAM L. editor *Western Manufacturers' Review and R. R. Journal* 30 S. Meridian, bds. 175 W. Alabama

Logan John, boilermkr. Sinker & Co.

Logan John, lab. r. ss. Sinker nr. Alabama

Logan John, lab. bds. 55 Eddy

Logan M. wks. Kingan & Co.

Logan Matthew, porter, r. 23 Fayett

Logan Michael, lab. r. ss. Sinker nr. Alabama

Logan Patrick, bds. 260 W. Washington

Logan Patrick, lab. r. 321 S. Missouri

Logan Reuben D. (Logan & Brown) r. 422 N. East

Logan Thomas, wks. Emerson, Beam & Thompson, r. 171 Meek

LOGAN & BROWN (Reuben D. Logan and Benjamin F. Brown) lawyers 4 W. Washington

Lonergan John, grocer 154 Pine

Loney Wesley, student, r. Vine bet. Broadway and Jackson

Long ——, grocer, r. 268 S. Illinois

Long David D. (Long, Snyder & Co.) r. 249 S. New Jersey

Long Edward F. salesman Pettis, Dickson & Co. bds. 60 W. Market

Long Eli C. grainer 7½ Massachusetts av. r. 289 W. Michigan

Long Frederick, porter Browning & Sloan, r. 75 S. California

Long Gabriel, bds. 430 S. Illinois

Long George, clergyman, r. 202 E. Market

Long Granville G. shoemkr. Dury & Hawk, r. 236 Blake

Long H. wid. J. W. r. 392 S. Tennessee

Long Henry C. r. 202 E. Market

Long Isaac S. (Long & Joseph) r. 264 Blake

Long James, plasterer, r. 159 High

Long Joseph, shoemkr. r. es. Western av. bet. Christian av. and Forest Home av.

Long Joseph T. news and city editor Indianapolis *Journal*, bds. Palmer House

Long Mathew (Long & Kregelo) bds. Circle se. cor. Market

Long Robert, cabinetmkr. (Long & Kregelo) r. 180 E. Vermont

Long Thomas F. clk. Ripley & Gates, r. 160 S. Illinois

Long William, lab. r. 268 S. Illinois

LONG, SNYDER & CO. (D. D. Long, A. Snyder and M. Munday) malt mnfrs. 214–216 S. Delaware

LONG & JOSEPH (Isaac S. Long and George W. Joseph) saw mill and dealers in lumber, yard LaFayette R. R. bet. Walnut and St. Clair

Long & Kregelo, (Matthew Long, David Kregelo) undertakers, carriages and hearses 15 Circle

Longa Frederick, lab. J. M. & I. R. R.

Longrich Edward, tailor, r. 282 E. North

Longsdorff Henry, r. 156 E. St. Joseph
Longsdorf W. H. (Longsdorf & Co.) bds. 88 W. Ohio
Longsdorf & Co. (W. H. Longsdorf, W. M. Aughinbaugh) news depot 26 N. Pennsylvania
Longtree George, lab. r. 98 N. Railroad
Loomis Geo. B. professor of music, r. 312 E. North
Loomis William H. r. 29 School
Looney Edward, lab. George F. Adams
Lord John M. prest. Indianapolis Rolling Mill Co. r. 297 N. Pennsylvania
Lord John P. clk. Indiana Banking Co. r. 297 N. Pennsylvania
Lord Samuel P. lab. Rolling Mill
Lorillard Fire Ins. Co. of New York, J. S. Dunlop & Co. agts. 2 W. Washington
Losse Charles, fireman C. C. & I. C. R. R. r. 326 E. Georgia
Losee Samuel, engineer C. C. & I. C. R. bds. 58 Benton
Losee Thomas V. master mechanic C. C. & I. C. R. R. machine shops, r. 326 E. Georgia
Losey John, cooper 102 S. East, r. 112 S. East
Losey Marquis D. bookkeeper Mitchell & Rammelsberg Furniture Co. r. 112 S. East
Losey R. C. actor Academy of Music
Losey Robert C. r. 112 S. East
Lothland James, lab. r. 55 Fayette
Loucks Christopher, carpenter, r. 186 Bates
Loucks George W. (Reynolds & Loucks) r. 87 N. Delaware
Loucks J. fireman C. C. & I. C. R. R.
Loucks James, groceries, &c., Broadway sw. cor. Cherry, r. 398 N. New Jersey
Loucks James, stovemoulder A. D. Wood
Loucks Joseph W. moulder, r. 186 Bates
Loucks William, varnisher Spiegel & Thoms
Loucks William W. carpenter, r. 341 N. Alabama
Louden A. A. r. 44 N. East
Louden A. J. bookkeeper, r. 44 N. East
Louden A. M. bookbinder, r. 44 N. East
Louden Andrew, binder W. & J. Braden, r. East sw. cor. Market
Louden Henry A. clk. Journal office, bds. East sw. cor. Market
Loughlan Dennis, lab. r. 40 Ellen
Louis Frederick, pianomaker, bds. Globe House
Louis G. W. machinist, bds. 20 S. Pennsylvania
Louney Edward, blacksmith, r. 111 Huron
Louney Michael, policeman and carpenter, r. 111 Huron
Louney William, lab. r. 111 Huron
Lout Henry, cabinetmaker, r. 168 S. Noble
Lout Reinhart, r. 168 S. Noble
Louthan David K. baker Parrott, Nickum & Co. bds. 121 Massachusetts av.
Love John, (gen.) office 24½ E. Washington, r. 81 N. Tennessee
Love Samuel, watchman, r. 163 S. East
Love William, (William Love & Co.) r. 506 E. Washington

Love William & Co. (William Love and Jacob P. Dunn) real estate brokers, room 1 Talbot and New's blk.

Lovecraft Joseph, (McKendry & Lovecraft) r. N. Mississippi bet. 1st and Pratt

Lovecraft Joshua, book keeper McKendry & Lovecraft, r. N. Mississippi bet. 1st and Pratt

Lovejoy John H. printer Indianapolis Printing and Publishing House, r. 35 S. West

Lowa Ernst, cabinet maker, Western Furniture Co.

Lowe Albert, (col'd) lab. r. Rhode Island nr. Blake

Lowe Charles, salesman, r. 318 N. Liberty

Lowe George, r. 467 S. New Jersey

Lowe George, r. 321 N. Pennsylvania

Lowe George (Mrs.) r. 321 N. Pennsylvania

Lowe Jennie, wid. r. 89 Iidiana av.

Lowe John, bds. 30½ N. Pennsylvania

Lowe Nahum H. (N. H. Lowe & Son) r. 308 E. North

Lowe Nahum H. Jr. (N. Lowe & Son) r. 308 E. North

Lowe Thomas, hostler William E. Wood

LOWE WILLIAM A. attorney at law and notary public, 16½ E. Washington, r. 44 Christian av. cor. Jackson

Lowe N. H. & Son, (Nahum H. Lowe and Nahum H. Lowe, Jr.) carpenters and builders, 30 S. New Jersey

Lowes Albert, errand boy I. Davis & Co. bds. 386 N. Delaware

Lowes John, carpenter, r. 386 N. Delaware

Lowes John W. salesman Coburn & Jones, r. 386 N. Delaware

Lowmon James, lab. r. 112 E. St. Clair

Lowmon William, blacksmith, bds. 112 E. St. Clair

Lowrie E, wid, r. 492 N. Mississippi

Lowry Wiley M. druggist, 65 Massachusetts av. r. 73 Massachusetts av.

Loy David M. tinner, r. 449 N. New Jersey

Lozier John H. agt. Conference Aid Society, r. E. Washington out of limits.

Lucas Benjamin F. brakeman, r. 82 Benton

Lucas Charles H. (col'd) barber, 29 N. Illinois, r. 66 N. Missouri

Lucas James (col'd) whitewasher, r. 67 N. Missouri

Lucas John, carpenter, bds. Nagel House

Lucas John G. mill-wright S. Taggart

Lucas Mary (col'd) wid. r. 194 W. 2d

Lucas Walter A. bookkeeper W. P. & E. P. Gallup, bds. 78 N. Tennessee

Lucas William, (col'd) waiter billiard hall, r. 165 Indiana av.

Lucid Morris, lab. r. 336 S. West

Lucitt John, lab. r. 358 S. West

Lucitt Morris, lab. r. 341 S. Missouri

Lucky Christopher F. lab. Coburn & Jones, r. 474 E. Washington

LUCKY GEORGE W. brick layer and contractor, 75 E. Washington, bds. 60 W. Market

Lucky Willis porter Illinois House, r. 179 S. Illinois

Luddington W. H. H. publisher, r. 80 S. Mississippi

Ludevick Francis, teamster, r. 253 Union
Ludlow George, carpenter, r. Court bet. New Jersey and East
Ludlow George L. carpenter Warren Tate, r. Virginia av. bet.
    Elk and Buchanan
Ludlow Jason C. foreman Warren Tate, r. 136 N. New Jersey
Ludlow Josiah, r. 268 S. New Jersey
LUDLOW SILAS, fine art gallery, 16½ E. Washington, and trav.
    salesman, r. Jackson se. cor. Christian av.
Ludlow Stephen W. mail clerk P. O. bds. Macy House
Ludlum Joseph E. clk. Howard A. Johnson, r. 49 Chatham
Ludorff Louis, (L. Ludorff & Co.) r. 320 S. Meridian
LUDORFF L. & CO. (L. Ludorff and R. E. Thompson) notions
    and fancy goods whol. 42 S. Meridian
Ludwig James, dyer Hoosier Woolen Factory, r. 27 Blake
Ludwig Louis, carver, 182 S. Delaware, r. same
Lueders Catherine, (Misses Lueders) r. 484 N. Mississippi
Lueders Cornelia, (Misses Lueders) r. 484 N. Mississippi
Lueders Eliza, (Misses Lueders) r. 484 N. Mississippi
Lueders Louisa, (Misses Lueders) r. 484 N. Mississippi
LUEDERS MISSES, (Catherine, Eliza, Louisa and Cornelia) mil-
    linery, stamping, embroidering, dress and cloak making,
    74½ E. Market and room 1, 40 S. Illinois
Lueders Thomas C. r. 484 N. Mississippi
Luemann Charles, grocer and saloon, 380 Virginia av. r. same
Luke Andrew, clerk, bds. 268 E. St. Clair
Luken Thomas G. moulder, r. 318 S. Delaware
LUKENS RICHARD L. agricultural impliment warehouse, 81 W.
    Washington, r. 281 Virginia av.
LUKENS R. L. & CO. (R. L. Lukens, W. B. Cox and William
    Gause) mnfrs. ditching machines, 81 W. Washington
Lumberman's Fire Ins. Co. of Chicago, Snyder & Hays agts. 17
    N. Meridian
Lunt Amos, supt. bridges C. C. & C. R. R. r. 98 W. Walnut
LUNT J. M. genl. supt. P. C. & St. L. R. R. C. C. and I. C. div.
    r. 98 Walnut, ne. cor. Tennessee
Lunt J. W. asst. engineer C. & I. C. R. R. r. 217 W. South
Luoney Amanda, wid. Dennis, r. Georgia se. cor. West
Lupton Elizabeth, wid Thomas, r. N. Pennsylvania n. of limits
Lupton G. dentist, r. 21 Indiana av.
Lupton William C. (William C. Lupton & Co.) r. 250 East nw.
    cor. Michigan
LUPTON W. C. & CO. (W. C. Lupton, A. Mosely and William Liv-
    ingston) painters, 24 Virginia av.
Luther Robert, wagonmaker, r. 15 S. Mississippi
Luthy William, tanner, bds. 18 S. Delaware
Lutz George, shoemaker George Fisher, r. 400 Virginia av.
Lutz Theodore, driver J. Butsch, bds. 68 W. South
Luwhurn Reuben, (col'd) physician and surgeon, 163 Indiana av.
    r. same
Luzingler George, (col'd) lab. r. 75 S. Missouri
Lybrand C. C. machinist, r. 223 S. Tennessee

LYD   208   McC

Lyden Thomas, lab. r. 388 S. Missouri
Lynch C. r. 376 E. Market
Lynch Jacob, lab. r. 374 S. West
Lynch John, lab. r. 349 S. Missouri
Lynch Martin, turner, bds. al. bet. East and Liberty and Georgia and Railroad
Lynch Mary, dressmkr. Mrs. N. M. Allen, r. 362 E. Market
Lynch Michael, bricklayer, r. 669 N. Illinois
Lynch Michael, lab. r. 278 S. Tennessee
Lynch Michael P. traveling agt. Kiefer & Vinton, bds. Palmer House
Lynch Patrick, engineer, r. 109 Harrison
Lynch Patrick, lab. frt. depot T. H. & I. R. R.
Lynch Patrick, lab. bds. 115 N. Noble
Lynch Patrick, machinist, Sinker & Co.
Lynn P. A. clk. Star Union Line bds 294 N. Tennessee
Lynn W. C. frt. agt. C. & I. J. R. R. bds. Pyle House
Lynn William A. jointer, A. L. Furgason, bds. 114 S. Noble
Lynn Winfield S. clk. Browning & Sloan, bds. Spencer House
Lyon M. A. wid. A. E. r. 500 N. Tennessee
Lyon R. puddler Indianapolis Rolling Mill
Lyons Charles, engineer C. C. C. & I. R. R. r. 263 Davidson
Lyons Daniel, fireman Gas Works, bds. 217 S. Illinois
Lyons George W. foreman J.C. Ferguson & Co. r. 298 Madison av.
Lyons Isaac, bricklayer, r. 291 N. Liberty
Lyons John, lab. r. 243 S. Missouri
Lyons John, traveling agt. r. 22 W. Georgia
Lyons Mary, wid. Timothy, r. Merrill cor. Missouri
Lyons Patrick, engineer Gas Works
Lyons Patrick, lab. bds. 217 S. Illinois
Lyons Timothy, fireman Gas Works
Lyons Timothy, lab. r. 372 S. Delaware
Lyons William, r. 100 S. East
Lyttle Maggie Miss, capmaker, r. 9 Draper
Lyttle Phoebe, stamper Barker, Williams & Co.

Mc

McAdams Belle, r. Douglas al. bet. New York and Ohio
McAdams Andrew, painter, bds. 128 S. East
McAlpine Alexander, machinist, r. 163 N. Spring
McAlpine Alexander, machinist, r. 265 Davidson
McAndrew C. blacksmith J. M. & I. R. R.
McAndry Walter, clk. J. McBride, bds. 161 W. Washington
McArthur John B. r. 270 N. West
McBride John, saloon, 161 W. Washington, r. same
McBride Michael, peddler, r. 274 N. Liberty
McCabe Matthew, saloon, 320 E. Washington, r. 9 Forrest av.
McCain ——, school teacher, W. Indianapolis, r. same
McCall Hugh, gardener J. M. Ray, bds. 112 N. Meridian

McCallian John, machinist, r. 62 Huron
McCally J. wheel rimmer Osgood, Smith & Co.
McCann James, painter Ryan Brothers
McCann John, lab. Rolling Mill
McCann Patrick, watchman, r. 100 S. East
McCann Samuel D. physician, 69 N. East, r. same
McCarey Robert, (col'd) barber, r. 190 N. Missouri
McCarthy John, salesman Prenatt & O'Connor
McCarthy John, turner, bds. al. bet. East and Liberty, Georgia
    and Railroad
McCarthy Simon, saloon, bds. Bates House
McCarthy William, lab. r. 533 E. Georgia
McCarty Charles, lab. r. 190 Harrison
McCarty Jerre, boilermaker Sinker & Co.
McCarty Nicholas, Washington sw. cor. Meridian, r. 122 N.
    Pennsylvania
McCarty Orrin, clk. bds. 73 W. Maryland
McCarty Stephen, lab. r. 393 E. Michigan
McCarty Thomas, wks. Rolling Mill
McCARTY THOMAS B. Ex Auditor of State and Indianapolis
    Cotton Manufacturing Co. State bldg. r. 194 N. Illinois
McCarty Timothy, lab. r. 57 Wyoming
McCarty William, moulder, r. 137 N. Davidson
McCARTY & BRIGHT, (Thomas B. McCarty and R. J. Bright)
    real estate agents, office, No. 4 *Sentinel* bldg.
McCash Charles, med. student, 135 N. Alabama
McCaslin William S. (McCaslin & Masters) r. 228 N. East
McCaslin & Masters, (William S. McCaslin and John H. Masters)
    new and secondhand furniture, 82 E. Washington
McCauley Thomas, bookbinder W. & J. Braden, bds. 148 Indi-
    ana av.
McCaw William D. painter Ryan Bros. bds. 150 E. St. Joseph
McChesney Edward, baggage master I. C. R. R. r. 454 N. Ten-
    nessee
McChesney Jacob B. treas. C. C. & I. C. R. R. r. 454 N. Tennessee
McChesney Sarah, wid. J. r. 133 N. Pennsylvania
McChesney William L. bookkpr. J. E. Robertson & Co. bds. 462
    E. Georgia
McClellan J. C. carpenter, r. 113 E. St. Joseph
McClellan John, clerk, r. 331 W. Maryland
McClellan Mary, works Cotton Factory
McClellan Robert C. carpenter C. C. & I. C. R. R. r. 378 E.
    Market
McClinton William, lab. r. 323 S. East
McCloskey John, carpenter, r. 88 S. Mississippi
McCloskey John H. baggage recorder Union depot, r. 121 N.
    Tennessee
McClure Alexander, lab. boiler shop, r. 227 N. Merrill
McClure Charles R. student Bryant & Stratton College, bds.
    Market cor. Pennsylvania
McClure Dock, (col'd) wks. John T. Pressly. r. 75 Missouri

McC   210   McC

McClure Frank, carpenter, r. es. Mississippi nr. 3d
McClure J. E. r. 61 Fort Wayne av.
McClure Joseph F. carpenter, r. 642 N. Mississippi
McClure Monticue, foreman Rolling Mill, bds. 347 S. Alabama
McClure Theopilus, printer *Journal* job room, r. 272 W. Vermont
McConnel Stephen, blksmith Phoenix Machine Works
McCool William, carpenter, r. 62 Greer
McCool William, carpenter H. H. Wheatly, r. 309½ S. East
McCord Benjamin R. (McCord & Wheatly) r. Laramie, Oregon
McCORD & WHEATLY, (B. R. McCord and W. M. Wheatly) lumber dealers and planing Mill, 186 S. Alabama
McCormick Ephram, teamster Union Starch Factory, r. 308 E. Washington
McCormick George, r. 157 W. Maryland
McCormick J. C. lab. Osgood, Smith & Co.
McCormick James A. r. 203 S. Missouri
McCormick Jediah R. carpenter, r. 400 N. Mississippi
McCormick John, nurseryman, W. Indianapolis, r. same
McCormick John L. carpenter, 726 N. Tennessee
McCormick W. H. conductor, r. 181 S. New Jersey
McCoupery Thomas, moulder D. Root & Co.
McCoy Charles D. r. California ne. cor. Michigan
McCoy Robert P. photographer, 139 W. Washington, r. 299 E. New York
McCoy Theodore W. clerk Supreme Court State Building, r. es. California bet. Michigan and North
McCraw Michael, varnisher Spiegel & Thoms
McCrea Rollin N. (Frahnley & McCrea) bds. Sherman House
McCready Frank, tailor, bds. 135 E. Washington
McCready James, bookkeeper Indiana National Bank, bds. Mrs. Mason's, Kentucky av.
McCrews Sarah, wid. r. 126 S. Tennessee
McCrouse M. boilermaker Sinker & Co.
McCrubary Thomas, moulder, r. 414 S. East
McCue Dennis, lab. Rolling Mill, r. 33 Maple
McCue Elida, wid. George, r. 301 W. Market
McCule Henry W. clerk, r. 159 N. Mississippi
McCullongh Jacob S. bookkeeper Hibben, Tarkington & Co. r. 325 E. New. York
McCune T. carpenter Builders & Mnfrs. Association
McCune Thomas, machinist Phoenix Machine Wks. bds. 366 W. Washington
McCurdy George W. auction and com. mer. Washington cor. Virginia av. r. 214 N. Alabama
McCurdy W. W. H. lawyer, bds. 172 W. Ohio
McCutcheon Allen, watchman frt. depot C. C. & I. C. R. R. r. 93 S. Noble
McCutcheon John C. bookkeeper Crossland, Hanna & Co. bds. 526 N. Meridian
McCutchon Elizabeth J. wid. Samuel, r. 93 S. Noble
McCutchon George, yardmaster Peru R. R. r. 93 S. Noble

McDermott James, boilermaker, r. 133 W. Maryland
McDermot Joseph, stove mounter, r. 159 S. Alabama
McDermott Mary, wid. John, r. 133 W. Maryland
McDermott Thomas, lab. r. 321 S. Missouri
McDevitt Edward, finisher Sinker & Co. bds. Ray House
McDole Osa, conductor construction train T. H. & I. R. R. r. 79 W. Louisiana
McDonald Alice, r. 139 W. Market
McDonald Curran E. deputy Marshal, r. 300 E. Market
McDonald David, Judge, 203 N. Pennsylvania
McDonald E. M. (McDonald, Roache & McDonald) r. 228 N. Meridian, nr. Michigan
McDonald James, foreman Indianapolis Paper Co. r. West ne. cor. Maryland
McDonald John, salesman Pettis, Dickson & Co. bds. 54 S. Pennsylvania
McDonald Joseph E. (McDonald, Roache & McDonald) r. 229 N. Pennsylvania
McDonald Patrick, lab. r. 20 Willard
McDonald Patrick, teamster Levi Clark, r. 133 S. New Jersey
McDonald Robert, lab. D. Root & Co.
McDONALD, ROACHE & McDONALD, (J. E. McDonald, A. L. Roache and E. M. McDonald) lawyers, room 3 Ætna bldg.
McDONOUGH D. B. dealer in coal, lime, cement and lath, 144 S. Alabama, r. 123 E. Vermont
McDougal Louisa, wid. George, r. 59 W. Maryland
McDougal R. brickmaker, r. 165 Huron
McDougal William, fireman C. C. C. & I. R. R.
McDowell John, lawyer, bds. 17 Kentucky av.
McDowell Joseph, bookkeeper Bowen, Stewart & Co. bds. 88 W. Ohio
McElroy Frank, porter, bds. Macy House
McElvano John, (Cornelius & McElvano) r. 67 W. New York
McElvano Mary, dressmaker 67 W. New York, r. same
McElwe John, machinist, r. 217 N. Mississippi
McEnally Martha E. Miss, teacher Colony School 5th Ward, bds. 333 S. Alabama
McEnally Terry, lab. r. 323 S. East
McFadden Lewis L. court bailiff, r. 195 N. Davidson
McFarland Cary A. (Bowker & Co.) r. 130 Virginia av.
McFarland Charlotte Miss, teacher, r. 26 E. St. Clair
McFarland Henry, pressman Indianapolis Printing and Publishing House, bds. 20 S. Pennsylvania
McFarland J. L. (Bowker & Co.) r. 130 Virginia av.
McFarland Laura W. Miss, teacher, r. 26 E. St. Clair
McFarland Robert, (D. M. Ross & Co.) r. 164 E. Daugherty
McFarland William M. compositor *Sentinel* news room, bds. Palmer House
McFARLANE W. K. baker 12 S. Meridian, r. same
McGarahan Thomas, porter, r. 195 N. Tennessee
McGaughey Charles, r. 82 Indiana av.

McGaw J. A. tobacconist 16 Bates House blk.r. 182 N. Mississippi
McGee Edward, porter Crossland, Hanna & Co. r. 215 S. Alabama
McGee John, lab. r. 94 Fayette
McGee Richard, physician 77 Massachusetts av. r. same
McGiffin Samuel, broommaker, r. 74 E. St. Clair
McGill ——, insurance agt. bds. 31 W. Ohio
McGill Margaret, wid. Robert, r. ws. McGill bet. Louisiana and South
McGill William, grocer, r. 801 N. Tennessee
McGilliard Martin V. (J. S. Dunlop & Co.) r. 82 N. East
McGinnis Edward, r. 41 Virginia av.
McGinniss Eliza, wid. William, r. 41 Blake
McGinniss Frank, clk. Murphy, Johnston & Co. r. 41 Virginia av.
McGINNISS GEORGE F. County Auditor, office County Bldgs. Court House Square, r. Perry township New Bethel rd. 4½ miles se. city
McGinniss Thomas, r. 41 Blake
McGinnis Hiram, cabinetmaker, bds. 65 S. East
McGinnis Herman, machinist Spiegel & Thoms
McGinnis John, groceries and saloon, 280 E. Washington, r. same
McGinnis Nicholas, tailor A. Kelley, r. 83 S. West
McGinnis Owen, r. 41 Virginia av.
McGinnis Rose, folder Caledonian Paper Mill
McGinnis Thomas, lumberdealer, r. 547 Mississippi
McGlen Thomas, book agt. r. 316 S. West
McGlynn Michael, wheeler Rolling Mill
McGordon Maggie, wid. George, r. 77 Indiana
McGowan Lansford, grocer 251 N. Illinois, r. 485 N. Alabama
McGrath John, tailor A. Kelley, r. 215 N. Mississippi
McGrath M. wks. Kingan & Co.
McGrath Thomas, machinist Burk, Earnshaw & Co. r. 329 S. Pennsylvania
McGrath Thomas W. sawyer Burk, Earnshaw & Co. r. 329 S. Pennsylvania
McGraw Daniel, lab. r. 294 E. Georgia
McGraw Dennis, lab. r. 474 E. Georgia
McGraw John, tailor, r. 215 N. Mississippi
McGruder Moses, (col'd) r. Douglas alley nw. cor. Michigan
McGuffin Patrick, brakeman. r. es. West 2 s. Georgia
McGuire Hannah, wid. r. 408 Indiana av.
McGuire Richard, gasfitter, bds. 88 S. Mississippi
McGynty Martin, flagman R. R. r. 243 Kentucky av.
McHenry ——, traveling agent, r. 80 N. Mississippi
McHugh Dennis, heater Rolling Mill
McHugh Thomas, lab. r. 104 Cherry
McHutchon Peter, clk. Trade Palace 26 and 28 W. Washington
McIlhenney M. A. Mrs. dealer in fancy goods, notions, etc. 58 N. Illinois, r. 31 Indiana av.
McIlvain M. E. publisher, r. 682 N. Illinois
McIlvain Robert, shoemaker ns. Nat. rd. w. of bridge, r. same
McIntire James, auctioneer, r. 71 Indiana av.

McIntire Lucius, heater Rolling Mill, r. 18 Henry
McIntire Nellie, operator Howe Sewing Machine, bds. 71 Indiana av.
McIntire Robert, tobaconist, r. 121 W. New York
McIntire William, street car driver, r. 79 W. South
McIreland David, tinner Gardner & Decker, bds. 220 S. East
McIVER JOHN C. hats, caps and furs 22 E. Washington, r. 148 N. East sw. cor. New York
McKaw William, painter, bds. 160 E. St. Joseph
McKay David, lab. D. Root & Co.
McKay James, gasfitter, r. 282 S. East
McKay John, lab. r. 35 Wyoming
McKay Moses H. (John Furnas & Co.) r. north city limits
McKeand John, engineer A. D. Wood, r. 228 Noble
McKeeby Dyer S. conductor, r. 195 S. Alabama
McKeeby Frank, conductor, r. 272 Railroad
McKeeby John, brakeman, bds. 195 S. Alabama
McKeehan Benjamin, track master, r. 333 S. Pennsylvania
McKeehan Benjamin N. clk. Adjt. General's office, r. 333 S. Pennsylvania
McKeehan James, R. R. bds. 333 S. Pennsylvania
McKeehan John, stock agt. r. 61 S. Noble
McKelvie Jerome, painter, bds 27 S. New Jersey
McKendry John E. (McKendry & Lovecraft) r. 276 N. West
McKENDRY & LOVECRAFT (John McKendry and Joseph Lovecraft) mnfrs. of kiln-dried staves and headings and dealers in hoops and barrels, LaFayette R. R. w. end Pratt. (See advt.)
McKenna Denis, lab. r. 124 Meek
McKeon Michael A. engraver H. C. Chandler & Co. r. 55 Bates
McKernan David S. clk. P. O. r. 117 W. New York
McKernan James H. real estate dealer No. 2 Blake Blk. bds. Palmer House
McKernan Joseph, clk. J. H. McKernan, bds. 117 W. New York
McKernan Michael, expressman, r. 39 Jones
McKibbon Joshua R. carpenter 402 N. East, r. same
McKinley Alexander, expressman, r. 150 Fort Wayne av.
McKinney John A. engineer Ind. Agricultural Works, r. 271 E. St. Joseph
McKinney John A. lab. r. 167 E. St. Joseph
McKinney John C. teacher, r. 332 E. Ohio
McKinney William, wks. Cotton Factory
McKinney William (col'd) porter Knotts & Co. bds. 72 W. Washington
McKinnick Frank, student, bds. 381 N. Delaware
McKinzie Rachel, wid. Duncan, r. ws. Blake 2 n. Vermont
McKinzie William, carpenter, r. ws. Blake 2 n. Vermont
McKnabe Hattie, milliner, J. W. Copeland & Co.
McKnight Mattie, r. 301 N. Market
McLaflin M. blacksmith, Phœnix Machine Works

McL	214	McO

McLaflin John, blacksmith, Eagle Machine Works, r. 309 S. Pennsylvania

McLane Annie, wid. David, r. Eckert nr Kentucky av.

McLain William C. carpenter, 162 N. Noble, r. 166 N. Noble

McLane Albert, painter and glazier, r. 12 W. North

McLANE MOSES G. State Librarian, bds. 346 N. Meridian

McLaren John, compositor *Journal* news room, r. 350 N. Noble

McLaughlin John, apprentice, r. 278 S. Tennessee

McLaughlin William, saloon, 324 S. West, r. same

McLene J. (McLene & Herron and H. Salsbury & Co.) r. 139 N. Pennsylvania

McLENE & HERRON, (J. McLene & F. M. Herron) watches and jewelry, 1 Bates House blk.

McLeod Mahala (col'd) wid. Thomas, r. 68 N. Missouri

McMacon M. painter Ind. Coach Works, bds. 41 Henry

McMahan Catharine, wid. Martin, r. 41 Henry

McMahan Dennis, lab. r. 205 Meek

McMahan Timothy, cabinet maker, bds. 65 S. East

McManus Frank, clk. N. & G. Ohmer, bds. Union depot restaurant

McMasters Robert, plasterer, bds. 82 E. St. Clair

McMillen J. W. chair maker, r. 199 Huron

McMILLIN SAMUEL, (S. McMillin & Co.) r. 74 E. Vermont

McMillen William, wks. Mrs. S. F. Morrison, bds. same

McMillin Samuel & Co. (Samuel McMillin and ——) real estate agts. 17½ W. Washington

McMullen Henry, bookkeeper, r. 160 N. Meridian

McNabb Stephen, baggage master Union depot, r. 227 S. Mississippi

McNamara E. Mrs. bds. 36 W. Maryland

McNamara John, press boy *Sentinel* office

McNamara Michael yardmaster r. 165 E. South

McNamara William, pressman *Sentinel* office, r. 165 E. South

McNamara William, stonecutter T. S. James & Co. bds. 134 S. Meridian

McNeeley Charles, clerk, bds. Stanridge House

McNeely Charles H. salesman, 71 W. Washington, bds. Wiles House

McNeely Elisha E. cooper, 364 W. Washington, (Nat. Rd.) r. 232 N. Illinois

McNeeley John B. clerk, bds. 185 W. Maryland

McNeely John B. clerk frt. office C. C. & I. C. R. R. r. First bet. Illinois and Tennessee

McNutt Alonzo, bricklayer, r. 177 Meek

McOney Daniel, lab. C. C. C. & I. R. R.

McOuat Andrew W. (R. L. & A. W. McOuat) r. New York ne. cor. East

McOuat Ellen, wid. Andrew, r. 300 Pattison

McOuat George, r. East ne. cor. New York

McOuat Robert L. (R. L. & A. W. McOuat) r. 74 W. Market

McOUAT R. L. & A. W. stoves and tinware, 61 and 63 W. Washington

McPherson William M. house and sign painter, 14 W. Pearl, bds. 184 N. Tennessee

McQuade Patrick, express driver, r. 79 Fayette

McVey Calvin A. piano maker Indianapolis Piano Mnfrg. Co. r. 76 Kentucky av.

McVey David, blacksmith, 277 W. Washington, r. 58 S. California

McVey David, wks. Indianapolis Brewery

McVey Hugh O. clerk Indianapolis Piano Mnfrg. Co. r. 76 Kentucky av.

McVey Lavinia, wid. John, r. N. Illinois

McVey William, tax collector, r. 76 Kentucky av.

McVickers A. V. mer. tailor, r. 176 W. Ohio

McWhorter George P. salesman T. De Gray, bds. 59 N. Illinois

McWilliams James, salesman Wood & Boyd, bds. 25 W. St. Clair

McWorkman Henry, mail clk. P. O. bds. Macy House

McWorkman J. clk. bds. Macy House

M

Maas Louis, cigarmaker Charles Coulon, bds. Maryland nr. Turner Hall

Mabb Maria, dress maker, 186½ W. Washington, r. same

Mabel Nellie Miss, actress Academy of Music

Mabrey James A. blacksmith Ind. agricultural works, bds. 225 E. Market

Mabrey Randolph C. r. 285 Massachusetts av.

MACAULEY DANIEL, mayor, office 35½ E. Washington, r. 18 W. North

Macauley John, bookkeeper, r. 526 N. Illinois

Macauley John T. Indianapolis Paper Co. bds. Illinois nw. cor. First

Mace D. cooper, r. 407 S. East

Machett Robert M. carpenter and builder, 169 E. St. Joseph, r. same

MacIntyre Harriet N. teacher Indiana Deaf and Dumb Institute, r. E. Washington out of limits

MacIntire John, Indianapolis Paper Co. r. 25 S. West

MacIntire Thomas, Supt. Indiana Deaf and Dumb Institute (and Brett, Braden & Co.) also Indianapolis Paper Co. r. E. Washington out of limits

Mack Henry, conductor, bds. 177 Meek

Mack John, lab. r. 193 High

Mack Morris, lab. T. H. & I. frt. depot, r. 296 S. East

Mack Philip, wks. Hoosier State Mills, r. 300 W. Maryland

Mackmannan, Bryan, lab. r. 122 Stevens

Macktee Annie, wid. Charles, r. 301 E. Washington

MACY DAVID, pres. Indianapolis, Peru and Chicago Rw. r. 298 N. Delaware

Macy House, A. W. Melsheimer, propr. 45 N. Illinois

Macy William, I. C. & L. R. R. bds. Ray House

Madden Elizabeth, wid. James, r. 225 W. Merrill

MAD	216	MAL

Madden Josephus, plasterer, bds. 116 Elm
Madden Michael, lab. frt. depot T. H. & I. R. R.
Madden Thomas, r. 131 W. First
Maddron Jacob, r. Maryland ne. cor. Illinois
Madgain Dennis, stone cutter Scott & Nicholson
Madison Charles, (col'd) lab. r. 217 Minerva
Madison Samuel, (col'd) lab. r. 3d nr. LaFayette R. R.
Magness Jacob, bds. 250 S. Missouri
Maguire Charles, salesman Pettis, Dickinson & Co. bds. 112 N. Pennsylvania
Maguire David, helper rolling mill
Maguire Douglas, coffee and spice dealer r. 78 E. Ohio
Maguire Richard, gas-fitter A. F. Noble, bds. 88 S. Mississippi
Mahan W. H. bookkeeper Rikhoff & Bro.
Mahan William H. traveling agt. r. 596 N. Illinois
Mahaney William, hostler, r. 191 W. Maryland
Mahivenny George, watchman Rolling Mill
Mahoney ——, brakeman, r. 58 Benton
Mahoney Daniel, teamster, r. 51 Ellen
Mahoney James, clk. Thomas Redmond, bds. same
Mahoney James, gasfitter, r. 58 S. Alabama
Mahoney John, flagman, r. 10 Buchanan
Mahoney Michael, lab. r. 18 Buchanan
Mahoney Patrick, r. 298 S. Delaware
Mahoney S. C. cabinet maker Spiegel & Thoms
Mahoney William, lab. Citizens St. R. R. Co.
Mahorney Ann E. hair worker and braider, 235 Blake, r. same
Mahorney John T. (col'd) trav. salesman, r. 235 Blake
Maiden John, blacksmith Citizens' Street R. R. Co. bds. Neiman House
Maier Jacob, barber, r. Washington sw. cor. Alabama
Maigel Gustav, starch maker, r. 121 N. Spring
Main Harvey, miller Sohl, Gibson & Co. r. 359 W. Washington
Mains John, machinist, bds. 524 N. Mississippi
Mais John, cooper John Losey
Major Stephen, attorney at law, room 5, Vinton's blk. opp. P. O. r. LaFayette Gravel rd. 4 miles nw. of city
Major Stephen F. mailing clk. P. O. r. 221 E. North
Major William, cooper, r. 78 Eddy
Makepeace Horace B. salesman Daggett & Co. r. 201 E. St. Mary
Maker Thomas J. painter W. Whitridge, r. 319 N. East
Mallony M. J. (col'd) wid. David, r. 588 N. Mississippi
Malone Abner, r. 128 Virginia av.
Malone Abner J. machinist, r. 128 Virginia av.
Malone Louis, (col'd) carpenter, r. 141 Bright
Malone Patrick, blacksmith, bds. 88 S. Mississippi
Malone Patrick, lab. r. 27 Wyoming
Malone William L. clk. W. R. Hogshire & Co. r. 128 Virginia av.
Maloney James, carpenter, r. McCarty cor. Illinois
Maloney John, r. 257 S. Mississippi

Maloney John, horseshoer J. Hitchens, r. al. bet. Ohio and New York, Mississippi and Tennessee
Maloney Thomas, lab. r. 333 E. Louisiana
Maloney Thomas, moulder Sinker & Co.
MALOTT VOLNEY T. cashier Merchants National Bank, 48 E. Washington, and treas. I. P. & C. R. R. r. 280 N. Delaware
Maloy Frank, switchman, bds. 66 W. Maryland
Maloy James, stonecutter, r. 67 W. McCarty
Malpas Henry, bleacher and presser of straw, 17 and 18 Miller's blk. Illinois cor. Market, r. 81 W. Michigan
Malvin A. J. machinist Sinker & Co.
Manahan Timothy, shoemaker, r. 474 E. Georgia
Manchester Louis, clerk, bds. Pyle House
Manchester Luman, salesman J. W. Copeland & Co. r. 6 N. Meridian
Mangold F. sawmaker Sheffield Saw Works
Mangold Frederick, lab. r. 130 St. Mary
Mangold Joseph, driver Citizens' Street R. R. Co. bds. Globe House
Mangold Joseph, moulder, bds. Globe House, 166 S. Illinois
Manheimer D. r. 172 E. Ohio
Manheimer Joseph C. salesman Dessar Bros. & Co. bds. 172 E. Ohio
Manlove G. B. clerk Stanton & Manlove, bds. 192 W. Ohio
Manlove William R. (Stanton & Manlove) r. 192 W. Ohio
Mann Adaline, r. 128 E. Ohio
Mann Alexander, lab. r. 63 Dacotah
Mann Alfred J. carpenter, r. 157 Davidson
Mann Harvey, r. 303 E. Washington
Mann Henry C. (col'd) barber, 10 S. Delaware, r. 361 E. New York
Mann James B. grocer, 283 Virginia av. r. 149 S. East
Mann Loran, carriagemaker, r. 303 E. Washington
Mann Samuel, carpenter, r. 443 S. Illinois
Mann Samuel, carriagemaker, r. 303 E. Washington
Mann Samuel R. real estate dealer, r. 316 S. Illinois
Mann Stevenson, lab. Bunte, Dickson & Co.
Mannfeld George, (F. Goepper & Co.) r. 336 N. East
Mannfeld Julius, tailor, r. 26 Chatham
Manning T. S. painter Bremerman & Renner, r. 76 W. Ohio
Mansfield John L. r. 351 N. Alabama
Mansfield Oscar, clk. J. T. Layman & Co. r. 351 N. Alabama
Mansfield Thomas, blksmith J. G. Smith, r. 161 W. Maryland
Mansur Charles W. salesman J. H. Vajen & Co. r. 19 E. Ohio
Mansur Frank, (Wood & Mansur) r. 10 E. Vermont
Mansur Isaiah, r. 10 E. Vermont
Mansur Jeremiah, r. 18 E. Vermont
Mansur William, r. 19 E. Ohio
Many Adolph, carpenter J. B. Many & Son, r. 125 N. Noble
Many C. carpenter Builders' & Mnfrs. Association
Many Camel, carpenter, r. 214 Railroad

MAN	218	MAR

Many Charles, lab. r. 356 Winston

Many Charles, pianomaker George Trayser

Many Charles J. (Many & Son) bds. 125 N. Noble

Many Henry, brakeman, r. 214 Rail Road

Many Jerred, teacher of French, r. 125 N. Noble

Many John, (Many & Names) r. 314 Virginia av.

Many John B. (Many & Son) r. 125 N. Noble

MANY JOHN B. & SON, (John B. and Charles J. Many) carpenters and builders, 120 Spring

Many & Names, (John Many and John Names) grocers Virginia av. ne. cor. Noble

Maraharty Daniel, lab. r. 502 E. Georgia

March Walter, lawyer, room 4, Talbott & New's Blk. r. 168 E. St. Clair

Marchant Isaac, paper mill, r. ns. W. Washington near River

Marchant Isaac, Jr. bookkeeper Merritt & Coughlen, r. w. end Washington opp. Woolen Factory

Mardick James G. grocer, 399 E. Georgia, r. same

Marien John, stonecutter, r. 19 School

Marien Joseph, stonecutter, r. 19 School

MARION CO. AGRICULTURAL AND HORTICULTURAL SOCIETY, room 7 Hubbard's blk.

Market Building (East) ns. Market bet. Delaware and Alabama

Market Building (West) ss. Ohio bet. Tennessee and Mississippi

Market Fire Ins. Co. of New York, J. S. Dunlop & Co. agts. 2 W. Washington

Marklin Mathias, bds. Sheridan House

Marlatt F. M. moulder, r. 3 n. s. end of Missouri

Marlatt F. R. moulder Greenleaf & Co.

Marlatt Zara C. patternmaker B. F. Hetherington & Co. r. 17 Henry

Marley Samuel, feeder W. & J. Braden

Marley Thomas, yardmaster J. E. Fawkner r. S. Missouri

Marmont Hall, Hugo Marmont propr. 102 S. Illinois

Marmont Hugo, saloon 102 S. Illinois, r. same

Maron John, r. 145 W. Washington

Marooney Matthew, machinist Greenleaf & Co. r. 142 E. McCarty

Marot John R. furniture dlr. 87 E. Washington, r. 36 N. Delaware

Marot Lewis, comp. *Journal* newsroom, bds. Commercial Hotel

Marquis George, lab. Osgood, Smith & Co. r. 41 Maple

Marquis Joseph O. expressman, r. 232 Bluff rd.

Marrer John, stove moulder, r. 44 Greer

Marrs Christiana B. wid. James A. r. 23 E. St. Joseph

Mars Jacob, boardinghouse 18 Circle

Marsee John L. (J. Marsee & Son) r. New Jersey se. cor. South

Marsee Joseph, (J. Marsee & Son) r. New Jersey se. cor. South

Marsee Joseph W. medical student, r. 203 E. South

Marsee J. & Son, (Joseph and John L. Marsee) saw mill New Jersey bet. Washington and Railroad

Marsh Alfred, carriagetrimmer Ind. Coach Works, bds. Pattison House

MAR	219	MAR

Marsh D. C. brakeman J. M. & I. R. R. bds. Ray House

Marsh D. M. traveling agt. r. 370 N. West

Marsh Elijah H. comp. *Sentinel* book and job rooms, bds. 35 Circle

Marsh Harmon, (H. Marsh & Son) r. 519 N. Meridian

Marsh Henry B. (H. Marsh & Son) r. 515 N. Meridian

Marsh William, express messenger, r. 210 Huron

Marsh William S. saddle and harnessmaker 180 W. Washington, r. 185 W. Maryland

MARSH H. & SON, (Harmon and Henry B. Marsh) oculists, office 2 Miller's blk. r. 52 N. Illinois

Marshall Benjamin, porter Wiley & Van Buren, r. 342 N. Winston

Marshall C. driver Citizens' Street R. R. Co. r. 63 N. Missouri

Marshall Charles H. Rev. pastor Fourth Presbyterian Church 13 Blackford's blk. r. 104 St. Mary

Marshall Edward, driver Citizens' St. R. R. Co. r 81 N. Missouri

Marshall H. J. foreman paint shop Ind. Coach Works, bds. 24 W. Georgia

Marshall Isaac, r. 243 N. New Jersey

Marshall J. carriage builder, bds. 24 W. Georgia

Marshall James, blksmith ss. Washington bet. West and California, r. 175 W. Washington

Marshall James, gardener, r. 432 E. St. Clair

Marshall James H. harnessmaker Daniel Sellers, r. 43 Chatham

Marshall James M. bookkeeper Martin, Hopkins & Ohr, r. 54 Massachusetts av.

Marshall James T. r. 322 Winston

Marshall John W. driver steamer No. 2, r. 120 E. New York

Marshall Joseph, carpenter, bds. 38 S. Tennessee

Marshall Levi, carpenter C. C. C. & I. R. R. r. 344 Winston

Marshall Lydia Mrs. (Marshall & Sweeney) bds. 16 S. Mississippi

Marshall N. Frank, paperhanger, r. 15 Indiana av.

Marshall W. W. (Smith & Marshall) r. Noble se. cor. Fletcher av.

Marshall William S. teacher Indiana Deaf and Dumb Institute

Marshall & Sweeney, (Mrs. Lydia Marshall and Mrs. Hettie Sweeney) dressmkrs. 58 N. Illinois

Mart Henry K. millwright, r. 189 N. Noble

Martin August, salesman Charles Mayer & Co. bds. Macy House

Martin Bernhard, confectioner whol. and ret. 80 E. Washington, r. same

Martin C. W. H. brakeman, r. 170 Winston

Martin Charles, moulder Sinker & Co. r. 30 Circle

Martin Dennis, traveling agt. John Sweetser

Martin Edward P. clk. Chandler & Field, bds. Pyle House

Martin Emil, clk. Frank Erdelmeyer, bds. 111 E. Washington

Martin G. clk. bds. Macy House

Martin George W. painter, bds. 392 N. Alabama

Martin Gustav, clk. C. Frese & Co. r. Langsdale blk.

Martin Henry, brakeman, r 350 Spring

Martin Henry C. (Martin, Hopkins & Ohr also Martin & Hopkins) r. 203 N. Illinois

Martin Herman, upholsterer, r. 113 Indiana av.
Martin House, Jesse Martin propr. 33 W. Maryland
Martin James, bds. 27 Henry
Martin James O. bookkeeper Martin, Hopkins & Ohr, bds 203 N. Illinois
Martin Jesse, propr. Martin House, 33 W. Maryland
Martin John, wks. Cotton Factory
Martin John, Woolen Mill, r. 33 Blake
Martin John cabinetmkr. Cabinetmakers' Union
Martin John, telegraph operator, bds. 2 Indiana av.
Martin John, hostler. bds. Neiman House
Martin John, (col'd) drayman 570 N. Mississippi
Martin John T. special agt. Charter Oak Life Ins. Co. bds. Pyle House
Martin Joseph T. (Martin & Myers) r. 41 Kentucky av.
Martin Louis, salesman Henry Reese, bds. 113 W. Washington
Martin Louisa, wid. Enos, r. 27 Henry
Martin Lucius, bds. 314 N. Alabama
MARTIN LUTHER R. real estate broker also stock and land-warrant broker and commissioner of deeds, 10 E. Washington, r. 97 E. Michigan
Martin Lyman, watchman, r. 128 E. St. Joseph
Martin Mary J. wid. Robert, r. 266 S. Tennessee
Martin Preston H. carpenter T. J. Morse, bds. 144 N. Tennessee
Martin Robert, (col'd) cook Oriental House
Martin Robert L. delivery clerk E. L. Hutton & Co. r. 496 N. Mississippi
Martin Rudolph, bl'ksmith helper C. C. C. & I. R. R. r. 13 Walter
Martin William, r. 220 Noble
Martin William, bell boy Bates House
Martin William, wks. J. S. Carey & Co. r. Helen ne. cor. Georgia
Martin William, wood turner, r. 492 N. Mississippi
Martin William H. teamster, r. 755 N. Mississippi
MARTIN, HOPKINS & OHR, (H. C. Martin, H. C. Hopkins, John H. Ohr) Fire Ins. agts. Market ne. cor. Circle, *Journal* bldg.
MARTIN & HOPKINS, (H. C. Martin & H. C. Hopkins) state agts. Indiana and Kentucky North Western Mutual Life Ins. Co. of Milwaukee, Wis. and agts. Railway Passengers Assurance Co. of Hartford, Conn. also publishers *North Western*, Market ne. cor. Circle, *Journal* bldg.
MARTIN & MEYERS, (Joseph T. Martin and John A. Meyers) dealers in stoves and tinware, 117 W. Washington
Martindale Charles, salesman S. Kaufman, r. 83 Bradshaw
MARTINDALE ELIJAH B. (Martindale & Tarkington, also W. I. Haskit & Co.) ins. agt. room 1, 2d floor Martindale's blk. r. 663 N. Meridian north of city limits
Martindale Julia A. Mrs. dressmaker, 194 W. Georgia, r. same
Martindale William, bookkeeper Lines, Smelser & Co. r. 83 Bradshaw
Martindale's Block, Pennsylvania ne. cor. Market

MARTINDALE & TARKINGTON, (Elijah B. Martindale, John S. Tarkington) attys. at law, 1 and 2 (2d floor) Martindale's blk.

Martz Sarah, wid. Peter, r. 90 S. East

Marvin Thomas G. printer *Journal* job room, bds. 84 Massachusetts av.

Maschall James, baker A. Balls, bds. 178 S. Illinois

Maskill Dennis, lab. r. 549 N. Tennessee

Maskill Michael, moulder Phœnix Machine Works

Mason B. clerk Am. U. Ex. Co.

Mason Benjamin, retired, bds. Sherman House

Mason Fannie R. r. 201 Meck

Mason Hampton, (col'd) barber M. Mason, r. 209 W. North

Mason Johnson, (col'd) lab. r. 177 St. Mary

Mason L. A. wid. Louis, boarding house, 17½ Virginia av. r. same

Mason Madison, (col'd) barber Palmer House, r. 209 W. North

Mason William B. joiner Warren Tate, bds. Little's Hotel

Mason William C. stamp clerk P. O. bds. 17½ Virginia av.

Masonic Hall, Washington se. cor. Tennessee

Masonic Secretary's Office Masonic Hall, entrance S. Tennessee

Massan William, lab. Rolling Mill, r. 302 S. West

Massey Jackson, (col'd) coachman C. J. Brackebush, bds. 220 N. Tennessee

Massey M. S. Mrs. r. 500 N. Tennesse

Massing Morris, pastor Hebrew Congregation, r. 229 E. Ohio

Masson James P. salesman Alford Talbot & Co. r. 407 N. East

Mast Edward, painter D. C. Chapman

Masters John H. (McCaslin & Masters) bds. Ray House

Mather John, engineer, I. C. & L. Rw. r. 189 Bates

Mathews J. F. notary public, Hamlin & Wright, bds. Pennsylvania cor. Maryland

Matter Stephen, tobacconist, r. 314 E. Ohio

Matlock Charles, painter Bremerman & Renner

Matlock James M. clerk Murphy, Johnston & Co r. 328 N. Alabama

Matlock William, bookkeeper, r. 251 N. West

Matson Edwin T. moulder D. Root & Co. r. 534 E. Georgia

Mattern Jacob H. Eastern route agt. *Mirror* office, r. Maryland sw. cor. Illinois

Mattern Martha C. Mrs. (Kay & Mattern) r. Illinois cor. Maryland

Matthe Charles, blksmith, bds. 292 E. Market

Matthes Clemens, saloon, 92 E. Washington, r. same

Matthews A. works J. S. Carey & Co.

Matthews Charles, puddler, r. 276 S. West

Matthews Clemens, saloon, r. S. end New Jersey

Matthews Cyrus, (Hart & Mathews) r. 337 S. East

Matthews Edward, confectioner R. L. Smith & Co. bds. 167 N. Illinois

Matthews George, puddler Rolling Mill, bds. 270 S. West

Matthews Gotlieb, drayman, r. 233 Union

MAT   222   MAY

Matthews Indiana, wid. Thomas, r. 20 Douglas
Matthews James, sawmaker Am. Saw Works, r. 20 N. Douglas
Matthews Joseph F. notary public with T. E. Johnson, bds. sw. cor. Maryland and Pennsylvania
Matthias Jacob, plasterer, r. 515 N. Mississippi
MATZ JOHN, mnfr. boots and shoes, 182 W. Washington, r. same
Mauer Anton, lab. r. 475 E. Market
Mauer John P. wks. Wheat, Fletcher & Co. r. 71 Elizabeth
Maulsby James, physician, r. 441 E. St. Clair
Maulsby Silas B. patent rights, r. 441 E. St. Clair
Maurice John N. (Maurice & Spohr) r. 5 Dougherty
Maurice & Spohr, (John N. Maurice and George Spohr) boot and shoe mnfrs. and dealers, 8 Martindale's Block
Maus Albert, brewer C. Maus, bds. same
Maus Casper, brewer, west end New York, r. ½ square north
Maus Joseph, deliveryman C. Mauss, bds. same
Maus Mathias, brewer C. Mauss, bds. same
Mauss Frank, law student C. W. Smith. Jr. bds. Casper Mauss
Manzy James S. bookkeeper Lesh, Tousey & Co.
Max Samuel, rag dealer, r. 83 W. South
Maxfield Cora, works Caledonia Paper Mill
Maxwell H. bill clerk Wiles, Bro. & Co. bds. 21 E. St. Joseph
Maxwell J. M. (Maxwell, Fry & Thurston) r. 330 N. Meridian
Maxwell John C. contracting agt. I. C. & L. R. R. r. 29 First bet. Illinois and Meridian
MAXWELL, FRY & THURSTON, (J. M. Maxwell, William H. Fry and W. B. Thurston) iron, steel, nails, &c. 34 S. Meridian
May Alvin D. mail clerk *State Sentinel*
May Andrew, stave factory, r. 125 S. East
May August, carpenter Eagle Machine Works, r. 264 Madison av.
May Charles, carpenter Eagle Machine Works, r. 264 Madison av.
May David, policeman, bds. 128 E. Maryland
May Edwin, architect 173 N. Pennsylvania, r. same
May Fred, brewer City Brewery, r. 213 S. Pennsylvania
May John (Stolte & May) r. 360 S. Alabama
May Lorenz, tinner Jacob Voegtte
May Robert A. tobacconist r. 26 W. Pratt
Mayer Charles, (Charles Mayer & Co.) r. 285 N. Illinois
Mayer Chas. student National Business College
Mayer David, student National Business College
Mayer Joseph (Mayer & Rheinheimer) bds. 18 Circle
Mayer Leopold, clothing ret. 133 S. Illinois, bds. 18 Circle
Mayer Matthias, cigar and tobacco retail, 96 S. Illinois, r. same
Mayer Melchior, Rev. r. 180 N. Noble
Mayer William (H. Altman & Co.) r. 224 S. Union
MAYER CHARLES & CO. (Charles Mayer and William Haueisen) importers and whol. dealers toys, notions and fancy goods 29 W. Washington
Mayer & Rheinheimer (Joseph Mayer and N. Rheinheimer) clothing and gent's furnishing goods 3 Palmer House
Mayers David, bds. 275 S. Delaware

Mayers John, butcher, r. Bluff rd. s. of limits
Mayers Michael, Meat Market 220 S. Meridian, r. Bluff rd. s. of city limits
Mayhew Enoch C. (Mayhew & Branham) bds. Pennsylvania cor. Vermont
Mayhew James N. salesman L. W. Moses, r. 512 E. Washington
MAYHEW OSCAR F. asst. sec. State Board of Agriculture, office State House, and solicitor of patents, r. 186 W. Vermont
Mayhew Parish L. (Mayhew, Warne & Co.) r. 59 W. Maryland
Mayhew R. H. entry clk. Kennedy, Byram & Co. bds. 17½ Virginia av.
MAYHEW, WARNE & CO. (P. L. Mayhew and J. B. Warne and ——) whol. dealers in boots and shoes 8 W. Louisiana
MAYHEW & BRANHAM (E. C. Mayhew and Edward Branham) boots and shoes whol. 129 S. Meridian
Mayo Edward H. banker, r. 562 N. Pennsylvania
Mays Alfred, (col'd) barber 160 Indiana av. r. Howard se. cor. 3d.
Mays Philip, barber A. Mays, bds. Howard bet. 2d and 3d.
Mazelin Mary, dressmkr. Mrs. N. M. Allen, bds. 182 S. Illinois
Mead James, planer McCord & Wheatley
Mead William H. traveling salesman Mayhew & Branham, bds. Sherman House
Meader James, engineer, r. 160 Indiana av.
Meadowcraft John E. tinner W. T. Jennings, r. 763 N. Mississippi
Meadows William H. carpenter, r. 191½ W. Washington
Meads Peter, (col'd) lab. r. 94 Elm
Means Thomas A. (Willcox & Means) bds 277 Virginia av.
Means William C. r. 238 Madison av.
Meany John, lab. r. 31 Maple
Mears George W. (Mears, Lilly & Co.) and physician, Vermont nw. cor. Meridian, r. same
Mears Joseph F. bartender, bds. 82 S. Illinois
MEARS, LILLY & CO. (Henry B. Mears, John O. D. Lilly and George W. Mears) props. Capital City Varnish Works, office and factory, Kentucky av. cor. Mississippi
Mechaelis John B. carpenter r. N. Pennsylvania n. of limits
Medarris Amanda, r. 27 Massachusetts av.
MEDINA FRANK J. wigs, toupees, hair work, &c. 34 W. Washington, r. 40 S. Illinois
Medor Margaret, r. 208 W. Vermont
Medow William, fireman, r. 452 E. Georgia
Medsker William F. (Ward & Medsker) bds. 162 N. New Jersey
Meek Alonzo, engineer I. C. & L. Rw. r. 240 E. Louisiana
Meek Charles I. driver street cars, bds. 266 S. Illinois
Meek Lawrence S. bookbinder *Journal* office
Megge Diederich, (C. Helgemeyer & Co.) r. 38 Wyoming
Meginnis Thomas, lumber dealer, r. 547 N. Mississippi
Mei Fritz, brewer P. Lieber & Co.
Meier Ernst, bakery, 131 S. Illinois, r. same
Meier Henry, (Roeth & Meier), r. 31 S. New Jersey
Meier Joseph, (V. Meier & Brother) bds. 76 S. West

MEI	224	MER

Meier Lewis, (Lewis Meier & Co.) r. 489 N. New Jersey

Meier Valentine, (V. Meier & Brother) r. 76 S. West

Meier Lewis & Co. (Lewis Meier and William Buschmann) dry goods, 151 Fort Wayne av.

MEIER V. & BROTHER, (Valentine and Joseph Meier) lager beer bottlers and dealers in Madison Ale, 76 S. West

Meighan James, peddler, r. 280 Railroad

Meigs Charles D. bookkeeper Merrill & Co. bds. Market cor. Pennsylvania

Meikel Brothers, (J. M. and F. J. Meikel) book and job printers and book binders, Washington, sw. cor. Meridian

Meikel Charles P. printer, r. 500 N. West

Meikel Frederick J. (Meikel Bros.) r. Illinois cor. North

Meikel John M. (Meikel Bros.) r. 113 N. Mississippi

MEIKEL JOHN P. propr. Indianapolis Brewery, ss. W. Washington Nat. rd. junction, r. 213 W. Maryland

Meikel Philip, machinist Greenleaf & Co.

Mellar Martha, wid. Henry, r. 304 E. Ohio

Melsheimer A. W. propr. Macy House, 45 N. Illinois, r. same

Melville Robert B. cutter J. Mitchell, r. 79 California

Melville Robert J. (Moran & Melville) r. 79 N. California

Melvin Thomas E. salesman C. J. Brackebush, bds. 168 N. Noble

Mendenhall M. H. pastor Grace M. E. Church, r. 183 E. Ohio

Mengis Frank, tobacco and cigars, 153 E. Washington, r. 182 S Delaware

Montel Moses, clk. L. Mayer, bds. Circle Restaurant

Merchant Alfred, salesman H J. Prier, r. 691 N. Tennessee

Merchant C. Miss, dressmaker 257 N. West, r. same

MERCHANTS' DESPATCH, E. Cummings, gen'l supt. Samuel F. Scott, agt. 19 Virginia av.

Merchants' Insurance Co. of Chicago, Hopkins & Ohr, agents, Market, ne. cor. Circle, *Journal* bldg.

MERCHANTS' NATIONAL BANK, John S. Newman, pres. V. T. Malott, cashier, 48 E. Washington

Merchants' and Manufacturers' Exchange, W. C. Tarkington, pres. James Greene, sec. 10 Blackford's block

Meredith Edward, sawmaker Sheffield Saw Works, r. 235 S. Mississippi

Meredith Richard O. carpenter, r. 80 Oak

Meredith Samuel C. mail clerk *Journal* office, r. 212 Blackford

Meredith William M. asst. foreman *Journal* newsroom, r. 124 N. Missouri

Merl N. boot and shoe maker, 286 W. Washington, r. same

Merlan Lizzie Miss, dressmkr. Maryland ne. cor. Illinois, r. same

Merrick W. student National Business College

Merrick William, hostler Citizens' Street R. R. Co. bds. 193 S. Tennessee

Merrifield Charles E. general trav. agt. C. J. Brackebush, bds. Vermont nw. cor. California

Merrill D. H. broommaker I. L. Newman, bds. 82 E. St. Clair

Merrill Lucinda, wid. John F. r. 244 W. New York

Merrill Samuel, (Merrill & Co.) r. 299 S. Alabama cor. Merrill
Merrill William, plumber, r. 244 W New York
MERRILL & CO. (Samuel Merrill and Mrs. C. W. Moores) book-
    sellers, stationers and publishers, 5 E. Washington
Merritt George, (Merritt & Coughlen) r. 172 N. West
MERRITT & COUGHLEN, (George Merritt, William Coughlen)
    proprs. Ohio Premium Woolen Factory, also dealers in
    woolen machinery and findings, w. end Washington
Merrymon Ann, wid. William, r. 365 N. Alabama
Merryweather Cameron, (col'd) lab. r. 420 E. St. Clair
Mertz Frederick, news agent 170 E. Washington
Merz Chris. butcher J. Roos, bds. 137 S. Illinois
Merz David, butcher J. Roos, bds. 137 S. Illinois
Meskamp William, lab. r. 42 Elm
Meskell Joseph, car inspector C. C. C. & I. R. R.
Meskell William, bookbinder William Sheets
Meskill James B. painter Corneilus & McElvano
Messenger Lyman, carpenter, r. 5 Vine
Messick John F. bkper R. L. Smith & Co. bds. 31 Indiana av.
Messick Thomas B. money order clk. P. O. r. 231 W. Vermont
Metropolitan Theatre, V. Butsch propr. 84 W. Washington
Mette Samuel E. watchman Peru depot, r. 233 Huron
Metz John gluemaker Goas & Co.
Metzger Alexander, real estate, claim, insurance, foreign ex-
    change and gen. collecting agt. room 6 Odd Fellows' Hall,
    r. 385 N. Pennsylvania
Metzger Catherine, wid. George, r. 382 E. Michigan
Metzger Charles, tailor Becker & Huber, r. 147 Vincent
Metzger Conrad, shoemaker George Shaub, r. 146 N. Vincent
Metzger D. lab. Sinker & Co.
Metzger E. J. editor *Daily Telegraph*, r. 79 N. East
Metzger Henry, brewer Schmidt's Brewery, r. same
Metzgler John, clk. William Selking, bds. 31 N. East
METZNER ADOLPH, drugs and medicines 127 E. Washington,
    r. same
Metzner Emil, lithogrpr. W. & J. Braden, r. 316 N. New Jersey
Meurer Frederick M. shoemaker 22 Virginia, r. 192 Virginia av.
Meyer C. framemaker H. Lieber & Co.
Meyer Caroline, wid. r. 110 W. Vermont
Meyer Charles, merchant, r. 285 N. Illinois
Meyer Charles, bartender Fred Dietz, r. 255 E. Washington
Meyer Christ. brass moulder Stierle & Looper, r. 70 S. Liberty
Meyer Christ. F. carpenter, r. 227 N. Liberty
Meyer Christian, carpenter, r. 275 E. Ohio
Meyer Christian, chairmkr. r. 31 S. New Jersey
Meyer Christian, porter Charles Mayer & Co. r. 21 Coburn
Meyer Emile, bkpr. Merchants' National Bank, bds. 126 E. Ohio
Meyer Fred. A. supt. Indiana Transfer Co. r. 141 Union
Meyer Frederick, wks. Indiana Transfer Co. r. 141 Union
Meyer Frederick, carpenter F. Diekmann, r. 326 E. Vermont
Meyer Frederick, porter Holland, Ostermeyer & Co.

MEY 226 MIL

MEYER GEORGE F. mnfr. and whol. dealer in cigars and tobac-co, 35 W. Washington, r. 180 N. Delaware
Meyer Henry, salesman S. Kahn & Bro. r. 641 N. Tennessee
Meyer Henry, teamster Indiana Transfer Co.
Meyer Henry, varnisher, r. 331 E. Ohio
Meyer Jacob, barber, r. 149 E. Washington
Meyer Jacob, clk. G. Beisdorfer
Meyer James, lab. Bunte, Dickson & Co.
Meyer John, baker Fred. C. Bollman
Meyer John F. umbrellamkr. 69 E. Washington, r. 123 E. St. Joseph
Meyer Joseph, clk. Adolphus Kahn, bds. 184 Virginia av.
Meyer Ludwig, drayman, r. 98 N. Davidson
Meyer Martin, turner 29 S. Alabama, r. same
Meyer W. student National Business College
Meyer William, blksmith C. C. & I. C. R. R. r. 426 E. Georgia
Meyer William, grocer, r. 224 Union
Meyers Christian, brassmoulder, r. 70 S. Liberty
Meyers Frank, moulder, r. 2 Meek
Meyers George E. printer, r. 222 N. New Jersey
Meyers H. F. stove mounter A. D. Wood
Meyers Jacob C. carpenter, r. 321 N. Liberty
Meyers John, moulder D. Root & Co.
Meyers Leonard, baker, r. 322 N. New Jersey
Meyers William H. agt. *Sentinel*, r. 322 N. New Jersey
Mezel A. pork packer, r. 167 W. Washington
Mezger David, lab. r. 501 S. East
Michael F. J. bookbinder, r. 323 N. Illinois
Michael Gustavus, lab. Union Starch Factory, r. 121 Spring
Michael Philip, machinist, r. Missouri s. of McCarty
Michaelis John, carpenter, r. 656 N. Tennessee
Michaelson Philip, r. 139 Virginia av.
Michel Mary C. wid. Jacob P. r. 113 N. Mississippi
Michel Martin, watchmaker, r. 113 N. Mississipi
Michelfelder John, teamster Cabinetmakers' Union
Mick James F. com. mer. and dealer in feathers, 21 W. Mary-land, r. 170 Jackson
Mick William E. (William E. Mick & Co.) r. Christian av. se. cor. Plum
MICK WILLIAM E. & CO. (William E. Mick and David Geyer) real estate agents, brokers and dealers, room 7 (2d floor) Martindale's blk. Pennsylvania ne. cor. Market
Miconi Dennis, lab. r. 80 Elm
Middaugh George, r. 58 Huron
Middeg John, r. 335 E. New York
Mie August, lab. r. 264 Madison av.
Mierhoff Mary, wid. Henry, r. 242 S. Alabama
Miflan James H. (col'd) barber W. Artis, r. 46 West Alley
Migelfelder John, teamster, r. 377 E. New York
Milburn Charles F. clk. lunch stand union depot, r. 197 N. Ill's
Millard E. checkman frt. office C. C. & I. C. R. R.

Milender Wm. B. painter, 12 S. Pennsylvania, r. 132 N. Liberty
Miles Antony, (col'd) lab. r. 32 Bradshaw
Miles James, carpenter, r. 538 N. Mississippi
Miles Oscar, foreman *Journal* job rooms, r. 267 N. Noble
Miles T. C. propr. Commercial Hotel
Miley John, r. 321 N. New Jersey
Miley John, lumber dealer, r. W. Indianapolis
Miller ——, dyer, bds. 174 W. New York
Miller A. J. wood dealer, r. 395 N. West
Miller Ada V. wid. J. F. bds. 68 Plum
MILLER ADAM R. photographic and oil painting studio, 45 E. Washington, r. 143 N. Delaware
Miller Albert, clk. bds. 339 N. Pennsylvania
Miller Anthony, carpenter, r. 227 E. Vermont
Miller August, principal Zion's School (German) Fletcher av.
Miller B. W. internal revenue, bds. Littles Hotel
Miller Carey W. messenger First National Bank of Indianapolis, r. 373 N. Delaware
Miller Charles, carpenter Fred. Stelkorn, r. E. Washington out of limits
Miller Charles, coppersmith W. Langenkamp, bds. 187 E. Washington
Miller Charles, clk. Gall & Rush
Miller Charles, brakeman, bds. 29 Meek
Miller Charles, lab. Bunte, Dickson & Co.
Miller Charles, lab. C. C. C. & I. Rw.
Miller Charles, lab. J. M. & I. R. R.
Miller Charles E. r. 133 N. Mississippi
Miller Charles F. clk. r. 27 N. California
Miller Charles F. clk. Kennedy, Byram & Co. bds Oriental House
Miller Charles L. tailor, r. 412 S. Illinois
Miller Christ, carpenter, r. 230 Davidson
Miller Christ, lab. C. C. C. & I. R. R.
Miller Christian, carpenter and builder, 489 S. East, r. same
Miller Christian, varnishes Spiegel & Thoms
Miller Christopher, watchmaker A. R. Miller, r. Plank road
Miller Corwin, fireman, C. C. & I. C. R. R.
Miller Daniel, brick moulder, r. 278 Railroad
Miller Dora Miss, teacher 9th Ward school, r. 25 S. Delaware
Miller E. S. Mrs. teacher 6th Ward school
Miller E. W. drayman, r. 170 Madison av.
Miller E. W. wid. H. W. r. 373 N. Delaware
Miller Edward, starch mnfr. r. 305 E. Market
Miller Edward T. (Miller & White) and druggist, 49 S. Illinois, r. 30 Indiana av.
Miller Elizabeth, wid. Jacob, r. 12 Indiana av.
Miller Emily, wid. Alexander, r. 293 Indiana av.
Miller Ernst, cabinetmaker Spiegel & Thoms
Miller Frank, clerk Emmerich & Co.
Miller Frank, cooper J. S. Carey & Co. r. 7 Cary's Row
Miller Fred. carpenter, r. 21 Biddle

| MIL | 228 | MIL |

Miller Frederick, blksmith Louis Miller, r. 172 S. Noble
Miller Frederick, supt. Indianapolis Hair and Bristle Works, s. end of S. West, r. same
Miller G. fireman C. C. & I. C. R. R.
Miller George, (Miller, Mitchell & Stough) r. 88 Kentucky av.
Miller George, apprentice Greenleaf & Co.
Miller George F. butcher, bds. Ray House
Miller George L. foreman Starch Factory, r. 290 N. Winston
Miller George P. blksmith Ind. Agricultural Works. r. 187 W. South
Miller George W. miller, r. 83 Ann
Miller George W. wheelmaker Ind. Agricultural Works, r. 666 N. Mississippi
Miller H. J. merchant tailor, r. 73 Kentucky av.
Miller H. S. gasfitter, r. 372 E. New York
Miller Henry, currier Mooney & Co. r. Illinois nr. McCarty
Miller Henry, lab. r. 206 W. Vermont
Miller Henry, lab. r. 254 E. Michigan
Miller Henry, lab. C. C. C. & I. R. R.
Miller Henry, lab. r. Coburn bet. East and Virginia av.
Miller J. F. bookkeeper G. F. Meyer, bds. Macy House
Miller J. W. cabinetmaker, r. 324 S. Meridian
Miller Jacob, cigars and tobacco whol. and ret. 140 S. Illinois, r. 61 S. Russell
Miller Jacob, shoemaker F. Schrader, bds. California House
Miller Jacob, Jr. cigar stand Spencer House, r. 61 Russell av.
Miller Jacob V. shoemaker J. A. Chiver, r. 63 Indiana av.
Miller James, conductor, bds. 58 Benton
Miller James, conductor, r. 29 Meek
Miller Joel, bartender, r. 293 Indiana av.
Miller John, brewer, r. 230 S. Pennsylvania
Miller John, machinist Sinker & Co.
Miller John, lab. Osgood, Smith & Co.
Miller John, propr. Boston House, 123 S. Illinois
Miller John A. bookkeeper Vinnedge, Jones & Co. bds. Pattison House
Miller John H. finisher, r. 50 Fayette
Miller Joseph, bar keeper M. Welsh
Miller Kate, wid. John, r. 573 E. St. Clair
Miller Kate, wid. W. B. r. 246 Blake
MILLER LAWRENCE, ornaments, architectural and furniture carver, factory rear of 84 E. Market, r. 133 E. Washington
Miller Lewis, blacksmith, r. Michigan rd. nr. junc. Washington
Miller Louis, plow and wagon manfr. E. Washington cor. Benton, r. east of limits
Miller Louisa, wid. William, r. 116 N. Noble
Miller Mark D. brakeman, r. 272 E. New York
Miller Mat. melter A. D. Wood
Miller Milton R. machinist C. C. & I. C. R. R. r. Grant out of limits

T. B. PERRINE, Engraver on Wood and Metal, 34 Virginia av.

MIL   229   MIL

Miller Mollie, dressmkr. Marshall & Sweeny, r. 25 N. New Jersey
Miller Ozias S. printer, r. 12 Indiana av.
Miller Patrick, bds. Jefferson House
Miller Peter, carpenter, r. 135 N. Noble
Miller R. A. watchmkr. and jeweler 268 E. Washington, r. same
Miller L. melter D. Root & Co.
Miller S. S. plasterer, r. rear 175 E. Market
Miller Sarah, r. 218 N. Missouri
Miller Sebastian, cigar maker J. Miller, bds. 61 S. Russell
Miller Sidney, teamster, r. 102 Elm
Miller Simon R. (Moffitt & Miller) r. 68 Plum
Miller Thomas, fireman, r. alley bet. East and Liberty and Georgia and R. R.
Miller Thomas, lab. J. M. & I. R. R.
Miller Thomas P. r. 372 E. New York
Miller Valentine, currier John Fishback, r. 140 N. Davidson
Miller William, bds. Jefferson House
Miller William, clk. Berg & Waterman, bds. 193 S. Tennessee
Miller William, engineer C. C. C. & I. R. R.
Miller William, hackdriver, r. ss. Nat. Road, west of the bridge
Miller William, sawmkr. Sheffield Saw Works, r. 124 Duncan
Miller William, teacher German-English school, r. 64 S. New Jersey
Miller William, varnisher Spiegel & Thoms
MILLER, MITCHELL & STOUGH (George Miller, William M. Mitchell and Charles A. Stough) proprs. Union Coach Shop cor. Kentucky av. and Georgia
Miller & White (E. T. Miller and Ninevah White) Central Nursery, Market nw. cor. Delaware
Millerman Charles, cabinetmkr. Spiegel & Thoms, Furniture Co.
Millerman Christian, cabinetmkr. Spiegel & Thoms Furniture Co.
Millerman Frank, (col'd) waiter Moffitt & Miller, bds. 46 S. Meridian
Milligan George A. lab. Barker, Williams & Co.
Milling Charles, teamster, r. 47 Douglass
Millner William J. (Millner & Sherwood) bds. National Hotel
MILLNER & SHERWOOD (W. J. Millner and F. W. Sherwood) whol. tea dealers, 27 McNabb opp. Union Depot
Millroy F. M. lab. Osgood Smith & Co.
Mills Agnes Miss, bds. 497 N. Meridian
Mills David, (Mills & Hollingsworth) r. 323 W. Washingtnn
Nills J. S. foreman machine shop J. M. & I. R. R.
Mills Layton, sale stable, r. 180 Massachusetts av.
Mills Thomas, grocer, r. 305 E. New York
Mills & Hollingsworth, (David Mills, Zeph Hollingsworth) sale and feed stable, es. Washington bet. California and West
Millspaugh Oscar, painter, bds. 30½ N. Pennsylvania
Milner Davis, mail clerk *Journal* office, r. 178 Dougherty
Milner J. lawyer, 94 E. Washington, bds. Little's Hotel
Milton E. packer Barker, Williams & Co.

MIL	230	MIT

Milton Emma Miss, ruler W. & J. Braden, bds. 338 Indiana av.
Milton Hiram T. carpenter, Builders and Mnfrs. Association, r. 338 Indiana av.
Milton M. packer Barker, Williams & Co.
Minchan Andrew, lab. r. 167 Madison av.
Miner Cornelius, saw mill, r. 325 E. Ohio
Miner L. lab. bds. 82 Benton
Miner Maggie Mrs. dressmaker, 30 W. Washington (up stairs) bds. 22 S. Mississippi
Miner Margaret, wid. William S. r. 32 S. Mississippi
Miner S. lab. Bunte, Dickson & Co.
Miner Wilford H. carpenter, r. 257 N. West
Miner Willis R. bkpr. Wiles Bro. & Co. r. 431 N. Mississippi
Minger Christopher, line repairer W. U. T. Co. r. 266 S. Delaware
MINICK DAVID C. real estate agt. 17½ W. Washington, r. same
Minick Hiram, policeman, r, 256 S. Meridian
Minteith John, carpenter, r. 127 E. South
Minthorne John J. carpenter, bds. 268 E. St. Clair
MIRROR, (daily and weekly evening) Harding, Morton & Finch publishers, 19 N. Meridian
Miscoll Joseph, lab. r. 30 John
Mitchell Adolphus O. clerk Samuel Taylor, r. 115 E. Ohio
Mitchell Bryant, (col'd) lab. r. 158 Douglas Alley
Mitchell Burrell, (col'd) porter Daggett & Co. r. 230 N. Missouri
Mitchell David M. r. 26 S. Mississippi
Mitchell David N. grocer, 52 Indiana av. r. 28 N. Mississippi
MITCHELL GEORGE M. D. barber shop and bath house, 21 N. Meridian, bds. Washington sw. cor. Mississippi
Mitchell J. merchant tailor, 2 Bates House blk. r. 174 E. Ohio
Mitchell James C. clerk Corbaley & Cossel
Mitchell James L. (Newcomb, Mitchell & Ketcham) r. E. Market city limits
Mitchell James T. (Jamison & Mitchell) r. 138 Bluff rd.
Mitchell Kate, (col'd) wid. John, r. 156 Douglas Alley
Mitchell Mary J. wid. Henry B. r. ss. Washington Nat. rd. 1 e. the bridge
Mitchell Morton, carriage builder, r. 81 W. Georgia
MITCHELL NELSON C. Patentee Buckeye Bee Hive and Bee Apiary, Tennessee cor. St. Clair, r. same
Mitchell Robert S. brickmaker, r. Michigan rd. nr. junc. Washington
Mitchell S. J. grocer ret. ws. Mississippi bet. 4th and 5th, r. 297 N. Mississippi
Mitchell William, (Miller, Mitchell & Stough) r. 81 W. Georgia
Mitchell Woodford, wks. J. C. Ferguson & Co.
MITCHELL & RAMMELSBERG, FURNITURE Co. furniture manufacturers and dealers, salesroom 38 E. Washington
Mittay H. A. clerk J. G. Fahrion, bds. 92 E. South
Mittay J. C. deliveryman Capital Ale Brewery
Mittay John C. r. 347 E. New York
Mitts John W. gluemaker, r. ss. Mayhew nr. Michigan rd.

MIX	231	MOO

Mix Lyman W. produce dealer, 43 S. Delaware, bds. 218 E. Market
Mock Frederick, lab. Bunte, Dickson & Co.
Mock L. G. brakeman, r. 153 Meek
Mock Martin, tailor Joseph Staub, r. 127 Davidson
Mock Sarah H. wid. George, r. 153 Meek
Mode Michael, (Christ Karle & Co.) r. 229 N. Noble
Moffat Charles A. musician, r. 70 Fletcher av.
Moffit John, r. 250 Minerva
Moffitt John, job printer W. & J. Braden, r. 237 S. New Jersey
Moffitt Oliver I. (Moffitt & Miller) r. 237 S. New Jersey
Moffitt Sarah, wid. John, r. 237 S. New Jersey
Moffitt William, clerk Browning & Sloan, r. 177 N. Tennessee
MOFFITT & MILLER, (C. I. Moffitt and S. R. Miller) dining hall and restaurant, 46 S. Meridian
Mohr George, cabinet maker, wks. Cabinet Maker's Union
Moloney John, office boy, bds. McCarty se. cor. Tennessee
Monaghan C. wid. John, r. 368 S. Tennessee
Monaghan Patrick T. shoemaker, r. 351 E. McCarty
Monaghan Timothy, cutter L. Siersdorfer, r. 474 E. Georgia
Mondon America T. Miss, r. 36 Henry
Monfort Cornelius B. carriagemaker, r. 39 W. St. Joseph
Moniarty Thomas, boilermkr. Eagle Machine Works, r. 248 S. Delaware
Monnahan Charles, hooker Rolling Mill, bds. 300 S. Tennessee
Monnahan John, lab. Rolling Mill, r. 300 S. Tennessee
Monnahan William, lab. r. 319 E. Merrill
Monninger C. saloon, 167 W. Wasington, r. 292 W. Maryland
Monninger Daniel, saloon, 20 Kentucky av. r. 386 N. Tennessee
Monroe Felix T. compositor *Commercial*, r. 32 S. Mississippi
Monroe John, (Monroe & Johnson) r. 330 E. Vermont
Monroe John L. carpenter, r. 431 E. St. Clair
Monroe & Johnson, (John Monroe and A. W. Johnson) carpenters and builders, 40 W. Market
Montague Martha, wid. William, r. 105 S. New Jersey
Montague Mollie, tailoress H. Small, bds. 105 S. New Jersey
Montaney Annie, (Wonnell & Montany) r. 31 Indiana av.
Montgomery Andrew, shoemaker, r. 505 N. Meridian
Montgomery Annora, wid. James, r. 233 W. South
Montgomery Edward, moulder, bds. Illinois House
Montgomery S. (col'd) wks. J. S. Carey & Co.
Montgomery William, cooper, W. Indianapolis, r. same
MOODY BROS. (C. W. and E. R. Moody) whol. and ret. druggists, Indiana av. cor. Tennessee, and 160 Indiana av.
Moody Charles C. switchman C. C. & I. C. R. R.
Moody Charles W. (Moody Bros.) bds. Pyle House
Moody Edward R. (Moody Bros.) r. 126 W. Vermont
Moody George A. clerk Moody Bros. bds. 144 N. Tennessee
Moon C. carpenter Builders & Mnfrs. Association
Moon John, sewing machine agt. r. 323 W. Washington
Mooney James E. (Mooney & Co.) bds. 152 N. Mississippi

MOO	232	MOO

MOONEY & CO. (James E. Mooney and A. S. Mount) mnfrs. and dealers leather, findings, belting, oil, etc. 147 S. Meridian

Moore Aaron, (col'd) lab. r. 245 W. Ohio

Moore Charles, carpenter, bds. 84 Massachusetts av.

Moore Clara J. ladies' underwear, 253 W. Washington, r. same

Moore Debora, wid. Joseph, r. 23 E. Michigan

Moore Edmund, (col'd) lab. r. 142 Elm

Moore Emma, dressmaker La Shears, r. 10 S. Mississippi

Moore Frank, foreman I. L. Franklin & Co. r. 394 Virginia av.

Moore George, lab. John Gorsch

Moore George, C. C. & I. C. R. R. r. 222 E. Louisiana

Moore George T. sec. and treas. Indianapolis Wagon and Agricultural Works, r. 387 N. Illinois

Moore George W. clerk, r. 222 E. Louisiana

Moore Granville C. clerk Dep't of Public Instruction, bds. Little's Hotel

Moore Harvey A. supt. Union Novelty Wks. Mnfg. Co. office St. Clair cor. Canal, r. Tennessee cor. 7th

Mooore Henry H. physician, 298 E. Ohio, r. same

Moore J. wks. J. S. Carey & Co.

Moore J. L. (Hoyle & Moore) r. Louisiana, bet. Liberty and Noble

Moore J. W. clk. bds. Oriental House

Moore James, engineer C. C. & I. C. R. R. bds. 61 S. Noble

Moore James, lab. r. 59 Jones

Moore James, pumpmaker, r. 312 E. Louisiana

Moore John, salesman Pettis, Dickson & Co. bds. Oriental House

Moore John, salesman, bds. 66 W. New York

Moore John A. grocery, r. W. Indianapolis

Moore John G. ale bottler, r 191 N. Noble

Moore John L. bkpr. Kingan & Co. r. 10 Bates House block

Moore John M. carpenter Shover & Christian

Moore Joseph, huckster, r. 31 Bright

Moore Joseph A. (Patterson, Moore & Talbot and Alfred Talbot & Co.) r. 433 N. Pennsylvania

Moore Joshua, fruit peddler, r. 246 S. Missouri

Moore Mary J. wid. John, r. 267 W. Merrill

Moore Michael, lab. r. 388 S. Missouri

Moore Michael H. trimmer S. W. Drew, r. 211 N. Davidson

Moore Nicholas, lab. r. 15 Dougherty

Moore P. H. pianomaker and tuner, r. 25 Ellsworth

Moore R. wks. J. S. Carey & Co.

Moore Richard, tailor, r. 67 S. West

Moore Samuel H. physician 37 Virginia av. bds. 84 Mass. av.

Moore Thomas, foreman cooper shop J. S. Carey & Co. r. 1 Carey's Row, Helen st.

Moore Thomas, soapmaker W. Indianapolis, r. same

Moore Thomas C. blksmith se. end Virginia av. r. 553 Virginia av.

Moore Thomas C. bookkeeper, Murphy, Johnston & Co. r. 23 E. Michigan

Moore William, cooper John Losey, r. 375 W. Washington

Moore William, plasterer, r. 387 Massachusetts av
Moore William, sale stables, r. 185 N. Noble
Moore Z. E. Mrs. wid. r. 164 W. Washington
Moores C. W. Mrs. (Merrill & Co.) r. Merrill sw. cor. Alabama
Moores Julia M. wid. Charles W. r. 145 E. Merrill
MOORHOUSE ROBERT, grocer 52 Indiana av. r. 392 N. West.
Moran Ellen, wid. Thomas, boardinghouse, r. 38 S. Tennessee
Moran George, cabinetmaker, bds. 65 S. East
Moran J. engineer C. C. & I. C. R. R.
Moran John, lab. r. 92 S. Liberty
Moran Patrick, lab. r. 294 S. East
Moran Patrick, lab. r. 80 Garden
Moran Patrick A. lab. Rolling Mill
Moran Samuel, (Moran & Melville) r. 140 W. Vermont
Moran & Melville, (Samuel Moran and Robert J. Melville) sign
    painters 18 S. Meridian
Moraski H. lab. J. Fishback
Morbach Charles, student National Business College
Morbach Charles, shoemaker P. Morbach, bds. 301 S. Delaware
Morbach Josephine, milliner M. A. Kunz, r. 301 S. Delaware
Morbach Peter, boot and shoe maker 301 S. Delaware, r. same
Moreau Jeremiah, machinist B. F. Haugh & Co. r. 216 Blackford
Moreland William W. actor Academy of Music, r. 75 N. Illinois
Moreton Alfred, (col'd) gardener, r. opp. City Hospital
Moreton James, (col'd) lab. r. Howard sw. cor. 3rd
Morgan Benj. F. pastor United Brethren Church, r. 216 N.
    Noble
Morgan Daniel, switchman J. M. & C. R. R. r. 131 E. Merrill
Morgan Daniel B. millwright G. Taggart
Morgan David, lab. r. Tennessee cor. 6th
Morgan David E. heater Rolling Mill, r. 248 S. Missouri
Morgan Dennis, egg packer, r. 316 E. New York
Morgan G. clergyman, r. 527 N. Mississippi
Morgan Jane, dressmaker Mrs. E. Spring, r. 316 E. New York
Morgan Jessie Mrs. r. 55½ S. Illinois
Morgan John W. bookbinder *Journal* office, r. 33 McCarty
Morgan Lawrence, cooper, r. 305 E. Washington
Morgan Pauline, wid. John, r. 33 E. McCarty
Morgan R. S. lab. Osgood, Smith & Co.
Morgan Samuel C. sewing machine agt. r. 322 N. Alabama
Morgan Stephen W. (Stewart & Morgan) r. 502 N. Illinois
Morgan William L. student, r. 33 E. McCarty
Morgenveck Valentine, grocer, 21 Chatham, r. same
Moriarty Daniel, lab. r. 248 S. Delaware
Moriarty James R. bricklayer, r. 493 S. East
Moriarty Jerry, lab. Bunte, Dickson & Co.
Moriarty Michael, plasterer, r. Coburn nr. foot New Jersey
Moriarty Patrick, lab. r. 23 Bates
Moriarty Thomas, lab. frt. depot C. C. & I. C. R. R.
Moriarty Willian C. bkpr. *State Sentinel,* r. 255 N. Mississippi
Moriarty William, flagman, r. 279 S. West

MOR   234   MOR

Moritz Bros. (Solomon and Mayer Moritz) clothiers and merchant tailors, 19 W. Washington

Morritz Mayer, (Moritz Bros.) r. New York city

Moritz Solomon, (Moritz Bros.) bds. Bates House

Morley Edward R. constable, r. 303 Indiana av.

Morley Thomas, lab. r. 226 S. Missouri

Morning Watch, W. W. Dowling editor and propr. Meridian se. cor. Circle

Morrell Lewis, student Bryant & Stratton's College, bds. 84 Massachusetts av.

Morrell Rachel, wid. W. S. r. 11 S. Meridian

Morris A. pattern maker Sinker & Co.

Morris A. W. Mrs. r. 115 S. Meridian

Morris Alfred, machinist Sinker & Co.

Morris Artemus, carpenter, r. 339 S. Delaware

Morris Austin G. bds. 79 Norwood

MORRIS CHARLES G. drugs and medicines, 521 N. Illinois, r. 112 Jackson

Morris Harmony, (H. Morris & Co.) r. 330 Indiana av.

Morris Harry W. salesman F. M. Brown, r. 28 S. Mississippi

Morris H. & Co. (Harmony Morris and ———) dyers and repairers, 22 W. Maryland

Morris James M. R. R. ticket agt. r. 219 N. New Jersey

Morris James W. clk. frt. depot I. C. & L. R. R. r. 112 Jackson

Morris John, shoemaker, r. 5 Dougherty

Morris John, lab. Rolling Mill

Morris John D. frt. agt. I. C. & L. R. R. r. 112 Jackson

Morris John I. (H. F. West & Co.) r. Ft. Wayne rd. n. of limits

Morris John S. librarian State House, bds. 311 S. East

Morris Joseph C. fireman R. R. bds. 79 Norwood

Morris Mary C. wid. r. 55 Mayhew

Morris Samuel B. city sealer, r. 79 Norwood

Morris Sanford, clk. Boston store, r. 275 W. Vermont

Morris Sarah A. wid. James, r. 17 Cherry

MORRIS THOMAS A. President Indianapolis and St. Louis R. R. office 53 S. Alabama, r. Western av. n. of limits

Morris William, (col'd) barber W. Porter

Morris William H. heater Rolling Mill, r. 159 Union

Morris William J. plasterer, r. 169 Fort Wayne av.

Morrison Alexander F. bookkeeper George K. Share & Co. r. St. Mary cor. Fort Wayne av.

Morrison Anna O. wid. A. F. r. Pennsylvania nw. cor. Market

Morrison Charles, asst. bookkeeper Alford, Talbot & Co. r. St. Mary cor. Fort Wayne av.

Morrison Hetty A. Mrs. clerk P. O. bds. 39 Virginia av.

Morrison John B. porter Wiles, Bro. & Co. r. 298 N. Tennessee

Morrison John I. (Wiles, Bro. & Co.) r. 298 N. Tennessee

Morrison Michael, r. 135 Union

Morrison Robert I. deputy State treas. State Bldg. r. 298 N. Tennessee

Morrison Samuel J. clerk Alford, Talbot & Co. r. St. Mary cor
    Fort Wayne av.
Morrison W. Lewis, bookkeeper Stewart & Morgan, bds. St. Ma-
    ry cor. Western av.
Morrison William, teamster, r. 270 Railroad
Morrison William, railroadman, r. Pennsylvania nw. cor. Market
Morrison William H. (Patterson, Moore & Talbot, and Alford,
    Talbot & Co.) r. 63 Circle
Morrison William H. bookbinder *Journal* office, bds. 144 N. Ten-
    nessee
Morrison William H. civil engineer, office 46 E. Washington
Morrison's Block, Meridian nw. cor. Maryland
Morrison's Opera Hall, Meridian ne. cor. Maryland, William H.
    Morrison propr.
Morroske Henry, tanner, r. 4th nr. Howard
Morrow R. lab. McKendry & Lovecraft
Morrow Thomas, carpenter, r. 217 Coburn
Morrow Thomas, lab. frt. depot C. C. & I. C. R. R. r. 327 W.
    Market
Morrow William, works J. S. Carey & Co.
Morrow Wilson, (Morrow & Trusler) r. 282 N. Pennsylvania
MORROW & TRUSLER, (Wilson Morrow and Nelson Trusler)
    attys. at law, room 6 Vinton's Block opp. P. O.
Morse Charles A. machinist, r. 204 Winston
MORSE THOMAS J. carpenter and builder, es. West bet. Ver-
    mont and New York, r. 199 N. West. See advt.
Mortland, Alexander M. saloon and restaurant, 23 N. Illinois,
    r. 227 N. Illinois
Morton Edward, carpenter, r. 325 Davidson
Morton George T. lawyer, room 1 Talbott & New's Blk. bds.
    Pyle House
Morton John brickmason, r. 67 Norwood
Morton John R. (Harding, Morton & Finch) r. 344 N. Alabama
Morton Joseph, (col'd) lab. r. 89 N. West
Morton Robert, teamster, r. 32 Bicking
Morton Thomas R. clerk Adj. Gens. Office, r. 215 W. Ohio
Moseley Alfred, (W. C. Lupton & Co.) r. 326 W. Maryland
Moser George, meat market, 295 S. Missouri, r. same
MOSES LUCIUS W. optician, 50 E. Washington, r. 87 E. Michigan
Mosher Theodore, foreman I. C. & L. Rw. shop, r. 101 Bates
Moss Louis, cigarmaker, r. 142 E. Maryland
Moss Martha, wid. Lewis, dressmaker, 188 N. Tennessee, r. same
Mossler A. J. mnfr. of hoopskirts, 59 S. Illinois, r. East cor.
    Vermont
Mossler Liebermann I. (Mossler L. I. & Bro.) r. 250 E. Vermont
Mossler Morris L. bookkeeper L. I. Mossler & Bro. bds. Circle
    Restaurant
Mossler Soloman (L. I. Mossler & Bro.) r. 35 N. East
Mossler L. I. & Bro. (Lieberman I. and Soloman Mossler) cloth-
    ing whol. and ret. 37 E. Washington
Moster Francis, shoemkr. bds. California House

Mothershead J. L. (Greenleaf & Co.) r. 10 W. Louisiana
Mothers' Monitor, Mrs. M. M. B. Goodwin editor and proprietor Meridian se. cor. Circle
Mott Charles E. (Elliott & Mott) bds. Dr. T. B. Elliott w. end Michigan
MOTTERY FERDINAND, propr. Concordia House, 200 S. Meridian, r. same
Moulton Charles W. engineer, r. 26 Fletcher av.
Moulton Daniel S. clk Express office
Mounden Benjamin, teamster, r. 300 S. Illinois
Mount Algeron S. (Mooney & Co.) r. 455 N. Tennessee
Mount Francis G. dressmkr. r. 148 Indiana av.
Mount G. A. wid. boarding house, 148 Indiana av.
Mount William P. currier Mooney & Co. bds. 455 N. Tennessee
Mount William T. clk. r. 455 N. Tennessee
Mountain Michael, lab. r. 17 Willard
Mounts Henry M. clk. J. M. & I. R. R. bds. 207 W. Maryland
Move Frank, carpenter, r. 84 S. Liberty
Move Henry, carpenter, bds. 84 S. Liberty
Moyer Joseph, carpenter Shover & Christian, r. Morrison 1 e. Delaware
MOZART HALL (J. Grosch) entrance 39 S. Delaware
Muckenberger John, cigar box maker, r. 152 Madison av.
Muecke William, r. 74 S. Delaware
Muecke William, (Egger & Muecke) bds. 135 E. Washington
Muehlenbeck Albert, clk. r. 198 E. Washington
Muehlenbeck August, hats, caps and furs, also (Muehlenbeck & Obermeyer) 198 E. Washington, r. Terre Haute, Ind.
Muehlenbeck William, clerk. Aug. Muehlenbeck, bds. 198 E. Washington
Muehlenbeck S. wid. Frederick, r. 294 South
Muehlenbeck & Obermeyer (August Muehlenbeck and W. M. Obermeyer) dealers in hats, caps and furs 2 Palmer House
Mueller Charles G. saloon 25 S. Delaware, r. same
MUELLER CHARLES L. tailor and repairer 53 S. Illinois, r. 412 S. Illinois
Mueller Christian, lab. Bellefontaine frt. depot, r. 219 Union
Mueller Edward, bookkeeper Starch Factory, r. 305 E. Market
Mueller John, importer and whol. dealer in wines, liquors and cigars 306 E. Washington, r. Madison road
Mueller John A. meat market 237 S. Alabama, r. 235 S. Alabama
Mueller Louis H. druggist 187 E. Washington, r. same
Mueller M. lab. Wood's Foundery, bds. 169 Stevens
Mueller Valentine, tanner, r. 140 N. Davidson
Mueller William, school teacher, bds. 238 S. New Jersey
Muerman Frederick, cooper, r. 70 Elm
Muhlemann Christian, cabinetmkr. r. 488 S. New Jersey
Muiller Anthony, r. 244 S. Tennessee
Muir James O. r. 121 N. Mississippi
Muir James W. salesman M. H. Spades, bds. Pyle House
Mulbarger William H. carriage maker, r. 175 Maple

Mulchay Margarett, wid. David, r. 488 E. Georgia
Mulchay Michael, lab. r. 87 S. Noble
Mull Jacob, route agt. R. R. r. 273 N. Tennessee
Mullaley Edward, porter P. O. r. 52 Huron cor. Noble
Mullany Dennis F. salesman Ryan & Holbrook, r. 355 N. Illinois
Mullany Mary, wid. Patrick, r. 355 N. Illinois
Mullaney Patrick J. salesman T. F. Ryan, r. 355 N. Illinois
Mullen Annie, wid. Roger, r. 20 Dougherty
Mullen John, driver Citizens' St. R. R. Co. r. 369 S. Illinois
Mullen William, blacksmith, bds. 10 W. Georgia
Mullen William, clerk H. F. West & Co. r. 521 N. Tennessee
Muller Charles, r. 330 Madison av.
Muller E. Mrs. teacher Sixth Ward School, bds. 88 Union
Muller Frederick, cabinet maker Cabinet Makers' Union
Muller Henry, stairbuilder, r. 360 N. East
Muller John, brewer City Brewery
Muller John, r. Madison rd. s. of limits
Muller John E. D. saw mill, r. 468 N. East
Muller Peter, cabinetmaker Cabinet Makers' Union
Muller Stephen, lab. D. Root & Co. r. 169 Stevens
Mulliken John, agt. r. 71 N. Davidson
Mulliken S. A. dress and cloak maker, 7 Martindale's blk. N.
    Pennsylvania, r. 71 Davidson
Mulry Thomas, lab. City Hospital, r. same
Munday M. (Long, Snyder & Co.) r. Dayton, Ohio
Mundon Jesse, salesman Wischart & Calvert, bds. 379 N. West
Mungar Christ, telegraph repairer, r. 266 S. Delaware
Munhall Lea W. dentist, 35½ E. Market, bds. Macy House
Muncey James, wks. S. S. Smith, bds. Ray House
Muncey L. switchman T. H. & I. R. R. r. 183 W. South
Munsell Ezra, wagonmkr. ns. St. Clair bet. Broadway and Mas-
    sachusetts av. r. 63 Peru
Munsell Henry, engineer C. C. C. & I. R. R.
MUNSELL HENRY, wagonmkr. Massachusetts av. cor. Plum, r.
    71 N. St. Charles
Munson Charles H. (Munson & Johnston) r. 286 N. Alabama
MUNSON DAVID, propr. Indianapolis Lightning Rod Works, 62
    E. Washington, r. 228 E. Market
Munson Lewis, r. 286 N. Alabama
Munson William G. clk. Munson & Johnston, bds. 228 E. Market
Munson William L. ret. grocer, 51 N. Alabama, r. 286 N. Ala-
    bama
MUNSON & JOHNSTON, (Charles H. Munson and William J. John-
    ston) stoves, tinware and house furnishing goods, 62 E.
    Washington
Muntz James, plasterer, r. 404 Virginia av.
Muntz Michael, plasterer, r. 440 Virginia av.
Muntz Thomas, plasterer, r. 111 Elm
Murdock Frank, actor Academy of Music, r. 75 N. Illinois
Murdock Joseph, moulder D. Root & Co. r. 385 S. Illinois
Murer Frederick, shoemaker, r. 192 Virginia av.

Murks Martin, engineer Helwig & Co.
Murphy B. H. r. 157 N. Mississippi
Murphy Chloe A. Miss, teacher First Ward School. r. 144 N. East
Murphy Daniel E. groceries ret. 396 W. North, r. same
Murphy George W. clk. Murphy, Johnston & Co. bds. Virginia av.
Murphy James, conductor, bds. 177 Meek
Murphy James r. 17 Elizabeth
Murphy James, lab. r. 278 E. Louisiana
Murphy James, wks. Kingan & Co. bds. 199 W. Maryland
Murphy Jesse T. policeman, r. 176 N. Spring
Murphy John cigar maker, bds. 15 Massachusetts av.
Murphy John, expressman, r. 26 Pitt
Murphy John lab. Rolling Mill, r. ws. Maple nr. limits
Murphy John W. (W. J. Holiday & Co. and Murphy, Johnston
    & Co.) r. 166 N. Meridian
Murphy John W. clerk David E. Murphy, bds. 396 W. North
Murphy Lizzie J. teacher Sixth Ward School, r. 42 Fletcher av.
Murphy Michael, lab. Rolling Mill, r. Alley bet. Pennsylvania
    and Delaware, South and McCarty
Murphy Michael, night policeman, r. 190 Blackford
Murphy Milton, engineer Starch Factory, r. 150 N. Winston
Murphy Morris, wks. Simms & Hoskins, r. 146 Meek
Murphy P. M. delivery clerk Express office
Murphy Patrick, lab. frt. depot T. H. & I. R. R.
Murphy Patrick, lab. r. 499 E. Georgia
Murphy Rebecca, wid. Jonathan, r. 85 N. Davidson
Murphy Samuel, farmer, r. 42 Fletcher av.
Murphy Timothy, shoemaker, 15 Massachusetts av. r. same
MURPHY TOBIAS M. gen'l agt. Home Life Ins. Co. of New York,
    and Aurora Fire Insurance of Covington, Ky. also real es-
    tate agt. room 9, 2d floor Martindale's blk. Pennsylvania ne.
    cor. Market, r. 321 E. Georgia
Murphy William, clerk W. H. Roll
Murphy William, (col'd) lab. r. 276 E. North
Murphy William, lab. Rolling Mill
MURPHY, JOHNSTON & CO. (J. N. Murphy, W. W. Johnston &
    W. J. Holiday) whol. dealers in dry goods and notions, Me-
    ridian, cor. Maryland
Murray Charles W. lumber dealer, r. 440 N. East
MURRAY JAMES A. agt. Empire Fast Frt. Line, 96 Virginia av.
    bds. Bates House
Murray Robert, tobacconist, r. es. Illinois bet. 3d and 4th
Musgrave Moses, woolen mnfr. A. L. Clark, r. 65 S. California
Musser Wm. A. compositor *Mirror* news room, r. 43 Dougherty
Mussmann Diedrich, (W. & D. Mussmann) r. 244 Bluff rd.
Mussman Louisa, wid. Henry, r. rear 269 S. Alabama
Mussmann William, (W. & D. Mussmann) r. 244 Bluff rd.
Mussmann W. & D. (William and Diedrich) grocers, 244 Bluff rd.
Mutchett Charles, carpenter, r. 461 N. Alabama
Mutchett Richard E. brakeman, 128 N. Spring
Muth Peter, saloon 8 S. Delaware, r. 132 St. Joseph

MUT	239	NAT

Mutual Benefit Life Ins. Co. of Newark, New Jersey, Nutting & Wood agts. 19 W. Washington

Mutual Life Ins. Co. of New York, E. B. Martindale agt. rooms 1 and 2 (2nd floor) Martindale's blk.

Mutz Antony, barber Sherman House, r. 315 S. Delaware

Muzza Barnett, lab. r. 70 N. Delaware

Myers Benjamin, student National Business College

Myers Catherine, wid. Peter, r. 244 S. Delaware

Myers Daniel M. pumpmaker, r. 225 S. Tennessee

Myers Frank, stove moulder A. D. Wood

Myers George, (col'd) barber Henry Byrd, bds. 63 S. Illinois

Myers H. F. stove mounter, r. 322 S. Delaware

Myers Henry, varnisher Cabinetmakers' Union

Myers Irvin M. clk. H. W. Caldwell, r. 168 W. Michigan

Myers James M. real estate agt. 30½ W. Washington, r. 258 N. Tennessee

Myers Jesse D. miller, r. 45½ N. Tennessee

Myers John, carpenter, r. 327 Winston

Myers John A. (Martin & Myers) r. 119 W. Washington

Myers John G. (Myers & Daubenspeck) r. 485 N. Alabama

Myers John W. principal School No. 10, r. ss. 5th bet. Tennessee and Mississippi

Myers Josephine, wid. r. 64 N. Tennessee

Myers Lewis, machinist Eagle Machine Works, r. 89 N. Davidson

Myers Mikel, butcher, r. ss. Kansas w. of Bluff rd.

Myers Smith H. clk. Hill & Vinnedge, r. 422 N. Illinois

Myers Thomas, varnisher Spiegel & Thoms

Myers William, machinist Eagle Machine Wks. r. 89 N. Davidson

Myers William M. salesman H. J. Prier

MYERS & DAUBENSPECK, (John G. Myers, N. Daubenspeck) real estate and house agts. 27 Massachusetts av.

Myhan James, spinner Hoosier Woolen Factory, r. ws. Douglass 8 S. New York

N

Nagel August, propr. Nagel House 272 W. Maryland

Nahn William, shoemaker Hill & Vennedge, r. 266 N. Noble

Nale Kate, wks. Indianapolis Paper Co.

Nale Mary, wid. Isaac, r. 90 Maple

Naltner Aegidius, (A. Seidensticker & Co.) bds. National Hotel

Naltner Martin, saloon and boarding-house 134 S. Meridian

Names John, (Many & Names) r. 314 Virginia av.

Nar Charles, heater Rolling Mill

Nardin Ethan T. piano tuner, 28 N. Delaware, r. same

Nartg John, bds. Jefferson House

Nash Martha A. wid. Philander, r. 113 Massachusetts av.

Natcher Charles, agent, r. 191½ W. Washington

Nathan Joseph, (col'd) porter Macy House, bds. same

National Art Association, M. O. Tracy gen'l supt. room 21 Talbott & New's blk.

NAT   240   NEL

National Hotel, W. P. Thatcher propr. ss. McNabb opp. Depot
Naughton Patrick, grocer 210 E. Washington, r. 101 S. New Jersey
Naughton Peter, clk. Patrick Norton, bds. 101 S. New Jersey
Navin John N. veterinary surgeon, 208 W. Washington, r. same
Naylor Mary D. Miss, teacher Indiana Institute for the Blind
Neab Conrad, plumber, steam and gas-pipe fitter, 70 N. Illinois, (Miller's blk.) bds. Palmer House
Neal Augustus C. printer Indianapolis Printing and Publishing House, r. 286 Virginia av.
Neal Jonathan, produce dealer, r. 218 E. Market
Neal William, (col'd) pastor Shelbyville African Church, r. 165 Elizabeth
Near George, r. 210 Madison av.
Nebirgall John, carpenter, r. 266 Winston
Neeb Charles, saloon 20 N. Delaware, r. Washington
Neeb Jacob, peddler, r. room 8, 77¼ E. Market
Needham William, (Crain & Needham and Indianapolis Banking Co.) r. Franklin, Ind.
Neeks William, driver Citizens' St. R. R. Co.
Neeld Nathan N. (J. C. Ferguson & Co.) r. 145 N. Meridian
Neely Jennie, teacher (A.) Intermediate Grade High School r. 115 Massachusetts av.
Neermann Christian, shoemaker 271 Massachusetts av. r. same
Neermann Christian, lab. r. 70 Lockerbie
Neff Albert, cooper, r. 19 Maria
Neff Charles, cooper D. Burton & Co.
Neff Edward, cooper, r. 19 Maria
Neffle E. F. Miss, r. 275 S. West
Neffle Fred. r. 275 S. West
Neffle Frederick, butcher J. A. Mueller, bds. 235 S. Alabama
Negley Peter L. law student Elliott & Holstein
Neidigh Catharine, wid John, r. ws. Blake 2 n. New York
Neidling Louis, house fitter D. Root & Co.
Neighbors Charles, express agent, r. 241 S. Mississippi
Neighbors Robert, drayman, r. 151 Union
Neiman Barbara, tailoress Henry Small, bds. 42 N. Douglas
Neiman Daniel, clerk Neiman House
Neiman House, (Mrs. L. Neiman) 130 S. Illinois
Neiman Jacob S. lab. r. 260 N. Noble
Neiman John S. clerk, bds. Neiman House
Neiman Joseph, carpenter, r. 42 Douglas
Neiman Laha Mrs. propr. Neiman House, 130 S. Illinois
Neiman Maggie, tailoress H. Small, bds. 42 N. Douglas
Neimaster Adam, shoemaker J. Stein
Neimeyer Henry, lab. C. & I. J. R. R.
Nelson Edward F. engineer, r. 500 E. Georgia
Nelson F. actor Academy of Music
Nelson Frank, bookkeeper, bds. 242 N. Illinois
Nelson H. N. r. 146 W. Vermont
Nelson Henry H. carpenter, r. 125 N. Mississippi

Nelson Horatio L. watchmaker W. P. Bingham & Co. r. 146 W. Vermont

Nelson James, (col'd) r. 385 N. New Jersey

Nelson Samuel, (col'd) lab. r. 126 N. Missouri

Nelson Thomas A. cashier New York Store, r. 54 S. Penn.

Nerney Alfred G. silverplater W. B. Higgins, r. Plum bet. Vine and Cherry

Nerse Thomas, coachman S. Taggart, r. 118 N. Mississippi

Nesler George, cabinetmaker Spiegel & Thoms, Furniture Co.

Netiron Charles C. basketmaker, r. 216 W. New York

Netiron Mary, fortune teller r. 216 W. New York

Nettler Louis, cook, r. 45½ N. Tennessee

Neu Barney, chairpainter II. Schilling & Bro.

Neubacher Louis, (Schneider & Co. r.) 269 S. Alabama

Neuerburg Leonard, clerk Edward Beck, bds. 44 W. Washington

Neusban Nicholas, works G. S. Smith, bds. Ray House

Neusle Charles, lab. Spiegel & Thoms

Neven Charles, watches, jewelry and ornamental hair worker, 51 Massachusetts av. r. same

Nevill James, physician, 114 N. Railroad, r. same

New Barney, chairpainter, r. 348 S. Delaware

New England Mutual Life Ins. Co. of Boston, Snyder & Hays agents, 17 N. Meridian

New George W. physician and surgeon, office 15 Miller's Block, Illinois cor, Market, r. 426 N. Illinois

NEW J. B. pastor 4th Christian Church, r. 82 N. Illinois

New Jersey Mutual Life Ins. Co. T. R. Bryant agt, 17½ W. Washington

New John C. cash. First National Bank of Indianapolis, r. 248 N. Pennsylvania

New Valentine, packer J. Woodbrige

New Valentine, porter, r. 472 S. East

New York Central Ins. Co. of N. Y. M. Child, Jr. agt. 25 W. Washington

New York Fur Mnfy. D. Leleuer & Bro. proprs. 39½ S. Meridian

New York Life Ins. Co. of New York, Byington & Erringer, state agents, 11 S. Meridian

NEW YORK ONE PRICE CLOTHING HOUSE, (L. I. Mossler & Bro.) 37 E. Washington

New York Store, Pettis, Dickson & Co. proprs. Glenn's blk.

New's Block, 10, 12 E. Washington

Newcomb H. C. Jr. jeweler r. 384 N. New Jersey

Newcomb Horatio C. (Newcomb, Mitchell & Ketcham) r. 243 N. East

Newcomb Richard II. salesman H. C. Newcomb, r. 48 W. North

Newcomb William C. salesman H. C. Newcomb, r. 446 N. New Jersey

NEWCOMB, MITCHELL & KETCHAM, (H. C. Newcomb, J. L. Mitchell and W. A. Ketcham) attys. at law, office 21 and 23 E. Washington

16

| NEW | 242 | NIC |

NEWCOMER FRISBY S. physician and surgeon No. 6 Blake blk r. 82 W. North
Newell J. V. salesman T. F. Ryan
Newell L. S. music teacher, Vinton's blk.
Newell Robert A. carpenter, bbs, 74 E. North
Newland Alexander, hostler Wood & Foudray bds. 30½ N. Penn.
Newland G. M. Dallas, prof. of music Indiana Institution for the Blind, r. same
Newland Robert A. prof. of music Indiana Iustitution for the Blind, r. same
Newman David, clk. Raugh Brothers, r. 139 Virginia av.
Newman Henry C. clk. A. V. Lawrence, bds. 80 S. Mississippi
NEWMAN JOHN S. prest. Merchants' National Bank 48 E. Washington, r. 243 N. Pennsylvania
Newman Isaac L. broommaker, 372 N. East, r. same
Newman Paulina, wid. Solomon, hoopskirt manfr. 95 E. Washington, r. 140 Virginia av.
Newman Peter, lab. r. 305 S. Missouri
Newmeyer Julius A. (Kettenbach, Newmeyer & Co.) r. 33 Noble
Newsom Lysias, r. 441 W. Mississippi
Newton Delos, cooper E. McNeely, r. 19 Fayette
Newton George A. clk frt. office C. C. & I. C. R. R. r. 210 S. Alabama
Newton J. Jesse, (Cramer & Newton) bds. Bates House
Newton Jennie Miss, teacher 9th Ward School, r. 240 S. Alabama
NEWTON MARIA MRS. milliner and dressmaker 110 S. Illinois, r. same
Newton Philo A. bleacher and presser of straw, r. 27 Fayette
Newton S. E. Mrs. teacher Indianapolis Female Institute, r. same
Ney Michael W. porter, r. 149 N. California
Neydecker Frederick, cabinetmaker Burk, Earnshaw & Co.
Neymiers Henry, frt. hand, r. 223 Buchanan
Nichol James M. teller Indiana National Bank, r. 357 N. Illinois
NICHOL JOSEPH W. lawyer, room 2 Ætna Bldg. bds. 519 N. Meridian
Nicholas Addison, r. 201 N. Liberty
Nicholas John S. clk. r. 550 N. Tennessee
Nichols Alvani V. teach. 8th Ward Dist. School, r. 201 N. Liberty
Nichols C. T. actor, bds. Oriental House
Nichols Catherine, wid. William, r. 66 Indiana av.
Nichols Harry T. operator W. U. T. Co. r. 66 Indiana av.
Nichols J. S. salesman William Eccles, r. Tennessee 4 n. 1st
Nichols Robert, (col'd) lab. r. 4th nr. La Fayette R. R.
Nichols Thomas, driver Street R. R. Co. bds. Illinois House
Nichols Thomas M. dentist 25 W. Washington, r. Bethel Gravel rd. se. city limits
Nichols Willard, comp. *Mirror* newsroom, r. 73 E. St. Clair
Nichols Willard C. clerk State Library, r. 73 E. St. Clair
Nichols William L. (col'd) porter J. H. Vajen & Co. r. 224 N. Missouri
Nicholson David, (Scott & Nicholson) r. 166 W. Georgia

Nicholson Edwin, r. 124 Blackford
Nicholson William, lab. r. 22 Lord
Nicholson William, lab. I. C. & L. R. R.
Nickum Joel G. blacksmith, r. 53 Maple
Nickum John R. (Parrott, Nickum & Co.) r. 155 N. Tennessee
Nicoli C. saddle and harness maker, 326 E. Washington, r. same
Nicoli Henry, butcher John Thorn, bds. 87 N. Noble
Nicoli Lewis, (Jackson & Nicoli) bds. 222 W. Ohio
Nieger Jacob, lab. r. al. bet. Washington and Market, Alabama and New Jersey
Niehaus Joseph L. (Zimmer & Niehaus) r. 349 S. Delaware
Nieman Charles, blacksmith, r. 231 N. Davidson
Nieman Christopher, carpenter, r. 231 N. Davidson
Niemann Gerhard, shoemkr. N. Merl, bds. 123 S. Illinois
Niemann Henry, (Boedeker & Niemann) bds. Winston bet. North and Michigan
Niemeyer William, grocer, 102 S. Noble, r. same
Niemeyer William C. brakeman, r. 165 S. Tennessee
Niermeyer F. T. student National Business College
Niermeyer Henry, boot and shoe maker, 126 Ft. Wayne av. r. 128 Ft. Wayne av.
Nies Lewis, grocer, 460 N. East, r. same
Nifeing Nicolas, lab. r. 760 N. Tennessee
Nihlson John, coachman J. H. Talbott, bds. 94 N. Meridian
NILIUS CHARLES, tailor and repairer, 134 S. Illinois, r. rear 65 W. South
Ninth Ward District School, Miss Mary E. Perrett, prin. Vermont, nw. cor. Davidson
Nissen Rudolph, cigarmkr. Chas. C. Hunt, bds. 13 S. Mississippi
Noble A. Frank, Ward's Gas Generator for Indiana, 28 Kentucky av. r. 80 S. Tennessee
Noble Nannie, Mrs. teacher 9th Ward School, r. Pennsylvania bet. Delaware and Meridian
Noble Samuel C. pastor Third Street Mission Church, (Methodist) r. 623 N. Illinois
NOBLE WILLIAM H. L. gen'l agt. I. C. & L. R. R. depot, Louisiana cor. Delaware, r. Madison av. nr. city limits
Noble Winston P. r. E. Market e. of limits
Noe Andrew J. carpenter C. C. & I. C. R. R.
Noe Andrew J. painter, r. 21 N. East
Noe Marshall, carpenter, r. 280 N. Alabama
Noe Mary, dressmaker, 21 N. East, r. same
Noel E. L. (Noel & Son) r. 252 S. New Jersey
Noel Edmond B. (Noel & Son) r. 252 S. New Jersey
Noel M. F. shoemaker, 252 N. Illinois, r. same
Noel Samuel V. B. (Noel & Son) r. 252 S. New Jersey
Noel Smallwood, clk. Noel & Son, r. 252 S. New Jersey
NOEL & SON, (E. L., E. B. and S. V. B. Noel) grain dealers and forwarding and com. mers. 86 Virginia av.
Noerr George, lab. Western Furniture Co.
Nofsinger Frank B. (Nofsinger, Kingan & Co.) r. 49 Indiana av.

Nofsinger William R. (Nofsinger, Kingan & Co.) r. National rd. e. of city limits

NOFSINGER KINGAN & CO. (William R. and Frank B. Nofsinger, Thomas D. and Samuel Kingan, and Joseph D. Pattison,) pork packers and commission merchants w. end Maryland st.

Nolan ——, brakeman, bds. 58 Benton

Nolan Ann, wid. Thomas, r. rear 65 N. Missouri

Nolan Joseph, shoemaker, r. 122 E. Merrill

Nolan Lavenia Mrs. boarding house, 198 S. Illinois, r. same

Nolan Michael, shoemaker A. Scherer, r. 132 S. West

Noland Thomas, lab. bds. Ray House

Nolting Charles, r. 127 E. St. Joseph

Nolting William, wks. *Journal* book bindery, bds. 127 St. Joseph

Nooan Michael, lab. r. 246 S. West

Nooe Daniel M. carriage maker, r. 121 S. Delaware

Nooe Martha, wid. Aquilla, r. 119 S. New Jersey

Nordman Frederick, cooper, r. 263 S. West

Nordman Henry, cooper r. 269 S. West

Norman James A. brush maker Schmedel & Fricker, r. 230 W. Georgia bet. West and the canal

Norris James C. salesman Fahnley & McCrea, r. 93 Broadway

Norris John, boots and shoes, 23 E. Washington, r. 56 S. Penn.

Norris John C. r. 9 Cherry

Norris Thomas, tanner Frenzell & Simon, bds. 518 E. Washington

North American Fire Ins. Co. of Hartfort Conn. Snyder & Hays agts. 17 N. Meridian

North American Fire Ins. Co. of New York, Snyder & Hays agts. 17 N. Meridian

North America Life Ins. Co. New York, William A. Bradshaw gen'l agt. room 14 Talbot and New's blk.

North British & Mercantile Fire Ins. Co. of London and Edinburgh, E. B. Martindale agt. rooms 1—2 (2d floor) Martindale's block

North Myron, depot master L. & I. R. R.

NORTHROP WILLIAM W. gen'l agt. Security Life Ins. and Annuity Co. of New York, No. 2, Blake blk. r. 310 N. Illinois

Northway George M. plasterer, r. 186 N. New Jersey

Northway John, plasterer, r. 306 E. North

Northwestern (monthly) Martin & Hopkins editors and proprs. Market, nc. Circle, Journal building

North Western Christian University, Ovid Butler pres. A. V. Cole sec. and treas. bet. College av. and University av. North and Forest Home av.

North Western Farmer, Bland and Taylor editors and props. 19 N. Meridian

North Western Mutual Life of Milwaukee Wis. Martin & Hopkins state agt. Indiana and Kentucky, Market nc. cor. Circle Journal building

Norton Frederick, piano maker, r. 50 Fletcher av.

Norvell H. C. r. 10 and 11, 85½ E. Market

Norton James, hostler Wood & Mansur, bds. 38 S. Tennessee

Norton Luther, carpenter, r. 417 E. St. Clair
Norton William H. baggageman Bellefontaine R. R. r. 234 S. Alabama
Norwood Block ws. Illinois bet. W. Washington and Market
Norwood George, retired, r. 129 N. Illinois
Norwood John L. R. R. r. 121 E. Ohio
Norwood M. A. wid. Newton, r. 121 E. Ohio
Nottmeyer Christian, carpenter Warren Tate, r. 293 E. Ohio
Nowland John H. B. traveling agt. r. 283 E. South
Nowland P. B. L. printer Indianapolis Printing and Publishing House, bds. 283 E. South
Noyes Albert, brakeman, bds. 58 Benton
Null Thomas E. bookbinder, r. 500 N. West
Nure Joseph (Goas & Co.) r. n. Mississippi city limits
Nutmier Christian, carpenter, r. 293 E. Ohio
Nutt James, carriagemkr. Bremerman & Renner
Nutting Rufus, Jr. (Nutting & Wood) r 368 N. East
NUTTING & WOOD (Rufus Nutting, Jr. and D. L. Wood) insurance agts. 19 W. Washington
Nutts Jacob, baker, Parrott, Nickum & Co. r. 121 Massachusetts av
Nutzel John, meat market 175 Madison av. r. same
Nydegger Fred, carpenter, r. 30 S. Alabama
Nydegger Fred C. turner, r. 30 S. Alabama

O'

O'Brien Christopher H. mail clk. P. O. r. 759 N. Mississippi
O'Brien Jerry, tinsmith Munson & Johnston, r. 28 Wyoming
O'Brien John, r. 82 Bates
O'Brien John, lab. r. 225 S. West
O'Brien John, lab. Parrott, Nickum & Co. r. East nw. cor. McCarty
O'Brien John, lab. r. 343 S. Delaware
O'Brien Joseph, lab. Rolling Mill, r. 73 McCarty
O'Brien Michael, car insp. C. C. C & I. R. R.
O'Brien Michael, carpenter C. C. C. & I. R. R.
O'Brien Michael, puddler Rolling Mill, bds. 300 S. Tennessee
O'Brien Richard, r. 397 S. East
O'Brien T. hostler Express Co.
O'Brien Thomas, r. es. Clinton alley bet. E. Ohio and New York
O'Brien Thomas, stonecutter, r. 59 S. California
O'Brien Timothy, traveling agt. I. C. R. R. r. 282 S. Delaware
O'Connell Daniel, lab. r. 191 Meek
O'Connell Ellen T. Mrs. N. M. Allen, r. 266 Huron
O'Connell James, drayman Andrew Wallace, r. 40 S. Lord
O'Connell Murty, lab. r. 290 S. Delaware
O'Conor Cornelius, varnisher Western Furniture Co.
O'Connor Daniel, lab. r. 36 N. Douglas
O'Connor John, r. 167 Meek
O'Connor John, hostler Citizens' St. R. R. Co.
O'Connor Michael, (Prenatt & O'Connor) r. 28 W. Pratt

O'Connor Michael, lab. r. 245 S. Tennessee
O'Connor Michael, lab. r. Minerva west end Vermont
O'Connor Michael, lab. r. 237 Coburn
O'Connor Michael J. agt. Sands' cream and stock ale 54 S. Illinois, r. same
O'Connor Peter, lab. bds. 130 S. Noble.
O'Connor Thomas, boot and shoe mkr. 294 S. Delaware, r. same
O'Donan Cornelius, lab. r. 579 E. St. Clair
O'Donnell Patrick, salesman John Dorian, bds Oriental House
O'Driscoll John, printer *Journal* job room, bds. 30½ N. Penn.
O'Farrell Edward, boilermaker, r. ss. Sinker nr. Alabama
O'Flarerty Thomas, clerk Schetter & Simpson, bds. 99 E. South
O'Haire Matthew, tailor, r. 233 S. West
O'Hanlon Francis, r. 179 N. Tennessee
O'Hare John, shoemaker, r. 386 S. West
O'Harra Michael, lab. r. 331 S. Missouri
O'Haver Anna, wks. Cotton Factory
O'Haver Eva, wks. Cotton Factory
O'Haver Mary, wid. George, r. ws. Blake 2 n. New York
O'Haver Patterson, lab. r. ws. Blake 3 n. New York
O'Haver Samuel, wks. Cotton Factory
O'Keane Patrick J. clerk R. Simpson, bds. Ray House
O'Keefe Cornelius, saloon 267 S. Tennessee, r. same
O'Keefe Timothy, lab. r. 18 Willard
O'Key Philip, carpenter, r. 77 Oak
O'Laughlin John, moulder D. Root & Co.
O'Leary Daniel, employee A. M. U. Ex. Co. r. 345 S. Meridian
O'Leary Jeremiah, saloon 103 S. Illinois, r. same
O'Leary John, clerk J. O'Leary, bds. 103 S. Illinois
O'Leary Michael, lab. r. 288 S. Delaware
O'Leary Mollie, bleacher H. Malpas. r. 103 S. Illinois
O'Malley Patrick, auctioneer, r. 327 W. Maryland
O'Mara James, lab. bds. 101 S. Illinois
O'Mara James, wks. Ex. Office, r. Minerva west end Vermont
O'Mara James, puddler Indianapolis Rolling Mill
O'Mara Jerry, (O'Mara & Hartnett) bds. 101 S. Illinois
O'Mara P. boilermkr. Sinker & Co. r. ss. Sinker near Alabama
O'Mara Richard, r. Minerva west end Vermont
O'Mara Richard, expressman, r. 101 S. Illinois
O'Mara & Hartnett, (J. O'Mara and P. E Hartnett) saloon, 101 S. Illinois
O'Neal Amanda Mrs. r. 320 E. Washington
O'Neal Charlotte, wid. Richard, r. 130 Virginia av.
O'Neal Etta Miss, milliner, r. Maryland nc. cor. S. Illinois
O'Neal J. G. lab. Osgood, Smith & Co.
O'Neal John, wks. J. C. Ferguson & Co.
O'Neal Patrick, lab. r. 190 Harrison
O'Neal Timothy, lab. C. C. & I. C. R. R.
O'Neal William H. sawyer, r. 372 S. West
O'Neil Edward, r. 140 E. St. Joseph
O'Neill John, lab. r. 211 E. Market

O'Neil Michael, r. 164 Meek
O'Neil Michael, cutter J. & P. Gramling, r. 143 E. McCarty
O'Neil Michael, lab. r. 199 Meek .
O'Neil Robert, teamster, r. 155 Meek
O'Neil Thomas, lab. r. 164 Meek
O'Neil Timothy, lab. r. 168 Meek
O'Reily John, shoemaker, bds. 414 S. Tennessee
O'Reily Michael, shoemaker W. P. Wasson, r. 414 S. Tennessee
O'Reily Thomas W. trader, bds. Ray House
O'Shea Patrick, lab. I. C. & L. Rw. r. 109 Huron
O'Val Joseph, miller Hoosier State Mills

O

Oaleslagher Benjamin, machinist Phœnix Machine Works
Oatman Merritt J. agent Singer Mnfg. Co. 16 N. Delaware, r. 712 N. Tennessee
Obenchain Timothy L. r. 417 N. Tennessee
Obergfell Isadore, checkman C. C. I. C. frt. depot, r. 392 S. Delaware
Obergfell M. carpenter, r. Madison rd. s. limits
Obergfell Philip, lab. frt. depot C. C. & I. C. R. R.
Oberly A wks. Caledonia Paper Mill, bds. 261 W. Washington
Oberman Robert, carpenter, r. 266 Blake
Obermeyer M. A. Mrs. dressmaker, 79 W. Ohio, r. same
Obermeyer W. M. (Muehlenbeck & Obermeyer, r. 79 W. Ohio
Obiren R. pianofortemaker J. H. Kappes & Co.
Obony Alexander, carpenter, r. 111 Massachusetts av.
Obrecht John, teacher, bds. 32 S. Alabama
Odd Fellows' Hall and Building, ne. cor. Washington and Penn.
Odd Felllows' Talisman, R. J. Strickland pub. 30 S. Meridian
Odell Charles, agent Wheeler & Wilson Sewing Machine, r. 576 N. Mississippi
Odell J. lab. C. C. & I. C. R. R.
Odell James, machinist, r. 147 Huron
Odell James M. solicitor Wm. Sumner & Co. r. 576 N. Mississippi
Odell Risdon M. compositor *Commercial,* bds. 30 S. Meridian
Odell Thomas B. solicitor Security Life Ins. and Annuity Co. of New York, bds. Pattison House
Odell William S. clk. Wm. Sumner & Co. bds. 576 N. Mississippi
Oechsle Kate Miss, teacher 9th Ward School, r. 171 N. Davidson
Oehler Andrew, watches and jewelry, 20 S. Delaware r. same
Oehler David, saloon, 84 Russell av. r. same
Oehler Romon, watchmkr. and jeweler, 183 W. Washington
Oehri Louis, engineer, wks. Cabinet Makers' Union
Ofer Frederick, tailor, bds. Washington House
Off Christian, (Christian Off & Brothers) r. 297 N. Noble
Off Gottliob (Christian Off & Brothers) r. 305 N. Noble
Off Jacob G. (Christian Off & Brothers) r. 291 N. Noble
OFF CHRISTIAN & BROTHERS, (Christian, Jacob G. and Gottleob Off) lumber dealers and mnfrs. St. Clair cor. Peru

OFF	248	ORP

Offutt James, carpenter, r. 181 S. Tennessee

Ogden Mary L. wks. Merritt & Coughlen, bds. ns. Blake 2 n. New York

Ogden William S. clerk gen'l frt. office T. H. & I. Rw. r. 522 N. Meridian

Ogle Nannie Miss, r. 704 N. Tennessee

Oglesby J. E. clerk C. C. C. & I. R. R. r. 476 N. Illinois

Oglesby J. H. r. 476 N. Illinois

Oheri Louis, engineer, r. 525 E. Market

Ohleyer George, basket maker, r. 156 Bluff rd.

Ohmer George, (N. & G. Ohmer) r. Dayton, Ohio

Ohmer Nicholas, (N. & G. Ohmer) r. Dayton, Ohio

OHMER N. & G. (Nicholas and George Ohmer) proprs. Union depot dining hall and restaurant, Union depot bldgs.

Ohr Aaron D. asst. ticket agt. Union depot, r. 431 N. Meridian

Ohr Henry, r. 126 N. Delaware

Ohr John H. (Martin, Hopkins & Ohr) also foreign exchange and passage agency, *Journal* bldg. r. 448 N. Meridian

Oiler Philip H. wks. Osgood & Smith, r. 180 N. Missouri

Okey Edward H. carpenter, r. 359 N. New Jersey

Okey Joseph, patent right agt. r. 326 N. East

Old Oaken Bucket, Cowen & Protzman publishers & proprs. 16½ E. Washington

Olds Henry, carpenter, r. 137 W. Michigan

Olds Lizzie, tailoress H. Small, bds. 580 N. Mississippi

Olin Chauncey C. gen'l agt. Travelers Ins. Co. 2 W. Washington, r. Tennessee n. of Tinker

Olin Edwin D. (Ohlin & Foltz) bds. Pyle House

OLIN & FOLTZ, (Edwin D. Olin, Howard M. Foltz) gen'l agts. of the Howe Sewing Machine, 12 N. Pennsylvania, opp. Odd Fellows Hall

Oliver C. cigars and tobacco ret. 288 W. Washington, r. same

Oliver D. H. physician and surgeon, 58½ E. Market, r. 28 Gregg

Oliver G. W. painter Bremerman & Renner

Oliver Theodore, lab. r. 315 S. Missouri

OLIVET PRESBYTERIAN CHURCH, McCarty cor. Union

Olsen Peter, bricklayer, r. Union opp. 6th Ward School

Omalia Patrick, porter Daggett & Co.

Opera Saloon, 79 E. Washington

Orbison William H. clerk, r. 126 N. Tennessee

Oren S. A. Mrs. teacher City Academy, r. 134 Broadway

Oriental House, Frank Costigan propr. 71 to 75 S. Illinois

Orm Charles, (C. Orm & Bro.) r. Country

Orm Henson E. (C. Orm & Bro.) r. Country

Orm J. S. M. clerk C. Orm & Bro. bds. 212 Bluff rd.

Orm Sanford, miller, bds. 212 Bluff rd.

Orm Charles & Bro. (Charles and Henson E. Orm) proprs. Indianapolis Flouring Mills, s. of city limits nr. Canal

Ormsby Emma, dresser Barker, Williams & Co.

Orphan Asylum, Mrs. Anna M. Johnson matron, 711 N. Tennessee cor. 5th

Orr Andrew, compositor W. S. Cameron, bds. 278 N. Alabama
Orr D. (col'd) boot and shoe mkr. 523 N. Illinois, r. same
Orr James F. r. 29 Grant
Orr John E. salesman J. N. Conklin, bds. Commercial House
Osborn ——, (col'd) expressman, r. 170 Douglas alley
Osborn David M. teacher. r. 150 Fort Wayne av.
Osborn Elizabeth, wid. John, r. 78 N. Pennsylvania
Osborn John H. cashier G. E. Gordon, r. 225 N. Liberty
Osgood Judson R. (Osgood, Smith & Co.) r. 84 E. Michigan
OSGOOD, SMITH & CO. (J. R. Osgood, S. F. Smith, J. Woodburn and J. S. Yost) manf. Sarven's patent wheel and wagon and carriage materials, 230 S. Illinois
Ossenforgh Frederick, lab. Starch Factory, r. 316 N. Winston
Osterman John, Emmerich & Co. r. 72 State
Ostermeyer C. wid. Louis, r. 263 N. Liberty
Ostermeyer C. F. dry goods and groceries 350 E. Ohio, r. same
Ostermeyer Fred, dry goods, r. Washington out of limits
Ostermeyer Frederick (Holland, Ostermeyer & Co.) r. E. Washington e. of city limits
Ostermeyer Louis, drayman, r. 9 Charles
Oswald Godfred, painter, r. 336 Railroad
Oswell William, turner Spiegel & Thoms
Otis Clark, photographer A. A. Barnes, r. 138 S. East
Otis William H. r. 421 N. Tennesee
Otstott Daniel, moulder, bds. 169 S. Tennessee
Ott John, r. w. of Dacota nr. limits
Otto August, foreman Lithographing dept. W. & J. Braden, r.81 N. Plum
Otto Frederick, porter, Bowen, Stewart & Co. r. 64 E. McCarty
Otto Philip, r. 230 S. New Jersey
Ott William, carpenter C. C. & I. C. R. R. r. 190 N. Noble
Ott William, upholster 71 W. Washington
Otten Diederich, r. 127 N. Spring.
Otwell Francis, policeman, r. 295 N. East
Otwell Frank A. salesman R. L. Lukens r. 277 Virginia av.
Otwell Joseph S. salesman R. L. Lukens, r. 295 N. East
Otwell Thomas, clk. r. 295 N. East
Otwell William, clk. r. 295 N. East
Over Ewald (E. Over & Co.) r. 79 N. Alabama
OVER E. & CO. (Ewald Over and Henry Schnull) whol. dealers in bar, hoop and sheet iron and hardware 82 and 84 S. Meridian
Overhall Thomas (col'd) lab. J. Landis, r. 30 S. Pennsylvania
Overholser Jacob, dealer in patent rights, r. 349 S. Pennsylvania
Overmyer Nelson F. carriagemkr. r. 213 Massachusetts av.
Overstreet James M. lab. Osgood, Smith & Co. r. 301 S. Penn.
Overstreet John, wks. Osgood, Smith & Co. bds. 301 S. Penn.
Owen Henry C. wks. Osgood, Smith & Co. r. 341 S. Meridian
Owen Mary E. clk. Sumner & Co. bds. 353 N. New Jersey
Owens Benjamin F. (Ebert & Owens) also with A. D. Streight, r. 580 N. Mississippi

OWE	250	PAR

Owens E. porter Davis & Jones
Owens Elijah, teamster S. Le Fervor, bds. 145 W. South
Owens Henry, (col'd) lab. r. 7 Ellsworth
Owens James M. plasterer, r. 175 Bluff rd.
Owens John, hostler Wood & Foudray, bds. 30½ N. Pennsylvania
Owens John, lab. r. Rockwood nr. River
Owings James, bds. 139 E. South
Owings Joseph T. clerk C. C. C. & I. R. R. bds. 139 E. South
Owings Nathaniel, r. 139 E. South
Owsley William A. carpenter, r. 24 Douglas

P

Pacific Fire Ins. Co. of San Francisco, Cal. E. B. Martindale
   agent, room 2, 2d floor Martindale's Block
Paesler Samuel, driver, r. 191¼ W. Washington
Paetz Wm. physician, 127 E. Washington, r. 67 N. New Jersey
Paff Hugh, carpenter W. H. Henschen, r. 173 Stevens
Paff Mathew, carpenter W. H. Henschen
Paff Samuel, lab. Osgood, Smith & Co.
Page W. H. clerk Scott, West & Co. bds. National Hotel
Paine Daniel L. foreman *Mirror* news room, r. 71 E. St. Clair
Painter Edward, printer, r. 370 W. Vermont
Painter J. R. painter, r. 82 W. Market
Painter John, clerk, r. N. Illinois se. cor. 2d
Painter Mary, bds. 297 N. Meridian
Paisley Samuel, driver Citizens' Street R. R. Co.
Palace Saloon, William E. Carter propr. 87 S. Illinois
Palmer Benjamin G. jeweler, r. 176 E. South
Palmer Charles C. retired, r. 67 W. Maryland
Palmer Edward L. bookseller and stationer, 60 S. Illinois, r. same
Palmer Harry B. salesman J. W. Adams, r. 401 N. Pennsylvania
PALMER HOUSE, (Jeff. K. Scott) . Illinois se. cor. Washington
Palmer John J. asst. assessor r. 401 N. Pennsylvania
Palmer Margaret A. wid. Daniel C. r. 337 Virginia av.
Palmer Marshall E. retired, r. 57 W. Maryland
Palmer Mary, wid. Charles C. r. 124 N. Liberty
Palmer Mary J. clerk R. Sedgwick, r. 124 N. Liberty
Palmer Nathan B. retired, r. 57 W. Maryland
Palmer Sylvanius F. painter, r. 124 N. Liberty
PALMER TRUMBLE G. deputy State Auditor, dept. of Public
   Accounts, office State bldg. r. 156 N. Illinois
Panard H. ins. agent, r. 419 N. Illinois
Pardieck Hermann, carpenter, r. ns. Stevens, 2 w. Virginia
Paris George, (col'd) lab. r. 185 W. 2d
Parisette Joseph, confectionery and ice cream saloon, 25 N. Illi-
   nois, r. same
Parker A. G. piano tuner, r. 93 N. New Jersey
Parker Catherine E. tailoress, r. 44 Virginia av.
Parker Columbus, bds. 163 S. Tennessee

PAR	251	PAT

Parker Eben A. (Parker & Bloomer,) r. 75 N. California
Parker Ellis L. student, bds. 320 E. Vermont
PARKER GEORGE W. Sheriff of Marion County, office County Building, Court House Square, r. same
Parker Jackson, (col'd) teamster, r. 4th nr. LaFayette R. R.
Parker James, harness maker Daniel Sellers, r. 44 Virginia av.
Parker Jonas F. (Case, Parker & Co.) r. 600 N. Illinois
PARKER R. R. ladies and gents furnishing goods, 30 W. Washington, r. 90 N. Mississippi
Parker Robert P. (Griffin & Parker) r. Shelbyville rd.
Parker Sarah J. dress maker, 156 E. Market, r. same
Parker W. C. clk. C. C. & I. C. R. R. bds. Pyle House
Parker Wilson, brick mason, r. 163 S. Tennessee
PARKER & BLOOMER, Eben A. Parker and Isaac L. Bloomer, attorneys at law and notaries public, 32½ E. Washington
Parkinson Patrick, blacksmith, r. 21 Maple
Parkman C. B. sec. Indianapolis Rolling Mill Co. r. 230 N. West
Parks Anna Mrs. bds. 255 S. New Jersey
Parks Hiram J. (col'd) cook, r. 122 S. Benton
Parlee Alexander, piano maker Indianapolis Piano Mfg. Co. bds. Pattison House
Parmelee John R. trav. agt. Kiefer & Vinton, bds Palmer House
PARMELEE W. H. agt B. & O. R. R. 10 Virginia av. r. 317 E. Ohio
Parr Henry, brickmaker, r. 384 E. Market
Parrott Horace, (Parrott, Nickum & Co.) r. 349 N. Delaware
Parrott Samuel, r. 34 S. West
PARROTT NICKUM & CO. (Horace Parrott, John R. Nickum and John A. Harter) steam cracker bakery 188 E. Washington
Parry Edward, bds. 12 Henry
Parry Roger, car inspector, r. 12 Henry
Parsley Berry, teamster, r. 545 N. Mississippi
Parsons Charles A. roadmaster, r. 234 W. New York
Parsons William S. traveling agt. bds. Martin House
Pascoe James E. boiler maker, r. 450 E. Georgia
PARVIN THEOPHILUS, physician and surgeon 435 N. Alabama, r. 143 Alabama se. cor. New York
Pasquier John B. carpenter Many & Son, r. es. Michigan nr. cor. Davidson
Passwater Matthew, hostler Citizens R. R. Co. bds. Neiman House
PATTERSON A. W. physician and surgeon 135 N. Alabama, r. 206 E. Ohio
Patterson Frank D. salesman J. Senour & Co. bds. Walnut sw. cor. Meridian
Patterson James, currier Deitz & Reissner, bds. 16 Delaware
Patterson John, carpenter, r. 29 Massachusetts av.
Patterson John Mrs. dress and cloak maker, 29 Massachusetts av.
Patterson John, carpenter, r. 362 S. Illlinois
Patterson John P. (Patterson, Moore & Talbot) and Alfred Talbot & Co. r. 163 N. New Jersey
Patterson Kate M. wid. James M. r. 140 Massachusetts av.
Patterson M. A: W. wid. Robert, r. 140 Massachusetts av.

PAT	252	PEA

Patterson R. M. city engineer, office Glenn's blk. r. 122 N. Illinois

Patterson Samuel, farmer, r. Elizabeth w. of Patterson

Patterson Sam'l W. feed and sale stable, 278—80 W. Washington, r. 332 W. Washington

Patterson Scott, clerk George Davis, r. 260 N. Noble

PATTERSON WILLIAM, lawyer, 98 E. Washington, (up stairs) r. 280 E. Ohio

Patterson William A. lab. Kingan & Co. bds. 169 S. Tennessee

Patterson William H. clk. S. Kahn & Bro. r. 520 N. Mississippi

Patterson William O. clerk P. O. r. 140 Massachusetts av.

Patterson William T. foreman stable Citizens Street R. R. Co. r. 193 S. Tennessee

PATTERSON, MOORE & TALBOT, (John P. Patterson, Joseph A. Moore, Richard L. Talbot and W. H. Morrison) wholesale druggists, 3 Morrison's Opera Hall S. Meridian

Pattison Augustus E. (Hibben, Tarkington & Co.) r. 429 N. New Jersey

Pattison Coleman B. (Hibben, Tarkington & Co.) r. 413 N. Illinois

Pattison House, J. B. Bell propr. r. 63 N. Alabama

Pattison Joseph D. (Nofsinger, Kingan & Co.) r. 404 N. Illinois

Pattison T. T. N. stock dealer, r. 416 N. Meridian

Pattison Terrell, salesman Hibben, Tarkington & Co. bds. 416 N. Pennsylvania

Pattison William A. gen'l agt. Indianapolis Wagon and Agricultural Works, bds. Pattison House

Patton Albert, r. 266 N. Alabama

Patton Albert Jr. student Bryant & Stratton's College, bds. 266 N. Alabama

Patton C. B. cabinetmaker Spiegel & Thoms

Patton Charles, varnisher, bds. 70 E. Market

Paul Henry, lieut. of police, r. 17 E. McCarty

Paul John, bds. Jefferson House

Pauli Henry, carpenter, r. 181 Davidson

Paulin Otto, bookkeeper Western Furniture Co. r. ns. E. Washington bet. Liberty and Noble

Pauling George, salesman, bds. 135 W. New York

Paulon J. H. lab. Osgood, Smith & Co.

Paver John M. route agt. Am. U. Ex. Co. r. 229 E. Vermont

Paxton Elizabeth Mrs. r. 22 Circle

Payne Daniel L. foreman *Mirror*, r. 71 E. St. Clair

Payton William, (col'd) lab. r. 187 W. 2d

Peabody John, stock trader r. 424 N. Delaware

Peacock James, bookkeeper L. Q. Sherwood, r. 196 W. Ohio

Peacock Mary H. Mrs. r. 354 W. North

Peacock William, shoemaker, r. 6th cor. Canal

Peak David, carpenter, r. 302 W. Maryland

Pearsall P. R. P. music teacher, r. 24 W. Georgia

Pearson C. (col'd) (Pearson & Harper) r. 325 E. Washington

Pearson Charles, fireman I. C. & L. Rw.

Pearson Charles D. physician and surgeon, 39½ W. Washington, r. 204 N. Illinois

T. B. Perrine, Engraver on Jewelry & Silver Ware. 34 Virginia av.

| PEA | 253 | PER |

Pearson Charles D. jr. clerk J. C. McIver, bds. 204 N. Illinois
Pearson John, (Pearson & Co.) bds. 135 E. St. Joseph
Pearson Joseph, stonecutter, Blackford, nw. cor. Vermont
PEARSON JOHN & CO. (John Pearson and John G. Hunning) proprs. House of Lords Saloon, 78 W. Washington
Pearson & Harper, (Charles Pearson and James Harper) (col'd) barbers, 325 E. Washington
Pease Louis, carpenter, r. 75 N. Davidson
Pease Sidney W. farmer, r. James sw. cor. 1st
Pease T. W. market master
Pease Theodore, lab. 163 Fort Wayne av.
Peck Edward A. r. 465 Virginia av.
Peck Edwin J. pres. Union Depot Co. and (Greenleaf & Co.) r. 59 W. Maryland
Peck Thomas H. S. supt. D. Root & Co. r. 488 N. Tennessee
Peck William, butcher, r. 225 E. Market
Peckham Caleb H. architect, 6 Blake blk. 55 W. Washington, r. 380 N. Delaware
Peckham C. S. salesman W. P. & E. P. Gallup, bds Palmer House
Peden Joseph S. tender A. Christy, r. 314 E. Ohio
Pedlow Robert J. moulder D. Root & Co. r. 20 Coburn
Pee Emmett, salesman, bds. 81 W. Ohio
Pee George W. (Stoneman, Pee & Co.) r. 81 W. Ohio
Peebles Nancy, wid. John, r. 295 N. Alabama
Peek Frank, tobacconist, r. 150 N. Tennessee
Peine Henry, currier J. Fishback, r. 548 N. Alabama
Pell Harry, steward Moffitt & Miller, bds. 46 S. Meridian
Pell Isaac, painter, r. W. Indianapolis
Pellett William A. conductor, r. Cady bet. Georgia and Bates
Peltier Eugene, stonecutter F. L. Farnam, r. 55 Hosbrook
Peltier Leon, stonecutter F. L. Farnam, r. 55 Hosbrook
Pence Ahiga, carpenter, r. S. Illinois nr. cor. Wilkins
Pence Caroline, wid. John, dressmaker, r. 151 Union
Pendleton Ralph C. J. clk. supt. office C. C. & I. C. R. R. r. 97 Buchanan
Pendrey N. S. physician, 10 and 11, 85½ E. Market, r. same
Penley R. S. brakeman C. C. &. I. C. R. R.
Penley Rufus, engineer, bds. 58 Benton
Penn George W. bookkeeper and sec. Eagle Machine Works, r. 331 S. Pennsylvania
Pennfield ——, printer, bds. 30½ N. Pennsylvania
Pennicke Morris, grocer, 191 W. South, r. same
Penseck William, painter, r. Wabash nr. cor. Noble
Pentecost Hugh O. compositor *Sentinel* news room, bds. 119 Maryland, sw. cor. Tennessee
PEOPLES DESPATCH, J. Chittenden, gen'l supt. Samuel T. Scott, agt. 19 Virginia av.
Pepper Edward, machinist Greenleaf & Co. r. Missouri s. of McCarty
Perdue George W. fireman C. C. C. & I. R. R. r. 7 Peru
Perdue Rebecca, wid. Milton, r. 7 Peru

Perhamus John, traveling agt. r. 27 W. 1st
Perine Peter R. deputy county appraiser, r. 293 N. Alabama
Perk Mary Ann, wid. Lewisbark, r. ws. Broadway bet. Cherry and Christian av.
Perkins Amos G. machinist Greenleaf & Co. r. 244 N. East
Perkins Charles, currier J. K. Sharpe, r. E. Michigan rd.
Perkins Elsbury H. comp. *Mirror* newsroom, r. 67 Dougherty
PERKINS J. A. gen. frt. and ticket agt. C. & I. J. R. R. r. 121 N. Illinois
Perkins J. H. salesman H. Rothschild, bds. 97 S. Illinois
Perkins James, boilermaker Sinker & C. r. 3 Elm
Perkins Samuel E. (Perkins & Perkins) r. New York nw. cor. California
Perkins Samuel E. Jr. (Perkins & Perkins) r. 276 W. New York
PERKINS & PERKINS, (S. E. and S. E. Jr. Perkins) lawyers, room 4 Ætna Bldg.
Perkinson Patrick, blacksmith Sinker & Co.
Perrett Mary E. prin. 9th Ward District School, r. 34 S. West
PERRIN GEORGE K. lawyer 45 E. Washington, r. 293 N. New Jersey
Perrine Minnie, drsmkr. Mrs. N. M. Allen, r. 169 N. Mississippi
Perrine Peter R. r. 293 N. Alabama
PERRINE TRUEMAN B. engraver 34 Virginia av. r. 169 N. Mississippi
Perrott Mary E. Miss, teacher 9th Ward School
Perry James H. carpenter, 70 W. North, r. 427 N. Mississippi
Perry John, printer, bds. 60 W. Market
Perry John C. (J. E. Robertson & Co.) r. 235 E. Michigan
Perry Mary E. Miss, teacher City Academy, bds. 410 N. Penn.
Perry Matthew, frmn. foundry Sinker & Co. r. 405 S. Delaware
Perry Roger, foreman smithshop T· H. & I. R. R.
Peru & Indianapolis Elevator, (Lawyer & Hall) 49 S. New Jersey
Pete Frank, roller Barker, Williams & Co.
Peters Chas. W. bkpr. J. C. Ferguson & Co. bds. Palmer House
Peters Elizabeth, (col'd) r. 173 Douglas Alley
Peters Joseph, r. 315 Massachusetts av.
Peterson Anders H. wks. Rolling Mill
Peterson Chris. lab. Rolling Mill, r. 233 W. South
Peterson James, engineer Burk, Earnshaw & Co.
Peterson James, tailor, bds. 259 S. Delaware
Peterson John, carpenter Eagle Machine Works, bds California House
Peterson L. (Thompson & Peterson) r. 351 S. Pennsylvania
Peterson Peter, lab. Rolling Mill, bds. 430 S. Tennessee
Peterson Peter, lab. Rolling Mill, r. 302 S. West
Peterson Peter, lab. Rolling Mill, r. 237 W. South
Peterson Rasmus, shoemaker, bds. 259 S. Delaware
Peterson Taylor, law student, bds. Ballard House, 70 E. Market
Pettis A. P. (Pettis, Dickson & Co.) r. New York
Pettis John, (col'd) mason, r. 224 Huron

PETTIS, DICKSON & CO. (A. P. Pettis, Andrew Dickson and ————) whol. and ret. dealers in dry goods and notions, Glen's block

Pettis Willis A. teller Citizens' Nat. Bank, bds Palmer House

Petty Calvin, driver J. Butsch, bds. 68 W. South

Petty James, lab. George T. Adams

Petty James, teamster, r, 131 Bates

Petty John W. cooper, r. 352 Indiana av.

Petty Julius, farmer, r. 350 Indiana av.

Peyton Elisha, car inspector C. C. & I. C. R. R.

Pfaendler Nicholas, Pfaendler & Zogg) r. Fourth Presbyterian Church, cor. Delaware and Market

PFAENDLER & ZOGG, (Nicholas Pfaendler and Ferdinand Zogg) box mnfrs. opp. Terre Haute frt. depot, Louisiana st.

Pfaff Jacob L. clk. bds. 153 N. West

Pfaff Lucius, clk. bds. cor. New York and West

Pfaff William A. (John C. Burton & Co.) r. 153 N. West

Pfafflin Theodore, salesman F. Smith, r. 25 W. North

Pfafflin William, salesman C. Mayer & Co. bds. California House

Pfau George, salesman Prenatt & O'Connor, bds. 487 N. Illinois

Pfeiffer John G. lab. r. 150 E. St. Joseph

Pfeiffer William, printer *Telegraph* office, Guttenberg Co. r. 335 S. Delaware

Pfening William, gilder H. Lieber & Co. r. 191 N. East

Pfingst Charles, clerk William Haerle, bds. 4 W. Washington

Pfingst George, clerk William Haerle, bds. 342 N. Illinois

Pfitzer George, tailor, r. 160 Coburn

Pfleger George, r. 18 Vinton

Pfleger Jacob, tailor r. 121 N. Davidson

Pfleger Peter, r. 18 Vinton

Phelan Catharine, wid. Patrick, r. 361 Virginia av.

Phelan James, lab. r. 138 Maple

Phelan Mary E. Miss, clk. Frank J. Medina, 34 W. Washington

Phelan William, boilermaker Sinker & Co.

Phelps A. painter Bremerman & Renner, r. 276 N. Mississippi

Phelps S. machinist C. C. C. & I. R. R.

Phelps Simon B. engineer, r. 330 E. Louisiana

Phelps Suel, chairmkr, r 282 S. Missouri

Phenyer Andrew, moulder, r. 320 S. Delaware

Philabaum Lucinda, vestmaker, r. 117 N. West

Philharmonic Band, 20½ N. Delaware

Philistine H. boilermaker Sinker & Co.

Phillips E. J. Mrs. actress Academy of Music, bds Macy House

Phillips Jesse, (col'd) lab. r. ws. Missouri nr. 1st

Phillips John R. carpenter, r. 255 S. West

Phillips Thomas, tailor, r. 174 W. Ohio

Phillips Wesley, hostler Wood & Foudray

Phillips William H. fireman C. C. & I. C. R. R. bds. 153 Meek

Phipps Brothers, (Edwin R. and Charles R.) watches, clocks and jewelry, 14 N. Pennsylvania

Phipps Charles R. (Phipps Bros.) r. Nat. Rd. e. city limits

PHI	256	PIN

Phipps Edwin R. (Phipps Bros.) r. 286 N. Pennsylvania

Phipps John M. physician, r. 233 N. Noble

Phipps Joseph B. bkpr. W. & J. Braden, bds. 224 E. Market

Phipps L. M. revenue clerk, r. 187 N. Alabama

Phipps William C. county appraiser, room 6, 20½ N. Delaware, r. Centre Township

Phœnix Bell and Brass Foundry, Schneider & Co. propr. 26 Union R. R. track

Phœnix Fire Ins. Co. of Hartford, Conn. Snyder & Hays agts. 17 N. Meridian

Phœnix Machine Works, (Chandler & Taylor) 370 W. Washington

PHŒNIX MUTUAL LIFE INS. CO. of Hartford, Conn. E. S. Folsom gen. agt. room 14 Talbott & New's Block

Phole William H. clerk Browning & Sloan, bds. Pyle House

Pickerill Frank, trav. salesman, r. 110 N. Delaware

Pickerill George W. (Pickerill & Co.) r. 104 Plum ne. cor Cherry

PICKERILL & CO. (George W. Pickerill and Zina Cole) physicians and surgeons, 30½ N. Pennsylvania. See card Business Directory

Pickett Henry, (col'd) lab. J. Landis, r. 30 S. Pennsylvania

Piel Henry, blksmith, r. 787 N. Illinois

PIEL WILLIAM F. manager Union Starch Factory, r. National Rd. o. of limits

Piele Herman, r. 130 E. McCarty

Pierce ——, clerk, bds. 204 N. Illinois

Pierce Albert, engineer I. C. & L. Rw. bds. 47 Bates

Pierce Charles, carpenter, bds. 64 W. Maryland

Pierce Charles, carpenter, r. 41 Huron

Pierce Converse, driver J. Carlisle, r. 307 W. Market

Pierce Dock, (col'd) r. 179 Douglas alley

Pierce Harrison, (col'd) lab. r. Cherry nw. cor. Ash

PIERCE HENRY D. atty. at law and notary public, 24½ E. Washington, bds. 570 N. Meridian cor. 2d

Pierce James, teamster, r. 177 N. Liberty

Pierce William, brickmoulder, r. 290 Massachusetts av.

Pierce William, engineer McKendry & Lovecraft

Pierce Winslow S. physician and surgeon, r. N. Meridian cor 2d

Pierson Charles C. trav. salesman Strong, & Smith, 48 N. Pennsylvania, bds. 231 N. East

Pierson Emily, wid. Samuel, r. 65 N. Missouri

Pierson I. J. cutter Moritz Bros. bds. Macy House

Pierson James, carpenter, r. 432 E. St. Clair

Pierson John C. mason, r. ss. 2d bet. Tennessee and Mississippi

Pierson Jouas O. machinist, r. 295 Indiana av.

Pierson Joseph L. lab. r. rear Rolling Mill

Pierson Lewis, (col'd) barber J. Britton, bds. 181 W. Washington

Pig John, pumpmaker, r. 232 E. Louisiana

Pig Sarah, wid. David, r. 232 E. Louisiana

Pilbam Sarah C. wid. George W. r. 279 Kentucky av.

Pinney Frank W. (King & Pinney) r. 186 E. McCarty

Pinney W. H. H. bds. 176 S. New Jersey

Piper Horatio N. salesman L. Q. Sherwood, bds. 242 N Illinois

Piscator August, mnfr. of surgical instruments 12 S. Delaware, r. same

Piscator Christian, file grinder Drotz & Steinhaur, bds. 281 S. Meridian

Pitry Eliza, wid. John, r. 302 N. New Jersey

Pittman Green S. sawyer McCord & Wheatley, r. 437 E. Georgia

Pittman Robert C. 208 W. Ohio

Pitts Fredonia, wid. Francis, r. 182 E. Washington

Pitts George W. ice dealer, r. 370 N. Tennessee

Pitts Harvey, switchman J. M. & I. R. R. r. 290 Madison av.

Pitts Mary A. wid. Albert, r. 166 Buchanan

Place D. N. clk. I. & St. L. Sleeping Car Co. bds. Sherman House

Plank August, machinist Eagle Machine Works, bds. California House

Plank Isaac, switchman, r. 384 E. Market

Plank John, conductor, bds. 61 S. Noble

Plant Charles, machinist Spiegel & Thoms

Plant George, engineer C. & I. J. R. R. r. 258 S. Delaware

Plant John W. lab. r. 261 E. Washington

Platt Carrie Miss, teacher Indianapolis Female Institute, r. same

Platt William, machinist C. C. C. & I. R. R. r. 207 Winston

Pleslin Charles F. piano mkr. Indianapolis Mnfrg. Co. bds. Pattison House

Plessner Otto, blacksmith, r. 435 Virginia av.

Plogsterth Henry, painter C. C. C. & I. R. R.

PLOGSTERTH VICTOR, grocer and dealer in flour and feed 207 N. Davidson, r. same

Plumb Hiram H. salesman J. H. Baldwin & Co. bds. 89 N. Delaware

Plummer E. wid. Hiram. r. 216 E. Market

Plummer Edward, painter, bds. Western av. se. cor. Christian av.

Plummer Edward, painter, Indpls. Coach Works, r. 19 Cherry

Plummer Edwin, painter, bds. 216 E. Market

Plummer Hiram, wks. R. R. bds. 216 E. Market

Plummer Peter, drayman, r. 480 E. Georgia

Plummer William M. conductor, r. 297 Winston

PLYMOUTH CONGREGATIONAL CHURCH, Meridian nw. cor. Circle, E. P. Ingersoll, pastor

Plympton Charles H. checkman frt. depot C. C. & I. C. R. R. r. 393 E. Georgia

Poe John M. (J. M. Poe & Co.) r. 213 N. Pennsylvania

POE J. M. & CO. (John M. Poe and Thomas J. Breedlove) real estate agents, brokers and dealers 24½ E. Washington

Pœhler Henry, r. 375 S. Illinois

Pœhler Louis, grocer, Bluff road se. cor. Ray, r. same

Pohler Chris. drayman, r. 385 Virginia av.

Pohler Henry, lab. J. M. & I. R. R.

Poister Henry, carpenter C. C. C. & I. R. R.

Pokemeyer John, drayman, r. 116 N. Winston

Poland John (Poland & Wiseman) r. 432 W. Washington (Nat. rd.)

J. ARDEN, keeps the best workmen in town, 65 S. Meridian st.

17

POL	258	POT

Poland & Wiseman, (John Poland, Simon S. Wiseman) meat market, 432 W. Washington National rd.

POLICE HEADQUARTERS. Glenn's blk. Thomas S. Wilson chief

Pollard Edwin M. salesman J. H. Cropper, r. 776 N. Tennessee

Poller Peter, painter, r. 282 Winston

Pollitt John, draughtsman J. Hodgson, bds. 144 N. Tennessee

Pollock John G. operator W. U. T. Co. r. 258 Mississippi ne. cor. Michigan

Ponder Milton, stock agt. B. & O. R. R. r. 144 N. East

Ponder Thomas M. repairer McCaslin & Masters, r. 235 Louisiana

Pontus John, fireman C. & I. J. R. R.

Pool Adoniram, engineer C. C. & I. C. R. R. r. 73 N. Davidson

Poorman Daniel S. drayman, r. 476 Virginia av.

Pope —— Mrs. wid. r. 195 W. Ohio

Pope Abner, retired, r. 74 W. North

Pope Alson G. clk. W. J. Holliday & Co. r. 179 Massachusetts av.

Pope Christian, brickmaker, r. 68 Harrison

Pope Henry, chairmaker H. Schilling & Bro. bds. 383 Virginia

Pope Henry T. carpenter T. J Morse, r. 199 N. West

Pope William, (Hotz & Co.) bds. California House

Popenhaus Henry, porter Union depot, r. 17 Meek

Poppenseeker Gottlieb, lab. Buute, Dickson & Co. r. 100 Huron

Porter Albert G. (Porter, Harrison & Fishback) r. 257 Delaware ne. cor. Michigan

Porter Amanda, wid. John, r. 393 S. Missouri

Porter George T. r. 257 N. Delaware

PORTER OMER T. produce and commission merchant and flour dealer 6 Martindale's blk. r. 164 E. St. Clair

Porter Omer T. salesman, r. es. Tennasse 3 s. 1st

Porter Theodore R. custom tailor 24½ W. Washington, r. same

Porter William H. J. M. & I. R. R. r. 361 S. Delaware

Porter William, (col'd) barber 140 S. Illinois (Spencer House) r. 130 W. New York

PORTER, HARRISON & FISHBACK, (Albert G. Porter, Benjamin Harrison, William P. Fishback) attorneys and counselors at law, room 6 Yohn's blk. Meridian ne. cor. Washington

Posey John, wks Indianapolis Paper Co.

POST CLARENCE C. western pass. agt. P. Ft. W. & C. R. R. bds. Bates House

POST OFFICE. Charles F. Holloway postmaster, Pennsylvania se. cor. Market

Pottage Benjamin, hardware merchant 77½ W. Washington, r. 127 W. Market

Pottage Charles E. salesman B. Pottage, r. 9 N. Ellsworth

Pottage Thomas W. salesman, r. 127 W. Market

Potter John L. carpenter, r. Dacotah cor. Jones

Potter John L. sawfiler, etc. 312 Indiana av. r. 77 Jones

Potter Nathaniel C. (Whitcomb & Potter) bds. 172 N. New Jersey

Potter R. (col'd) lab. McKendry & Lovecraft

Potter Richmond, (col'd) whitewasher, r. 198 W. 2nd

The latest styles of Hats & Caps at I. Davis & Co. 12 E. Wash'n.

POT   259   PRE

Potter Charles, dry goods retail 100 E. South, r. same
Potts Charles, Jr. clk Charles Potts, bds. 100 E. South
Potts John T. cigarmaker Thomas Forsha, bds. Clinton bet. New York and New Jersey
Potts Mary A. wid. Alfred, rooms 7–9 (3d floor) Martindale's blk.
Potts Silas, r. 138 W. 6th
Pound Will. city editor *Journal*. r. 222 N. Delaware
Pound William, correspondent *Cincinnati Gazette*, bds. 126 E. Ohio
Powell David, boilermaker Sinker & Co. r. 434 N. New Jersey
Powell George W. clerk, r. 434 N. New Jersey
Powell John H. student, r. 434 N. New Jersey
Powell M. M. salesman, r. 284 E. Market
Power Jacob B. r. 71 N. East
Power Stephen, lab. r. 65 Maple
Powers James, lab. bds. 267 E. Washington
Powers John, lab. r. 507 S. Tennessee
Powers John, wks. Phœnix Machine Works
Powers Michael, cigarmaker Jacob Garratt, bds 90 S. Illinois
Powers Patrick, boilermkr. Sinker & Co. r. 271 S. Pennsylvania
Powers Peggy, wid. r. 55 Fayette
Powers Thomas, boilermkr. Sinker & Co. r. 273 S. Pennsylvania
Powers Thomas, lab. r. al. bet. East and Liberty and Georgia Railroad
Powers William, cook Moffit & Miller, bds. 46 S. Meridian
Powl Charles, lab. C. C. C. & I. R. R.
Prail Fred. J. brickmason, r. 214 Winston
Pramus Samuel, porter Will. W. Wallace, bds. rear 441 N. Illinois
Prange Anton F. (Charles Prange & Co.) r. 318 E. Washington
Prange Charles, (Charles Prange & Co.) r. Michigan rd. near junction of Washington
Prange Frederick, carpenter, rear 289 S. Illinois, r. 289 S. Illlnois
Prange Fred. expressman, r. 193 Davidson
Prange Charles & Co. (Charles and Anton F. Prange and Henry Buddenbaum) groceries and dry goods, 318 E. Washington
Prasse Henry, grocer, 446 Virginia av. r. same
Prather Austin, r. 82 N. Mississipi
Pratt Julius F. bkpr. Osgood, Smith & Co. bds 188 S. Mississippi
Pratt O. C. machinist B. F. Hetherington & Co. r. 244 S. Penn.
Prauer Fred. baker Adam Knauf, bds. 257 Massachusetts av.
Pray Enos G. physician and pastor Friends' Church, r. 102 Broadway
Pray Joseph J. clk. D. E. Wilkinson
Pray William, (Gates, Pray & Co.) r. 79 N. Alabama
Preggea Henry, stonemason, r. 330 Railroad
Prenatt F. J. (Prenatt & O'Connor) r. Madison, Ind.
PRENATT & O'CONNOR, (F. J. Prenatt and Michael O'Connor) whol. liquor dealers, 141 S. Meridian
Prentice Lena Miss, actress Academy of Music
Pressel Albert, clerk E. Over & Co. r. 110 Plum
Pressel Anna, tailoress, r. 102 Oak
Pressel Charlotte, wid. Philip, r. 110 Plum

PRE	260	PUR

Pressel George, bricklayer, r. 102 Oak

Pressel John, carpenter, bds. 110 Plum

Pressel Mary, wid. Henry, r. 236 Blake

Pressell Oliver, book-binder W. & J. Braden, bds. 110 Plum

Pressell Thomas, carpenter, r. 164 Pattison

Pressell William, carpenter, r. Broadway se. cor. Cherry

PRESSLY JOHN T. saw mill, also manfr. and dealer in lumber, es. West bet. Louisiana and Georgia, r. 119 S. East

Preston Alexander, employee Am. Ex. Co. r. 447 S. Tennessee

Preston Alfred, clk. r. 335 N. East

Preston Elliott M. porter Am. M. U. Ex. r. 447 S. Tennessee

Preston Margaret, wid. Alfred, r. 335 N. East

Preston S. N. bkpr. Byington & Erringer, bds. 65 W. Michigan

Prezel Henry, lab. r. 125 Stevens

Price Darra, r. 46 Massachusetts av.

Price E. J. teacher N. W. C. University

Price John, wks. Caledonia Paper Mill, bds 175 W. Washington

Price William, teamster, r. 379 N. West

Priegnity William, carpenter, r. 327 E. Georgia

PRIER HENRY J. ge'l agt. McCormick's Reaper and Mower, and dealer in agricultural implem'ts, 230 E. Washington, bds. 691 N. Tennessee

Prier Louis, (col'd) lab. r. 298 E. Michigan

Prime C. B. engineer McKendry & Lovecraft, r. 301 Indiana av.

Prinz John D. salesman Alford, Talbot & Co. r. 83 N. Noble

Pritzer John, blacksmith N. Kimball

Pritznits William, carpenter C. C. & I. C. R. R.

Privett Willis, bricklayer, r. 719 N. Mississippi

Prosser John, dyer and scourer, 50 N. Illinois, r. same

Protzman Ferdinand, (Cowen & Protzman) r. 48 S. Illinois

Protzman John H. r. 48 S. Illinois

PROVIDENT LIFE & TRUST INS. CO. of Philadelphia, Charles M. A. Hess special agt. 8 E. Washington—see margin side lines

Pruitt Sarah Mrs. r. 73 W. Georgia

Prunk ——, wks. Rolling Mill, bds. 169 N. Tennessee

Prunk Daniel H. physician and surgeon, 30 N. Mississippi, r. 372 W. New York

Pryan Edward S. miller, r. 45 Virginia av.

PRYOR RICHARD, propr. Little's Hotel, Washington se. cor. New Jersey, r. same

Pugh Wm. R. painter C. C. C. & I. R. R. r. Vine ne. cor. Plum

Pullam John W. bricklayer, bds. Western House

Purcell George W. auctioneer, r. 74 S. Mississippi

Purcell Michael, picture dealer, 122 N. East bds. East cor. Ohio

Purcell Peter, foreman Munson & Johnston, r. 2 Douglas

Purcell Peter, lab. Bunte, Dickson & Co.

Purcell Sarah, (col'd) wid. Daniel, r. 215 W. 2d

Purcell T. A. salesman H. T. West & Co. bds. Union Depot

Pursel Jonathan H. shoemaker A. Knodle, r. 115 W. New York

Pursel Peter, tinner, r. 26 Douglas

Pursel Theodore W. salesman Kennedy, Byram & Co. bds. Sherman House
PURSELL ABNER E. dentist, rooms 1 and 2 (3d floor) Martindale's blk. r. 278 N. Mississippi
Putnam Benjamin, varnisher Helwig & Co.
Putnam Fire Ins. Co. of Hartford, Conn. E. B. Martindale, agt. room 2, 2d floor, Martindale's blk.
Puttenden James, porter, r. 289 E. New York
Pyburn Agnes, r. es. West, 3 s. Georgia
Pyle House, John Pyle, propr. 95 N. Meridian
Pyle John, propr. Pyle House, 95 N. Meridian, r. same
Pyle John E. bkpr. J. W. Sulgrove & Co. r. 79 Massachusetts av.

Q

Quamby Joseph, stonecutter Goddard & Sons, r. 316 E. North
Queisser Frederick, butcher Julius Quiesser, r. 336 Virginia av.
Quiesser Julius, meat market, 131 Massachusetts av and 148 N. Tennessee, r. 336 Virginia av.
Quigley Bridget, wid. Patrick, r. 52 Eddy
Quillan William, roller Barker, Williams & Co.
Quillins William, tobacconist, bds. Ray House
Quinius Herman, pastor German Evangelical Zions Church, r. 36 W. Ohio
Quinius John, clk. Todd, Carmichael & Williams, r. 32 W. Ohio
Quinlin John, tailor A. Kelley
Quinn D. bds. Jefferson House
Quinn David, r. 312 S. Illinois
Quinn Edward, shoemaker Christ Karle & Co. r. 54 Virginia av.
Quinn James, watchman, r. 300 S. East
Quinn John, foreman H. Allen's livery, r. 303 S. Pennsylvania
Quinn John, saloon, 245 W. Maryland, r. same
Quinn Michael, wks. Terre Haute R. R. bds. 245 W. Maryland
Quinn Thomas, wks. Kingan & Co. bds. 245 W. Market
Quinn William, carpenter, r. 248 W. Market
Quinnell Isaac, confectioner, 79 E. Market, r. same

R

Raab Sebastian, shoemaker, r. 242 S. Delaware
Rabb ——, Mrs. r. 29 S. West
Rabb Mary A. Mrs. confectioner, 35 S. Illinois, r. same
Raby William, lab. Osgood, Smith & Co. r. ws. Blake 1 s. New York
Racker Gertrude, wid. Godfried, r. 269 E. Ohio
Raday Patrick, lab, r. 240 S. Missouri
Raenaker Jacob, r. s. end S. Missouri
Rafert A. F. carpenter and builder, 75 E. Walnut, r. 447 N. West
Rafert Antony, carpenter, r. 374 N. West

RAF	262	RAN

Rafert C. checkman Peru frt. depot, r. 139 E. Merrill
Rafert C. F. carpenter and builder, 83 E. Pratt, r. same
Rafert Charles, check clerk I. P. & C. Rw. r. 189 Maryland
Rafert Ernst, drayman, r. 93 Union
Rafert William, drayman, r. 242 Madison av. or Railroad St.
Raferty Michael J. wks. Osgood, Smith, & Co. bds. Ray House
Ragan Charles, lab. r. 283 E. Georgia
Ragan David J. bookkeeper, r. 81 W. Walnut
Ragen Martin, bds. Ray House
Ragin Michael, marble polisher, r. 77 W. McCarty
Rahe Hermann, carpenter F. Diekmann, r. 124 Davidson
Raible Charles, carpenter, r. 518 E. Washington
Raible John, tailor, ns. Wabash alley bet. New Jersey and East
Raible Louis, cabinetmaker Long & Kregelo, 132 N. Spring
Rail Jacob, lab. r. 391 S. Missouri
RAILROAD CITY PRINTING CO. (L. G. & J. F. Dynes, W. C. West, L. C. Heins) 35½ E. Market, Vinton's blk.
Railsback Adaline, wid. David, r. 186 Blake
Railsback Martha, r. 223 W. Washington
Railway Passengers Assurance Co. of Hartford, Conn. Martin & Hopkins agts. Maket ne. cor. Circle, *Journal* bldg.
Railway Passenger Assurance of Hartford, Conn. R. E. Beardsley agt. 11 N. Meridian
Rains Mary V. (Holmes & Rains) r. 16 Center
Raisner Christian, shoemaker Charles Rehling
Rakestraw Mattie, cloak and dressmaker, 17 Massachusetts av.
Rakestraw Thomas M. (Rakestraw & Co.) r. 17 Massachusetts av.
Rakestraw & Co. (Thomas M. Rakestraw, Frank J. Clark) boot and shoe manufactuers, 64 N. Pennsylvania
Ralph Alfred J. clk. Scott, West & Co. bds. 244 S. New Jersey
Ramsay J. W. bookkeeper Wiley & Van Buren, bds. N. Illinois
Ramsey J. F. r. 260 N. Illinois
Ramsey John, lab. Sinker & Co.
Ramsey Mary, (col'd) wid. Barton, r. 171 Blake
Ramsey Samuel, (col'd) lab. r. Rhode Island nr. Blake
Ramsey Thomas, shoemaker James E. Davis, r. 46 Elm
Ramsey Thomas A. bricklayer, r. 46 Elm
Ramsey W. H. B. grocer, r. 118 W. Vermont
Ramsey Walter L. plumber John G. Hanning, r. 135 E. St. Joseph
Ramsey William, student Bryant & Stratton's College, bds. 135 E. St. Joseph
Ran Benjamin, blksmith, r. 289 Indiana av.
Ran Kate, (col'd) wid. Bryant, r. 171 Indiana av.
Rand Frederick, (Rand & Hall) r. 270 N. Illinois
RAND & HALL, (Frederick Rand and Reginald H. Hall) attorneys at law, 24½ E. Washington
Randall Berry, oyster saloon, 29 S. Illinois, r. same
Randall George, carpenter, r. 784 N. Illinois
Randall H. P. deputy assessor, r. 19 E. St. Joseph
Randolph Lot, teamster, r. W. Indianapolis
Randolph Reuben, lab. r. W. Indianapolis

Ranihan James, undertaker, r. 212 Indiana av.
Rankin Albert, plasterer, r. 422 N. New Jersey
Rankin Hamilton, carpenter, r. 142 Douglas
RANSDELL DANIEL M. city clerk, office 8 Glenn's Block, bds. 346 N. Meridian
Ransford W. P. (Ransford & Denton) r. Laporte, Ind.
Ransford & Denton, (W. P. Ransford and A. B. Denton) state agents Continental Life Ins. Co. of Hartford, Conn. Washington. sw. cor. Meridian
Raper George, pressman *Journal* office
Rapp Carl, veterinary surgeon, room 4, 104 S. Illinois, r. same
Rapp Fritz, bds. Jefferson House
Rapp Fritz, brewer City Brewry, r. 213 S. Pennsylvania
Rariden John, painter C. C. C. & I. R. R. r. 201 N. Davidson
Rariden Mary C. teacher N. W. C. University
Raschig Charles M. whol. and ret. dealer in cigars and tobacco, 13 West Washington, r. 200 N. Tennessee
Raschig Edward, auditor A. M. U. Ex. Co. office 42 E. Washington, r. 126 E. North
Rasener F. William, groceries, drygoods, &c. 288 E. Washington, r. E. Michigan road
Rasener Henry, car inspector C. C. & I. C. R. R.
Rasener Herman, r. 231 N. Liberty
Rasener William, tallyman C. C. C. & I. Rw. r. 155 Union
Rasner Henry, (Reed & Rasner) r. W. 6th
Rassel Frank, gluemaker Goss & Co.
Rassel Margaret, wid. Nicholas, saloon, ws. Michigan rd. above 1st, r. same
Rassel Nicholas, lab. r. Michigan rd. above 1st
Rathut William, student, National Business College
Ratti Francis A. r. 318 N. East
Ratti Francis A. Jr. r. 318 N. East
Ratti Frank A. foreman *Sentinel* press room, r. 318 N. East
Ratti Joseph, foreman *Sentinel* book and job room, r. 318 N. East
Rau Benjamin, blksmith Ind. Ag. Wks. r. 289 Indiana av.
Raugh B. (B. L. & S. Raugh) r. 1 Palmer House
Rauh Bernhard, merchant, r. 165 N. Tennessee
Raugh Brothers (B. L. & S. Raugh) clothiers, Palmer House Blk.
Raugh John, teamster, r. 238 Bluff road
Raugh L. (B. L. & S. Raugh) Cincinnati, Ohio
Raugh S. (B. L. & S. Raugh) Cincinnati, Ohio
Rauschen Henry, lab. r. 366 S. Illinois
Rauschen William, lab. Rolling Mill
Raushenbah Edward, wagonmkr. r. 275 E. New York
Rauser George, bakery 68 S. West, r. same
Rautter William, gardener, r. 23 Ellsworth
Ravenscroft Francis M. cooper, r. es. Douglas 1 s. New York
Rawlings ——, bds. Pennsylvania nw. cor. Market
Rawlings Clay, bds. 169 S. Tennessee
Rawlins B. F. presiding elder M. E. Church, r. 89 Christian av.

RAW	264	REA

Rawzell Jacob T. cooper A. L. Furgason, r. 168 Union
Ray ——. bds. Pennsylvania nw. cor. Market
Ray A. S. com. mer. r. 147 Buchanan
RAY CHARLES A. Chief Justice of the Supreme Court, State Building, r. 140-144 N. Illinois
Ray H. C. lawyer, room 12 Talbott and New's Block, r. N. Pennsylvania cor. 7th
Ray House, South se. cor. Delaware, J. M. Lambert, propr.
Ray Isaac, clk. J. Y. Mardick, r. 44 Forrest av.
RAY JAMES M. pres. Franklin Life Ins. Co. office Illinois cor. Kentucky av. r. 112 N. Meridian
Ray John, cabinet maker N. S. Baker & Co. r. 270 N. Noble
Ray John W. lawyer and register in bankruptcy 24½ E. Washington, r. E. Washington, city limits
Ray Mary, wid. r. 34 W. Ohio
Ray Samuel, carpenter, r. 325 E. Merrill
Ray Sarah, wid. George W. r. 163 N. Noble
Ray T. J. check clerk C. & I. J. R. R. r. 109 S. New Jersey
Raymond Henry, bookkeeper, r. 47 Coburn
Raymond Samuel, blacksmith 60 E. Maryland, r. Pennsylvania ne. cor. Maryland
Raynor Jacob, (col'd) porter Hume, Adams & Co. r. 3d bet. Tennessee and Mississippi
Raynor C. A. salesman, r. 523 N. Tennessee
Read Enoch, marble worker B. O. Carpenter, bds. 419 N. East
Read George D. M. machinist I. C. & L. Railway, r. 185 Bates
Read George H. r. 185 Bates
Read George L. boss weaver Hoosier Woolen Factory
Read Samuel B. r. 185 Bates
Reading T. C. supt. Indpls. Coach Works, r. 126 E. Maryland
Reading William, carriage trimmer Indianapolis Coach Works, bds. 126 E. Maryland
Ready Michael, lab. r. 345 S. Meridian
Ready Patrick, wks. Scott & Nicholson, r. 240 S. Missouri
Reagan David J. bookkeeper Donaldson & Stout, r. 81 W. Walnut
Reagan Lot, physician and surgeon 12 S. Mississippi, r. same
Reagan Michael, polisher La Dow & Calvert
Reak Henry, machinist Eagle Machine Works, bds. Globe House
Realy Frederick, lab. J. M. & I. R. R. r. 232 Madison av.
Ream Laura Miss, r. 25 Virginia av.
Reams Robert L. shoemaker Rakestraw & Co. bds. 17 Mass. av.
Reamy James, r. W. North nw. cor. Mississippi
Reany William, r. W. North nw. cor. Mississippi
Reasner Anthony, drayman, r. 23 E. McCarty
Reasner Charles, teamster Indianapolis Transfer Co.
Reasner Fred. W. grocer, r. Michigan rd. nr. junc. Washington
Reasner Henry, shoemaker 370 Virginia av. r. 368 Virginia av.
Reasner Henry F. carpenter, r. 235 Winston
Reasner William F. (Reasner & Shiltmeyer) r. Michigan rd. e. of limits

Reasner & Shiltmeyer, (William F. Reasner and Antony Shilt-
meyer) grocers, Washington e. of limits
Reaume John, r. Louisiana cor. McGill
Reaume John A. clerk R. R. Parker
Reaume Joseph, clerk, bds. Pyle House
Reaume W. clk. Anderson Bullock & Schofield, bds. Pyle House
Rebber Ford, stonecutter Scott & Nicholson
Rebentish Charles, shoemaker, r. 187 E. South
Reber Godfred, stonecutter, r. 268 S. Delaware
Rebi George A. carpenter, r. Elizabeth nw. cor. Blake
Rebstock Sarah N. wid. George, r. 235 E. Michigan
Rech George, clerk A. Bretz, bds. 118 S. Illinois
Rech John, clerk Adam Bretz, bds. 118 S. Illinois
Rech Mattie, wid. George, r. 77 W. 1st
Rechter Henry, blksmith, r. 261 S. Mississippi
Recke Edward, r. 126 E. North
Reckenouer Lydia, dressmaker r. 273 S. New Jersey
Recker Charles, cigarmaker Buck & Wenken
Recker Godfrey, clerk H. Lieber & Co. r. 238 S. New Jersey
Recker Hubert, carpenter, 219 E. Washington, r. 507 E. Market
Recketts John D. driver Street R. R. Co. r. 253 Madison av.
Records Isaac, janitor County Buildings
Records Isaac, medical student, bds. 197 N. Illinois
Red Edward, (col'd) lab. Osgood, Smith & Co. r. 79 Ann
Reddick Thomas, foreman Barker, Williams & Co. r. 121 W.
New York
Redfield David A. publisher, r. 71 W. Michigan
Redford John E. (W. W. Barker & Co.) r. 80 N. Pennsylvania
Redford John E. Mrs. cloak and dressmaker, 80 N. Pennsylvania
Redforin James, lab. r. 409 S. Delaware
Redman Henry, sexton High School, r. 31 W. St. Clair
Redman John, works Root's Foundry, bds. 243 W. Maryland
Redman Margaret, wid. John, r. 243 W. Maryland
Redman O. A. printer *Journal* job room, bds Commercial Hotel
Redman Patrick, wks. Root's foundry, bds. 243 W. Maryland
Redmon Dennis, r. 179 W. South
REDMOND THOMAS, produce dealer and saloon W. Washington
(Nat. Rd.) ne. cor. Blake, r. 25 N. Bright
Reece C. K. compositor *Journal* news room, r. 127 Meek
Reed Anson (A. Reed & Co.) r. 225 W. Washington
Reed B. F. mail agt. r. 31 W. Michigan
Reed Elilabeth, wid. William K. r. 293 Indiana av.
Reed Emma, wks. Cotton Factory
Reed Erastus R. engraver Bingham & Co. r. 17 W. Maryland
Reed Frank, wks. A. Reed & Co. bds. 225 W. Washington
Reed George, lab. Russell & Kasberg, r. 186 Bates
Reed Harry A. (Reed & Rasner) Illinois cor. Indiana av.
Reed Howard, surveyor, r. 31 W. Michigan
Reed Jerry, (col'd) lab. Osgood, Smith & Co. r. 2 Ann
Reed John F. salesman L. I. Mossler & Bro. r. 134 N. East
Reed Julian, wid. Nathaniel, r. 298 S. Illinois

REE	266	REI

Reed Michael, porter Bates House, r. 218 W. Georgia
Reed Rachel, (col'd) wid. Niles, r. 161 Indiana av.
Reed Sarah A. wid. Benjamin, boarding-house 30½ N. Penn.
Reed Thadeus, surveyor, r. 31 W. Washington
REED & RASNER, (Harry A. Reed and Henry Rasner) house and sign painters, Illinois cor. Indiana av.
REED A. & CO. (Anson Reed and James J. Boyle) mineral and soda water mnfrs. 225 W. Washington
Roeder E. C. groceries ret. 298 E. Washington, r. same
Rees E. clerk Samuel Taylor
Rees Henry, physician, r. 315 Virginia av.
Rees Kate, wid. John, r. Cherry se. cor. Oak
Rees Mary, boarding-house 89 N. Delaware, r. same
Reese August, varnisher Cabinetmakers' Union
Reese Charles, cabinetmaker, bds. 188 N. Noble
Reese Charles Jr. bds 188 N. Noble
Reese Henry, grocer 113 and 115 W. Washington, r. same
Reese William, boxmaker Pfaendler & Zogg, r. 95 E. Oak
Reeves Albert, student, bds. 268 E. St. Clair
Reeves Sarah, wid. William, r. 469 N. Meridian
Reeves Thomas, lab. r. 17 Dacotah
Regan E. foreman boiler shop Sinker & Co. r. 132 S. Tennessee
Reger Charles W. carpenter, r. 79 N. Davidson
Reger William, cabinetmaker, Cabinetmakers' Union
Regula Conrad, salesman F. M. Brown, r. 59 W. Washington
Rehling C. grocer, bds. 106 N. Spring
Rehling Charles, shoemaker, 218 E. Washington, r. same
Rehling W. C. student Bryant & Stratton's bds. 257 S. Delaware
Rehling William, shoemkr. 257 S. Delaware, r. 259 same
Reht Joseph, lab. Evert Everts, bds. 139 Ft. Wayne av.
Reich Gideon S. policeman, r. 83 Elm
Reichardt Philip, cabinetmaker Speigel & Thoms
Reichardt John, carpenter, r. 425 N. East
Reichel Adolph, carpenter, r. 125 N. Spring
Reichel Edward, patternmaker Eagle Machine Works, r. 123 Spring
Reichter F. B. (F. B. Reichter & Co.) r. Illinois, junc. Russel av.
Reichter F. B. & Co. (F. B. Reichter and John Schroerbuck) grocers, S. Illinois, junction Russell av.
Reick Augustus, policeman, r. 490 Virginia av.
Reid Earl, (W. R. Hogshire & Co.) bds. Oriental House
Reid John W. r. 231 Virginia av.
Reid Johnson, r. 156 Stevens
Reiert Gottlieb, butcher, 153 W. Washington r. same
Reifert William, r. 268 S. Alabama
Reiley Henry H. lab. B. F. Haugh & Co. r. 43 Bluff rd.
Reinard Louis, stone cutter, r. 80 Elm
Reinacker Jacob, barkeeper, r. 78 W. Washington
Reinacher Jacob, lab. r. 330 N. New Jersey
Reinacher Jacob, puller Rolling Mill,
Reinchwein John, lab. r. 199 Davidson

Reinchwein Philip, saloon and propr. Noble St. Gardens, 50 N. Noble, r. same
Reinecke Frederick, lab. r. ns. McCarty, 1 w. of Virginia av.
Reinfels Henry, lab. r. 272 Union
Reinhardt Frederick, tinner, r. 131 W. 4th
Reinhardt Michael, moulder, r. 12 N. New Jersey
Reinhardt P. J. saloon and restaurant, and locksmith, 81 S. Illinois, r. same
Reinhardt Vallentine, wks. Burk, Ernshaw & Co. r. 277 Bluff rd.
Reinker Albert, plasterer, r. 754 N. Tennesse
Reinker Henry, cigars and tobacco, 266 E. Washington, r. same
Reinken Henry J. clk. Henry J. Roy, bds. 266 E. Washington
Reinken John, cigarmkr. H. Reinken, bds. 266 E. Washington
Reising Louis, gas-fitter Joseph W. Davis, r. 388 S. Delaware
Reisner George A. salesman A. W. Bronson, r. 170 Winston
Reisner Hermann, lab. Osgood, Smith & Co.
Reisner L. wid. Christ, r. 240 S. Tennessee
Reisner William, lab. r. 155 Union
Reissmer Albert, news depot, r. ws. Blake 5 n. New York
Reissner Albert, (Dietz & Reissner) r. ws. Blake bet. New York and Vermont
Reitch Augustus, deputy City Marshall
Reitz Charles, machinist Singer Mnfg. Co. r. 287 S. Pennsylvania
Reitz Frank A. r. Washington, cor. Michigan rd.
Reitzel Christ, machinist Sinker & Co. r. 417 S, Illinois
Renard Eugene, saloon, 299 E. Washington, r. same
Renard Eugene, stonecutter F. L. Farnam, r. 323 E. New York
Renard John B. stonecutter F. L. Farman, r. 323 E. New York
Renner Christian, blacksmith 123 Bluff rd. r. 127 Bluff rd.
Renner George, cigarmaker, r. 127 Bluff rd.
Renner Henry, student National Business College
Renner Jacob, (col'd) porter, r. 129 W. 4th
Renner John B. (Bremerman & Renner) r. 34 S. Alabama
Rennett George F. r. 70 E. Maryland
Rennihan Joseph, lab. r. 12 Center
Reno R. S. millwright, r. 136 N. Winston
Rensman Herman, dyer 28 Virginia av. r. same
Rentsch Edward, grocer 172 S. Illinois, r. same
Rentsch Ferdinand, clk. Severen & Schnull, r. New Jersey cor. New York
Rentsch Herman, grocer 145 E. Washington, r. same
Rentschler moulder, r. 213 N. Mississippi
Rentschler Frederick, clk. Charles Helwig, r. 106 N. Spring
Reutschler J. blacksmith, bds. 106 N. Spring
Rentschler Martin, blacksmith, r. 304 E. Ohio
Renz Ferdinand, clk. bds. 185 E. New York
Renzenbrink William, lab. Eagle Machine Works, r. 94 Eddy
Replogle John, (Lee & Replogle, r. 161 S. Spring
Republic Fire Ins. Co. of Chicago, J. S. Dunlop & Co. agts. 2 W. Washington
Resch Joseph, brewer Schmidt's Brewery, r. 328 S. Delaware

RES	268	RHO

Resener Charles, blacksmith, r. Arch nw. cor. Broadway
Resener Christian F. carpenter and builder in rear of 100 E. New York, r. 161 N. New Jersey
Resener Fred, (F. &. W. Resener) r. 179 N. East
Resener Frederick W. clk. F. & W. Resener, r. 179 N. East
Resener Henry, carpenter C. F. Resener, r. 235 N. Winston
Resener William, (F. & W. Resener) r. 331 E. Ohio
Resener F. & W. (Fred and William Resener) grocery and dry goods, 179 N. East
Revein Henry, blacksmith Bremerman & Renner
Revel William, engineer C. C. & I. C. R. R. r. 303 E. Georgia
Rexford Eugene M. express messenger, r. 155 N. Illinois
Reyer George, salesman, r. es. Meridian bet. 2nd and 3rd
Reynolds Charles E. clk. Merchts' Despatch, r. 323 N. Delaware
Reynolds Charles H. (Reynolds & Loucks) r. 278 E. Michigan
Reynolds Chesley, expressman, r. 79 Ash
Reynolds Clarkson, yardmaster, r. 323 N. Delaware
Reynolds David, cigarmaker N. W. Reynolds, r. 278 E. Michigan
Reynolds Frank, ydmaster C. C. C. & I. Rw. r. 156 N. Liberty
Reynolds James M. cigarmaker, r. 278 E. Michigan
Reynolds John, r. 92 W. Ohio
Reynolds John, city assessor, 35½ E. Washington, r. 287 N. Alabama
Reynolds John B. r. 160 Virginia av.
Reynolds John W. cigar boxmnfr. 174 E. Washington, r. 78 Benton
Reynolds Lizzie, wid. Thomas, r. 278 E. Michigan
Reynolds M. lab. Builders and Manufacturers Association
Reynolds Madison, cigarmkr. N. W. Reynolds, r. 278 E. Michigan
REYNOLDS NELSON W. cigar mnfr. 174 E. Washington, r. 278 E. Michigan. See adv't
Reynolds S. agt. bds. 456 Virginia
Reynolds Samuel, carpenter, r. 323 N. Delaware
Reynolds Silas S. trav. agt. r. 278 E. Michigan
Reynolds Thomas, carpenter Builders and Mnfrs. Association
Reynolds Thomas E. (Wiles & Reynolds) r. 160 Virginia av.
Reynolds Thompson, carpenter, r. ns. E. St. Clair bet. Broadway and Plum
Reynolds W. L. fruit stand, 20 S. Meridian, r. Ash nr. Christian
Reynolds W. tobacconist, r. ns. Ash bet. Cherry and Christian av.
Reynolds William, clerk C. C. & I. Rw. r. 323 N. Delaware
REYNOLDS & LOUCKS, (C. H. Reynolds and G. W. Loucks) whol. dealers in leaf tobacco, 22 N. Delaware
Rheinheimer Nathan, (Mayer & Rheinheimer) r. 275 S. Delaware
Rhinehold Jacob, carpenter, 373 W. Vermont, r. same
Rhoads Charles W. r. 231 W. New York
Rhoads Hiram R. teamster, r. 37 Vinton
Rhoads William, farmer, r. 43 Dacotah
Rhodes James, (col'd) waiter r. 79 W. Missouri
Rhodes James H. clerk Patterson, Moore & Talbot
Rhodes John W. real estate agt. bds 82 E. St. Clair

Buy your Hats, Caps and Furs at I. Davis & Co. 12 E. Washington.

RHO   269   RIC

Rhodes Milton L. compositor *Journal* news room, bds. 74 N. Pennsylvania
Rhodes Miranda, wid. Mountain, r. 285 Blake
Rhodes Thomas L. prof. of music, r. ss. Michigan bet. East and New Jersey
Rhodius Mary, wid. George, Circle Restaurant, 15 N. Meridian, r. same
Rice Alexander, salesman G. Rice, r. 164 W. Washington
Rice George H. pump maker, r. 69 W. New York
Rice Gustav, dry goods, 164 W. Washington, r. same
Rice Isaac, cabinet maker, r. 167 Winston
Richard Eliza, carder Hoosier Woolen Factory
Richard John, bds. 325 N. Liberty
Richard Mary, carder Hoosier Woolen Factory
Richard Philip, cabinetmaker, r. 461 N. Alabama
Richards Edward, (Richards & Thomas) r. 30 W. Pratt
Richards Frank, stonecutter, r. 485 E. Georgia
Richards Fred, compositor *Journal* news room
Richards George B. porter J. H. Baldwin & Co. bds. 31 Hosbrook
Richards Lizzie, bookbinder J. H. C. Smith
Richards Richard, engineer Goddard & Sons, r. 176 N. Missouri
Richards Sarah, r. 176 N. Missouri
Richards Thomas, carpenter, r. 314 E. Market
Richards & Thomas, (Edward N. Richards and Oliver E. Thomas) grocers, 213 E. Washington
Richardson Benjamin, clerk Indianapolis Gas. Light Co. r. 351 Pennsylvania cor. Warren
Richardson Daniel A. (Geisendorff, Richardson & Co.) bds. Palmer House
Richardson Daniel A. teamster, r. 378 N. West
Richardson Francis M. lab. r. 9 Elizabeth
Richardson Frank, trav. agent, r. 444 N. New Jersey
Richardson G. O. trav. agt. L. Q. Sherwood, bds. 556 N. Illinois
Richardson John W. teamster, r. 122 Maple
Richer Julius, tinner, r. 324 S. Delaware
Richer William, works Capital Ale Brewery
Richey Charlotte, wid. John, r. 124 N. Missouri
Richey Edward, clerk Charles Mayer & Co. bds. 31 Indiana av.
Richey James, moulder, bds. 80 S. Mississippi
Richey Julius, tinsmith, 223 S. Delaware, r. 324 S. Delaware
Richmann Charles, chief Fire Dept. r. 16 Fletcher av.
Richman John, lab. r. 233 S. East
RICHMOND TEMPERANCE HOUSE, (Joseph G. Collins) 35 W. Georgia
Richter Anthony, stonemason, r. Lord sw. cor. Benton
Richter August, Street Commissioner, r. 310 Virginia av.
Richter Fred, painter, r. es. Camp nr. 1st
Richter Henry, blksmith helper C. C. C. & I. R. R.
Richter Herman, (Western Furniture Co.) r. 265 N. Winston
Richter Herman, undertaker, r. 256 Winston
Richter Joseph, shoemaker, 217 E. Washington, r. same

RIC   270   RIL

Richter Simon, brickmason, r. 146 Huron

Richter William, clerk, bds. Lord sw. cor. Benton

Richter William, grocer, saloon and meat market, 416 Virginia av. r. 414 Virginia av.

Richwea J. lab. I. C. & L. Rw.

Rickard Henry, (Rickard & Talbott) bds. Bates House

RICKARD & TALBOTT, (Henry Rickard & Charles H. Talbott) hats, caps and furs whol. and ret. 78 S. Meridian

Rickards Thomas, carpenter and builder, 127 E. Maryland, r. 314 E. Market

Ricker Frank, advt. agent *State Sentinel*, bds. 143 N. Alabama

Ricker H. carpenter, r. 507 E. Market

Ricker Sarah H. Mrs. boardinghouse, 47 N. East r. same

RICKETTS DILLARD, pres. J. M. & I. R. R. r. S. Delaware, (Madison rd.) near city limits

Ricketts John D. bds. 256 Madison av.

Ricketts William H. foreman *State Sentinel* bookbindery, bds. 24 W. New York

Riddick Thomas, foreman Barker, Williams & Co. r. 121 W. New York

Riddick W. E. roller Barker, Williams & Co.

Riddle Mary, wid. John, r. ws. Minerva, 3 s. New York

Riddle William, plasterer, r. ws. Minerva 3 s. New York

RIDENOUR JONATHAN M. (James Thayman & Co.) and vice-pres. C. C. & I. J. R. R. office 64 E. Washington, r. ns. Michigan road one-half mile beyond city limits

Rider Isaiah, prof. of Penmanship, bds. 440 N. New Jersey

Ridgeway Otis N. watchmaker George Davis, r. 119 W. Maryland, bds. 44 S. Tennessee.

RIDGWAY JOHN F. physician and surgeon 88 E. Market, r. 151 N. New Jersey

Ridgway William, bds. 18 W. Georgia

Riebel Fred, cigar mkr. George F. Meyer

Riemenschneider H. (Krouse & Reimenschneider) r. 83 N. New Jersey

Riesenier L. wid. Christ, r. 240 S. Tennessee

Rifle Abraham, wks. Rolling Mill

Rifle Martin, file cutter Dartz & Steinhauer, r. 36 Union

Rifles Peter, r. 36 Union

Rigger Joseph, carpenter, r. 7 Charles

Riggs John, butcher, bds. 214 Union

Rihl Charles H. bricklayer, r. 30 N. New Jersey

Rihl Emma, dressmkr. Mrs. M. Miner, bds. 30 N. New Jersey

Rihl Henry S. r. 30 N. New Jersey

Rikhoff Bernard, carpenter, r. 351 N. Noble

Rikhoff Herman (Rikhoff & Bro.) r. 278 E. South

Rikhoff J. G. (Rikhoff & Bro.) r. Cincinnati, Ohio

RIKHOFF & BRO. (Herman and J. G. Rikhoff) whol. liquor dealers 77 S. Meridian

Riley Benjamin F. deputy county treasurer, office Court House, r. 37 Kentucky av.

| RIL | 271 | RIZ |

Riley Edward, lab. r. 167 Madison av.
Riley Ellen Miss, capmkr. r. 66 Eddy
Riley Henry H. candymkr. r. 43 Russell av.
Riley Hugh, lab. r. 340 Winston
Riley Hugh, watchman C. C. & I. C. R. R.
Riley James, waiter Depot Dining Hall, r. ns. New York 6 e. Minerva
Riley John, porter A. M. U. Ex. Co. r. 414 S. Tennessee
Riley John H. r. 66 S. Eddy
Riley Michael, wks. Rolling Mill
Riley Patrick, lab. r. 96 N. Railroad
Riley Thomas, lab. r. Chespeak bet. West and the Canal
Riley Timothy, teamster, r. 287 s. Tennessee
Riley William, lab. Osgood, Smith & Co.
Rinderknicht Charles, wks. Eagle Machine Works, r. 21 Wyoming
Riner Russell, bricklayer, r. 549 N. Mississippi
Reinert Frederick, foreman J. Fishback
Ring John, fireman Gas Works
Ring John, lab. r. 183 Dougherty
Ringen John, upholster 71 W. Washington
Ringosky H. lab. r 123 W. McCarty
Rinkle A. lab. r. 406 S. Tennesse
Rinkle David, barber 94 E. South r. same
Rinn Thomas, contractor, r. Tennessee cor. Norwood
Ripley William (Ripley & Gates) r. 225 W. New York
Ripley & Gates (William Ripley and Alfred B. Gates) groceries and provisions, 47 and 49 N. Illinois ·
Risby Thomas, machinist, r. 149 S. New Jersey
Rising Sun Ins. Co. of Rising Sun, Ind. T. A. Goodwin, agent, 35 E. Market
Risner Chris. H. chairmaker, r. 511 S. New Jersey
Ritchey Arnold, r. 470 S. New Jersey
Ritchey James W. bds. 55 Maple
Ritchey Sarah, dress and cloakmaker, r. 22 Douglas
Ritchie Edward, clerk, bds. 31 Indiana av.
Rittenhouse George L. grocer, r. 479 N. Meridian
Ritter August, teamster, r. 496 S. New Jersey
Ritter Eli F. (Ritter & Irvin) and notary public, 24½ E. Washngton, bds. cor. College av. and Butler
RITTER & IRVIN, (Eli F. Ritter and William Irvin) attorneys at law 24½ E. Washington
Rittew John P. painter, r. W. North nw. cor. Mississippi
Ritzinger Augustus W. bookkeeper J. B. Ritzinger's Savings Bank, bds. 226 E. Ohio
Ritzinger Frank L. teller S. A. Fletcher & Co. bds. 226 E. Ohio
Ritzinger Frederick, sec. German Mutual Fire Ins. Co. r. 226 E. Ohio
RITZINGER JOHN B. savings Bank, 14 E. Washington, r. 240 E. Ohio
Rizer Socrates, bds. 2 Indiana av.

ROA	272	ROB

Roache Addison L. (McDonald, Roache & McDonald) r. 613 N. Pennsylvania

ROACH ALVA C. publisher of subscription books, also of the *Jolly Hoosier*, and Roach's *Western Museum*, Market ne, cor. Circle, (*Journal* bldg.) r. 555 N. Illinois

Roach Charles, engineer, r. 297 S. East

Roach John, teamster, r. W. Indianapolis

Roach Milton E. sawer Warren Tate, bds. 297 S. East

Roach Nicholas, engineer, r. 25 Bright

Roach Sarah, wid. Daniel, wks. Paper Mill, r. 373 W. Washington

Roach's *Western Museum*, (monthly) A. C. Roach, editor and publisher, *Journal* bldg.

Roane Martin, lab. r. 241 S. Tennessee

Roark Thomas, steward Spencer House, r. 72 W. Louisiana

Roback Albert G. railroadman, r. 26 S. West

Roback Eli, bookbinder *Sentinel* bindery, r. 231 N. Mississippi

Roback Sarah, wid. r. 231 N. Mississippi

Roberts —— Mrs. r. 223 W. Washington

Roberts A. B. S. pump maker, r. 574 N. Mississippi

Roberts A. J. lab. r. es. Douglas, 2 s. New York

ROBERTS CHAPEL, (Methodist E.) F. C. Holliday, pastor, Vermont ne. cor. Delaware

Roberts E. L. student Bryant & Stratton's College, bds. 84 Massachusetts av.

Roberts Edward, boiler maker, r. 3 Willard

Roberts H. W. salesman B. Davis, r. same

Roberts Hannah, dressmaker, r. 10 Bates House Block

Roberts John, engineer, r. 454 E. Michigan

Roberts John, student, r. Vine bet. Broadway and Jackson

Roberts Joseph, jr. street car driver, r. 375 W. Washington

Roberts Silas, hostler Sullivan Drew

Roberts Thos. B. hostler Wood & Mansur, r. 223 W. Washington

Roberts Turner W. (col'd) clergyman, r. 244 N. Mississippi

Robertson Alexander M. (A. M. Robertson & Bro.) r. 96 E. Washington

Robertson Fount, (A. M. Robertson & Bro.) r. 96 E. Washington

Robertson George, (col'd) lab. r. 434 N. East

Robertson Jas. E. (J. E. Robertson & Co.) r. 177 N. Alabama

Robertson Mary S. wid. John M. r. 38 Henry

Robertson Thomas, bds. 75 S. Pennsylvania

Robertson William, machinist Eagle Machine Wks. r. 223 Union

ROBERTSON A. M. & BRO. (Alexander M. and Fount Robertson) dry goods, 96 E. Washington

ROBERTSON J. E. & CO. (James E. Robertson, Amos Birchard and John C. Perry) whol. grocers, 74 and 76 S. Meridian

Robinius Francis P. clk. F. Robinius, bds. same

Robinius Frank, boot and shoe manfr. and dealer, 223 W. Washington, r. 222 W. Maryland

ROBINS CHARLES J. meat market 34 N. Pennsylvania, r. 393 W. New York

Robins Charles J. Jr. butcher C. J. Robins, Sr. bds. same

Robinson Benjamin, (col'd) sexton Asbury Chapel, r. ws. Missouri bet. New York and Vermont

ROBINSON BROS. (Lafe and Bruce Robinson,) trunk manufrs. 20 Virginia av.

Robinson Bruce, (Robinson Bros.) r. 318 Massachusetts av.

Robinson C. fireman C. C. & I. C. R. R.

ROBINSON CHARLES B. supt. Union Rw. Co. office Union depot r. 381 S. Alabama

Robinson G. painter, r. 402 S. Illinois

Robinson George A. comp. *Sentinel* news room, bds. 213 N. Penn.

Robinson H. I. watchman C. C. C. & I. Rw. r. 432 E. North

Robinson Henry, engineer, r. 182 E. McCarty

Robinson Horace, watchman, r. Davidson nw. cor. Michigan

Robinson J. packer Barker Williams & Co.

Robinson James W. plasterer, r. 339 S. Alabama

Robinson Jane, wid. Robert W. r. 110 N. Missouri

Robinson John, mattrass maker, r. 280 W. Market

Robinson John R. mattrass maker, r. 85 N. Missouri

Robinson Joseph (col'd) lab. r. 163 Indiana av.

Robinson Lafe, (Robinson Bros.) r. 318 Massachusetts av.

Robinson Martha A. Miss, teacher, Sixth Ward School, r. 291 S. New Jersey

Robinson Martis S. clk. frt. office T. H. & I. R. R. bds, 188 S. Mississippi

Robinson Matthew B. r. 318 Massachusetts av.

Robinson Ruben D. presiding elder M. E. Church, r. 303 N. New Jersey

Robinson Sarah, wid. John L. r. 176 N. East

Robinson W. J. H. piano maker Indianapolis Piano Manuf'g Co. r. 163 E. Washington

Robison E. D. runner Commercial Hotel, bds. same

Robison Harry, wks. paper mill, bds. 261 W. Washington

Robison John, map agt. bds. 73 Kentucky av.

Robison Minta (col'd) wid. Harris, r. 239 N. West

Robison William, carpenter, r. 319 W. Merrill

Robson Charlotte, wid. William, r. 209 N. Pennsylvania

Rocap F. B. carpenter C. C. C. & I. R. R. r. 201 N. Davidson

Rock Adam, baker Charles Ferger, bds. 96 E. South

Rocker Peter, saloon, 290 W. Maryland, r. same

Rockey H. S. r. 202 E. Ohio

Rockwell James, fireman C. C. C. & I. R. R. bds. 454 E. Michigan

Rockwell Jones S. (Sanders & Rockwell) r. 62 S. Pennsylvania

Rockwell Silas, boarding house, 62 S. Pennsylvania, r. same

Rockwood William O. r. 276 N. Illinois

Rodenberger Samuel, carpenter, r. 321 E. North

Rodewald Henry, groceries ret. 441 Virginia av. r. same

Rodgers Harvey, physician, 293 Kentucky av. r. same

Rodgers James, lab. r. 293 Kentucky av.

Rodius Andrew, barber G. Ferling, bds. South

Roeback Amanda, weaver Hoosier Woolen Factory

Roeback Hellen, weaver Hoosier Woolen Factory

Roesener Charles, blacksmith, ns. St. Clair, bet. Broadway and Massachusetts av. r. Arch nw. cor. Broadway
Roesener Christian, chairmaker H. Schilling & Bro.
Roesener H. carpenter Eagle Machine Works, r. 23 E. McCarty
Roesener Henry, lab. Union Starch Factory, bds. 292 N. Winston
Roeth Adam, tailor Roeth & Meier, r. 207 E. Washington
Roeth John, (Roeth & Meier) r. 329 E. Michigan
Roeth & Meier, (John Roeth and Henry Meier) merchant tailors, 207 E. Washington
Rogers B. F. switchman, r. 247 N. Davidson
Rogers Birt, lab. Bunte, Dickson & Co.
Rogers Daniel W. conductor, bds. 58 Benton
Rogers G. F. ins. agt. r. 409 N. East
Rogers Isaac, watchman J. S. Carey & Co. r. 38 Helen
Rogers. J. N. bookkpr. L. H. Tyler & Co. bds. 154 S. New Jersey
Rogers James, wks. J. S. Carey & Co.
Rogers James C. city editor *Daily Sentinel*, bds. 30 W. Maryland
Rogers James H. salesman A. F. Coors, bds. 14 S. Mississippi
Rogers John, wks. J. S. Carey & Co.
Rogers John F. salesman L. H. Tyler & Co. bds. 218 E. Market
Rogers Kate Mrs. mnfr. of yeast cakes, r. 188 Virginia av.
Rogers Mary, wks. Indianapolis Paper Co.
Rogers William C. fuel agt. C. C. C. & I. R. R. 53 S. Alabama, bds. Oriental House
Rogge Rudolph, tailor Hotz & Co. r. 92 Russell
Rogge Rudolph, tailor and repairer, 335 Virginia av. r. same
Roland John, machinist Phœnix Machine Works
Roland Julia, wid. Patrick, r. 239 S. Tennessee
Roland Samuel, (col'd) r. Benton nr. cor. Maryland
Roland Thomas, cooper, r. 423 W. New York
Rolen Cloe, cigar stand Bates House, bds. same
Roll Rebecca, wid. Joseph, r. 351 N. New Jersey
ROLL WILLIAM H. dealer in carpets, wall paper, etc. 38 S. Illinois, r. 117 W. Maryland
Rolling Mill Coal Co. Tennessee nw. cor. South, D. Titcomb agt.
Romaine Charles H. teacher Indiana Telegraphic Institute, bds. 188 S. Mississippi
Roman Patsey, wid. William, r. 126 N. Missouri
Romerill Charles E. plasterer, r. 342 N. East
Romerill James H. chairmkr. r. 342 N. East
Ronan Michael, lab. r. 131 S. Tennessee
Ronevalt J. H. chair mkr. Spiegel & Thoms
Roney Charles, r 133 Harrison
Roney Charles S. cistern builder and street paver. r. 173 N. East
Roney Elias, teamster, r. 133 Harrison
Roney Felix, puddler Indianapolis Rolling Mill, bds. 26 Willard
Roney Henry (Haywood & Co.) r. 172 E. Washington
Rooker Alfred J. painter, r. 37 Douglas
Rooker Calvin F. deputy county clerk, r. 778 N. Illinois
Rooker Cameron F. r. 778 N. Illinois
Rooker George L. D. painter, r. 104 N. California

Roop John A. wagonmkr. Ind. Agal.Works, r. 48 N. New Jersey
Roos Jacob, Meat Market 137 S. Illinois, r. same
Root Deloss (D. Root & Co.) r. 441 N. Meridian
Root Emma Miss, teacher Third Ward School
Root Jerome B. (D. Root & Co.) r. 511 N. Illinois
Root Julia Miss, r, 429 N. Meridian
Root L. E. Miss, teacher, bds. 60 N. California
Root Louis, bartender, r. 122 N. Mississippi
Root Robert, clerk P. Fahrbach, bds. Washington Hall
Root Samuel, painter, bds. 314 E. George
ROOT D. & CO. (Delos & Jerome B.) stoves and castings 66
   E. Washington, foundry and machine shop 183–185 S.
   Pensylvania
Ropkey H. F. peddler, r. 457 E. Georgia
Ropke Helene, grocery store, McCarty sw. cor. Madison av. r same
Rorex Mary E. wid. Martin, r. 81 W. McCarty
Rorick Thomas, steward Spencer House
Rose A. fireman C. C. C & I. R. R.
Rose A. D. r. 19 W. Pratt
Rose David G. bds. Macy House
Rose Frank B. agt. *Evening Commercial*, r. 67 Madison av.
Rose Fred, lab. C. C. & I. C. R. R.
Rose Henry, carpenter W. H. Henschen
Rose John ex-postmaster, r. 35 W. Market
Rose John N. manufacturer of ladies' and gents' fine boots, shoes
   and gaiters 90 E. Market, r. 242 Coburn
Rose Margarett, dress maker 181 Virginia av. r. same
Rose Robert, shoemaker J. N. Rose, bds. same
Rose Thomas, shoemaker J. N. Rose, bds. same
Rosebrock, F. W. grocer 486 Virginia av. r. same
Rosebrock John F. grocer 201 Virginia av. r. same
Rosenbaum Chris. teamster, r. 21 Elm
Rosenbaum William, porter Institute for the Blind, r. same
Rosenberg John, cutter A. J. Gerstner, r. 308 E. Washington
Rosener E. W. Henry, carpenter, r. 110 N. Noble
Rosengarten Albert, bds. 30½ N. Pennsylvania
Rosengarten Charles, entry clerk Anderson, Bullock & Schofield,
   bds. Pyle House
Rosengarten Louis, junk dealer, r. 33 N. Noble
Rosenthal Henry, (Hays, Rosenthal & Co. r. 160 N. East
Rosenthal Moses, (Hays, Rosenthal & Co.) r. 212 E. Market
Roser John, boilermaker C. C. & I. C. R. R.
Ross Alfred, student, bds. 81 W. 2d
Ross Amos P. insurance agt. r. 284 N. New Jersey
Ross David M. (D. M. Ross & Co.) r. 81 W. 2d
Ross Frank, clerk J. Hauck & Co. r. 65 Indiana av.
Ross Friend D. carpenter, r. 36 Helen
Ross H. J. r. 65 Indiana av.
Ross Henry, saloon, r. 105 Buchanan
Ross Jacob, (col'd) lab. r. ws. Missouri nr. 1st
Ross James, painter, r. 62 Huron

ROS	276	ROW

Ross James, wagon maker, r. 333 S. Delaware

Ross James J. cooper W. Baird, r. 335 W. Maryland

Ross Johnson H. coal dealer, 24 E. Pearl, r. 294 N. Tennessee

Ross Maria, wid. Jehiel, r. 10 Walter

Ross Mary, wid. William A. r. 146 E. McCarty

Ross Oliver L. clerk E. B. Martindale, bds. Martindale's Block

Ross T. wks. J. S. Carey & Co.

Ross W. R. salesman H. H. Lee, r. New York nw. cor. Meridian

Ross William W. trimmer Bremerman & Renner, bds. Dells Hotel

ROSS D. M. & CO. (David M. Ross and Robert McFarland) flour, feed and com. mers. 155 W. Washington

Rossater J. L. machinist Greenleaf & Co.

Rossiter Lyola, machinist, r. 72 Bicking

Rossman Belle Miss, saleslady Wiley & VanBuren, bds. 20 S. Pennsylvania

Rost August, cigarmkr. N. W. Reynolds, r. 23 Massachesetts av.

Roswinkel Fred, cigarmaker George Roswinkel

Roswinkel George, cigar mnfr. es. Massachusetts av. bet. North and Michigan, r. same

Rotebaugh Omer, clerk, bds. Illinois cor. 6th

Roth Adam, student National Business College

Rothert John, clerk Frederick Jasper, bds. 333 Virginia av.

Rothfuss Paul cigarmaker, bds. 135 E. Washington

Rothgery J. F. velocipede smith Miller, Mitchell & Stough, bds. Bicking House

Rothgery Peter, helper Miller, Mitchell & Stough, bds. Bicking House

Rothrock Valentine, supt. Osgood, Smith & Co. bds. Ray House

Rothschild Henry, clothing store, 125 W. Washington, r. 207 S. Illinois

Rothschild Samuel A. clerk, bds. Oriental House

Rotter Frank M. (Frauer, Beiler & Co.) bds. Union Hall, 135 E. Washington

Rouhette A. bookkeeper, r. 300 E. Washington

Rourke John, puller Rolling Mill

Rouse John C. butcher C. J. Robins, bds. 31 Indiana av.

Rouse R. R. gen. agt. Am. Driving Well, office 30 Kentucky av. r. 17 S. Mississippi

Rout Thomas, bookkeeper, r. 22 Lockerbie

Routh Edward F. clk. Pettis, Dickson & Co. r. 54 S. Pennsylvania

Routier A. B. carpenter P. Routier

ROUTIER PETER, carpenter and builder Virginia av. cor. Cedar, r. 394 Virginia av.

Rouzer Charles, clk. lunch stand Union dpt. bds. same

Rowan John, wks. Kingan & Co. r. 327 W. Market

Rowe Alice, wid. Matthew, r. w. end Rose

Rowe Austin, engineer C. C. & I. C. R. R. r. Benton nr. cor. Maryland

Rowe Eliza, wid. Titus, r. 311 S. Missouri

Rowe George, asst. engineer Rolling Mill

Rowe Samuel P. clk. James T. Lyman & Co. r. 284 E. Michigan

ROWE WILLIAM, (W. H. Close & Co.) and treas. Indianapolis Cotton Mnfg. Co. and bkpr. Indianapolis Rolling Mill, r. 5 Madison av. nr. se. cor. Meridian and South

Rowe William E. yardmaster C. C. & I. C. R. R. r. 230 N. East

Rowland John, watchman Hoosier Woolen Mill, r. 30 Douglas

Rowland Michael, r. 30 Douglas

Rowland Peter, wks. Hoosier State Mills

Rowland Timothy, wks. Caledonia Paper Mill

Rowland William E. H. bds. 366 N. Alabama

Rowley Fayette R. trav. agt. L. Q. Sherwood, r. 242 N. Illinois

Rowlson Margaret, wid I. L. r. 82 Indiana av.

Roxford E. M. express messenger, r. 135 N. Illinois

Roy Henry J. saloon and billrd. hall, 274 E. Washington, r. same

Royer George, fireman C. C. C. & I. R. R.

Royer George W. lab. r. 245 N. Liberty

Royse William T. (Greene & Royse) bds. Pyle House

Rozier Aaron, (H. H. Langenberg & Co.) r. 146 Blackford

Rozier George, printer H. C. Chandler & Co. r. 146 Blackford

Rozier Percy, printer H. C. Chandler & Co. r. 146 Blackford

Rubus Alexander, bricklayer Gas Works

Rubush George A. r. 75 S. Noble

Ruckersfeldt Charles, clk. Gapen, Catherwood & Co. r. 183½ W. New York

Ruckle Nicholas R. foreman *Commercial*, bds. 17 W. Maryland

Rucklos Jacob, r. 340 E. Market

Ruddell James H. lawyer 35½ E. Washington, r. 62 S. Pennsylvania

Rudibaugh Omer, clk. J. Tarlton

Rudisall Maggie Miss, bds. Martin House

Rueck Henry, machinist, bds. Globe House

Ruemely Joseph, newsdealer, r. 389 S. East

Rufus Conrad, carpenter, r. 356 N. West

Ruley Frederick, watchman J. M. & I. R. R.

Rumell Jacob F. catcher Rolling Mill

Rumell Jacob W. lab. Rolling Mill, r. 162 Bluff rd.

Rummell John, tie roller Rolling Mill

Rummell John A. Rolling Mill, r. 250 S. Tennessee

Rummele George, books and stationery, 153 E. Washington, r. 389 S. East

Runge Christian, butcher Fred Heargt, bds. 345 E. Washington

Rupert Frederick, runner Oriental Hotel

Rupp John, grocer, Kentucky av. cor. West, r. same

Rupp William F. mer. tailor, 38 W. Washington, r. 131 E. Washington

Ruschhaupt August, (A. Ruschhaupt & Wands) r. 56 Massachusetts av.

RUSCHHAUPT FREDERICK, pres. Eagle Machine Works, r. 270 N. Delaware

Ruschhaupt A. & Wands, (August Ruschhaupt and Alexander Wands) saloon and restaurant, 81 E. Washington

Rush Charles, (Gall & Rush) r. 115 N. New Jersey

RUS	278	RYA

Rush Fred P. flour, grain, seed, storage and com. mer. 99 S. Delaware, r. 105 N. Meridian
Rush Peter, prompter, r. 275 S. Tennessee
Rushton John, cigarmaker Jacob Garratt, bds. 2 Indiana av.
Rusk Francis, (col'd) wid. Isaac, r. rear 241 W. Ohio
Ruske Henry A. carpenter Warren Tate, r. 86 S. East
Russe Charles, wks. Schneider & Co. r. 417 E. Washington
Russe Conrad, stonemason, r. 417 E. Washington
Russe George, fireman C. C. C. & I. R. R.
Russell Alexander W. clerk P. O. r. 15 Fletcher av.
Russell Annie E. Mrs. clerk P. O. bds. 204 N. Illinois
Russell Bell, r. 75 W. South
Russell David, student National Business College
Russell David, (Russell & Kosserg) r. 391 Market cor. Davidson
Russell George, (col'd) barber J. B. Cropper
Russell Henry C. r. 23 W. Georgia
Russell James N. dist. clerk P. O. r. 296 S. Meridian
Russell James, contractor, r. 291 N. Alabama
Russell James, cooper, r. 272 Union
Russell James, hostler Citizens' Street R. R. Co.
Russell John S. carpenter, r. 254 S. Delaware
Russell John, wood worker J. W. Whitney, r. 68 Bicking
Russell John S. carpenter. r. 354 S. Delaware
Russell Joseph, r. 291 N. Alabama
Russell Loren M. policeman, r. 82 S. Noble
Russell Lot, (col'd) farmer, r. 239 N. Tennessee
Russell Samuel, lab. C. C. & I. C. R. R. r. 130 Blackford
Russell Thomas, lab. r. 299 S. Missouri
Russell William, (Russell & Gulliver) r. 212 W. Vermont
Russell & Gulliver, (William Russell and William Gulliver) barbers, 50 E. Washington
RUSSELL & KASBERG, (David Russell and Peter Kasberg) foundry, Market no. cor. Benton
Russwinkle Fred. cigarmaker, r. 377 E. St. Clair
Rust Conrad, lab. Spiegel & Thoms
Ruth Adolph A. clerk Louis Lang, bds. 122 N. Mississippi
Ruth Charles, clerk Louis Lang, r. 188 Virginia av.
Ruth Louis G. barkeeper P. Fahrbach, r. 122 N. Mississippi
Ruthard Charles, carver Spiegel & Thoms, r. 23 Buchanan
Rutner Santo, carpenter, r. 98 Fletcher av.
Ryan Bros. (John B. & George W. Ryan) house and sign painters, 18 S. Meridian
Ryan Dennis, driver Citizens St. R. R. Co. bds. Neiman House
Ryan Ellen B. wid. John, r. 75 S. Mississippi
Ryan Francis D. decorator Gall & Rush, r. 126 Indiana av.
Ryan Frank, wid. John, r. 2 Union
Ryan George W. (Ryan Bros.) r. 31 E. Coburn
Ryan James, porter Sherman House, bds. same
Ryan James, lab. r. 88 Garden
Ryan James B. (Ryan & Holbrook) r. 158 N. Mississippi
Ryan John, r. 28 Willard

Ryan John, lab. r. 278 S. Delaware
Ryan John, machinist Sinker & Co. r. 277 E. Georgia
Ryan John, wks. Simms & Hoskins
Ryan John A. driver Citizens St. R. R. Co. bds. 266 S. Illinois
Ryan John B. (Ryan Bros.) r. 481 S. New Jersey
Ryan M. B. Mrs. dressmaker, 209 Virginia av. r. same
Ryan Margarett, wid. r. 277 E. Georgia
Ryan Martin, lab. C. C. C. & I. R. R.
Ryan Michael (1) wks. Kingan & Co. r. 32 Helen
Ryan Michael (2) wks. Kingan & Co. r. 34 Helen
Ryan Michael, puddler Indianapolis Rolling Mill
Ryan Michael, lab. r. 358 Winston
Ryan Richard J. lawyer, r. 355 N. Illinois
RYAN T. F. whol. liquor dealer, 143 S. Meridian, r. 355 N. Illinois
Ryan Thomas, clerk, r. 75 S. Mississippi
Ryan Thomas, lab. r. 280 E. Washington
Ryan Walter G. cooper D. Burton & Co. r. 39 Blake
Ryan Walter jr. cooper D. Burton & Co. r. 39 Blake
Ryan William, blacksmith Ind. Coach Works, bds. Pyle House
Ryan William J. clerk P. O. r. 75 S. Mississippi
RYAN & HOLBROOK, (James B. Ryan & H. C. Holbrook) wine
    and liquors whol. 48 S. Meridian
Rynders J. C. F. entry clk. J. H. Vagen & Co. r. 128 N. Meridian
Rysing Louis, gas-fitter, r. 338 S. Delaware

S

Sabel Henry, lab. r. 32 Ann
Sackett Cyrus O. printer H. C. Chandler & Co. bds. 74 N. Penn.
Sacket Frank E. salesman D. Root & Co. bds. 510 N. Delaware
Sacks John P. cooper W. Baird, r. 77 N. Illinois
SAGE CHARLES, druggist 172 W. Washington, r. 327 same st.
Sage John, core maker D. Root & Co. r. 363 S. Tennessee
Sagehorn James, r. 125 E. Washington
Sager Alfred B. teamster, r. 135 W. Michigan
Sager William, wks. Western Furniture Co. r. 556 N. Alabama
Sahm Louis, carpenter, r. ss. E. St. Joseph nr. Fort Wayne av.
Sahm Ludwig, grocer, 142 Fort Wayne av. r. same
Sailors H. C. bookkeeper Coburn & Jones, bds. Palmer House
SAILORS JAMES L. dry goods 156 W. Washington, r. same
Sailors Mason P. salesman J. L. Sailors, bds. 156 W. Washington
Sain H. A. N. clk. G. W. Despatch, bds. Bates House
St. Clair Charles G. prof. of music rooms 4–5, 77½ E. Market, r. same
St. Clair Mission Sabbath School (Congregational) E. St. Clair
    nr. cor. East
St. Clair William, yard man T. H. & I. R. R. r. nr. same
ST. JOHN'S CATHOLIC CHURCH, (German) ss. Maryland bet.
    Delaware and Pennsylvania
ST. JOHN'S CHURCH, Augustus B. Eessinones pastor ns. Georgia
    bet. Illinois and Tennessee

St. J	280	SAN

St. John's Home for Invalids, under charge of Sisters of Providence, 127 and 129 S. Tennessee

St. John's School (for boys) Brothers of the Sacred Heart in charge, ns. Georgia, bet. Illinois and Tennessee

St. John's School (for girls) S. Tennessee ne. cor. Georgia, Sisters of Providence in charge

ST. LOUIS MUTUAL LIFE INSURANCE CO. of St. Louis, Mo. E. A. Whitcomb state agt. No. 4 Yohn's Block

ST. MARY'S GERMAN CATHOLIC CHURCH, Rev. Father S. Siegrist, pastor, ss. Maryland bet. Delaware and Pennsylvania

St. Mary's German School, Sister Stanislas, superior, rear St. Mary's Church

ST. PAUL'S CHURCH (Episcopal) N. Illinois se. cor. New York

ST. PETER'S CHURCH (Catholic) Joseph Petit, pastor, Dougherty nr. Virginia av.

St. Peter's School (Catholic) Miss Lucy Keating, principal, Dougherty nr. Virginia av.

Salcours Theodore, lab. Bunte, Dickson & Co.

Salge Henry, engineer Frd. C. Bollman

Salisbury P. carpenter, bds. 449 N. New Jersey

Salsbury Henry, (II Salsbury & Co.)

SALSBURY H. CO. (J. McLene, A. E. Vinton and W. H. Talbott) mnfrs. of news and book paper, w. end of Maryland

Saltcorn Theodore, cooper, r. 567 E. St. Clair

Salter William H. r. 222 N. New Jersey

Sammons A. clerk Express Office

Samson Charles, stonecutter Scott & Nicholson

Sanborn Abraham J. painter J. M.VanBlaricum, r. 176 Blackford

Sanders E. G. painter, r. 27 Vine

Sanders G. (col'd) lab. r. Peru nr. cor. St. Clair

Sanders John, Express Messenger

Sanders John, (col'd) porter W. Bucksot, r. 60 N. Missouri

Sanders John, (col'd) teamster Caledonia Paper Mill, r. rear 265 W. Washington

Sanders John B. carpenter, r. 282 N. Liberty

Sanders John E. (Sanders & Rockwell) saloon and propr. Palmer House, r. 185 W. South

Sanders Richard, (col'd) lab. r. rear 264 Massachusetts av.

Sanders Theodore, (Western Furniture Co.) r. 25 S. Delaware

Sanders William, blksmith, r. Ellen nw. cor. Elizabeth

Sanders William, (col'd) blksmith G. M. Davis, (col'd) r. Blake cor. Elizabeth

Sanders & Rockwell, (John Sanders and Jones S. Rockwell) dealers in pumps, &c. 30 Kentucky av.

SANDERSON CHARLES J. sect. and treas. I. & St. L. Sleeping Car Co. office Union Depot, r. Tennessee cor. Walnut

SANDERSON H. Q. pres. I. & St. L. Sleeping Car Co. office Union Depot, r. Tennessee cor. Walnut

Sands Mary, wid. Isaac, r. 76 Maple

Sangamo Fire Ins Co. of Springfield, Ill. F. W. Blair agent, 44 N. Pennsylvania

Sanger Joseph, car reporter I. C. & L. Rw. r. 113 S. New Jersey
Santo Edward, grocer, 204 Indiana av. r. same
Santo Henry, watchman, r. rear 266 N. West
Sapf Edward, cabinetmaker, r. 126 Maple
Sapp George W. watchman Street R. R. Co. bds. Globe House
Sapp John, blacksmith N. Kimball
Sapp John, r. 497 S. New Jersey
Sarden James, currier Dietz & Reissner
Sargent Francis L. blacksmith Ind. Ag. Wks. r. 336 N. West
Sass B. porter Hays Rosenthal & Co. bds California House
Sater James A. salesman Trade Palace, r. 9 Cherry
Satoriess John, (Vondergotten & Satoriess) r. 321 E. Ohio
Sauer John, brewer Schmidts Brewery, r. E. McCarty bet. Meridian and Illinois
Sauley Charles, harnessmaker Ad. Hereth
Sauley Daniel, lab. R. R. bds. 235 Madison av.
Saunders Enoch, painter W. B. Milender
Saunders John, propertee and costumer Academy of Music
Saunders John, bds. 144 N. Tennessee
Saunders John, (col'd) barkeeper, r. 66 N. Missouri
Saunders Philip, blacksmith, r. Michigan rd. above 8th
Savings Bank, (J. B. Ritzinger,) 14 E. Washington
Sawyer Clara J. Miss, teacher Indianapolis Female Inst. r. same
Sawyer Corwin, stone cutter Goddard & Sons, bds. Western House
Sawyer Edward, presser H. Malpas, r. Washington
Sawyer John S. clk. Crossland, Hanna & Co. r. 170 W. Market
Saxton Richard J. r. 47 S. Illinois
Sayer Philip, blacksmith Ind. Coach Wks. r. 431 E. Vermont
Sayers H. A. lab. Sinker & Co.
Sayers John, flagman Union depot, bds. 426 S. Tennessee
Sayers John, lab. R. R. r. 276 S. Delaware
Sayers Thomas, lab. r. 118 Meek
Sayers Thomas, yard master, r. 426 S. Tennessee
Sayers Thomas, sen. flagman C. C. & I. C. R. R.
Sayles Charles F. bkpr. J. H. Baldwin & Co. bds. Sherman House
Saylor Jackson, supt. Rolling Mill, r. 285 S. Illinois
Saylor William, wks. Rolling Mill, bds. 285 S. Illinois
Scanlon Bridget, (Field, Locke & Co.) r. 263 W. Washington
Scanlon Patrick, foreman Caledonia Paper Mill, r. 271 W. Washington
Schaaf Able, lab. r. 103 N. Noble
Schaaf Conrad, packer, wks. Cabinet Makers Union
Schaaf Valentine, carpenter, r. 313 E. Market
Schaat George, varnisher Helwig & Co.
Schad Christian, tailor T. R. Porter, bds. 331 E. Vermont
Schad George, varnisher, 101 N. Davidson
Schad Gottlieb, carriage maker, r. 101 N. Davidson
Schade F. wid. r. 89 W. Georgia
Schaefer Adam, cabinet maker Helwig & Co.
Schafer Henry, watchman, r. 106 N. Spring

SCH	282	SCH

Schafer John, butcher, 92 N. Illinois, r. Bluff rd.
Schaffer Andrew, cooper M. Seiter, bds. California House
Schaffer August, machinist Eagle Machine Works, r. 124 S. Ills.
Schaffer Charles, carpenter Eagle Machine Works, r. 123 E. Mc-
    Carty
Schaffer Mayer, basket maker, r. 251 Bluff rd.
Schaffner Jacob, lab. r. 361 N. Noble
Shakel Frederick, lab. McCord & Wheatley, r. 53 Coburn
Schallenberg Frederick, chair maker, r. 510 S. East
Schalor J. helper T. H. & I. R. R. r. Kentucky av. opp. Cemetery
Schaub C. fireman C. C. & I. C. R. R.
Schaub, George, shoemkr. 170 E. Washington, r. 77 S. Liberty
Schaub Henry, saloon, 168 W. Washington, r. same
Schaub Henry, jr. bowling saloon, 334 Virginia av. r. same
Schaub Jacob, shoemaker George Schaub, r. 191 N. Noble
Schaub John, painter, r. 497 N. Alabama
Schaub John, r. 225 N. Noble
Schaub Joseph, lab. Bunte, Dickson & Co.
Schaub Peter, r. 158 Huron
Schaub Peter, expressman, r. 217 N. Noble
Schaub William, cash boy J. H. Baldwin & Co. bds. 222 Noble
Schaumle John, baker, r. 340 Virginia av.
Sched Mathias, tailor, r. 331 E. Vermont
Scheele Frederick, helper T. H. & I. R. R.
Scheessler Conrad, r. 93 N. New Jersey
Scheid, Charles, cooper, r. 333 W. Maryland
Scheigert Frederick, policeman, r. 264 S. Illinois
Scheigert Henry, carpenter, bds. Washington House
Scheigert William, lab. Rolling Mill
Scheiter Henry H. machinist Helwig & Co.
Scheldmeir Christian, engineer, r. 195 Meek
Scheley George J. clerk, bds. Macy House
Schell Christ, teamster, r. 575 S. Illinois
Schell Christopher, lab. Osgood, Smith & Co.
Scheller Max, physician, 210 E. Ohio, r. same
Schellschmidt Adolph, music teacher, r. 244 E. Ohio
Schellschmidt Ferdinand, musician, r. 511 E. Market
Schendel Frederick, carpenter, r. 33 N. East
Schenk Chris. cabinetmaker Helwig & Co.
Scherer Adam, boot and shoe mnfr. 34 N. Illinois, r. 23 Grand
Scherrer John, brewer P. Lieber & Co. r. 220 S. Meridian
Schetter Christopher, (Schetter & Simpson) r. 283 S. Pennsylvania
SCHETTER & SIMPSON, (C. Schetter & John Simpson) groceries
    whol. & ret. 99 E. South
Schierling Harmann, clerk Henry Syerup, r. 292 N. Liberty
Schildmeier Fred. tailor, 182 E. Washington, r. 310 E. Market
Schildmyer Anthony, boot and shoemaker, 313 E. Washington,
    r. 375 E. Michigan
Schille Lawrence, baker, 314 N. New Jersey, r. same
Schilling Diedrich, (H. Schilling & Bro.) r. 134 E. McCarty
Schilling Frederick, teamster, r. 487 S. New Jersey

SCH	283	SCH

Schilling Henry, H. (Schilling & Bro.) r. 134 E. McCarty

SCHILLING H. & BRO. (Henry and Diedrich Schilling) chair mnfrs. 134 E. McCarty

Schillinger George, porter Kennedy, Byram & Co. r. 167 N. Spring

Schimberg Minnie, student National Business College

Schindler R. clk. A. M. Robertson & Bro. bds. 184 E. Washington

Schisler Cooney, lab. Bunte, Dickson & Co.

Schisselle Christian, lab. r. 15 Russell av.

Schley George J. comp. *Mirror* newsroom, bds. Macy House

Schley John, night editor *State Sentinel*, r. 70 N. Mississippi

Schliebitz Frederick W. watchmaker and jeweler 147 E. Washington, r. 173 E. Washington

Schloer Christian, r. 128 Fort Wayne av.

Schlosser Michael, brewer Schmidt's Brewery, r. Madison av.

Schlotzhauer Adam, grocer 248 N. Liberty, r. same

Schlotzhauer Valentine, cabinetmaker, r. 152 E. New York

Schlusher Heury, watchmaker, r. rear 302 W. Maryland

Schmalholz Caspar, clk. John Huegele, r. Noble bet. Market and Ohio

Schmalholz Rudolph, harnessmaker John Andra, r. 64 N. Noble

Schmalholz Simon, cigarmaker Back & Wenken

Schmedel Hiram, (Schmedel & Fricker) r. 77 Lockerbie

SCHMEDEL & FRICKER, (Hiram Schmedel and Jacob Fricker) brush mnfrs. 194 E. Washington

Schmehl E. moulder, r. 109 Stevens

Schmertz Jacob, varnisher Cabinetmakers' Union, bds. Jackson bet. Arch and St. Clair

Schmidt Charles, lab. r. 203 Union

Schmidt Charles, clk. Indianapolis Soap Factory, r. 215 Union

Schmidt Chris. city scavenger, r. 120 Dacotah

SCHMIDT CHRISTIAN F. propr. Schmidt's Brewery, s. end Alabama, r. same (See card front cover)

Schmidt Fred, grocer, r. 468 N. Tennesse

Schmidt Frederick, blacksmith, r. 46 Walter

Schmidt George, r. 78 S. Delaware

Schmidt George, lab. Union Starch Factory

Schmidt George, varnisher Cabinet Makers' Union

Schmidt Harald, bookkeeper John Mueller, r. 246 E. Washington

Schmidt Henry, lab. Union Starch Factory, r. e. end Michigan

Schmidt Hermann, clerk, r. 31 N. Liberty

Schmidt Jacob, cigarmaker Louis Young, r. 32 Jones

Schmidt Leonard, lab. r. 29 W. McCarty

Schmidt Leopold, turner Cabinet Makers' Union

Schmidt Lorenz, clerk A. Seidensticker & Co. r. Washington cor. East

Schmidt Peter, carpenter Hubert Ricker, r. 394 E. Market

Schmidt Robert, tanner and drumhead mnfr. 96 S. East, r. same

Schmidt Rudolph, wines and liquors whol. 269 E. Washington, r. same

Schmidt Sylvanius, cabinetmaker Burk, Earnshaw & Co.

SCH	284	SCH

Schmidt William, blksmith, r. 330 S. Alabama
Schmidt William, butcher, r. 23 Charles
Schmidth Leonard, brewer Harting & Bro. r. 29 W. McCarty
Schmidth William, carpenter, r. 24 Jones
Schmit Christena, wid. Henry, r. Michigan rd. nr. junc. Washington
Schmit Henry, baker Fred C. Bollman
Schmitt George, painter, r. 191 N. Liberty
Schmitt George, lab. r. 220 Railroad
Schmitt Jacob, baker J. G. Klein
Schmitt J. painter, r. 78 S. Delaware
Schmitt Joseph, carpenter, r. 294 N. Noble
Schmitts William H. grocer, 389 N. Noble, r. same
Schneider Conrad, sawmkr. Sheffield Saw Wks. r. 67 Wyoming
Schneider Conrad P. carpenter A. F. Rafert, r. 247 N. Liberty
Schneider John, (Schneider & Co.) r. 195 S. East
Schneider Louis, moulder D. Root & Co. r. 125 Stevens
Schneider Nicholas, bricklayer, r. 33 Buchanan
SCHNEIDER & CO. (John Schneider, Louis Neubacher and Chris. Karle) props. Phoenix Bell and Brass Foundry 26 Union
Schnull Henry (Severin & Schnull & E. Over & Co.) and Indianapolis Cotton Manufacturing Co. r. 124 N. Alabama
Schnull's Block, Meridian sw. cor. Maryland
Schorn —— Mrs. r. 307 W. Market
Schœn Andrew, finisher Smith's Chemical Dye Works 62 E. Market, r. 196 E. Washington
Schœttle Christian, clk. Hugo Marmont, r. 102 S. Illinois
Schofield James B. salesman Anderson, Bullock & Schofield, bds. Bates House
Schofield N. N. (Anderson, Bullock & Schofield) r. Franklin, Ind.
Scholta Frank, tanner, r. alley bet. Washington and Market, Alabama and New Jersey
Scholtzbauer Valentine, treas. Cabinet Makers' Union, r. Davidson nw. cor. New York
Scholz John, blacksmith Sinker & Co.
Schomberg F. W. shoemaker, 23 N. New Jersey, r. 131 Davidson
Schonacker A. R. wid. Hubert, r. 134 N. Illinois
SCHONACKER CLARA, hairworker 134 N. Illinois, r. same
Schonacker Louis, asst. ticket agt. Union depot, r. 134 N. Illinois
Schonacker Mary, hairworker C. Schonacker, r. 134 N. Illinois
Schooley Thomas, farmer, r. 520 N. Illinois
Schoonemaker Peter H. with A. A. Barnes, r. 228 W. Maryland
Schopp George, shoemkr C. Friedger, r. 140 S. Union
Schoppenhorst W. wid. William, r. 48 Lockrbie
Schott Charles wiper T. H. & I. R. R.
Schove William, lab. r. Vine bet. Broadway and Jackson
Schovie Frederick, lab. I. C. & L. R. W.
Schovie Jacob, lab. I. C. & L. R. W.
Schowe Fred. E. blacksmith B. F. Haugh & Co. r. 1 N. Water
Schowe Fred. lab. r. 350 Virginia av.
Schowe Henry J. lab. r. 9 Walter

The latest styles of Hats & Caps at I. Davis & Co. 12 E. Wash'n.

SCH   285   SCH

Schowe William, carpenter, r. 338 S. Alabama
Schowe William, machinist, r. 350 Virginia av.
Schnabel Aug. bookbinder W. & J. Braden, r. 507 N. Mississippi
Schrader Andrew, **lab.** I. P. Evans & Co. r. 276 N. Liberty
Schraker Charles, grocer, r. 133 E. Merrill
Schrader Christena, wid. Frederick, r. 221 S. Alabama
Schrader Christian, clk. J. Woodbridge, r. 127 N. Mississippi
Schrader Christian, (Schrader & Kruger) r. 355 E. McCarty
Schrader Fred, boots and shoes, 85 W. Washington, r. 126 N.
    Mississippi
Schrader John H. r. 126 N. Mississippi
Schrader Rudolph, machinist, r. 332 E. Market
Schrader & Kruger, (Christian Schrader and Christian Kruger)
    groceries ret. 401 Virginia av.
Schrake Mary, wid. Christopher, r. 253 N. Noble
Schramm Charles, bookkeeper, r. 223 E. Vermont
Schramm John C. A. sec. Spiegel & Thoms' Furniture Co. r. 223
    E. Vermont
Schreier Charles, millwright, r. 25 Bright
Schrewsbury S. C. clk. Maxwell, Fry & Thurston, bds. Pyle House
Schreyer Emma, milliner S. B. Conaty, r. 159 Bluff rd.
Schreyer John, heater Rolling Mill, r. 159 Bluff rd.
Schreyer William, piler Rolling Mill
Schroeder Christian, machinist Eagle Machine Works, r. 124 E.
    McCarty
Schroeder Frederick, cooper Bernhard Keohring, r. 322 N. Noble
Schroeder John, machinist Sinker & Co.
Schroeder William, (Klare & Schroeder) r. ns. Bluff rd. 3 n. of
    limits
Schroener William, porter Stewart & Morgan
Schroerluck Bernard, tailor, r. 356 S. Alabama
Schroerluck John, (F. B. Reichter & Co.) r. 165 Stevens
Schrotz Joseph, lab. McCord & Wheatley, r. 30 Coburn
Schroyer Charles F. millwright S. Taggart, r. 25 Bright
Schuer John, cistern builder, r. 382 E. New York
Schuer Paul, r. 431 E. Vermont
Schuerle Frederick, r. es. Illinois 1 s. Wilkins
Schuessler Elizabeth, saleswoman Wm. H. Close & Co.
Schuh John, grocer, 322 Virginia av. r. same
Schuler Fedal, carpenter, r. 301 Winston
Schulmeyer Fred, gas lighter, r. 109 St. Mary
Schulmeyer Henry, butcher Peter Spitzfaden, bds. 252 S. Delaware
Schulmyer Louis C. clk. Stewart & Morgan, bds. sw. cor. Fort
    Wayne av. and New Jersey
Schuls Isaac, lab. r. 471 E. Georgia
Schulte Hermann, flagman, r. 436 S. East
Schultheis Jacob, carpenter Many & Sons, r. 78 S. Delaware
Schultheis John, carpenter, r. 410 S. Illinois
Schultz George, billiard hall, bds. Morrison 2 east of Delaware
Schultz John, blacksmith, r. Morrison 2 east of Delaware
Schulz August, machinist, r. 361 S. Alabama

Schulz Henry, cigars and tobacco, 36 Virginia av. r. 176 S. Delaware

Schulz John, currier J. K. Sharpe, r. 431 E. Georgia

Schumacker Louis, cabinet maker Spiegel & Thoms

Schumaker O. lab. r. 311 E. St. Clair

Schurich Frederick, saloon and grocery, ns. Nat. rd. west of bridge, r. same

Schurman Charles, student, National Business College

Schurr Albert, watchman T. H. & I. R. R.

Schurr Charles, tinner Jacob Voegtte

Schurr Henry, wiper, T. H. & I. R. R.

Schurr John, cistern builder, r. 382 E. New York

Schurr Leonhard, r. 74 Indiana av.

Schurr Leonhard J. jeweler, 74 Indiana av. r. same

Schurr Paul, r. 431 E. Vermont

Schuster Joseph, tailor, r. 521 E. Market

Schutt Charles, lab. round house, r. 525 S. Illinois

Schutter Christian, grocer, 239 S. Meridian, r. same

Schuvert George, r. 328 N. West

Schwab Joseph, r. Cumberland, bet. New Jersey and Alabama

Schwab Leonard, r. Cumberland, bet. New Jersey and Alabama

Schwabacher Joseph, (Schwabacher & Selig) bds. Bates House

SCHWABACHER & SELIG, (Joseph Schwabacher & Abram Selig) wines and liquors, rectifiers and whol. dealers, 41 S. Delaware

Schwartz Charles, clerk G. E. Gordon, r. 173 E. Washington

Schwartz Frederick, painter, r. 339 N. Noble

Schwartz Joseph, (Glick & Schwartz) r. 161 Massachusetts av.

Schwartz Peter, teamster, r. 206 Winston

Schwartzer Joseph, cap maker, 151 E. Washington, r. Coburn

Schwarz Henry, tailor, r. 289 E. Ohio

Schwarz John G. engineer W. Furniture Co. r. 465 N. Alabama

Schwear Christian, student National Business College

Schwear Christian H. (Schwear & Spier) r. 576 E. Washington

Schwear & Spier, (Christian H. Schwear and Frederick Spier) groceries, dry goods, and flour and feed, 574 & 576 E. Washington

Schwegel Daniel, horse collar mnfr. 261 S. Pennsylvania, r. same

Schweinhart Daniel, bricklayer, r. 299 N. East

Schweinhart Edmond, shoemaker, 195 Massachusetts av. r. 68 or 132 St. Mary

Schweinhart Susan, wid. Peter, r. 299 N. East

Schweinsberger William, meat market, 329 S. Delaware, r. same

Schweitzer ——, printer, bds. 83 N. Pennsylvania

Schwicho Charles, grocery and saloon, 224-6 Bluff rd. r. same

Schwinge A. H. salesman H. H. Lee, bds. Patterson House

Schwomeyer Charles H. grocer, 397-9 S. Meridian, r. same

Schwomeyer Christian, drayman, r. 280 E. Michigan

Schwomeyer, Henry, cooper, 308 N. Noble, r. same

Schwomeyer William, cooper Henry Schwomeyer, r. 309 N. Noble

Scofield Sabra A. Miss, teacher Indiana Institution for the Blind

| SCO | 287 | RIZ |

Scollen Edward, puddler Indianapolis Rolling Mill
Scollen Patrick, puddler Indianapolis Rolling Mill
Scott Adam, (Scott & Nicholson) r. 118 N. East
Scott Almond A. salesman G. G. Holman, r. 472 N. East
Scott Amos, lab. r. 229 Winston
Scott Avery G. (Wherrett & Scott) r. 142 N. Mississippi
Scott Charles, carriage trimmer, r. 472 N. East
Scott Charles S. blacksmith Indpls. Coach Works, r. 472 N. East
Scott E. P. (Anderson & Scott) r. New Palestine
Scott Erastus, binder W. & J. Braden, bds. Macy House
Scott George, farmer, r. 304 E. Walnut
Scott Harvey, r. 222 S. East
Scott Harvey, teamster J. Marsee & Son
Scott James P. clk. Pettis, Dickson & Co. bds. Little's Hotel
Scott James W. (Scott, West & Co.) r. Richmond, Ind.
Scott James W. (cold) lab. r. 77 Ann
SCOTT JEFF K. propr. Palmer House, Illinois se. cor. Washington, r. same
Scott John, bkpr. C. E. Geisendorff & Co. r. 59 N. Fayette
Scott John, (col'd) lab. r. 592 N. Mississippi
Scott John, baker W. K. McFarlane, bds. 12 S. Meridian
SCOTT JOHN N. lawyer 32½ E. Washington, r. 179 W. Alabama
Scott Joseph, (col'd) porter, r. 229 Elizabeth
Scott L. E. wid. Erastus, r. 77 Indiana av.
Scott Robert H. engineer, r. 28 N. Noble
SCOTT SAMUEL T. agent Merchants' and People's Despatch, office 19 Virginia av. 271 E. Ohio
Scott Thomas, carpenter J. Marsee & Son, bds. 222 S. East
Scott W. H. clk. C. C. C. & I. Rw. r. 271 E. Ohio
Scott William, carpenter., r. 415 S. Tennessee
Scott William, lab. bds. 198 S. Illinois
Scott William R. farmer, r. 59 Dacotah
SCOTT, WEST & CO. (James W. Scott, J. C. West and John A. Burbank) china, glass and queensware, table cutlery, etc. 127 S. Meridian
SCOTT & NICHOLSON, (Adam Scott and David Nicholson) mnfrs. building stone and contractors, ws. Kentucky av. bet. West and Louisiana
Scovill George W. r. 353 N. Noble
Scraffen James, fireman Gas Works
Scribner George B. (Scribner and Smith) r. 142 Blackford
SCRIBNER & SMITH, George B. Scribner and William Smith) mineral water mnfrs. 64 E. Market. See advt.
Scudder H. M. Mrs. dressmaker. 85 N. New Jersey, r. same
Scudder Henry, miller, r. es. Douglas 1 N. New York
Scudder John, foreman Exchange stables, r. 29 E. Ohio
Scudder Michael R. deputy city marshall, r. 77 E. Washington
Scully Michael, works Kingan & Co. r. al. rear. 75 S. West
Seaman Charles, brakeman, bds. 243 E. Louisiana
Seaman Edwin, (Seaman & Co.) bds. 80 S. Mississippi

SEAMAN & CO. (Edwin Seaman and David H. Strickland) general paper dealers, 74 W. Washington

Seamore Conrad, upholsterer, r. 181 Meek

Sears Martin, watchman T. H. & I. R. R. r. 269 S. Pennsylvania

SEATON E. A. hats, caps, and furs, 25 N. Pennsylvania, r. 25 Gregg

Seaton James, clerk E. A. Seaton, bds. 25 Gregg

Seaton William D. clerk E. A. Seaton, bds. Pyle House

SECOND PRESBYTERIAN CHURCH, Hanford A. Edson pastor, Pennsylvania nw. cor. Vermont

SECOND UNIVERSALIST CHURCH, ns. Michigan bet. Illinois and Tennessee

Second Ward School, ws. Delaware bet. Vermont and Michigan

Secor Sidney B. printer *Journal* job room

Secrest Alice, teacher 7th Ward School, r. 317 S. Alabama

SECREST CHARLES, justice of the peace, 45 E. Washington, r. 317 S. Alabama

Secrest John, watchman, J. M. & I. R. R.

Secrest Nathan, r. 317 S. Alabama

Secrist H. A. confectioner Daggert & Co. r. Hasbrook cor. Cedar

Security Fire Ins. Co. of New York, J. S. Dunlop & Co. agents, 2. W. Washington

SECURITY LIFE INS. AND ANNUITY CO. of New York, William W. Northrop gen. agt. for Ind. and Southern Ill. office No. 2 Blake, block

Seddelmeyer M L. clk. Henry Greenewald, bds. 500 N. Alabama

Sedgewick James, marblecutter LaDow & Calvert

Sedgewick Rodwick, dealer in fancy goods and notions, 68 N. Illinois, r. 129 N Mississippi

Sedenburg Martha A. Mrs. boardinghouse, 24 W. Pearl, r. same

Seeber Sylvanus S. clk. Trade Palace, bds. Palmer House

Seeberger Louisa teacher Sixth Ward School, bds. 207 S. Illinois

Seele Frederick, helper blacksmith, r. 37 Henry

Seele Henry, lab. r. 308 N. Liberty

Seeman Christian, grocer, Washington e. of limits, r. same

Sees Mary, wid. William, r. 136 N. Tennessee

Seger John M. carriage builder, 178 Indiana av. r. 267 N. West

Segar Levi, clothing secondhand, 243 E. Washington, r. same

Scheller Max, physician, 210 E. Ohio, r. same

Sebler Henry, striker, r. 225 S. Alabama

Sebler Henry, jr. wks. Washington Foundry, r. 225 S. Alabama

Sehling Henry, machine hand Cabinet Maker's Union

Seibel Peter, cooper Bernhard Koehring, r. 114 S. Noble

Seibert Cicero, fireman Steamer No. 2

Seibert George W. groceries and provisions, 51 N. Noble, r. same

Seibert Hiram, street contractor, 143 S. East, r. same

Seibert Samuel M. blacksmith, 302 E. Washington, r. 11 N. Liberty

Seidensticker Adolph, (A. Seidensticker & Co.) and pres. German Mutual Fire Ins. Co. 14 S. Delaware, bds. National Hotel

Seidensticker F. saloon, 176 S. Illinois, r. same

Seidensticker Louis, tailor Charles Nilius, r. 145 S. Illinois
SEIDENSTICKER A. & CO. (Adolph Seidensticker and Aegidius Naltner) lawyers and real estate agts. 14 S. Delaware
Seiders M. C. milliner and millinery goods, 3 Martindale's blk.
Seiders William H. state agt. Ins. Co. of North America or Philadelphia, Market ne. cor. Circle, (*Journal* bldg.) r. 426 N. Mississippi
Seidler Gustav, machinist Sinker & Co.
Seifert Augustus, clerk Joseph Smith, r. 13 N. Illinois
Seig George B. r. 91 E. Michigan
Seiter Christoph, cooper M. Seiter, bds. California House
Seiter Kasimir, cooper, Union cor. McCarty, r. 183 Madison av.
Seitz ——, cooper J. S. Carey & Co. r. 55 S. California
Seitz Charles, confectioner, 112 S. Illinois, r. same
SEITZ EREDERICK, saloon and boarding house, 117 S. Illinois
Self Berry (Isaac Davis & Co.) r. 169 Massachusetts av.
Seilig Abram (Schwabacher & Selig) bds. Circle Restaurant
Selking William, tobacconist and saloon 33 N. Pennsylvania, r. 35 S. Delaware
Sell Peter, wagonmkr. bds. Stanridge House
Sellers Daniel, harness and saddle manfr. 17 Virginia av. bds. 17½ Virginia av.
Sellers John H. blacksmith N. Kimball, r. 400 S. Missouri
Sellers Richard, lab. r. 362 E. New York
Sells Michael, stock broker, r. 176 S. New Jersey
Selman Andrew G. physician 21 Virginia av. r 222 E. South
Selman John r. 222 E. South
Selman Thomas, student, r. 222 E. South
Semer Conrad, upholster, Wilkens & Hall, r. 181 Meek
Semon Charles, carpenter, r. Arch bet. Broadway and Jackson
Senior William T. piano forte maker J. H. Kappes & Co. r. 104 W. Vermont
Senour John (J. Senour & Co.) r. 24 W. Michigan
Senour William (J. Senour & Co.) bds. Pyle House
SENOUR J. & CO. (John and William Senour) proprs. City Shoe Store 5 W. Washington
Senn Hannah, wid. Moritz, r. 398 S. Delaware
Sergension J. puddler Indianapolis Rolling Mill
Server A. wks. Kingan & Co.
Server Granville, carpenter, Shover & Christian, r. 114 Plum
Serviss Wilber, bookkeeper J. S. Carey & Co. bds. 191 N. Delaware
Sess Michael, tailor, r. 388 E. Market
Setbert Fred, painter, r. 286 N. Noble
Seute Frederick, lab. C. & I. J. R. R. r. 182 Bates
SEVENTH PRESBYTERIAN CHURCH, C. M. Howard pastor, Cedar cor. Elm
Seventh Ward School, ns. East bet. Louisiana and Georgia
Severin Henry,(Severin & Schnull) r. New Jersey cor. New York
SEVERIN & SCHNULL, (Henry Severin, Henry Schnull and Berg Applegate) wholesale grocers 137 and 139 S. Meridian

19

SEW	290	SHA

Sewall Elmer C. salesman Mayhew & Branham
Sexaner Edward, grocer 125 E. Washington, r. same
Sexton John, comp. *Journal* newsroom, bds. 69 W. Market
Seybold Anton, beam hand J. Fishback
Seybold J. H. marble dealer, r. 233 E. Ohio
Shackelford John S. r. 94 W. 1st
Shackleton Joseph, patternmaker, r. 283 S. East
Shackleton Sarah, bookbinder *Journal* Bookbindery
Shafer August, shoemaker, r. 191½ W. Washington
Shafer Adolphus, shoemaker 327 E. Washington, r. Noble cor. Market
Shafer Carrie P. Miss, r. 351 E. Market
Shafer Henry, watchman, r. 106 N. Spring
Shafer L. J. carpenter Hill & Wingate, r. 276 S. East
Shafer Mellie Miss, r. 351 E. Market
Shaffer G. sawer McKendry & Lovecraft
Shaffer James, shoemaker, r. 161 W. South
Shaffer John, butcher, bds. ns. Kansas nr. Canal
Shaffer John, shoemaker, r. 161 W. South
Shaffer Nancy A. wid. Jacob, r. 308 E. Ohio
Shaffer Susey V. bds. 308 E. Ohio
Shaffer William, porter Andrew Wallace, r. alley bet. Tennessee and Mississippi 3d and 4th
Shako Charles, machinist Greenleaf & Co.
Shaler Henry, blksmith helper C. C. C. & I. R. R.
Shaler Henry, boilermaker Eagle Works, r. 225 S. Alabama
Shaler John, engineer, r. es. Kentucky av. 3 s. of West
Shaler Joseph, boilermaker Eagle Machine Works, r. Massachusetts av. nr. toll house on Pendleton rd.
Shallenberger Alexander, carpenter, r. 468 N. Delaware
Shaneberger David, trav. agt. Howe Sewing Machine, r. ss. New York bet. Delaware and Alabama
Shaneberger William A. carpenter, r. ss. New York bet. Delaware and Alabama
Shank Benjamin, teamster, r. 219 N. Davidson
Shannon Charles T. law student, bds. 92 E. New York
Shannon James, botanist, r. 121 W. New York
Shannon Sarah, boardinghouse, 126 E. Ohio
Shannon Thomas A. jeweler William H. Craft, bds. Market nw. cor. Pennsylvania
Share George K. (George K. Share & Co.) r. 332 N. Alabama
SHARE GEORGE K. & CO. (George K. Share and ——) whol. saddlery, hardware and carriage material, 49 S. Meridian
Sharff Nathan, clerk, r. 178 Virginia av.
Sharpe Mrs. wid. r. 110 Union
Sharpe Andrew W. cigars and tobacco, 28 N. Pennsylvania and 73 E. Market, r. 193 S. New Jersey
Sharpe Calvin L. clerk A. W. Sharpe, bds. 193 S. New Jersey
Sharpe Ebenezer (H. L. Benham & Co.) and banker, r. 564 N. Pennsylvania
Sharpe George, cigarmaker Back & Wenken, r. 123 Meek

Sharpe James, r. 441 S. Illinois
Sharpe John, blacksmith Bremerman & Renner
Sharpe John S. clerk, r. 193 S. New Jersey
Sharpe Joseph K. hide and leather dealer, 47 and 49 S. Delaware, r. N. Pennsylvania nr. corporation line
Sharpe Stephen, engineer I. P. Evans & Co. r. 255 S. Alabama
Sharpe Thomas H. cashier Indianapolis Branch Bankidg Co. (F. & S.) r. 239 N. Pennsylvania
Sharpless Pennell, (Case Parker & Co.) r. 71 N. Califorma
Shattuck David J. engineer C. C. C. & I. R. R. r. 393 Massachusetts av.
Shatz Christian (Shatz & Stortz) r. 369 S. Delaware
Shatz & Stortz, (Christian Shatz and John M. Stortz) meat market, 369 S. Delaware
Shaughnessy Catherine, wid. Thomas, r. 179 Madison av
Shaughnessy James, hooker Rolling Mill
Shaughnessy John, tender P. Welch, r. 46 S. Bicking
Shaughnessy John, roller Rolling Mill
Shaughnessy Peter, lab. r. 311 Merrill
Shaughnessy Thomas, lab. r. 41 Dacotah
Shaver Peter, drayman, r. 567 E. St. Clair
Shaw ——, sawyer, r. 526 N. Mississippi
Shaw Augustus T. brakeman, r. 222 Winston
Shaw Benjamin C. (Shaw, Lippincott & Conner,) r. Illinois ne. cor. Pratt
Shaw Edward, r. McGill ne. cor. South
Shaw Frank, fireman C. C. & I. C. R. R.
Shaw Griffin M. clk. G. B. Williams, bds. 30 W. Maryland
Shaw Henry, carriage trimmer Indianapolis Coach Works, r. Pratt ne. cor. Illinois
Shaw James C. wood-worker Indianapolis Coach Works, r. 219 Buchanan
Shaw Lucien, law student Ritter & Irvin, bds. 320 N. East
Shaw Melinda, r. 146 E. McCarty
Shaw Thomas, banker, r. 239 N. Pennsylvania
SHAW, LIPPINCOTT & CONNER, (Benj. C. Shaw, Samuel R. Lippincott and James H. Conner,) proprs. Indianapolis Coach Works, 26, 28 and 30 E. Georgia
Shawver A. P. saddlemaker James W. Sulgrove & Co. r. 297 Indiana av.
Shawver Christopher J. saddler, 297 Indiana av. r. same
Shay B. wks. J. S. Carey & Co.
Shay Cornelius, lab. r. 187 w. New York
Shay Ellen, r. 16 E. Michigan
Shay James, lab. Rolling Mill, r. 345 S. Missouri
Shay John, lab. I. & T. H. depot, r. 276 S. Delaware
Shay Mary, wid. John, r. 162 Meek
Shay Patrick, lab. r. Georgia sw. cor. Helen
Shay Patrick, wks. J. C. Ferguson & Co.
Shay Timothy, lab. r. 497 E. Georgia
Shay Timothy, lab. r. 501 E. Georgia

Shea James R. court bailiff, r. 520 N. Delaware

Shea James W. bookkeeper Greenleaf & Co. bds. Spencer House

Shea John, actor, bds. 74 N. Pennsylvania

Shea Michael, contractor, r. 520 N. Delaware

Shea Thomas, blacksmith, r. 343 Winston

Shead C. woodworker S. W. Drew, r. 101 Davidson

Sheaff William, brakeman, r. 308 E. Louisiana

Shear Lou, dressmaker, 10 S. Mississippi, r. same

Shearer Frederick, teamster, r. 518 S. Illinois

Shearer John W. carpenter, r. 456 E. Georgia

Sheerer Adam, shoemaker, r. 23 Grant

Sheerer John, brewer, r. 220 S. Meridian

Sheesley Eli, (Heckman & Sheesley) r. 317 E. Washington

Sheets David, grocery, 241 W. McCarty, r. same

SHEETS WILLIAM, blank book mnfr. printer, stationer, 79 W. Washington, r. N. Pennsylvania se. cor. Ohio

Sheets William H. H. r. Westfield Pike

Shehan Daniel, lab. r. 237 S. West

Shehan Dennis, lab. r. 72 N. Railroad

Shehan Jerry, lab. r. 90 N. Railroad

Shehan Timothy, lab. r. 72 Benton

Shelburn Richard, (col'd) lab. r. es. Douglas 4 s. New York

Shelladay Isham, (col'd) lab. r. 288 Railroad

Shellenberger John, gardener, r. 298 N. New Jersey

Shellman Harry J. agt. A. Frank Noble, r. 174 E. New York

Shelly Thornton, (col'd) lab. Palmer House

Shelt William W. salesman Dessar, Bro. & Co. bds. Bates House

Sheltmeyer Christian, engineer C. C. & I. C. R. R. bds. Stanridge House

Sheltmier Christopher, wks. King & Pinney, bds. Wyle House

Shenaman William, lab. r. 148 Bluff rd.

Shepard James E. clk. J. M. & I. R. R. r. 270 S. Alabama

Shepard Jonathan F. carpenter, r. Kentucky av. cor. Merrill

Shepard M. wid. David, dress maker, r. 331 N. New Jersey

Shepard Thomas L. carpenter, r. Kentucky av. cor. Merrill

Shepherd James M. agt. J. P. Meikel, r. 213 W. Maryland

Shepherd James McB. saloon and garden 156 E. Washington, r. W. Maryland bet. West and Canal

Shepherd John, (col'd) lab. r. Rhode Island nr. Blake

Sheridan Barney, moulder Union Novelty Works

Sheridan Eliza, weaver Merritt & Coughlen, bds. W. Blake

Sheridan John, lab. Union Novelty Works

Sheridan John, driver Citizens' Street R. R. Co.

Sheridan John, lab. A. D. Wood

Sheridan John, bellboy Bates House

Sheridan John, lab. r. 20 Maria

Sheridan Peter H. clk. Pettis, Dickson & Co. bds. 60 W. Market

Sherman Charles H. salesman Trade Palace, bds. Pyle House

Sherman De Roy, trav. agt. James F. Mick, r. 243 W. McCarty

Sherman Gustavus, r. 258 N. Pennsylvania

SHERMAN HOUSE, (W. M. Hawkins) Louisiana opp. Union depot

Buy your Hats, Caps and Furs at I. Davis & Co. 12 E. Washington.

SHE   293   SHO

Sherman Paul harnessmaker Ad. Hereth, r. 62 Indiana av.
Sherman S. H. clk. bds. Pyle House
Sherwood Frederick W. (Millner & Sherwood) bds. Nat. Hotel
SHERWOOD LYMAN Q. general southwestern agt. for Russell's reapers and mowers and Massillon thresher, 79, 81 N. Illinois (Academy of Music blk.) r. 556 N. Illinois
Sherwood William O. carpenter and builder, r. 23 N. West
Shick Gottfred, butcher J. Ross, bds. 137 S. Illinois
Shields Cain, lab. r. 406 S. West
Shields James, r. 26 Biddle
Shields K. moulder Sinker & Co.
Shields William, works J. C. Ferguson & Co. r. 228 W. Georgia
Shildmeyer Anthony, r. 375 E. Michigan
Shilling C. D. trunkmaker R. L. Shilling, bds. 299 N. New Jersey
Shilling Nicholas, porter P. O. r. 292 N. Liberty
SHILLING RICHARD L. trunk mnfr. 55 W. Washington, r. 299 N. New Jersey
Shilling R. W. trunkmaker R. L. Shilling, r. 120 N. Tennessee
Shilling William, engineer City Laundry, r. 109 N. Illinois
Shiltmeyer Antony, (Reasner & Shiltmeyer) r. country
Shindler Oscar, clerk Clemens Vonnegut, r. 154 E. Washington
Shine John, lab. r. 116 Stevens
Shinners Ella, milliner J. B. Conaty, bds. 44 S. Illinois
Shipp Joseph P. clk. Landers, Conduitt & Co. r. 30 W. Maryland
Shipp S. Milton bookkeeper Rickard & Talbott, bds. 30 W. Maryland
Shippey John, wks. Rolling Mill, r. 273 S. Tennessee
Shissler David, clerk M. Burton, bds. Stanridge House
Shivers William, puller Rolling Mill
Shlott Sarah, wid. William H. r. 88 N. California
Shmrlsegarg Mathias, tinner, r. 76 Garden
Shoe John, moulder, bds. 174 W. New York
Shoemaker Amanda J. teacher 9th Ward School, r. 171 N. Davidson
Shoemaker Charles, trunkmaker M. Burton, r. 45 Fletcher av.
Shoemaker Fred, real estate agent, r. 45 Fletcher av.
Shoemaker George, teamster, r. 149 E. Washington
Shoemaker George, clerk H. Rentsch
Shoemaker John, cabinetmaker, r. 45 Fletcher av.
Shoemaker Otto, trunkmaker M. Burton, r. 45 Fletcher av.
Short William, paperhanger W. H. Roll, bds. Ohio House
SHORTRIDGE ABRAHAM C. (Shortridge & Alden) supt. Public Schools, also (Indianapolis Printing and Publishing Co.) office High School, r. 195 Jackson
Shortridge & Alden, (A. C. Shortridge and John B. Alden) publishers of the *Little Chief*, 18 S. Pennsylvania
Shover Charles, carpenter Shover & Christian, bds. 30½ N. Pennsylvania
Shover James E. (Shover & Christian) r. 318 N. Delaware
SHOVER & CHRISTIAN (J. E. Shover and W. F. Christian) carpenters and builders 124 E. Vermont

SHO	294	SIM

Showalter Samuel, groceries 258 Indiana av. r. same
Showe William, lab. Union Starch Factory, r. east end Michigan
Showergt Michael, wagonmkr. r. 22 E. Ray
Shrewsbery ——, hardware clk. bds. Pyle House
Shriner William, porter drug store, r. 307 S. Pennsylvania
Shrœder Charles, grocer 299 S. Delaware, r. same
Shrœnluk John, grocer, r. 165 Stevens
Shrœr Henry H. grocer 260 S. Alabama, r. same
Shue Wolf, moulder Union Novelty Works
Shughraw Michael, lab. r. 130 Meek
Shuh John, engineer D. Root & Co.
Shuh Samuel, moulder, B. F. Hetherington & Co. bds. 19 Madison av.
Sheelmyer Louis, druggist, r. New Jersey junc. Fort Wayne av.
Shulo Amelia, wid. Henry, r. 175 Union
Shultise Michael, carpenter, r. 468 S. Illinois
Shultz John P. lab. Greenleaf & Co. r. 228 Spring
Shultz Lawrence, bds. 191 W. South
Shumacher John cabinetmkr. P. Dohn
Shurman William, tally clk. J. M. & I. R. R.
Shute Alfred, patent right dealer, r. 249 N. Mississippi
Shute Mary, weaver Hoosier Woolen Factory
Shutts C. cooper J. S. Carey & Co.
Shutts John, cooper J. S. Carey & Co. r. 6 Carey's Row (Helen st.)
Sibings William, engineer ns. Georgia bet. Liberty and Noble
Sibird David, r. 205 E. Market
Sickels William W. Rev. r. 351 N. East
Siddall James H. student, r. 227 E. Louisiana
SIDDALL JAMES P. physician and surgeon, 166 Virginia av. r. 227 E. Louisiana
Sides David T. ins. agt. r. 74 E. Pratt
Sides Thomas, ins. agt. r. 74 E. Pratt
Sidney Amos (col'd) waiter, r. opp. City Hospital
Siecrist John, watchman, r. E. Ohio, e. of city limits
Siegrist S. pastor St. Mary's Catholic Church, r. 75 E. Maryland
Sielking Louis, clerk H. Lieber & Co. bds. 467 N. Delaware
Siemon Anthony, lab. r. Washington east of limits
Siepold A. tinner, bds. Tennessee cor. 7th
Sier Nettie, wid. Frederick, r. 200 Bates
Siersdorfer Louis, mnfr. and dealer in boots and shoes, 41. E. Washington, r. 187 Virginia av.
Sihmehl Henry, moulder D. Root & Co.
Sikes Joseph, (col'd) lab. Budd & Hensley, bds. Michigan cor. West
Silvers Angeline, dressmaker Anna Silvers, r. 305 E. Washington
Silvers Anna, milliner & dressm'kr. 305 E. Washington, r. same
Silvers Emma, dressmaker Anna Silvers, r. 305 E. Washington
Silvers Luvenia, dressmaker Anna Silvers, r. 305 E. Washington
Silvers Lucretia, dressmaker Anna Silvers, r. 305 E. Washington
Simcox John W. saddler, r. 120 Massachusetts av.
Simcox Samuel, machinist, r. 35 Ellen

Simmelink Mary, wid. William, r. 299 E. Ohio
Simmerman Gotlieb, butcher, r. 211 W. Michigan
Simmons Hermann, optician, 43 S. Illinois, r. same
Simms Addison, wks. Simms & Hoskins, r. 423 N. Mississippi
Simms James A. tar roofer, r. 433 N. Mississippi
Simms John, carpenter, r. 25 W. St. Clair
Simms John M. (Simms & Hoskins) r. 423 N. Mississippi
SIMMS & HOSKINS, (John M. Simms and Robert S. Hoskins)
  composition roofers, agts. State of Indiana for Burns patent
  Concrete Paving, ws. Canal bet. Georgia and Louisiana
Simon Andrew, porter Holland, Ostermeyer & Co. r. E. Wash-
  ington e. of city limits
Simon Charles, carpenter W. H. Henschen
Simon Christian, lab. r. 263 N. Noble
Simon Frederick, grocer, 188 N. Noble, r. same
Simon James C. carpenter, r. 52 Cherry
Simon John P. Frenzel & Simon) r. 344 E. Market
Simonds Gustavus B. supt. White River Iron Co. r. 552 S. Me-
  ridian
Simons Louisa, (col'd) wid. John, r. 202 W. 2d
Simpson Charley, stonecutter, r. 33 Grant
Simpson J. P. carpenter, r. 183 Meek
Simpson James, lab. Noel & Son, r. 103 S. New Jersey
Sympson Jeptha E. bookkeeper W. I. Haskit & Co. bds. Pyle
  House
Simpson John, (Schetter & Simpson) r. 99 E. South
Simpson John, lab. r. ns. Nat. rd. w. of bridge
SIMPSON JOHN E. asst. supt. T. H. & I. R. R. office Louisiana av.
  sw. cor. Tennessee, bds. Virginia av. cor. Alabama
Simpson Nicholas, grocer, 235 S. Delaware, r. 263 S. Delaware
Simpson Oliver, clerk E. E. Case, bds. 520 N. Illinois
Simpson Oliver, lab. r. 459 E. Georgia
Simpson Richard, flour and feed, 19 S. Delaware, r. 325 S. Del-
  aware
Sincox Samuel, machinist Phœnix Machine Works
Sindlinger Gotfred, meat market, 194 S. Illinois, r. same
Singel Abdon, saloon, 176 E. Washington, r. same
Singer Mnfg. Co. M. J. Oatman, agt. 16 N. Delaware
Singleton William, (col'd) expressman, r. 131 Bright
Sinker Edward T. (Sinker & Co.) r. 84 W. Vermont
SINKER & CO. (Edward T. Sinker, Daniel and George B. Yandes)
  proprs. Western Machine Works, 125 S. Pennsylvania
Sinkes Alfred T. sawmnfr. r. es. Western av. bet. Butler and
  Forrest Home av.
Sinks Frank, teamster, r. ns. Wabash al. bet. New Jersey and
  N. East
Sinks James, carpenter, r. 69 W. Market
Sinks Laura, wid. George, r. 75 W. First
Sipf Minnie Miss, baker Institute for the Blind, r. same
Sipp C. machinist Phœnix Machine Works r 512 N. Mississippi
Sipple James, wks. J. S. Carey & Co.

SIP	296	SMA

Sipple John, wks. J. S. Carey & Co.

Sisco Henry C. foreman Osgood, Smith & Co. r. 445 S. Illinois

Sisco Joel, r. 445 S. Illinois

Sisco Joseph, lab. Osgood, Smith & Co.

Sixth Ward School, Union bet. Maryland and McCarty, Ellen A. Davis, principal

SKILLEN JAMES, propr. Ætna Flour Mill 356–358 W. Washington, r. 48 N. West

Skillen Wm. M. bookkeeper James Skillen, bds same

Skinner Ellison E. tailor, 62 S. Illinois, r. 124 W. Sixth

Skinner John, brick layer, r. 1 Cumberland

Skinner John, clk. W. De Ruiter & Bro. bds. 65 S. Illinois

Slate Benjamin F. teamster McCord & Wheatley, r. 215 Coburn

Slate Henry, lab. McCord & Wheatly

Slater R. mail agt. r. 41 Bradshaw

Slatterry William, lab. frt. depot C. C. & I. C. R. R. r. 3 Bates

Slaughter James L. teller First National Bank of Indianapolis, r. 352 N. Meridian

Slaughter Milton, carpenter, r. 203 Meek

Slaven Ann Mrs. r. 131 N. East

Sleith James, harnessmkr. W. S. Marsh, bds. 185 W. Maryland

Slevin Mariah, wid. James r. 82 E. South

Slife John, watchman F. Wright's Brewery, r. es. Minerva 2 s. New York

Slinger Henry, pedler, r. 293 E. Market

Sloan Andrew J. wood yard, bds. 163 N. Noble

Sloan George W. (Browning & Sloan) r. 350 N. Illinois

Sloan J. carpenter, Gilkey & Jones

Sloan John, r. 230 N. Tennessee

Sloan Maggie, dressmaker 50 S. Illinois, bds. 113 Massachusett av.

Sloan Maggie Miss, milliner, bds. 173 Jackson

Sloan Robert, wrapper L. H. Tyler & Co. bds. 230 N. Tennessee

Sloan Sarah, Miss, teacher 6th Ward School, r. 230 N. Tennessee

Sloan William G. r. 142 Bates

SLOANE EDWARD W. supt. A. M. U. Ex. Co. 42 and 44 E. Washington, r. 451 N. Tennessee cor. Pratt

Sloane James K. carpenter, r. 638 N. Mississippi

Sloniger Christian, teamster, r. Cumberland bet. New Jersey and Alabama

Sloninger John, planer Warren Tate, r. Cumberland alley bet. New Jersey and Alabama

Sloss Robert, pastor 3d Presbyterian Church, r. 198 N. Illinois

Slosser Henry, huckster, r. 432 S. West

Slusher Henry, jeweler, 172 W. Washington, r. 119 Blake

Slusser Michael, brewer, r. 185 Madison av.

Smalezergang Mathias, currier Mooney & Co. r. 76 Garden

Small B. F. printer, bds. Palmer House

Small Charles A. r. Michigan rd. nr. junc. Washington

Small David, carpenter, r. 89 Jackson

Small Elizabeth, wid. Rody A r. Michigan rd. nr. junc. Washington

Small Henry, custom tailor, 8 E. Washington, r. 144 W. N. York
Small Jerome N. engineer I. C. & L. Rw. r. 111 Mock
Small Louisa, dressmkr. Mrs. M. A. Obmeyer, r. 83 E. Michigan
Smallholtz John, r. 64 N. Noble
Smallwood William, lab. r. 121 N. Noble
Smelser Frank, (Lines, Smelser & Co.) r. 188 S. Mississippi
SMITH see SCHMIDT, SCHMIT, SCHMITT, SCHMIDTH, SMIDT, SMYTHE.
Smith ——, (col'd) lab. r. 190 N. Missouri
Smith —— Mrs. r. rear 116 Ash
Smith —— Mrs. wid. r. 7. Ellsworth
Smith —— Mrs. works Paper Mill, r. 423 W. Washington (Nat. rd.)
Smith A. machinist C. C. & I. C. R. R.
Smith Albert, (col'd) hair worker Charles Neven, r. Minerva bet. North & Michigan
Smith Alexander, student rooms, 110 Massachusetts av.
Smith Amos B. coachmkr. J. B. Hampton, bds. 365 W. Vermont
Smith Andrew, bartender Peter E. Doman, bds. 18 S. Delaware
Smith Andrew, engineer, r. 96 Bates
Smith Arthur H. checkman frt. office T. H. & I. R. R. r. 299 N. New Jersey
Smith August, (A. & C. Smith) r. 23 Charles
Smith Augustus, machinist, bds. 61 S. Noble
Smith Aurelius, printer Indianapolis Printing and Publishing House, r. 70 N. Mississippi
Smith Benjamin W. engineer W. & J. Braden, r. 301 S. East
Smith Butler K. (Butler, Smith, & Harlan) r. 319 E. North
Smith C. wks. J. S. Carey & Co.
Smith C. M. with Singer Mnfrg. Co; bds. 112 N. Pennsylvania
Smith Charles, (A. & C. Smith) r. 23 Charles
Smith Charles, yardman T. H. & I. R. R.
Smith Charles, carpenter S. W. Cochrane
Smith Charles, R. roller Rolling Mill
SMITH CHARLES W. Jr. attorney at law and notary public, No. 5 Yohn's Block, Meridian ne. cor. Washington, bds. Pyle House
SMITH CHEMICAL DYE WORKS, 32 N. Missouri, office 62 E. Market, see advt. Index
Smith Christian, r. 120 Dacotah
Smith Christian, (Smith, Ittenbach & Co.) r. 131 Stevens
Smith Clara, school teacher, bds. 144 N. Tennessee
Smith Columbus, (col'd) lab. r. Missouri nr. Tinker
Smith David, lab. r. 446 Indiana av.
Smith David, wks. Kingan & Co. r. 35 Blake
Smith E. Athlee, Dancing Academy, Yohn's blk. r. 146 Buchanan
Smith E. M. physician, office 40 N. Pennsylvania, r. same
Smith Eben, (Strong & Smith) r. 76 N. New Jersey
Smith Ebenezer, bds. Pyle House
Smith Elizabeth B. wid. Caleb B. r. 296 W. New York
Smith Eliza J. wid. Isaac, r. 70 N. Mississippi
Smith Ellen, wid. Michael, r. 285 S. East

Smith Elen, wid. Washington, r. 171 S. Alabama
Smith Emily, (col'd) wid. William, r. rear 241 W. Ohio
Smith Emma, bookbinder J. H. C. Smith
Smith Enoch H. teamster, r. 11 S. Alabama
Smith F. J. carpenter, r. 60 N. Railroad
Smith Francis, (F. Smith & Co. r. Tennessee nw. cor. 3d
Smith Frank, compositor *Sentinel* book and job room, r. 70 N. Mississippi
Smith Frank, lab. Rolling Mill, r. 493 S. Tennessee
Smith Frank E. (Smith & Marshall) r. Noble se. cor. Fletcher av.
Smith Fred, blacksmith C. C. C. & I. R. R.
Smith Frederick, grocer, 200 N. Mississippi, r. 468 N. Tennessee
Smith Fisk, puddler Indianapolis Rolling Mill
SMITH FULLER, Citizens' Carriage and Wagon Mnfy., Liberty, se. cor. Washington, r. 138 Virginia av.
Smith George, lab. Union Novelty Works
Smith George F. engineer I. C. & L. Rw. r. 524 N. Mississippi
Smith George M. drayman, r. Elizabeth n. of Patterson
Smith George T. clerk, E. A. Seaton, bds. 229 N. New Jersey
Smith George W. B. printer Indianapolis Printing and Publishing House, r. 39 Virginia av.
Smith H. B. lab. Osgood, Smith & Co.
Smith Harriett, wid. William, r. 467 S. Illinois
Smith Harris, r. 296 W. New York
Smith Harry Rev. editor Indiana *Standard*, r. 400 N. New Jersey
Smith Henry, clk. William Selking, r. Alabama, se. cor. Market
Smith Henry, fireman J. M. & I. R. R.
Smith Henry, saloon, r. 47 N. Alabama
Smith Henry B. freight agt. I. P. & C. Rw. bds. Pyle House
Smith Henry C. brakeman, bds. 62 Bates
Smith Herman, r. 282 N. Liberty
Smith Horace B. r. 20 W. Georgia
Smith Hubert H. carpenter, r. Morrison nr. cor. Alabama
Smith Hugh H. shoemaker, r. 49 N. Alabama
Smith Isaac, peddler, r. 325 S. Tennessee
Smith J. H. shippingclk. Crossland, Hanna & Co. bds. Sherman House
Smith J. W. (Smith & Foster) and agt. Florence Sewing Machine, r. 123 N. Illinois
Smith Jacob, (col'd) lab. r. North nr. cor. Blackwell
Smith Jacob, (col'd) lab. r. 102 Howard
Smith Jacob W. ruler W. & J. Braden, bds. 86 N. California
Smith James, salesman Pettis, Dickson & Co. r. 50 W. New York
Smith James, lab. J. Fishback
Smith James, r. 62 Bates
Smith James, supt. Home of the Friendless, r. N. Pennsylvania n. of limits
Smith James C. carpenter, r. 394 S. Delaware
Smith James H. trav. agent. r. 219 Virginia av.
Smith James H. V. clerk Merrill & Co. r. 225 S. New Jersey
Smith James L. brakeman I. C. & L. R. R. bds. Ray House

Smith James W. telegraph oporator, r. 368 E. New York
Smith John, (col'd) barber Knox & Embers
Smith John, lab. Street Car Stables, r. 70 Fayette
Smith John, (col'd) lab. r. 217 W. 2d
Smith John, shoemaker, r. 69 Bright
Smith John, stonecutter Scott & Nicholson
Smith John, works Emerson, Beam & Thompson
SMITH JOHN B. Chemical Dye Works, 32 N. Missouri, oflice 62
  E. Market and 307 E. Washington, r. 307 E. Washington
Smith John C. (Rev.) agt. Globe Mutual Life Ins. Co. of N. Y.
  11 N. Meridian, r. 229 N. New Jersey
Smith John C. carpenter, r. 86 James
Smith John C. yardmaster, r. 171 S. New Jersey
Smith John G. blacksmith 36 S. Penn. r. 162 N. New Jersey
Smith John P. r. 320 E. Vermont
SMITH JOHN T. publisher *Hotel Register* and blankbook mnfr.
  27 S. Meridian
Smith John W. cigar maker, N. W. Reynolds, r. 273 E. North
Smith John W. clk. John Furnas & Co. bds. Pattison House
Smith John W. lab. r. 62 Bates
Smith John W. medical student J. F. Ridgway
Smith Jonah, real estate agt. r. 385 W. New York
Smith Jonathan, printer, rooms 39 Virginia av.
Smith Joseph, fruits and confectionary, 13 N. Illinois, r. same
Smith Joseph W. merchant, r. 123 N. Illinois
Smith Josiah, (J. Smith & Co.) r. 385 W. New York
Smith Julius H. C. book-binder, mnf'r blank books and paper
  boxes, Circle sc. cor. Meridian, r. 329 N. Illinois
Smith Lawrence, porter, r. 72 N. Davidson
Smith Lizzie Mrs. milliner, 40 S. Illinois, bds. Pyle House
Smith M. r. 127 Indiana av.
Smith Maria, wid. Edward, r. 141 W. Washington
Smith Martha, wid. Stephen, r. 162 N. Mississippi
Smith Mary, wid. Henry, r. 276 W. Washington
Smith Mary, saleslady Mrs. E. I. Fisk, r. 84 Michigan Row
Smith Mary A. wid. Joseph, r. 35 Blake
Smith Matthew, lab. r. es. Douglas, 3 s. New York
Smith Matthew, painter Phœnix Machine Works
Smith Mattie, bookbinder J. H. C. Smith
Smith Nathaniel, currier J. R. Sharpe, r. 368 E. New York
Smith Norton R. (N. R. Smith & Co.) r. 203 N. Illinois
Smith Octivi, wid. James, r. 335 N. Liberty
Smith Peter C. carpenter, r. 231 W. Ohio
Smith Patrick H. foreman, r. 232 S. Tennessee
Smith Patrick, Jr. helper Rolling Mill
Smith Richardson, lab. r. Michigan rd. cor. 8th
Smith Richard, (col'd) lab. bds. 172 W. Georgia
Smith Robert drug clerk, bds. 230 W. Ohio
Smith Robert, printer, rooms 39 Virginia av.
Smith Robert A. compositor *Sentinel* job room, bds. Webb
  House

SMI	300	SMI

Smith Robert L. (R. L. Smith & Co. confectioners) r. 167 N. Ilinois

Smith Robert L. (R. L. Smith & Co. trunk mnfrs.) r. 385 W. New York

Smith Samuel, shoemaker, bds. Fatout's Block

Smith Samuel F. (Osgood, Smith & Co.) r. 28 Fort Wayne av.

Smith Samuel S. lab. r. 22 E. Ray

Smith Samuel S. mnfr. of plug tobacco, 312 S. Delaware, r. 121 E. Duncan

Smith Sarah J. Mrs. city missionary, r. Home of the Friendless

Smith Senator, (col'd) mason, r. 107 Howard

Smith Socrates, lab r. Missouri nr. Tinker

Smith Sophia, r. 148 E. Pratt

Smith Sophia, wid. James, r. 196 Bates

Smith Squire, salesman John Jordan, r. 230 W. Ohio

Smith Susan, dressmaker Mrs. F· Jarrell, r. 377 N. Illinois

Smith Susan A. wid. John, r. es. Winston, 4 n. New York

Smith Thomas, r. 162 N. Mississippi

Smith Thomas, lab. r. 113 N. West

Smith Thomas R. catcher Rolling Mill

Smith W. A. saloon 40 W. Louisiana, r. same

Smith William, r. 97 N. Delaware

Smith William, baker W. K. McFarlane, bds. 12 S. Meridian

Smith William, blksmith John J. Gates, r. 330 S. Alabama

Smith William, bookbinder, r. 162 N. Mississippi

Smith Willam, lab. I. C. & L. R. R.

Smith William, (Scribner & Smith) bds. Wabash alley bet. New Jersey and East

Smith William, watchman, r. 195 Bates

Smith William W. r. 203 W. South

Smith William C. harnessmaker J. M. Huffer & Son, bds. 341 N. Alabama

Smith William H. bookbinder Julius H. C. Smith, r. 162 N. Mississippi

Smith William H. bkpr. Mooney & Co. bds. 162 N. New Jersey

Smith William J. foreman, r. 121 E. Duncan

Smith William P. surveyor, r. 248 N. East

Smith William S. fruit dealer, r. 619 N. Illinois

Smith William Q. foreman Osgood, Smith & Co. r. 20 W. Georgia

Smith William Q. (Smith & Goodhart) r. 180 N. East

Smith A & C. (August and Charles Smith) meat market 221 Massachusetts av.

SMITH FRANK & CO. (Francis Smith and M. W. Boyles) real estate and ins. agents, room 4 Odd Fellows' Hall

SMITH, ITTENBACH & CO. (Christian Smith, Gerhard Ittenbach and Frank Ittenbach) stoneyard two squares east of Noble, bet. Harrison and Lord

Smith Josiah & Co. (Josiah Smith and ———) real estate agts. 16½ S. Meridian

SMITH N. R. & CO. (N. R. Smith and G. A. Eaton) dry goods whol. and ret. Trade Palace, 26 and 28 W. Washington

SMITH R. L. & CO. (Robert L. Smith and ———) confectioners whol. 40 W. Washington

SMITH R. L. & CO. (R. L. Smith and ———) trunk mnfrs. 16½ S. Meridian

SMITH & FOSTER, (J. W. Smith and Wallace Foster) mnfrs and dealers in gents' furnishing goods, 27 N. Pennsylvania

SMITH & GOODHART, (W. Q. Smith and B. F. Goodhart) storage and com. mers. Delaware se. cor. Virginia av.

SMITH & MARSHALL, (Frank E. Smith and W. W. Marshall) grocers Noble se. cor. Fletcher av.

Smither James W. (Daggett & Co.) r. 24 W. North

Smither John, livery stable 149 S. Mississippi, r. 184 N. Tennessee

Smither John N. bookkeeper, Chandler & Taylor

Smithers Henry, com. mer. r. 368 N. Mississippi

Smithers William, grocer, r. 34 W. North

Smithson Issac, lab. r. W. Indianapolis

Smock C. wks. J. S. Carey & Co.

Smock Charles, lab. Osgood, Smith & Co.

Smock Charles, teamster, bds. 266 S. Illinois

Smock George W. auctioneer D. B. Taylor & Co. r. 22 Fletcher av.

Smock Huston, express messenger

Smock James, wks. J. S. Carey & Co.

Smock John, wks. J. S. Carey & Co.

Smock Marcellus, express messenger

Smock Mattie, dressmaker, r. 38½ S. Illinois

Smock Newton, express messenger, r. 40 Huron

Smock Peter, bookkeeper Davis & Jones, r. 229 Virginia av.

Smock Peter, Quartermaster State of Indiana, r. cor. Market and Tennesse

Smock Peter, teamster, bds. 271 Virginia av.

Smock Richard, cooper, r. 68 S. California

Smock Richard M. depty. county clerk, r. Western av. bet. Butler and Forest Home av.

Smock Samuel J. r. 36 N. New Jersey

Smock W. switchman C. C. C. & I. Rw.

Smock William, lab. r. ss. Bates bet. Noble and Benton

SMOCK WILLIAM C. County Clerk office, County Bldg. Court House square, r. 410 N. Delaware

Smock William H. conductor, r. 344 N. Noble

Smucker Louis, cabinetmaker, r. 253 N. Noble

Snaghble John, lab. r. 507 N. Mississippi

Snell Louis, teamster, r. 339 S. East

Snider R. J. clerk Snider & Lackey, r. Virginia bet. Dougherty and Coburn

Snider Adam, porter D. Root & Co. r. 106 St. Mary

Snider Charles D. (Snider & Lackey) r. 85 Bradshaw

Snider Fred bds. 217 S. Illinois

Snider George W. bkpr. Anderson, Bullock & Schofield, bds. Pyle House

SNIDER WILLIAM H. drugs and medicines ret. South cor. East, r. 199 S. East

Snow William H. machinist, r. 282 N. Alabama

Snider & Lackey, Charles D. Snider and Joseph Lackey) grocers 200 Virginia av. cor. East

Snyder A. (Long, Snyder & Co.) r. Dayton, Ohio

Snyder Conrad, carpenter, r. 247 N. Liberty

Snyder David E. (Snyder & Hays) r. 454 N. Tennessee

Snyder David W. farmer Virginia av. nr. corporation line

Snyder Elizabeth, r. 33 W. McCarty

Snyder Frederick, collarmaker D. Schurgel, r. 33 W. McCarty

Snyder Fred, foreman Greenleaf & Co. r. 204 Union

Snyder Henry, r. 600 N. Mississippi

Snyder James F. driver City R. R. r. 338 E. Washington

Snyder John, lab. Long & Joseph

Snyder John F. carpenter and confectioner, 143 W. Washington, r. same

Snyder Louis, stove moulder A. D. Wood

Snyder Paul, watchman, r. 203 Madison av.

Snyder Peter, porter Alford, Talbot & C. r. ws. Spring 1 s. Michigan

Snyder Stephen, lab. Osgood, Smith & Co. r. 137 S. Illinois

Snyder Thomas, brakeman, bds. 58 Benton

SNYDER & HAYS, (David E. Snyder, Isaac C. Hays) gen. ins. agts. 17 N. Meridian

Sobbe Charles, carpenter, r. Winston se. cor. Michigan

Sobbe Ernst, carpenter, r. 231 N. Davidson

Sobbe Henry, salesman J. Karney, bds. 307 S. Delaware

Socks Philip, cooper, r. 77 N. Illinois

Soewell Henry M. grocer, 232 E. Washington, r. 266 E. Market

Soehner Charles, (Soehner & Benham) r. 86 N. Illinois

Soehner Charles, Jr. clerk Fahnley & McCrea, bds. 86 S. Illinois

SOEHNER & BENHAM, (Charles Soehner and Azel M. Benham) pianos, organs and melodeons, stools and covers, 36 E. Washington

Sogemuer William, (H. Altman & Co.) r. Bluff rd. cor. Ray

Sohl Afnd J. (Sohl, Gibson & Co.) r. Hamilton Co.

Sohl Levi, (Sohl, Gibson & Co.) and (D. Burton & Co.) r. ws. West bet. Washington and Market

SOHL, GIBSON & CO. (Levi and Alfred J. Sohl and David Gibson) proprs. White Rose Flour Mills, 352 W. Washington

Solomon Charles, cigarmaker, r. 22 W. Georgia

Solomon Henry, tobacco and cigars, 27 S. Illinois. r. same

Solomon Mary, works Indianapolis Paper Co.

Solomon Morris, (J. & M. Solomon) r. 211 E. Ohio

Solomon Joseph, (J. & M. Solomon) r. 40 N. East

SOLOMON J. & M. (Joseph and Morris Solomon) pawnbrokers, 25 S. Illinois

Somer August, drayman, r. Union opp. 6th Ward School

Sommallard Christopher, varnisher, 77 Washington, r. 212 S. New Jersey

Sommers Martin, (col'd) engineer, r. 144 Douglas

Sonderegger Frank, painter, r. 126 N. Spring

SON   303   SPE

Sonnifield William, teamster, r. 64 S. Noble
Soper Solon R. com. mer. r. 28 Henry
Soubrock Frank, lab. r. 227 N. Davidson
Souer John, lab. r. 27 W. McCarty
Soule Charles E. compositor *Sentinel* news room, r. es. Blake 4 s. New York
Soule Eliza M. wid. Joshua. r. es. Blake 4 s. New York
SOUTHARD ALBERT B. sec. and gen. ticket agt. I. P. & C. R. R. r. 80 W. St. Clair
SOUTHARD A. LEMON, teacher the Bryant & Stratton Business College, rooms 10 E. Washington
Southard George, tel. operator I. P. & C. Rw. r. 399 N. Alabama
Southard James P. bookkeeper r. 399 N. Alabama
Southard James W. carpenter, r. 123 Meek
Southard M. R. r. 49 Chatham
Southern Christopher, carpenter, r. 62 Grant
SPADES MICHAEL H. dry goods, notions and human hair goods, 20 E. Washingtin, bds. Palmer House—see margin side lines
Spahr Frank L. bkpr. Fahnley & McCrea, bds. Sherman House
Spahr George W. lawyer, r. 21 Lockerbie
Spahr William, horse dealer r. 326 W. Washington
Spall Timothy, r. 365 E. Market
Spann John M. student Greylock Inst. r. 163 N. Pennsylvania
Spann John S. (John S. Spann & Co.) r. 163 N. Pennsylvania
Spann Peter, cabinet makur Spiegel & Thoms, r. 293 E. Ohio
Spann Thomas H. student Williams College, r. 163 N. Penna.
SPANN JOHN S. & CO. (John S. Spann, John B. Cleaveland and John Carter, real estate agts. brokers, and dealers, 50 E. Washington (Brown's bl'k.)
Sparkling Gem, A. Q. Goodwin publisher, 30 S. Meridian
Sparks John, street car driver, r. 223 W. Washington
SPAULDING J. L. propr. Indianapolls Steam Laundry 22 and 24 S. New Jersey and Velocipede School, 26 and 28 S. Tennessee bds. Pattison House
Spaulding Ralph, (col'd) r. 307 W. Market
Spaulding Rufus (col'd) lab. Aldrich & Gay
Spear Frederick (Schwear & Spear) r. 580 E. Washington
Speelman Samuel, (S. Speelman & Co.) r. 111 S. Illinois
SPEELMAN & CO. (Samuel Speelman and C. Aaron,) auction and commission, 111 S. Illinois
Speer Henry P. (T. S. James & Co.) r. 229 S. Alabama
Spelmann Frederick, lab. Union Starch Factory, r. 84 S. Liberty
Spellman John, police, r. 340 R. R.
Speckman Henry, cigars and tobacco whol. and retail, 108 S. Illinois, r. same
Speckman Henry, Jr. cigar maker H Speckman, bds. 108 S. Illnois
Spencer A. J. carpenter, bds. Little's Hotel
Spencer Andrew, fireman, bds. 61 S. Noble
Spencer C. C. turner Burk, Earnshaw & Co.
Spencer Charles F. clerk L. H. Tyler & Co. bds. 40 S. Illinois

| SPE | 304 | SPR |

SPENCER HOUSE, (John W. Canan) Illinois ne. cor. Louisiana
Spencer James, (col') restaurant, under 1st Nat. Bank, r. 225 N. Tennessee
Spencer Lewis, (col'd) restaurant, r. 225 N. Tennessee
Spencer Milton, clerk J. B. Hill, r. 188 E. Washington
Spencer William, r. ss. 2d bet. Illinois and Meridian
Spengel Philip, butcher, r. 21 N. New Jersey
Spicer Alfred S. conductor, bds. 67 and 69 N. Davidson
Spicer Bloomfield, real estate agt. r. 67 and 69 N. Davidson
Spicer E. M. carpenter, r. 67 and 69 N. Davidson
Spicer William, lab. Bunte, Dickson & Co.
Spickelmeyer Francis, (Spickelmeyer & Bird) r. 17 Center
SPICKELMEYER & BIRD, (Francis Spickelmeyer and John C. Bird) grocers ret. 217 Indiana av.
Spiegel Augustus, foreman Spiegel & Thoms Furniture Co. r. 219 N. Liberty
Speigel Augustus, turner, r. 310 N. East
Spiegel Christian, treas. Spiegel & Thoms Furniture Co. r. 310 N. East
Spiegel Edward, cabinetmkr. Spiegel & Thoms, r. 310 N. East
Spiegel Fred A. turner Spiegel & Thoms
Spiegel Henry, carver Spiegel & Thoms
Spiegel William, porter, 71 W Washington, r. 310 N. East
Spiegel William C. cabinetmkr. Spiegel & Thoms
SPEIGEL & THOMS FURNITURE CO. H. Frank, pres. C. Schram sec. C. Spiegel treas. office 71 and 73 W. Washington
Spielhoff H. carver Spiegel & Thoms, r. 285 S. Illinois
Spitl John, painter, r. Wisconsin opp. Mill
Spittle Joseph, machinist C. C. C. & I. R. R. r. 203 N. Delaware
Spitzfadan Peter, meat market, 97 E. Washington, r. 252 S. Delaware
Spitznagle Leopold, barber, 154 Bluff rd. r. same
Splane James, teamster J. E. Fawkner, r. 89 S. West
Splane Michael, lab. r. 95 S. West
Splane Thomas, lab. r. 340 Winston
Splane Timothy, teamster J. E. Fawkner, r. 77 S. West
Spohr George, (Maurice & Spohr) bds. 8 Martindale's blk.
Sponable M. J. wid. Philip, r. 175 N. Tennessee
Sponsel Conrad, (Sponsel & Bolz) r. Madison rd. nr. Dunlop
Sponsel Henry, grocer, 355 S. Delaware, r. same
SPONSEL & BOLZ, (Conrad Sponsel and Peter Bolz) proprs. Union Brewery, Madison rd. nr. Dunlop
Spooner P. L., U. S. Marshal, bds. Bates House
Spratt John E. salesman W. H. Sullivan, bds. 126 N. Tennessee
Spratt Simon D. jeweler Wm. H. Craft, bds. 126 N. Tennessee
SPRATT T. B. supt. Union Depot dining rooms and restaurant, r. same
Spray Jennie Miss, clk. W. H. Valentine, 34 W. Washington
Spray Jessie, bds. 60 S. Pennsylvania
Spray Joseph, hostler Kolyer & Caffey
Spray Lizzie Miss, clk. W. H. Valentine, 34 W. Washington

SPR   305   STA

Spreng Adam, stonecutter Scott & Nicholson, r. 128 N. Liberty
Spriggs Jerome, lab. Long & Joseph
SPRING ELLEN MRS. millinery and dressmaking 50 S. Illinois
Springer Daniel M. foreman foundry Greenleaf & Co. r. 418 S. Illinois
Springer David, (D. Springer & Son) r. 13 Chatham
Springer Edward (D. Springer & Son) r. 13 Chatham
Springer Hiram, woolen worker, r. 167 Ft, Wayne av.
Springer Howard, porter Chas. Mayer & Co. r. 167 Ft. Wayne av.
Springer James E. special traveling agent Security Life Ins. Co. r. 115 Meek
Springer John M. carpenter Greenleaf & Co.
Springer John M. machinist, r. 103 Bates
Springer Joseph M. carpenter Greenleaf & Co.
Springer Levi, woolen worker, r. 167 Ft. Wayne av.
Springer M. B. moulder B. F. Haugh & Co. r. 103 E. Meek
Springer Morris woolen worker, r. 167 Ft. Wayne av.
Springer D. & Son, (David & Edward Springer) carpenters and stair builders, 260 Massachusetts av.
Springfield Fire & Marine Ins. Co. of Springfield, Mass. Frank Smith & Co. agts. room 4 Odd Fellows Hall
Springstein A. builder, r. 268 E. Market
Springstein Abraham, student National Business College
Springstein Jeff. dept. marshall Union depot, r. 117 N. Spring
Sprole James E. groceries and provisions ret. Illinois sw. cor. Ohio, r. 92 S. Mississippi
Sproudle George, saw mill, r. 11 Ellsworth
Sproule Robert S. *Sentinel* office, r. 36 N. California
Sprow George W. machinist Warren Tate, r. 466 S. East
Sprow Louisa, wid. Jacob, r. 464 S. East
Spurrier James B. horse dealer, r. 87 Ann
Squires O. H. bds. Macy House
Staats George, janitor, r. 10 E. Michigan
Stable Michael, teamster, r. 133 N. Spring
SACY HENRY, supt. Indianapolis Gas Light & Coke Co. r. 155 S. Delaware
Stacy James, rimmer Osgood, Smith & Co.
STACY MAHLON D. watches, clocks and jewelry, No. 1 Martindale's blk, ne. cor. Pennsylvania and Market, r. 42 N. New Jersey
Stacy Milton H. finisher Merritt & Coughlen, r. 321 Blake
Stagg Charles W. lawyer, r. 269 W. Vermont
Stagg Eliza P. wid. r. 146 W. New York
Stagg John R. traveling agt. Osgood, Smith & Co. r. 287 S. East
Stahl Louis, artist, r. 263 S. Delaware
Stahlhut F. collar maker, r. 71 S. Pennsylvania
Stahlhut Fred, carpenter, r. 228 Railroad
Stake Chas. engineer C. C. & I. C. R. R. bds. 149 S. New Jersey
Stake Joseph, chair painter, r. 19 Meek
Staley Eugene, clk. bds. 259 N. Illinois
Staley F. J. sawer W. North nr. La Fayette frt. depot

| STA | 306 | STE |

Staley Jerome, sawer Long & Joseph
Stalhead Charles, carpenter, r. 28 W. 1st
Stalhead Fred, saddler, r. 664 N. Tennessee
Stallwagan John, meat market 442 S. Illinois, r. same
Stam Jacob, r. ns. New York 2 e. Minerva
Stanley H. M. wid. William, r. 153 Huron
Stanton Ambrose P. (Stanton & Manlove) r. 357 N. East
Stanton Ann, Mrs. bds. 151 High
STANRIDGE HENRY J. propr. Stanridge House 41 W. Maryland
Stanridge House, Henry J. Stanridge propr. 41 W. Maryland
Stanton John, moulder D. Root & Co.
STANTON & MANLOVE, (Ambrose P. Stanton and William R.
  Manlove) lawyers 87 E. Market
Staples Joshua, r. 368 N. New Jersey
Stapp Henry B. S. (col'd) barber Knox & Embers
Stapp James H. lawyer 12 S. Pennsylvania, r. 71 Mississippi
  cor. 5th
Stapp Thomas B. r. 110 N. Missouri
STAR UNION FAST FREIGHT LINE, S. F. Gray, agt. 85 Virgi-
  nia av.
Stark Christian, wagonmaker, r. 38 S. Alabama
Stark Evila J. wid. Abner, r. 140 Massachusetts av.
Stark G. C. rag dealer, r. 389 S. East
Stark George, lab. S. S. Smith, r. 12 Mullen
Stark Gustavus, secy. Cabinetmkrs. Union, r. 121 Ft. Wayne av.
Stark Herman, shoemaker 148 Virginia av. r. 230 S. New Jersey
Stark John C. wagonmaker 26 S. New Jersey, r. 38 S. Alabama
Stark Joseph, filecutter Drotz & Steinhauer, bds. 260 S. Penn.
Starr Ellen D. Miss, teacher Indiana Inst. for the Blind, r. same
Starr John, carpenter, r. 25 Henry
Starr William, wks. Rolling Mill, bds. 25 Henry
Starts William, teamster, r. 12 N. California
State Board of Agriculture, A. J. Holmes, sec. office State House
STATE BUILDING, (state offices) W. Washington bet. S. Illinois
  and Tennessee
State Fire Ins. Co. of Cleveland, Ohio, J. Barnard, agt. Vinton's
  Blk. Pennsylvania sw. cor Market
State Library, M. G. McLain, librarian, State House
STATE OFFICES (State Buildings) Washington sw. cor. Tennessee
State Sentinel, (daily and weekly,) R. J. Bright, editor and pro-
  prietor, 16½ E. Washington
Staton John D. wks. Rolling Mill, bds. 20 Douglas
Staton Mary A. wid. Washington, r. 20 Blake
Staton Samuel, wks. Cotton Factory
Staub Alexander, tinner Wolfrom Bros.
Staub Joseph, mer. tailor 2 Odd Fellows' bldg. r. 200 N. Noble
Staubrake George, r. 321 W. Market
Stauck John. lab. r. 272 Blake
Stealy Israel, physician, 78 S. Illinois, bds. same
Steanaker Ernst, drayman, r. 167 Union
Stebbins Sarah, wid. John, r. 33 Henry

Stechban L. upholster 71 W. Washington, r. 173½ E. Washington
Stecker Fred, painter, r. Michigan road near junc. Washington
Stedman Elkanah P. clk. frt. depot I. C. & L. R. R. r. 52 Bates
Stedman Henry S. clk. H. L. Benham & Co.
Stedman Percival, clk. frt. depot I. C. & L. R. R. r. 174 Jackson
Steeg Philip W. r. 226 Dougherty
Steele Edward, stonecutter F. L. Farman, bds. 76 S. Missouri
Steele Elmer R. chief clk. Bland & Taylor
Steele Oliver, cooper, r. 33 S. West
Steele Thomas J. printer, r. 187 N. Liberty
Steele William H. carpenter John Fearnley, r. 187 N. Liberty
STEFFENS CHARLES, saloon 192 N. Mississippi, r. same
Steffens E. Ferdinand, mathematical and philosophical instrument maker, Washington sw. cor. Meridian, r. 183 Blake
Steffon George, butcher R. Essigke, bds. 170 S. Illinois
Stegall Jerry, blksmith, r. 120 W. Maryland
Stehlin Caroline, wid. r. 496 N. West
Steidler John, bookbinder *Sentinel* bindery, r. 341 N. Liberty
Steierberg Charles, car repairer, r. 279 S. Delaware
Steiert John B. machinist, r. 332 S. Delaware
Steiger George, cooper M. Seiter, r. 288 E. Michigan
Stein Abram, meat market, 177 Virginia av. r. same
Stein F. barber, 276 E. Washington, r. same
Stein Herman J. salesman Trade Palace, bds. 231 E. Washington
Stein Joseph, shoemaker, 106 Bluff rd. r. same
Steinbau Leonard, brewer City Brewery, r. 16 Dougherty
Steinbauer L. brewery, r. 16 Dougherty
Steiner John, upholsterer N. S. Baker & Co. r. 62 W. South
Steinhauer Fred, filecutter Dortz & Steinhauer, r. 323 S. Penn.
Steinhauer GeorgeC. boot and shoemkr. 72 W. Maryland, r. same
Steinhauer Michael, (Drotz & Steinhauer) r. 260 S. Pennsylvania
STEINHAUSER B. A. bookbinder and paperbox maker, 168 E. Washington, r. 194 E. Washington
Steinhilber Anna, wid. Martin, r. 316 Railroad
Steinmann John, (Steinmann & Bernauer) r. 139 Virginia av.
Steinmann & Bernauer, (John Steinmann and Benedict Bernauer) mer. tailors, 43 Virginia av.
Steinmeyer William, porter W. J. Holliday & Co. r. 225 Bluff rd.
Steinwenter Catherine, wid. Andrew, r. 128 E. St. Joseph
Stelhorn Christian, carpenter F. Diekmann, r. 306 N. Noble
Stelhorn Frederick, carpenter, 175 Davidson, r. same
Stelsel John, barber J. G. Klein, r. 376 E. Ohio
Step ——, clerk, 30½ N. Pennsylvania
Stephens A. J. shoemaker Maurice & Spohr, bds. Bicking House
Stephens Alexander D. compositor *Sentinel* news room, r. 213 N. Pennsylvania
Stephens Edward, clk. bds. 154 S. New Jersey
Stephens James, boilermaker C. C. & I. C. R. R. r. 93 S. Benton
Stephens James, policeman, r. 115 E. St. Joseph
Stephens John F. boilermaker C. C. & I. C. R. R. r. 118 S. Benton

STE	308	STE

Stephens Sarah, wid. Joshua, r, 348 N. Alabama
Stephens Thomas D. confectioner 104 Indiana av. r. same
Stephenson John W. carpenter, r. 252 Bluff rd.
Stephenson Walter, student, bds. 268 E. St. Clair
Sterberg Charles, car inspector I. C. & L. Rw.
Stern M. G. I. pastor German Evangelical Church, r. 30 Chatham
Sterrete Ann Maria Mrs. bds. 405 N. Pennsylvania
Steubing Philip, lab. r. 211 N. Noble
Stevens A. D. compositor, r. 213 N. Pennsylvania
Stevens A. G. r. 241 Virginia av.
Stevens A. S. salesman Pettis, Dickson & Co. bds. 60 W. Market
Stevens Benjamin F. tinsmith, r. 190 N. Davidson
Stevens Edward, clk. Wm. H. Close & Co. bds. 154 S. New Jersey
Stevens Harry C. paperhanger, r. 516 N. Mississippi
STEVENS HATTIE M. MRS. Ladies' Exchange store 32 S. Illinois, r. same
Stevens James N. policeman, r. 165 E. St. Joseph
Stevens Julia M. teacher 8th Ward School, r. 15 S. New Jersey
Stevens Levi B. brickmaker, r. 87 Union
Stevens Marinda Mrs. r. 213 N. Pennsylvania
Stevens P. E. tinsmith Munson & Johnston
Stevens T. M. physician, bds. 255 New Jersey
Stevenson David, r. 442 N. Illinois
Stevenson David, cooper, r. 213 N. Missouri
Stevenson John, cooper, r. 213 N. Missouri
Stevenson W. W. carpenter, bds. 144 N. Tennessee
Stewart A. C. (col'd) cook, r. 229 N. Tennessee
Stewart Adoniram J. tinner Gardner & Decker, r. 129 E. Merrill
Stewart Anna, wid. William, r. 226 N. Meridian
Stewart Caroline Miss, (col'd) teacher Allen Chapel Day School, r. 229 N. Tennessee
Stewart Charles G. (Bowen, Stewart & Co.) r. 141 N. Alabama
Stewart Daniel, (Stewart & Morgan) r. 265 N. Illinois
Stewart David, teamster, r. 311 Indiana av.
Stewart Elizabeth, wid. Andrew, r. 311 Indiana av.
Stewart Frank, wks. Rolling Mill
Stewart Frederick S. clerk Bowen, Stewart & Co. r. 198 N. East
Stewart George, (col'd) barber Hill & Carter, bds. 66 N. Missouri
Stewart George H. W. (col'd) teacher 4th Ward dist. School, es. Market bet. West and California, r. 175 Blake
Stewart Harriett, (col'd) wid. Henry, r. 158 Douglas al.
Stewart Jacob, lab. r. 72 Wilkins
Stewart James, wks. Rolling Mill
Stewart James, (col'd) lab. r. 237 W. Michigan
Stewart James, (col'd) lab. r. Rhode Island nr. Blake
Stewart James, (col'd) porter r. 237 W. Michigan
Stewart John, (col'd) barber Russell & Gulliver, bds. 229 N. Tennessee
Stewart John, cigarmaker N. W. Reynolds
Stewart John, driver Express Co.
Stewart John, fireman C. C. C. & I. Rw. r. 71 Peru

Who is your Hatter? Try Davis at No. 12 E. Washington.

| STE | 309 | STO |

Stewart John, turner, r. 55 E. McCarty
Stewart Nellie, saleslady Glick & Schwartz, r. 311 Indiana av.
Stewart Robert M. carpenter, Vermont nr. cor. Massachusetts av. r. 115 Massachusetts av.
Stewart Sophia W. wid. William, (Bowen, Stewart & Co.) r. 117 N. Illinois
Stewart William, printer, bds. Commercial Hotel
Stewart William, teamster, r. 311 Indiana av.
STEWART & MORGAN, (Daniel Stewart and Stephen W. Morgan) druggists, 40 E. Washington
Stibing Philip, lab. C. C. & I. C. R. R.
Stibing William, engineer C. C. & I. C. R. R.
Stich Floribert, carpenter, r. 281 S. New Jersey
Stiedel George, r. 216 N. Noble
Steigmann Charles, general store, 150 Madison av. r. 144 same
Stierle Charles, (Stierle & Loeper) bds. National Hotel
STIERLE & LOEPER, (Charles Stierle and Jacob W. Loeper) 94 S. Delaware
Stiers P. Jane, Mistress tailor shop Deaf and Dumb Institute, r. E. Washington out of limits
Stiles Daniel J. (Kimble, Aikman & Co.) r. 335 N. East
Stiles E. C. bricklayer, bds. Ray House
Stiles Jacob, cigarmaker N. W. Reynolds, bds. 77½ E. Market
Stiles James, shoemaker L. Siersdorfer, bds. Martin House
Stiles John, baker Lawrence Shille, bds. 314 N. New Jersey
Stillsmith Simon, r. 512 N. Mississippi
Stilting Charles, mechanic, r. 86 Railroad
Stilwell George, r. 336 E. North
Stilwell George W. lawyer, 61½ E. Washington, bds. Little Hotel
Stilwell J. D. bookkeeper Munson & Johmston, bds. Little's Hotel
Stilwell W. M. sec. and steward Indiana Institution for the Blind, r. same
Stilz Frederick, clerk J. H. Baldwin & Co.
Stilz J. George, whol. and ret. dealer in agricultural implements seeds &c. 78 E. Washington, r. s. of limits nr. Virginia av.
Stilz John G. clerk Frank Erdelmeyer, r. 131 Fort Wayne av.
Stindin Thomas, wheeler Rolling Mill
Stirk David P. (Stirk & Allaire) r. East bet. New York and Ohio
Stirk & Allaire, (David P. Stirk and Andrew Allaire) blacksmiths, East bet. South and Louisisana
Stivert J. machinist Sinker & Co.
Stockman George W. foreman Nofsinger, Kingan & Co.
Stoddard William. hostler Citizens' R. R. Co.
Stoeling Charles, stationary engineer T. H. & I. R. R.
Stofer John, ink mnfr. r. 19 N. East
Stokely Benjamin, machinist, r. 164 Winston
Stokes James, (col'd) lab. r. 450 S. Tennessee
Stokes R. M. foreman M. Byrkit & Sons, bds. 126 N. Tennessee
Stolte Henry, student Bryant & Stratton, bds. 365 S. Delaware
Stolte William, (Stolte & May) r. 365 S. Delaware

STO	310	STO

STOLTE & MAY, (William Stolte & John May) groceries, and flour and feed, 365 S. Delaware

Stoltz John, belt maker Mooney & Co. r. S. Meridian

Stoltz Charles, boot and shemaker, 118 Bluff rd. r. same

Stolz Frank, basket maker, r. 118 Bluff rd.

Stone Charles, clerk, bds. 20 S. Pennsylvania

Stone Oscar, salesman, r. 113 N. Illinois

Stone T. S. (Hendricks, Edmonds & Co.) r. Worcester, Mass.

Stone Thomas, fireman, r. 145 Virginia av.

Stone Thomas, lab. r. W. Indianapolis

Stone Willian O. bookkeeper Hendricks, Edmonds & Co. r. 113 N. Illinois

Stoneman William H. (Stoneman, Pee & Co.) bds. 363 N. Alabama

STONEMAN, PEE & CO. (W. H. Stoneman, George W. Pee and Samuel Alward) whol. dealers in groceries and notions, 2 W. Louisiana

Stoner Abram S. carpenter, r. 237 N. Noble

Stoner Charles, actor, bds. 242 N. Illinois

Stoner J. P. actor Academy of Music

Stopher F. engineer C. C. & I. C. R. R.

Storer Emil, clerk C. Friedgen, bds. 36 N. East

Storm John, lab. r. ns. Kansas nr. the Canal

Stortz John M. (Shatz & Stortz, r. 369 S. Delaware

Storz John, milkman, r. 504 S. East

Storz William, piano maker, bds. 18 S. Delaware

Storz William D. student Bryant & Stratton's College

Stott Josiah, heater Rolling Mill, r. 216 Bluff rd.

Stott Jonathan, wks. Phœnix Machine Works, r. 293 W. Vermont

Stouck Franklin, barkeeper Bates House, bds. same

Stouck William, lab. Osgood, Smith & Co.

Stough Charles A. (Miller, Mitchell & Stough) r. 202 W. Maryland

Stout B. G. (Stout & Bro) r. 144 N. Mississippi.

Stout Carhart, clk. J. H. Ross, r. 133 W. South

Stout D. L. salesman B. G. Stout & Bro. bds. Palmer House

Stout David E. (Donaldson & Stout) r. 169 N. Illinois

Stout Furman (F. Stout & Son) r. 331 W. Washington

Stout George (W. F. Stout & Son) r. 331 W. Washington

Stout Harriet, wid., Dr. O. H. r. 144 N. Mississippi

Stout Hiram, engineer T. H. & I. R. R.

Stout I. wks. J. S. Carrey & Co.

Stout John, printer Wm. Sheets, bds. 133 W. South

Stout John R. salesman B. G. Stout & Bro. r. 246 N. Illinois

Stout O. B. salesman B. G. Stout & Bro. r. 173 W. Market

Stout R. C. (Stout & Bro.) r. 173 W. New York

Stout Remson, employee A. M. U. Ex. Co. r. 382 S. Illinois

Stout Thos. student National Business College

STOUT B. G. & BRO. (B. G. and R. C. Stout) grocers whol and retail 6 and 8 Bates House Blk.

STOUT F. & SON (Furman and George W. Stout) liquor dealers 160 W. Washington

STOWEL MYRON A. musical Instruments, pianos, melodeons, organs &c. 46 N. Pennsylvania, r. 78 W. Michigan, (See front paster and back cover.)

Strabel Jacob, lab. r. New Jersey s. of limits

Strahan George C. salesman F. Deitch, r. 26 N. Fayette

Strang G. L. master shoe shop Indiana Deaf and Dumb Institute, r. 195 Harrison

STRANGE CHAPEL (Methodist Episcopal Church) George W. Tell, pastor, 183 N. Tennessee

Strangmeier Frederick, porter Murphy, Johnson & Co. r. 412 S. Delaware

Strasner Fred. clk. r. 479 N. Alabama

Strater Charles, varnisher Spiegel & Thoms

Stratmann Henry, lab. r. 609 E. Washington

Strattan Elwood H. bookkeeper, r. 48 Cherry

Stratton A. bookkeeper L. Ludorff & Co.

Straw John, hostler H. Allen, r. 27 E. Pearl

Straub Elizabeth, wid. Albert, r. 247 W. Maryland

Straub John, tanner, Robert Schmidt

Straub John A. carpenter, r. 33 Fletcher av.

Straub Vinzeng, shoemaker, 10 Bates House, blk. r. same

Strauch John, tanner, bds. Washington House

Strauss Leopold, clk. M. Griesheimer & Bro. bds 15 N. Meridian

Strauss Samuel, **r.** 79 E. Michigan

Strauss Solomon, with Moritz Bros. bds. Bates House

Straussner Frederick, cutter, F. Goepper & Co. r. 479 N. Alabama

Strawbridge Hannah, wid. Benjamin, r. 350 Winston

Strawbridge William, clk. H. M. Loewell, r. 350 Winston

Street Charles, cabinet maker, r. 194 W. Vermont

Street Herman, turner, Builders and Manfrs. Association

Street Nathaniel, carpenter, r. 41 John

Streeter Noble R. salesman, Hume, Adams & Co. bds. 31 W. Maryland

Streicher Barbara, wid. Jacob, r. 169 Ft. Wayne av.

Streicher Jacob, cigar maker, r. 169 Ft. Wayne av.

Streif David, lab. J. Fishback

STREIGHT A. D. book publisher, Yohn's blk. Meridian ne. cor. Washington, r. Nat. rd. two miles east of city

Stretcher Elmira, wid. J. I. r. 421 N. Tennessee

Striblen Mary Mrs. r. 506 N. Delaware

Strickland David H. (Seaman & Co.) bds. 213 W. Market

Strickland Harry, dyer Merritt & Coughlen, bds. 252 W. Market

Strickland Joseph, bookbinder, bds. 252 W. Market

Strickland R. J. editor and publisher *Odd Fellows' Talisman*, 30 S. Meridian, r. Centerville, Ind.

Striebeck Charles, baker 319 N. West, r. same

Strieger Gabriel, brewer Schmidt's brewery, **r.** same

Strider Talfero P. pattern and trimming store, branch of Madame Demorest of New York, 46 S. Illinois, r. same

Stringer William, r. 22 W. North

STR	312	STY

Stringfellow H. J. pastor St. Paul's Episcopal Church, r. 216 N. Delaware

Stringfellow James, bds. 216 N. Delaware

Stringmeyer Frederick, porter, r. 412 S. Delaware

Stroble Alice, dressmkr. Mrs. N. M. Allen, r. 112 N. Noble

Stroble John, boot and shoemkr. 554 E. Washington, r. same

Stroble Mary, r. Maryland ne. cor. West

Stroele Frederick, cabinetmkr. wks. Cabinetmakers' Union

Strong Melville, (Strong & Smith) r. 231 N. East

STRONG & SMITH, (Melville Strong and Eben Smith) dealers in artificial teeth, gold foil, dental instruments and material of every description, depot 2-3 Vinton's block, 48 N. Penn.

Strother William, lab. bds. 213 W. McCarty

Struble John, bartender, bds. 112 N. Noble

Strubbe Philip, carpenter Many & Sons, r. 112 N. Noble

Struckman Frederick, machinist Helwig & Co. r. 173 Union

Struckman William, tailor Rudolph Rogge, bds. 335 Virginia av.

Stuber John, huckster, r. 384 S. Missouri

Stuck David, bds. 337 W. Maryland

Stuck James W. sawer, r. 55 Maple

Stuck John, r. 337 W. Maryland

Stuck Matthias, boilermkr. Sinker & Co. r. 24 Elm

Stucker William, dyer r. Mayhew nr. Brooks

Stuckey Charles, cooper, r. 111 N. Spring

Stuckmeyer John, grocer, and meat market 362 Virginia av. r. 358 Virginia av.

Stump Frank C. paperhanger, r. 17 Kentucky av.

STUMPF HENRY A. tinsmith 94 Indiana av. bds. 178 N. Mississippi

Stumpf John, stone mason, r. 317 N. Alabama

Stumpf John B. (Tobias, Bender & Co.) r. 459 E. Market

Stumpf John G. stone mason, r. 221 John

Stumpf John H. lab. r. 344 N. East

Stumph John J. carpenter, r. 91 Buchanan

Stumpf John W. tinner H. A. Stumpf, r. 459 E. Market

Stumpf Joseph, blacksmith, Massachusetts av. cor. Plum, r. 344 N. East

Stumpf Louis, brick mason, r. 171 N. Noble

Stumph Louis, brewer Schmidt's Brewery

Stundon Patrick, driver Express car, r. 367 N. West

Stundon Patrick, lab. r. 14 Buchanan

Stundon Thomas, tallyman C. C. C. & I. Rw. r. 391 N. West

Sturdevant Melora, asst. teacher Indianapolis Female Institute

Sturges Levick, shoemkr. r. 37 Blake

Sturges William, shoemkr. J. W. Adams

Sturk Porter, blacksmith, bds. 124 N. East

Sturley ——, carpenter, r. 237 Madison av.

Sturm George, tailor, J. & P. Gramling, bds. 34 N. Pennsylvania

Sturr William G. wizard oil mnfr. r. 362 N. West

Sturz William, piano forte maker J. H. Kappes & Co.

Styner John H. brakeman, r. 68 S. Noble

Suart John, turner Osgood, Smith & Co.
Suart John B. grocer and shoe mkr. 219 Massachusetts av.
Suart Miles, moulder Eagle Machine Works, r. 55 E. McCarty
Suber Chris. clerk H. Altman & Co. bds. Bluff road cor. Ray
Sudbrink Minna, weaver Merritt & Coughlen, bds. N. West
Sudbrock Henry, carpenter, r. 316 N. Noble
Suddith George, fish dealer 107 S. Illinois, r. 193 W. South
Suer Louis, sawfiler, r. 28 Wyoming
Suess Charles A. tailor W. Sweinhart, bds. Choptank alley
Suesy Godfried, shoemaker, r. 310 E. Ohio
Suguiough Patrick lab. R. R. r. 179 Maple
Suhre Albert, watchmn. T. H.& I. engine house, r. 231 Bluff rd.
Suhre E. Henry, r. 178 Winston
Suhre Fred, driver P. Dohn, bds. 246 S. Meridian
Suhre Frederick, driver city express, bds. 178 N. Winston
Suhre Henry, wiper round house, r. es. N. Illinois 3 n. limits
Suhre Henry, Jr. carpenter, r. 178 Winston
Suhre L. sawmaker Sheffield Saw Works
Suitt James B. supt. Eagle Machine Works. r. 251 S. Meridian
Sulgrove Berry R. editor-in-chief Indianopolis *Journal*, r. 125 W. South
Sulgrove Eli, saddler, r. 16 W 1st
Sulgrove George, salesman James W. Sulgrove & Co. bds. 20 W. Washington
Sulgrove Henry, harnessmaker James W. Sulgrove & Co. bds. 20 W. Washington
Sulgrove John, harnessmaker, bds. 27 Henry
Sulgrove James W. (James W. Sulgrove & Co.) r. 137 W. New York
Sulgrove Jerome B. with James W. Sulgrove & Co. r. 190 N. Mississippi
Sulgrove Joseph B. harnessmaker James W. Sulgrove & Co. r. 235 W. Vermont
Sulgrove Milton, harnessmaker James W. Sulgrove & Co. r. Indiana av. cor. Illinois
SULGROVE JAMES W. & CO. (James W. Sulgrove and ———) saddlery hardware and coach trimmings, 20 W. Washington
Sullivan Bev. W. dentist 76½ E. Market, r. 172 N. Delaware
Sullivan C. boilermaker C. C. & I. C. R. R.
Sullivan Cornelius, lab. r. 142 Meek
Sullivan Cornelius, lab. r. 335 Winston
Sullivan Daniel, hostler H. Allen, r. 27 E. Pearl
Sullivan Daniel, lab. r. 112 Meek
Sullivan Daniel, lab. r. 27 S. Alabama
Sullivan Dennis, hackman, bds. 161 S. Illinois
Sullivan F. r. 276 S. Delaware
SULLIVAN GEORGE T. agt. South Shore Fast Freight Line, r. 321 S. Alabama
Sullivan James, lab. Georgia sw. cor. Helen
Sullivan James, roller Rolling Mill, r. Merrill cor. Missouri
Sullivan John, lab. r. 5 Bates

Sullivan John, lab. frt. depot C. C. & I. C. R. R.
Sullivan John, lab. r. 498 E. Georgia
Sullivan John, lab. r. 175 Meek
Sullivan John, lab. r. 364 W. North
Sullivan John, moulder Sinker & Co. bds. 38 S. Tennessee
Sullivan John, night watchman LaFayette freight depot
Sullivan John B. (Sullivan & Drew) r. 83 E. Pratt
Sullivan Michael, lab. r. 152 Meek
Sullivan Nancy, car cleaner C. C. & I. C. R. R.
Sullivan Peter, lab. frt. depot I. C. & L. R. R. r. 217 S. Illinois
Sullivan Thomas, lab. r. 3 Bates
Sullivan Timothy, car inspector C. C. C. & I. R. R.
Sullivan Timothy, lab. Rolling Mill, r. ws. Maple nr. limits
Sullivan Timothy, lab. r. 335 Winston
Sullivan Timothy, plasterer, r. 22 Buchanan
Sullivan William Sr. carpenter, r. 427 N. Tennessee
Sullivan William, heater's helper Rolling Mill
Sullivan William, lab. r. 456 S. East
Sullivan William, lawyer 45 E. Washington, r 410 N. Meridian
Sullivan Wm. H. grocer 76 W. Wash'ton, bds. 60 N. California
SULLIVAN & DREW, (John B. Sullivan and John A. Drew) proprs. Citizens' Livery Stable, 10 E. Pearl
Summers A. B. carpenter, r. 83 James
Summitt Benjamin, (col'd) mason, r. opp. City Hospital
Summons George, (col'd) lab. r. es. Clinton al. bet. E. Ohio and New York
Summons Martin, (col'd) engineer H. C. Chandler & Co.
Sumner E. patent dry kiln, bds. 70 E. Market
Sumner William, (William Sumner & Co.) r. Cincinnati, Ohio
SUMNER WILLIAM & CO. (William Sumner, John R. Wright and Alva S. Walker) agents Wheeler & Wilson's sewing machines, 10 W. Washington
Sunbeam, Wm. Travis, editor and propr. Meridian se. cor. Circle
Sunday Spottongyell, Gutenberg Co. publishers, 23 W. Maryland
Sun Ins. Co. of Cleveland, Ohio, J. Barnard, agt. Vinton's blk. Pennsylvania sw. cor. Market
Surbey Jacob S. (Baker & Surbey) r. 275 E. South
Surface John M. med. student B. Ward, bds. 357 N. New Jersey
Surface John M. watchman Spiegel & Thoms
Surface Lydia, wid. John R. r. 40 Christian av.
Surgeson Joseph, lab. Rolling Mill, r. 441 S. Illinois
Susz Godfrey, shoemaker Charles Rehling
Sutbrink Winie, weaver Woolen Factory, r. 117 N. West
Sutherland Andrew, lab. r. 783 N. Illinois
Sutherland James W. machinist, r. 58 Greer
Sutherland Levi, wks. Osgood, Smith & Co. r. 59 E. McCarty
Sutter Frederick, physician 63 E. Wash'ton, r. 290 Virginia av.
Sutter George, gardener, r. 6th cor. Canal
Sutter James, clerk, r. 9 Cherry
Sutton Daniel, (col'd) lab. r. 173 Eddy
Sutton Joseph M. plasterer, r. 82 Massachusetts av.

Sutton Peter, machinist King & Pinney, bds. Wyle House
Sutton S. L. engineer C. C. C. & I. R. R. r. 360 N. Noble
Swabb Kate, wks. Caledonia Paper Mill
Swain David F. bkpr. John C. Burton & Co. bds. Sherman House
Swain E. W. engineer Long & Joseph
Swain Edward, lab. r. West Indianapolis
Swain George, clerk, bds. Macy House
Swain George H. carriage painter, 36 S. Pennsylvania, r. Vine nr. Broadway
Swain George H. clerk Merchants Despatch, r. 41 N. Illinois
Swain George H. real estate agt. r. 25 Vine
Swain J. bds. Macy House
Swain Louis, lab. bds. 267 E. Washington
Swain Mary J. wid. Rufus, r. 41 Fletcher av.
Swain Sallie, saleslady R. Sedgewick, r. 240 N. Illinois
Swain William M. fireman, bds. 129 Bates
Swales John S. stonecutter, r. 42 Henry
Swan George, wks. brewery, r. 55 California
Swan John, brewer Indianapolis Brewery
Swanerberger L. J. toll gate keeper White River Bridge, r. same
SWANK M. cancer physician, 76 N. Pennsylvania, see card Business Directory
Swarm Francis M. teamster, r. 64 Bicking
Swartz Andrew, lab. r. 19 Lord
Swartz Andrew jr. lab. r. 19 Lord
Swartz Joseph, notions, 340 N. Noble
Sweeney Eugene, lab. r. 347 Winston
Sweeney Hettie Mrs. (Marshall & Sweeney) 58 N. Illinois
SWEENEY HUGH, saloon, 116 S. Illinois, r. same
Sweeney Jerry, drayman Scott & Nicholson, r. ws. Kentucky av. bet. West and Louisiana
Sweeney John, cigar maker A. W. Sharpe, r. 16 S. Mississippi
Sweeney Sarah, wid. Patrick, r. 268 S. Tennessee
Sweeney Thomas, machinist, r. 51 E. McCarty
Sweet George M. clk. P. O. bds. N. Pennsylvania n. of limits
Sweet James N. lawyer, bds. N. Pennsylvania n. of limits
Sweet Rebecca, wid. Philip, r. N. Pennsylvania, n. of limits
Sweetser Geo. M, city distributing clk. P. O. r. N. Pennsylvania nr. city limits
Sweetser James N. lawyer, 21 E. Washington, r. Pennsylvania s. of city limits
SWEETSER JOHN, whol. dealer in liquors and wines, 30 S. Meridian r. 242 N. Meridian
Sweinhart Andrew, painter, S. W. Drew
Sweinhart Charles E. clk. W. Sweinhart, bds. 379 N. Alabama
Sweinhart W. merchant tailor, 21 S. Meridian, r. 379 N. Alabama
Sweinhart William T. r. 379 N. Alabama
Swigert Joseph, harness maker E. Edwards, r. 40 N. Douglas
Swindler John H. traveling agt. r. 232 N. Noble
Swing William W. (Swing & Dennis) bds. 248 N. West

Swing & Dennis, (William W. Swing and Charles C. Dennis,) drugs and medicines, 4 Martindale's blk.

Swoboda Joseph, cabinet maker Western Furniture Co.

Syerup Henry, grocer and dry goods, 199 Massachusetts av. r. 197 Massachusetts av.

Sylvester David, street contractor, r. 26 Lockerbie

Sylvia Marion, coachman J. F. Hill, bds. 84 N. Alabama

Sym James, machinist Sinker & Co. r. 346 S. Alabama

T

Tackett Frank M. painter, r. 313 S. Delaware

Tachan William, r. 156 Huron

Taffe George, Lieut. of Police, r. 175 Spring

Taffe Hanibal, policeman, rooms McQuat's Blk.

Taggart Daniel, woodworker Indiana Coach Works

TAGGART SAMUEL, millwright and mill furnisher, 132 S. Pennsylvania, r. 118 N. Mississippi

Tailor Dorsey (col'd) lab. r. 6th nr. La Fayette R. R.

Talbert William (col'd) hostler Mills & Hollingsworth

Talbert William (col'd) r. 245 W. Ohio

Talbot Gabriel, cooper, F. Wright, r. ws. Blake 4 n. New York

TALBOT RICHARD L. (Patterson, Moore & Talbot, and Alfred Talbot & Co.) r. 136 E. North

Talbot Willliam, cooper John Losey

Talbot William, cooper, bds. ws. Blake 4 n. New York

Talbot William F. cooper W. Baird

Talbott Charles H. (Rickard & Talbott) r. 28 N. Mississippi

Talbott F. (col'd) hod carrier, r. Arch ne. cor. Broadway

Talbott Henry (col'd) bds 63 S. Illinois

Talbott John M. r. 114 N. Tennessee

Talbott W. H. (H. Salsbury & Co.) r. Meridian sw. cor. Ohio

Talbott Washington H. office 24½ E. Washington, r. 94 N. Meridian

Talbott William A. tinner Martin & Myres, r. 33 N. Liberty

Talbott & New's Block, es. Pennsylvania bet. Washington and Market

Tallerday Caroline G. Mrs. nurse Institution for the Blind

TALMAGE A. A. asst. supt. Indianapolis and St. Louis R. R. office 53 S. Alabama

Tangley Mary, wid. Dennis, r. 151 S. Alabama

Tann H. piano forte maker J. H. Kappes & Co.

Tanner D. F. lab. Long & Joseph

Tanner Emily, wid. David, r. 9 Elizabeth

Tanner Isaac W. (col'd) lab. Builders and Mnfrs. Association

Tanner James, hackdriver, r. 69 Elizabeth

Tanner John, mattress maker Wilkens & Hall, 84—86 E. Market

Tanner Samuel, lab. r. ns. New York 5 e. Minerva

Tanner Thomas, lab. Long & Joseph

Tanner William F. boot and shemaker, 166 Indiana av. bds. same

Buy your Hats, Caps and Furs at I. Davis & Co. 12 E. Washington.

TAP   317   TAY

Tapking John F. machine hand Cabinetmakers Union, r. 133 N. New Jersey

Tapking Minnie, wid. Frederick H. r. 189 S. Alabama

Tarkington John S. (Martindale & Tarkington) notary public, room 2, 2d floor Martindale's blk. r. 272 N. Meridian

Tarkington W. W. clerk P. O. r. 77 W. North

Tarkington William C. (Hibben, Tarkington & Co.) r. 77. W. North

Tarkington William S. doorkeeper Senate, bds. Bates House

Tarlton James A. grocer ret. Illinois se. cor. Sinker, r. ws. Illinois above 8th

Tarlton John, merchant, r. 492 N. Tennessee

Tate Robert, blacksmith John J. Gates, bds. Cumberland alley bet. New Jersey and Alabama

TATE WARREN, sash, doors and blinds mnfr. 38 S. New Jersey, bds. Pattison House

Tate William, r. 410 N. Tennessee

Tatgen Charles, carpenter Bodeker & Niemann

Tattersall Fannie, tailoress H. Small, bds. 186 Virginia av.

Tattersall Joseph, stonecutter, r. 186 Virginia av.

Taylor Mrs. bds. 62 S. Pennsylvania

Taylor Charles, fireman, bds. 58 Benton

Taylor Charles O. (col'd) cook Knotts & Co. r. 225 W. Ohio

Taylor Charles P. clk. Snyder & Hayes, bds. 357 N. Pennsylvania

Taylor Clay, engineer T. H. & I. R. R.

Taylor Clinton, stock dealer, r. 125 E. North

Taylor D. B (D. B. Taylor & Co.) r. 63 N. Alabama

TAYLOR DANIEL M. cashr. Ind. Nat. Bank, r. 680 N. Illinois

Taylor Dorsey, (col'd) porter J. H. Cropper, r. cor. 6th and the Railroad

Taylor Edwin, law student N. B. Taylor, bds. 251 N. Alabama

Taylor Franklin, (Chandler & Taylor) r. 290 W. Vermont cor. California

Taylor George, (col'd) coachman, r. 68 N. Missouri

Taylor George, (col'd) r. 198 Minerva

Taylor Howard, r. E. Market e. of limits

Taylor I. J. auction and com. mer. bds. Pattison House

Taylor Isaac, architect, room 5, 14 N. Delaware, r. 209 N. Liberty

TAYLOR ISAAC J. lawyer, 85 E. Washington, bds. Pattison House

Taylor Isaac H. traveling agt. r. 185 Bluff rd.

Taylor Israel, bookkpr. Harrison's Bank, r. 397 N. Pennsylvania

Taylor J. M. brakeman, bds. 248 E. Louisiana

Taylor James B. foreman foundry Eagle Machine Works, r. 250 S. Meridian

Taylor James B. pianomkr. Indianapolis Piano Mnfg. Co. r. 79 N. New Jersey

Taylor Jesse D. B. r. 185 Bluff rd.

Taylor John, lab. Osgood, Smith & Co.

TAYLOR JOHN F. plaster supplies ornamental, 80 Massachusetts av. r. 61 N. New Jersey

TAY	318	TEM

Taylor Julia A. teacher Indiana Deaf and Dumb Institute, r. E. Washington out of limits

Taylor Lizzie M. wid. Richard, r. 389 Virginia av.

Taylor M. J. Mrs. milliner and millinery goods, 6 W. Washington, r. same

Taylor Mary Miss, teacher 3d Ward School

Taylor Mary C. wid. Joseph, r. 45 Huron

Taylor Mary E. wid. Abijah, r. 76 Ft. Wayne av.

TAYLOR NAPOLEON B. attorney at law and notary public, 4 Brown's Block, Pennsylvania nr. cor. Washington, r. 251 N. Alabama

Taylor Oliver, (col'd) cook, r. 225 W. Ohio

Taylor Pierson T. switchman J. M. & I. R. R. r. 250 Madison av.

Taylor Quartus, confectioner, 42 Indiana av. r. same

Taylor Stephen, (col'd) lab. r. Rhode Island nr. Blake

Taylor Samuel L. groceries, 77 E. Market, r. 153 N. Tennessee

Taylor Thomas J. r. 139 Union

Taylor Timothy B. (Bland & Taylor) r. 125 E. Vermont

Taylor William A. salesman Mooney & Co. r. 266 S. New Jersey

Taylor William M. salesman Mayhew & Branham, r. 168 N. Illinois

TAYLOR D. B. & CO. (D. B. Taylor and ——) auction and commission merchants, 85 E. Washington

Teal Edward, carpenter John Fearnley, bds. same

Teal Nathaniel, physician, room No. 5 Blake blk. 53 W. Washington, r. 84 S. Illinois

Tarny Thomas, puddler Indianapolis Rolling Mill

Tebbee Charles, lab. r. 39 Meek

Teckenbrock Christopher, blacksmith T. H. & I. R. R. r. 16 Henry

Teckenbrock H. Wm. car inspector T. H. & I. R. R. r. 145 Bluff rd.

Tedron David F. carpenter, r. east end Christian av.

Tedron Joseph T. clerk Strong & Smith, bds. David F. Tedron

Tedron Vina Miss, teacher 2d ward school, bds. David F. Tedron

Teepe Harmon, blacksmith Sinker & Co. r. 330 Virginia av.

Teetus J. lab. Greenleaf & Co.

Teetus George W. lab. Greenleaf & Co.

Teetus Richard, lab. Greenleaf & Co.

Teezle George, grafter, r. 174 N. Davidson

Teichman Frederick, cigar maker, bds. Union Hall

Teina Charles G. lab. r. 563 E. St. Clair

Teina Christian, cigar maker, r. 553 E. St. Clair

Telegraph Daily, Gutenberg Co. publisher, 23 W. Maryland

TELEGRAPH OFFICES, (Branch City) M. U. T. Co. Union depot bldg.

Telle George W. pastor Strange Chapel, (Methodist) r. 183 N. Tennessee

Tellkamp Henry, cigar maker, bds. 117 S. Illinois

Tellkamp J. H. F. cigar maker, r. 117 S. Illinois

Tellkamp John, carriage blacksmith, r. 232 S. New Jersey

Teman William, gardiner, r. 500 E. Washington

Temple William, brakeman, r. 62 Bicking

Templer James, carpenter, r. 2 Dougherty

| TEM | 319 | THA |

Temporley John, carpenter bds. 82 E. St. Clair
TenEyck Edward, fireman J. M. & I. R. R. r. 29 W. Georgia
TenEyck James, wks. A. Reed & Co.
TenEyck Jeremiah A. (J. A. and R. F. TenEyck,) r. 340 W. Washington
TenEyck John, fireman, bds. 111 W. South
TenEyck John, shoemaker, r. 124 Indiana av.
TenEyck R. F. (J. A. and R. F. TenEyck,) bds. 111 W. South
TenEyck Sarah Mrs. r. 29 W. Georgia
TenEyck J. A. & R. F. (Jeremiah A. and Richard F. TenEyck,) boot and shoe makers 340 W. Washington
Terberville Robert, propr. Farmers and Drovers Hotel, ss. Nat. rd. west of bridge
Torr Philip, lab. r. 579 E. St. Clair
Terra William, stone mason, r. 467 S. East
TERRE HAUTE & INDIANAPOLIS R. R. W. R. Mc Keen, prest. C. R. Peddle, supt. R. A. Morris, gen. ticket agt. H. W. Hibbard, gen. frt. agt. Office Louisiana sw. cor. Tennessee. George B. Engle, agt. Frt. Depot Louisiana sw. cor. Tennessee. Machine Shops, West bet. Georgia and South, C. Idler, foreman
Terrell Eliza B. wid. Henry L. r. 175 N. New Jersey
TERRELL WILLIAM H. H. adjutant gen. of Indiana, office State bldg. bds. Bates House
Terreney Thomas, puddler Rolling Mill, bds. 300 S. Tennessee
Terry George D. carpenter Osgood Smith & Co. bds. Ray House
Terry Joel N. marble worker Dame & Greenlee, r. 164 Buchanan
Terry William, (col'd) lab. r. 16 Douglas Alley
Tersey Amelia, r. W. Indianapolis
Tersey Eliza, weaver Merritt & Coughlen, r. W. Indianapolis
Tetus Jerry, (col'd) lab. r. 580 S. Tennessee
Teutonia Fire Ins. Co. of Cleveland O., C. A. Beidenmeister, agt. 96 E. Washington
Tewell E. Y. tuner A. G. Willard & Co. r. 69 N. East
Tewes Henry, cooper Henry Schwomeyer, r. 351 N. Noble
Tezas Lewis, huckster, r. 323 N. Alabama
THACHER W. P. propr. National Hotel, r. same
Thacher William, engineer Hill & Wingate, r. Meek nr. city limits
Thalman Isaac, student Bryant & Stratton's College, bds. 75 N. Alabama
Thalman Isaac, piano manufacturer, r. 324 E. Ohio
Thalman Isaac, Jr. (Geisendorff, Richardson & Co. C. E. Geisendorff & Co.) and sec and treas. Indianapolis Piano Manufacturing Co. r. 336 W. New York
Tharp Andrew J. lab. r. ws. Geisendorff 2 s. New York
Thatcher James, spoke turner Osgood, Smith & Co. r. 59 Eddy
Thatcher, Jasper H. lab. Osgood, Smith & Co. r. 270 Noble
Thatcher Louis, moulder Eagle Machine Works, r. 182 Meek
Thatcher Rebecca, wid. Amos, r. 184 Meek
Thayer Frank, bds. 309 E. Market

THA	320	THO

Thayer George V. (Thayer & Frauer) r. 309 E. Market
Thayer Mary A. wid. Daniel, r. 309 E. Market
Thayer Selden, salesman Rickard & Talbot
THAYER & FRAUER (George V. Thayer and Albert G. Frauer) grocers 248 E. Washington
The *Indiana Teacher,* John B. Alden, publisher, 18 S. Pennsylvania
The *Inventor and Mechanic,* Charles Werbe propr. 81 E. Market
The *Little Chief,* Shortridge & Alden, publishers, 18 S. Pennsylvania
Theobald F. china, glass and queensware 94 E. Washington, r. same
Theodore Thomas, bricklayer, r. 285 N. East
Thinler Fred, baker, bds. 68 S. West
THIRD PRESBYTERIAN CHURCH, Illinois ne. cor. Ohio, Rev. Robert Sloss, pastor
THIRD STREET MISSION CHURCH (Methodist) ns. 3d bet. Illinois and Tennessee
THISTLETHWAITE JOHN P. publisher, r. 24 W. New York
Thistlethwaite Rachel wid. r. 24 W. New York
Thomann John, saloon 44 Massachusetts av. r. same
Thomas Albert, blacksmith Samuel Raymond, r. 25 S. New Jersey
Thomas Benj. finisher Hoosier Woolen Factory, r. 26 N. Douglas
Thomas Caleb, butcher Poland & Wiseman, r. W. Indianapolis
Thomas Charles (C. Thomas & Bros.) r. 115 N. Noble
Thomas H. Connor, grocer, bds. 115 N. Noble
Thomas Charles & Bros. (Charles, John C. and W. A. Thomas) ret. grocers 250 E. Ohio
Thomas D. L. student, r. 76 Ash
Thomas Dudley, (col'd) lab. r. 192 w. 2d
Thomas Edwin, grocer, r. 69 N. Liberty
Thomas George, r. 115 N. Noble
Thomas George Jr. policeman, r. 115 N. Noble
Thomas Henry, roller Barker, Williams & Co.
Thomas Henry P. Capt. Mer. Police, r. 463 E. Georgia
Thomas J. E. clk. ns. Georgia bet. Liberty and Noble
Thomas James, bricklayer, r. 301 Indiana av.
Thomas James E. bkpr. W. U. T. Co. r. Georgia 2 e. of Liberty
Thomas Jefferson, tobacconist, r. 121 W. New York
Thomas John, supt. Rolling Mill, r. 319 S. Meridian
Thomas John C. (C. Thomas & Bros.) r. 115 N. Noble
Thomas John Q. student, bds. 76 Ash
Thomas John M. teamster, r. 179 S. Tennessee
Thomas John P. lab. r. Cumberland bet. the Canal and West
Thomas Lewis A. clk. E. L. Hutton & Co. r. 176 Virginia av.
Thomas Lewis L. carpenter, r. 176 Virginia av.
Thomas Mary Mrs. millinery goods 8 W. Washington, r. 704 N. Tennessee
Thomas Newton, telegraph operator C. C. C. & I. R. R. bds. ws. Michigan bet. Winston and Railroad
Thomas Olive P. wid. James, r. New York se. cor. West
Thomas Oliver E. (Richards & Thomas) r. 69 N. Liberty

I. Davis & Co., dealers in Hats, Caps, Furs and Straw Goods.

THO   321   THO

Thomas Richard, carpenter Rolling Mill, bds. 319 S. Meridian
Thomas Scott, fireman I. M. & I. R. R. bds. 146 Madison av.
Thomas William, (col'd) shoemaker, r. 226 W. Vermont
Thomas William A. (C. Thomas & Bros.) r. 115 N. Noble
Thomas William II. carpenter, r. 195 W. Maryland
Thomas William II. street car driver, r. 146 Madison av.
Thomas William M. bookkeeper, r. 463 E. Georgia
Thomas Zachary, wks. J. M. Van Blaricum, bds same
Thompson A. B. clerk Bates House, bds. same
Thompson Anna, wid. Thomas, r. 131 N. Alabama
Thompson Augustus, lab. r. 138 Elm
Thompson Daniel I. stonemason, r. 69 E. McCarty
Thompson David, teamster, bds. 151 Bluff rd.
Thompson Edwin P. money order clk. P. O. r. 430 N. Tennessee
Thompson Eli, (Emerson, Beam & Thompson) r. 125 N. West
Thompson George, lab. Rolling Mill, r. 272 S. Missouri
Thompson George, sr. patcher Rolling Mill
Thompson Gideon B. ("Snacks") printer *Journal* job room r. 256 N. Alabama
Thompson Henry, (col'd) r. 233 W. Ohio
Thompson I. C. asst. supt. I. P. & C. R. R. r. Peru
Thompson James L. clerk Clem & Bro. r. country
Thompson John, (Thompson & Peterson) r. 351 S. Pennsylvania
Thompson John, carpenter Shover & Christian, r. es. Illinois bet. 3d. and 4th
Thompson John, blksmith, r. 14 Dougherty
Thompson John, (col'd) lab. r. 428 E. St. Clair
Thompson John F. (Cartwright & Thompson) bds. Oriental House
Thompson John H. r. 430 N. Tennessee
Thompson John W. wagon painter Ind. Agricultural Wks. r. 65 S. California
Thompson Joseph, stonecutter, r. 37 S. West
Thompson Joseph, stove moulder, r. 54 Greer
Thompson Louis, (col'd) barber 107 S. Illinois, r. Meridian cor. Georgia
Thompson Mary E. wid. Fehling, r. 309 E. New York
Thompson Philip, jeweler, bds. 24 E. Washington
Thompson Thomas, driver Citizen's Street R. R. Co.
Thompson Thomas, lab. bds. 266 S. Illinois
Thompson W. A. C. tailor, r. 35 Henry
Thompson W. Clinton, (Thompson & Woodburn) r. 75 W. Ohio
Thompson William II. A. trav. agt. Indiana Masonic Home *Advocate*, r. 294 N. Pennsylvania
Thompson William J. stonecutter F. L. Farnam, r. 31 S. West
Thompson William O. clk. B. & O. R. R. bds. Ray House
Thompson William S. clk. D. B. McDonough, bds. 84 Mass. av.
Thompson & Peterson, (John Thompson and L. Peterson) saloon and beer garden, 351 S. Pennsylvania
THOMPSON & WOODBURN, (W. Clinton Thompson and James H. Woodburn) physicians and surgeons, office, 90 N. Illinois

Thoms Frederick, manager Spiegel & Thoms Furniture Co. r. 76 N. East

Thoms Henry, cabinetmaker Spiegel & Thoms Furniture Co.

Thomson Addie Mrs. bookseller and stationer, 13 N. Pennsylvania, r. 131 N. Alabama

Thomson Franklin, (col'd) lab. r. 2 Ann

Thomson George, (col'd) lab. Meikel Bros.

Thomson James, painter, bds. 726 N. Tennessee

Thomson William, physician, 66 and 68 Virginia av. r. same

Thoney G. W. cabinet maker Spiegel & Thoms

Thonssen Broder E. (L. Lndorff & Co.) r. 257 N. Mississippi

Thorn John, meat market, 141 N. Delaware, r. 87 N. Noble

Thorn William, blacksmith helper C. C, C. & I. R. R.

Thorn William, lab. r. es. Jackson bet. Cherry and Christian av.

Thorn William F. (col'd) lab. r. 13 Blake

Thornbraugh Allen, policeman, r. 194 N. Mississippi

Thornbraugh John M. clk. W. A. Briston, r. Washington nw. cor. Mississippi

Thornberry Joseph P. clk. E. T. Miller, bds. 30 Indiana av.

Thornley C. wks. J. S. Carey & Co.

Thornley Jasper, machinist D. Root & Co. r. 66 Forrest av.

Thornton Edwin C. clk. L. H. Tyler & Co. r. 139 N. Alabama

Thorp Caleb P. brickmason, r. 103 Ft. Wayne av.

Thorp Thomas, salesman John Woodbridge & Co. r. 86 E. Pratt

Thorp's Block & Hall, ss. Market bet. Pennsylvania & Delaware

Thrasher W. M. teacher N. W. C. University

Throne David, upholster Hume, Adams & Co. bds. Pyle House

Thudium George, clerk Indianapolis Nat. Bank, bds. National Hotel

Thurston, Charles P. trav. agt. Maxwell, Fry & Thurston, r. 79 W. North

Thurston Veloras, foreman lumberyard Emerson, Beam & Thompson, bds. 239 W. Market

Thumlert William, shoemaker J. W. Adams, r. 1 W. Washington

Thurston William B. (Maxwell, Fry & Thurston, r. 79 W. North

Thurston William B. jr. clk. Empire fst. frt. line, r. 79 W. North

Tibbetts James I. drug clerk, bds. 258 N. Tennesse

Tibbi Charles, lab. frt. depot C. C. & J. C. R. R.

Tick R. harnessmaker Ad. Hereth

Tieman Charles, porter Lesh, Tousey & Co.

Tierney Martin, lab. r. 152 Madison av.

Tiezel Adam, expressman, r. 156 Davidson

Tilbury Naham, cooper, r. 308 Indiana av.

Tilford Joseph M. (Greene & Tilford) r. College av. opp. N. W. C. University

Tilford Samuel E. mail agt. from Indianapolis to Michigan City, r. College av. opp. N. W. C. University

Tilly Herman, compositor Gutenberg Co. r. 17 N. East

Tilly Joseph, r. 17 N. East

Tilt Thomas C. clk. Pettis, Dickson & Co. r. 86 N. Mississippi

Tilt Thomas C. clerk, bds. Oriental House

TIM   323   TRA

Timmons Patrick, delive   man Capital Ale Brewery, r. es. Minerva 1 s. New York
Tindall Norman, photographer, 164 E. Washington, r. 83 Jackson
Tiner Fred. carpenter, r. 803 N. Tennessee
Tipton Lorenzo G. r. ns. New York 4 e. Minerva
Tisdale T. P. (Burnham & Tisdale) bds. Bates House
Titcomb D. agt. Rolling Mill Coal Co. r. 107 W. South
Tobin Thomas, boilermaker Eagle Machine Works, r. 1 Ann
Tobin Thomas H. lab. Rolling Mill, r. 421 S. West
Tobin William, clk. Treat & Claflin, bds. 421 S. West
Todd Charles N. (Todd, Carmichael & Williams) r. 228 N. Tennessee
Todd Henry H. presser Barker, Williams & Co. r. 164 W. Wash.
Todd John M. real estate agt. r. 312 Indiana av.
Todd Mary A. wid. r. 78 W. Market
Todd Robert N. (Todd & Bigelow) r. 78 W. Market
Todd S. A. tender J. C. Cropper
TODD, CARMICHAEL & WILLIAMS, (Charles N. Todd, Jesse D. Carmichael and Daniel G. Williams) booksellers and stationers wholesale and retail, Glenn's blk.
TODD & BIGELOW, (R. N. Todd and James R. Bigelow) physicians and surgeons, office No. 3 McOuat's blk. Kentucky av.
Tohlman Charles, baker 75 N. Alabama, r. same
Toledo Antonia, tailor, bds. 73 N. Illinois
Tomlinson James M. (Tomlinson & Cox) r. 410 N. Meridian
Tomlinson Stephen D. retired, r. 23 W. Ohio
Tomlinson & Cox, (James M. Tomlinson William C. Cox) drugs and medicines 18 E. Washington
Tompkins J. H. F. bkpr. Ind. Coach Wks. r. Pendleton Pike
Toohey James F. collector State Sentinel
Toole John H. wks. Osgood, Smith & Co. bds. 177 S. New Jersey
Toole Martin, lab. C. C. C. & I. R. R. r. 281 S. East
TOUSEY GEORGE, pres. Indiana National Bank, Washington cor. Meridian, r. 415 N. Meridian cor. St. Clair
Tousey Joseph H. switchman, bds. 75 Kentucky av.
Tousey Oliver, (Kennedy, Byram & Co.) r. 182 N. Meridian
Tousey Omer, salesman Kennedy, Byram & Co. r. 786 N. Illinois, n. of city limits
Tousey Ralph, r. Tennessee cor. 3rd
Tousey Wood G. (Lesh, Tousey & Co.) r. 359 N. Illinois
Tout Wilkson, bricklayer, r. 625 N. Meridian
Townley George E. bookkeeper F. P. Rush, bds. Bates House
Townsend A. G. wid. Horace, r. 321 E. Washington
Townsend William, r. 142 S. East
Tracy Henry, lab. C. C. & I. C. R. R.
Tracy Kate, pastry cook Oriental House, bds. same
Tracy M. O gen'l supt. National Art Association, 21 Talbott & New's block. r. same
Tracy Nancy, wid. r. 25 Maple
TRADE PALACE, (N. R. Smith & Co.) 26 and 28 W. Washington

Trask George K. driver Express Co.

Trask John, merchant policeman, r. 25 Greer

Traub Charles, printer, r. es. Jackson bet. Christian av. and Forest Home av.

Traub Conrad, cistern builder, r. 111 Fort Wayne av.

Traub Israel, grocer 500 N. Alabama, r. 490 N. Alabama

Traub Jacob, painter, r. 500 N. Alabama

Travan William, (col'd) pastor African Methodist Church, r. 244 N. Mississppi

Travelers' Accident Ins. Co. of Hartford, Conn. J. S. Dunlop & Co. agents, 2 W. Washington

TRAVELERS' LIFE AND ACCIDENT INS. CO. of Hartford, Conn. C. Colin, gen'l agent, 2 W. Washington

Traver George M. (L. H. Tyler & Co.) r. 475 N. Meridian

Travis Albert, wks. Emerson, Beam & Thompson, r. cor Washington and Mississippi

TRAYSER FREDERICK L. piano mnfr. and tuner 82 E. Market, r. same. See card business directory

Trayser George, piano mnfr. New York ne. cor. Davidson, r. 90 N. East

Trayser P. piano maker, r. 41 Russell av.

Treat A. A r. 25 W. Pratt

Treat Atwater J. (Treat & Claflin) r. 118 W. Vermont

TREAT & CLAFLIN,(Atwater J. Treat and Charles C. Claflin) merchant tailors, 30 N. Pennsylvania

Trebe Henry, turner P. Dohn

Treher Hiram R. compositor *Sentinel* news room, bds. 213 N. Pennsylvania

Treiter John, stonemason, r. ss. Lockerbie bet. Liberty and Noble

Treitschke William, clk. Charles Mayer & Co. bds. 31 W. Ohio

Trendelman Christ, lab. r. 312 N. Noble

Trendelman Fred. lab. r. 312 N. Noble

Treol Kate, wid. Peter, r. 316 W. Washington

Tretton Eugene, stonecutter, r. Chespeak bet. West and the Canal

Trigg Spencer C. miller Sohl Gibson & Co. r. 29 N. Blake

Trindle Samuel, conductor Terre Haute and Ind. R. R. r. 419 W. New York

TRINITY METHODIST EPISCOPAL CHURCH, Rev. J. M. Crawford, pastor, E. North nw. cor. Alabama

Triplett James, lab. r. Oak sw. cor. Vine

Trefz Gottlob, pastor German M. E. Church, r. 224 E. Ohio

Troost ——, stonemason, r. 247 S. Delaware

Trott John, confectioner R. L. Smith & Co. r. 138 E. McCarty

Trotter John, lab. 65 N. East

Trouse Henry, butcher, r. 12 Willard

Troutman J. B. express messenger A. M. U. Ex. Co.

Troy J. lab. frt. depot C. C. & I. C. R. R. r. 267 E. Washington

Trucks John (Trucks & Ray) r. 60 Kentucky av.

Trucks & Ray (John Trucks and Robert Ray) wagonmakers and blacksmiths 60 Kentucky av.

True Russell H. agt. Bartram & Fanton Sewing Machine 18 S. Pennsylvania, bds. same
Trueblood James, r. 347 N. Delaware
Trueblood Lindley D. clerk J. T. Huff, r. 347 N. Delaware
Trueblood Newton A. with A. C. Roach, r. 483 N. Mississippi
Trueman Alexander, butcher, r. Tennessee cor. Wilkinson
Trulex Henry, hackdriver, bds. 132 Maple
Trump Jacob, brickmason, r. 135 Fort Wayne av.
Trump Jacob, brickmason, r. 356 Wintson
Trusler Nelson (Morrow & Trusler) r. 162 N. Illinois
Trusler Thomas J. deputy sec. State, office State Building, r. Western av. out of limits
Trussell William, boilermkr. Sinker & Co.
Truxlex Jane, wid. r. 271 W. Merrill
Tubough John, clk. Eugene Renard, bds. 299 E. Washington
Tucker Duane H. traveling agt. Stoneman, Pee & Co. r. 780 N. Illinois
Tucker Hannibal S. clk. Trade Palace, r. 80 N. Mississippi
Tucker Joshua, salesman T. F. Ryan, r. 114 W. Vermont
Tucker Maggie, r. Cumberland bet. New Jersey and Alabama
Tucker Richard S. locksmith, r. 27 Grant
Tucker Samuel, r. 549 N. Mississippi
Tucker Tolfero, plasterer, r. 128 S. Tennessee
Tull John H. house and sign painter, r. 37 Rose
Tully Eliza A. wid. William, boardinghouse, r. 60 W. Market
Tune Mariah, wid. Josiah B. r. 191 S. New Jersey
Turk John, lab. Gas Works, r. 3 Thomas
Turn ——, chairmkr. Spiegel, Thoms & Co. r. 16 Chadwick
Turner A. (col'd) barber, 4 N. Meridian, r. 99 W. Georgia
TURNER ANDREW H. state agt. for Indiana of the Anchor Life Ins. Co. of New York, office No. 1 Wiley's blk. ws. Pennsylvania nr. Washington, r. 6 W. Washington
Turner Augustus, (col'd) barber, r. 99 W. Georgia
Turner Burton, (col'd) carpenter, r. 172 Douglas al.
Turner Chauncey L. with Indianapolis *Journal*, bds. 97 Delaware
Turner Hall, ns. Maryland bet. Delaware and Alabama
Turner James H. (Burke, Earnshaw & Co.) r. Moseville rd.
Turner John R. engineer, r. 214 Railroad
Turner Nathan, (col'd) cook, r. 232 Blackford
Turner Robert, (col'd) lab. r. 185 W. 2d
Turner William, bricklayer, r. 416 N. New Jersey
Turner William H. (W. H. Turner & Co.) r. nw. cor. Circle and Meridian
TURNER W. H. & CO. miners, manufacturers, whol. and ret. dealers in coal and coke, office 19 Circle. See card front cover
Turney Martin, lab. Greenleaf & Co.
Tuschong Michael, shoemaker R. Schildmyer, r. 239 Blake
Tuschong Michael, jr. shoemaker 368 W. Washington, r. 239 Blake
TUTEWILER BROS. (John W., Henry W. and Charles W. Tutewiler) stoves and tinware and house furnishing goods 74 E. Washington

TUT	326	UNI

Tutewiler Charles W. (Tutewiler Bros.) r. 85 Massachusetts av.

Tutewiler Henry, plasterer, r. 85 Massachusetts av.

Tutewiler Henry W. (Tutewiler Bros.) r. 166 N. Alabama

Tutewiler John W. (Tutewiler Bros.) r. 85 Massachusetts av.

Tuttle B. F. whol. grocer, r. 496 N. Meridian

Tuttle Orrin, driver hose reel steamer No. 1, bds. 261 W. Washington

Tylee James D. machinist, r. 225 W. Vermont

Tyer George W. conductor, r. 139 S. East

Tyler Anna Miss, teacher Fourth Ward School

Tyler Charles, r. 241 N. Illinois

Tyler Charles D. (L. H. Tyler & Co.) bds. 346 N. Meridian

Tyler John, carriage maker, bds. 124 S. Meridian

Tyler John, helper Indianapolis Coach Wks. bds. 141 S. Meridian

Tyler Lewis H. (L. H. Tyler & Co.) r. New York City

TYLER L. H. & CO.)Lewis H. Tyler, George M. Traverand and Charles D. Tyler,) "Tyler's Bee Hive," dry goods whol. and retail, 2 W. Washington

Tyre Charles W. machinist C. C. & I. C. R. R. bds. 139 S. East

Tyre Madison, machinist C. C. & I. C. R. R. bds. 139 S. East

Tyrrell W. Brindley, wood engraver H. C. Chandler & Co. bds. Little's Hotel

Tysen Ella S. Mrs. principal Second Ward School, bds. 199 N. Pennsylvania

U

Uhl John, butcher, r. ns. Kansas nr. Bluff rd.

UHL MATTHEW, physician 52 S. Pennsylvania, r. same

Uhl Peter, clk. C. M. Raschig, r. 118 E. Pratt

Uhl Peter, cigarmaker, r. 118 E. Pratt

Uhl & Durham, (Peter Uhl and H. E. Durham) tobacconists, 22 N. Pennsylvania

Underhill Ann E. wid. Frank, r. 355 N. Alabama

Underhill John W. special traveling agt. *Indiana Masonic Home Advocate,* and Brooklyn Life Ins. Co. bds. F. M. Blair

Underwood John M. r. 27 N. California

Underwriters' Agency of New York, C. A. Biedenmeister, agt. 96 E. Washington

Unger Julius, cigarmkr. r. 101 N. Noble

Union Fire Co. No. 3, engine House 125 E. South

Union House, George Ilg, propr. 202 S. Illinois

Union Mission Chapel, es. Blackford bet. Vermont and Michigan

UNION MUTUAL LIFE INS. CO. of Boston, Mass. A. S. White, gen'l agt. 39½ W. Washington

UNION NOVELTY WORKS MANUFACTURING CO. S. C. Frink, pres. R. S. Dorsey, sec and treas. office and works W. St. Clair cor. Canal

UNION STARCH FACTORY, W. F. Piel, manager, e. end New York

UNITED BRETHREN CHURCH, New Jersey se. cor. Ohio

UNITED PRESBYTERIAN CHURCH, ns. Ohio bet. Delaware and Pennsylvania

UNITED STATES EXPRESS CO. J. Butterfield agt, 42–44 E. Washington

United States Fire Ins. Co. of Baltimore, J. Barnard agt. Vinton's block, Pennsylvania sw. cor. Market

United States Life Ins. Co. of New York, J. N. Wright & Son, agents Northern Indiana, 10 E. Washington

Universalist Church, 80 W. Michigan. No pastor or service

University Square, bet. Meridian and Pennsylvania and New York and Vermont

Unversagt A. wks. Kingan & Co.

Unversal Andrew, butcher, r. 125 E. Merrill

Unversau John, r. 345 S. Alabama

Ulrich John G. clk. Hume, Adams & Co. bds. Bicking House

Updike John, plasterer, r. 154 S. Noble

Updike Samuel H. plasterer, r. 107 Meek

Upfold George, Bishop Diocese of Indiana, r. 477 N. Penn.

Urban John, lab. r. 502 N. West

Urey William B. carpenter, r. 398 S. Tennessee

Urich John, clk. bds. 101 S. Illinois

Urlaub William, cigarmkr. Henry Speckman, bds. 108 S. Illinois

Ussenfort Fred. wks. Starch Factory, r. 316 Winston

Utz Frederick, r. 187 Davidson

V

Vacker John, lab. foundry, r. 315 S. Pennsylvania

Vaeland Christian, switchman Central R. R. r. 134 Union

Vahling William, lab. r. 53 Harrison

Vail Ella, packer Barker, Williams & Co.

Vail Sidney Jr. teacher Indiana Deaf and Dumb Institute, r. Washington out of limits

Vajen John H. (J. H. Vajen & Co.) r. 128 N. Meridian

VAJEN J. H. & CO. (J. H. Vajen, J. S. Hildebrand and J. L. Fugate) whol. and ret. dealers in hardware and cutlery, 21 W. Washington

VALENTINE W. H. hoopskirt and corset mnfr. 34 W. Washington, r. 115 N. Illinois

Van Antwerp Geo. W. (Van Antwerp & Dryer) r. 175 N. East

Van Antwerp & Dryer, (G. W. Van Antwerp and Peter Dryer) blacksmiths 287 E. Washington

Van Benthuisen James H. r. 145 Virginia av.

Van Blaricum Mrs. r. 225 W. Washington

VAN BLARICUM JESSE M. carriage and wagon maker, 231 W. Washington r. 233 W. Washington

Van Buren Fred A. (Wiley & Van Buren) r. 287 E. Market

Van Burgen William H. carpenter J. L. & M. K. Fatout r. 75 W. Michigan

Van Buskirk Byron r. 128 E. Maryland

VAN	328	VAN

Van Buskirk Byron clerk W. D. Wyatt, bds. 128 E. Maryland
Van Buskirk Elias real estate agt. room 8, 30 W. Washington r. 128 E. Maryland
Van Camp Courtland, bookeeper (Van Camp & Jackson,) bds. 222 W. Ohio
Van Camp Gilbert C. (Van Camp & Jackson) r. 222 W. Ohio
Van Camp John carpenter, r. 239 E. Louisiana
VAN CAMP & JACKSON, (Gilbert C. Van Camp & Thomas B. Jackson) commission merchants, 69 W. Washington
Vance Lawrence M. jr. r. Washington cor. Cady
Vance Mary J. widow Lawrence M. r. Washington cor. Cady
Vance Rebecca, milliner J. W. Copeland & Co.
Vance Samuel C. (Indiana Banking Co.) r. East end Market
Vance Thomas, cabinet maker r. 327 E. Vermont
Vance Thomas P. clerk r. ss. Vine, bet. Broadway and Plum
Vancleve B. carpenter, r. 178 N. Mississippi
Vancleve Joseph, woodsawer, bds. 199 W. Maryland
Vandegrift Harry, mail transfer agt. Union dpt. r. 562 N. Tennessee
Vandegrift Wm. H. operator W. U. T. Co. bds. 562 N. Tennessee
Vandervort James O. P. miller Starch Factory r. Michigan rd.
Vandervort Perry, r. Michigan rd. nr. Washington
Van Dusan Chauncey, roadmaster I. C. & L. R. R. office depot Louisiana cor. Delaware, r. 288 E. South
Van Dyke William, salesman, bds. 89 Indiana av.
Van Dyne George, clk. Hume, Adams & Co. r. 38 W. North
Vanetten Martha Mrs. r. 129 N. Liberty
Van Horn Nicholas, (Harvey & Van Horn) r. 85 Ash se. cor. Cherry
Van Houten Cornelius W. r. 272 N. East
Van Houten Isaac H. clk. J. J. Graham, r. 272 E. North
Vankeuren Edward, carpenter and builder, r. Ohio ne. cor. Mississippi
Vankeuren William J. salesman Wherrett & Scott
Van Laningham C. W. clk. James Loucks, bds. 398 N. New Jersey
Van Laningham Elizabeth, wid. Wm. r. Broadway nw. cor. Vine
VAN LANINGHAM LEMUEL, secy. Indianapolis Gaslight and Coke Co. r. 274 N. Alabama
Van Laningham Minerva Miss, bds. Broadway nw. cor. Vine
Vannoy Warder, plasterer, bds. 158 E. Michigan
Van Pelt Louis, auctioneer D. B. Taylor & Co. r. 18 Fletcher av.
Van Sielen Alexander, ins. agt. with E. B. Martindale, bds. R. B. Duncan
Vanstan John, shoemaker 15 Virginia av. r. 239 S. Alabama
Van Syckle Henry, bds. 135 E. Washington
Van Syckle John, farmer, National rd. W. Indianapolis
Van Tuyle Abraham, foreman C. & I. J. R. R. machine shops, r. 328 E. Georgia
Van Vleet Druciler, dressmaker 30 N. Delaware, r. same
Van Way Walter, r. 181 S. Tennessee
Van Way Warren G. lab. freight depot I. C. & L. R. R.

VAR	329	VIN

Varnitt Thomas, watchman, r. 390 N. Mississippi
Varney Catharine, wid. Thadeus, r. 291 E. Ohio
Vater Thomas J. builder, r. 339 N. Tennessee
Vaughan Jacob, carpenter, r. 548 N. Mississippi
Vaughn Dennis, carpenter, r. 75 N. Louisiana
Vaughn Dennis, car inspector I. C. & L. Rw.
Vaughn W. N. student Bryant & Stratton's College, bds. 26 N. Mississippi
Vawter John A. huckster, r. 275 Bluff rd.
Veazey William, brakeman, r. 62 Bicking
Vehle Henry, watchman Express office, r. 313 N. Noble
Vehling Frederick, grocer, 195 E. South, r. same
Vehling Frederick, tailor Becker & Heuber, r. 195 S. New Jersey
Vehling Henry, chair maker Spiegel & Thoms
Veith Christian J. (Barker, Williams & Co.) r. 126 Duncan
Veizer Frederick, driver Helwig & Co.
Verity Lauretta, wks. Cotton Factory
Verity Stephen T. piano maker, 42 Huron, r. same
Vert Addie Miss, bds. Martin House
Vert Elizabeth, wid. Daniel, r. 282 S. Missouri
Verp Lou Miss, bds. Martin House
Vert Reasner, painter Corneilus & McElvano, r. 282 S. Missouri
Vert William, lab. frt. depot T. H. & I. R. R.
Vesseler John, lab. r. 133 N. Railroad
Vest William A. driver Citizens St. R. R. Co.
Vestal John N. compositor *Journal* news room, r. 131 Blackford
Vetters John, cabinetmaker, r. 211 S. Pennsylvania
Vickers Edwin, salesman Scott, West & Co. bds. National Hotel
VICKERS WILLIAM B. local editor *Mirror*, r. 120 N. Mississippi
Victor Catherine, wid. r. 166 N. Mississippi
Victor Celia Mrs. cook Institute for the Blind, r. same
Victor Julius A. (Leonard & Victor) r. 65 W. Washington
Victor Marshie, bookbinder J. H. C. Smith
Vielhaber Daniel, boot and shoe mkr. 204 E. Washington, bds. Little's Hotel
Vielhaber Gustave, shoemaker Daniel Vielhaber
Vieweg August, tailor, r. 125 E. Washington
Villant Frederick, lab. C. & I. J. R. R.
Vincent William A. conductor Indiana Central R. R. bds. 61 Russell av.
VINCENT WILLIAM H. carpenter and builder 178 N. Delaware, r. same
Vinnedge George W. (Hill & Vinnedge) r. 245 N. Illinois
Vinnedge John A. (Wright & Vinnedge) r. 704 N. Illinois
Vinnedge Joseph D. (Vinnedge, Jones & Co.) r. Pennsylvania nw. cor. W. Ohio
VINNEDGE, JONES & CO. (Joseph D. Vinnedge, Agilla Jones, Jr. and William S. Armstrong) boots and shoes whol. 66 S. Meridian
Vinton Almus E. (Kiefer & Vinton and H. Salisbury & Co.) r. N. Meridian n. of limits

VIN	330	WAG

Vinton's Block, Pennsylvania sw. cor. Market
Vinyard Thomas, R. R. r. 9 Draper
Vinyard Wm. H. cash boy L. H. Tyler & Co. bds. 213 S. West
Violland Eugene L. clk. P. O. bds 47 N. East
Virgil Isaac H. supt. Express Co. stable, r. 164 N. Alabama
Virnickel Joseph, baker 285 E. Washington, r. same
Virt William P. frt. hand, r. 8 N. Liberty
Vocker John, lab. D. Root &. Co.
VOEGETTE JACOB, stoves and tin ware 103 E. Washington, r. 473 N. Delaware
Vogel Fred lab. r. 260 Winston
Vogel Frederick lab. Rolling Mill, r. 446 S. West
Vogel Henry, carpenter, 523 E. Market, r. same
Voght B. J. leader Academy of Music, r. 242 E. Ohio
Voght Frederick J. (H. H. Langenberg & Co.) r. 246 W. Washington
Voight David, belt maker J. Fishback, r. 235 Bluff rd.
Voight Frederick, city express office, 26½ N. Pennsylvania, r. 111 N. Noble
Voight Henry W. (W. J. Holliday & Co.) r. 225 N. Mississippi
Volland Frederick, clk. C. Frese & Co. bds. N. Alabama
Vollmar Charles, mason Rolling Mill
Vollmar Gotfried, butcher Charles Kuhn, bds. same
Vollmar John, stone mason, r. 50 S. West
Vollrath Charles, cabinet maker, P. Dohn
Vondergotten Henry, (Vondergotten & Satorius) r. 279 N. Liberty
Vondergotten & Satorius, (H. Vandergotten and John Satorius,) barbers, 37 S. Illinois
VONDERSAAR WENDELL, blacksmith and wagon maker 144 Ft. Wayne av. r. 146 Ft. Wayne av.—see advt.
Vonnegut Clemens, hardware and cutlery, 184 E. Washington, r. 508 E. Market
Voorhees Jacob, plasterer, r. ns. Arch bet. Broadway and Plum
Voorhees Mary J. wid. A. L. r. 135 N. Illinois
Voss Gustavus H. (Voss & Davis,) r. 590 N. Illinois
VOSS & DAVIS, (G. H. Voss and Edward Davis,) lawyers, room 3 Talbot and New's blk.
Vumby Charles, lab. Rolling Mill, bds. 272 S. Missouri

W

Wachtstetter Charles, bartender, 154 W. Washington, bds. same
Wachtstetter Jacob, saloon, 154 W. Washington, r. same
Wachtstetter Mathias, r. 154 W. Washington
Wade Samuel, (col'd) barber, 249 E. South, r. same
Wade Walker, (col'd) lab. r. 140 Elm
Wade William R. comp. *Sentinel* news room, bds. 83 N. Penn.
Waegeman Gustavus, (Weinberger & Co.) r. 88 Union
Waggerman John, porter, r. 46 Coburn

Waggonet Geo. W. car inspector J. M. & I. R. R. r. 123 E. Merrill

Wagner Charles, r. 81 S. Illinois

Wagner David, fireman C. C. C. & I. R. R. bds. 315 E. New York

Wagner George M. porter W. I. Haskit & Co. r. 39 Georgia

Wagner George W. loan office, 66 N. Illinois, r. same

Wagner Louis, (col'd) cooper, r. al. bet. Noble and Benton, Georgia and Meek

Wagner Louisa Mrs. r. 261 Bluff rd.

Wagner Louisa, wid. r. Tennessee cor. 7th

Wagner Theodore A. clk. J. A. Heidlinger, bds. Emminiger Hotel

Waiest Christoph A. r. 187 E. South

Waijand John, policeman Union Depot, r. 147 Bluff rd.

Wainwright Samuel, tinsmith 18 W. Maryland, r. 278 N. Mississippi

Wainwright William, r. 23 W. St. Joseph

Waite Annie Miss, actress Academy of Music

Wakes George, machinist Spiegel & Thoms

Walden William, (col'd) whitewasher, r. 223 N. West

Waldo Azel, carpenter, r. es. McGill bet. Louisiana and South

Waldo George, tinsmith Munson & Johnston, r. 115 W. New York

Waldie James, agt. r. 105 N. Noble

Waldo Mary, wid. r. 258 N. Mississippi

Waldo William P. painter, r. 31 Vine

Walk Anthony, shoemaker, r. 336 E. Market

Walk Charles, clk. Lake & Co. r. Bluff rd.

Walk Julius C. watchmkr. W. P. Bingham & Co. r. ss. Michigan bet. Illinois and Tennessee

Walk Louis, boardinghouse, 26 and 28 W. Georgia, r. same

Walker Alva S. (William Sumner & Co.) r. 81 W. Vermont

Walker Andrew, engineer, r. 128 St. Mary

Walker Austin, (col'd) billiard hall, 195 W. Washington, r. Missouri nr. cor. Washington

Walker Edward, stencil cutter, 25 W. Washington, r. same

Walker Frank, (col'd) lab. r. Missouri nr. Tinker

Walker Henry, (col'd) lab. r. Rhode Island nr. Blake

Walker Henry, r. 41 Elm

Walker Henry, sawer McCord & Wheatley

WALKER HENRY H. state agt. Home Ins. Co. of New York, room 3, 2d floor Martindale's blk. Pennsylvania ne. cor. Market, r. es. Western av. bet. Butler and Forrest Home av.

Walker Isaac L. brakeman, r. 170 Winston

Walker John, carpenter, r. 418 N. East

Walker John, (col'd) waiter billiard saloon, r. 169 Indiana av.

Walker John, carpenter C. F. Rofert

Walker John C. painter, r. Bright sw. cor. Vermont

Walker Lizzie, wid. George, r. 172 W. Washington

Walker Noah A. pastor Christian Evangelist Church, r. 88 Christian av.

Walker S. W. engineer I. C. & L. R. R. bds. Ray House

Walker Thomas R. clk. Mahew & Branham, bds. Spencer House

WAL	332	WAL

Walker Webster, spoke turner Ind. Agricultural Works, bds. 211 S. Illinois

Wall Arthur H. sawer, r. 382 S. West

Wall Cora, bookbinder J. H. C. Smith

Wall Daniel, lab. r. 49 Ellen

Wall George, lab. r. al. bet. East and Liberty, Georgia and R. R.

Wall Gertrude, bookbinder J. H. C. Smith

Wall Harrison, lab. r. rear 47 Ellen

Wall William, flagman, r. 154 Stevens

WALLACE ALEXANDER G. Justice of the Peace 74 E. Washington, r. 105 Ash

Wallace Andrew, wholesale grocer and commission merchant Delaware sw. cor. Maryland, r. 86 N. Delaware

Wallace Andrew, stonecutter Scott&Nicholson, bds.258 S.Missouri

Wallace Catherine, wid. William, r. 358 Winston

Wallace David, clk. I. P. & C. R. R. r. New Jersey cor. Massachusetts av.

Wallace Frank, wks. Paper Mill, r. Geisendorff bet. Washington and New York

Wallace Henry, stonecutter, r. 167 S. Alabama

Wallace James, copyist, r. 219 N. Davidson

Wallace James, stonecutter F. L. Farman, r. 167 S. Alabama

Wallace James H. clk. Reasner & Shiltmeyer, bds. Michigan rd. e. of limits

Wallace John W. bookkeeper W. J. Wallace and dealer in flour and feed 43 S. Delaware, r. 391 E. Market

Wallace Johnson, stonecutter, bds. 258 S. Missouri

Wallace Joseph A. clk. Alexander G. Wallace, r. 105 Ash

Wallace Joseph W. salesman Andrew Wallace, r. 86 N. Delaware

Wallace Lydia, (col'd) wid. Zacariah, r. 170 W. Georgia

Wallace Oliver, brickmaker, r. 219 N. Davidson

Wallace Samuel, bricklayer, r. Vine nr. cor. Plum

Wallace W. lab. Sinker & Co.

Wallace William, lawyer room 4 Odd Fellows' Hall, r. 285 N. Delaware

Wallace William, lab. Rolling Mill, r. 258 S. Missouri

Wallace William, lab. Bunte, Dickson & Co.

WALLACE WILLIAM J. produce and commission merchant 43 S. Delaware, r. 391 E. Market

Wallace William P. mnfr. and dealer in cigars and tobacco 28 W. Louisiana, r. 160 E. Market

WALLACE WILL. W. grocer 441 N. Illinois, r. same

Wallace William W. r. 560 N. Illinois

Wallace's Hall, 54 S. Delaware

Walle John, blacksmith, r. 244 S. Delaware

Walle Mathew, blacksmith John J. Gates, r. 73 S. Liberty

Waller Bernhard, boot and shoe maker 151 Indiana av. r. same

WALLICK JOHN F. supt. Western Union Telegraph Co. Union depot, r. 36 W. Michigan

Wallingford Catharine, wid. Estes, r. 456 N. Delaware

Wallner Fred, clk. John Miller, bds. Boston House, 123 S. Illinois

WAL   333   WAR

Walls Henry M. confectioner, r. 21 E. North
Walls Wesley, printer *Journal* job rooms, bds. 277 N. East
Walpole Esther, wid. Thomas D. r. 410 N. Illinois
Walpole Luke, r. 410 N. Illinois
Walsh James, lab. r. 335 N. Noble
Walsh Luke, lab. Rolling Mill
Walsh M. boiler maker Sinker & Co.
Walsh Margaret, wid. r. 334 S. Alabama
Walsh Michael, lab. r. 334 S. Alabama
Walsh Robert B. salesman P. M. Culliny, bds. 40 N. Pennsylvania
Walsman Frederick, pastry cook Union Depot Restaurant, r. 133 N. Liberty
Walsmann James H. locksmith C. Kindler, r. 133 N. Liberty
Walson Charles, wks. Wood & Foudray
Walter Charles, cabinet maker, r. 200 N. Mississippi
Walker George, cook, Palmer House
Walters James W. spoke turner Osgood, Smith & Co.
Walters L. M. pastor Ames M. E. church, r. 309 S. Meridian
Walton John F. piano maker Indianapolis Piano Manufg. Co. bds. Patterson House
Walton William W. heater Rolling Mill, r. 265 S. Mississippi
Waltz Frank, drayman Indianapolis Paper Co.
Wampler David, r. 47 Bates
Wampler William, conductor, r. 47 Bates
Wamsley Harvey, carpenter, r. 354 N. West
Wanan John, puddler Indianapolis Rolling Mill
Wands A. machinist Sinker & Co.
Wands Alexander, (A. Ruschhaupt and Wands,) r. 359 N. Pennsylvania
Wands John, boot and shoe maker, 28 S. Delaware, r. Grear ne. cor. McCarty
Wands John jr. shoemaker John Wands, r. 73 Huron sw. cor. Noble
Wands William, county physician and surgeon, 66 E. Market, r. 330 E. Vermont
Wann Henry L. millright S. Taggart
WARD BOSWELL, physician and druggist, 397 N. New Jersey, r. 357 N. New Jersey
Ward D. L. Express messenger
Ward Daniel, lab. r. 9 Peru
Ward Gabriel, toy mnfr. r. 395 N. West
Ward Harry, brakeman, bds. 262 E. Washington
Ward Homer, conductor St. Louis & Terre Haute R. R. r. 43 Kentucky av.
Ward James E. r. Geisendorff bet. W. Washington & New York
Ward John, lab. r. 62 S. West
Ward Michael, lab. bds. Ray House
Ward Michael J. salesman Pettis, Dickson & Co. r. 74 Fayette
Ward Patrick A. salesman Prenatt & O'Connor, r. 195 W. South
Ward Peter H. (Ward & Medsker) bds. 162 N. New Jersey
Ward T. wks. J. S. Carey & Co.

Ward Thomas, lab. bds. Ray House
Ward Thomas, salesman Pettis, Dickson & Co. room 54 S. Penn.
WARD & MEDSKER, (P. H. Ward and W. F. Medsker) lawyers, 83½ E. Washington
Ware Kate, wid. Robert, r. 111 W. South
Wareham Annie Miss, clerk N. & G. Ohmer, bds. Union Depot Restaurant
Warfield Charles, (col'd) porter, r. ws. Ash nr. cor. Cherry
Warfield William, (col'd) lab. r. 288 Railroad
Waring Isaac, bookkeeper Ind. Fire Ins. Co. bds. 140 N. Alabama
Warne Joseph B. (Mayhew, Warne & Co.) r. 59 W. Maryland
Warne Timothy, lab. bds. 217 S. Illinois
Warner Charles, bartender Wm. E. Carter, bds. Bicking House
Warner Charles, bookbinder Julius H. C. Smith, r. 35 Ellsworth
Warner Charles G. printer *Journal* job room, r. 35 Ellsworth
Warner Charles L. book binder Meikel Bros. r. 35 Ellsworth
Warner Edward W. printer, r. 35 Ellsworth
Warner George, barkeeper Knotts & Co. r. 72 W. Washington
Warner Simeon, (Wilson & Warner,) r. 213 N. Liberty
Warner Thomas D. printer, r. 226 W. New York
Warner William W. brickmason, r. 511 N. Mississippi
Warns Joseph, lab. r. 155 High
Warpole S. B. Mrs. r. 137 N. Meridian
Warren C. F. clk. J. H. Baldwin & Co. bds. 162 N. New Jersey
Warren George S. (J. H. Baldwin & Co.) bds. Spencer House
Warren J. Mrs. r. 66 s. Alabama
Warren John, blacksmith, Rolling Mill
Warren Michael, lab. r. alley bet. East and Liberty and Georgia and Railroad
Warren Michael, foreman Gas Works
Warren S. M. wid. George W. r. 167 W. Washington
Warren Timothy, fireman Gas Works
Warrenburg Wellington, lab. r. 216 Winston
Warrenburg William, teamster, r. 149 N. Noble
Warriner M. bds. Palmer House
Washburn Calvin, carpenter, r. 346 Winston
Washington Edward, whitewasher, r. Pattison bet. North and Michigan
Washington George, (col'd) lab. Union Novelty Works
Washington Hall, (Philip Fahrbach) 78 and 80 W. Washington
Washington Henry, (col'd) lab. r. 223 E. Michigan
WASHINGTON HOUSE, Peter Dietz propr. 181 S. Meridian
Washington Insurance Co. of New York, J. Barnard agt. Vintons' block Pennsylvania, sw. cor. Market
Washington J. M. patent medicines, r. 77 Jackson
Washington Lewis, (col'd) conductor sleeping car, r. Benton near Maryland
Wason A. W. veterinary surgeon, r. 85 S. Pennsylvania
Wasson Charles K. moulder Phœnix Machine Works, bds. 175 S. Tennessee
Wasson Ethelburt, telegraph operator, bds. 177 S. New Jersey

Wasson H. E. telegraph operator I. C. & L. R. R.
Wasson Hiram P. salesman L. H. Tyler & Co. r. 175 S. Tenn.
Wasson Joel, blacksmith N. Kimball, r. 218 W. Georgia
Wasson John, blacksmith, Bremermann & Renner
Wasson William G. machinist Rolling Mill, r. 177 S. Tennessee
Wasson William P. shoemaker 175 S. Tennessee, r. same
Wate Abbie, Miss, teacher, r. 290 E. Ohio
Wate Annie, teacher German-English 'School, r. 290 E. Ohio
Waterman Christian, (Berg & Waterman) r. W. South nr. Tenn.
Waterman Henry, moulder, Greenleaf & Co.
WATERMAN LUTHER D. physician and surgeon, 68 N. Pennsylvania, r. 377 N. Delaware
Waters ——, (col'd) lab. r. 188 N. Missouri
Waters John G. deputy City Clerk, r. 86 N. Mississippi
Waters Morris, lab. frt. depot T. H. & I. R. R.
Waters Samuel, lab. r. 166 S. East
Wathers Michael, lab. r. rear 242 S. Mississippi
Watkins Eward, painter W. B. Milender, bds. 266 S. Illinois
Watson Elmer W. artist, bds. 607 E. Washington
Watson G. T. cutter Barker, Williams & Co.
Watson James, enginer, r. 92 Bates
Watson John M. machinist, r. 607 E. Washington
Watson John C. lab. r. al. bet. East and Liberty and Georgia and Central Railroad
Watson Joseph S. printer Wm. Sheets, r. 207 W. Maryland
Watson Louisa, r. 117 N. Missouri
Watson M. Mrs. packer Barker, Williams & Co.
Watson Robert H. machinist I. C. & L. Rw. r. 393 E. Georgia
Watson Samuel W. bkpr. Harrison's Bank. r. 504 N. Delaware
Watson William P. gen'l bookkeeper First National Bank of Indianapolis, r. 421 N. Illinois
Watters Morris, lab. r. 27 Rose
Watts William, grate setter, r. 458 E. Georgia
Waugh Daniel, bolt cutter C. C. C. & I. R. R.
Waugh Henry, lab. C. C. C. & I. R. R.
Way Alfred, guitar teacher, r. es. Illinois above 6th
Way Amanda Miss, editress, bds. 20 S. Pennsylvania
Way Louisa, wid. Joseph, r. es. Illinois above 6th
Way Robert, boardinghouse, 20 S. Pennsylvania, r. same
Way Truman, switchman, r. 296 S. Alabama
Way William W. baggage master I. & C. R. R. r. 296 S. Alabama
Waymus Mary, wks. Paper Mill, r. ws. Minerva, 3 s. New York
Wayne C. foreman D. Yandes, jr. r. 51 S. New Jersey
Wayne Minnie Miss, clk. Frank J. Medina, r. 34 W. Washington
Weakly Jerry A. trav. agt. J. H. Cropper, r. 179 W. New York
Weakley Robert, tinner W. T. Jennings, bds. 70 E. Market
Weakman Charles, painter, r. ss. Wabash al. bet. New Jersey and East
Weaks Richard, porter, r. E. Wabash nr. cor. East
Weaner John, (Geis & Weaner) r. 292 S. East
Weathers A. barber Russell & Gulliver, bds. 66 N. Missouri .

WEA	336	WEB

Weaver David, moulder D. Root & Co.
Weaver Frank, bookbinder, bds. 233 N. Illinois
Weaver George, bricklayer, r. 323 N. Liberty
Weaver H. shoemkr. 299 N. East, bds. N. Liberty nr. cor. North
Weaver James P. bookbinder, bds. 233 N. Illinois
Weaver Orange R. salesman Sanders & Rockwell, r. 43 S. Illinois
Weaver Sarah Miss, teacher Sixth Ward School, bds. 244 S. New Jersey
Weaver Thomas J. plasterer, r. 280 S. Missouri
Weaver William W. undertaker, 39 N. Illinois, r. 233 N. Illinois
Webb Alfred L. (Webb & Bates) r. 59 Indiana av,
Webb Charles, (col'd) teamster N. S. Baker & Co. r. 162 Elm
Webb Jennie, saleslady J. Webb, r. 416 W. Washington
Webb John W. carpenter, r. 65 Bright
Webb Joseph P. carpenter, r. 291 N. Liberty
Webb Joshua, baker and confectioner, 56 N. Illinois, r. 312 Indiana av.
Webb L. A. D. Mrs. physician 65 Bright, r. same
Webb Laura Mrs. boarding house 64 W. Maryland, r. same
Webb Sidnor, r. 91 S. Pennsylvania
Webb Willis S. (Hibben, Tarkington & Co. and Indian Banking Co.) r. 440 N. Meridian
WEBB & BATES (Alfred L. Webb and Charles A. Bates) commission merchants and agricultural implemets, 83 W. Washington
Weber Adam, wks. Smith, Ittenback & Co. r. 340 S. Delaware
Weber David, cabinet mkr. Western Furniture Co.
Weber David, moulder Union Novelty Works, r. 278 Winston
Weber Erhard, porter Crossland, Hanna & Co. r. 53 S. California
Weber Fred, carpenter, r. 277 Massachusetts av.
Weber Fred. watchmkr. Andrew Œhler, bds. Globe House
Weber Frederick, clk William Hærle, bds. California House
Weber Frederick, machine hand, wks. Cabinet Makers' Union, r. 366 N. Noble
Weber George H. tinsmith 130 Bluff rd. r. same
Weber Henry, moulder, Schneider & Co.
Weber Henry, lab. r. 354 Railroad
Weber Henry, lab. D. Root & Co.
Weber John A. r. 29 Chatham
Weber Lizzie, candymkr. Daggett & Co. r. N. Noble
Weber Louis, barber 182 S. Illinois, r. same
Weber Mary, candymkr. Daggett & Co.
Weber Michael, sr. & jr. wks. J. S. Carey & Co. r. 2 Carey's row, Helen st.
Weber Peter F. r. 391 N. New Jersey
Webber W. F. student National Business College
Weber William, blacksmith William Hillman, r 105 Huron
Webster A. r. 706 N. Illinois
Webster C. B. wagon repairer, 291 Kentucky av. r. 235 N. Merrill

WEB	337	WEI

Webster George C. (Daggett & Co.) r. 140 N. East

Webster George C. Jr. salesman Daggett & Co. r. 224 E. Michigan

Webster George S. machinist Sinker & Co. r. 88 W. James

Webster Harvey D. salesman Daggett & Co. r. 140 N. East

Webster J. H. fireman, Hook and Ladder Co. r. 29 N. New Jersey

Weegmann C. H. music teacher, r. 259 E. New York

Weekly Telegraph, Gutenberg Co. publishers, 23 N. Maryland

Weekly Zukemft (The Future) Gutenberg Co. publishers, 23 W. Maryland

Weeks George, machinist, r. 174 E. Washington

Weeks William, bookkeeper, bds. 147 W. Maryland

WEGHORST HENRY, nurseryman and florist cs. Japan bet. Nebraska and South, city limits, r. same. See adv.

Wegorst Hermann, gardner, r. 467 S. East

Wehle Gregor, clk. G. Korniger, bds. 338 S. Meridian

Wehle Lucas, boot and shoe maker, 235 E. Washington, r. same

Wehling Charles, wagon and blacksmith shop, 234 S. Delaware, r. 236 S. Delaware

Wehling William, cooper E. McNeely, r. Elm, bet. North and Indiana av.

Wehn Christian, tanner, r. 451 S. New Jersey

Weibel John E. barber, F. Stein, r. 376 E. Ohio

Weibke Henry, drayman, J. E. Robertson & Co.

Weichman ——, baker, r. al. bet. Washington and Market, East and Liberty

Weidman John, brakeman, bds. 58 Benton

Weigant John, deputy Marshall Union depot, r. Bluff rd.

Weigle Gotlieb, tanner, r. 85 N. Noble

Weiker Henry, teamster, J. Marsee & Son

Weikert Alonzo, clk. W. I. Haskit & Co. bds. 127 Duncan

Weikert Joseph carpenter, L. H. Daniels, r. 127 Duncan

Weilacher John, barkeeper, D. Moninger, r. 386 N. Tennessee

Weiland August L. tailor, N. Tennessee, 2 s. McCauley

Weiland Christopher, switchman, C. C. & I. C. R. R.

Weiland Ernest, machinist Greenleaf & Co.

Weiland William C. clk. C. H. Schromeyer, bds. 558 S. Illinois

Weinberger Ernst, (Weinberger & Co.) r. 297 N. East

Weinberger Hermann, (Weinberger & Co.) r. 138 S. Meridian

WEINBERGER & CO. (Hermann and Ernst Weinberger and Gustavus Waegemann) restaurant, 10 W. Louisiana

Weinderger John, bds. 88 Union

Weinrich William G. bartender James McB. Shepherd, r. 156 E. Washington

Weir James L. salesman Pettis, Dickson & Co. bds. Macy House

WEIR WILLIAM, marble worker and dealer, 42 and 44 Virginia av. rooms 75 Virginia av.

Weismire John, wks. Rolling Mill

Weiss George, tailor G. H. Heitkam, bds. 8 W. Washington

Weiss Henry, barber, 143 E. Washington, r. 401 E. Washington

Weiss John, bricklayer, r. 343 N. Delaware

	WEI	338	WEN

Weiss John L. saloon, E. Washington cor. Benton
Weiss Peter, r. McCarty sw. cor. East
Welch A. J. switchman Union Depot Co. r. 83 W. Louisiana
Welch B. D. painter, bds. 74 State
Welch James, shoemkr. John G. Kisner, bds. 199 W. Maryland
Welch John, puddler Rolling Mill, r. 232 S. Missouri
Welch John, lab. r. 374 S. Delaware
Welch Luke, blacksmith, r. 5 Willard
Welch Michael, clerk, r. 80 Fayette
Welch Patrick, engineer C. C. & I. C. R. R. bds. 58 Benton
Welch Patrick, wks. Kingan & Co. r. 30 Helen
Welch Patrick, saloon, 23 W. Washington, r. 355 S. Meridian
Welch William, tinner R. L. & A. W. McOuat, r. 355 S. Meridian
Weldon James, miller Brett, Braden & Co. r. at Mill
Weller James, r. Blake, nw. cor. New York
Weller Levi, mail carrier, r. 651 N. Tennessee
Weller William, blacksmith Sinker & Co. r. 281 N. Mississippi
Wellman Hirain B. patent agt. r. 29 Vine
Well Frederick shoemkr. r. 96 N. Noble
Wells Andrew J. policeman, r. 240 N. Illinois
Wells Charles, (col'd) coachman, r. opposite City Hospital
Wells Charles, delivery clk. J. F. Wingate
Wells E. shoemkr. John Wands, r. 191 S. New Jersey
Wells Graham A. dentist, 15 E. Washington, r. 181 N. New
    Jersey
Wells James, engineer Judson & Dodd, r. alley bet. East and
    Liberty, Georgia and the Railroad
Wells John II. carpenter, r. 786 N. Tennessee
WELLS MERIT, dentist, room 2 Yohn's block, Meridian, ne.
    cor. Washington, r. 112 Plum
Wells Peter, (col'd) lab. r. 201 Minerva
Wells Thomas, boot and shoemaker, 57 N. Illinois, r. 52 W. Ohio
Wells William F. carpenter, r. 40 Cherry
Welsh Anthony, carpenter, C. C. C. & I. R. R.
Welsh B. D. painter, r. No. 3. Blake Block
Welsh Edward, wks Hoosier Woolen Factory
Welsh James, lab. C. C. C. & I. R. R.
Welsh John, lab. r. 109 N. Railroad
Welsh John, watchman C. C. C. & I. R. R.
Welsh John, puddler, Indianapolis Rolling Mill
Welsh Maurice, propr. Senate Saloon 80 W. Washington, r. 355
    S. Meridian
Welsh Michael, lab. Bunte, Dickson & Co.
Welsh Michael, porter John C. Burton & Co. r. 80 Fayette
Welsh Patrick, saloonkeeper, r. 355 S. Meridian
Wempner William, lab. r. 59 Harrison
Wener Elizabeth, wid. Adam. r. 292 S. East
Wener John, saloon, r. 292 S. East
Wenger Frank, bartender George Geis, bds. 62 S Delaware
Wengers M. saloon and boarding house, 60 S. Delaware, r. same
Wenken Ernst (Back & Wenken) r. 178 N. Noble

Buy your Hats, Caps and Furs at I. Davis & Co. 12 E. Washington.

WEN   339   WES

Wenken William, pianomkr. Indianapolis Piano Mnfrg. Co. r. 178 N. Noble

Wenner J. J. varnisher Helwig & Co.

Wensing Hermann, tailor, r. 357 S. Delaware

Wensler Simeon, lab. r. 323 W. Market

Wentworth William H. fresco painter, 321 E. Washington, bds. same

Wentz C. A. farmer r. 319 Massachusetts av.

Wentz William W. conductor, r. 165 S. Alabama

Wenz Elizabeth, wid. William, r. 226 Dougherty

Wenz George W. carpenter, r. 226 Dougherty

Werbe Charles, United States patent agt. and propr. of *The Inventor and Mechanic*, 81 E. Market, r. Alabama cor. Court

Werbe Ferdinand L. grocery and notions 249 W. Washington, r. same

Werbe Henry G. watchmkr. W. P. Bingham & Co. r. 249 W. Washington

Wernbeck George (Holzwar & Wernbeck) r. 285 E. Washington

Werner Sandrook, driver. J. Carlisle

Wert Benjamin, clk. Clem & Bro.

Wert Edwin A. travelling agt. James W. Sulgrove & Co. r. 127 N. Alabama

Wert J. William, bookkeeper D. Yandes, Jr. bds. 127 N. Alabama

Werther William, meat market, Noble ne. cor. New York, r. 358 E. New York

Wesbey Charles, painter Ryan Bros.

Wesbey Ephram, cooper W. Baird, r. 324 W. Maryland

Wesbey William, compositor *Sentinel* news room

Wesling Conrad, drayman, r. 330 N. Noble

Wessler John, lab. Bunte, Dickson & Co.

Wesselhœft Emma Miss, assistant Indiana Normal Academy of Music, r. 263 Meridian

West Charles M. trav. salesman Stewart & Morgan, bds. Bates House

West Clinton, printer, r. 248 S. Alabama

West George, wks. J. S. Carey & Co.

West George E. (H. F. West & Co.) r. 483 N. Tennessee

West Henry F. (H. F. West & Co.) r. Cincinnati

West John, cabinetmaker, r. 143 Ft. Wayne av.

West John C. (Scott, West & Co.) r. 33 W. St. Clair

West Joseph, r. 127 N. Alabama

West William, (col'd) lab. r. 130 N. East

West William C. Railroad City Printing Co. r. 248 S. Alabama

WEST H. F. & CO. (Henry F. & George H. West, John I. Morris and A. W. Gorrell) importers and dealers in china, glass and queensware, 37 S. Meridian

Westenfeld Conrad, driver A. Balls, bds. 178 S. Illinois

Western Fireside, (monthly) F. C. Holliday, DD. editor, R. R. City Printing Co. proprs. 35½ E. Market

WES	340	WHI

WESTERN FURNITUBE CO. (John Weiest, John Deshler, Herman Richter, Christ. Fahrion, Charles Wilhelm, Daniel Willig, Andy Ackermann, Siezfried Hahnenstein, Theodore Sander) furniture mnfrs. and dealers, factory 461 N. Alabama, salesroom 105 E. Washington

Western House, Clawson & Woods proprs. 127 S. Illinois

Western Ins. Co. of Buffalo, A. I. Harrison agt. 79 W. Washington

WESTERN MACHINE WORKS, Sinker & Co. proprs. 125 S. Pennsylvania

Western Manufacturers Review and R. R. Journal, A. L. Logan editor, 30 S. Meridian

Western Musical Review (Monthly) H. L. Benham & Co. editors and publishers, No. 1 Martindale's blk. Market ne. cor. Penn.

WESTERN UNION TELEGRAPH OFFICE, 11 S. Meridian, Charles C. Whitney manager

Weston W. S. shoemaker, bds. Stanridge House

Westover Jonathan, moulder D. Root & Co. r. 124 E. Merrill

Westpfhal Theodor, lab. Bellfontaine frt. depot, r. 150 Union

Wexler Daniel, butcher, r. 424 S. Illinois

Weymouth Amos, blacksmith, ns. Nat. rd. west of the bridge, r. same

Wetzel Henry, bookkeeper Chas. Mayer & Co. r. 285 N. Illinois

Wetzel Peter C. gardner, r. s. end of S. West

Whalen Dennis, lab. r. 126 Meek

Whalen Timothy, flagman frt. depot C. C. I. C. R. R.

Whaling William, cooper, r. 45 Ellen

Wharton John C. student minister, r. 175 E. St. Clair

Wheat William C. (Wheat, Fletcher & Co.) r. Franklin, Ind.

WHEAT, FETCHER & CO. (William C. Wheat, L. W. Fletcher, Barnabas Coffin) pork packers, Blake n. Washington, office room 1 Vinton's blk. opp. Postoffice

Wheatly Henry H. mnfr. doors, sash and blinds and boxes, South cor. Delaware, r. 311 S. East

Wheatly Jerry, lab. Long & Joseph

Wheatley John M. bkpr. McCord & Wheatley, r. 309 S. East

Wheatley William W. (McCord & Wheatley and H. Daumont & Co.) r. 202 E. Ohio

Wheeler Albert W. tinner, bds. 31 W. Ohio

Wheeler Charlotte, wid. r. Maryland ne. cor. West

Wheeler Daniel Y. clerk Browning & Sloan, bds. Pyle House

Wheeler Henry H. carpenter, r. 311 S. East

Wheeler John, fireman, bds. 58 Benton

Whelan Edward, r. 245 W. South

Whelan Joseph K. bds. Massachusetts av. sw. cor. St. Clair

Whentling L. L. bds. Macy House

Wherrett William H. (Wherrett & Scott) r. 246 N. West

WHERRETT & SCOTT, (William H. Wherrett and Avery G. Scott) groceries and provisions 150 N. Tennessee

Whetzel Henry, clerk, bds. 285 N. Illinois

Whipple Charles W. machinist D. Root & Co. r. 315 S. East

Whisler Henry, miller Hoosier State Flour Mills

The latest styles of Hats & Caps at I. Davis & Co. 12 E. Wash'n.

WHI   341   WHI

WHITCOMB EDWARD A. (Whitcomb & Potter) also state agent St. Louis Mutual Life Ins. Co. Yohn's blk. r. 172 N New Jerey

Whitcomb James, saloon opp. Union Depot, bds. 18 W. Georgia

WHITCOMB JEROME G. agt. Jeffersonville, Madison & Indianapolis R. R. office ss. South bet. Delaware and Pennnsylvania, r. 162 E. Market

WHITCOMB & POTTER, (Edwin A. Whitcomb and Nathaniel C. Potter) gen'l ins. agts. room 4 Yohn's block, Meridian ne. cor. Washington

White A. M. r. 377 N. East

WHITE A. S. general agent Union Mutual Life Ins. Co. of Boston Mass. 39½ W. Washington, bds. Bates House

White Alfred (col'd) lab. r 77. Ann

White Allen C. paperhanger C. P. Wilder, r. 102 Bates

White Azariah S. ins. agt. bds. Bates House

White Charles, physician and surgeon, 80 Indiana av. r. same

White Charles H. (Coulter & White) r. 365 E. New York

White Charles M. ins. agt. r. 415 N. Tennessee

White Daniel, physician and surgeon 12 Indiana av. r. same

White Ferdinand G. actor Academy of Music, r. 329 Virginia av.

White G. W. salesman L. Ludroff & Co. bds. Martin House

White H. wks. B. F. Hetherington & Co. bds. 120 S. New Jersey

White Hiram, (col'd) farmer, r. opp. City Hospital

White Hughes W. merchant tailor, 11 S. Meridian, r. 36 Massachusetts av.

White J. lab. Sinker & Co.

White James, lab. bds. 23 Willard

White James W. gardner, r. 584 N. Mississippi

White Jane Mrs. boarding house 75 S. Pennsylvania, r. same

White John, teamster, r. 174 N. Davidson

White K. N. Miss, township librarian rooms 1 and 3 14 N. Delaware, r. 62 Bicking

WHITE LINE TRANSPORTATION CO. M. M. Landis agt. Alabama cor. Union R. R. track

White Margaret (col'd) wid. Stepen, r. ws. Douglas alley 2 s. New York

White Mary H. dressmaker Mrs. N. M. Allen, r. 102 Bates

White Newton, (col'd) lab. r. 3d nr. LaFayette R. R.

White Minerva, (Miller & White,) r. Orient nr. Deaf and Dumb Asylum

White Robert B. r. 251 E. St. Clair

White Roda, wid. Charles, r. Illinois opp. Macy House

White S. J. wks. W. P. Gibbs

White Sarah, wid. Samuel, r. 117 N. Mississippi

White Susan, wid. r. 494 Virginia av.

White Thomas, lab. r. 340 S. Alabama

White Thomas, moulder Sinker & Co.

White William, carpenter, bds. 325 E. Walnut

White William, bds. 59 Eddy

White William A. (cold) wks. John W. King, bds. same

White William H. carpenter, r. 72 Maple
White William M. lab. Osgood, Smith & Co.
Whitehead John, clk. Adam Gold, bds. same
Whitehead Lucy, weaver Hoosier Woolen Factory
Whitehead Thomas, miller, r. 420 W. Washington, (Nat. rd.)
Whitehead Thomas, sashmkr. M. Byrkit & Son, r. 160 Fort Wayne av.
Whitehead William, clerk Adam Gold, r. 415 W. Washington, (Nat. rd.)
Whiteman Peter, lab. r. 326 Railroad
Whiteside Joel G. bookkeeper Wm. H. Turner, bds. 31 W. Ohio
Whitman L. M. receiver Sinnissippi Ins. Co. 87 E. Market, r. 493 N. East
Whitmore Oliver, printer, bds. 30½ N. Pennsylvania
WHITNEY CHARLES C. manager W. U. T. Co. 11 S. Meridian, r. 94 S. Noble
Whitney Jonathan W. wagonmnfr. 46 S. Pennsylvania, r. 71 E. Maryland
Whitney Theopholis D. carpenter, r. 309 Indiana av.
Whiting Timothy M. straw bleacher, 26 Kentucky av. r. 42 Kentucky av.
Whitney William, agt. Junction R. R. r. 160 N. Meridian
Whitney William, boot and shoemkr. 119 S. Illinois, r. same
Whitridge Samuel, painter W. Whitridge, r. N. Illinois, n. of city limits
WHITRIDGE WILLIAM, house and sign painter, 60–62 E. Market, r. 363 N. New Jersey
Whitsit Benjamin F. bricklayer, bds. 291 Virginia av.
Witsit Courtland E. bricklayer and contractor, Washington sw. cor. Meridian, r. 291 Virginia av.
Whitsit Jessie, bricklayer, bds. 291 Virginia av.
Whitsit John A. brickmaker, r. 293 Virginia av.
Whitsit John B. engineer C. C. & I. C. R. R. r. 43 Bates
Whittaker J. W. carpenter, r. W. North nw. cor. Mississippi
Whittaker John, (col'd) lab. r. 530 S. Illinois
Whittaker Thomas T. clk, R. L. Shilling, r. 126 W. Michigan
Whittemore Elizabeth C. wid. John B. boardinghouse 58 Benton
Whitten Elijah Rev. r. 418 N. East
Whitton Robert L. clk. Stewart & Morgan, bds. 258 S. Meridian
Wicham Charles C. L. carriage painter with Fuller Smith, r. 216 E. Market
Wichmann Charles, coach painter, 229 E. Washington, r. Wabash bet. East and New Jersey
Wickenhucker Ernst, tailor Rudolph Rogge, bds. 335 Virginia av.
Wickliffe Charles, (col'd) lab. r. 67 Eddy
Wickliffe Peter, (col'd) fireman Bates House
Wickliffe Peter, (col'd) lab. r. 452 S. Tennessee
Wicks Richard, clerk Munson & Johnston, r. Wabash bet. East and Liberty
Wield Adolph, baker, r. 376 East Ohio
Wiebel Edward, barber, r. 376 E. Ohio

Wiedman George, clerk M. H. Spades, r. 71 Railroad st.

WIEGAND ANTHONY, florist and nurseryman, cor. Kentucky av. and the Canal, r. same, see card

Wiegand Michael, lab. r. 75 Coburn

Wieman William, lab. I. P. & C. R. Way, r. 476 E. Georgia

Wier J. S. clerk, bds. Macy House

Wierer Charles, brush maker Schmedel & Fricker, bds. Jefferson House

Wiesee Andrew, carpenter C. C. & I. C. R. R.

Wiese Andrew, student National Business College

Wiese Charles, carpenter, r. 283 E. Ohio

Wiese M. F. pastor Danish Lutheran Church, r. 66 Huron

Wieschan Augustus. baker A. Balls, bds. 178 S. Illinois

Wiest Christian, bartender Christopher Wiest, bds. Washington ne. cor. East

Wiest Christopher, saloon, Washington ne. cor. East, r. same

Wiggins Benjamin, porter Oriental House, bds. same

Wiggins Benjamin H. (col'd) r. 223 N. West

Wiggins George W. tinner C. Zimmerman, r. 36 S. Alabama

WIGGINS JOSEPH P. Pension agt. 54 S. Delaware, and (Foster & Wiggins) r. 325 N. Pennsylvania

Wiggins Lizzie Mrs. r. 268 N. Washington

Wiggins Percival E. clerk Joseph P. Wiggins, r. 38 W. St. Clair

Wigman Christian, baker Fred C. Bollman

Wikehart Henry, lab. M. Byrkit & Sons

Wikert Henry, lab. bds. 81 S. Illinois

Wiker Henry, teamster, r. 274 E. Louisiana

Wilch Catharine, wid. Christian, r. 152 E. New York

Wilcox Thomas, machinist, r. 31 Douglas

Wilcox David, driver Citizens' Street R. R. Co.

Wilcox Thomas, lab. Bunte, Dickson & Co.

Wilcoxin George, pressman *Journal* office, r. 73 N. Illinois

Wilcoxon William B. cabinetmaker, r. 9 Vine

Wilde John H. sawmaker Sheffield Saw Works, r. 274 Bluff rd.

Wilde Urban, huckster, bds. 274 Bluff rd.

WILDER CHARLES P. bookseller and stationer, 26 E. Washington, r. 374 N. Tennessee

Wilding Charles, clerk J. Norris, r. 183 N. Tennessee

Wilding William, shoemaker C. Friedgen, r. 183 N. Tennessee

Wildman Charles, brewer, r. 72 W. South

Wiles Charles H. clerk Thomas Wiles, r. 224 E. Market

Wiles Daniel H. (Wiles, Bro. & Co.) r. 53 Fort Wayne av.

Wiles T. S. salesman Thomas Wiles, r. 224 E. Market

Wiles Theodore, bds. Stanridge House

WILES THOMAS, stoneware and fruit jars whol. 25 E. Georgia, r. 224 E. Market

Wiles William D. (Wiles, Bro. & Co.) r. 394 N. New Jersey

WILES WILLIAM M. (Wiles & Reynolds) and Assessor Internal Revenue, office room 14 P. O. bldg. r. 281 N. Pennsylvania

WILES, BRO. & CO. (W. D. and D. H. Wiles, D. W. Coffin and John I. Morrison) whol. grocers, 149 S. Meridian

WIL   344   WIL

WILES & REYNOLDS, (William M. Wiles and Thomas E. Reynolds) druggists whol. and ret. Vinton's blk. opp. P. O.

Wiley Delaney, physician and surgeon 68 E. Market, r. 30 (old No.) N. Delaware

Wiley Emory W. (Wiley & Van Buren) bds. 287 E. Market

Wiley H. W. teacher N. W. C. University

Wiley William, storekeeper Arsenal, bds. Bates House

Wiley's Block, ws. Pennsylvania bet. Market and Washington

WILEY & VAN BUREN, (E. W. Wiley and F. A. Van Buren) state agts. for the Grover & Baker Sewing Machine, 21 E. Washington

Wileyman John, porter Maxwell, Fry & Thurston

Wilgus Jacob, lab. Greenleaf & Co.

Wilgus Jacob, enginner, r. 302 S. Illinois

Wilgus William, lab. Osgood, Smith & Co.

Wilharm Christian, lab. Central frt. depot, r. 265 S. Alabama

Wilhelm August, machinist McCord & Wheatley

Wilhelm Charles (Western Furniture Co.) r. St. Mary av. nr. cor. Alabama

Wilhoff George, teamster Schmidt's Brewery, r. 212 Madison av.

Wilie Andrew, clk. Mrs. Addie Thomson, bds. 131 N. Alabama

Wilie Charles, clk. Mrs. Addie Thomson, bds. 131 N. Alabama

Wilkening Charles, expressman, r. 283 Davidson

Wilkens Elnora, wid. John A. r. 80 E. Market

Wilkens John A. (Wilkens & Hall) r. 80 E. Market

WILKENS & HALL (John A. Wilkens, Thomas Q. Hall) bed and mattrass mkrs. upholsters and manufacturers of Streit's extension sofa lounge, 84–86 E. Market

Wilkes T. A. harness mkr. Frauer, Bieler & Co.

Wilkes Thomas A. artist, r. 390 S. Tennessee

Wilking Henry, shoemkr. 248 W. Washington, r. 20 S. West

Wilkins Clark L. belt mkr. Mooney & Co. bds. 31 W. Ohio

WILKINSON DAVID E. groceries and provisions 44 N. Pennsylvania, r. 412 N. Delaware. (See card.)

Wilkinson Frank M. clk. C. & I. J. R. R. r. 258 S. Meridian

Wilkinson John, clk. bds. 73 N. Illinois

Wilkinson William, compositor *Sentinel* news room, bds. 73 N. Illinois

Wilkison Henry (col'd) porter, r. 251 N. Liberty

Wilkison William, r. 85 N. Delaware

Will Adolph, clk. Gall & Rush, r. 96 N. Noble

Will Frederick, lab. r. 99 N. Noble

Will John F. r. 96 N. Noble

Willard Albert B. (Willard & Co.) r. 148 New York nw. corner Alabama

Willard Albert G. (Willard & Co.) r. 138 Massachusetts av.

Willard H. mnfr. of office furniture, 73 E. Market, r. same

Willard Isaac, brickmaker, r. 311 E. St. Clair

Willard M. F. wid. William, dressmkr. 264 S. Tennessee, r. same

WILLARD A. G. & CO. (A. G. and A. B. Willard and C. B. Wilson) dealers in pianos, music, etc. 4 and 5 Bates House blk.

WIL   345   WIL

Willcox Charles D. (Willcox & Means) r. 64 Fletcher av.

Willcox William H. speculator, r. 154 N. West

WILLCOX & MEANS, (Charles D. Willcox and Thomas A. Means) state agts. DeSoto Mutual Life Ins. Co. of St. Louis, Mo. rooms 3 and 4 Wiley's blk. opp. Odd Fellows Hall

Williams —— Mrs. r. 34 Helen

Williams A. Ford, cash. Indianapolis National Bank, r. 170 E. Michigan

Williams Alexander, (col'd) lab. r. Rhode Island nr. Blake

Williams Angeline, wid. Thomas, r. 131 Huron

Williams Anna M. wid. Jacob T. r. 88 N. California

Williams August, moulder, r. 172 W. New York

Williams B. (col'd) lab. Barker, Williams & Co. r. 228 Huron

Williams B H. gen'l trav. agt. G. W. Ex. Co. r. 298 E. Market

Williams C. lab. freight depot C. C. & I. C. R. R.

Williams Charles, cabinetmkr. r. Alabama se. cor. St. Mary

WILLIAMS CHARLES, undertaker, 10 Bates House sq. r. 20 W. Michigan

Williams Charles C. traveling agt. r. 748 N. Illinois

Williams Charles C. student National Business College, bds. 20 W. Michigan

Williams Curtis, paperhanger Gall & Rush

Williams Daniel, student, bds. Jackson sw. cor. Cherry

Williams Daniel, plasterer, r. 277 E. New York

Williams Daniel, (col'd) fireman Bates House

Williams Daniel G. (Todd, Carmichael & Williams) r. 512 N. Tennessee

Williams David, blacksmith, r. 237 W. Merrill

Williams Edgar H. bookkeeper H. C. Chandler & Co. bds. 84 Massachusetts av.

Williams Edgar L. asst. bookkeeper Browning & Sloan, r. 226 N. Illinois

Williams Edward, (col'd) cook Sherman House

Williams Elizabeth, wid. William, r. 438 S. Illinois

Williams F. C. paperhanger, r. 299 S. East

Williams George, lab. r. 195 W. Ohio

Williams George, lab. r. ws. Bright 2 s. New York

WILLIAMS GEORGE B. supervisor int. rev. for the State of Ind. office No. 4 Vinton's blk. opp. P. O. bds. Bates House

Williams Gibbon Mrs. bds. 475 N. Pennsylvania

Williams Gottlieb, blacksmith F. Smith, r. ns. New York bet. Mississippi and Canal

Williams Griffith, blacksmith C. C. & I. C. R. R.

Williams Horace, (col'd) lab. Lesh, Tousey & Co.

Williams Isaac M. (col'd) clergyman and teacher, 642 N. Mississippi, r. Howard bet. 2d and 3d

Williams James, miller John Carlisle, r. 210 W. Ohio

Williams James M. regst. clk. P. O. r. 287 N. Delaware

Williams James T. machinist Phœnix Machine Works, r. 88 N. California

23

WIL	346	WIL

Williams Jefferson, special agt. Charter Oak Life Ins. Co. bds. Pyle House

Williams Jennie R. bds. 201 Meek

Williams John, lab. r. 374 S. Illinois

Williams John C. (col'd) whitewasher, r. 85 W. Georgia

Williams John R. lab. Rolling Mill, r. 363 S. Missouri

Williams John X. heater Rolling Mill, r. 260 S. Missouri

Williams Joshua, r. 249 S. New Jersey

Williams Oris, (col'd) butcher, r. 140 Elm

Williams Owen, deputy county appraiser, room 6, 20 N. Delaware, r. 226 N. Illinois

Williams P. wks. J. S. Carey & Co.

Williams R. R. engineer Rolling Mill, r. 7 Willard

Williams Robert, hostler Exchange Stable

Williams S. A. Mrs. dressmaker, 37 W Market, r. same

Williams Sandy, (col'd) lab. r. Tinker cor. Missouri

Williams Silas W. (J. S. Davenport & Co.) r. 82 N. East

Williams Susan Mrs. r. 281 E. New York

Williams Thomas T. bricklayer, r. ws. Broadway bet. Cherry and Christian av.

Williams W. S. traveling agt. Lines, Smelser & Co. bds. Oriental House

Williams Wallace, (col'd) lab. r. Missouri nr. 7th

Williams William, (Barker, Williams & Co.) r. 204 N. Illinois

Williams William, lab. r. 397 Massachusetts av.

Williams William, policeman, r. 299 East cor. Merrill

WILLIAMS WILLIAM B. agt. Atlantic & G. W. Despatch, office, 80 Virginia av. r. 238 S. Alabama

Williams William D. salesman Trade Palace, bds. Palmer House

Williams William G. blacksmith C. C. & I. C. R. R. r. 70 Meek

Williams William R. asst. receiver Citizens Street R. R. Co. r. 13 N. West

Williamson Asher, lab. Osgood, Smith & Co. r. 128 E. Merrill

Williamson Hiram farmer, r. West Indianapolis

Williamson L. L. engineer Greenleaf & Co. r. Merrill bet. Delaware and Alabama

Williamson Levi B. finisher D. Root & Co. r. 317 S. East

Williamson M. D. lumber dealer, r. 460 N. Delaware

Williamson P. S. carpenter, r. 115 N. Tennessee

Willich Chas. cabinetmkr. Western Furniture Co. r. 163 St. Mary

Willich D. (Western Furniture Co.) r. 163 St. Mary

Willis Gaorge, express messenger Am. M. U. Ex. Co. r. 376 E. New York

Willis John, moulder James Hamilton

Willis Jonathan, tinsmith, 166 Indiana av. r. Smith sw. cor. Maria

Wills James, livery man, r. 164 W. Washington

Wills Thomas, (Thomas Wills & Co.) r. 305 E. New York

WILLS THOMAS & CO. (Thomas Wills and William M. Bone) grocers, 105 Massachusetts av.

Wilmington Edwin M. deputy auditor, r. 122 1st (St. Mary)

Wilmington Levi F. mail agt. I. & V. R. R. r. 311 N. Alabama

Wilson Alice B. Miss, teacher 5th Ward school, r. 97 W. Maryland
Wilson Ann, wid. William, groceries, 88 E. South, r. same
Wilson B. T. student National Business College
Wilson Benjamin, r. 686 N. Illinois
Wilson Charles, cashier H. H. Lee, bds. 178 S. New Jersey
Wilson Charles, clk. William Lee, bds. 173 S. Tennessee
Wilson Charles G. carriage painter, r. 266 S. Mississippi
Wilson Charles G. Jr. bookbinder, bds. 266 S. Mississippi
Wilson Charles P. (Willard & Co.) r. 337 S. Meridian
Wilson E. G. wid. r. 236 N. Illinois
Wilson Ebenezer, clk. Clem & Bro.
Wilson Elisha E. medical student with Dr. Atlem, r. 9 McOuat Block
Wilson Frank, actor, bds. 74 N. Pennsylvania
Wilson Frank, apprentice W. & J. Braden, bds. 30½ N. Pennsylvania
Wilson Frank, compositor *Sentinel* news room, r. Vermont nw. cor. Tennessee
Wilson Frank, hostler Citizens' St. R. R. Co.
Wilson Fred, bds, 69 W. Market
Wilson Frederick, mantlesetter Munson & Johnston, r. W. Market bet. Illinois and Tennessee
Wilson George W. (Gordon & Wilson) r. 409 N. New Jersey
Wilson George W. r. 174 W. Michigan
Wilson Grace D. Miss, teacher Sixth Ward School, r. 97 W. Maryland
Wilson Henderson Miss, wks. Indianapolis Paper Co.
Wilson J. C. manager telegraph office Union depot, r. 236 N. Illinois
Wilson James, carpenter, r. 477 W. Michigan
Wilson James, brakeman, r. 189 S. Illinois
Wilson James, carriage painter, bds. 75 Kentucky av.
Wilson James, clk; F. R. Baldwick, r. 32 W. Louisiana
Wilson James G. r. 418 Indiana av.
Wilson James H. clk. J. E. Robertson & Co. r. 324 N. Delaware
Wilson James H. hostler Citizens' St. R. R. Co. r. 18 N. Noble
Wilson James S. receiver Citizens' St. R. R. Co. bds. Globe House
Wilson James W. (Wilson & Warner) r. 300 E. North
Wilson John, lab. r. 188 W. Georgia
Wilson John, huckster, r. ns. Arch bet. Broadway and Plum
Wilson John, clk. James T. Layman & Co. r. N. Delaware cor. Ft. Wayne av.
Wilson John, clk. bds 392 N. Alabama
Wilson John, marble cutter, bds. 64 W. Maryland
Wilson John McC. baker, Parrott, Nickum & Co. r. 274 S. Mississippi
Wilson John S. carpenter, r. 68 N. East
Wilson John T. plasterer, r. 117 Benton
Wilson John W. tailor 55 Massachusetts av. r. 226 S. Noble
Wilson Joseph, miller Brett Braden & Co. r. 758 N. Mississippi
Wilson L. B. clk. Star Union Line, r. 97 W. Maryland

WIL	348	WIN

Wilson Lizzie, r. 167 W. Washington
WILSON LORENZO D. lawyer, 68 E. Washinton, r. same
Wilson M. piano forte maker J. H. Kappes & Co.
Wilson Margaret, wid. Patrick, r. 276 S. Delaware
Wilson Martha, wid. George, dress maker, r. 119 W. Vermont
Wilson Martin B. r. 253 Bluff rd.
Wilson Mary E. Miss, teacher Sixth Ward School, bds. 214 Union
Wilson Mary J. tailoress John W. Wilson, r. 226 S. Noble
Wilson Napoleon, (col'd) farmer, r. Rhode Island nr. Blake
WILSON OLIVER M. lawyer, room 2 Ætna bldg. r. 73 S. Tennessee
Wilson Richard, (col'd) lab. r. ns. Missouri nr. First
Wilson S. A. wid. James B. r. 239 E. Louisiana
Wilson Sanford B. r. Washington east of limits
Wilson Stephen, chair bottomer, r. 159 Elizabeth
Wilson Stephen B. salesman Wiles Bro. & Co. r. 126 E. Walnut
Wilson Stephen V. plasterer, r. 325 S. Alabama
Wilson Theodore, local editor *Sentinel*, bds. 27 W. Ohio
WILSON THOMAS S. chief of police r. 178 S. New Jersey
Wilson William, bookkeeper, Kimble Aikman & Co. r. 324 N. Delaware
Wilson and Warner, (James W. Wilson and Simeon Warner) lumber merchants, 27 Massachusetts av.
Wilte August, tripe cleaner, r. ss. Nat. Rd. west of the bridge
Winans Jennie, wid. r. 115 N. Missouri
Winchen Elizabeth, wid. Peter, r. 137 N. Noble
Winchenbach E. D. picture dealer, bds. 426 N. Mississippi
Winder Alfred, chief operator W. U. T. Co. r. ns. Georgia 4 e. Liberty
Winder Annie Miss, teacher 5th Ward School
Winder John W. ferreotype gallery 33 W. Washington, r. Cincinnati, Ohio
Windsor Lydia, wid. Elan F. r. 186 Bates
Winesley Simon, carpenter Indianapolis Brewery
Wing T. R. conductor C. C. & I. C. R. R. bds. Spencer House
Wingate Joseph F. groceries and provisions 42 N. Pennsylvania, r. 306 N. Delaware
Wingate William L. (Hill & Wingate) r. 122 Virginia av.
Wingle William F. clerk, r. 194 Davidson
Wink Theressa Mrs. wid. John, r. 194 E. Washington
Winkle William F. clerk J. R. Blake & Co. r. 194 N. Davidson
Winn Cynthia, wid. r. 136 E. St. Joseph
Winner Jacob, varnisher, r. 484 S. New Jersey
Winnesheik Ins. Co. of Freeport Ill. M. Child, jr., state agent, 25 W. Washington
Winns A. J. dressmaker, r. 164 W. Washington
Winslow Alonzo B. bookkeeper J. D. Condit,r. 8 old P. O. bldg.
Winslow Ann, (col'd) wid. Jacob, r. 219 N. West
Winston John, (col'd) lab. r. rear 237 Massachusetts av.
Winter Anthony, wks. J. C. Ferguson & Co. r. 171 St. Mary
Winter David, painter, r. nr. cor. Jackson and Vine
Winter F. W. broommaker, r. 219 Coburn

Winters Henry F. machinist, r. 172 W. Washington
Winters Henry S. machinist r. 172 W. Washington
Winter J. N. tailor 27 N. Illinois, r. 43 Ellsworth
Winter John A. painter, r. 345 N. Nobie
Winter Philip, malster Long, Snyder & Co. bds. Ray House
Winter Philip C. malster Long, Snyder & Co. r. 240 S. Delaware
Winter R. J. ragdealer, r. 244 S. Meridian
Wirer Charles, bds. Jefferson House
Wirmer Frank, teamster, r. Arch bet. Broadway and Jackson
Wirt John, bds. 244 S. New Jersey
Wirth John R. clerk Bruner & Comer, bds. Tennessee cor. 4th
Wirt Sarah C. Mrs. 1st asst. teacher 8th Ward District School
Wirtz Henry, blacksmith Ind. Coach Works, r. 503 S. East
Wirtz Jacob, veterinary surgeon, r. 503 S. East
Wirtz John, bds. 73 N. Illinois
Wise August, lab. B. F. Haugh & Co. r. 573 St. Clair
Wise William T. (col'd) barber, 223 Massachusetts av. r. same
Wisehart Benjamin, (Wisehart & Calvert,) bds. 375 N. West
WISEHART & CALVERT, (Benjamin F. Wisehart and Redmon
    Calvert) flour and feed dealers, 185 Indiana av.
Wiseman Barbara A. wid. Jacob J. r. 199 N. Pennsylvania
Wiseman John, weaver, r. 347 W. Washington
Wiseman Joseph, spinner, r. 347 W. Washington
Wiseman Simon, teamster, r. 355 W. Washington
Wiseman Simon S. (Poland & Wiseman) r. 353 W. Washington
Wiseman Theophilus, student, r. 347 W. Washington
Wiseman William, Mrs. wid. r. 391 W. Washington
Wiseman William, watchman C. C. & I. C. R. R. r. 114 Meek
Wishmeyer C. with Union Starch Factory, r. 292 N. Winston
Wishmeyer Christian, lab. Starch Factory, r. 292 N. Winston
Wishmeyer Henry, fireman Starch Factory, r. 176 N. Winston
Wishmeyer Michael C. clerk Hay & Co. bds. 345 McCarty
Wishmier Anthony, lab. r. 274 E. Ohio
Wishmier Charles F. Starch Factory, r. 292 Winston
Wishmier Christian F. saw mill, ss. North bet. Railroad and Da-
    vidson, r. 258 Davidson
Wishmier Christian F. wks. Starch Factory, r. 292 Winston
Wishmier Christopher, teamster, r. W. Indianapolis
Wishmier John, lab. r. 345 E. McCarty
Wishmier William, wks. Starch Factory, r. 292 Winston
Wissert John, boarding house, 180 S. Meridian, r. same
Withorn Benjamin, upholster Wilkens & Hall, 84–86 E. Market
Witking Henry, drayman, r. 293 Davidson
Witman H. N. carpenter Builders and Mnfrs. Association, r.
    101 Bradshaw
Witman Harrison T. physician and surgeon, 39 Ind. av. r. same
WITT BENNETT F. lawyer, war claim agt. and supervising agt.
    Franklin Life Ins. Co. Washington sw. cor. Meridian r. 364
    N. New Jersey
WITT & ARBUCKLE, (B. F. Witt and M. Arbuckle) real estate
    agts. Washington sw. cor. Meridian

WIT	350	WOO

Witte Edward, groceries ret. 300 Blake, r. same

Wittenberg Charles, r. 217 E. Ohio

Wittenbrink Henry, cigar maker Henry Reinken, bds. 266 E. Washington

Witthoeft Frederick, grocer and saloon, 329 Indiana av. r. 325 Indiana av.

Witthoeft Henry, carpenter. r. 82 S. East

Witthoeft William, cabinetmaker Helwig & Co.

Wittlinger Jacob, grocer, 100 S. Noble, r. same

Witzmann John, teamster, r. 162 Winston

Wocher John, stonecutter Smith, Ittenbach & Co. r. 21 Meek

Wocher Julius, student National Business College

Woelz Charles A. confectioner, 149 N. Delaware, r. same

Wolder Victor, brush maker Schmedel & Fricker, bds. Morris bet. East and New Jersey

Wolf Catharine, wid. Philip, saloon and boarding house, 76 S. Delaware, r. same

Wolf Charles, collar maker, r. 149 E. Washington

Wolf Elisha, foreman machine shops J. S. Carey & Co. r. 8 Carey's row, Helen st.

Wolf Erastus, cooper D. Burton & Co. r. Geisendorff bet. Washington and New York

Wolf Isaac, cooper D. Burton & Co. r. ws. Minerva 2 s. N. York

Wolf Louisa, wid. Jacob, r. 246 Madison av.

Wolf Moses, salesman Hays, Rosenthal & Co. r. 144 Virginia av.

Wolf Philip, cigarmaker Henry Schulz, r. 176 S. Delaware

Wolf Samuel, r. 10 Harrison

Wolf Sophia, wid. John, r. ws. Minerva 2 s. New York

Wolf William, painter D. C. Chapman

Wolfrom Albert T. (Wolfram Bros.) r. 201 N. New Jersey

Wolfrom Bros. (Christian A. and Albert T. Wolfram) stoves and tinware, 197 E. Washington

Wolfrom Charles A. foreman *Journal* press room, r. 201 N. New Jersey

Wolfrom Christian A. (Wolfrom Bros.) r. 201 N. New Jersey

Wolfrom Ernst E. bookkeeper Ind. Banking Co. bds. 201 N. New Jersey

Wolfrom Sarah, wid. Charles, r. 201 N. New Jersey

Wompner Henry, lab. frt. depot C. C. & I. C. R. R.

Wonnell George, painter, r. 31 Indiana av.

Wonnell Mary E. (Wonnell & Montany) r. 31 Indiana av.

Wonnell & Montany, (Miss Mary E. Wonnell and Miss Annie Montany) dressmakers, 31 Indiana av.

Wonner Louis, groceries and provisions 46 Indiana av. r. same

Wood Albert, lab. r. 374 S. West

Wood Alexander, asst. City Engineer, r. 18 W. Vermont

Wood Andrew B. cooper, J. S. Carey & Co. r. 3 Carey's Row

WOOD AUGUSTUS D. propr. Hoosier Foundry and Stove Works 135-7 S. Delaware, r. 201 N. Delaware

Wood Cynthia, wid. Stephen S. r. 74 N. Liberty

Wood David, bookkeeper Dessar, Bro. & Co. r. east of limits

Wood Daniel L. (Nutting & Wood) r. 417 N. Pennsylvania
Wood Edmonson R. carpenter, r. alley bet. Noble and Benton and Georgia and Meek
Wood George, cooper J. S. Carey & Co. bds. 3 Carey's Row
Wood Heman, (Wood & Manson) r. 123 N. East
Wood Jacob, lab. r. West Indianapolis
Wood James W. carpenter, r. 124 Bates
Wood John, cooper D. Burton & Co.
Wood John F. asst. P. M. r. 393 N. Pennsylvania
Wood John G. carpenter, r. 124 Bates
Wood John M. (Wood & Foudray) r. 4 Massachusetts av.
Wood Levi, (Wood & Boyd,) r. 561 N. Mississippi cor. Second
Wood Lewis, cooper, r. 3 Carey's Row, Helen st.
Wood Louisa Miss, bds. 74 N. Liberty
Wood Mary, wid. James, r. 30 Circle
Wood Maurice G. clk, Nutting & Wood, bds. 417 N. Pennsylvania
Wood Morris, ins. agt. bds. 417 N. Pennsylvania
Wood N. H. conductor, C. C. & I. C. R. R. bds. Bates House
Wood Phœbe, wid. William, r. 70 Elizabeth
Wood Phœbe Miss, bds. 18 E. Michigan
Wood S. wks. J. S. Carey & Co.
Wood Sarah, wid John, r. 125 N. Pennsylvania
Wood Sylvia Ame Miss, bds. 18 E. Michigan
Wood William D. bds. 189 N. Illinois
Wood William E. propr. First National livery and board stable, ns. Court nr. cor. Pennsylvania r. 442 N. Pennsylvania
WOOD & BOYD, (L. Wood and Frank A. Boyd,) oils, paints, varnishes, etc. whol. 22 S. Meridian
WOOD & FOUDRAY, (John M. Wood and John E. Foudray,) livery, sale and feed stable, 16 and 18 N. Pennsylvania
WOOD & MANSUR, (Heman Wood and Frank Mansur,) livery and sale stable, 21 and 23 W. Pearl
Woodard Albert, brakeman, bds 58 Benton
Woodard Howard, car repairer C. & I. J. R. R.
WOODARD JAMES H. associate editor *Daily Evening Commercial*, r. 366 N. Alabama
Woodbridge Charles salesman John Woodbridge & Co. bds. 147 N. Pennsylvania
Woodbridge Charles A. r. 147 N. Pennsylvania
Woodbridge John, whol. dealer in queensware, lamps, looking glasses, etc. 36 S. Meridian, r. 147 N. Pennsylvania
WOODBRIDGE JOHN & CO. (John Woodbridge and ——,) china, glass and queensware, whol. and retail, 12 W. Washington
Woodburn Jacob, (Osgood, Smith & Co.) r. St. Louis, Mo.
Woodburn James H. (Thompson & Woodburn) r. 264 N. Illinois
Woodbury Uriah T. dentist, 39½ W. Washington, bds 60 W. Market
Woodfill George, grocer, 174 Bluff rd. r. same
Woodford James, bds. 160 N. West
Woodford Margaret, (col'd) wid. bakery 161 Indiana av. r. same
Woodin William M. comp. *Journal* news room, bds. Littles' Hotel

WOO	352	WRE

Woodman George E. (Charles Helwig & Co.) r. 223 N. Mississippi

Woodruff Myron, bds. 470 N. Pennsylvania

Woodruff William, R. R. conductor, bds. 237 E. South

Woods A. W. bds. 377 N. Illinois

Woods Albert, lab. Bunte, Dickson & Co.

Woods Albert R. stove moulder A. D. Wood

Woods Alice, r. 27 N. New Jersey

Woods B. F. wood dealer, r. 234 Huron

Woods C. wks. J. S. Carey & Co.

Woods Daniel, cutter, r. 89 S. Pennsylvania

Woods J. S. groceries, 382 Indiana av. r. 378 Indiana av.

Woods Maria, wid. P. r. 460 S. Missouri

Woods Nicholas, lab. r. 428 E. St. Clair

Woods Thomas, lab. r. 24 W. McCarty

Woods William (Clawson & Woods) r. Western House

Woods William, travelling agt. r. 308 E. Market

Woodson John S. (Woodson & Foxcroft) r. ss. 2d bet. Illinois and Meridian

Woodson & Foxcroft (John S. Woodson and Francis Foxcraft) house and carriage painters 25 S. East

Woodville Alexander, butcher, r. W. Indianapolis

Woollen Greenly V. physician 35½ E. Washington, r. City Hospital

Woollen Keziah, boarding house 10 W. Georgia, r. same

Woollen M. A. student Bryant & Stratton's College, bds. 288 N. Tennessee

Woollen Milton A. student, r. 248 N. West

Woollen Sarah, wid. Milton, r. 248 N. West

Woollen William M. grocer, 101 Indiana av. r. 288 N. Tennessee

WOOLLEN WILLIAM W. cashier Indiana Banking Co. r. 167 N. Tennessee

WOOLLEN WILLIAM W. jr. lawyer, 35½ E. Washington, r. 405 N. Pennsylvania

Woolley Thomas, r. 369 N. New Jersey

Woolson Charles, lab. r. 188 Winston

Workman Jennie Miss, actress Academy of Music

Worland William, grocer, 52 Virginia av. r. same

Worley John, teamster, r. West Indianapolis

Worley Valentine, farmer, r. West Indianapolis

Worley William, lab. r. 149 N. Noble

Worman Enoch, livery, r. 366 W. Vermont

Worman Jasper, farmer, Nat. rd. West Indianapolis

Worman W. clk. r. 79 E. Ohio

Worner Theodore, clk. J. H. Keeber, bds. 525 N. Mississippi

Worth Paul, cooper W. Baird

Worthington William H. trunk mkr. M. Burton, r. 266 N. West

Wortman ——, lab. r. 406 S. Delaware

Wortmann Charles, shoemaker H. Reasner

Wren Edmund, wagon maker, r. 99 S. New Jersey

Wren Mary, wid. John, r. 315 S. Delaware

Wren Michael, teamster, r. 273 S. Tennessee

Wriedt Charles, saloon, bowling alley and shooting gallery, 31 W Georgia, r. same

Wright Abram, engineer, bds. Ray House

WRIGHT ARTHUR L. county treasurer, office Court House, r. 426 N. New Jersey

Wright Asa, r. 71 E. McCarty

Wright Asbury P. lab. r. ns. Broadway nr. cor. Christian av.

Wright Benjamin C. clk. r. 275 N. Delaware

Wright Cage M. (Wright & Bro.) r. 230 S. Noble

Wright Charles E. (Fletcher & Wright) r. 236 E. Vermont

WRIGHT CHARLES W. gen'l agt. Hartford Life and Annuity Ins. Co. of Hartford, Conn. office 10 E. Washington, up stairs, r. 477 N. Meridian

Wright Elizabeth Miss, r. 71 E. McCarty

Wright Elizabeth, wid. Alonzo, r. 182 W. Georgia

Wright Frances, wid. Frank, r. ns. Washington bet. Mississippi and the Canal

WRIGHT FRANK, propr. Capital Ale Brewery and vinegar mnfr. Blake bet. New York and Washington, r. 160 N. West

Wright Frank, clerk G. E. Gordon, r. 189 E. Ohio

Wright Granville S. clk. Hamlin & Wright, r. 275 N. Delaware

Wright Hiram N. blacksmith Eagle Machine Works, r. 366 W. Washington

Wright Isaac, r. 426 N. New Jersey

Wright J. H. coachmaker, bds. Western House

Wright Jacob T. (Hamlin & Wright and Wright & Vinnedge) r. 275 N. Delaware

Wright James, engineer, bds. 58 Benton

Wright Jesse, farmer, r. W. Indianapolis

Wright John, (col'd) lab. r. Elizabeth nr. Blake

Wright John H. with J. N. Wright & Son, bds. 477 N. Meridian

Wright John N. (J. N. Wright & Son) r. 477 N. Meridian

Wright John R. (William Sumner & Co.) r. Cincinnati

Wright John S. r. 795 N. Tennessee

WRIGHT JONATHAN J. physician and surgeon, 58½ E. Market, r. 498 N. Pennsylvania

Wright Joseph, lab. Union Novelty Works

Wright Levi, grocer, 323 N. Alabama, r. 314 N. Alabama

Wright Mansur H. physician, r. 103 N. Meridian

Wright Richard shoemkr. James E. Davis, r. 32 Orient

Wright T. lab. Sinker & Co.

Wright Theodore F. printer, r. 361 W. Vermont

Wright Thomas, (col'd) lab. r. 135 Bright

Wright Thomas, watchman, bds. 75 S. Pennsylvania

Wright Wesley bartender, r. 440 Virginia av.

Wright William G. (Wright & Bro.) r. 271 Virginia av.

Wright William H. salesman Crossland, Hanna & Co. r. 83 E. Michigan

Wright Z. H. ins. solicitor E. S. Green, r. 320 N. Delaware

J. Arden, will make the best sewed boot in town, 65 S. Meridian.

24

WRIGHT J. N. & SON, (John N. and Charles W. Wright) gen'l agts. United States Life Ins. Co. of New York for Northern Indiana, 10 E. Washington

WRIGHT & BRO. (W. B. & C. M. Wright) pump mnfrs. 127 E. Maryland

WRIGHT & VINNEDGE, (Jacob T. Wright & John A. Vinnedge) real estate brokers, 62¼ E. Washington

Wuest John, (Western Furniture Co.) r. 143 Ft. Wayne av.

Wunderley Henry, bricklayer, r. 146 N. Davidson

Wunderley Mary Mrs. milliner, 146 N. Davidson, r. same

Wundram William, tailor, r. 406 S. Delaware

Wundrum Louis, shoemaker John G. Kistrer, r. 83 S. Illinois

Wunsh Frederick, stonemason, r. 139 Stevens

Wurgler Adolph, dairyman, r. West Indianapolis

Wveser Frederick, teamster, r. 53 N. Alabama

Wyant Oliver P. carpenter, r. 78 E. New York

Wyatt Jackson, (col'd) lab. r. 434 N. East

Wyatt Thomas, r. 83 S. Benton

Wyatt William D. grocer, 78 Virginia av. r. 83 Benton

Wychoff Samuel, switchman C. C. & I. C. R. R.

Wyland Ernest, machinist, r. nr. s. end S. Missouri

Wyland William C. bookkeeper, r. 558 S. Illinois

Wylie Andrew, clerk, bds. 131 N. Alabama

Wyman Charles, R. R. conductor, r. 78 Virginia av.

Wynn Cynthia C. Mrs. teacher German English School, r. 136 E. St. Joseph

Wynn Wilbur S. salesman Bowen, Stewart & Co. r. 138 E. St. Joseph

Wysong Christopher, bricklayer, r. 281 N. Noble

Wysong George, bricklayer, r. 281 N. Noble

Y

Yahrleng John P. tailor 3 Virginia av. r. 125 McCarty

Yaker Fred. lab. C. C. & I.C. R. R.

Yandes Daniel, sr. (Sinker & Co.) r. 84 W. Vermont

Yundes Daniel, jr. dealer in hides and leather 76 E. Washington, r. 179 E. New York

Yandes George B. (Sinker & Co.) bds. Bates House

Yandes Simon, lawyer 21 E. Washington, bds. Bates House

Yarbrough Peter, engineer C. C. & I. C. R. R. r. 153 Meek

Yaw James, lab. r. 302 W. Market

Yeager Christ. watchman frt. depot C. C. & I. C. R. R.

Yeager Gotfried, trunkmkr. M. Barton, r. 185 N. Noble

Yeager Henry, lab. D. Root & Co.

Yeager William, grocer ret. 282 N. Noble, r. 284 N. Noble

Yeaman Samuel H. marble worker, Dame & Greenlee, bds. Circle Restaurant

Yeaton Lendell B. supt. fire alarm telegraph r. 74 E. Ohio

Yelling Peter J. tailor, r. 125 E. McCarty
Yetter John, foreman Western Furniture Co.
Yewell Frank, baggage master, bds. 320 Madison av.
Yewell Solomon, book keeper Mears, Lilly & Co. r. 320 S. Chesnut (Madison av.)
Yewell Solomon, jr. supt. Parcell Express, R. 320 Madison av.
Yewell Thomas, (Graham & Yewell) r. Louisville, Ky.
Yohn Albert B. student, bds. 206 N. Delaware
Yohn Charles G. student, bds. 206 N. Delaware
Yohn James C. r. 206 N. Delaware
Yohn's Block, Meridian ne. cor. Washington
Yonkers and New York Ins. Co. of N. Y. Martin, Hopkins & Ohr, agts. Market ne. cor. Circle, *Journal* bldg.
Yorger Clemens, butcher, r. 215 N. Noble
Yorger Ignatz (John Yorger & Bro.) r. 323 E. Vermont
Yorger John (John Yorger & Bro.) r. out of city limits
YORGER JOHN & BRO. (John & Ignatz Yorger) Meat Market 245 E. Washington
York Edwin D. express messenger r. 216 E. South
York Frank, steward Ray House, bds. same
York Robert S. bookkeeper M. Child, jr. bds. 128 N. Tennessee
Yorker Charles, wood sawer, r. 327 S. Pennsylvania
Yost J. H. T. stonemason, r. 395 S. West
Yost James J. (Osgood, Smith & Co.) r. St. Louis, Mo.
Yost Thomas, stonemason, bds. 103 W. South
Yotz Peter, wagonmkr. J. M. Van Blaricum, r. Stringtown
YOUART JOHN M. physician and surgeon 39½ W. Washington, r. 564 N. Tennessee
Young G. r. 77½ Market
Young J. pianofortemaker J. H. Kappes & Co.
Young John, lawyer, 100 E. Washington (up stairs) r. Christian av ne. cor. Jackson
Young Julius, tailor, bds. Union Hall
Young Levi, (col'd) brickmaker, bds. 228 Huron
Young Louis, cigars and tobacco, 77 S. Illinois and 290 E. Washington, r. 290 E. Washington
YOUNG MEN'S CHRISTIAN ASSOCIATION, John B. Brandt supt. library and rooms, 16, 17, 18, and 19 Vinton's blk.
Young Richard, lab. r. 153 Huron
Young Richard, (col'd) lab. r. 228 Huron
Young Squire, (col'd) lab. r. 259 N. West
Young Taylor, (col'd) brickmaker, bds. 228 Huron
Young Thornton, (col'd) lab. r. 228 N. Noble
Young William, carpenter, r. 60 Anthony nr. City Hospital
Youngerman Mary P. wid. Conrad, r. 118 Massachusetts av.
Youngman John, carpenter, r. 23 Massachusetts av.
Younk John, lab. Osgood, Smith & Co.
Younk John, teamster, bds. 266 S. Illinois
Youtsey Thomas, spoke turner Osgook Smith & Co. r. 57 Eddy
Youtsey William, lab. Osgood, Smith & Co. r. 43 Eddy

Z

Zabel Charles, cabinet maker, r. 185 Meek

Zahm Barnhard, engineer, C. C. & I. C. R. R.

Zambell A. fireman C. C. & I. C. R. R.

Zapf Edward, cabinet maker P. Dohn

Zapf Fred. clk. M. Rodius, bds. same

Zapf George, tanner Frenzel & Simon

Zapf Philip, clk. M. Rodius, bds. same

Zehringer Landiline, cabinet maker, r. 164 Davidson

Zeile Henry, clk. J. C. Ferguson & Co.

Zeller H. mattrass maker Spiegel & Thoms, bds. Macy House

Zenore Zacheus, shoemaker Thomas Duggan

Zepp George W. lab. Hair and Bristle wks. r. 172 W. McCarty

Zeigel Louis, saloon, Wyoming sw. cor. High, r. same

ZIEGELMUELLER HERMAN, saloon, 59 N. Alabama, r. 55 N. Alabama

Ziegler Charles, lab. Western Furniture Co.

ZEIGLER GEORGE H. military atty. and notary public, room 6 Talbott and New's blk. r. 202 N. West

Zimmer Ferdinand, barber, r. 260 S. Delaware

Zimmer Peter, (Zimmer & Niehaus,) r. 321 S. Delaware

Zimmer & Niehaus, (Peter Zimmer and Joseph L. Niehaus,) grocers, 323 S. Delaware

Zimmerle Amos B. carpenter, r. 253 S. Mississippi

ZIMMERMAN C. slate and metal roofer, also dealer in stoves and tinware, 35 S. Alabama, r. E. Washington out of city limits

Zimmerman Harry C. roofer C. Zimmerman, r. 130 Spring

Zimmerman Henry, driver Boston Bakery, bds. 285 E. Washington

Zimmerman J. B. roofer C. Zimmerman, r. 422 E. Georgia

Zimmerman John K. roofer C. Zimmerman, r. 130 Spring

Zimmerman Mary, wid. William, r. 130 N. Spring

Zimmerman Silas, (col'd) barber, r. 66 N. Missouri

Zink Henry, barber, r. 343 S. Delaware

Zion's Church School, (German) August Miller principal, rear Zion's Church

Zismer P. M. salesman Charles Mayer & Co. r. rear 174 E. Washington

Zogg Ferdinand, (Pfaendler & Zogg,) r. 4th Presbyterian Church, cor. Delaware and Market

Zoncada Charles, music teacher, bds. 20 S. Pennsylvania

Zph Sebastian, varnisher Burke, Earnshaw & Co. r. 19 Meek

Zschech Frederick, carpenter, r. 90 Union

Zschech Gustavus, supt. Eagle Machine Wks. r. 251 S. Meridian

Zumbusch Theodore, watches and jewelry, 93 E. Washington, r. 61 E. Maryland

SCHEDULE OF STAMP DUTIES.

AGREEMENT OR CONTRACT, not otherwise specified; **any appraisement** of value or damage, or for other purpose; for each agreement, or for each sheet of each agreement, &c., or renewal of same............................... $0.05

ASSIGNMENT.—See Conveyance.

BANK CHECK, DRAFT, OR ORDER for the payment of any sum of money drawn upon any bank, banker, or trust company, or for any sum exceeding $10, drawn upon any other person, companies, or corporations, at sight or on demand... .02

BILL OF EXCHANGE, (*Inland*,) DRAFT OR ORDER, for the payment of money, not at sight or on demand, or any PROMISSORY NOTE, (except bank notes issued for circulation, and checks made and intended to be forthwith presented, and which shall be presented to a bank or banker for payment,) or any memorandum, check, receipt, or other written or printed evidence of money to be paid on demand, or at a time designated, for every $100 or part thereof.................... .05

BILL OF EXCHANGE, (*Foreign*,) OR LETTERS of CREDIT, drawn in but payable out of the United States:
    If drawn singly or in duplicate, same as Inland Bills of Exchange.
    If drawn in sets of three or more, every bill of each set, for every $100, or the equivalent thereof, in any foreign currency in which the bill is expressed........ .02

BILL OF LADING or RECEIPT, (other than charter party,) for any goods &c., exported to a foreign port............... .10

BILL OF SALE OF VESSEL, or any part thereof, consideration of value not over $500......... .... .50

    Every additional $500, or part thereof, 50 cents more.

BOND OF INDEMNITY, every $1000, or part thereof............ .50

BOND, for the execution of the duties of any office......... 1.00

BOND, other than required in legal proceedings, or used in connection with mortgage deeds, and not otherwise charged .... .25

CERTIFICATE OF STOCK, in incorporated company............ .25

CERTIFICATE OF PROFITS, or any certificate or momorandum
showing an interest in the property or accumulations
of any incorporated company, if for $10 and not
over $50...... 10

    Over $50 and not over $1,000.............................   .25

Every additional $1,000 or part thereof, 25 cents more.

CERTIFICATE OF DAMAGE, or otherwise, and all other certificates or documents issued by any port warden, marine surveyor, or person acting as such..................   .25

CERTIFICATE OF DEPOSIT, $100, or less..........................   .02

    Over $100..   .05

(Certificates of measurement or weight of animals,
wood, coal, or hay; certificate of the record of a deed
or other instrument in writing, or of the acknowl-
edgement or proof thereof, by attesting witnesses,
require no stamp.)

CERTIFICATE, of any other description..........................   .05

CHARTER PARTY, (or renewal, &c. of same,) contract or
agreement for charter of vessel or steamer of registered tonnage, not over 150 tons...........................   1.00

    Over 150 and not over 300 tons.........................   3.00

    Over 300 and not over 600 tons.........................   5.00

    Over 600 tons...   10.00

CONTRACT, or renewal, Broker's note, or memorandum of
sale of merchandise, exchange, real estate, or other
property issued by brokers, or persons acting as such,
each...   .10

CONVEYANCE.—Deed or writing, whereby any lands, tene-
ments, or other realty sold is granted, assigned, or
transferred, for every $500, or part thereof...........   .50

ENTRY OF GOODS, &c., at any custom house, for consump-
tion or warehousing, of value not over $100...........   .25

    Over $100 and not over $500............................   .50

    Over $500.......... ....   1.00

WITHDRAWAL from bonded warehouse........................   .50

INSURANCE (*Life*). —Policy, (for assignment &c. of same)
not over $1,000...... 25

    Over $1000 and not over $5000.........................   .50

    Over $5000..   1.00

INSURANCE (*Marine, Inland and Fire*).—Each policy or renewal, (or assignment &c. of same) on which premi-
um is $10, or less..   .10

    Over $10 and not over $50..............................   .25

    Over $50..   .50

INSURANCE against accidental injury to persons...............exempt

LEASE, agreement, memorandum, or contract, for the hire, use, or rent of any land, tenement, or portion thereof, when rent or rental value is not over $300 per annum..... .... .50

Every additional $200 or part thereof, 50 cents more

LEASE, ASSIGNMENT OF—A stamp duty equal to that imposed on the original instrument, increased by a stamp duty on the consideration or value of the assignment equal to that imposed upon the conveyance of land for similar consideration or value. (See Conveyance.)

LEGAL DOCUMENTS.—Writ, or other original process, by which any suit, either criminal or civil, is commenced in any Court, either of law or equity.. ....exempt

Confession of judgment, or cognovit ....exempt

Writs or other process on appeals from justice courts or other courts of inferior jurisdiction to a court of record............. ....exempt

*Warrant of distress...*exempt

Affidavits in suits or legal proceedings........................exempt

MANIFEST, for custom house entry or clearance of vessel's cargo for foreign port, (except to British North America,) tonnage not over 300 tons.................... 1.00

Over 300 and not over 600 tons............ .... 3.00

Over 600 tons.. .... 5.00

MORTGAGE, Trust Deed, or Personal Bond, for the payment of money, over $100 and not over $500......... .50

Every additional $500 or part thereof, 50 cents more
Upon each assignment or transfer of a mortgage, a stamp duty equal to that upon a mortgage for the amount remaining unpaid.

TRUST DEED conveying estate to uses, to be stamped as a conveyance

ORDER for the payment of money.—See Bank Check.

PASSAGE TICKET, to foreign port, (except British North America,) costing $35 or less................................ .50

Over $35 and not over $50................................ 1.00
Every additional $50, or part thereof, $1 more.

PAWNER'S CHECKS.. .05

POWER OF ATTORNEY, to sell or transfer any stock, bond, or scrip, or for the collection of any dividend, or interest thereon..... .... .25

To vote by proxy for officers of any corporation or society, (except religions, charitable, literary societies, or public cemeteries................................... .10

To sell or rent real estate................................... 1.00

To collect rents....... .... .25

To perform any act not herein mentioned................. .50

PROBATE OF WILL, OR LETTER OF ADMINISTRATION, value of estate not over $2000................................... 1.00

Every additional $1,000 or part thereof, 50 cents more

PROMMISSORY NOTE.—See Bill of Exchange, Inland.

PROTEST, of note, check, draft, &c............................... .25

RECEIPT, for payment of money or debt, over $20, not being for the satisfaction of any mortgage or judgment, and for the delivery of property, (except receipts issued by persons, firms, or companies doing business as an express, or express company, on the delivery of property for transportation............................. .02

WAREHOUSE RECEIPTS, exempt

——o——

☞The indiscriminate use of all kinds of stamps (except postage or proprietary) is permitted, care being taken to affix a stamp or stamps of the proper amount.

Documents made in any foreign country, to be used in the United States, shall pay the same duty as when made here.

Powers of Attorney, or other papers relating to applications for bounties, arrearages of pay, or pensions, require no stamp; neither do indorsement of negotiable instrument, nor any warrant of attorney accompanying a bond or note, when such bond or note shall be stamped; and whenever any bond or note shall be secured by mortgage, but one stamp duty is required, provided the stamp duty placed thereon is the highest rate required for said instrument, or either of them.

The person using or affixing the stamp or stamps, shall write thereupon the initials of his name and the date upon which the same shall be attached or used, so that the same shall not be used again, under a penalty of $50; or they may be otherwise cancelled as the Commissioner of Internal Revenue may prescribe.

Violations of these stamp duties will be punished as the law directs.

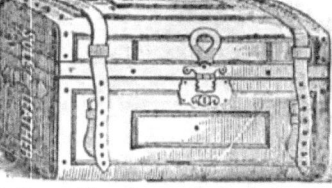

25

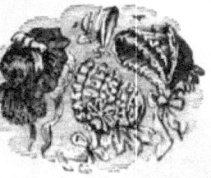

INDIANAPOLIS

Steam Stone Works

S. GODDARD & SONS,

DEALERS IN

LIMESTONE & FREESTONE,

In blocks and slabs, Window Sills, Lintels, Flagging, and sawed Stone in general always on hand at prices that defy competition. BUILDERS are especially invited to give us a call.

All Cut Stone Work executed at the Shortest Notice.

OFFICE AND MILL: KENTUCKEY AVENUE, CORNER GEORGIA.

MERIDIAN STREET

BATH HOUSE

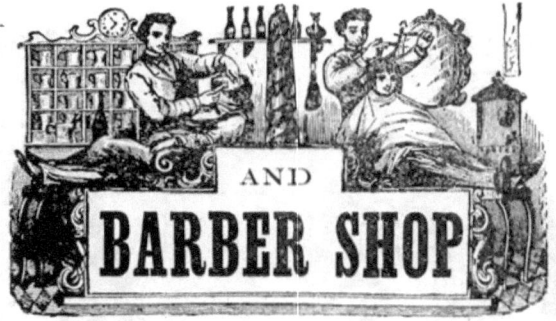

AND

BARBER SHOP

In Basement of the Tilford Building, cor. Meridian & Circle Sts

HOT, COLD AND SHOWER BATHS

All hours of the day and until 12 o'clock at night—Sundays excepted.

EDWARDS'

BUSINESS DIRECTORY,

EMBRACING

A Classified List of all Trades, Professions and Pursuits in
the City of Indianapolis, for the Year 1869, arranged
Alphabetically for each Trade, thus exhibiting
at a glance, the full address and Special Business of her Citizens.

Abstract of Titles.

Elliott Joseph T. office Recorder's office,
Court House Square

Academies, Schools, Etc.

(*See City Register.*)

Agricultural Hardware.

BRACKEBUSH C. J.
75 and 77 W. Washington. (See advt.
index)

Agricultural Implements.

(*Manufacturer.*)

Indianapolis Wagon and Agricultural Works,
W. A. Pattison, agt. 172 S. Tennessee

Agricultural Implements.

BRACKEBUSH C. J.
75 and 77 W. Washington
Case, Parker & Co. 84 W. Washington

CROPPER JAMES H.
169 and 171 W. Washington. (See adv't
Index)
Dickson & Co. 47 and 49 N. Tennessee
LUKENS RICHARD L.
81 W. Washington. (See adv't Index)
Prier Henry J. 230 E. Washington
Stilz & George. 78 E. Washington
WEBB & BATES,
83 W. Washington. (See adv't Index)

Agricultural Seed Stores.

BRACKEBUSH C. J.
75 and 77 W. Washington. (See adv't
Index)
CROPPER JAMES H.
169 W. Washington. (See adv't Index)
Emmerich & Co. 86 W. Washington
LUKENS RICHARD L.
Agent D. M. Ferry & Co.'s seeds, 81 W.
Washington. (See adv't Index)
WEBB & BATES,
83 W. Washington. (See adv't Index)

· 26

Agricultural Warehouses.

BRACKEBUSH C. J.
75 and 77 W. Washington. (See adv't Index)

Case, Parker & Co. 84 W. Washington

LUKENS RICHARD L.
81 W. Washington. (See adv't Index)

Ale and Porter Depots.

(See also Breweries.)

Baker Charles, 211 Massachusetts av.

MEIER V. & BROTHER,
76 S. West. (See advt. Index)

O'Conner, Michael J. agent Sands' pale cream ale, 54 S. Illinois

Amusements.

(Places of.)

ACADEMY OF MUSIC,
W. H. Leake lessee, Ohio se. cor. Illinois.

INDIANAPOLIS SKATING
RINK, Tennessee nw. cor. Georgia

METROPOLITAN THEATRE,
W. H. Leake, lessee, 84 W. Washington

Morrison's Opera House, Meridian, cor. Maryland, William H. Morrison propr.

MOZART HALL,
(J. Grosch) 39 S. Delaware

Amusements.

(Resort.)

MOZART HALL RESTAU-
RANT, J. GROSH, prop. CHOICEST WINES, LIQUORS, CIGARS, etc., etc., 39 S. Delaware

Apothecaries.

(See Drugs and Medicines.)

Architects and Superintendents.

Bohlen Diederick A. room 19 Talbott & New's Block

Curzon Joseph, 55 W. Washington

DAGGETT ROBERT P.
room 6 Wiley's Block Pennsylvania nr. Washington. (See card opp.)

ENOS & HUEBNER,
1 and 2 Eden's Block, 77½ E. Market. (See adv't Index)

HODGSON ISAAC,
room 2 Brown's Block, Washington nw. cor. Pennsylvania

Johnes Eugene, room 33, Blackrord's block

May Edwin, 173 N. Pennsylvania

Peckham Caleb H. M. Blake blk. 55 Washington

Taylor I. room 5, 14 N. Delaware

Architectural Carver and Modeler.

MILLER LAWRENCE,
rear of 84 E. Market. (See advt. Index)

Artificial Limbs.

AMERICAN LEG & ARM CO.
Haywood & Co. proprs. 172 E. Washington

Artists.

(See also Painters, Portrait; also Photographers)

Cox Jacob, 26 and 28 W. Washington

Kendrick Robert, 73 N. East

Artists' Materials.

LIEBER H. & CO.
21 N. Pennsylvania

Attorneys at Law.

(See Lawyers.)

Auction and Commission.

(See also Commission Merchants.)

Davis & Jones, 88 E. Washington

Featherson William E. 194 and 196 W. Washington

McCURDY GEO. W.
Washington cor. Virginia av.

McIntyre James, 190 W. Washington

Spellman S. Co. 111 S. Illinois

Taylor D. B. & Co. 85 E. Washington

Awning Manufacturers.

Gorham William H. (slate) 16 E. Washington

Bakeries.

(See also Confectioners.)

AEREATED BREAD BAKERY,
G. W. Caldwell & Co. proprs. 14 and 16 E. South. (See advt index)

Balls Antony, 178 S. Illinois

Beck Henry, 88 Fort Wayne av.

Bossart John. 112 Bluff rd.

Boston Bakery, Joseph Virnickel propr. 285 E. Washington

Bower Jacob, 147 W. Washington

Cincinnati Bakery, Fred. C. Bollman propr. 107 E. Washington

De Gray Thomas, 59 N Illinois

Ferger Charles, 96 E. South

Genter Charles, 233 E. Washington

Grine Charles, 264 E. Washington

Hespelt & Co. 150 W. Vermont

Hofacker Charles, 277 N. Noble

Indiana Bakery, William Kuhn propr. 150 N. East

Kestler Rosa Mrs. 173 W. Washington

Knauf Adam, 257 Massachusetts av.

R. P. DAGGETT,

ARCHITECT

—AND—

SUPERINTENDENT.

OFFICE:

No. 6 Wiley's Block, opp. Odd Fellows Hall,

PENNSYLVANIA STREET,

INDIANAPOLIS, INDIANA.

O. F. MAYHEW,

SOLICITOR OF

AMERICAN & FOREIGN PATENTS.

Agencies in Washington City and London. Office with Secretary State Board of Agriculture, State House, Indianapolis, Ind. Send for Circular, Post Office Box, 385.

A. F. JENISON & CO.

Staple & Fancy Groceries

FOREIGN AND DOMESTIC FRUITS,

WINES AND LIQUORS,

WHOLESALE AND RETAIL.

Produce solicited from country merchants.

No. 89 North Illinois, Academy of Music Building.

Dont forget Davis, 12 E. Washington, when you want a new Hat.

BAN 372 BEE

WILLIAM K. McFARLANE, (Successor to Quinton & Thomson) Manufacturer and Wholesale Dealer in Crackers, Bread, Pies and Cakes, 12 South Meridian.

McFarlane W. K. 12 S. Meridian
Meier Ernst, 131 S. Illinois
Rauser George, 68 S. West
Shille Lawrence. 314 N. New Jersey
STEAM CRACKER BAKERY, Parrott, Nickum & Co. proprs. 188 E. Washington
Striebeck Charles, 319 N. West
Tholman Charles, 75 N. Alabama
Webb Joshua, 56 N. Illinois
Woodford Margaret, (col'd) 161 Indiana av-

Bands.

Philharmonic, 20½ N. Delaware

Bankruptcy.

(*Register in*)
Ray John W. 24½ E. Washington

Banks and Bankers.

(*See also Banks Saving.*)

CITIZENS' NATIONAL BANK, W. C. Holmes, pres. Joseph R. Haugh, cashier, 4 E. Washington
First National Bank of Indianapolis, William H. English, pres. John C. New, cashier, Washington se. cor. Meridian
Fletcher's Bank, (S. A. Fletcher & Co.) 32 E. Washington
Harrison A. & J. C. S. 15 E. Washington
Indiana Banking Co. W. W. Woolen, cashier, 28 E. Washington
Indiana National Bank, George Tousey, pres. D. M. Taylor, cashier, 2 E. Washington

INDIANAPOLIS BRANCH BANKING CO. (Fletcher & Sharpe) Thomas H. Sharpe, cashier, Washington sw. cor. Pennsylvania
Indianapolis National Bank, Theodore P. Haughey, pres. A. F. Williams, cashier. Washington ne. cor. Pennsylvania

MERCHANTS' NATIONAL, John S. Newman, pres. V. T. Mallott, cashier, 48 E. Washington

Banks, Saving.

INDIANAPOLIS INSURANCE CO'S SAVINGS BANK, William Henderson, pres. Alex. Jameson, sec. cor. Virginia av. and Pennsylvania
RITZINGER JOHN B. 14 E. Washington

Bar, Hoop and Sheet Iron.

(*Wholesale.*)
OVER E. & CO.
82 and 84 S. Meridian

Barbers.

Artis William, (col'd) 197 W. Washington
Britton John, (col'd) 181 W. Washington
Byrd Henry, (col'd) 63 S. Illinois
Cropper J. B. 16 W. Pearl
Crosson John D. (col'd) 395 N. New Jersey
Davis John, (col'd) 14 S. Pennsylvania
Deitz Adam, 116 Fort Wayne av.
Elff Frank, 135 S. Illinois
Ferling George, Washington se. cor. Meridian
Fisher Benedict, Union Depot bldg.
Fisher John, 374 Virginia av.
Frankenstein Jacob, 326 S. Delaware
Guetig Henry, Washington ne. cor. Penn.
Gulliver A. (col'd) Washington sw. cor. Kentucky av.
Harding Richard, (col'd) 255 W. Washington
Hill & Carter, (col'd) 14 N. Illinois
Johnson G. C. 267 W. Washington
Johnson John, (col'd) 303 E. Washington
Jones & Hall, (col'd) 16 S. Meridian
Klein John G. 2 Martindale's Block
Knox & Embers, Washington ne. cor. Meridian
Lucas Charles H. (col'd) 29 N. Illinois
Marin Henry C. (col'd) 10 S. Delaware
Mason M. under Palmer House
Mays A. 160 Indiana av.
MITCHELL GEORGE M. D. 21 N. Meridian
Mutz Antony, Sherman House
Pearson & Harper. (col'd) 325 E. Washingt'n
Rinkle David, 94 E. South
Russell & Gulliver, 50 E. Washington
Spencer House, (William Porter) 140 S. Illinois
Spitznagle Leopold, 154 Bluff rd.
Stein F. 276 E. Washington
Thompson Louis, (col'd) 107 S. Illinois
Vandergotten & Satorius, 37 S. Illinois
Wade Samuel, (col'd) 249 E. South
Weber Louis, 182 S. Illinois
Weiss Henry, 143 E. Washington
Wise William T. (cold) 223 Massachusetts av.

Bath Houses.

City Bath House, 16 W. Pearl
MERIDIAN STREET BATH HOUSE, 21 N. Meridian. (See adv't Index)

Bed and Mattrass Makers.

(*See also Upholsters.*)
Wilkens & Hall, 84 and 86 E. Market

Beer Gardens.

Appolo Garden, Kentucky av. cor. S. Tennessee
Inwalle's Garden Benjamin J. Inwalle propr. 367 Virginia av.

Noble Street Gardens, Phil. Reichwein propr. 50 N. Noble
Shepherd James McB. 156 E. Washington

Bees.
(Dealer in.)
Mitchell Nelson C. Tennessse cor. St. Clair

Bell Hangers.
Isensee, Albert, 24 N. Pennsylvania
KINDLER CHARLES, 60 N. Pennsylvania. (See adv't Index)

Bell Manufacturers.
(See also Brass Foundries.)
Phœnix Bell and Brass Foundry, 26 Union (R. R. track)

Belting.
(Rubber and Leather.)
Mooney & Co. 147 S. Meridian

Billiard Halls.
(See also Saloons.)
Asmus Louis, 199 Indiana av.
Cramer & Newton, 63 N. Illinois
Gem Billiard Hall, W. Bucksot propr. 9 W. Washington
Gymnasium Billiard Hall, 46 S. Meridian
Huegele John, 39 E. Washington
Ray Henry J. 274 E. Washington
Walker Austin, (col'd) 195 W. Washington

Bird Cages.
Baldwin J. H. & Co. (Fancy Bazar) 6 E. Washington
Henninger G. & E. 115 S. Illinois

Bird Dealers.
Speckman Henry, 108 S. Illinois

Blacksmiths.
(See also Horse Shoers.)
Affantranger S. J. 191 Indiana av.
Buechner Frederick, Virginia av. nw. cor. Dougherty
Davis G. M. (col'd) 252 Indiana av.
EWALD HENRY, 299 Massachusetts av. (See adv't Index)
Fleitz Charles, 187 Bluff rd.
Gates John J. 26 S. New Jersey
Gibson Harry, 291 Kentucky av.
Hammel A. ss. 7th bet. Tennessee and Mississippi
Hillman William, 377 Virginia av.
Holzwart & Werubeck, N. Alabama bet. Washington and Market
Kurts H. P. 178 Indiana av.
Marshall James, ss. Washington bet. West and California
Moore Thomas C. se. end Virginia av.
Raymond Samuel, 60 E. Maryland
Renner Christian, 123 Bluff rd.

ROESENER CHARLES, ns. St. Clair bet. Broadway and Massachusetts av.
Siebert Samuel M. 302 E. Washington
Smith John G. 36 S. Pennsylvania
Stirk & Allaire, East bet. South and Louisiana
STUMPF JOSEPH, Massachusetts av. cor. Plum. (See advt. Index)
Trucks & Kay, 60 Kentucky av.
VAN ANTWERP & DRYER, 287 E. Washington
VONDERSAAR WENDELL, 144 Fort Wayne av. (See advt. index)
Wehling Charles, 234 S. Delaware
Weymouth Amos, ns. Nat. Rd. west of the bridge

Blacksmiths' Tools.
Holliday W. J. & Co. 59 S. Meridian
Maxwell, Fry & Thurston, 34 S. Meridian

Blank Book Manufacturers.
(See also Book Binders.)
Braden W. & J. 24 W. Washington
Journal Book Bindery, (Douglass & Conner) Market ne. cor. Circle (*Journal* bld.)
Sheets William, 79 W. Washington
Smith Julius H. C. Circle se. cor. Meridian
State Sentinel Book Bindery, R. J. Bright, 16½ E. Washington

Bleachers and Pressers.
County J. B. 44 S. Illinois
Dunn & Franco, 85 N. Illinois, Academy of Music
Green A. Mrs. 162 N. Delaware
Maples Henry, 17 and 18 Miller's blk. Illinois cor. Market
Whiting Timothy M. 26 Kentucky av.

Blinds.
(Manufacturer of.)
Barr Jacob, 424 N. Delaware

Boarding Houses.
(See also Hotels)
Adams Alexander, 268 E. St. Clair
Bagley Jane Mrs. 36 W. Maryland
Ballard Samuel, 70 E. Market
Base Ernst, 65 S. East
Boston House, J. Miller propr. 123 S. Illinois
Coen John, 169 S. Tennessee
CHICAGO HOUSE, (F. Seitz) 117 S. Illinois
DELL WILLIAM, 135 E. Washington
Doerr George, 267 E. Washington
Dunmeyer Christian, 217 S. Illinois
Edwards Martha Mrs. 75 Kentucky av.
Everson Margaret Mrs. 98 E. New York
Fenton J. Mrs. 124 S. Meridian

BOI	374	BOO

Ferree J. Mrs. 83 N. Pennsylvania
Ford P. Mrs. 78 S. Illinois
Fox Mrs. 191 W. Maryland
Fry R. M. Miss, 204 N. Illinois
Gruenert John H. 61 E. South
Hamilton C. Mrs. 89 Indiana av.
Hubbard William, 266 S. Illinois
Jack M. W. 74 N. Pennsylvania
King John W. Mrs. Circle se. cor. Market
Kitchel M. 18 W. Georgia
Kobb William, 23 Kentucky av.
Kreglo M. Mrs. 82 E. St. Clair
Mars Jacob, 18 Circle
Mason L. A. Mrs. 17½ Virginia av.
Moran Ellen Mrs. 38 S. Tennessee
Mount G. A. Mrs. 148 Indiana av.
Naltner Martin, 134 S. Meridian
Nolan L. Mrs. 198 S. Illinois
O'Mara Richard, 101 S. Illinois
Quinn John, 245 W. Maryland
Reed Sarah A. 30½ N. Pennsylvania
Reese Mary, 89 N. Delaware
Ricker Sarah H. 47 N. East
Rockwell Silas, 62 S. Pennsylvania
Sedenburg Martha A. 24 W. Pearl
Shannon Sarah Mrs. 126 E. Ohio
Sherwood W. O. Mrs. 23 N. West
Sinks James, 69 W. Market
Tuly Eliza A. 60 W. Market
Walk Louis, 26 and 28 W. Georgia
Way Robert, 20 S. Pennsylvania
Webb House, Mrs. L. Webb propr. 64 W. Maryland
Wenger M. 60 S. Delaware
White Jane Mrs. 75 S. Pennsylvania
Whittemore Elizabeth C. 58 Benton
Wissert John, 180 S. Meridian
Wolf Catharine Mrs. 176 S. Delaware
Woolen Keziah. 10 W. Georgia
Wright Hiram Mrs. 366 W. Washington

Boiler Makers.

(See also Foundries and Machine Shops.)

COX & BROTHERS,
  24 E. Georgia
EAGLE MACHINE WORKS,
  Louisiana se. cor. Meridian
WESTERN MACHINE WORKS
  Sinker & Co. proprs. 125 S. Pennsylvania

Book Binders.

JOURNAL BOOK BINDERY,
  (Douglass & Conner) Market ne. cor. Circle, *Journal* bldg.
Meikel Bros. Washington sw. cor. Meridian
SENTINEL BOOK BINDERY,
  (R. J. Bright) 16½ E. Washington
Sheets William, 79 W. Washington
Smith Julius H. C. Circle se. cor. Meridian
STEINHAUSER B. A.
  168 E. Washington

Booksellers and Stationers.

Aftung Anton, 26 S. Delaware

BOWEN, STEWART & CO.
  18 W. Washington
Braden W. & J. 24 W. Washington
Gehring Conrad, 147 E. Washington
Kummüle George, 153 E. Washington
Merrill & Co. 5 E. Washington
Palmer Edward L. 60 S. Illinois
Thompson Addie Mrs. 13 N. Pennsylvania
TODD, CARMICHAEL & WILLIAMS, Glenn's Block
WILDER C. P.
  26 E. Washington

Boot and Shoe Manufacturers.

(And Retail Dealers.)

Adams J. W. 49 and 53 W. Washington
ALBERSHARDT HENRY F.
  139 E. Washington
ALDAG CHARLES,
  175 E. Washington
ARDEN J.
  65 S. Meridian. (See bottom lines)
Baker John H. 63 Massachusetts av.
Bannwuarth B. 48 Massachusetts av.
Beasler Thomas, 137 N. Tennessee
Bristor William A. 75 E. Washington
Bronson A. W. 17 W. Washington
Burk Henry, 68½ E. Market
Busch Christian, 248 W. Washington
Cady D. & Co. 9 Odd Fellows' bldg.
Chives James A. 63 Indiana av.
Davis James E. 239 E. Washington
Dugan Thomas, 136 S. Illinois
Engelhardt W. 286 E. Washington
Eymenn John H. 9 N. Illinois
Farrar James, 191 W. Washington
Fisher George, 119 Fort Wayne av.
FRIEDGAN C.
  36 W. Washington
Gilbrecht Jacob, 168 Virginia av.
Halterman Charles, 168 S. Illinois
Hanson Mat, 359 S. Delaware
Hill & Vennedge, 3 W. Washington
Hofecker Gottlob, 6 S. Delaware
Hoffman Henry, 122 S. Illinois
HOGSHIRE W. R. & CO.
  25 W. Washington
Karle Christ & Co. 83 E. Washington
Karle J. J. 160 Bluff rd.
Keleper James, Coburn bet. East and Virginia av.
Killgore John, 64 S. Delaware
King J. H. 156 Indiana av.
King James, 105 Indiana av.
Kistner John G. 83 S. Illinois
Kline Nicholas, 283 Massachusetts av.
Knodle A. 32 E. Washington
Lintner Charles H. 184 Indiana av.
McIlvaine Robert, ns. National rd. w. of bridge
Matz John, 182 W. Washington
Maurice & Spohr, 8 Martindale's Block
Merl N. 286 W. Washington
Meurer Frederick M. 22 Virginia av.
Morbach Peter, 301 S. Delaware
Murphy Timothy, 15 Massachusetts av.

Neermaner Christian, 271 Massachusetts av.
Neirmeyer Henry, 126 Fort Wayne av.
Noel M. F. 252 N. Illinois
Norris John, 23 E. Washington
O'Connor Thomas, 294 S. Delaware
Orr D. 523 N. Illinois
Rakestraw & Co. 64 N. Pennsylvania
Reasner Henry, 370 Virginia av.
Rehling Charles, 218 E. Washington
Rehling William, 257 S. Delaware
Richter Joseph, 217 E. Washington
Robinius Frank 223 W. Washington
Rose John N. 90 E. Market
Scherer Adam, 34 N, Illinois
Schildmyer Anthony, 313 E. Washington
Schomberg F. W. 23 N. New Jersey
Schrader Fred, 85 W. Washington
Schweinhart Edmund, 195 Massachusetts av.
Senom J. & Co. 5 W. Washington

SHAFER ADOLPHUS,
327 E. Washington
Shaub George, 170 E. Washington

SIERSDORFER LOUIS,
41 E. Washington
Stark Herman. 148 Virginia av.
Stein Joseph. 106 Bluff rd.
Steinhauer George E. 72 W. Washington
Stolz Charles, 118 Bluff rd.
Straub Vingeng. 10 Bates House Square
Strohle John, 654 W.
Suart John B. 219 Massachusetts av.
Tanner William F. 166 Indiana av.
TenEyck J. A. & R. F. 340 W. Washington
Tushong Michael. 368 W. Washington
Vanstan John, 15 Virginia av.
Vielhaber Daniel, 204 E. Washington
Waller Bernhard, 151 Indiana av.
Wands John, 28 S. Delaware
Wasson William P. 175 S. Tennessee
Weaver Henry, 299 N. East
Wehle Lucas, 235 E. Washington
Wells Thomas, 57 N. Illinois
Whitney William, 119 S. Illinois

Boots and Shoes.
(*Wholesale.*)

BURTON JOHN C. & CO.
114 S. Meridian

HENDRICKS, EDMUNDS & Co.
56 S. Meridian
Mayhew, Warne & Co. 8 W. Louisiana
Mayhew & Branham, 129 S. Meridian
Vinnedge, Jones & Co. 66 S. Meridian

Boots and Shoes.
(*Wholesale and Retail.*)

BRONSON A. W.
17 W. Washington
Dury & Hawks, 3 E. Washington

Bottlers.
Knotts & Co. 72 W. Washington

MEIER V. & BROTHER,
76 S. West.   (See adv't Index)

Bowling Alleys.

KLARE & SCHROEDER,
Bluff rd. cor. city limits
Wriedt Charles, 34 W. Georgia

Box Manufacturers.
Pfaendler & Zogg. Louisiana opp. Terre
Haute Freight Depot
Wheatly Henry H. South cor. Delaware

Brandies, Wines, and Liquors.
(*See Liquor Dealers also Wines and Liquors.*)

Brass Foundry.
Eagle Brass Works, Stierle & Loeper, proprs.
94 S. Delaware

Brewers.

CAPITAL ALE BREWERY,
Frank Wright, propr.   Blake bet. New
York and Washington
City Brewery, P. Lieber & Co. proprs. 213 S.
Pennsylvania
Harting & Bro. 7 Norwood
Indianapolis Brewery, John P. Meikel, propr.
ss. W. Washington, junction National rd.
Maus Casper, (Ale) west end New York

SCHMIDT'S BREWERY,
C. F. SCHMIDT, propr., south end Alabama   (See advt. front cover)

SPONSEL & BALZ,
(UNION) Madison rd. nr. Corporation
line.

Bricklayers and Contractors.

LUCKY GEORGE W.
75 E. Washington
Whitsit Courtland E. Washington sw. cor.
Meridian

Brick Moulds.
(*Manufacturer of.*)

HARDIN R. E.
237 E. Washington

Brokers.
(*Merchandise.*)
Connely Robert. 27 S. Meridian
Hasselman Otto H. 30 S. Meridian

Brokers.
(*Note, Stock and Bond.*)
Goodwin T. A. 35 E. Market
Martin Luther R. 10 E. Washington

Broom Maker.
Newman I. L. 372 N. East

Brush Manufacturers.

HEISSER J. H.
(Agent for Moulin, N. Y.) 24 N. Pennsylvania

SCHMEDEL & FRICKER,
194 E. Washington   (See advt. Index)

Builders.

(*See Carpenters and Builders. Also Architects and Superintendents. Also Contractors.*)

Builders Materials.

Frese C. & Co. 27 W. Washington

Butchers.

(*See also Meat Markets.*)

Balz Philip, 427 N. Illinois
Heid F. 59 N. Noble
Kelly Thomas, 34 Kentucky av.
Lake & Co. 22 N. Illinois
Quisser Julius, 148 N. Tennessee
Reinert Gottlieb, 153 W. Washington
Shafer John, 92 N. Illinois

Butter and Eggs.

(*Packer and Dealer.*)

Lawyer & Hall, 49 S. New Jersey

Cabinet Makers.

(*See also Furniture Manufacturers and Dealers.*)

Greer James, 49 S. Mississippi

KELLER PAUL,
21 Circle   (See advt. Index)

Cancer Physicians.

Howard Edward, 92 S. Illinois

SWANK M. 76 N. PENNSYLVANIA,
DR. SWANK is a Graduate of one
of the best American MedICal Colleges, and having practiced more
than twenty-five years, always
giving special attention to Cancers. His success in the treatment
of this disease is generally known.
Send for Circular.

Cap Makers.

Schwartzer Joseph, 151 E. Washington

Carpenters and Builders.

Anderson George, al. in rear 177 E. Market
Berry Marion, 23 N. Noble
Boedeker & Niemann, 418 E. North
Brouse Andrew, 130 E. New York
Bullard William, ns. Washington bet. Canal
and Mississippi
Cochrane Samuel W. Tennessee cor. Michigan
Cosley Richard M. 32 Christian av.

DANIELS LEWIS H.
129 S. New Jersey

Denny John, 50 Kentucky av.
Dickey Thomas W. 34 Pennsylvania

DIEKMANN FREDERICK,
Wabash nr. cor. East

Ebert John, 44 Kentucky av.
Ewing William, 2 Indiana av.

FATOUT J. L. & M. K.
LaFayette nr. old LaFayette Freight Depot

Fearnley John, 23 Circle
Feary Jeremiah E. rear 318 E. North
Freitaz John M. 264 Railroad
Garrett David, 353 E. Market
Gilkey & Jones, 48 Kentucky av.
Hardon R. E. 237 E. Washington
Hart & Mathews, Maryland se. cor. Pennsylvania

HELM ADAM,
North nr. cor. Liberty

Henschen William H. 252 E. South
Jacobs Richard, Maryland e. of Illinois
Kellenger John G. 326 E. Market

KEMPER JOHN M.
184 E. South.   (See adv't Index)

Knighton C. J.
Lowe N. H. & Son, 30 E. New Jersey
McKibben Joshua R. 402 N. East
McLain William C. 164 N. Noble
Muchett Robert M. 169 E. St. Joseph

MANY JOHN B. & SON,
120 Spring

Miller Christian, 489 S. East
Monroe & Johnson, 40 W. Market

MORSE THOMAS J.
es. West, between New York and Vermont.   (See adv't. Index)

Prange F. rear 289 S. Illinois
Rafert A. F. 75 E. Walnut
Rafert C. F. 83 E. Pratt

RESENER C. F.
rear 100 E. New York

Rickard Thomas, 127 E. Maryland
Ricker Hubert, 219 E. Washington
Rhinehold Jacob, rear 373 W. Vermont
Routier Peter, Virginia av. cor. Cedar

SHOVER & CHRISTIAN,
124 E. Vermont.   (See adv't. Index)

Springer D. & Son, 260 Massachusetts av.
Stelhorn Frederick, 175 Davidson
Stewart Robert M., ss. Vermont nr. cor.
Massachusetts av.
Vincent William H. 178 N. Davidson
Noall Henry, 523 E. Market

Carpetbags, Valises, &c,

(*See Trunks, Traveling Bags and Valises.*)

Carpets and Oil Cloths.

(*Wholesale and Retail.*)

GALL & RUSH,
101 E. Washington cor. Delaware

HUME, ADAMS & CO.,
26 and 28 W. Washington

Roll W. H. 38 S. Illinois

Carriage Builders.
(Blow Lamp.)
HEISSER J H., Agent,
24 N. Pennsylvania

Carriage Manufacturerers.
(See also Wagon Makers.)
BREMERMAN & RENNER,
133 E. Washington
CITIZENS CARRIAGE AND WAGON MANUFACTORY, Fuller Smith, Prop. Liberty se. cor. Washington. (See adv't. Index.)
Drew S. W. E. Market Square, bet. Deleware and Alabama
Hampton Jehiel B. 186 W. Market
Indianapolis Coach Works, Shaw, Lippincott & Conner, proprietors, 26, 28 and 30 E. Georgia
MILLER, MITCHELL & STOUGH. Kentucky av. cor. Georgia. (See adv't. Index.)
Seger J. M. 178 Indiana av.
Van Blaricum Jesse M. 231 W. Washington

Carriage Materials.
Osgood, Smith & Co.
SARVEN'S PATENT WHEEL,
230 S. Illinois
Share Geo. K. & Co. 40 S. Meridian

Carriage Trimmings.
Holliday W. J. & Co. 59 S. Meridian

Castings.
D. Root & Co. 66 E. Washington

Coach Manufacturers.
MILLER, MITCHELL & STOUGH, Kentucky av. cor. Georgia

Coach Trimmings.
Sulgrove James W. & Co. 20 W. Washington

Constables.
Carson Pryor G. 83½ E. Washington
Davis Edward, 83½ E. Washington
Delano Joel A. Yohn's Blk.

Cemeteries.
(See City Register.)

Chair Manufacturers.
(See also Furniture Manufacturers.)
SCHILLING H. & BRO.
134 E. McCarty

Chandeliers and Lamps.
HOLLIDAY W. & C. F.
16 S. Meridian

China, Glass and Queensware.
(Wholesale and Retail.)
HOLLWEG LOUIS,
90 S. Meridian
Johnson E. & Co. 108 S. Delaware
Scott, West & Co. 127 S. Meridian
Theobald F. 94 E. Washington
West H. F. & Co. 37 S. Meridian
Woodbridge John, 36 S. Meridian
WOODBRIDGE JOHN & CO.
12 W. Washington

Cigar Box Manufacturers.
Reynolds J. W. 174 E. Washington

Cigars and Tobacco.
(Manufacturers and Retail Dealers. See also Tobacco Manufacturers.)
Back & Wenken, 209 E. Washington
Barker W. W. & Co. 22 N. Pennsylvania and 19 Massachusetts av.
Beltz Harvey A. Spencer House
Bond Edward, 262 E. Washington
Coulon Charles, 11 Pennsylvania
Ferree & Cantrill. 11 N. Illinois
Forsha Thomas. 66 Massachusetts av.
Garratt Jacob, 257 E. Washington
Heidlinger John A. 39 W. Washington
Hohmann V. 74 Virginia and 51 S. Illinois
Jameson Lillie Mrs. 33 S. Illinois
Koster C J. M. 141 E. Washington
Kretsch Peter, 141 S. Illinois
McGaw J. A. 16 Bates House blk.
Mayer Matthias, 96 S. Illinois
Menkes Frank, 153 E. Washington
MEYER GEORGE F.
35 W. Washington. (See advt. index.)
Oliver Charles, 288 W. Washington
Raschig Charles M. 13 W. Washington
Reinken Henry, 266 E. Washington
REYNOLDS N. W.
174 E. Washington. (See advt. index)
Roswinkel George, es. Massachusetts av. bet. North and Michigan
Schulz Henry, 36 Virginia av.
Setking William, 32 N. Pennsylvania
Sharpe A. W. 73 E. Market
Sharpe Andrew W. 28 N. Pennsylvania
Solomon Henry, 27 S. Illinois
Turkish Cigar Store, Charles C. Hunt propr. 61 E. Washington
Uhl & Durham, 22 N. Pennsylvania
Young Louis, 77 S. Illinois and 290 E. Washington

Cigars and Tobacco.
(Wholesale. See also Tobacco Manufacturers.)
BARKER, WILLIAMS & CO.
42 W. Washington. (See adv't Index)

MEYER GEORGE F.
35 W. Washington. (See adv't Index)
Miller Jacob, 110 S. Illinois
Speckman Henry, 108 S. Illinois
Stout F. & Son, 160 W. Washington
Wallace William P. 28 W. Louisiana

Cistern Builders.

Homan W. J. & J. 82 W. Washington

Claim Agents.

Denny Robert, 98 E. Washington. (up stairs)
Hamlin A Wright, 62½ E. Washington
HANNAMAN WILLIAM,
Agent Indiana State Military Claims, 56
N. Tennessee opp. State House
Mirrick David C. 17¾ W. Washington
WITT B. F.
Washington sw cor. Meridian

Clairvoyant.

Lewis F. C. Mrs. 70 E. Ohio

Clothing.
(Mens' and Boy's.)
GRAMLING J. & P.
35 E. Washington

Clothing.
(Wholesale.)
DESSAR BRO. & CO.
70 S. Meridian
Hays, Rosenthall & Co. 64 S. Meridian
MOSSLER L. I. & BRO.
37 E. Washington

Clothing.
(Wholesale and Retail.)
Gundelfinger Benjamin, 6 W. Washington
MOSSLER L. I. & BRO.
37 E. Washington
Speelman S. & Co. 111 S. Illinois

Clothing.
(Retail.)
Goeppert F. & Co. 17 E. Washington
Griesheimer M. Bro. 1 W. Washington
Kahn Adolphus, 95 S. Illinois
Kaufmann P. 24 W. Louisiana
Levy Henry, 199 E. Washington
Mayer Leopold, 133 S. Illinois
Mayer & Rhienheimer, 3 Palmers House
Moritz Bros. 19 W. Washington
Raugh Brothers, 1 Palmer House
Rothschild Henry, 125 W. Washington

Clothing.
(Second Hand.)
Garratt A. & Son, 257 E. Washington
Segar Levi, 213 E. Washington

Coach Manufacturers.

MILLER, MITCHELL &
STOUGH, Kentucky av. cor. Georgia

Coach Trimmings.

Sulgrove James W. & Co. 20 W. Washington

Coal Mining Companies.

INDIANAPOLIS MINING,
COAL AND COKE CO. W. H. Turner &
Co. lessees, office 19 Circle
Rolling Mill Coal Co. office Tennessee nw.
cor. S uth, D. Titcomb agt.

Coal and Coke Dealers.
(See also Wood and Coal Yards.)
Burk John, 23 Virginia av.
BUTSCH, DICKSON & DELL,
27 E. Georgia
Fawkner John E. 24 W. Maryland
Ingle Mark W. 28 S Meridian
McD nough D. R. 144 S. Alabama
Ross J. H. 24 E. Pearl

TURNER WILLIAM H. &
CO. Wholsale and Retail
Dealers in Coal and Coke, 19
Circle. See card front cover.

Coffee and Spice Mills.

Judson A Dodd, 251 and 253 E. Washington

Collar Makers.
(Horse.)
Schwegel Daniel, 261 S. Pennsylvania

Collection Agents.

Blake John W. 45 E. Washington
Goodwin T. A. 35 E. Market
Poe J. M. & Co. 24½ E. Washington

Colleges, Institutes and Universities
(See City Register.)

Commercial Colleges.

Bryant & Stratton's Business College, C. E.
Hollenbeck, principal, Washington, S. E.
cor Meridian
National Business College, (A. Hollingsworth
& Co.) Hendrix & Koerner in charge,
entrance 24½ E. Washington

Commission Merchants.

Bigham Heyden S. 149 E. Washington cor.
Alabama
Blake J. R. & Co. 15 S. Delaware
Bowker H. & Co. 50 Virginia av. cor. Dela-
ware
Caldwell H. W. 149 Indiana av.
Caldwell J. W. 61 S Illinois

Harper Henry, 180 Bluff rd.

KOEHRING BERNHARD,
  287 N. Liberty
Kruger Charles D. rear 362 W. New York.
Coble D. & G. 152 W. Washington

COORS AUGUST,
  151 W. Washington—see bottom lines
Daggett & Co. 26 N. Meridian
Davis & Donovan, 342 E. Washington
Elliott & Mott. 37 E. Market
Gallup W. P. & E. P. 43 and 45 N. Tennessee
Glazier Charles, 146 S. Pennsylvania

HOLMAN G. G.
  6 Bates House Block
Karney John, 56 S. Illinois

LUKENS RICHARD L.
  81 W. Washington   (See advt. Index)
Mick James F. 21 W. Maryland
Noel & Son, 86 Virginia av.

PORTER OMER T.
  6 Martindale's Block
Ross D. M. & Co. 155 W. Washington
Taylor D. B. & Co. 85 E. Washington

VAN CAMP & JACKSON.
  69 W. Washington   (See advt. Index)
Wallace Andrew, Delaware sw. cor. Maryland
Wallace William J. 43 S. Delaware

WEBB & BATES,
  83 W. Washington.   (See advt. index)
Wherrett & Scott, 150 N. Tennessee

WISEHART & CALVERT,
  185 Indiana av.   (See advt. Index)

Commission Merchants.
(*Pork.*)

Ferguson J. C. & Co. west end Georgia
Kingan & Co. west end Maryland
Nofsinger, Kingan & Co. west end Maryland
Wheat, Fletcher & Co. pork house, Blake bet.
  New York and Washington, office Vinton's Block, opp. P. O.

Commissioner of Deeds.

Martin Luther R. 10 E. Washington

Commissioner.
(*United States.*)

Kimball Eben W. 46 E. Washington

Concrete Paving.
(*Burns' Patent.*)

SIMMS & HOSKINS,
  ws. the Canal, bet. Louisiana and Georgia
                (See advt. index)

Confectionery and Fruit Stores.

Balls Anthony, 178 S. Illinois
Bower Jacob, 147 W. Washington
DeGray Thomas, 59 N. Illinois
Genter Charles, 233 E. Washington
Graves Richard, 50 Kentucky av.

Hespelt & Co, 150 W. Vermont
Holt Alexander, 3 Indiana av.
Parisette Joseph, 25 N. Illinois
Quinnell Isaac, 79 E. Market
Rabb Mary A. Mrs. 35 S. Illinois
Seitz Charles, 112 S. Illinois
Smith R. L. & Co. 40 W. Washington
Snyder John F. 143 W. Washington
Stephen Thomas D. 164 Indiana av.
Taylor Quartus, 42 Indiana av.
Webb Joshua, 66 N. Illinois
Weinberger & Co. 10 W. Louisiana
Woelz Charles A. 149 N. Delaware

Confectioners.
(*Wholesale and Retail.*)

BECKER F. P. & BRO
  17 N. Pennsylvania

DAGGETT & CO.
  26 S. Meridian
Martin Bernhard, 80 E. Washington

Constables.

Carson Pryor G. 83½ E. Washington
Davis Edward, 83½ E. Washington
Delano Joel A. Yohn's Blk.

Contractors and Builders.
(*See also Carpenters and Builders.*)

Roedeker & Niemann, 418 E. North
Daniels Lewis H. 129 S. New Jersey

MORSE THOMAS J.
  es. West bet. New York and Vermont
                (See advt. index)
Resener C. F. rear 100 E. New York
Scott & Nicholson, ws. Kentucky av. bet.
  West and Louisiana
Seibert Hiram, 143 S. East

SHOVER & CHRISTIAN,
  124 E. Vermont   (See advt. Index)

Conveyancers.

Dial Frank A. 8 E. Washington
Martin Luther R. 10 E. Washington

Coopers.

**BAIRD WILLIAM, Cooper,
Manufacturer of Tight Barrels, Pork Barrels, Bacon Hogsheads, Butter Firkins, and all kinds of Iron Bound Work. Orders Promptl Filled.**

Brenker William, ss. Walnut bet. East and
  New Jersey
Burton D. & Co. w. end New York
Carey J. S. & Co. Georgia bet. West and the river

FURGASON ALBERT L.
  321 E. Georgia

COP   380   DRE

Losey John, 102 S. East.

McKENDRY & LOVECRAFT,
Shops Lafayette R. R. w. end Pratt (See adv't. Index.)

McNeely E. 364 W. Washington, (Nat. road)

Montgomery William, W. Indianapolis

SCHWOMEYER HENRY,
308 N. Noble

Seiter Kasimar, McCarty cor. Union.

Copper Dealers.

Cottrell & Knight, 108 S. Delaware

Coppersmiths.

LANGSENKAMP WILLIAM,
96 S. Delaware.

Corn Shellers.

(Mills Patent.)

Fearnley John, 23 Circle

Cotton Factory.

Indianapolis Cotton Manufacturing Co. Robert P. Duncan, Supt., w. end Washington (Nat. road,) n. of the bridge

Cutlery.

(Importers of.)

WOODBRIDGE JOHN & CO.
12 W. Washington

Cracker Bakery.

Parrott Nichum & Co. 188 E. Washington

Dancing Academy.

Smith A. Yohn's Block

Dental Depot.

Strong & Smith, 23 Vinton's block. 4 N. Pennsylvania

Dentists.

Burgess & Faries, room 1, Odd Fellows Hall

Griffith Edward, room 3, 77½ E. Market

Heiskell William L., rooms 13-14-15-16 (2d floor) Martindales block

HUNT PHILLEAS G. C.
76½ E. Market

Johnston John F. 19 W. Maryland

Munhall Lea W. 35½ E. Market

Nichols F. M. 25 W. Washington

PURSEL A. E.
rooms 1-2, (3d floor) Martindales block.

Wells Graham A. 15 E. Washington

WELLS MERIT,
room 2, Yohn's block, Meridian ne. cor. Washington

Woodbury U. T. 39½ W. Washington

Dining Rooms.

(See also Eating Houses ; also Restaurants.)

UNION DEPOT DINING-ROOMS. T. B. Spratt, Supt. Union Depot bldgs.

Distillers.

(See Rectifiers and Distillers.)

Ditching Machine.

GAUSE'S DITCHING MACHINE. R. L. Luckens & Co. proprietors, 81 W. Washington.

Dress Trimmings.

HAERLE WILLIAM,
4 W. Washington

Smith N. R. & Co. Trade Palace, 26 and 28 W. Washington

Dress and Cloak Makers.

(See also Milliners.)

ALLEN N. M. MRS.
36½ E. Washington

Anders E. S. Mrs. 36 Rose

Austin Margaret, 32 N. Delaware

Baine Jennie Mrs. 20 W. Maryland

Barker Kate, 19 Massachusetts av.

Barnet Frances, 11 Massachusetts av.

Beckley Misses S. & M. 258 Bluff rd.

BENTLEY & CHANDLER,
44 Indiana av.—(See advt. Index)

Blalock Mattie, 9 Massachusetts av.

Bramley Mary Mrs. 196 E. Washington

Bramley & Chapman, 28 N. East

Campbell Mary F. 113 Massachusetts av.

Clark Sarah Miss. 199 N. Illinois

Coles Susie, 199 N. Illinois

Daugherty E. Miss, room 12 (2d floor) Martindale's blk.

Dorland A. Mrs. 9 E. New York

Enwic J. H. Mrs. 161 W. Maryland

Fletcher Mary, 309 E. New York

Forby S. L. Mrs. 34 S. Illinois

Foster Emma, 323 E. Washington

Gaston Mrs. Frank E. 35 N. Alabama

Harper Laura Mrs. 69 E. Maryland

Holmes Mrs. Mary M. 30 S. Delaware

Huntley Nellie Mrs. 19 E. North

Hukins Mrs. Jennie, 186½ W. Washington

Hutchison Annie, 299 N. East

Jarrell F. E. Mrs. 36 N. Illinois

Jencks Mary A. 21d E. Washington

Johnson Ann E. 231 Massachusetts av.

Johnson Jennie Mrs. 68 S. Illinois

Jordan Ella, 186½ W. Washington

KAY & MATTERN,
68½ E. Market—(See advt. Index)

Kissell Jacob W. Mrs. 22 S. West

McElvano Mary, 67 W. New York

Mabb Maria, 186½ W. Washington

Marshall & Sweeney, 58 N. Illinois

Martindale Julia A. Mrs. 194 W. Georgia

Martz Clara, 90 S. East

Merchant C. Miss, 27 N. West

I. Davis & Co., dealers in Hats, Caps, Furs and Straw Goods.

DRU 381 DRY

Merlau Lizzie Miss, Maryland, ne. cor. Illinois
Miner Maggie Mrs. 30 W. Washington
Moss M. Mrs. 188 N Tennessee
Mulliken S. A. 7 Martindale blk. N. Pennsylvania
NEWTON MARIA MRS.
110 S. Illinois, up stairs. (See advt. Index)
Noe Mary Miss, 21 N. East
Obmeyer M..A. Mrs. 79 W. Ohio
Parker Sarah J. 156 E. Market
Patterson John Mrs. 29 Massachusetts av.
Rakestraw Mattie, 17 Massachusetts av.
Redford John Mrs. 80 N. Pennsylvania
Ritchey Sarah, 22 Douglass
Robinson Emma B. Mrs. 402 S. Illinois
Rose Margaret, 181 Virginia av.
Ryan M. B. Mrs. 209 Virginia av.
Scudder H. M. Mrs. 85 N. New Jersey
Shears Lou, 10 S. Mississippi
Shepard M. 331 N. New Jersey
Smith L. Mrs. 40 S. Illinois
Swindler Rebecca A. 232 N. Noble
Van Vleet Druciler, 30 N. Delaware
Willard M. F. Mrs. 264 S. Tennessee
Williams S. A. Mrs. 37 W. Market
Wilson M. Mrs. 119 W. Vermont
Wonnell & Montany, 31 Indiana av.

Druggists.
(Wholesale.)
Browning & Sloan, 7 and 9 E. Washington
HASKIT W. I. & CO.,
14 W. Washington
Kiefer & Vinton, 68 S. Meridian
Patterson, Moore & Talbot, 3 Morison's Opera Hall, S. Meridian
STEWART & MORGAN,
40 E. Washington
Wiles & Reynolds, Vinton's blk. opp. post office

Drugs and Medicines.
Bell John S. 212 E. Washington
Bell Miletus, 261 Massachusetts av.
Black Eagle Pharmacy, A. Metzner, propr. 127 E. Washington
Browning & Sloan, 7 and 9 E. Washington
Bazan James W 48 W Louisiana
Campbell & Green, Hoosier Drug Store, 149 W. Washington
Capitol Drug Store, F. A. Bryan, propr. Massachusetts av. cor. Vermont
Dryer James W. 344 E. Washington
Erdelmeyer Frank, 91 E. Washington
Frauer I. C. 246 E. Washington
Gerhardt L. J. 96 Russel av.
German Pharmacy, L. H. Mueller, propr. 187 E. Washington
Green J. C. & Co. 100 E. Washington
Hay & Co. 48 W. Washington
Lee H. H. 18 and 20 Bates House blk.
Lowry Wiley M. 65 Massachusetts av.
METZNER, ADOLPH
(Black Eagle Pharmacy) 127 E. Washington
Miller Edward T. 49 S. Illinois
Moody Bros. Indiana av. cor. Tennessee and 180 Indiana av.

Morris Charles G. 521 N. Illinois
Sage Charles, prop. West End Drug Store, 172 W. Washington
Snider W. H. South cor. East.
STEWART & MORGAN,
40 E. Washington
Swing & Dennis, 4 Martindales block
Tomlinson & Cox. 18 E. Washington
Ward Boswell, 397 N. New Jersey
WILES & REYNOLDS,
Vinton's block, opp. Post Office

Drum Head Maker.
Schmidt Robert, 96 S. East

Dry Goods.
(Importer of.)
CULLINY PATRICK M.
98 E. Washington. (See card on back cover, and top lines)

Dry Goods.
(Retail.)
Boston Store (Wm. H. Close & Co.) 10 E. Washington
Brady O. H. P. 546 E. Washington
Cook William & Co. 249 E. Washington
Cussen Garret, 158 Indiana av.
Deitch Felix, 162 W. Washington
Eccles William 22 W. Washington
Greenewald Henry, 174 E. Washington
Kahn S. & Bro. 45 and 47 E. Washington
Kirlin James, 186 W. Washington
Lintner C. H., 184 Indiana av.
Meier Lewis & Co. 151 Fort Wayne av.
Ostermeyer C. F. 350 E. Ohio
Potts Charles, 100 E. South
Prange Charles & Co. 318 E. Washington
Rasener F. William, 288 E. Washington
Resener F. & W. 179 N. East
Rice Gustav, 164 W. Washington
Robertson N. M. & Bro. 96 E. Washington
Sailors James L. 156 W. Washington
Schwear & Spear, 576 E. Washington
SPADES M. H.
20 E. Washington (See margin side lines)
Steignmann Charles, 150 Madison av.
Sverup Henry, 199 Massachusetts av.
TRADE PALACE,
N. R. Smith & Co. 26 and 28 W. Washington

Dry Goods.
(Staple and Fancy.)
DREHER & BOLINGER,
250 E. Washington
Kennedy, Byram & Co. 104 S. Meridian
Pettis, Dixon & Co. Glenn's blk.

Dry Goods.
(Wholesale.)
HIBBEN, TARKINTON & CO.
112 S. Meridian

Kennedy Byram & Co. 104 S. Meridian
LANDERS, CONDUITT & CO.
58 S. Meridian
Murphy, Johnston & Co. S. Meridian, cor. Maryland

Dry Goods.
(Wholesale and Retail.)
CULLINY P. M.
10 N. Pennsylvania, (See advt. Index)
Furnds John & Co. 68 E. Washington
Gordon George E. 3 Odd Fellows' bldg.
PETTIS, DICKSON & CO.
Glenn's blk.
Smith N. R. & Co. 26 and 28 W. Washington
Tyler L. H. & Co. 2 W. Washington

Dye Works.
SMITH'S CHEMICAL DYE
WORKS, (John B. Smith) 32 N. Missouri office 62 E. Market (See advt. index.)

Dyers and Scourers.
(See also Tailors and Repairers.)
BOUCHET SOPHIA MRS.
42 Kentucky av.
Fette George, 38 Virgininia
Heaf August, propr. New York Dye House, 65 N. Illinois
Morris H. & Co. 22 W. Maryland
Prosser John, 50 N. Illinois
Rensman Herman, 28 Virginia av.
SKINNER ELLISON E.
62 S. Illinois
SMITH JOHN B.
32 N. Missouri, office 62 E. Market and 307 E. Washington. (See advt. index.)

Eating Houses.
See also Dining Rooms; also Restaurants.)
Bach John, 30 W. Louisiana
Baldwick Fred. R 32 W. Louisiana
Keppel Martin, 36 W. Louisiana

Edge Tool Manufacturers.
Kellog N. 411 W. Washington (Nat. Rd.)

Elevator.
(Grain.)
Peru & Indianapolis Elevator, Lawyer & Hall propr. 49 S. New Jersey

Embroidering and Stamping.
(See also Dress and Cloak Makers. Also Milliners.)
Forby S. L. 34 S. Illinois
Lemmert Sarah, 76 N. Pennsylvania
LUDERS MISSES,
74½ E. Market and room 1, 40 S. Illinois. (See advt. index)
Strider T. P. 46 S. Illinois

Engine Builders.
WESTERN MACHINE WORKS
Sinker & Co. proprs. 125 S. Pennsylvania

Engines, Portable and Stationary.
EAGLE MACHINE WORKS,
Louisiana se. cor. Meridian
Greenleaf & Co. 325 S. Tennessee

Engravers.
Beckmann J. W. 46 Virginia av.
Bingham W. P. & Co. 50 E. Washington

Engravers, Wood and Metal.
Chandler H. C. & Co. 25 and 27 S. Meridian
PERRINE TRUMAN B.
34 Virginia av. (See top lines)

Engravings.
(Steel.)
National Art Association, M. O. Tracy, gen'l supt. room 21 Talbott & New's blk.

Exchange Dealers.
(See Banks and Bankers)

Express Companies.
(See also Fast Freight Lines.)
American Merchants' Union, E. W. Sloan, supt. J. Butterfield, agt. 42-44 E. Washington
Great Western Express Co. T. A. Lewis, supt. 82 Virginia av.
United States, J. Butterfield, agt. 42-44 E. Washington

Family Medicines.
(Manufacturer of.)
BUELL C. H.
75 E. Market

Fancy Goods.
Aughinbangh & Bro. 7 Martindale's blk. n. P. O.
BALDWIN J. H. & CO.
(Fancy Bazaar) 6 E. Washington
Boston Store (Wm. H. Close & Co.) 10 E. Washington
FAIRBANKS & CO
22 W. Washington
Fisk E. I. Mrs. 62 N. Illinois
Glick & Schwartz, Miller's blk. 54 N. Illinois
Kahn S. & Bro. 45 and 47 E. Washington
Langbein Joseph, 200 E. Washington, cor. New Jersey
McIlhenney M. A, Mrs. 58 N. Illinois
Miller Edward T. 49 S. Illinois
Sedgewick R. 68 N. Illinois

Fancy Goods.
(Wholesale.)
Fahnley & McCrea, 131 S. Meridian

Ludolff L. & Co. 42 S. Meridian

MAYER, CHARLES & CO.
29 W. Washington

Farm Machinery.
(*See also Agricultural Implements.*)

Farmers and Mechanics Tools and Hardware.

CROPPER JAMES II.
169 and 171 W. Washington. (See adv't index)
Dickson C. & Co., 47 and 49 N. Tennessee

Fast Freight Lines.
(*See also Express Companies.*)

Empire Line J. A. Murray, agt. 96 Virginia av.
Great Western Despatch, D. A. Lewis, agt. 82 Virginia av.

MERCHANT'S DESPATCH,
S. T. Scott, agt. 19 Virginia av.

PEOPLES DESPATCH,
S. T. Scott, agt. 19 Virginia av.

STAR UNION LINE,
S. F. Gray, agt. 85 Virginia av.

White Line Transportation Co. Alabama. cor. Union R. R. track

Feathers.
(*Wholesale.*)

Mick James F. 21 W. Maryland

File and Rasps.
(*Manufacturers.*)

Drotz & Steinhauer, 136 S. Pennsylvania.

Fish Dealers.

Johnson C. R. 397 Virginia av.

Fishing Tackle.

Ballweg A. 123 W. Washington

Florists.
(*See Nurserymen and Florists.*)

Flour and Feed Stores.
(*See also Flour Mills.*)

ANDERSON & SCOTT,
180 E. Washington
Avels J. H. 61 N. Illinois
Bigham Heyden S. 149 E. Washington cor. Alabama

BLAKE J. R. & CO.
15 S. Delaware

BOWKER & CO.
146 Virginia av.
Brown F. M. 59 W. Washington
Caldwell H. W. 149 Indiana av.

Case Elmer E. 523 N. Illinois
Corbaley & Cossel, 414 W. Washington
Craig William & Co. 78 Massachusetts av.

CROPPER JAMES II.
169 and 171 W. Washington. (See adv't. Index)

DAVIS BENJAMIN,
Indiana av. cor. West
Delue & Bro. 300 E. Washington
Emmerich II. & Co. 86 W. Washington
Fahrion J. George, 90 and 92 E. South
Gallup W. P. & E. P. 43 and 45 N. Tennessee
Goth, Brown & Co. 489 N. New Jersey
Graham J. J. & Co. 62 N. Pennsylvania
Henderson & Bass, 145 N. Delaware
Keever John II. 525 N. Mississippi

LANGENBERG II. II. & CO.
244 W. Washington
Lawyer & Hall, 19 S. New Jersey
Mitchell David N. 52 Indiana av.
Moorhouse Robert, 52 Indiana av.
Newcomb II. C. 302 N. Illinois
Plogsterth Victor, 207 N. Davidson
Porter Omer T. 6 Martindale's blk.
Rentsch Edward, 172 S. Illinois
Ross O. M. & Co. 155 W. Washington
Rush Fred P. 99 S. Delaware
Schuh John 322 Virginia av.
Schwear & Spear, 576 E. Washington
Simpson Richard, 19 S. Delaware
Sohl, Gibson & Co. 352 W. Washington
Smith & Goodhart, Delaware cor. Virginia av.
Smith & Marshall, Noble se. cor. Fletcher av.
Stolte & May, 365 S. Delaware
Wallace Will W. 441 N. Illinois

WEBB & BATES,
83 W. Washington

WISEHART & CALVERT,
185 Indiana av. (See adv't. Index)
Worland W. 52 Virginia av.

Flouring Mills.

ÆTNA, JAMES SKILLEN,
propr. 356–358 W. Washington
Brett, Braden & Co. Michigan rd. nw. cor. Mill

CARLISLE HENRY D.
Maryland cor. Canal (See adv't. Index)
Carlisle's Model Mills. John Carlisle, propr. Market cor. Canal

CITY MILLS, HECKMAN & SHEESLEY, propr. 354 E. Washington
Hoosier State, Geisendorff, Richardson & Co. proprs. ns. W. Washington, (Nat. rd.) nr. the Bridge
Indianapolis Mills. C. Orm & Bro. proprs. s. of limits, bet. Bluff rd. and Canal

SKILLEN JAMES,
(Ætna) 356–358 W. Washington

SOHL, GIBSON & CO.
(White Rose) 352 W. Washington

Dont forget Davis, 12 E. Washington, when you want a new Hat.

FOU   384   GEN

Foundries and Machine Shops.

(See also Engine Builders also Boiler Makers)

EAGLE MACHINE WORKS,
Frederick Ruschaupt, pres. Meridian cor. Louisiana, e. end Union depot

GREENLEAF & CO.
325 S. Tennessee

Hamilton James, Kentucky av. cor. Mississippi

Hetherington B. F. & Co. 244 S. Pennsylvania

Hoosier Foundry and Stove Works, A. D. Wood, propr. 135-137 S. Delaware

Johnson Isaac B. 24 N. East

King & Pinney, Kentucky av. cor. Mississippi

Phœnix Bell and Brass Foundry, Schneider & Co. 26 Union R. R. track

Phœnix Machine Works, 370 W. Washington

Root D. & Co. 183 and 185 S. Pennsylvania

Russell & Kasberg, Market nr. cor. Benton

Fruit House.

INDIANAPOLIS FRUIT HOUSE, VanCamp & Jackson, proprs. 69 W. Washington   (See advt. Index)

Fruit Jars.

Wiles Thomas, 25 E. Georgia

Fruits, Green and Dried.

Conti Antonia, 22 N. Illinois

Daggett & Co. 26 S. Meridian

JENISON A. F. & J. H.
89 N. Illinois   (See advt. Index)

Moorhouse Robert, 52 Indiana av.   (See advt. Index)

Smith Joseph, 13 N. Illinois

Stout B. G. & Bro. 7 and 8 Bates House blk.

VAN CAMP & JACKSON,
69 W. Washington   (See advt. Index)

Wallace Will W. 441 N. Illinois

Furniture.

(Church.)

MILLER LAWRENCE,
rear 84 E. Market.

Furniture Manufacturers and Dealers.

APPLEBY ROBERT,
83 N. Illinois   (See advt. Index)

Baker N. S. & Co. 73 E. Washington

Burk, Ershaw & Co. salesroom 67 and 69 W. Washington, factory 251 S. Pennsylvania

CABINET MAKERS' UNION,
E. Market cor. Winston

CROPPER JAMES H.
169 and 171 W. Washington   (See advt. Index)

DOHN PHILIP,
246 S. Meridian

GEBHARD AUGUST,
67 E. Washington

Gibbs W. P. 78 E. Market

Helwig Charles & Co. factory cor. New York and the canal, salesroom 115 and 117 E. Washington

Jose N. S S. Delaware

Marot John R. 87 E. Washington

Mitchell & Rammelsberg Furniture Co. 38 E. Washington

SPIEGEL & THOMS' FURNITURE CO. salesrooms 71 and 73 W. Washington

WESTERN FURNITURE CO.
Factory 161 N. Alabama, salesroom 105 E. Washington

Furniture.

(New and Second Hand.)

APPLEBY ROBERT,
83 N. Illinois   (See advt. Index)

McCASLIN & MASTERS,
82 E. Washington

Furs.

(Wholesale and Retail.)

Bamberger H. 16 E. Washington

Lelewer D. & Bro. 394 S. Meridian

McIver J. C. 22 E. Washington

Muehlenbeck August, 198 E. Washington

Gas Fixtures.

Hanning John G. 82 W. Washington

Neab Conrad, 70 N. Illinois

Gas Generator.

Noble Frank A. 28 Kentucky av.

Gas Light and Coke Co.

Indianapolis Gas Light and Coke Co. S. A. Fletcher Jr. Prest., S. A. Fletcher Sen. Treas., L. Van Laningham Sec. Pennsylvania ne. cor. Maryland.

Gas and Steam Pipe Fitters.

(See also Plumbers.)

Hanning John G. 82 W. Washington

Neab Conrad, 70 n. Illinois

Gents Furnishing Goods.

(See also Tailors Merchant, also Clothiers Retail.)

Baldwin J. H. & Co. (Fancy Bazaar) 6 E. Washington

Davis Isaac & Co. 12 E. Washington

GRAMLING J. & P.
35 E. Washington

Griesheimer M. & Bro. 1 W. Washington

Holtz & Co. 124 S. Illinois

Ladorf L. & Co. 42 S. Meridian

PARKER R. R.
30 W. Washington

Dont forget Davis, 12 E. Washington, when you want a new Hat.

GLU   385   GRO

Roeth & Meier, 207 E. Washington
Smith & Foster, 27 N. Pennsylvania

Glue Manufacturer.

Goss & Co. Michigan rd. opp. Camp Carrington

Grain Dealers.

(*See also Commission Merchants.*)

Emmerick & Co. 86 W. Washington
LANGENBERG H. H. & CO.
   244 W. Washington
Noel & Son, 86 Virginia av.

Grain Elevators.

(*See Elevators.*)

Grainers.

(*See also Painters.*)

JAMES M. FUGIT, Grainer,
18 S. Meridian. Orders
Promptly Attended to.

Long E. C. 7½ Massachusetts av.

Groceries Fancy.

Jenison A. F. & J. H. 89 N. Illinois (See adv't.

Grocers.

(*Wholesale.*)

Alford Talbot & Co. 2 Morrison's blk. S. Meridian
CROSSLAND, HANNA & CO.
   Meridian se. cor. Maryland
FOSTER & WIGGINS,
   68 and 70 Delaware
Holland, Ostermeyer & Co. 27 and 29 E. Maryland
Robertson J. E. & Co. 74 and 76 S. Meridian
Severin & Schnull, 137 and 139 S. Meridian
STONEMAN, PEE & CO.
   2 W. Louisiana
Wallace Andrew, Maryland sw. cor. Delaware
WILES BRO. & CO.
   119 S. Meridian

Grocers.

(*Wholesale and Retail.*)

COORS AUGUST F.
   151 W. Washington.   (See bottom lines)
LAWRENCE ARTHUR B.
   173 W. Washington.   (See advt. Index)
MOORHOUSE ROBERT,
   52 Indiana av. cor. Tennessee and New York.   (See adv't. Index)
Reese Henry, 113 and 115 W. Washington
Schetter & Simpson, 99 E. South
Stout B. G. & Bro. 7 and 8 Bates House block

Groceries and Provisions.

(*Retail.*)

Altman H. & Co. Bluff rd. cor. Ray
Baker & Surbey, 199 Virginia av. cor. South
BARR M. J.
   233 S. Tennessee
Baxter & Davis, 250 W. Washington
Berg & Waterman, 193 S. Tennessee
Blatz Katy Mrs. 108 Bluff rd.
BOSWELL & FLEMING,
   211 Massachusetts av.
Bothwell Henry, 536 N. Mississippi
Bowker H. & Co. 50 Virginia cor. Delaware
Brady O. H. P. 546 E. Washington
Bretz Adam, 118 S. Illinois and 44 W. Louisiana
Brinker August, 174 W. New York.
Brooker Thomas, 774 N. Tennessee
Brown Albert, 387 S. Delaware
Brown F. W. 59 W. Washington
Brown I. I. 292 E. Washington
Brown John G. 300 N. New Jersey
Bruner & Comer, Tennessee sw. cor. 4th
Buchter George, 54 S. California
Bulsterbaum E. Mrs. 312 N. Meridian
BURCH LEONARD B.
   223 W. Ohio
Butler, Smith & Harlan, Massachusetts av. ne. cor. New Jersey
Cady E. E. 523 N. Illinois
Caldwell H. W. 149 Indiana av.
Carr Thomas, 276 S. Missouri
Clem & Bro. junction Massachusetts av. and Delaware
City Grocery, J. N. Conklin propr. 31 W. Washington
Coble D. & G. 152 W. Washington
Cook William & Co. 249 E. Washington
Corbaley & Cossel, 414 W. Washington (Nat. Rd.
Cusick Joseph, 73-75 S. West
DAMMEYER ANTHONY,
   E. Washington, out of limits
Davis Benjamin, Indiana av. cor. West
Davis & Donovan, 342 E. Washington
Donnelly Francis, 347 S. Delaware
Douglass George, 157 W. Washington
Eagle & Son, 340 N. Delaware
Elder E. A. 32 N. Illinois
Fawkner John E. 338 W. Washington
Farmers' Grocery, John Hauck & Co. 11 W. Washington
Francis James, 99 Massachusetts av.
Frech Henry, ns. Nat. Rd. west of bridge
Frick John, St. Clair, junction Massachusetts av. and Plum
Gahn John, 196 Indiana av.
Gembal Michael, 329 S. East
George Robert, 184 W. Washington
Goe H. N. Illinois se. cor. St. Clair
Gold Adam, 405 W. Washington (Nat. Rd.)
GOTH, BROWN & CO.
   489 N. New Jersey
HAGERHORST CHRISTIAN L.
   223 W. Ohio

J. Arden, will make the best sewed boot in town, 65 S. Meridian.

28

GRO	386	GRO

Haneman J. & T. 135 Massachusetts av.
Hanna David, 203 Massachusetts av.
Harmeniger Chris, 283 S. Delaware
Helm John, 272 Winston
Henuinger G. & E. 115 S. Illinois
Hill J. B. 192 E. Washington
Hill James, New York ne. cor. Douglas
Hilgemeyer C. & Co. 367 S. Delaware
Hiltebrand Malissa, 46 Massachusetts av.
Hofmann M. 170 Bluff rd.
Hofman Philip, 775 N. Tennessee
Hofmeister Nicholas, 150 N. Noble
Holowell Edwin, 430 W. Washington, Natl. rd
Howard Azel B. Virginia av. cor. New Jersey
Huff J. T. 298 N. Pennsylvania
Hutchins H. S. 407 N. Alabama
Hutton E. L. & Co. 94 N. Illinois

JACKSON & NICOLI, Dealers in Groceries, Provisions and Fresh Meats, 221 W. Ohio.

Jasper Frederick, 333 Virginia av.
JENISON A. F. & J. H. 89 N. Illinois. (See advt. Index)
JOHNSON HOWARD A. 399 N. New Jersey
Johnson Sidney H. 143 N. Delaware
Jordan John, 158 W. Washington
Kalb Fred. 310 Winston
Karney John, 56 S. Illinois
Kattmann Ernst, 1 Buchanan
Keever John H. 525 N. Mississippi
Kenzie George, 233 W. McCarthy
Kettenbach, Newmeyer & Co. 273, 275 and 277 Massachusetts av.
Koch Henry H. 192 S. Noble
Koehl Peter, 188 S. Illinois
Kohler John, 247 N. Noble
Kothe William 130 N. Davidson
KRUG G. C. & CO. Georgia cor. Liberty
Kuhn Philip J. Ft. Wayne av. junction New Jersey
Laugbein Joseph, 200 E. Washington, cor. New Jersey
LANGENBERG H. H. & CO. 216 W. Washington
Lawless & Curran, 138 S. Noble
Lehr Philip, 246 N. Noble
Lemon Daniel A. 187 W. Washington
Lentzen William, 219 W. McCarty
Lexauer Edward, 125 E. Washington
Lindemann Frank, 206 E. Washington
Lintner Amos H. 182 Indiana av.
Lintner Daniel H. 400 W. North
Lauergan John, 154 Pine
Loucks James, Broadway sw. cor. Cherry
Luemann Charles, 380 Virginia av.
McGinnis John, 280 E. Washington
McGowan L. 251 N. Illinois
Mann James B. 283 Virginia av.
Many & Names, Virginia av. cor. Noble
Mardick James G. 399 E. Georgia
Mitchell David N, 52 Indiana av.
Mitchell S. J. ws. Mississippi bet. 4th and 5th

Morgenveck Valentine, 21 Chatham
Munson W. A. 51 N. Alabama
Murphy Daniel E. 396 W. North
Massmann W & D. 244 Bluff rd.
Naughton Patrick, 210 E. Washington
Newcomb H. C. 302 N. Illinois
NIEMEYER WILLIAM, 102 S. Noble
Nies Lewis, 460 N. East
Ostermeyer C. F. 350 Ohio
Pennicke Morris, 191 W. South
Plogsterth Victor, 207 N. Davidson
Pochler Lous, Bluff rd. se. cor. Ray
Prange Charles & Co. 318 E. Washington
Prasse Henry, 446 Virginia av.
Rasener F. William, 288 E. Washington
Reasner & Shiltmeyer, Washington east of limits
Reeder E. C. 298 E. Washington
Reese Henry, 113 and 115 W. Washington
Reichter F. B. & Co. S. Illinois junction Russell av.
Rentsch Edward, 172 S. Illinois
Rentsch Herman, 145 E. Washington
Resener F. & W. 179 N. East
Richards & Thomas, 213 E. Washington
Richter William, 416 Virginia av.
Ripley & Gates, 47 and 49 N. Illinois
Rodewald Henry, 441 Virginia av
Ropke Helen Mrs. McCarty sw. cor. Madison av.
Rosebrock John S. 201 Virginia av.
Rosebrook F. W. 485 Virginia av.
Rapp John, Kentucky av. cor. West
SAHN LUDWIG, 142 Fort Wayne av.
Santo Edward, 204 Indiana av.
Schlotzhauer Adam, 248 N. Liberty
Schmitts William H. 389 N. Noble
Schrader & Kruger, 401 Virginia av.
Schuh John, 322 Virginia av.
Schutter Christian, 239 S. Meridian
Schwear & Spear, 576 E. Washington
Schwicho Charles, 224-6 Bluff rd.
Schwomeyer Charles H. 397-9 S. Meridian
Seeman Christian, Washington east of limits
Seibert George W. 51 N. Noble
SEVENTH WARD GROCERY, Azel B. Howard propr. Virginia av. cor. New Jersey
Sheets David, 241 W. McCarty
Showalter Samuel, 235 Indiana av.
Shroeder Charles, 299 S. Delaware
Shroer Henry H. 2-0 S. Alabama
Simon Frederick, 188 N. Noble
Simpson N. 235 S. Delaware
Smith F. 200 N. Mississippi
Smith & Marshall, Noble se. cor. Fletcher av.
Snider & Lackey, 200 Virginia av. cor. East
Sockwell H. M. 232 E. Washington
Spickelmeyer & Bird, 247 Indiana av.
Sponsel Henry, 355 S. Delaware
Sprole James E. Illinois sw. cor. Ohio
Stiegmann Charles, 150 Madison av.
Stolte & May, 365 S. Delaware
Stuckmeyer John, 362 Virginia av.
Suart John B. 219 Massachusetts av.
SULLIVAN WILLIAM H. 76 W. Washington

SYERUP HENRY,
  199 Massachusetts av.
Tarlton James A. Illinois cor. Tinker
Taylor Samuel, 77 E. Market
Thayer & Frauer, 248 E. Washington
Thomas C. & Bros. 250 E. Ohio
Traub Israel, 500 N. Alabama
Vehling F. 195 E. South
Wallace Will. W. 441 N. Illinois
Werbe Ferdinand L. 249 W. Washington
Wherrett & Scott, 150 N. Tennessee
Whittlinger Jacob, 100 S. Noble
WILKINSON D. E.
  44 N. Pennsylvania (See advt. index)
WILLS THOMAS & CO.
  105 Massachusetts av.
Wilson Ann Mrs. 88 E. South
Wingate Joseph F. 42 N. Pennsylvania
Witte Edward, 300 Blake
Witthoeft Frederick, 329 Indiana av.
Woods J. S. 382 Indiana av.
Woollen William M. 101 Indiana av.
Wonner Louis, 46 Indiana av.
Woodfill George. 174 Bluff rd.
Worland W. 52 Virginia av.
Wright Levi, 323 N. Alabama
Wyatt W. D. 78 Virginia av.
Yeager William, 282 N. Noble
Zimmer and Niehaus, 323 S. Delaware

Guns and Pistols.

Ballweg A. 129 W. Washington
Vajen J. H. & Co. 21 W. Washington

Gunsmiths.

Ballweg A. 129 W. Washington
Beck Christian, 12 S. Pennsylvania
BECK SAMUEL,
  63 E. Washington

Hair Workers and Braiders.

  (See also Human Hair Goods.)
Mahorney Ann E. 235 Blake
MEDINA FRANK J.
  34 W. Washington
Neven Charles, 51 Massachusetts av.
SCHONACKER CLARA,
  134 N. Illinois
Spades M. H. 20 E. Washington

Hair and Bristle Works.

Indianapolis Hair and Bristle Works, F. Miller, supt. office and works south end of S. West

Hardware--Heavy.

  (Wholesale.)
OVER E. & CO.
  82 and 84 S. Meridian

Hardware and Cutlery.

  (Wholesale.)
Anderson, Bullock & Schofield, 62 S. Meridian

KIMBLE, AIKMAN & CO.
  198 S. Meridian
Layman James T. & Co. 64 E. Washington
OVER E. & CO.
  82 and 84 S. Meridian

Hardware and Cutlery.

  (Wholesale and Retail.)
CROPPER JAMES H.
  169 and 171 W. Washington. (See adv't index)
Frese C. & C. 27 W. Washington
Pottage Benjamin, 77½ W. Washington
VAJEN J. H. & CO.
  21 W. Washington
Vonnegut Clemens, 184 E. Washington

Harness and Saddle Makers.

Andra John, 178 E. Washington
ARNHOLTER HENRY & BRO.
  225 E. Washington
CARR JAMES M.
  9 Bates House blk   (See advt. index)
Carr R. S. & J. M. 9 Bates House blk.
Edwards Edward, 16 W. Maryland
Hereth Ad. 24 N. Delaware
Huffer J. M. & Son, 23 S. Meridian
Jamison & Mitchell, 138 Bluff rd.
Marsh William S. 180 W. Washington
Nicolai C. 326 E. Washington
SELLERS DANIEL,
  17 Virginia av.
Shawver Christopher J. 297 Indiana av.

Harness and Saddles.

  (Manufacturer and Whol. Dealer.)
FRAUER, BIELER & CO.
  109 E. Washington

Hat Manufacturer.

Brown William P. 61 E. Washington

Hat and Bonnet Frames.

Copeland J. W. & Co. 39 S. Meridian

Hats, Caps and Furs.

BAMBERGER HERMAN,
  10 E. Washington
DAVIS, ISAAC & CO.
  12 E. Washington. (See margin lines)
German Hat Store, August Muehlenbeck proprietor, 198 E. Washington
Goldsberry B. S. 32 W. Washington
Kaufman S. 16 W. Washington
Lintner Charles H. 184 Indiana av.
McIver J. C. 22 E. Washington
Muehlenbeck & Obermeyer 2 Palmer House
SEATON E. A.
  25 N. Pennsylvania

Hats, Caps and Furs.

(Wholesale.)

CARR & ALVEY,
  6 W. Louisiana, opp. Union Depot
DONALDSON & STOUT,
  54 S. Meridian
Rickard & Talbott, 78 S. Meridian
Seaton E. A. 25 N. Pennsylvania

Hearses and Carriages.

(See also Livery Stables.)

Long & Kregel, 15 Circle

Hides and Leather.

(See also Tanners.)

Dietz & Reissner, 17 S. Delaware
FISHBACK JOHN,
  125 S. Meridian
Frenzel J. P. 104 S. Illinois
Sharpe Joseph K. 47 and 49 S. Delaware
Yandes D. J. 76 E. Washington

Hoop Skirts and Corsets.

(Manufacturers and Dealers. See also Dry Goods.)

Fisk E. I. Mrs. 62 N. Illinois
Fortner Floyd & Co. 75 S. Meridian
Glick & Schwartz, Miller's Block, 54 N. Illinois
Mossler A. 1. 59 S. Illinois
Newman Pauline Mrs. 95 E. Washington
VALENTINE W. H.
  34 W. Washington

Horse Powers.

EAGLE MACHINE WOKRS,
  Louisiana se. cor. Meridian

Horse Shoers.

(See also Blacksmiths.)

Clark John T. 27 N. Tennessee
HITCHENS JOHN,
  44 E. Maryland

Hosiery.

PETIS, DICKSON & CO.
  Glenns Block

Hot Air Furnaces.

Frankem I. L. & Co. 34 E. Washington
MUNSON & JOHNSTON,
  62 E. Washington

Hotels.

(See also Boarding Houses.)

BATES HOUSE,
  (N. D. Keneaster,) Washington nw. cor. Illinois
Bicking House, (W. Hebble) 89 S. Illinois
California House, (A Kestner) 184 S. Illinois
Commercial Hotel, (T. C. Miles) Illinois ne. cor. Georgia
Concordia House, (F. Mottery) 200 S. Meridian
Globe House (H. Gruenard) 166 S. Illinois.
Emeneggers Hotel, 111 and 113 E. Washington
Grant House, (H. Doefer) South ne. cor. Illinois
Illinois House, (W. Essmann) 183 S. Illinois
LaFayette House, (George Hoppe) 179 S. Meridian
Littles Hotel, (Mrs. R Pryor,) Washington, se. cor. New Jersey
Macy Hause, (A. W. Melsheimer,) 45 N. Illinois
Martin House, (Jesse Martin,) 33 W. Maryland
Nagel House, (August Nagel,) 272 W. Maryland
National Hotel, (W. P. Thacher,) S. McNabb opp. Union depot
Neiman House, (Mrs. L. Neiman,) 130 S. Illinois
Oriental House, (Frank Costigan,) 71 to 75 S. Illinois
PALMER HOUSE,
  (Jeff. K. Scott,) Illinois, se. cor. Washington
Pattison House, (J. B. Bell) 63 N. Alabama
Pyle House, (John Pyle,) 95 N. Meridian
Ray House, (J. M. Lambert,) South, se. cor. Delaware
RICHMOND TEMPERANCE
  HOUSE, (J. G. Collins,) 35 W. Georgia
SHERMAN HOUSE,
  (W. M. Hawkins,) Louisiana, opp. Union Depot
SPENCER HOUSE,
  (J. W. Canan,) S. Illinois, ne. cor. Louisiana
STANRIDGE HOUSE, (HENRY
  J. STANRIDGE, 41 W. Maryland
Union House, (George Hz.) 202 S. Illinois
Washington House, (Peter Deitz,) 181 S. Meridian
Western House, (Clawson & Woods,) 127 S. Illinois

House Furnishing Goods.

Frankem I. L. & Co. 34 E. Washington
Kimble, Aikman & Co. 108 S. Meridian
MUNSON & JOHNSTON,
  62 E. Washington
TUTEWILER BROS.
  74 E. Washington
West H. F. &. Co. 37 S. Meridian
Voegtte Jacob, 103 E. Washington

Human Hair Goods.

(See also Hair Workers and Braiders.)

Copeland J. W. & Co. 39 S. Meridian

MEDINA FRANK J.
34 W. Washington

SPADES M. H.
20 E. Washington

Ice Cream Saloons.
(*See also Confectioners*)
Becker F. P. & Bro. 17 N. Pennsylvania
Parisette Joseph, 25 N. Illinois

Ice Dealers.
BURKHART ANDREW J.
Mississippi sw. cor. Michigan   See adv't. index

Insurance Agents.
Abromet A. room 1 Ætna Bldg.

BARNARD J.
Vinton's block, Pennsylvania sw. cor. Market

BEARDSLEY R. E.
11 N. Meridian
Biedenmeister C. A. 96 E. Washington
Blair F. M. 44 N. Pennsylvania
Bradley Joseph, 25 W. Washington
Bradshaw William A. room 14. Talbott & New's block
Bryant Theodore R. 174 W. Washington
Byington & Erringer, 11 S. Meridian

CHILD M. Jr.
25 W. Washington
Childers John R. 4 Blackford's blk.

COPELAND W. J. & CO.
5 Martindale's block. (See margin bottom lines)
Davis C. B. room 6, Odd Fellows Hall
Douglass R. L. room 1, Ætna bldg.

DUNLOP J. S. & CO.
2 W. Washington
Emrich Nicholas, 4 Blackford's blk.
Ewing R. H. Market ne. cor. Circle. (Journal bldg.)
Folsom E. S. room 14 Talbott & News block
Gilbert Edward, 2 and 4 Blackford's blk.

GREEN E. S.
room 4 Martindale's block, Pennsyvania ne. cor. Market
Greene & Royse, 10 Blackford's blk.

GREENE & TILFORD,
21 N. Meridian
Grubbs Daniel W. 7 Blackford's blk.

HAEHL & ANKER, LIFE,
FIRE AND ACCIDENT INSURANCE AGENTS, 20 S. Delaware
Harrison A. Irwin, 79 W. Washington

HESS CHARLES M. A.
8 E. Washington. See side margin lines.

JONES CYRUS G.
No. 7 Vintons block
Joseph R. C. 81 E. Market

MARTIN, HOPKINS & OHR,
Market ne. cor. Circle. (Journal bldg.)

MARTINDALE E. B.
room 2, (2d floor) Martindales blk.
Metzger Alexander, room 6, Odd Fellows Hall

MURPHY TOBIAS M.
room 9 (2 floor) Martindales blk. Pennsylvania ne. cor. Market

NORTHROP WILLIAM W.
No. 2. Blake Block.
Nutting & Wood, 19 W. Washington
Olin C. C. 2 W. Washington
Ransford & Denton, Washington sw. cor. Meridian
Seiders William H. Market ne. cor. Circle (Journal Bldg.)
Smith Frank & Co. room 4 Odd Fellows Hall
Smith John C. 11 N. Meridian

SNYDER & HAYS,
17 N. Meridian
Turner A. H. No. 1 Wiley's block
Walker Henry H. room 3 (2d floor) Martindale's block, Pennsylvania ne. cor. Market

WHITCOMB & POTTER,
room 4 Yohn's blk. Meridian ne. cor. Washington
White A. S. 394 W. Washington

WILLCOX & MEANS
room 3 and 4 Wiley's blk. opp. Odd Fellows Hall
Wright Charles W. 10 E. Washington
Wright J. N. & Son, 10 E. Washington

Insurance Companies.
Accident.
Railway Passengers Assurance Co. of Hartford Conn. R. E. Beardsly, Agt. 11 N. Meridian.

TRAVELERS OF HARTFORD,
CONN. J. S. Dunlop & Co. agts. 2 W. Washington

Insurance Companies.
(*Fire and Marine.*)
Ætna. of Hartford, Conn. A. Abromet, agt. room 1, Ætna bldg.

ALBANY CITY, of NEW YORK
R. E. Beardsley, State agt. 11 N. Meridian

AURORA, OF COVINGTON,
KENTUCKY, Tobias M. Murphy, agt. room 9, 2d floor. Martindale's blk.

BUCKEYE, OF CLEVELAND,
OHIO. J. S. Dunlop & Co. agts. 2 W. Washington
Buffalo City, of Buffalo, New York, J. Barnard, agt. Vinton's blk. Pennsylvania sw. cor. Market
Cleveland, of Cleveland, Ohio, J. Barnard, agt. Vinton's blk. Pennsylvania sw. cor. Market

INS   390   INS

Commerce, of Albany, New York, Martin. Hopkins & Ohr. agts. Market, ne. cor. Circle, (Journal bldg.)

Continental of New York, Martin. Hopkins & Ohr. agts. Market ne. cor. Circle, (Journal bldg.)

Enterprise, of Cincinnati, Ohio, Martin. Hopkins & Ohr, agts. R. H. Ewing, State agt. Market ne. cor. Circle, (Journal bldg)

German Mutual. of Indianapolis, Adolph Seidensticker, pres. Valentine Butsch. vice-pres. Fred Ritzinger, sec. 16 S. Delaware

GERMANIA, OF CINCINNATI,
OHIO. J. S. Dunlop & Co. agts. 2 W. Washington

Girard, of Philadelphia, J. Barnard. agt. Vinton's blk. Pennsylvania sw. cor. Market

HARTFORD, OF HARTFORD,
CONN. Snyder & Hays, agts. 17 N. Meridian

Home, of New Haven, Conn. C. A. Biedenmeister, agt. 96 E. Washington

Home, of New York, E. B. Martindale, agt. room 1 and 2, 2d floor, Martindale's blk.

HOME, OF NEW YORK,
Henry H. Walker, State agt. room 3, 2d floor, Martindale's blk. Pennsylvania ne. cor. Market

Home Mutual, of Indianapolis, Charles W. Smith, jr. receiver, No. 5 Yohn's blk. Meridian ne. cor. Washington

Howard, of New York, A. Abromet, agt. room 1. Ætna bldg.

Imperial, of London, C. B. Davis, gen. agt. room 6, Odd Fellows' Hall

INDIANA, OF INDIANAPO-
LIS, J. S. Harvey, pres. W. T. Gibson, sec. room 5, Odd Fellows' Hall

INDIANAPOLIS, OF INDIAN-
APOLIS, William Henderson, pres. Alex C. Jameson, sec. Virginia av. cor. Pennsylvania

Insurance Co. of North America, of Philadelphia. Martin, Hopkins & Ohr, agts. W. H. Seiders, State agt. Market ne. cor. Circle, (Journal bldg.)

International of New York. Martin. Hopkins & Ohr, agts. Market ne. cor. Circle, (Journal bldg.)

LORILLARD, OF NEW YORK,
J. S. Dunlop & Co. agts. 2 W. Washington

LUMBERMAN'S, OF CHICA-
GO, Snyder & Hays, agts. 17 N. Meridian

MARKET, OF NEW YORK,
J. S. Dunlop & Co. ag'ts. 2 W. Washington

Merchants' of Chicago. Martin, Hopkins & Ohr, agents, Market ne. cor. Circle (Journal bldg.)

NEW YORK CENTRAL,
of New York, M. Child. jr. agt. 25 W. Washington

NORTH AMERICAN OF
HARTFORD, CONN. Snyder & Hays, agts. 17 N. Meridian

NORTH AMERICAN OF
NEW YORK, Snyder & Hays, agents, 17 N. Meridian

North British and Mercantile- of London and Edinburgh, E. B. Martindale, agent, rooms 1 and 2 (2d floor) Martindale's block

Pacific and San Francisco, California, E. B. Martindale, agt. room 2 (2d floor) Martindale.s block

PHŒNIX OF HARTFORD,
Snyder & Hays, agts. 17 N. Meridian

Phœnix of New York, Greene & Royse, agts. 10 Blackford's Block

PUTNAM OF HARTFORD,
CONN. E. B. Martindale, agt. room 2 (2d floor) Martindale's block

Queen of Liverpool and London, Greene & Royse, agts, 10 Blackford's block

REPUBLIC OF CHICAGO,
ILLINOIS, J. S. Dunlop & Co. agents. 2 W. Washington

Rising Sun of Rising Sun. Ind. T. A. Goodwin, agt. 35 E. Market

Sangamo of Springfield, Ill. F. M. Blair agt. 44 N. Pennsylvania

SECURITY OF NEW YORK,
J. S. Dunlop & Co. agts. 2 W. Washington

SPRINGFIELD OF SPRING-
FIELD, MASS. Frank Smith & Co. agts. room 4 Odd Fellows' Hall

State. of Cleveland, Ohio, J. Barnard, agent, Vinton's blk. Pennsylvania sw. cor. Market

Sun. of Cleveland. Ohio. J. Barnard. agent, Vinton's blk. Pennsylvania sw. cor. Market

Tentonia, of Cleveland, Ohio, C. A. Biedenmeister, agt. 96 E. Washington

UNDERWRITERS' AGENCY
OF NEW YORK, C. A. Biedenmeister, agt. 96 E. Washington

United States, of Baltimore, J. Barnard. agt. Vinton's blk. Pennsylvania sw. cor. Market

Washington, of New York, J. Barnard. agt. Vinton's blk. Pennsylvania sw. cor. Market

Western, of Buffalo, A. I. Harrison, agt. 79 W. Washington

WINNESHEIK, OF FREE-
PORT, ILL. M. Child, jr. state agt. 25 W. Washington

YONKERS AND NEW YORK,
OF NEW YORK, Martin, Hopkins & Ohr, agts. Market ne. cor. Circle (Journal bldg.)

Insurance Companies.
(Life.)

Ætna, of Hartford, Conn. A. Abmomet, agt. room 1 Ætna bldg.

ANCHOR, OF NEW YORK, A. H. Turner, state agt. room 1 Wiley's blk. ws. N. Pennsylvania near Washington

BERKSHIRE OF PITTSFIELD, MASS. Greene & Tilford, state agents, 21 N. Meridian

Brooklyn of Brooklyn New York F. M. Blair state agent, 47 N. Pennsylvania (Vinton's blk.)

CHARTER OAK of HARTFORD CONN., W. H. Hay genl. agent, 6 Blackford's blk.

CINCINNATI MUTUAL LIFE INSURANCE CO., Cyrus G. Jones Gen. Agt. No. 7 Vinton's block, opp. Post Office

COMMONWEALTH of NEW YORK. Gibson Bros. agt-, room 5 Odd Fellows' Hall

Connecticut General of Hartford, Conn. Cowen & Protzman, agts. Central Indiana, 16¼ E. Washington

CONNECTICUT MUTUAL of HARTFORD, CONN. E. S. Green state agt. room 4 (2d floor) Martindale's blk.

Continental of Hartford, Conn. Ransford & Denton state agts. Washington, sw. cor. Meridian

Continental of New York, D. W. Grubbs genl. agt. 7 Blackford's blk.

DeSOTO MUTUAL of ST. LOUIS. MO. Wilcox & Means state agts. rooms 3 and 4 Wiley's blk. opp. Odd Fellows' Hall

EQUITABLE of NEW YORK, J. S. Dunlop, genl. agt. for Indiana, 2 W. Washington

FRANKLIN of INDIANAPOLIS, Ind. E. P. Howe, secy. Illinois cor. Kentucky av.

GLOBE MUTUAL of N. Y. R. E. Beardsley, state agt. J. C. Smith, local agt. 11 N. Meridian

Guardian Mutual of New York, Edward Gilbert, genl. agt. 2 and 4 Blackford's blk.

HAHNEMANN OF CLEVELAND, OHIO, W. J. Copeland, state agt. 5 Martindale's blk.

Hartford Life and Annuity of Hartford, Conn. Chas. W. Wright, genl. agt. office 10 E. Washington (up stairs)

HOME of NEW YORK. Tobias M. Murphy, genl. agt. room 9 (2d floor) Martindale's blk.

MUTUAL BENEFIT of NEWARK, N. J., Nutting & Wood, agts. 19 W. Washington

Mutual of New York, E. B. Martindale, agt. rooms 1 and 2 (2d floor) Martindale's blk.

NEW ENGLAND MUTUAL of BOSTON, Snyder & Hays, agts. 17 N. Meridian

New Jersey Mutual, Theodore R. Bryant agt. 17¼ W. Washington

New York of New York, Byington & Erringer, state agts. 11 S. Meridian

North America of New York, William A. Bradshaw genl. agt. room 14 Talbott and New's blk.

North Western Mutual of Milwaukee, Wis. Martin & Hopkins, state agts Indiana and Kentucky, Market ne. cor. Circle, Journal building

PROVIDENT LIFE & TRUST of PHILADELPHIA, Charles M. A. Hess special agt. 88 E. Washington. See margin side lines

PHŒNIX MUTUAL of HARTFORD, CONN. E. S. Folsom genl. agt. room 14 Talbott and New's blk.

ST. LOUIS MUTUAL of ST. LOUIS, MO. E. A. Whitcomb state agt. room 4 Yohn's blk.

SECURITY LIFE & ANNUITY of NEW YORK. W. W. Northrop genl. agt. for Indiana and Southern Illinois, room 2 Blake blk.

Standard of New York, Greene & Royse agts. 10 Blackford's blk.

UNION MUTUAL of BOSTON, Mass A. S. White agt. 39¼ W. Washington

United States, of New York. J. N. Wright & Son, agts. Northern Indiana, 10 E. Washington

Insurance.
(Life and Accident.)

TRAVELERS', OF HARTFORD, CONN. C. C. Olin, gen'l agt. 2 W. Washington

Iron Foundry.

(See also Foundries and Machine Shops.)

Union Novelty Works Manufacturing Co. S. C. Frink, pres. R. S. Dorsey, sec. and treas. St. Clair cor. Canal

Iron and Steel Warehouses.

Holliday W. J. & Co. 59 S. Meridian

Maxwell, Fry & Thurston, 34 S. Meridian

JEW 392 LAW

Jewelers.

(See also Watches, Clocks and Jewelry.)
Bingham W. P. & Co. 50 E. Washington
Craft William H. 36 E. Washington
Dietrichs Charles, 66 N. Pennsylvania
French Charles G. 13 N. Meridian
Phipps Brothers, 14 N. Pennsylvania
Stacy M. D. 34 Virginia av.
Stevens H. M. Mrs. 32 S. Illinois

Justices of the Peace.

CURTIS ANDREW,
83½ E. Washington
Doepfner Charles F. 139½ E. Washington
Fisher Charles, room 3 Yohn's blk. Meridian ne. cor. Washington
Secrest Charles, 45 E. Washington
Wallace Alexander G. 74 E. Washington

Knitting Machines.

Lamb's Knitting Machine, Austin W. Allen, agt. 18 N. Delaware

Ladies' Exchange Store.

STEVENS H. M. MRS.
32 S. Illinois. (See advt. index)

Ladies' Furnishing Goods.

Bentley & Chandler, 44 Indiana av

Lamp Trimmings.

HOLLIDAY W. & C. F.
15 S. Meridian

Lamps and Chandeliers.

Scott, West & Co. 127 S. Meridian

Lamps and Lanterns.

HOLLIDAY W. & C. T.
15 S. Meridian (See adv't index)

Land Agents.

(See also Real Estate Agents, Brokers, and Dealers.)
Elder John R. 21 S. Pennsylvania

Land Warrant Brokers.

Martin Luther R. 10 E. Washington

Lath Machines.

(Manufacturer of.)
Learned Charles, 30½ W. Washington

Lath and Shingles.

(See also Lumber Merchants.)
Builders' and Manufacturers' Association, C. Eden, pres. J. L. Avery, treas. James Hasson sec. 225 N. Delaware
McCord & Wheatley, 186 S. Alabama
McDonough D. B. 144 S. Alabama

Laundries.

INDIANAPOLIS STEAM
LAUNDRY. J. L. Spaulding, propr. 22 and 24 S. New Jersey

Lawyers.

Adams Samuel, 19 W. Washington
BARBOUR & JACOBS,
14 N. Delaware
Bartholomew P. W. room 1, 20½ N. Delaware
Beck Albert T. 4 Brown's blk. Pennsylvania nw. cor. Washington
Bills J. M. room 2, 20½ N. Delaware
Blake John W. 45 E. Washington
Bowles Thomas H. 4 W. Washington
Brown Ignatius, 10½ E. Washington
Buell J. R. 68 E. Washington
BURNS & CARTER,
74 E. Washington
Denny A. F. 94 E. Washington
DUNCAN R. B. & J. S.
3 Brown's blk. Pennsylvania nw. cor. Washington
Dye & Harris, rooms 8 and 9 Talbott & New's blk.
ELLIOTT & HOLSTEIN,
2½ E. Washington
FINCH & FINCH,
room 6 Talbott & New's blk.
Fitzgerald Nathan, room 5 Vinton's blk.
Goodwin Robert M. room 6 Vinton's block, Pennsylvania sw. cor. Market
Gordon George E. room 6 Odd Fellows' Hall
Gordon J. W. room 4 Talbott & New's blk.
GUFFIN & PARKER,
rooms 10 and 11 Talbott & New's blk.
Hamlin Carlin, 62½ E. Washington
Hammond Upton J. 8 E. Washington
Hanna & Kueller, room 4, 20½ N. Delaware
Harrison R. E. 17½ W. Washington
Harrison Temple C. 17½ W. Washington
HARVEY & VAN HORN,
101 E. Washington, cor. Delaware
HENDERSON WILLIAM R.
Indianapolis Ins. Co.'s bldg. es. Pennsylvania bet. Washington and Maryland
HENDRICKS, HORD & HENDRICKS, 24½ E. Washington
HOWLAND LIVINGSTON,
8 E. Washington
Holman John A. room 12 Talbott & New's blk.
IGOE & JOHNSTON,
83½ E. Washington
JOHNSON T. E.
42 E. Washington
Johnson Thomas E. room 9 Blackford's blk.
Jordon Lewis, room 1 Talbott & New's blk.

KIMBALL EBEN W.
46 E. Washington
Klingensmith Israel, 115 E. Washington
Leary Patrick C. 85 E. Market

LEATHERS & CARTER,
room 3 Odd Fellows' Hall
Logan & Brown, 4 W. Washington
Lowe William A. 16½ E. Washington
McCurdy W. W. H. 172 W. Ohio
McDonald, Roache & McDonald, room 3, Ætna bldg.
Major Stephen, room 5, Vinton's blk. opp. Post Office
March Walter, room 4, Talbott & New's blk.

MARTINDALE & TARKINGTON, rooms 1 and 2, 2d floor, Martindale's blk.
Milner J. 94 E. Washington

MORROW & TRUSLER,
room 6, Vinton's blk. Pennsylvania sw. cor. Market
Morton George T. room 1, Talbott & New's blk.

NEWCOMB, MITCHELL & KETCHAM. 21 and 23 E. Washington
Nichol Joseph W. room 2, Ætna bldg.
Parker & Bloomer, 32⅝ E. Washington
Patterson William, 98 E. Washington, (up stairs)
Perkins & Perkins, room 4, Ætna bldg.
Perrin George K. 45 E. Washington

PIERCE HENRY D.
24½ E. Washington

PORTER, HARRISON & FISHBACK, No. 6 Yohn's blk. Meridian ne. cor. Washington
Rand & Hall, 24½ E. Washington
Ray H. C. room 12, Talbott & New's blk.
Ray John, register in bankruptcy, 24½ E. Washington

RITTER & IRVIN,
24½ E. Washington
Ruddell James H. 35½ E. Washington
Sage Henry, 172 W. Washington
Scott John N. 32½ E. Washington
Seidensticker A. & Co. 14 S. Delaware

SMITH CHARLES W. Jr.
No. 5 Yohn's blk. Meridian ne. cor. Washington
Stanton & Manlove, 87 E. Market
Stepp James H. 12 S. Pennsylvania
Sullivan William, 45 E. Washington
Sweetser James N. 21 E. Washington
Taylor Isaac J. 85 E. Washington

TAYLOR NAPOLEON B.
4 Brown's blk. Pennsylvania, ne. cor. Washington

VOSS & DAVIS,
room 3 Talbott and New's blk.
Wallace William, room 4 Odd Fellows' Hall

WARD & MEDSKER,
83½ E. Washington
Wilson L. D. 68 E. Washington

Wilson O. M. room 2 Ætna Building
Witt B. F. Washington sw. cor. Meridian

WOOLEN WILLIAM W. Jr.
35½ E. Washington
Young John, 110 E. Washington (up stairs)

Lead Pipe and Sheet Lead.

Cottrell & Knight, 108 S. Delaware

Leather and Findings.

Mooney & Co. 147 S. Meridian

Leather and Hides.

FISHBACK JOHN,
125 S. Meridian

Leather and Rubber Belting.

FISHBACK JOHN,
125 S. Meridian

Leather and Gum Belting.

Vajen J. H. & Co. 21 W. Washington

Lightning Rod Manufacturer.

INDIANAPOLIS COPPER LIGHTNING ROD WORKS, David Munson propr. 62 E. Washington

Lime, Plaster and Cement.

(See also Lumber Merchants.)

BUTSCH, DICKSON & DELL,
27 E. Georgia
Fawkner John E. 24 W. Maryland
McDonough D. B. 141 S. Alabama

Linen.

(Importers of.)

CULLINY P.
98 E. Washington. See card back cover
Dorian John 69 S. Illinois

Linseed Oil Manufacturer.

Evans J. P. & Co. 124 S. Delaware

Liquor Dealers.

(Wholesale. See also Wines and Liquors.)
Hahn & Bais, 25 S. Meridian
Prenatt & O'Connor, 141 S. Meridian

RIKHOFF & BRO.
77 S. Meridian
Ryan T. F. 143 S. Meridian
Ryan & Holbrook, 48 S. Meridian
Sweetser John, 30 S. Meridian

Lithographer.

Braden W. & J. 24 W. Washington

Livery, Sale and Feed Stables.

Allen Henry, 25 and 27 E. Pearl

Silk and Paisley Shawls in Endless Variety, at CULLINY'S.

LOC   394   MAC

Brinkman Charles, 23 S. Delaware

BRUNDAGE EDWARD C.
223 E. Washington

Exchange Stables, William Hinesley, propr. 35 N. Illinois

Fletcher T. A. ns. Court bet. Pennsylvania and Delaware

Gates, Pray & Co. F. Market Square, bet. Delaware and Alabama

Hetselgesser L. W. & Co. Illinois nw. cor. South

Holmes & Rains, 163 W. Washington

Kolyer & Caffey, Wabash al. bet. Pennsylvania and Delaware

Landis Jacob, 30 S. Pennsylvania

Mills & Hollingsworth, ss. Washington bet. West and California

Patterson Samuel W. 278 and 280 W. Washington

Smither John, 149 S. Mississippi

Sullivan & Drew, 10 E. Pearl

Whitney J. W. 44 S. Pennsylvania

Wood William E. ns. Court nr. cor. Pennsylvania

Wood & Fondray, 16 and 18 N. Pennsylvania

WOOD & MANSUR,
21 and 23 W. Pearl

Locks.

HEISSER J. H. (Agent),
24 N. Pennsylvania

Locksmiths and Bell Hangers.

Isensee Albert, 24 N. Pennsylvania

KINDLER CHARLES,
60 N. Pennsylvania (See advt. index)

Koser John, 18 Virginia av.

Reinhardt P. J. 81 S. Illinois

Looms.

(*Stafford's.*)

Howe & Converse mnfrs. Merritt & Coughlen, gen'l western agts. west end Washington

Looking Glasses.

Crapo R. P. 196 E. Washington

Daumont H. & Co. 45 W. Washington

LIEBER H. & CO.
21 N. Pennsylvania

Scott, West & Co. 127 S. Meridian

Woodbridge John, 36 S. Meridian

Lounge.

(*Street's Extension Sofa.*)

Wilkins & Hall, 84 and 86 E. Market

Lumber Manufacturers & Dealers.

(*See also Saw Mills.*)

ADAMS GEO. F.
169 Bates

Builders & Manufacturers' Association, 343 Massachusetts av.

BUNTE & DICKSON,
387 E. Washington. (See advt. index)

Coburn & Jones, north of Terre Haute depot

Ebert & Owens, 44 Kentucky av.

Emerson, Beam & Thompson, 225-229 W. Market

HILDEBRAND, KEPPELE &
CO. Indiana av. cor. Canal. (See advt. index)

Hill & Wingate, East se. cor. Georgia

Isgrigg & Bracken, 180 W. Market

King Eli, 448 E. St. Clair

Long & Joseph, LaFayette R. R. bet. Walnut and St. Clair

McCord & Wheatley, 186 S. Alabama

Marsee J. & Son, New Jersey bet. Washington and Railroad

OFF CHRISTIAN & BROS.
St. Clair cor. Peru

PRESSLY JOHN T.
es. West, bet. Louisiana and Georgia

TATE WARREN,
38 S. New Jersey. (See advt. Index)

Wilson & Warner, 27 Massachusetts av.

Machine Cooperage.

Carey J. S. & Co. Georgia bet. West and the river

Machine Shops.

(*See also Foundries and Machine Shops.*)

Cincinnati and Indianapolis Junction R. R. Machine Shops. A. VanTuyle, foreman. E. Maryland at city limits

Cleveland, Columbus, Cincinnati & Indianapolis R. R. L. W. Durgin, foreman. North cor. Winston

Columbus, Chicago & Indiana Central R. R. Thomas V. Losee, master mechanic. Noble nr. cor. Washington

EAGLE MACHINE WORKS,
Louisiana se. cor. Meridian

Hetherington B. F. & Co. 244 S. Pennsylvania

Indianapolis, Cincinnati & LaFayette Railway Theodore Mosher, foreman, Louisiana, e. of limits

King & Pinney, Kentucky av. cor. Mississippi

Root D. & Co. 183 and 185 S. Pennsylvania

Terre Haute & Indianapolis R. R. C. Idler, foreman, West bet. Georgia and South

WESTERN MACHINE WORKS
Sinker & Co. proprs. 125 S. Pennsylvania

Machine Works.

EAGLE MACHINE WORKS,
Louisiana se. cor. Meridian

Phoenix Machine Works, 370 W. Washington

Western Machine Works, Sinker & Co. proprs. 125 S. Pennsylvania

Machinery and Castings.

Greenleaf & Co. 325 S. Tennessee

I. Davis & Co., dealers in Hats, Caps, Furs and Straw Goods.

MAC   395   MIL

Machinists.

(See Foundries, also Machine Shops.)

GREENLEAF & CO.
325 S. Tennessee

Maltsters.

(See also Brewers.)

Long, Snyder & Co. 214 and 216 S. Delaware

Mantles and Monuments.

(See also Marble Workers and Dealers.)

Indianapolis Marble Works, LaDow & Calvert, proprs. 120 S. Illinois

Marble Workers and Dealers.

Carpenter Benjamin O. 36 E. Market

DAME & GREENLEE,
69 E. Washington

JAMES T. S. & CO.
136 S. Meridian

La Dow & Calvert, 120 S. Illinois

MUNSON & JOHNSTON,
62 E. Washington

Weir William, 42 and 44 Virginia av.

Mathematical Instruments.

(Manufacturer of.)

STEFFENS E. F.
Washington sw. cor. Meridian

Mattrasses.

(See also Upholsters also Furniture Dealers.)

Baker N. S. & Co. 73 E. Washington
Wilkins & Hall, 83 and 86 E. Market

Meat Markets.

(See also Butchers.)

Barker Samuel, ss. St. Clair bet. East and New Jersey
Barthel & Kaufmann, 32 Virginia av.
Becher Henry, 122 Bluff rd.
Beck Frederick, Meridian sw. cor, McCarty
Bodmer Charles, 276 W. Market
Brooker Thomas, 774 N. Tennessee
Coleman Herman, 267 N. East

DAVIS HARVEY D.
71 E. Washington

Essigke August, 295 E. Washington

GASS ANDREW,
118 E. St. Joseph

Gold Adam, 407 W. Washington
Grafenstein Frederick, 660 N. Tennessee
Hahn Louis, 229 S. Tennessee
Hargt Fred. 234 E. Washington
Hist Louis, 71 S. Noble
Howes C. & H. 150 Virginia av. cor. New Jersey
Hust George C. 564 E. Washington
Jackson & Nicoli, 221 W. Ohio

JOACHIM JOHN C.
88 Fort Wayne av.

Kaeser Charles, 4th bet. Tennessee and Mississippi
Kaufman Moritz, North cor. West
Kramer Henry, 80 Ft. Wayne av.
Kramer William C. 306 Virginia av.
Kuhn Charles, 207 W. Michigan
Mayers Michael, 220 S. Meridian
Moser George, 295 S. Missouri
Mueller John A. 237 S. Alabama
Nutzel John, 175 Madison av.
Poland & Wiseman, 432 W. Washington, (Nat. rd.)
Qnisser Julius, 131 Massachusetts av.
Richter William, 416 Virginia av.

ROBINS CHARLES J.
34 N. Pennsylvania

Roos Jacob, 137 S. Illinois
Schweinsberger William, 329 S. Delaware
Shatz & Stortz, 369 S. Delaware

SINDLINGER G.
194 S. Illinois

Smith A. & C. 221 Massachusetts av.
Spitzfaden Peter, 97 E. Washington
Stallwagan John, 442 S. Illinois
Stein Abram, 177 Virginia av.
Stuckmeyer John, 362 Virginia av.
Thorn John, 141 N. Delaware
Werther William, Noble ne. cor. New York

YORGER JOHN & BRO.
245 E. Washington

Melodeons.

SOEHNER & BENHAM,
36 E. Washington

STOWELL M. A.
46 N. Pennsylvania. (See front paster and back cover)

Metals and Tinner's Goods.

OVER E. & CO.
82 and 84 S. Meridian

Midwives.

Beyer F. Mrs. 78 N. Noble
Bohne P. Mrs. 70 E. Maryland
Despa Minna, 50 Leckerbie
Jochmann A. Mrs. 312 E. Washington
Rauschen H. Mrs. 366 S. Illinois
Wink Theresa Mrs. 194 E. Washington

Military Attorneys.

Ziegler George H. room 6, Talbott & New's blk.

Mill Furnishing Goods.

TAGGART SAMUEL,
132 S. Pennsylvania

Millwrights.

TAGGART SAMUEL,
132 S. Pennsylvania

Millers.

(See Flour Mills.)

Milliners.

(See also Millinery and Millinery Goods.)

Baker A. Mrs. 42 S. Illinois
Brauer Maggie, 129 Massachusetts av.
Clark Sarah Miss, 199 N. Illinois
Copeland J. W. & Co. 8 E. Washington
Davis Mary, (col'd) Mrs. 252 Indiana av.
KAY & MATTERN,
  69½ E. Market. (See advt. Index)
KUNZ M. A. MISS,
  9 S. Alabama
Lane Mary J. 428 N. East
Livering Matilda Miss, 140 Bluff rd.
LUEDERS MISSES,
  74½ E. Market. (See advt. Index)
NEWTON MARIA MRS.
  110 S. Illinois, (up stairs.) (See advt. Index)
Snyder Susan C. Mrs. 143 W. Washington
Wunderly Mary Mrs. 146 N. Davidson

Milliners and Dress Makers.

(See also Dress and Cloak Makers, also Milliners.)

Silvers Anna, 305 E. Washington
SPRING ELLEN MRS.
  50 S. Illinois. (See advt. Index)

Milliners and Millinery Goods.

(See also Milliners.)

Baker Bertha, 244 E. Washington
CATLIN M. J. MRS.
  46 W. Washington
Conaty J. B. 44 S. Illinois
Copeland J. W. & Co. 8 E. Washington
Dunn & Franco, 85 N. Illinois, Academy of Music
Hinsdale E. 197 W. Washington
Kirk E. Mrs. 75 N. Pennsylvania
Sieders M. C. 3 Martindale blk. N. Pensylvania
Smith L. Mrs. 40 S. Illinois
Taylor M. J. Mrs. 6 W. Washington
Thomas M. J. Mrs. 8 W. Washington
WINK ISABELLA MISS,
  152 E. Washington

Millinery Goods,

(Wholesale.)

Copeland J. W. & Co. 39 S. Meridian
FAHNLEY & McCREA,
  131 S. Meridian

Mineral Water Manufacturers.

REED A. & CO.
  225 W. Washington
SCRIBNER & SMITH,
  64 E. Market. (See advt. Index)

Model Maker.

Leavette Gilbert M. 5 Blake blk.

Mouldings.

(Gilt and Rosewood.)

Daumont H. & Co. 15 W. Washington
Emerson, Beam & Thompson, 225-229 W. Market
Hill & Wingate, East se. cor. Georgia

Mowers and Reapers.

(See also Reapers and Mowers. Also Agricultural Implements.)

EXCELSIOR REAPER AND MOWER, Webb & Bates, gen'l agts. 83 W. Washington

Music Publisher.

BENHAM H. L. & CO.
  No. 1 Martindale's blk. Market ne. cor. Pennsylvania

Music.

(Sheet.)

Benham H. L. & Co. No. 1 Martindale's blk. Market ne. cor. Pennsylvania

Music Teachers.

Bergstein Carl, room 11 (2d floor) Martindale's blk.
Chitian R. 198 E. Washington
Loeper Max, 192 E. Washington
Neivill L. S. Vinton's blk.
St. Clair Charles G. 4 and 5, 77¾ E. Market

Music and Musical Instruments.

BENHAM H. L. & CO.
  No. 1 Martindale's blk. Market ne. cor. Pennsylvania
SOEHNER & BENHAM,
  36 E. Washington
STOWELL M. A.
  46 N. Pennsylvania. (See front paster and back cover)
Willard A. G. & Co. 4 and 5 Bates House blk.

Musical Institute.

BLACK J. S. PROFESSOR,
  rooms 25, 26, 27 and 28 Talbott & New's blk.

Musical Instrument Repairer.

FREDERICK L. TRAYSER, Pianos, Organs and Melodeons. All Musical Instruments Tuned and Repaired; also Pianos Bought and Sold, 82 E. Market.

Nails.
(*Wholesale.*)

OVER E. & CO.
82 and 84 S. Meridian

Newspaper and Periodical Depots.

Beltz Harvey A. Spencer House
Fisk E. I. Mrs. 62 N. Illinois
Ganter Daniel, 338 E. Washington
Langsdorf & Co. 26 N. Pennsylvania
Palmer Edward L. 60 S. Illinois

Newspapers and Publications.

American Housewife, Mrs. M. M. B. Goodwin Editor and proprietor. Meridian se. cor. Circle
Beharrell's Bibical Biography (3d edition) Downey & Brouse, publishers, Meridian se. cor. Circle
DAILY EVENING COMMERCIAL. M. G. Lee editor and proprietor. Illinois ne. cor. Washington
Heart and Hand, (monthly) Rev. E. P. Ingersoll, editor, A. A. Barnes & Co. publishers, office 83 E. Washington
Independent, (monthly) S. T. Montgomery, editor, 10½ S. Pennsylvania
Indiana Masonic Home Advocate (monthly) J. M. Blair editor and publisher, 44 N. Pennsylvania
Indiana School Journal, (monthly) G. W. Hoss & Thomas Charles, editors and proprietors, Meridian se. cor. Circle
Indiana Teacher, (monthly) John B. Allen, editor and proprietor, issued by the Indianapolis Printing and Pub. House
Indiana Volksblatt, (German) Julius Boetticher, editor and proprietor. 164 E. Washington
Indianapolis Journal, (Republican) daily except Sunday, weekly Friday. Douglass & Conner publishers, Market ne. cor. Circle, (Journal bldg.)
Inventer and Mechanic, Charles Werbe proprietor, 81 E. Market
Jolly Hoosier, (monthly) A. C. Roach Editor and publisher. Market ne. cor. Circle. (Journal Bldg.)
Ladies Christian Monitor, (monthly) Mrs. M. M. B. Goodwin, editor and proprietor, Meridian se. cor. Circle
LADIES OWN MAGAZINE, Mrs. M. Cora Bland, editor. Bland & Taylor publishers, 19 N. Meridian
Little Chief, (monthly) Shortridge & Alden, publishers, 18 S. Pennsylvania
Little Sower, (weekly) W. W. Dowling editor and proprietor. Meridian se. cor. Circle
MIRROR, (Daily evening) (weekly, Saturday,) Harding, Morton & Finch publishers, 19 N. Meridian
Morning Watch (monthly) W. W. Dowling editor and proprietor, Meridian se. cor. Circle

Mothers Monitor (monthly) Mrs. M. M. B. Goodwin, editor and proprietor, Meridian se. cor. Circle
Northwestern (monthly) Martin & Hopkins publishers, Market ne. cor. Circle
NORTH WESTERN FARMER, Bland & Taylor editors and proprietors, 19 N. Meridian
Odd Fellows Tallisman, (monthly) R. J. Strickland editor and publisher, 30 S. Meridian
OLD OAKEN BUCKET, (monthly) Cowen & Protzman editors and proprietors, 10½ E. Washington
Roach's Western Museum, (monthly) A. C. Roach, editor and publisher, Journal bldg.
Sparkling Gem, (monthly) A. Q. Goodwin, publisher, 30 S. Meridian
Spottongel, (Sunday paper) 23 W. Maryland
State Sentinel, Daily, and Weekly, R. J. Bright, propr. J. J. Bingham, editor-in-chief, 16½ E. Washington
Sunbeam, (monthly) Wm. Travis, editor and propr. Meridian se. cor. Circle
TELEGRAPH, Daily and Weekly, (German) 23 W. Maryland
Western Fireside, (monthly) published by R, It. City Printing Co. Rev. F. C. Holliday, editor, office 35½ Market
Western Manufacturers' Review and Railroad Journal, (semi-monthly) A. L. Logan, editor and publisher, 30 S. Meridian
WESTERN MUSICAL REVIEW, monthly, H. L. Benham & Co editors and publishers, No. 1 Martindale's blk,
Zukunft, (The Future) 23 N. Maryland

Notaries Public.
(*See also Lawyers.*)

Anderson George P. 2 Wiley's blk. ws. Pennsylvania nr. Market
Arbuckle Matthew, Washington sw. cor. Meridian
Beck Albert T. 4 Brown's blk. Pennsylvania nw. cor. Washington
Cale Howard, room 6 Yohn's blk. Meridian ne. cor. Washington
Copeland W. J. 5 Martindale's blk. (ground floor)
Corbaley Will. H. Washington sw. cor. Meridian
Denny Robert, P. O. box 204
Elliott Joseph T. office Recorder's office, Court House Square
Fitzgerald Nathan, room 5 Vinton's blk.
Goodwin Robert M. room 6 Vinton's blk. opp. Postoffice
Greenawalt John G. N. Tennessee opp. State House
Hammond Upton J. 8 E. Washington
HENDERSON WILLIAM R. Indianapolis Ins. Co's. Bldg. es. Pennsylvania bet. Washington and Maryland.
Howland Livingston, 8 E. Washington

NOT	398	PAI

Jamison Alex. C. Virginia av. cor. Pennsylvania
Johnson T. F. room 1, 42 E. Washington
KIMBALL EBEN W.
46 E. Washington
Lindley & Co. 8 E. Washington
Lowe William A. 16½ E. Washington
Martin Luther R. 10 E. Washington
Matthews J. F. 42 E. Washington
Parker & Bloomer, 32½ E. Washington
PIERCE HENRY D.
24½ E. Washington
Ritter Eli F. 24½ E. Washington
Sage Henry, 172 W. Washington
Smith Charles W. jr. No. 5 Yohn's blk. Meridian ne. cor. Washington
Stapp James H. 12 S. Pennsylvania
Tarkington John S. rooms 1 and 2, 2d floor, Martindale's blk.
Taylor Napoleon B. 4 Brown's blk. Pennsylvania nw. cor. Washington
Witt B. F. Washington sw. cor. Meridian
Ziegler George H. room 6, Talbott & New's blk.

Notions.
(*Wholesale.*)
Fortner, Floyd & Co. 75 S. Meridian
Hibben, Tarkington & Co. 112 S. Meridian
Kennedy, Byram & Co. 108 S. Meridian
Landers, Conduitt & Co. 58 S. Meridian
Ludorff L. & Co. 42 S. Meridian
Murphy, Johnston & Co. Meridian cor. Maryland
Stoneman, Pee & Co. 2 W. Louisiana

Notions.
(*Wholesale and Retail.*)
Baldwin J. H. & Co. (Fancy Bazaar) 6 E. Washington
Fairbanks & Co. 22 W. Washington
PETTIS, DICKSON & CO.
Glenn's Block

Notions and Fancy Goods.
Badger Theodore, 175 W. Washington
Deitsch Felix, 162 W. Washington
Fisk E. L. Mrs. 62 N. Illinois
Glick & Schwartz, Miller's blk. 54 N. Illinois
Greenewald Henry, 174 E. Washington
Haupt Robert, 151 E. Washington
Jacob Joseph, 131 E. Washington
Sailors James L. 156 W. Washington
Sedgewick R. 68 N. Illinois
Spades M. H. 20 E. Washington

Nurserymen and Florists.
Beechwood Nurseries, John F. Hill, propr. Michigan rd. e. of city
Central Nursery, Miller & White, proprs. Market nw. cor. Delaware
McCormack John, West Indianapolis
WEGHORST HENRY,
es. Japan bet. Nebraska and city limits. (See advt. Index)

WEIGAND ANTHONY,
cor. Kentucky av. and the Canal. (See advt. Index)

Oculist.
Marsh H. & Son, office No. 2, Miller's blk. 52 N. Illinois

Office Furniture Manufacturers.
KELLER PAUL,
21 Circle. (See advt. Index)
Mitchell & Rammelsberg Furniture Co. 38 E. Washington
Willard H. 73 E. Market

Oil Dealers.
Wood & Boyd, 22 S. Meridian

Opticians.
Moses L. W. 50 E. Washington
Simmons H. 43 S. Illinois

Organs.
SOEHNER & BENHAM,
36 E. Washington
STOWELL M. A.
46 N. Pennsylvania, Vinton's blk. (See front paster and back cover)

Oyster, Fish and Game Depot.
De Ruiter W. & Bro. 65 S. Illinois
Francis & Bro. 67 S. Illinois

Packers.
(*Pork.*)
Ferguson J. C. & Co. west end Georgia st.
KINGAN & CO,
west end Maryland
Lesh, Tousey & Co. 72 and 74 S. Delaware
Nofsinger, Kingan & Co. west end Maryland street
Wheat, Fletcher & Co. Blake nr. Washington, office room 1 Vinton's blk. opp. P. O.

Packers.
(*Produce and Provision*)
Foley J. W. & Co. 188 W. Washington

Painters
(*Biolamp.*)
HEISSER J. H. (Agent)
24 N. Pennsylvania

Painters.
(*Carriage.*)
Fletcher Charles, (col'd) 178 Indiana av.
Swain George H. 36 S. Pennsylvania
WICHAM CHARLES C. L.
Citizen's Carriage and Wagon Manufactory. Liberty se. cor. Washington
Wichmann Charles, 229 E. Washington

Painters.
(Fresco.)

FERTIG FRANK,
6 E. Washington. (See advt. index)
Wentworth William H. 321 E. Washington

Painters House and Sign.

Anhorn Elbert, ss. St. Clair bet. Noble and
Railroad
CHAPMAN DAVID C.
Virginia av. cor. Washington. (See
advt. index)
Cornelius & McElvano, 46 Kentucky av.
Egger & Muecke, 152 E. Washington, cor.
Alabama
Emile Max, 143 S. New Jersey
Feld G. 249 W. Maryland

FRANK FERTIG,

HOUSE, SIGN AND ORNAMENTAL
PAINTER,
No. 6 E. Washington St.
INDIANAPOLIS, IND.

All Work warranted, and orders Promptly attended to.

Guezet A. 298 S. Delaware
Helle Louis, 248 S. Pennsylvania
Imelli Max, 143 S. New Jersey
JENKINS E.
43 Massachusetts av. (See advt. Index)
Kelley John B. 19 Cherry
Lupton W. C. & Co. 24 Virginia av.
McPherson W. M. 14 W. Pearl
Milender W. B. 12 S. Pennsylvania
Rasner & Rittew, 61 Kentucky av.
REED & RASNER,
Illinois cor. Indiana av. (See advt. Index)
Ryan Bros. 18 S. Meridian
Whitridge William, 60 and 62 E. Market
Woodson & Foxcroft, 25 S. East

Painters.
(Portrad. See also Photographers; also Artists.)

Dennis James M. room 6, Wiley's blk. ws.
Pennsylvania nr. Washington
Hays B. S. room 24, Talbott & New's blk.

INGRAHAM'S ART GALLERY,
C. B. Ingraham, propr. 32½ E. Washington, opp. Glenn's blk. (See advt. index)

Painters.
(Scenic.)

Glessing Thomas B. 237 W. New York

Painters.
(Sign and Ornamental.)

Cook Thomas V. 58 N. Pennsylvania
Fertig Frank, 6 E. Washington
Howell J. W. 12 S. Pennsylvania
Moran & Melville, 18 S. Meridian

Paints, Oils and Glass.

Browning & Sloan, 7 and 9 E. Washington
Campbell & Green, 149 W. Washington
Morris Charles G. 521 N. Illinois
Sage Charles, 172 W. Washington
Wood & Boyd, 22 S. Meridian

Paper Bags.
(Wholesale.)

Chandler & Field, 24 S. Meridian

Paper Box Manufrs.

Smith Julius H. C. Circle se. cor. Meridian
STEINHAUSER B. A.
168 E. Washington

Paper Dealers.
(Wholesale.)

Chandler & Field, 24 S. Meridian
Seaman & Co. 74 W. Washington

Paper Hangers.
(See also Painters.)

Cornelius & McElvano, rear 72 W. Washington
Helle Louis, 248 S. Pennsylvania
Roll William H. 38 S. Illinois

Paper Manufactures.

CALEDONIA PAPER MILL
CO. Field, Locke & Co. proprs. E. Locke
supt. Office 265 W. Washington. Factory west end Market
Salsbury H. & Co. west end Maryland

Paper Stock.

Field, Locke & Co. 265 W. Washington
Salsbury H. & Co. west end Maryland

Parcel Express.

Graham & Jewel, 20 S. Meridian

Patent Right Agents and Dealers.

Anderson George P. 2 Wiley's blk. ws. Pennsylvania nr. Washington
Durfeld & Conklin, 16½ E. Washington
Taylor's Tube Well, Isaac J. Taylor, propr.
85 E. Washington
Werbe Charles, 81 E. Market

PAT	400	PHY

Patents.

(*Solicitors of.*)

Durfeld & Conklin, 16½ E. Washington

MAYHEW OSCAR F.

Office State House. (See advt. Index.)

Paving Concrete.

(*Burns' Patent.*)

SIMMS & HOSKINS,

ws. the Canal, bet. Louisiana and Georgia. (See advt. index)

Pawnbrokers.

Solomon J. & M. 25 S. Illinois
Wagner George W. 66 N. Illinois

Phonographer.

Drapier W. H. 21 N. Meridian

Photographers.

Andrews Samuel B. 94 E. Washington
Barnes A. A. 39 E. Washington
Bruening Edward & Joseph, 6 E. Washington

CITY ART GALLERY,

(J. PERRY ELLIOTT) 8 and 10 E, Washington. (See advt. index)

Crane James F. ns. Washington bet. Canal and West
Dryer G. W. 2 W. Washington
Photographic Temple of Art, Gordon & Wilson 36½ E. Washington
Hall Alfred, 16½ E. Washington

INGRAHAM'S ART GALLERY

(C. B. Ingraham) 32½ E. Washington, opp. Glenn' blk. (See advt. opposite)

Ludlow Silas, 16½ E. Washington
McCoy R. P. 139 W. Washington

MILLER ADAM R.

43 E. Washington. (See advt. index)

Winder John W. 33 W. Washington

Photographers' Stock.

Crapo R. P. 196 E. Washington

Physicians, Cancer.

(*See also Cancer Physicians.*)

Howard Edward, 92 S. Illinois

SWANK M.

76 N. Pennsylvania

Physician, Throat and Lung.

Hale Judson, office No. 1 Miller's blk. Illinois nw. cor. Market

Physicians and Surgeons.

Abbett L. & C. H. 35 Virginia av.
Aborn Orin, office 74 E. Market

Athon James S. rooms 5 and 7 26 Kentucky av.
Avery John P. 1 Massachusetts av.
Bacon E. H. Washington sw. cor. Meridian
Barnes Henry F. C. McOuats blk. Kentucky av.
Barnes R. A. 66 Virginia ave.
Barney Jacob J. 81 S. Illinois
Bobb John S. 15 E. Washington
Boyd J. T. 5 Martindale's blk.
Bryan A. H. 68 E. Market
Bullard William R. 72 E. Market
Burnham & Tisdale, 38 W. Market
Butterfield S. A. 366 N. East
Butterfield W. Webster, 382 N. East
Cameron John J. 15 E. Washington
Carpenter John. 31 N. Delaware
Clippinger G. W. 64½ E. Washington
Connugor John A. 1 Massachusetts av.
Cooper Joseph M. 160 Indiana av.
Corliss C. T. office No. 5 Miller's blk. Illinois nw. cor. E. Market
Dunlap J. M. room 77½ E. Market
Duzan W. N. 418 N. Tennessee
Eggert William, 75 E. Ohio
Ewing D. B. 33 Virginia
Farnsworth T. W. 21¾ W. Maryland
Ferrell Francis M. 31 N. Delaware
Fletcher & Wright, 107 N. Alabama
Foley W. W 53 Indiana av.
Gaston John M. 66 E. Market
Gillett Omer T. 64 E. Washington
Gustin Levi, 44½ W. Louisiana
Hall Sarah C. 248 N. Illinois
Harbin Thomas M. 26 N. Illinois
Harlan L. D. 142 Virginia av.

HARVEY THOMAS B.

58 E. Market

Homburgh K. 194½ E. Washington
Jameson & Frinkhouser, 19 E. Meridian
Kendrick W. H. 73 N. East
Kirkpatric John, 24½ N. Illinois
Kitchen John M. Vinton's blk. opp. Post-office
Larimore J. 172½ W. Washington
Lawhurn Reuben, (col'd), 63 Indiana av.

LEGRAND HUBERT L.

192 Massachusetts av.

Loeper F. W. 192 E. Washington
McCann Samuel, 69 N. East
McGee Richard, 77 Massachusetts av.
Mears George W. 210 N. Meridian
Moore H. H. 296 E. Ohio
Moore Samuel H. 37 Virginia av.
Nevill James, 114 N. Railroad
New George W. office No. 15 Miller's blk. Illinois cor. Market

NEWCOMER F. S.

No. 6 Blake blk.

Oliver D. H. 58½ E. Market

PAETZ WILLIAM,

127 E. Washington

Parvine Theophilus, 135 N. Alabama
Patterson A. W. 135 N. Alabama
Pearson C. D. 39½ W. Washington
Pendrey N. S. 10 and 11, 85½ E. Market

INGRAHAM'S
ART GALLERY!

INDIANAPOLIS, INDIANA.

32½ East Washington Street,

OPPOSITE GLENN'S BLOCK.

Photographs finished in India Ink, Oil & Water Colors.

Old Pictures Copied and Enlarged to any Size.

PICKERILL & COLE, Physicians and Surgeons, 30 1-2 N. Pennsylvania st. (nearly opp. and west of the Post-office,) Indianapolis, Indiana. Calls promptly attended to at all hours. They would respectfully inform the citizens of Indianapolis and vicinity that they have the exclusive right to the use of the VITALIZER, an improved Vacuum Apparatus for the treatment of Chronic Diseases, such as Paralysis, Shrunken Limbs, General Debility, Gout, Rheumatism, Neuralgia, Impotency, Deafness. Also of the Eye, Ear, Liver, Epileptic Fits, Lung and Throat affections, etc. There is no re-adjustment of clothing in taking the Vacuum Bath.

Prunk Daniel H. 30 N. Mississippi

Reagan Lot. 12 S. Mississippi

RIDGWAY JOHN F.
   88 E. Market

Rodgers Harvey, 291 Kentucky av.

SCHELLER MAX,
   210 E. Ohio

Selman Andrew G. 21 Virginia av.
Siddall James P. 166 Virginia av.
Smith E. M. 40 N. Pennsylvania
Stealy Israel, 78 S. Illinois
Sutter Frederick, 64 E. Washington
Teal N. No. 5 Blake blk. 55 W. Washington
Thompson William, 66 and 68 Virginia av.
Thompson & Woodburn, 90 N. Illinois

TODD & BIGELOW,
   room 3, McOuat's blk. Kentucky av.

Uhl Matthew, 54 S. Pennsylvania
Wands William, 66 E. Market
Ward Boswell, 397 N. New Jersey
Waterman Luther D. 68 N. Pennsylvania
Webb L. A. D. Mrs. 65 Bright
White Charles, 80 Indiana av.
White Daniel, 12 Indiana av.
Wiley Delaney, 68 E. Market
Witman Harrison T. 39 Indiana av.
Woolen Greenly V. 35½ E. Washington
Wright J. J. 58½ E. Market
Youart John M. 39½ E. Market

Piano Dealers.

SOEHNER & BENHAM,
   36 E. Washington

STOWELL M. A.
   46 N. Pennsylvania. (See front paster and back cover)

WILLARD A. G. & CO
   4 and 5 Bates House blk.

Piano Manufacturers.

INDIANAPOLIS MANUFACTURING CO. 159 and 161 E. Washington

KAPPES J. H. & CO.
   210 to 216 S. Illinois

Trayser Frederick L. 82 E. Market (See adv't. index)

TRAYSER GEORGE
   New York ne. cor. Davidson

Verity S. T. 42 Huron

Piano Tuners.

Narden Ethan T. 28 N. Delaware
Soehner & Benham, (Philip Herring) 36 E. Washington
Trayser Benedict L. 82 E. Market

Picture and Picture Frames.

Crapo R. P. 196 E. Washington
Daumont H. & Co. 15 W. Washington

LIEBER H. & CO.
   21 N. Pennsylvania

Purcell Michael 122 N. East

Planing Mills.

BYRKITT & SONS
   Tennessee nw. cor. Georgia. (See adv't index)

Builders & Manufacturers Association Charlton Eden, Prest. J. L. Avery. Treas. Jas. Hasson, Sec. 225 N. Delaware

Emerson, Beam & Thompson, 225-229 W. Market

Hill & Wingate, East se. cor. Georgia
McCord & Wheatley, 186 S. Alabama

TATE WARREN,
   38 S. New Jersey, (See adv't index)

Plasterers.

Dearenger Simeon 313 E. Georgia

HEISSER J. H.
   (Bushes and moulders tools) 24 N. Pennsylvania

Plasterers.
(*Ornamental.*)

TAYLOR JOHN F.
   80 Massachusetts av.

Platers.
(*Gold and Silver.*)

Alcon A. room 22, Talbott & New's blk.
Fulmer F. & Son, 30 Virginia av.
Gray George, 498 E. Washington
Higgins W. B. 8 W. Washington

Plow Dealers.

.LUKENS RICHARD L.
agt. for E. M. Doty's Sod Plow, 81 W. Washington. (See advt. Index)

WEBB & BATES,
83 W. Washington (See advt. Index)

Plow Handles.

(Manufacturer of.)
OSGOOD, SMITH & CO.
230 S. Illinois

Plow Manufacturers.

BUCHANAN & HOOVER,
25, 27 and 29 S. East

KIMBALL NATHAN,
es. S. Tennessee bet. Washington and Kentucky av. (See advt. Index)
Miller Louis, E. Washington cor. Benton

Plumbers.

(See also Gas and Steam Pipe Fitters.)
Coulter & White, 47 S Pennsylvania
Hanning John G. 82 W. Washington
Neab Conrad, 70 N. Illinois, Miller's blk.

Plumbers and Gas Fitters.

(Blow Lamps.)
HEISSER J. H.
24 N. Pennsylvania

Powder Dealers.

BECK SAMUEL,
63 E. Washington

Printers, Book and Job.

Boetticher Julius, 164 E. Washington
Braden W. & J. 24 W. Washington
Cameron W. S. 8 E. Pearl
Chandler H. C. & Co. 25 and 27 S. Meridian
Drapier W. H. 23 N. Meridian

GOODWIN A. Q.
30 S. Meridian
Harding W. P. 21 N. Meridian
Indianapolis Printing and Publishing House, W. W. Dowling, prest. Scott Butler, sec. Meridian se. cor. Circle
Journal, (Douglas & Conner) Market ne. cor. Circle, Journal Building
Mirror, (Harding, Morton & Finch) 19 N. Meridian
Meikel Bros. Washington sw. cor. Meridian.
Railroad, City Printing Co. (L. G. Dynes, W. C. West, L. C. Hunt & J. F. Dynes,) 35 E Market
Sheets William, 79 W. Washington.
State Sentinel, (R. J. Bright) 16½ E. Washington

Produce and Provision Dealers.

(See also Groceries and Provisions.)
Avels J. H. 61 N. Illinois
Budd & Hinsley, 18 W. Pearl
Cady E. E. 523 N. Illinois
Caldwell H. W. 149 Indiana av.
Clark Levi, 49 S. New Jersey
Elder E. A. 52 N. Illinois
Glazier Charles, 146 S. Pennsylvania
Hobbs Soloman, 49 S. New Jersey

JENISON A. F. & J. H.
89 N. Illinois. (See adv't index)
Johnson E. & Co. 108 S. Delaware
Jordon John 158 W. Washington

LAWRENCE A. V.
173 W. Washington. (See adv't index)
Lemon Daniel A. 187 W. Washington
McGowan Lunsford, 251 N. Illinois
Mitchell David, N. 52 Indiana av.
Mix Lyman W. 43 S. Delaware

MOREHOUSE ROBERT
52 Indiana av. (See adv't index)
Newcomb, H. C. 302 N. Illinois
Noel & Son, 86 Virginia av.
Porter Omer T. 6 Martindale's blk.

REDMOND THOMAS,
W. Washington (Nat. rd.) ne. cor. Blake
Smith & Marshall, Noble se. cor. Fletcher av.
Wallace Will W. 441 N. Illinois
Wallace William J. 43 S. Delaware
Warner Louis, 46 Indiana av.
Woolen William M. 101 Indiana av.

Publishers.

(See also Newspapers and Publications.)
Asher, Adams & Higgins, 76 E. Market

BLAND & TAYLOR,
19 N. Meridian
Cowen & Protzman, 16½ E. Washington
Gutenberg Co. Adolph Frey, supt. 23 W. Maryland
Merrill & Co. 5 E. Washington
R. R. City Printing Co. 35 E. Market
Roach A. C. Market ne. cor. Circle (Journal Bldg.)
Streight A. D. Yohn's blk. Meridian ne. cor. Washington
Western Publishing Co. 16½ E. Washington

Pump Makers and Dealers.

Dain Thomas, 57 Massachusetts av.
Davis W. H. 133 N. Tennessee
Durbon R. A. 97 and 99 S. Meridian
Hanning John G. 82 W. Washington

HOYLE & MOORE,
14 Virginia av.
Neab Conrad, 70 N. Illinois
Sanders & Rockwell, 30 Kentucky av
Wright & Bro. 127 E. Maryland

Railings.

(Wrought and Cast.)
Haugh B. F. & Co. 74 S. Pennsylvania

Railroad Companies and Offices.

Baltimore & Ohio Rw. S. P. Hazzard, western frt. agt. W. H. Parmelle, agt. Office Virginia av. cor. Alabama.

CLEVELAND, COLUMBUS, CINCINNATI & INDIANAPOLIS R. W. CO. L. M. Hubby, pres. O. Townsend, vice pres. E. S. Flint, genl. supt. R. W. Geiger, agt. J. L. Cozad, div. supt. ne. cor. Virginia av. and Alabama

Columbus, Chicago & Indiana Central R. R. Virginia av. cor. Delaware, J. M. Lunt, genl. supt.

INDIANAPOLIS CINCINNATI & LaFAYETTE R. R. W. H. L. Noble, genl. agt. A. E. Clark, genl. ticket agt. F. Richardson, supt. H. L. Hall, asst. supt. Office Louisiana cor. Delaware. (See R. R. Dept.)

Indianapolis, Peru & Chicago Railroad, genl. office 101 E. Washington. Frt. depot New Jersey nr. Washington

INDIANAPOLIS & ST. LOUIS R. R. T. A. Morris, pres. E. King, secy. and treas. J. D. Herkimer, supt. Office 53 S. Alabama. (See R. R. dept.)

JEFFERSONVILLE, MADISON & Indianapolis R. R. Horace Scott, gen. supt. J. G. Whitcomb, frt. agt. Frt. depot E. South nr. Delaware. (See R. R. Dept.

Railroad Companies.

(Street.)

Citizens Street Railway Co. office and depot ns. Louisiana bet. S. Illinois and S. Tennessee

Reapers and Mowers.

(See also Agricultural Implements.)

KNIFFEN MOWER & REAPER, C. J. Brackebush, genl. agt. 75 W. Washington. (See advt. Index)

LUKENS R. L. Agt. Bucyrus Reaper and Mower, 81 W. Washington. (See advt. Index)

McCORMICKS REAPER & MOWER, H. J. Prier, genl. agt. 230 E. Washington

Sherwood Lyman Q. genl. south western agt. for Russell's Reapers and Mowers, 79 and 81 N. Illinois, Academy of Music blk.

Rectifiers and Distillers.

Bender, Tobias & Co. 189 E. Washington

Brinkmeyer J. C. & Co. 80 S. Meridian

Hahn & Bals, 25 S. Meridian

Schwabacher & Selig, 41 S. Delaware

Restaurants.

(See also Eating Houses; also Dining Halls.)

Beck Edward, 44 W. Washington

Becker F. B. & Bro. 17 N. Pennsylvania Circle, (Rhodius Mary) 15 N. Meridian

Grobe Charles, 12 W. Louisiana

Holmes Sophia Miss, 75 S. Illinois

Knotts & Co. 72 W. Washington

Lauer Charles, 202 E. Washington

MOFFITT & MILLER, 46 S. Meridian. (See advt. index)

Mortland Alexander M. 23 N. Illinois

Mozart Hall Restaurant, (J. Grosch) 39 S. Delaware

Randall Berry, 29 S. Illinois

Reinhardt P. J. 81 S. Illinois

Ruschhaupt A. & Wands, 81 E. Washington

Spencer James, (col'd) under 1st. Nat. Bank

UNION DEPOT RESTAURANT, T. B. Spratt, supt. Union Depot bldgs.

WEINBERGER & CO. 10 W. Louisiana

Whitney William, 121 S. Illinois

Rolling Mills.

Greenleaf & Co. 325 S. Tennessee

Indianapolis Rolling Mill Co. J. M. Lord, pres C. B. Parkman, sec. A. Jones, treas. office No. 8 Blake Block

Roofers.

(Composition.)

SIMMS & HOSKINS, ws. Canal bet. Georgia and Louisiana. (See advt. index)

Roofers.

(Slate and Metal.)

ZIMMERMANN C. 35 S. Alabama. (See advt. index)

Real Estate Agents, Brokers and Dealers.

Alexander G. W. & Co. 2 W. Washington

Anderson George P. 2 Wiley's blk. ws. Pennsylvania near Washington

Barnitz Charles, 115 E. Washington

Burnham Samuel W. 17½ W. Washington

COLDEN JOHN E. room 11 Talbott & New's blk.

Copeland W. J. & Co. 5 Martindale's blk.

Cresp V. B. & Son, Washington nw. cor. Delaware

Du feld & Conklin, 16½ E. Washington

Eldridge J. room 8, 30 W. Washington

Frank James, 35½ E. Washington

Goodwin Thomas A. 35 E. Market

Joie. Jesse, 19 W. Washington

Lehr Ferdinand A. 83 E. Washington

LINDLEY & CO. 8 E. Washington

Lloyd Gideon, 45 E. Washington

Love William & Co. room 1, Talbott & New's blk.

McCARTY & BRIGHT,
office No. 4, Sentinel bldg.
McKernan J. H. room 2, Blake blk.
McMillin Samuel & Co. 17½ W. Washington

MARTIN LUTHER R.
10 E. Washington
Metzger Alexander, room 6, Odd Fellows Hall
Mick William E. & Co. room 7, 2d floor, Martindale's blk.
Minick David C. 17½ W. Washington

MURPHY TOBIAS M.
room 9, 2d floor Martindale's blk.

MYERS & DAUBENSPECK.
27 Massachusetts av.

Poe J. M. & Co. 24½ E. Washington
Seidensticker A. & Co. 14 S. Delaware

SMITH FRANK & CO.
room 4, Odd Fellows Hall
Smith Josiah & Co. 16½ S. Meridian

SPANN JOHN S. & CO.
50 E. Washington (Brown's blk.)
VanBuskirk E. room 8, 30 W. Washington
Witt & Arbuckle, Washington sw. cor. Meridian
Wright & Vinnedge, 62½ E. Washington

Saddle & Harness Makers.
See Harness and Saddle Makers.

Saddlery Hardware.
Share Geo. K. & Co. 40 S. Meridian
Sulgrove James W. & Co. 20 W Washington

Safes.
OVER E. & CO.
82 and 84 S. Meridian
Vajen J. H. & Co. 21 W. Washington

Saloons.
Altman H. & Co. Bluff rd cor. Ray
Armbruster Frank E. ss. W. Washington, 2 e. the Bridge, (Nat. rd.)
Armbruster John J. 215 W. Maryland
Asmus Lewis, 199 Indiana av.
Astor Saloon, (Joseph Deschler,) 15 N. Pennsylvania
Balke Charles, 231 E. Washington
Ballweg Ferderick, 131 W. Washington
Beck Edward, 44 West Washington
Behringer Joseph, 145 W. Washington
Beirsdorfer George, prop'r "Great Western" Illinois cor. Indiana av.
Bershea Daniel, 294 E. Washington
Bess William K. 284 W. Washington
Blodau John, 231 S. Delaware
Bothwell Henry, 526 N. Mississippi
Bourgonne S. & Co. 139 S. Illinois
Brown Albert, 387 S. Delaware
Brown T. B. 125 S. Illinois.
Bruner & Cumer, Tennessee sw. cor. 4th.

Bucksot W. 9 W. Washington
Buehrig Henry E. 37 E. South
Buress William, Washington se. cor. New Jersey
Burk George, 154 Indiana av.
Busch Jacob, 251 W. Washington
Buscher Henry, 89 E. South
Cabinet Saloon, Palmer House.

CAFE DU PUEPLE
Eugene Renard, prop'r, 299 E. Washington.
Carr Thomas, 276 S. Missouri
Carter & Bowman, 9 W. Washington

CARTWRIGHT & THOMPSON
33 N. Illinois. (See adv't index)
Christy Albert, 26 W. Louisiana
Corriden Thomas, 350 S. West
Cropper John B. 24 W. Pearl
Cusick Joseph, 73 and 75 S. West
Dell William, 135 E. Washington
Diekmann Charles, 208 E. Washington
Deitz Peter, 181 S. Meridian
Dietz Fred, 255 E. Washington
Dietz Fred & Co. 133 E. Washington
Doman Peter E. 18 S. Delaware
Dugan Neil, 53 S. Illinois
Eix Henry, 228 E. Washington
Enners William, 387 N. Noble
Eurich John, 17 N. Illinois

EVERTS EVERT,
137 Fort Wayne av.
Fahrbach Philip, propr. Washington Hall Saloon, 78 and 80 W. Washington
Fidel Siemon, 211 W. Washington
Frech Henry, ns. Nat. rd. west of the bridge
Frick John, St. Clair junc. Massachusetts av. and Plum
Frick John, 155 Ft. Wayne av.
Geis John, 62 S. Delaware
Geis & Weaner, 99 E. Washington
George Robert, 184 W. Washington
Ginz M. & H. 185 E. Washington
Gold Adam, 405 W. Washington
Griffin Timothy, 48 S. Pennsylvania
Gruenert John H. 61 E. South

HART EDWARD F.
Prop'r "Hearts Content Saloon," 132 S. Illinois. (See adv't Index)
Hartrott H. 249 W. South
Heiser Charles, 76 S. Delaware
Hennington Robert, 178 S. Delaware
Hofmann M. 170 Bluff rd.
Hofman Phillip, 775 N. Tennessee
Hollywood Richard, White House Saloon, 66 W. Maryland
Hoppe George, 179 S. Meridian
Hong Michael, 138 S. Pennsylvania
"House of Lords," John Pearson & Co. prop's 78 W. Washington
Howell Elizabeth ns. Nat. rd. w. Bridge
Huegele John, 39 E. Washington
Inwalle Benjamin J. 367 Virginia av.
Jasper Frederick, 333 Virginia av.
Kaestner A. 184 S. Illinois
Kamm Gotleib, 70 Virginia av.
Kattemann Ernst, 1 Buchanan
Kissel F. 98 Russel av.

KLARE & SCHRODER, Proprietors, Saloon & Bowling Alley, Bluff Road corner City Limits. Open all the time. A good place to enjoy yourself.

Knotts N. K. & Co. 72 W. Washington
Korniger George, 338 S. Meridian
Kohler John, 247 N. Noble
LaMotte Charles, 100 S. Illinois. (See adv't Index)
Lauer Charles, 202 E. Washington
Laupheimer August, 191 E. Washington
Lee William, 48 Virginia av.
Lee & Replogle. Noble nw. cor. Washington.
Lehr Philip, 248 N. Noble
Lehritter George, 143 E. Washington
Leonard & Victor, proprs. Emmett Saloon, 65 W. Washington
Luemann Charles, 380 Virginia av.
McBride John, 161 W. Washington
McCabe Matthew, 320 E. Washington
McLaughlin William, 324 S West
Marmont Hugo, 102 S. Illinois
Matthes Clemens, 92 E. Washington
Miller John, 123 S. Illinois
Monninger, Conrad, 167 W. Washington
Monninger Daniel, 20 Kentucky av.
Mortland Alexander M, 23 N. Illinois
Mottery F, 200 S. Meridian
Mueller Charles G. 25 S. Delaware
Muth Peter, 8 S. Delaware
Naltner Martin, 134 S. Meridian
Neel Charles, 20 N. Delaware
O'Keefe C. 267 S. Tennessee
O'Leary Jeremiah, 103 S. Illinois
O'Mara & Hartnett, 101 S. Illinois
Oehler David, 84 Russell av.

OPERA SALOON, Thomas J. Barlow, propr. 79 E. Washington
Palace Saloon, William E. Carter, propr. 87 S. Illinois
Quinn John, 245 W. Maryland
Russel Margaret, ws. Michigan rd. above 1st
Ray Henry J. 274 E. Washington

REDMOND THOMAS, 432 W. Washington, Nat. rd. cor. Blake
Reichwein Philip, 50 N. Noble
Reinhardt T. J. 81 S. Illinois
Rhodius M. 15 N. Meridian
Richter William 416 Virginia av.
Rocker Peter, 200 W. Maryland
Ruschhaupt A. & Wands, 81 E. Washington
Ruse John, 222 E. Washington
Schaub Henry, 168 W. Washington
Schaub Henry, jr. 334 Virginia av.
Schurich Fred. ws. Nat. Rd. west of bridge
Schwicho Charles, 224-6 Bluff rd.
Schwomeyer Charles H. 297 S. Meridian
Seidensticker F. 176 S. Illinois
Seitz Frederick, 117 S. Illinois
Selking William, 33 N. Pennsylvania
Shepherd James McB. 156 E. Washington
Sherman House Saloon, George B. Carter, clerk

impson & Dugan, 52 S. Illinois
Singel Abdon, 176 E. Washington
Smith W. A. 40 W. Louisiana
Spencer House Saloon, Henry Guetig, propr.
Steffens Charles. 192 N. Mississippi
Sweeney Hugh, 116 S. Illinois
Thomann John, 44 Massachusetts av.
Thompson & Peterson, 351 S. Pennsylvania
Wachtstetter Jacob, 154 W. Washington
Weiss John L. E. Washington cor. Benton
Welch Patrick, 23 W. Washington
Welsh Maurice, proprietor, Senate Saloon, 80 W. Washington
Wenger M. 60 S. Delaware
Whitcomb James, W. Louisiana opp. Union Depot
White Fawn, 33 W. Washington
Wiesh Christopher, Washington ne. cor. East
Wissert John, 180 S. Meridian
Witthoeft Frederick, 329 Indiana av.
Wolf Catharine Mrs. 176 S. Delaware
Wriedt Charles, 34 W. Georgia
Ziegel Louis, Wyoming, sw. cor. High
Ziegelmueller Herman, 59 N. Alabama

Salt Dealers.

Ingle Mark W. 28 S. Meridian

Sash, Doors and Blinds.

(*See also Planing Mills, also Lumber Dealers.*)

Builders and Manufacturers Association, C. Eden, pres. J L. Avery, Treas. James Hasson, sec'y, 225 N. Delaware

BYRKITT M. & SONS. Tennessee nw. cor. Georgia. (See adv't. Index)

Emerson, Beam & Thompson, 225 and 229 W. Market

HILDEBRAND, KEPPELE & CO. Indiana av. cor. Canal (See adv't. Index)

Hill & Wingate, East se. cor. Georgia

TATE WARREN 38 S. New Jersey. (See adv't Index)

Vajen J. H & Co. 21 W. Washington
Wheatley Henry H. South cor. Delaware

Saw Filers.

Foster William N. 71 Jackson
Heirmann Mathias, 63 S. Pennsylvania

Saw Manufacturers.

SHEFFIELD SAW WORKS, E. C. Atkins & Co. proprietors, 210 to 216 S. Illinois. (See adv't. index)

Saw Mills.

HILDEBRAND, KEPPELE & CO. Office Indiana av. cor. Canal. (See advt. Index)

Long & Joseph, LaFayette R. R. bet. Walnut and St. Clair

Marsee J. & Co. New Jersey bet. Washington and Railroad
PRESSLY JOHN T.
es. West, bet. Louisiana and Georgia
Wishmier C. F. es. North, bet. Railroad and Davidson

Saw Mills.
(Manufacturer of.)
WESTERN MACHINE WKS.
Sinker & Co. propr. 125 S. Pennsylvania

Saw Mills.
(Portable.)
EAGLE MACHINE WORKS.
Louisiana se. cor. Meridian

Saws.
(Cross Cut)
OVER E. & CO.
82 and 84 S. Meridian

Saws.
(Circular, Muley and Cross Cut.)
SHEFFIELD SAW WORKS,
E. C. Atkins & Co. propr. 310 to 316 S. Illinois. (See advt. index)

Scales and Balances.
Gallup W. P. & E. P. genl. agts. Fairbanks scales for Indiana, 43 & 45 N. Tennessee

School Apparatus.
Asher, Adams & Higgins, 76 E. Market

Second Hand Store.
Benson David S. 206 S. Illinois

Seed Stores.
(See Agricultural Seed Stores.)

Sewing Machine Agent.
True R. H. 18 S. Pennsylvania

Sewing Machines.
Florence Sewing Machine, J. W. Smith, agt. 27 N. Pennsylvania
Grover & Baker Sewing Machine Co. Wiley & VanBuren, state agts. 21 E. Washington
HOWE, (OLIVE & FOLTZ, agts.)
12 N. Pennsylvania
Singer Mnfg. Co. M. J. Oatman, agt. 18 N. Delaware
Wheeler & Wilson's. William Sumner & Co. agts. 10 W. Washington

Sheet Iron Dealers.
Cottrell & Knight, 108 S. Delaware
OVER E. & CO.
82 and 84 S. Meridian

Sheet Iron Workers.
(See also Tin, Copper and Sheet Iron Workers.)
COX & BROTHERS,
24 E. Georgia. (See advt. index)

Shingle Knives.
Kellogg N. 411 W. Washington, Nat Rd.

Shingle Machines.
(Sawing and Cutting.)
EAGLE MACHINE WORKS,
Louisiana se. cor. Meridian

Shoe Findings.
Sharpe Joseph K. 47 & 49 S. Delaware

Shooting Galleries.
Wriedt Charles, 34 W. Georgia

Show Case Manufacturers.
Berkhofer George, jr. 5 Virginia av.

Silver Plated Goods.
WOODBRIDGE JOHN & CO.
12 W. Washington

Silver Platers.
(See Platers Silver and Gold.)

Silver and Plated Ware.
Bingham W. P. & Co. 50 E. Washington
Craft William H. 36 E. Washington
Ferguson C. A. 7 W. Washington
West H. F. & Co. 37 S. Meridian

Soap Manufacturers.
Bergmann Frank, s. end S. West
Moon Thomas, W. Indianapolis

Soda Water Manufacturers.
(See Mineral Water.)

Spectacles.
(See also Opticians.)
Moses L. W. 50 E. Washington

Spring Bed Manufacturer.
HALL L. A.
83 E. Market

Stair Builders.
DES JARDINS JOSEPH,
191 Virginia av. (See adv't. Index)
SHOVER & CHRISTIAN,
124 E. Vermont. (See adv't index)
Springer D. & Son, 260 Massachusetts av.

STA	408	STR

Starch Manufacturer.

UNION STARCH FACTORY,
east end of New York

Staves.

(*Oil Barrel.*)

BUNTE & DICKSON,
387 E. Washington. (See adv't. Index)

Staves and Headings.

(*Manufacturers of.*)

BUNTE, DICKSON & CO.
Railroad north of Market. (See adv't. index)

Carey J. S. & Co Georgia bet. West and the river.

McKENDRY & LOVECRAFT,
works LaFayette Railroad, w. end Pratt (See adv't. index)

Steam Engines.

(*See Engine Builders.*)

Steam Pipe and Gas Fitters.

(*See also Plumbers, also Gas and Steam Pipe Fitters.*)

Davis Joseph W. 110 S. Delaware
Neab Conrad. 70 N. Illinois

Steamship Co.

CUNARD MAIL LINE,
bet. New York, Liverpool and Queenstown. Edward F. Hart, agt. office 132 S. Illinois. (See adv't. Index)

Steel Warehouse.

OVER E. & CO.
agts. Sanderson's Steel, 82 and 84 S. Meridian

Stencil Cutters.

Walker Edward, 25 W. Washington

Stock Yards.

Indianapolis, Cincinnati and LaFayette Cattle Yards. Vincent Fazen, Supt. Louisiana out of limits

Stocking Manufacturers.

Funke F. W. 99 E. Washington
Krause & Riemenschneider, 84 E. Washington

Stone Cutters.

(*Blow Lamps.*)

HEISSER J. H.
agt. 24 N. Pennsylvania

Stone Yards.

GODDARD & SONS,
Kentucky av. cor. Georgia (See advt. Index)

SMITH, ITTENBACH & CO.
two squares e. of Noble bet. Harrison and Lord. (See advt. Index)

SCOTT & NICHOLSON,
ws. Kentucky av. bet. West and Louisiana

Stone and Crockery Ware.

Wiles Thomas, 25 E. Georgia

Stone and Marble Cutters.

SMITH, ITTENBACH & CO.
two squares e. of Noble bet. Harrison and Lord. (See advt. Index)

Storage and Commission.

(*See also Commission Merchants.*)

Rush Fred P. 99 S. Delaware
Smith & Gerhart, Delaware se. cor. Virginia av.

Store Furniture.

Fearnley John, 23 Circle

KELLER PAUL,
21 Circle (See advt. Index)

Stove Manufacturers and Dealers.

ROOT D. & CO.
foundry 183 and 185 S. Pennsylvania. office and salesroom, 66 E. Washington

Wood A. D. 135 and 137 S. Delaware

Stoves and Tinware.

(*See also Tin, Copper and Sheet Iron Workers*)

Cox Charles, 57 W. Washington

CROPPER JAMES H.
169 and 171 W. Washington (See advt. Index)

Frankem I. L. & Co. 34 E. Washington
LaMotte Joseph & Son, 192 Massachusetts av.

McOUAT R. L. & A. W.
61 and 63 W. Washington

Martin & Myers, 117 W. Washington

MUNDSON & JOHNSTON,
62 E Washington

TUTEWILER BROS.
74 E. Washington

Voegtle Jacob, 103 E. Washington
Wolfrom Bros. 197 E. Washington

ZIMMERMANN C.
35 S. Alabama. (See adv't Index)

Straw Goods.

(*Wholesale.*)

Carr & Alvey, 6 Robert's blk, opp. Union Depot.
Copeland J. W. & Co. 39 S. Meridian

I. Davis & Co., dealers in Hats, Caps, Furs and Straw Goods.

STR   409   THR

Straw Goods.
(*Wholesale and Retail.*)

Bamberger H. 16 E. Washington
Davis Isaac & Co. 12 E. Washington
McIver J. C. 22 E. Washington

Surgical Instruments.

Browning & Sloan. 7 and 9 E. Washington
Piscator August, 12 S. Delaware

Tailors.
(*Merchant*)

BECKER & HUBER,
  77 E. Washington
Clark W. & W. H. 26 N. Illinois
Clark William, 31 S. Illinois
Crain & Needham, 3 Bates House blk.
Enggass H. 113 S. Illinois
GERSTNER ANTHONY J.
  173 E. Washington
Goepper F. & Co. 17 E. Washington
GRAMLING J. P.
  35 E. Washington
Green George, 32 N. Pennsylvania
HALL E. A.
  31 N. Pennsylvania
Hattendorf Henry, 317 E. Washington
Heitkam George H. 8 W. Washington
Cotz & Co. 124 S. Illinois
HURRLE I.
  168 E. Washington
Lenox Edward, 20 N. Pennsylvania
Mitchell J. 2 Bates House Blk.
Moritz Bros. 19 W. Washington
Roeth & Meier, 207 E. Washington
Rupp William F. 38 W. Washington
Sailors James L. 156 W. Washington
Schildmeier Frederick, 182 E. Washington
Staub Joseph, 2 Odd Fellow's Hall
Steimann & Bernauer, 43 Virginia av.
SWEINHART WILLIAM,
  21 S. Meridian
TREAT & CLAFLIN,
  30 N. Pennsylvania
White H. M. 11 S. Meridian

Tailors and Repairers.
(*See also Tailors Merchant.*)

Baar B. 174 E. Market
Ballman Hermann, 200 S. Illinois
Budenz Louis, 168 E. Washington
Fetty Conrad, room 16 Miller's blk. N. Illinois
FISHER SAMUEL A.
  26 Virginia av.
Friedgen C. H. 41 N. Illinois
Frink H. S. 28 S. Delaware
Gererdy Nicholas, 313 E. Washington
Gorbler William, 182 Bluff rd.
Gopp John, 284 N. Liberty
Gray George W. 27 Kentucky av
Gregoire August, 129 S. Illinois

Hilger Christian, 42 S. Liberty
Kelley Anthony, 28 S. Meridian
LIPP HENRY,
  13 Massachusetts av.
Longrich Edward, 282 E. North
Morris H. & Co. 22 W. Maryland
Mueller Charles L. 53 S. Illinois
NILIUS CHARLES,
  134 S. Illinois
Parker Catharine E. Mrs. 44 Virginia av.
Porter Theodore R. 244 W. Washington
Rogge Rudolph, 335 Virginia av.
Skinner Ellison E. 62 S. Illinois
Small Henry, 8 E. Washington
Wilson John W. 55 Massachusetts av.
Winter I. N. 27 N. Illinois
Yahrleng John P. 3 Virginia av.

Tanners' Oil.

Fishback John, 125 S. Meridian
Mooney & Co. 147 S. Meridian

Tanners and Curriers.

Fishback John, tannery Michigan rd. near McIntyre, salesroom 125 S. Meridian
Frenzel & Simon, Benton cor. Washington
Schmidt Robert, 96 S. East

Taxidermist.

Bernitz Jacob W. 115 E. Washington

Teacher.
(*Of Languages.*)

Lewis Frederick C. 70 E. Ohio

Teas.
(*Wholesale. See also Grocers.*)

COORS AUGUST F.
  (agt. American & China Tea Co.) 151 W. Washington. (See marginal bottom lines)
Lee H. H. 18 and 20 Bates House blk. and 7 Odd Fellows' Hall
MILLNER & SHERWOOD,
  27 McNabb, opp. Union Depot
Wiles Bro. & Co. 149 S. Meridian

Telegraph Company.

Western Union Telegraph Co. 11 S. Meridian, Branch Union Depot

Theatres.
(*See Amusements, places of.*)

Threshing Machines.
(*See also Agricultural Implements*)

EAGLE MACHINE WORKS,
  Louisiana se. cor. Meridian
Sherwood Lyman Q. "Massillon Thresher," 79 and 81 N. Illinois. (Academy of Music blk.)

TIN	410	VAR

Tin, Copper and Sheet Iron Workers.

Gardner & Decker, 308 Virginia av.
Frankem I. L. & Co. 34 E. Washington
Jennings William T. 60 E. Market
Johnson E. & Co. 108 S. Delaware
Richey Julius, 223 S. Delaware
Stumpf Henry A. 94 Indiana av.
Wainwright Samuel, 18 W. Maryland
Weber George H. 130 Bluff rd.
Willis Jonathan, 166 Indiana av.

Tobacco Manufacturers and Wholesale Dealers.

(See also Cigars and Tobacco.)

BARKER WILLIAMS & CO.
Propr's Capitol Tobacco and Cigar Works.
Factory 19, 21 and 23 N. Tennessee.—
Sales room 42 W. Washington. (See adv't Index)
Oliver Charles, Washington bet. California and West
Reynolds & Loucks, 22 N. Delaware
SMITH SAMUEL S.
312 S. Delaware
Wiles Bro & Co. 149 S. Meridian

Tobacco Works.

CAPITOL TOBACCO WORKS,
19, 21 and 23 N. Tennessee. Baker, Williams & Co. propr's. (See adv't Index)

Toys and Notions.

(Wholesale. See also Notions.)

Baldwin J. H. & Co. (Fancy Bazaar,) 6 E. Washington
Henninger G. & E. 115 S Illinois
MAYER CHARLES & CO.
29 W. Washington. (See adv't Index.)

Transportation Lines and Cos.

(See Express Co's. Also Fast Freight Lines. Also Railroads.)

Trunks, Traveling Bags and Valises,

(Manufacturers and Dealers.)

Baldwin J. H. & Co. (Fancy Bazaar) 6 E. Washington
Bogert James, 2 N. Meridian
BURTON M.
39 N. Illinois
Forby Charles H. 109 S. Illinois
ROBINSON BROTHERS
20 Virginia av. (See adv't index)
SHILLING R. L.
55 W. Washington and 12 Kentucky av.
Smith R. L. & Co. 16½ S. Meridian

Trunks, Traveling Bags and Valises.

(Wholesale.)

SHILLING R. L.
55 W. Washington and 12 Kentucky av.

Turners.

(Wood.)

LOUIS KOLB, Manufacturer of every Description of Job Turning. Stair Ballusters and Newell Posts Made to Order; also, all Kinds of Turning in Builders and Cabinet Makers' Line. All Orders Promptly Attended to. No. 23 East South St., bet. Meridian and Pennsylvania Sts., Indianapolis Indiana.

Meyer Martin, 19 S. Alabama

Umbrella Maker.

Meyer John F. 69 E. Washington

Undertakers.

Grinstelner George, 276 E. Market
HERRMANN F. J. & SON,
26 S. Delaware
Long & Kregelo, 15 Circle, e. Meridian
Weaver William W. 39 N. Illinois
Williams Charles, 10 Bates House Square

Undertakers' Trimmings.

Newton Maria Mrs. 110 S. Illinois (up stairs.)
(See advt. index)

Upholsterers.

(See also Furniture Manufacturers and Dealers.)

GEBHARD AUGUST,
67 E. Washington
Wilkins & Hall, 84 and 86 E. Market

Varnish Manufacturer.

(See also Glue Makers.)

Mears, Lilly & Co. proprs. Capital City Varnish Works, office and factory Kentucky av. cor. Mississippi

Velocipede Halls.

Guezet Alexander, 224 S. Delaware
Spaulding J. L. Velocipede Riding Hall, 26 and 28 S. Tennessee

Velocipede Manufacturer.

MILLER, MITCHELL & STOUGH, Kentucky av. cor. Georgia

Veterinary Surgeons.

Ellerby James, 10 E. Pearl
Navin John N. 208 W. Washington
Rapp Carl, room 4, 104 S. Illinois

Vinegar Manufacturer.

Wright Frank, Blake bet. New York and Washington

Wagon Makers.

(See also Carriage Builders.)

Berryman John, se. end Virginia av.
Bonse William, East bet. South and Louisana
Chapman John W. ns. Natl. rd. west of bridge
Drew S. W. E. Market Square bet. Delaware and Alabama

EWALD HENRY,
299 Massachusetts av. (See advt. Index)
Feil John, 123 Bluff road
Gregg J. A. 191 Indiana av.
Hartman Frederick, 377 Virginia av.
Horan James, bet. W. Washington and Nat. road
Indianapolis Wagon and Agricultural Works, W. A. Pattison, agt. 172 S. Tennessee
Job Alzire, Virginia av. nr. cor. Dougherty
Miller Louis, E. Washington cor. Benton

MUNSELL EZRA,
ns. St. Clair bet. Broadway and Massachusetts av. (See advt. Index)

MUNSELL HENRY,
Massachusetts av. cor. Plum. (See advt. Index)
Starke John C. 26 S. New Jersey
Trucks & Kay, 60 Kentucky av.
VanBlaricum Jesse M. 231 W. Washington

VONDERSAAR WENDELL,
144 Fort Wayne av. (See adv't index.)
Webster C. B. 291 Kentucky av.
Wehling Charles, 234 S. Delaware
Whitney J. W. 46 S. Pennsylvania

Wagon Yards.

(See also Livery, Sale and Feed Stables.)

Gates, Pray & Co. E. Market square, between Delaware and Alabama.
Patterson S. W. 278—80 W. Washington

Waggon and Buggy.

(Wood Work.)

OVER E. & CO.
82 and 84 S. Meridian

Waggon and Carriage Materials.

Case, Parker & Co. 84 W. Washington
Indianapolis Wagon and Agricultural Works, W. A. Patterson, ag't. 172 S. Tennessee.

OSGOOD, SMITH & CO.
230 S. Illinois

Wall Paper and Window Shades.

GALL & RUSH,
101 E. Washington cor. Delaware
Hume, Adams & Co. 26 & 28 W. Washington.
Roll William H. 38 S. Illinois

WILDER C. P.
26 E. Washington

Watches, Clocks and Jewelry.

Also Makers and Repairers. (See also Jewellers.)

Barfuss G. 79 S. Illinois
Beck S. T. 43 S. Illinois
Bingham W. P. & Co. 50 E. Washington
Carter John E. 125 W. Washington
Craft William H. 36 E. Washington
Daumont H. & Co. 15 W. Washington
Daumont P. A. 47 S. Illinois
Davis George, 37 W. Washington
Dietrichs Charles, 66 N. Pennsylvania
Feller George, 114 S. Illinois
Ferguson C. A. 7, W. Washington

FORBES JOSEPH R.
34 Virginia av. (See top margin lines.)
French Charles G. 13 N. Meridian
Kiefer L. F. & Son, 2 Odd Fellows' bldg.
Kingbury John E. 237 Massachusetts av.
McLewe & Herron, 1 Bates House blk.
Miller R. A. 268 E. Washington
Neven Charles, 51 Massachusetts av.
Oehler Andrew, 20 S. Delaware
Oehler Romon, 183 W. Washington
Phipps Brothers, 14 N. Pennsylvania
Schliebitz Frederick W. 147 E. Washington
Schurr Leonhard, Jr. 71 Indiana av.
Slusher Henry, 172 W. Washington
Stacy M. D. 34 Virginia av.
Zambusch Theodore, 93 Washington

Weavers.

Bush George, 20 and 22 S. East

Wigs, Toupees, &c.

Mahorney J. T. 233 and 235 Blake

MEDINA FRANK J.
34 W. Washington

Willow Ware.

(Wholesale. See also Grocers.)

MAYER CHARLES & CO.
29 W. Washington

Window Glass.

(*Wholesale.*)

Layman James T. & Co. 64 E. Washington
OVER E. & CO.
  82 and 84 S. Meridian

Wines and Liquors.

(*Wholesale. See also Liquor Dealers.*)

Bender Tobias & Co. 189 E. Washington
Brinkmeyer J. C. & Co. 80 S. Meridian
Conklin J. N. 31 W. Washington
GAPEN, CATHERWOOD & CO.
  118 S. Meridian
Hahn & Bals, 25 S. Meridian
Heymann Herman, 193 W. Washington
KAUFMAN S.
  116 S. Meridian
Kaufman M. & Bro. 42 W. Louisiana
Knotts & Co. 72 W. Washington
Lang Louis, 29 S. Meridian
Prenatt & O'Connor, 141 S. Meridian
RIKHOFF & BRO.
  77 S. Meridian
Ryan T. F. 143 S. Meridian
Ryan & Holbrook, 48 S. Meridian
Sage Charles, 172 W. Washington
Schmidt Rudolph, 269 E. Washington
Schwabacher & Selig, 41 S. Delaware
Stout F. & Son, 160 W. Washington
Sweetser John, 30 S. Meridian
Wallace Will. W. 441 N. Illinois

Wood Carvers.

Ludwig Louis, 182 S. Delaware
MILLER LAWRENCE,
  opp. 73 E. Market. (See advt. index)

Wood Yards.

(*See also Coal Dealers.*)

ALDRICH & GAY,
  Indiana av. cor. Canal (See advt. index

Wool Dealers.

Clark A. L. (woolen waste) rear 164 W. Maryland
Geisendorff C. E. & Co. ns. Washington (Nat. Rd.) near White river bridge
MERRITT & COUGHLEN,
  west end Washington

Woolen Mill Machinery and Findings.

Dickson C. & Co. 47 and 49 N. Tennessee
MERRITT & COUGHLEN,
  west en I Washington

Woolen Mills.

Geisendorff C. E. & Co. (Hoosier Mills) ns. Washington (Nat. Rd.) near White river bridge
MERRITT & COUGHLEN,
  (Ohio Premium Woolen Factory) west end Washington

TOO LATE FOR REGULAR INSERTION.

Billiard Saloons.

GEM BILLIARD SALOON,
  Carter & Bowman, props. 9 W. Wash'ton

Boarding Houses.

Rockwell Silas, 87 and 89 E. Market

Newspapers and Publications.

THE WESTERN FIRE SIDE.
  F. C. Holliday, D. D., editor, Dynes, West & Co. publishers, Vinton's Block

Saloons.

Carter & Bowman, 9 W. Washington

Saw Works.

AMERICAN SAW WORKS,
  Alfred T. Sinker, propr. Pennsylvania cor. Georgia

SMITH & CO.
DEALERS IN

TRADE PALACE
DRY GOODS
CARPETS

DE PALACE. 26

Dry Goods of Every Description,

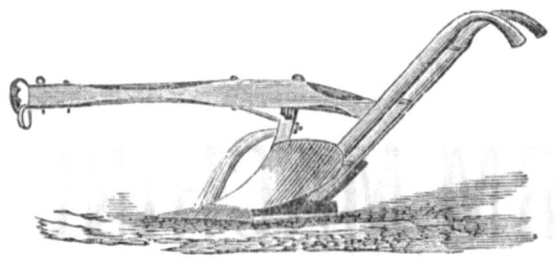

INDIANAPOLIS, CINCINNATI

—AND—

LAFAYETTE

RAIL ROAD!

The great through Express and Mail Route
from Indianapolis to and from all points East and West.

CINCINNATI TRAIN.

Three Trains Daily from the Union Depot for Cincinnati, and connecting at
Cincinnati with all the Great Eastern and Southern Rail Road Lines
and the Ohio Steamers.

---o---

LAFAYETTE AND CHICAGO TRAINS.

Two through Express Trains Daily for Chicago, with the most direct
connections in Chicago to and from all points in the North West.

---o---

Lafayette, Quincy and St. Joseph Trains.

Two through Trains Daily, via Lafayett for and from Springfield, Quincy,
Keokuk, St. Joseph and all points in Iowa, Kansas, Nebraska and
the Gold Regions.

SLEEPING CARS ON ALL NIGHT TRAINS.

Baggage Checked through to any point East or West.

A. E. CLARK, Gen'l Ticket Agt.,
    CINCINNATI.

W. H. L. NOBLE, Gen'l Agt.,
    INDIANAPOLIS.

H. L' HALL, Assistant Sup't.,
    LAFAYETTE.

J. F. RICHARDSON, Sup't.,
    CINCINNATI.

CINCINNATI, CONNERSVILLE

AND

INDIANAPOLIS JUNCTION

RAIL ROAD,

VIA

RUSHVILLE, CONNERSVILLE, OXFORD AND HAMILTON,

TO AND FROM CINCINNATI.

This road is completed from Rushville to Indianapolis
running

Two Passenger Trains Each Way Daily,

BETWEEN CINCINNATI AND INDIANAPOLIS,

Making all connections at both points, and also, via the Branch Road from
Connersville via Cambridge City to New Castle, Indiana, which
Branch will be extended to Muncie during summer
of 1869, which will constitute

THE GREAT CENTRAL ROUTE

From Cincinnati to the West and North-West,

Through the most desirable portion of Indiana, and on shorter time than
any other route in the directions indicated.

J. H. SHELDON,
Superintendent, Cincinnati, O.

J. M. RIDENOUR,
Vice-President, Indianapolis

Indianapolis & St. Louis

RAILROAD.

THE GREAT SHORT LINE

Between Indianapolis and the South and West.

THREE THROUGH EXPRESS TRAINS DAILY,

Making close connections for all points in Central and Southern Illinois, and points South of the Ohio River.

TWO THROUGH EXPRESS TRAINS

Leave St. Louis daily via Pacific and North Missouri Railroads for Kansas City, Leavenworth, Atchison, St. Joseph, Lawrence, Topeka, Junction City and Omaha, connecting with Express trains and Stage lines for all points in the Far West.

Luxurious Sleeping Coaches accompany all night trains.

Baggage Checked Through without Extra Charge.

Tickets for sale at all Principal Rail Road Offices.

JOHN S. GARLAND,   **J. D. HERKIMER,**

Gen'l Passenger Ag't., St. Louis, Mo.   *Gen'l Supt., St. Louis, Mo*